THE SOLACE OF HOPE

OTHER BOOKS BY DAVIS ASHURA

The Castes and the OutCastes:

A Warrior's Path

A Warrior's Knowledge

A Warrior's Penance

Omnibus Edition (only available on Kindle)

Stories for Arisa (short-story collection)

The Chronicles of William Wilde:

William Wilde and the Necrosed

William Wilde and the Stolen Life

William Wilde and the Unusual Suspects

William Wilde and the Sons of Deceit

William Wilde and the Lord of Mourning

Instrument of Omens

A Testament of Steel

Memoriwes of Prophecies

A Necessary Heresy

Bonds of Truths

The Eternal Ephemera

Blood of a Novice

Steel Sharpens

The Solace of Hope

THE ETERNAL EPHEMERA

◆ Book Three ◆

THE SOLACE OF HOPE

DAVIS ASHURA

To those who've kept with me on this journey so far.

ACKNOWLEDGEMENTS

As always, I have to give my humble thanks and gratitude to the members of my Patreon. Your support is so amazing!

There continues to be the wonderful people in my life, especially my wife and children, who give me the time and space to write. There are also the wonderful readers, who are willing to serve as my beta readers. Not sure how you put up with my typos.

And once again, to the members of my writers group, where we're the only writers in the building. They know what I mean.

THE TRIALS SO FAR

Cam Folde decides to dive an unknown Pathway to Grace with his childhood friends, Jordil, Lilia, and Tern. It is a chance for him to become something more than a no-good Folde, which is how most of the people of his small town of Traverse view him.

Within the strange world of the Pathway, Cam and his friends discover Saira Maharani, a powerful Crown, who helps them escape the deadly place in which they find themselves trapped. Nonetheless, disaster strikes. Tern dies, and Cam is gravely wounded. To save himself, he accepts Plasminia as his Primary Tang. It is a choice that leaves Cam physically disabled, and with a short, bitter life as his future. Over the ensuing years, he buries his guilt over Tern's death and sorrow over his infirmity in alcohol.

His sister, Pharis, helps Cam break free of his addiction, and more good news comes when he learns of a freshly discovered Pathway to help him fully heal. Jordil, Lilia, and Master Bennett—one of their teachers—accompany Cam to the Pathway. He dives it, and immediately discovers an oddity: an Awakened squirrel named Honor. She's injured and chooses to gift Cam with her Ephemera, allowing him to create a Kinesthia Tang.

However, on their way home from the Pathway, fresh tragedy occurs when their small group is attacked by rakshasas. Lilia is killed and many villagers blame Cam for her death. He is driven from his home where Cam eventually comes across Pan, an Awakened panda. They gain sponsorship through Master Winder to the Ephemeral Academy.

At the school, Cam and Pan are inducted into Light Squad with Avia Koravail, the Awakened orca daughter of a Sage-Duke, Jade Mare, the daughter of a fallen Crown, and Weld Plain, a commoner and a pain in Cam's backside. Surprisingly, amongst their instructors is also included Saira, who has regressed to Glory.

Cam finds his footing, becoming Light Squad's leader, where they destroy a boil in a small town named Surelend, earn great acclaim in the mid-year tournament, and defeat a challenge from the nobility, earning their respect.

All is going well, and Cam might even consider Victory Arta, a son of a Sage-Duke to be a friend. Another such child of nobility, Charity Kazar, teasingly flirts with him, and a third noble—the son of a Crown—Card Wolver, is so impressed by Light Squad that he forces his way into their unit.

But Light Squad is then tasked to aid Sidewinder Company, one of Master Winder's military units, in the eradication of a powerful boil. It is a close-fought battle, and afterward, Cam is troubled. This is the second time Master Winder has placed Light Squad in situations too dangerous for them. He and Saira talk about it and decide that perhaps Cam and Light Squad should break from the Wilde Sage and go their own way.

Cam's second year at the Ephemeral Academy is one that begins with confusion as Charity Kazar also forces her way into Light Squad. Later on, Cam discovers that Weld Plain, who has steadfastly refused to work as hard as the rest of the unit, has also intentionally kept necessary teachings from them. After the information is brought to Master Winder's attention, Weld is dismissed from Light Squad.

In addition, there is a new instructor, Cinder Shade, the husband to one of their other instructors, Eveangel Grey. Both are Glories, and both are sublime in their abilities. Their teachings inspire Cam and the rest of Light Squad. The instruction is necessary since Light Squad faces another challenge from the nobles.

Prior to the tournament, however, Weld makes his return to Nexus, having gained a new sponsor. Shortly after meeting him in order to ascertain Weld's motives, Light Squad is attacked by the rakshasa Sages Nailing and Nageena.

All seems lost, but Professors Shade and Grey somehow manage to fight off the Sages, but not before Nailing creates an anchor line that thrusts Light Squad and Saira into the Realm of Hearth. There, they are immediately attacked by the Jom-Strafes, powerful foes who entered Hearth when the Sages of that world were somehow trapped while battling an unknown foe.

Light Squad kills the Jom-Strafes but discover that the deadly enemy will now send fresh opponents after them, each time of greater Advancement. And the only means of survival is to reach Nylara, the city and home of Hearth's Sages.

Their travel is brutal, and the people of Hearth aren't always kind. Some are villainous. Nevertheless, Light Squad perseveres. They defeat each group of Jom-Strafes that come after them. However, when a single Jom-Strafe Crown is sent against them, all hope seems lost just as Light Squad reaches Nylara.

None can stand against the Jom-Strafe, and much of the city is destroyed in an ensuing battle between the creature and Nylara's defender, also a Crown. Meanwhile, Light Squad reaches the Temple of Gates, and there Cam manages to awaken Thor, one of Hearth's Sages. Thor destroys the Jom-Strafe Crown, and all is finally well as two voices speak to Light Squad within the temple, and in the process, destroy Rabisu, who had invaded Saira's mind, unbeknownst to her. The voices appear to have a special fondness for Cam.

Light Squad helps in the rebuilding of Nylara, and they all Advance to Adept and return home to Salvation where they plan their next step, which can't be to remain at the Ephemeral Academy. Cam believes there are traitors amongst the Sage-Dukes and nobility. There have been too many occasions where they've been placed in unnecessary danger, and as if in confirmation of his fears, Weld Plain is now an instructor at the school.

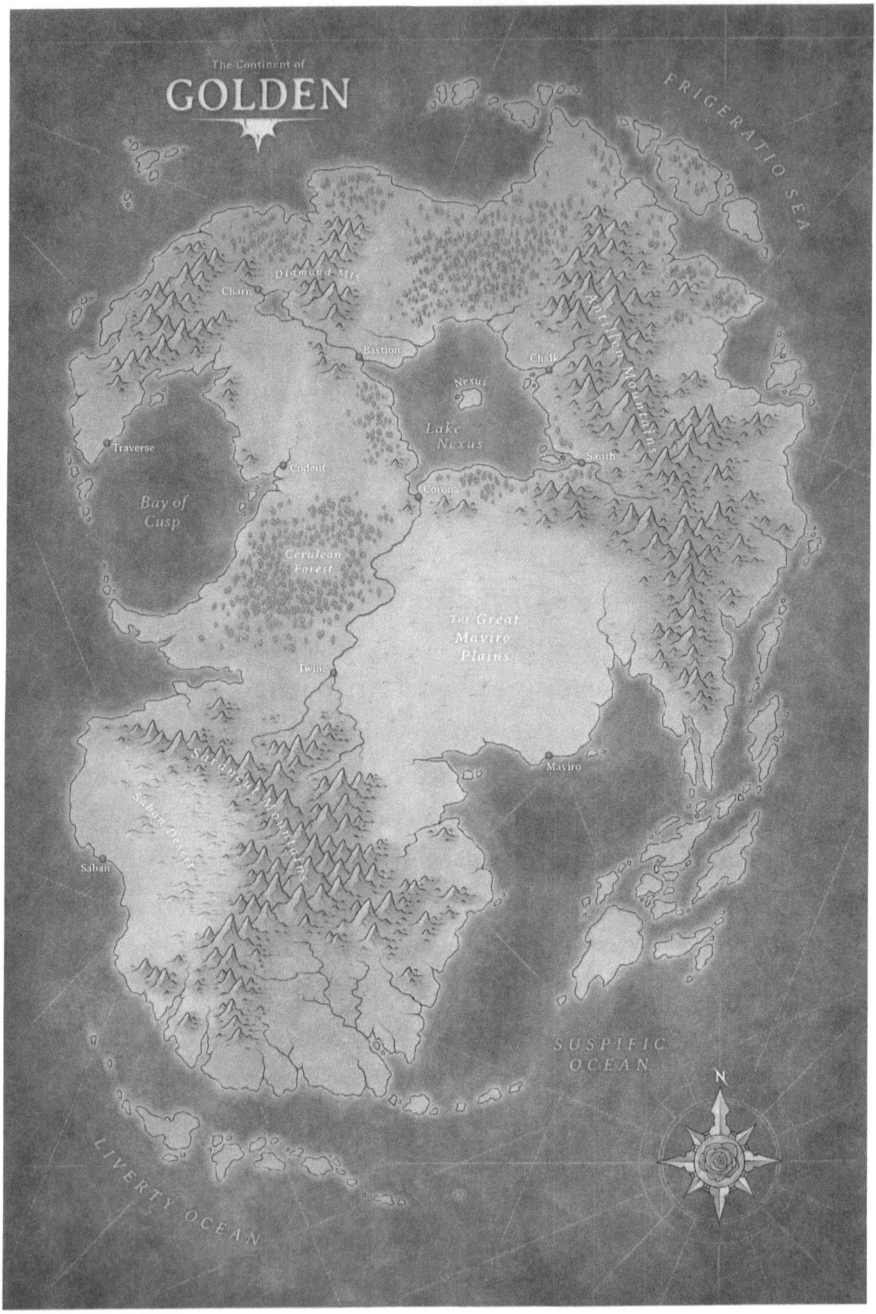

The Continent of
GOLDEN
FRIGERATIO SEA
Diamond Mts
Charn
Ancient Mountains
Bastion
Chalk
Nexus
Smith
Lake Nexus
Traverse
Codent
Corona
Bay of Cusp
Cerulean Forest
The Great Maviro Plains
Twine
Maviro
Saldrian Mountains
Saban Desert
Saban
SUSPIFIC OCEAN
N
LIVERTY OCEAN

1

Cam sat cross-legged within the front room of his quarters, eyes closed and seeking to Enhance his Tangs. He'd been at it for hours now—hard labor—but it was also work that went far faster and easier as an Adept than it had as an Acolyte. Of course, that wasn't on account of some greater skill that Cam had recently mastered but rather because of the perfection of Awareness taught to him and Light Squad by Rail Gristle, the mysterious old man they'd met in Hearth.

As a result of Rail's teachings, it had only taken Cam a week to Enhance his Tangs to Crystal upon getting home to Salvation, and all he was doing now was bringing them all to a mirror-perfect shine. Even better, rather than the fancy dancing and breathing exercises he'd been forced to use as an Acolyte, all that was required this time was to slow Plasminia's lightning-laced spinning to a crawl, extrude the yellow bile, and drive it down into his lower Tangs. It wasn't far off from what he'd done as a Novice, and the easy technique was on account of how he'd Advanced perfectly to the Stage of an Adept.

In addition, he'd made a small dent in learning the skills given to him by the voices who'd saved him from Rabisu. Likely it had been

Rukh and Jessira, and since they'd granted him a Sage's knowledge in the use of Ephemera, he wasn't about to waste their gift. Empathy loomed especially large in his focus since he figured that understanding how a person felt would be a good way to know how best to help them. Empathy didn't even need a True Bond. It only required the Delving of his Source and viewing a person through the woven world.

A moment later, Cam frowned, his pleasure over what he might be able to accomplish draining away. Thinking on Rail Gristle had brought about less pleasant recollections. Specifically, Hearth and everything he'd witnessed and endured in that Realm. The constant terror of being chased by the savage Jom-Strafes, the killing, and all those dead in Nylara. He still struggled with it all, the memories grabbing him unawares at times, leaving him sweating, heaving for breath, and his mind lost to horrors.

It was why he'd spent his week not only Enhancing his Tangs and learning the Holy Servants teachings, but also practicing the meditations taught to him by Saira. He regularly allowed his horrific memories to surface, letting himself feel and re-experience them, and when they became too painful, he shut them away.

It was a kind of torture, but one that was necessary for healing. His agitated emotions—sorrow, anger, and terror—often crept up on him like an icy wind or an unfriendly fellow fixing to do him harm, and that couldn't be ignored.

So, Cam didn't ignore them. Every morning, he did what was required, and slowly, surely, he was finding his bearings. More remarkably and of greater benefit for him, as his emotions settled, a way forward had appeared, one past the brambles of his fearful living and that would eventually lead to solace. He needed that blessed kind of living.

Solace. Cam considered the word. How little peace had he experienced in life since that fatal first Pathway where Tern had died? How much tragedy?

Pan wandered out of his bedroom just then, distracting Cam from his hard memories. The Awakened panda grabbed a stalk of bamboo, took a mighty crunch, and tossed a wink at Cam before settling down next to him, eyes closed and meditating.

Cam smiled at his friend. Yes, tragedy existed in his world, but so did wonder and joy. Cam had a loving family back in Traverse, but he'd found one here at the Ephemeral Academy, too. It began with Pan, an Awakened panda who Cam considered a brother. Then there was Avia, Jade, and Card—all of whom were also chosen siblings—and Saira, who he'd come to view as an auntie. Reciting the members of Light Squad ended on Charity Kazar. What did he think about her?

She'd come back to the Academy a few days ago, earlier than expected, and while Cam currently enjoyed her company, he had to wonder how long it would last. Possibly—hopefully—a long time, but then again, this was Charity Kazar, the woman who found needling him to be one of life's great pleasures.

Cam exhaled heavily and rose to his feet. He was supposed to meet Charity in a little while for breakfast, so it was best if he made himself presentable. After a quick shower and a change of clothes, he rejoined Pan in their front room where a quick glance outside told him what he expected to see, but nevertheless, he found the sight a mite disappointing. Bright sunshine blazed through the windows, and based on the cloudless haziness outside, it was sure to be another hot, humid one. Cam mentally sighed. He hated the heat.

An instant later, he turned his attention to Pan, who sat on the ground, reading what looked to be a letter and still munching on his stalk of bamboo.

"What are you reading?"

Pan displayed the missive. "It's a message from Lord Shoner, the dean. He says the others should be coming back soon."

Cam took in the words, blinking in surprise before grinning with excitement. He hadn't expected the rest of Light Squad to come back for another month. "Really? When?"

"The dean doesn't say." Pan took a big chomp of his bamboo. "But he thinks Card and Avia will be the first ones back and later on, Jade."

Cam continued to smile, but a missing name furrowed his brow. "Did he say when Saira is coming back?"

Pan shook his head. "She's a Crown. There's no place for her here."

"But she said she'd take us to that area where Ephemera was concentrated."

Another chomp of bamboo. "That was before Hearth, and by Salvation's time, it was four years ago. It's probably long since been emptied."

"There ain't no way to empty Ephemera out of a place," Cam said, getting sidetracked and falling into his country way of speaking. The truth was, he'd figured the same as Pan, but he had also hoped Saira *would* come back. Their unit would be incomplete without her. They needed her wisdom and counsel.

Pan scoffed at his comment. "Next you'll say All is Ephemera and Ephemera is All."

Cam grinned. "Why fixate on a new phrase when the old one will do just fine?"

"Why indeed?" Pan asked, offering a grin of his own, the cute kind that always made Cam feel better.

"What do you have going on today?" Cam asked, shifting the conversation.

Pan shrugged. "I'll Enhance. Get in some practice later on and then do some reading at the library in the afternoon. You want to join me?"

Cam hedged. "Maybe."

His answer earned him a head tilt of curiosity. "What else do you have to do?" Cam didn't answer at once, not wanting to say, but Pan was too perceptive, and a slow grin lit the panda's face. "You have plans with Charity, don't you?" He made kissing noises.

Cam controlled a flush by forcing a laugh. "What are you? Twelve?"

"Nine, actually, and that wasn't a denial. You're going on a date with Charity." More kissing noises followed.

"It's just for breakfast," Cam protested, not knowing why he was feeling so defensive.

"Which is when the two of you will finally declare your love for one another and share a passionate embrace."

"I think someone has been reading too many romance novels."

Pan shrugged. "So what if I have? You still haven't denied anything I've said." He waggled his eyebrows. "And the spicy kind of romance novels say a declaration of love leads to a certain kind of activity. The kind humans do at night."

Cam threw his hands in the air. The notion of kissing Charity—and other things—wasn't exactly unpleasant, and he even found himself wondering in a longing sort of way at how soft Charity's lips might be.

An instant later, he admonished himself for thinking on what he shouldn't expect. Charity was a noble, and he was common as dirt.

"Well?" Pan asked. "Are you going to kiss her?" He was apparently obsessed with the idea of Cam and Charity kissing.

Cam threw his hands in the air again. "Get your mind out of the gutter. Charity and I ain't going to declare our love for one another and share a passionate kiss."

"Yes, you are," Pan said. "You used 'ain't', and nowadays you only do that if you're flustered or distracted."

"I just said 'ain't' a few minutes ago."

"Because you were distracted." Pan folded his arms, appearing smug, like he'd won a debate.

His reaction had Cam scowling. "Why is this so important to you?"

For a wonder, Pan appeared abashed. "I like to be right about these kind of things."

Cam shook his head. "Well, you're wrong about it this time. I like Charity."

"Aha!"

"As a friend," Cam quickly added. But he flushed on adding the caveat and wished he hadn't. "She's been right pleasant since she's come back."

"Right pleasant. Another country phrase." Pan smirked in triumph. "Flustered and distracted."

Cam threw his arms in the air a third time. He didn't want to discuss this anymore, mostly because he didn't like where the conversation would undoubtedly lead: disappointment. "You're hopeless. There ain't…" Another flush. "I mean, whatever's between me and Charity is none of your business."

Pan's attitude shifted from playful to serious. "Yes, it is. As your guide—"

"My what?"

"Your guide." Pan flashed another of his cute smiles. "I think the prophecy about me—"

"Not this again," Cam muttered.

"—doesn't mean I'll do something wonderful. It's all about supporting someone else who'll do something wonderful." He pointed at Cam with his stalk of bamboo. "It means I'll support you."

Cam rolled his eyes. Pan and his stupid prophecy. For most of the panda's life, it had been nothing but an anchor around his friend's neck. Maybe one day, Pan would be done with it and end his devotion to that fragging prophecy.

"Anyway," Pan said, "as your guide, I believe you and Charity have unresolved feelings for one another. You want to kiss her, and she wants to kiss you." Another cute smile. "I'll even wager it will happen. If not today, then in the next week."

Cam glared at the grinning panda, but he was also smart enough not to take the wager.

The summer sunshine poured heat and humidity from a cloudless sky, and the light glinted like diamonds on the surface of Lake Nexus. Ships lined the harbor and crowding the air above the vessels and docks were a flock of seagulls, lofted by the stiff breeze swirling the water and shore. Distance, however, soothed that same wind until it was softer than a baby's breath by the time it reached the Ephemeral Academy where the air hung heavy, still, and sad. And although the sun had only risen several hours ago, the day already sweltered.

Cam wafted his shirt, disgusted with the mugginess. He would have figured that as an Adept, the discomfort wouldn't have bothered him as much, and it didn't. But that wasn't the same as saying it didn't bother him at all, which he was kind of wishing was the case, especially since Charity was walking so close.

He glanced at her sidelong, noticing again how the grotesque brew made from the pancreas of a Jom-Strafe and his own yellow bile had marked her, and in the process, saved her life. Of course, he'd imbibed the same loathsome drink, and it had changed him in the same general way it had Charity: darkening his skin, curling his hair, and granting him greater strength, stamina, and speed whether or not he held a True Bond.

So many changes in just a few short months. It had been a rough time that Cam didn't want to think about.

"What I wouldn't give for some snow," Charity sent telepathically to him.

Early on after her return, they'd discovered that their ability to speak mind-to-mind with one another had vastly increased upon their Advancement to Adept with no limits found to the distance. Oddly enough, the enhanced link was only with Charity. Cam didn't share a similar ability with anyone else, not even Pan, no matter how much the two of them practiced at stretching their telepathic skills with one another. He couldn't figure on why that was the case and had eventually chalked it up to another mystery of Hearth. Likely it was related to when they'd shared that nasty healing concoction that had saved them from the Jom-Strafes' poison.

Regardless, hearing Charity's mournful tone, Cam set aside his thoughts about the past and viewed her with uncertainty. Was she mocking him? Charity was from Maviro, a southern city, which was warm almost all year round. Why would she find snow to her liking?

"I know it sounds strange," Charity sent, apparently picking up on his unspoken question. *"But I was happy enough with the cold weather in Hearth."*

Cam didn't reply to her statement. Instead, his mind went back to that strange Realm where so much had changed for Light Squad. They'd all grown there, Advancing to Adepts and achieving a finer control of Ephemera than any of them had ever dreamed possible. It was also where Cam had begun wondering what it might be like to court a woman like Charity Kazar. Was there actually a future for them like Pan reckoned?

Until Hearth, Cam would have never figured such a possibility since Charity had always been a pain in his backside, poking fun at him, and making him squirm. In the face of that kind of treatment, her beauty hadn't mattered, and Cam had often unconsciously and unfairly compared her to Maria Benefield, the woman in Traverse that every boy had admired and lusted after. The same woman who had spent many years making Cam feel worthless before finally driving him away from his home.

But those comparisons of Charity to Maria had finally and fully died in Hearth, during a walk along the dock of some no-name river town. And where a Jom-Strafe Crown had nearly killed them both, ending the gentle stroll that had edged on being romantic.

There must have been something of his thoughts reflected in his features because Charity took his hand, squeezing it. "We're done with Hearth."

Cam squeezed her hand back. "Do you still dream about it?"

He didn't have to tell her what he was talking about. "I dream about it every night," Charity said, her voice small and her expression haunted. An instant later, she forced a bright smile. "Let's talk about something else."

"About what?"

Charity held silent for a beat, and Cam glanced her way. She was usually skilled at seemingly changing her emotions at will, but right now, the tightness in her features told of her strain. Hearth had marked her no less than it had him. "Us," she finally replied.

"Us," Cam repeated, knowing he sounded stupid but unable to help it. That word had a powerful connotation. What did she mean by it? A part of him didn't want to learn. Spending time with Charity these past few days after she'd come back to the Academy had been some of the finest Cam could recall, and he wasn't ready to ruin it yet.

As a result, he didn't want to talk about what *us* might mean, but this was clearly important to Charity, and he couldn't be a coward about it. He gathered his courage, feeling like talking to her in this moment was deadlier than battling the Jom-Strafe Glory. "What do you want us to be?"

Charity gave him a narrowed gaze. "I would have thought that was obvious." Her head tilted in question. "Have I been unclear?"

Cam barked low laughter. "You've been as clear as mud from the first time we met." He pressed into her personal space, giving her a low-lidded expression just short of a knowing leer. "Does this look familiar?"

Charity blushed, and it took her a few seconds to collect herself before she could address him again. "That was before experiencing everything that happened to us. Before Hearth. Before now."

Cam didn't respond at once. "That's the rub. *Now* has me feeling fearful. My heart ain't exactly experienced."

Charity stared at him, brows lifted in amazement, before she threw her head back in laughter. "Cam, I love your country drawl, but now isn't the time to pretend to be a yokel."

"I wasn't pretending," Cam said, flushing. "I'm just nervous about all this. That's all."

"All what?"

Cam gestured vaguely. "These questions. Us. I wasn't lying when I said my heart is inexperienced." He started rambling, and once the words started, he couldn't bring them to a stop. "I know you've had suitors pretty much your entire life, but I haven't. I've never courted anyone, and no one ever wanted me to court them."

Charity took both his hands in hers and stared at him. "Do you want to court me, Cam Folde? Is that what you're saying?"

Cam studied his emotions. Was that what he wanted? Remembrances of all the times Charity had feigned interest in him rose up but were swept away when he gazed at her, seeing her concern and honesty.

"We don't have to court," Charity said after a moment of quiet. "We were good friends in Hearth. We still can be. That doesn't have to change."

Cam continued to stare at her, pondering what he wanted. But any certainty at knowing his mind and emotions remained as elusive as a fish in hand. He wanted friendship with Charity, but did he also want more? He thought he might, but he couldn't yet find a way to push the answer past his lips. Instead, he vacillated. "What happens if we do court? Will your family accept me?"

"After everything you've already accomplished? You know they will." She peered at him with a frown. "What's really holding you back?"

Cam feared answering her, feared how she would react. His heart raced, and his throat clenched, but he managed to blurt out the question. "How can I trust you?"

Charity surprised him by not reacting with anger. Rather she continued to hold his hands, empathy writ large on her face. "Is it me you don't trust, or is it yourself?"

Cam scowled, pulling his hands free of hers, realizing even as he did so that she'd hit on the heart of his fears: he didn't trust himself. He didn't trust that he was worthy of her. It was the old lie that he had yet to fully overcome. His eyes narrowed as he looked inward. *No. In this moment, he would overcome it.* "I trust myself."

A challenging glint filled Charity's eyes. "Prove it."

Cam felt like he was standing upon a precipice. Take one step, and he'd launch himself off a cliff. Or maybe if he trusted himself, he'd soar to the sky. What to do?

The question answered itself. He took a leap into faith by moving close to Charity, holding her by the waist and bending low to kiss her. Her arms went around his neck, and she drew him closer. Their kiss deepened.

2

Cam wandered the paths of the Ephemeral Academy, struggling to believe what had just happened. Had he really kissed Charity Kazar? It felt like it must have happened to somebody else, but his arms still tingled from their embrace, and when he licked his lips, the taste of her—a fragrance of honeysuckle and hibiscus—remained.

Had it been a mistake, though? He searched his feelings, smiling as he discarded that unnecessary concern. No. Kissing Charity hadn't been a mistake. It had been one of the best decisions he'd ever made.

With a vague startlement, he realized his feet had led him back to his quarters, and he opened the door, finding Pan at the dining table. His friend sat in a pool of light from the late-morning sun shining in, reading a book, and—as usual—munching on a stalk of bamboo.

Cam glanced to the window. Shouldn't the day be almost done? The conversation with Charity had been so meaningful, so important. Surely it had taken more than just a couple of hours. He smiled again, thinking about her.

"What did you and Charity talk about?" Pan asked, looking up from his book. An instant later, his eyes narrowed with suspicion. "And why are you smiling like that?"

Cam tried to wipe off the expression and feign nonchalance. He loved Pan, but talking about what had happened with Charity wasn't something he was ready to discuss. "Smiling like what? I was just glad to see the sun shining."

Pan continued to stare at him, eyes lidded before they abruptly widened in understanding. He jumped to his feet, clapping his hands and bouncing up and down like an oversized bunny. "You kissed her, didn't you? You did! You did! Tell me everything."

Cam barely kept his jaw from dropping. How the fragging hells had Pan figured it out? A moment later, he regathered himself and forced a bland expression on his face. "We talked. That's all."

"I bet it was hard to talk with your lips stuck together," Pan said, going on to make smooching sounds.

A knock on the door saved Cam from having to answer. "It was nothing like that," he shot over his shoulder as he went to see who it was. He flung open the door and immediately sobered. All thoughts about answering Pan's irritating questions fled from his mind because standing on the stoop was Master Rainen Winder, Cam's and Pan's sponsor at the Ephemeral Academy. The Wilde Sage was old, hundreds of years in age, but no wrinkles marred his skin, no gray streaked his black hair, and his posture remained upright and straight. Lean and well-built, a neatly-trimmed beard framed a warm smile as he gazed at Cam.

"Hello, Cam," the Wilde Sage said. "It's been too long."

"Master Winder," Cam said, speaking loudly so Pan would take the hint and shut off his teasing. Thankfully, he did exactly that and a sense of sobriety fell over the room. "Come in."

The Wilde Sage entered, and Cam was struck anew at how much taller he was than the other man. He towered over Master Winder. Of course, that wasn't exactly important. Master Winder was a Sage, and his presence had a gravity beyond mere physical stature.

"You've grown. Both of you," Master Winder noted.

It took Cam a moment to recognize what the Wilde Sage was

talking about. The last time they'd been together, Cam and Pan had been Acolytes. Now, they were Adept Primes.

"I'm sorry I haven't been able to come by to see you before today," Master Winder continued. "Life has been… interesting."

Cam frowned, studying the Wilde Sage, who had initially appeared unchanged, as strong and indomitable as ever. But sighting him more closely, there were changes. Fresh worry lines creased his features—tiny crow's feet at the corners of his eyes—and whatever had him concerned seemed to slope his shoulders with fatigue, weighing him down and wafting off of him like a barely felt breeze.

"Why *are* you here?" Cam asked

Master Winder flashed a strained smile. "Straight to the point, I see." He exhaled slowly. "I've heard accounts about your time in Hearth, verified some aspects, which we can discuss if you wish, but I also recognize what you're considering. I recognized it the last time I saw you."

Cam cocked his head in confusion. "What do you mean? What was I considering?" This wasn't what he'd expected of his first conversation with Master Winder since returning from Hearth. Shouldn't the Wilde Sage want to debrief them?

"Not just you. Both of you," Master Winder said, indicating Pan, who stood in the center of their room, quiet and unassuming, looking like he didn't want to draw any attention to himself, which wasn't a surprise. Pan had always been intimidated to speechlessness by the Wilde Sage.

"What about us?" Cam asked, still not sure of the Wilde Sage's purpose.

"You're planning on leaving my sponsorship."

Cam momentarily pursed his lips, but he also didn't bother denying the charge. If Master Winder had figured out their intentions, there was no reason to lie about it. "Yes, sir. That's what we're figuring."

Master Winder grimaced. "Even before Hearth, correct?"

"Correct," Pan replied, having mastered his intimidation enough to straighten his shoulders and answer.

"May I know why?" the Wilde Sage asked.

By a bare margin, Cam kept from boggling at Master Winder in disbelief. Wasn't the answer obvious? It should have been. Nonetheless, Cam went on to explain about Light Squad's unhappiness with what had occurred in their Novice year, especially at Dander. "We should have never been asked to fight there."

Another grimace from Master Winder. "You are correct. I should have never asked you to fight there, but I also had no choice. Over the decades, my allies amongst the Sage-Dukes have grown thin. They mouth the proper promises of aid, but when Ephemera, steel, and hard fighting are required, their actions prove their lack of piety."

Cam frowned, parsing the Wilde Sage's words, inhaling sharply when understanding took hold. His suspicions about the Sage-Dukes being untrustworthy was right. But the confirmation simply led to further unsettling questions, including wondering why Master Winder was telling them this now. Why not earlier? Why not seek them out when they'd first come back from Hearth?

Something on his expression must have given away his feelings because Master Winder chuckled dryly and without humor. "You don't doubt my words, but you doubt my good intentions. I understand. Trust lost is not so easily regained." He inhaled deep. "If you leave my service, you know I cannot sponsor you here any longer. What will you then do?"

Cam shared a speculative glance with Pan. Should they tell the Wilde Sage their plans? Receiving a shrug of uncertainty, Cam held off from answering Master Winder's question, and instead asked one of his own. "Why didn't you offer to send me and Pan home after our first year?"

Master Winder's brows lifted. "You ask this now? Why? Is it truly that important?"

Cam nodded. Maybe his question sounded petty, but for all this time, what had been done for Weld after their shared first year at the Ephemeral Academy but not for him and Pan had lodged wrong in his craw.

Master Winder sighed. "I honestly didn't know you wanted to go home. I found it strange that you didn't, but Saira assured me that such was the case."

Cam blinked in surprise. Saira had said that?

"Rabisu," Pan whispered, providing the answer.

Master Winder's gaze sharpened. "Who is Rabisu?"

Cam offered a sour grimace. It seemed Master Winder hadn't learned everything about Light Squad's time in Hearth. Avia must not have told him when she'd come back. And apparently neither had Jade, Card, and Charity, unless… "I'm guessing you haven't spoken to the others in Light Squad?"

"You are the first two I've had a chance to talk to since returning from the Sinanes."

Cam's eyes widened. The Sinanes? Why would Master Winder have gone there?

"That's where I've largely been since your return. The islands have seen an increase in sea-borne rakshasa activity, more than they've noted in decades. Between that and the insistence of Sage Lysha—Saira's mother—who wasn't happy with what Saira endured in Hearth and largely blamed me for it, I've been busy."

"You weren't at fault," Cam replied. There were many things for which he could blame Master Winder, but Saira's regression and her possession by Rabisu weren't part of it.

Master Winder sighed. "I know that, and I think Lysha knows it, but she's a mother first, and I doubt she'll ever forgive me." He seemed to collect himself a moment later. "You were saying about Rabisu."

"Saira didn't tell you?" Pan asked.

Master Winder gazed from one of them to the other. "Should she have?"

Cam wasn't able to say one way or the other. Rabisu had been a violation and maybe Saira just didn't want to talk about it. But Cam could, felt like it was the right thing to do, and he ended up giving Master Winder a full explanation of what Light Squad had encountered and endured in Hearth.

However, before he could reach the end of his summation, Master

Winder interrupted when he heard about Rabisu's destruction. "You truly believe it was Rukh and Jessira who destroyed this Rakshasa of Dissolution?"

"We do," Cam confirmed, not mentioning that those same voices had singled him out for special attention. He wasn't ready to share that with anyone outside of Light Squad.

"I see," Master Winder said, appearing lost in thought. Moments later, he broke out of his reverie. "What happened next?"

Cam went on to tell about their last days in that Realm. "Thor was wonderful: kind, generous, and giving."

Master Winder wore a smirk. "Unlike me is what it sounds like you're leaving unsaid."

Cam shrugged, not bothering to deny the Wilde Sage's words.

"And this is why you are leaving my service?" Master Winder asked.

"You really expect us to learn under the tutelage of Weld Plain?" Pan asked.

"If he helps you Advance to Glory, then yes," Master Winder said, appearing genuinely confused.

"Weld Plain is a snake," Pan hissed.

"I asked for his removal from Light Squad for a reason," Cam added.

Master Winder's demeanor shifted to one of a thoughtful frown, and he stroked his chin. "I think I see it now. For you, only a few months have passed since your last encounter with Weld, while for him, it has been four years. You still harbor resentment toward him, while he has grown and become a far better person compared to when you last knew him."

"That would take a miracle," Cam replied.

Master Winder shrugged. "Miracles can happen. Witness Rabisu's death and your return to Salvation."

Cam shook his head. "That's not good enough for us to trust him. We were there when Nailing and Nageena attacked. We saw Weld. He seemed happy about it."

The Wilde Sage appeared troubled. "I won't try to change your mind, but I've spoken to Weld on occasion over the years. He seemed changed, truly regretful over his role in how his initial time here ended. But since the situation is irredeemable, what happens next for you two? For Light Squad?"

Again, Cam shared a look of speculation with Pan, and again, received nothing more than a mere shrug of a reply. Cam grimaced inwardly. Pan was no help. "Saira told us about an area of condensed Ephemera in the foothills of the Antilles Mountains. We were planning on going there to Advance to Glory."

Master Winder's eyes locked on his. "You have certainty in the answer? You understand the difference between giving and receiving?"

Cam hesitated. "I think so. It's not firm, but with meditation, I believe it will be by the time we get to there."

"You Advance so swiftly," Master Winder mused.

Cam shrugged. Light Squad's time in Hearth had been horrific, but it had also forced unexpected growth. Gaining a sense of the answer required to Advance to Glory had been one aspect of it.

"It won't do you any good," Master Winder eventually declared.

Cam frowned. "Why not?"

"That area has already been mined," Master Winder said. "Nothing useful remains there."

Cam slumped. Going to the area that Saira had found and promised for them was supposed to have been Light Squad's means of freedom, of unshackling themselves from those who didn't always have their best interests at heart.

"There is another place, though," Master Winder continued, smiling slightly now. "Perit Line, the Crown in charge of Sidewinder Company, discovered it several months ago and made its location known to me. An ancient temple, ruined and overrun by jungle."

"And you and Perit won't mind us using it for ourselves?" Cam asked, suspicions roused.

Master Winder chuckled. "I've seen the place myself. It has enough Ephemera for all your needs, even Sidewinder's." He nodded. "I don't mind sharing. Consider it my peace offering and penance for placing you in danger. I want to see you do well. You're special, and I hope one day, you'll think better of me. This world needs people like you. I need people like you. I can't fight the rakshasas on my own." He sighed. "I hope there will come a day when you'll trust me enough to let me fight by your side. Until then, one last piece of advice: you will need a Crown to guide and protect you. There are some dangerous Awakened Beasts who live close by, and for some reason, it's not possible to anchor line anywhere closer than several weeks' travel on foot." He shrugged. "Anchor lining out of there is no trouble, though."

"We'll have a Crown with us," Cam replied.

Master Winder's attention speared him once more. "Saira has been in contact?"

Cam tried not to shift under the intensity of the Wilde Sage's regard. "She promised she'd come back to the Academy." Of course, Saira hadn't said *when* she'd come back, but Cam figured it would be soon enough.

"Then you should be fine, especially since you'll also have Avia with you, and her father sent to me that she should soon Advance to Glory." He dipped his head to them. "I wish you good journeys—all of Light Squad—as well as good luck. And if you ever have need…" he offered them both an oval pendant, the size of an egg… "use these *nomasras*, and I will do whatever I can to help."

With that, he strode to the door, exiting. Upon his departure, the room fell into a contemplative silence. Master Winder had played such a large role in both their lives, and for Cam, it was strange to think he might be gone from it now.

Saira stood alone atop the large balcony extending off her quarters and stared at the aqua-blue waters of the Arylyn Ocean. A thigh-high balustrade, clever in its simplicity, edged the platform while the midday sun shone upon the ocean and cast glittering diamonds amongst the warm waters where a number of people frolicked. Saira watched it all, arms folded and lost in contemplation as the wind played with her braided hair, ruffled the pleats of her sari, and lofted the fragrance of the jasmine and rose bushes growing within the large terra cotta planters scattered across the balcony.

A lovely setting, but Saira's attention remained elsewhere, her eyes unfocused and only glancingly recognizing the haunting beauty of the Sinanes, such as how the lovely capital of Tulara wrapped about Solstice Palace—her mother's place of governance—like an oyster around a pearl. Nor did she take pleasure in how the island's many green hills melded seamlessly with the city's elegant whitewashed buildings and their brilliant copper-and-gold tiles before the city poured down to the Arylyn Ocean. The islands of Capricia and Warouni, forested gems lined by golden beaches and visible in the distance, barely registered in her mind either.

Rather, her contemplations were fixed upon Light Squad. They needed her. No doubt, Rainen would demand their aid in the endless battles against the rakshasas, and she couldn't allow it. Light Squad was special, but they also weren't ready. They needed to be cultivated and nurtured so their future greatness could help the world in ways even she couldn't imagine.

Of course, telling her amma—her mother—of her plans would be no easy task. Amma had been overjoyed when her oldest daughter had returned to the Sinanes, but she would be less pleased upon learning of that same child's intent to leave again so soon. Saira grimaced at the oft-delayed conversation. It wouldn't be pleasant, but it was necessary.

Saira glanced into her quarters when she heard the door open, unsurprised when her amma strode inside. A serious and unhappy expression carved her face, like she'd somehow already deduced the discussion to be had. And she likely had.

Amma was as tall as Saira and similarly lovely—ageless, actually—but with a maturity to her features that came from the weight of her responsibilities. Her blonde hair shimmered, appearing nearly white, and her blue irises—of the same hue as Saira's—sparkled with intelligence. Amma's, however, were curtained by the violet-Haunted sclerae of a Sage, whereas Saira's were merely the indigo of a Crown.

Saira smiled at the arrogance of her sentiment. *Merely a Crown.* She'd achieved this Stage of Advancement once before, but in comparison to the dull lantern of her prior Awareness, her current abilities felt as bright as a fully lit chandelier, especially with all her Tangs Enhanced to Crystal.

Amma joined her on the balcony. "You look pleased."

Saira explained, "I was thinking about expectations."

"Mine or yours?"

"Mine were always heavier than yours."

Amma lifted a hand, gently stroking the side of Saira's face, a pained expression on her own. "And I sense that those heavy expectations mean you'll be leaving us soon. Are you sure you have to go? Golden didn't treat you well."

Saira blinked back abrupt tears. She wanted to stay, and she already felt the pangs of missing her mother and her family, but duty impelled her. She kissed her amma's palm, pressing it against her face. "I've been here for over a month. It's time."

Amma inhaled deep, as if preparing herself for an unhappy topic. "Those young ones are truly worth your effort? I know about Cam Folde. He's a Plasminian, but what of the others?"

Saira held in a sigh. They'd already discussed this topic on multiple occasions. "The others are equally special in their own ways."

"If you truly believe so, then find a way for them to come to us. They will be safer in my service."

Saira didn't immediately agree to do as her amma asked. Light Squad included several nobles, and while Card Wolver and Jade Mare might be convinced to leave Golden, what about Charity Kazar? She was the daughter of a Sage-Duke, bred to her own responsibilities, and if what Saira hoped might have finally happened—Charity gaining the courage to speak her heart to Cam—then his future would be inextricably linked to hers. Where Charity went, Cam would follow.

Unsurprisingly, her amma guessed the cause of her silence since few had her level of perception. "Was it wise to have encouraged Cam to pursue a relationship with Charity Kazar?"

"I don't know if he has."

"Not beyond a shadow of a doubt, but you believe it's likely."

Saira nodded. "I considered trying to save him for Dru or one of the younger nieces, but Charity…" She smiled. "You'd like her. Cam does, even if he doesn't fully realize why. They are good for one another."

This time, it was her amma who sighed, followed by a wry chuckle. "You always were a romantic."

Saira offered a faint grin. "And whose fault is that?"

Her amma's lips twitched into a smile, then she let loose a full-throated laugh. Saira watched in wistful amazement. Amma loved and laughed so easily.

"I suppose I can't blame your father, can I?" Amma asked.

Saira shook her head. As much as she loved her nanna, his was a mind devoted to philosophy with nary a romantic bone in his body. "If I can bring them both with me, I will. The rest will follow."

"So long as you come back, that's all I care about," Amma said. "The dangers of Golden, this foreign Realm, Hearth, and then a powerful rakshasa hiding within you…" She shook her head, appearing simultaneously fearful and angry.

Saira, however, shrugged in response, having made her peace with the situation. "I survived."

"You were lucky."

"I like to think I was in the right place at the right time."

Her amma scoffed. "You think nearly dying at the hands of some monster, this Jom-Strafe, was being in the right place at the right time? Or nearly being undone by some terrible rakshasa?"

Put that way, Amma's questioning was appropriate. Nevertheless, Saira didn't have any different answer to offer. "Like I said, I survived," she repeated.

"Through an Act of Devesh."

"It wasn't Devesh."

Her answer silenced her amma. They'd spoken about the events in the Temple of Gates, of the two beings who had rid her of Rabisu's infection. Had they truly been Rukh and Jessira? In the weeks and months since the events in that faraway Realm, Saira had yet to come up with a better answer.

Which meant it had to be them, and for whatever reason, they had a special bond with Cam. It had likely even been Rukh who had severed the connection that Shimala had somehow placed on the boy, and it had likely been Jessira who had pretended to be a squirrel who had helped him heal from his Plasminian-induced weakness. And then there were Professors Shade and Grey. Were they also Rukh and Jessira? Had they been watching over Cam this entire time, doing enough to keep him safe but allowing him to struggle and grow stronger, to become more competent and self-confident?

"You're thinking about Cam?"

Saira nodded. "Not just him. Also Rukh and Jessira. Their relationship with him." She and her amma had discussed this on previous occasions as well.

"What do you suppose it means?"

Saira wasn't sure. "I don't know," she said after a moment of deliberation. However, an idea occurred to her that had the flavor of truth. She grew excited by it, but not enough to disregard safety. With a wave of her hand, she created a bubble of silence, making it impossible for anyone to overhear their conversation or even visualize their features and read their lips. "Their behavior was what I'd expect from a parent with their child."

Her amma's gaze sharpened. "You speak dangerous words. Careful where you repeat them."

Saira nodded, not needing the warning. Even in the Sinanes, the Great Rakshasas had their servants.

"You think he's their son?" Amma asked.

Saira smiled. "Who can say? But it's another reason for me to go back and keep an eye on him."

Her amma nodded. "So you shall, but you won't be alone." She drew forth a *nomasra* from her *null pocket.* "With this, I can anchor line to wherever and whenever you might need me, even into Nexus itself."

Saira fingered the *nomasra.* "Hopefully, I'll never need it."

3

Avia chewed on a strip of jerky as she hustled to where her father waited for her. It was at their usual meeting spot, a gazebo centered in a large pond stocked with koi and shaded by weeping willows, grassy reeds, and cattails. Some flowers, too, but Avia didn't have the inclination or patience to learn their names. Besides which, if she really needed to know, she could just ask a gardener.

She reached the pond, pausing to gather her breath and breathe in its beauty. While her heart longed for the ocean's expansive glory, any kind of water would do, and had she been alone, she would have slipped off her clothes and swum among the fishes—of which she wasn't one, no matter what her friends in Light Squad liked to say.

But she couldn't linger. Her father, Sage-Duke Kelse Vail of Saban, awaited her at the gazebo, arms folded behind his back and a welcoming smile on his face.

As Avia marched across the arching bridge leading to her father, she studied him. He was a Sage, but an old injury when he'd been a Crown had stunted his health. This meant that while he was still vigorous and hale, compared to the other Sage-Dukes, he was rather weak.

And maybe that should have mattered to Avia—would have when she'd swum the oceans as a predatory orca—but when she'd first arrived in the human world of land and stone, Sage-Duke Kelse had been kind to her, generous, understanding, and loving.

It hadn't taken long for Avia to call him father, and his nature continued to inspire her. As far as she was concerned, her father was the sort of person she wanted to mirror, including his cleverness, which he hid behind a facade of careless humor.

Still, it would have been far finer if her father had all his good qualities and also been stronger. In that regard, he would have been more similar to her mother, the matriarch of their pod. A brighter notion occurred to Avia, and she smiled. How much better would it have been if her father had been like Professors Shade and Grey?

She shivered thinking about those two, grinning now. Their power was delicious.

Her father chuckled. "And which heroes have you smiling this time?"

Avia's humor fell. "How did you know?"

Her father smiled, taking her hands in his. "Call it a father's intuition, and my intuition tells me that you plan on resuming your studies at the Ephemeral Academy. Am I wrong?"

Avia shook her head. "Light Squad has returned."

Her father grunted. "So they have. But are you sure it's wise to renew your attachment to them?" Left unsaid was that her father believed that while her friends didn't necessarily put her in danger, Karma had her hungry eyes set upon Light Squad, and those who accompanied them carried the same risk.

It was also a notion about which Avia wasn't overly concerned. She and her friends had survived many terrifying circumstances, but they'd also thrived. According to rumors, Hearth had been no different for Light Squad. They had Advanced to Adept, all of them at Crystal with their Tangs.

Avia was at the same level of Advancement and the same degree of Enhancement, although for her, it hadn't been easy. Far from it. She'd returned from Hearth as an Adept with all her Tangs at Silver, and everyone would have told her that Enhancing her Primary to Crystal would have been the best she could hope to accomplish, but they would have been wrong.

In this particular circumstance, Avia had been fortunate. Adept was the last Stage of Awareness where she could still relatively easily Enhance all of her Tangs beyond Primary to Crystal, and she'd managed the achievement. Although, it would have been far easier if Cam had been around. All of Cam's guidance from when they'd been Novices had been invaluable.

Avia nodded to herself, recognizing how much she owed Cam, how much she owed Light Squad. And beyond just her unpaid debts, the true reason she wanted to rejoin Light Squad was because she missed her friends. Despite being the daughter of a Sage-Duke and having a physical form others found pleasing, in the end Avia was still an Awakened Beast. No one let her forget it in Saban, and the only ones who hadn't cared had been Light Squad.

Besides which, on a more practical note, who could help her Advance and Enhance better than Light Squad?

"You need to be careful," her father said, drawing her out of her musings. "I don't know which Sage-Dukes I can trust. They might seek to harm you at the Academy."

Avia scowled, having an immediate answer. "You shouldn't trust Merit's mother."

"I don't."

"And the Sage-Dukes and Sage-Duchesses who supported her? Can you trust them?" It was a long-simmering argument, and while Avia preferred the direct approach, she also recognized that when it came to politics, a straightforward charge wasn't generally the best option. Of course, it generally wasn't the best option in a battle, either. Professors Grey and Shade had drilled that fact into her head, over and over again.

Her father sighed. "Our era isn't like the one several thousand years ago when the Sages of the day united and several of them Ascended to Divines. That was the last time the rakshasas nearly overran Golden."

"Where *are* the Divines?" It was a question Avia had often pondered. If Divines were as powerful as legend stated, then why had they abandoned their responsibilities?

"I don't know," her father said with a shrug. "We haven't heard from them in hundreds of years. Some believe they're disappointed with our lack of Ascension or that we're unworthy of their attention."

Avia scoffed. "How well any of us do at Advancing on the Way into Divinity shouldn't matter. We are their responsibility. They should help us, especially if things are as bad as you say."

Her father heaved a tired-sounding exhalation. "None of that matters now. Just remember what I taught you. You have it in you to eventually Advance to Crown or more. Do as you have been instructed, and you'll be fine."

It wasn't really a proper response to Avia's claim, but she knew when to drop a matter. Her father was kind, but he didn't think like an orca. Given the sea's viciousness, her people couldn't afford to coddle their young, but they did their utmost to defend them.

"Spend time with your friends," her father continued, "but Advance quickly and return home."

Avia didn't voice agreement. Her father meant well, but she couldn't live her life cowering behind his shield, not with the dangers facing the world. "I'll Advance to Glory, like we talked about, but I need to stay and protect my friends. Weld Plain is supposed to be an instructor this year at the Academy."

Her father's gaze sharpened. "Don't do anything foolish."

"I won't. But I also won't leave my friends unprotected from that unholy jackhole."

"Weld Plain has powerful allies," her father continued to caution, his tone hard. "Avoid him. Do nothing to antagonize him."

There it was: the slimy entrails of politics. The wisdom of her father's advice was obvious, but Avia couldn't find it in herself to follow through with what he had in mind. "No," she replied, her tone as equally unyielding as her father's. "I won't swim like a seal afraid of its own shadow if Weld comes after me." She offered a grin of sharp orca teeth, which she planned on keeping when she Advanced to Glory "If he does, I'll break him." A second later, she shrugged, affecting a less confrontational posture. "Besides, I have words to say to that man. He did something to allow Nailing and Nageena to nearly kill me and my friends. I won't let that go."

Her father grunted, not bothering to agree since he suspected the same. But he was also limited in what he could do because of the lack of evidence.

Avia scoffed at the idea of evidence in the human world. In the ocean and amongst her pod, evidence was obtained in blood.

Only minutes before, Card Wolver had arrived on the platform where Sages were able to open an anchor line into Nexus. But prior to striding off toward the Ephemeral Academy, he had halted his progress and gazed upon the sight in front of him. The city's glistening white buildings and indigo-tiled roofs reflected the late-day summer sun while white clouds as large as palaces paraded across a serene sky that reflected the blue hue of the lake. A breeze, drenched in humidity and lush with the scents of the city's wonderful street foods—chana masala, vada pav, and aloo tiki chaat—carried to him.

Maviro, where Card had spent much of the last few weeks since returning to Golden, was a fine enough city, but its menu of culinary options—beyond the wonderful tzatziki sauce and gyros—was somewhat lacking.

Another inhalation, and a new flavor wafted Card's way, and he inhaled deeply, appreciating a different aroma, that of wood-fired pizza. He'd tried it once and found it to his liking. He'd try it again.

Card smiled inwardly then, thinking on what an epicurean snob he had become over the years. In this, perhaps he was truly his mother's son. She refused to eat anything but the finest of foods.

The reminder of his mother tugged Card's lips into a frown. Once again and just like last time, due to his steadfast refusal to resign from

Light Squad, his mother had evicted him from the family home. An unsurprising action. By now, Card had given over any notion that his mother might have any sort of maternal bonds of affection for him—or any of her children, for that matter. She was a selfish bitch and likely always would be.

But in spite of his homelessness and lack of motherly caring, Card hadn't been bereft of options. He'd reached out to Sage-Duke Ahktav Kazar, Charity's father, and had spent the past few weeks with an acquaintance in Maviro until the time had come to return home to the Academy.

Card smiled, considering the word that had just flickered through his thoughts: home. It was true. For him, the Ephemeral Academy was as close to a home as any place that might exist. His time at the school had been where he'd experienced his greatest growth as a person, where he'd incorporated those learnings, and where he'd discovered what he wanted out of life. The Academy was the place where he felt his greatest peace, and now he was going back. He was going home.

Happy with his understanding, Card descended the platform and set off toward the Academy, noting the city's harbor and briefly pausing when his eyes alighted upon the towering statues of Rukh and Jessira out in the bay. Resting atop a pair of islands that served as plinths, they had been cast of alabaster marble and rose hundreds of feet into the blue sky: a man in an achkan and a pair of pants and a woman wearing a pleated sari. Both of them wore gentle smiles and had an arm extended across the water.

Staring at the statues, Card's memory was cast back to Hearth. Had he truly heard the voices of the Holy Servants there? Had it been real? It had certainly felt that way, and at one point, Card might have figured that his life's journey had been completed on that strange day of blood, toil, and death. After all, he had experienced the touch of the Holy Servants. What else was there to life?

Or perhaps his journey was just beginning. Was it not said that the Holy Servants asked a single devotion of their disciples: to serve in whatever capacity was best suited for them? If so, could Card claim to have truly and fully served in such a capacity? Did he not have much more to offer the world?

Card's thoughts lingered on his future expectations of himself as he made his way through the city's bustle and commotion, halting again when he came upon the park where Light Squad had been exiled into the Realm of Hearth. In the view of a fresh day, it was a fine enough green space, but in truth, it struck Card as a place of surpassing mediocrity. Nevertheless, there was an actual import to the park. This was where two Glories had defeated a pair of Sages. Had Cinder Shade and Eveangel Grey actually been Rukh and Jessira in disguise?

It seemed as likely an explanation as any, possibly a *more* likely explanation that hadn't initially occurred to Card. But after that hectic and deadly battle against the Jom-Strafe Crown, the awakening of Thor, and the final defeat of that terrible fiend, Rabisu, the truth had become obvious and evident.

If those whispering voices in the Temple of Gates had belonged to Rukh and Jessira, then couldn't Cinder Shade and Eveangel Grey be their avatars as well? True, the timbre of their voices had been different, but their phrasing, their manner of speech, and their specific intonation… those had been the same. Card simply hadn't noticed it until he'd fully rested and recovered here in Salvation.

But once he had, it told him something else equally important: the Holy Servants viewed Cam Folde in a particularly protective way. What that was, Card didn't know, and he didn't care to know. It wasn't necessarily information he needed to know, at least not now. All that currently mattered was that Card felt the calling to serve the man who the Holy Servants held in special esteem.

Thoughts on the Holy Servants and Cam, Card continued his journey to the Academy, striding swiftly since there was no reason to tarry, and passed through the front gates just as the sun lowered to setting. It was then that he slowed down. He had arrived. He was home, and he breathed deep, inhaling the scent of fresh-cut grass and flowers. The school was currently quiet, but it would come to life when the new students arrived. That would be soon enough, but what about the rest of Light Squad?

Cam and Pan had never left the Academy, and rumors in Maviro indicated that Charity had returned a few days prior, but what about the others? When would Jade come back? And would Avia rejoin their squad as well? Card hoped so. They were at their best when together.

Pondering these matters, it didn't surprise Card when his footsteps led him to Cam's quarters. He knocked on the door, and for once, it was Pan who answered. Card's favorite panda-person grinned in that adorable way of his, moving forward and offering a warm embrace before ushering Card inside.

Once within, Card frowned, staring about, even going so far as to poke his head into the bedrooms. "Where's Cam?"

Pan shocked Card by smirking. "He's with Charity For two people who insist that they find the other annoying, they sure spend a lot of time together."

"Charity never found Cam annoying. It was always the other way around," Card said, distracted and thrown off by the possibility of Cam and Charity together. Were they finally acting on their feelings for one another? It seemed unlikely. Those two were terrified of being hurt by the other, and it would probably take an Act of Devesh to get them to admit their feelings for one another.

"Regardless, that's where he is," Pan said. "And I must say, it's good to see you. There's so much to tell. You just missed Master Winder. He left a few hours ago."

"Master Winder? It seems there is much to tell. Did he talk to Cam?"

Pan wore a put-upon expression. "Cam was here, but then he left right afterward to be with Charity. They're inseparable."

Card's brows lifted. "Inseparable?" That was unexpected.

Pan nodded. "Inseparable." He continued to wear a long-suffering mien, but Card could see how deliriously happy the cute panda-person was for Cam and Charity.

The reaction had Card doing a double-take. "What exactly are they doing when they get together?"

Pan's put-upon expression became a delighted grin. "I imagine they kiss a lot."

Card didn't respond at once, closing his eyes and needing time to sort his thoughts. Cam and Charity *had* gotten together. He would have never imagined it. It was a good thing, though. He opened his eyes and smiled, happy for his friends but still needing a final confirmation. "You're sure about this? They kiss?"

"Yes! Cam admitted it."

Card laughed. "Why don't you start at the beginning then?"

4

After spending the afternoon with Charity, Cam had been delighted to find Card waiting for him in his quarters. They had some catching up to do, and they talked late into the evening. The truth was that while Card was the silent, gruff type, some might even call him a bit of a jackhole, he was actually a good sort. Cam liked the man, and given that several members of Light Squad had returned to the school, he decided they should meet at the cafeteria the next morning for breakfast. He had words.

Light Squad needed to get back into the grind, embrace the pain, so to speak. And as soon as breakfast was finished, Cam intended on having them do exactly that by heading over to the Kinesthia field for a few hours of hard training. Then would come a long lunch followed by more sparring—both armed and unarmed—before retiring to the library for studying. It was pretty much the same routine that Light Squad had followed during the school year, and if it had worked before, then why not now?

Cam and Pan were the first to arrive at the cafeteria, which was largely empty except for the staff who waited behind the single buffet line where breakfast was served. Upon loading their trays with a heaping pile of masala dosas, a couple of bowls of sambar poured over idlis, and a generous helping of upma, the two of them got themselves sorted at a table.

"I hope the food is as delicious as it smells," Pan said, inhaling deep.

"I don't doubt it will be," Cam replied in a vague sort of way since the majority of his attention was fixed on the plates of food before him. Eating was serious business, and he bent low to tuck in.

Card showed up a few minutes later and was courteous enough to not bother them with useless talking. He simply began eating. *Good man.*

"You didn't wait for me," Charity said, marching up to their table and sounding aggrieved.

Cam glanced up from his food, not sure what had her upset. However, based on her expression, he figured he better figure it out right quick. He gave his food a longing look before pushing away from the table and standing to face Charity. "I didn't know I was supposed to wait for you," he replied, although thinking it through, he could see how he maybe should have.

Charity tsked, arms folded. "Rather thoughtless, wouldn't you say?"

Cam made a noncommittal noise, his mind on what other expectations he might be facing. Were there other rules of courting that he didn't yet know but would be expected to follow? And what happened if he messed up again out of ignorance? Would that be the end for him and Charity?

His questions and worries evaporated when Charity leaned forward and gave him a soft kiss that ended too soon. Cam was just about to pull her close when she leaned away from him. Only then did he notice her pleased smile and Pan's sniggering. Card, of course, didn't react. He continued to eat, never slowing and never looking up.

"You're officially forgiven," Charity said, still wearing a smug grin.

A less pleasant voice broke in before Cam could respond. "If you're handing out free kisses, I'd be right happy to accept." It was Weld Plain. He stood close at hand and wore a leering sneer. This was the person

Master Winder claimed was a changed man? He didn't sound like it. Nonetheless, Cam did his best not to grimace. He'd known this meeting would eventually have to happen, but he'd also done his best to avoid the other man, honestly hoping to never see Weld again.

"The kisses aren't free," Cam said to the man he loathed above just about anyone in all of Golden. "And you shouldn't ask for them, *Instructor.*"

Weld whistled. "Well, look at that. You using proper grammar. I remember when you might have said 'kisses ain't free.' I like that way of talk."

"I've grown."

"So have I." Weld's smile left him, and his Glory-Haunted blue sclerae flashed. A moment later, the sneer returned, this one mocking and triumphant. "What do you think?"

Cam's jaw briefly clenched, and he wanted to punch the expression off the jackhole's face. He struggled at keeping his hands from curling into fists.

Charity squeezed his shoulder, her touch helping soothe his anger. "Asking for a kiss is inappropriate," Charity said to Weld. "You're an instructor."

"I'm an instructor, that's true," Weld agreed. "But that don't mean I'm not a man first. I remember you giving me the stink eye and the rough side of your tongue more than once. What do you say now? I'm a Glory and two shakes from making it to Crown. Ain't I worth a kiss?" He puckered his lips.

Cam glowered at the repulsive jackhole, while Card and Pan had gone quiet, staring hard at Weld.

Charity, however, merely smirked. "You're right. You are a Glory, and I'm only an Adept, but one day, that will change. What won't change, though, is you. You'll still be the same person you've always been: a pathetic weakling."

Weld threw his head back and laughed. "I'm going to enjoy instructing you. You'll learn more than you can ever imagine at my feet." He grinned. "Now simmer down some while me and the menfolk have a discussion about what I expect from you lot this coming year. I'll be teaching Kinesthia, and y'all weren't all-too skilled with it the last I saw."

Cam corralled his anger. It wouldn't help him any. "You're only our instructor if we agree to it."

"Maybe so, but just remember to call me Professor Plain," Weld said, his grin never breaking. "You don't get to name me nothing else until you've Advanced to Glory." He shrugged dismissively. "Of course, by then I'll be a Crown. A Sage later on. Then you'll be calling me 'Master.'"

"I'll never call you 'Master,'" Pan growled.

Weld snorted in derision. "You'd best learn to keep that hairy mouth shut, little panda. I'm an instructor, and I might take it in mind to teach you some lessons whether you figure to learn from me or not."

The threat was clear, but Pan didn't wilt. Instead, he continued to glare at Weld, not backing down an inch.

"You sure you want this?" Weld whispered as the two of them stared hard at one another.

Cam cleared his throat, quickly intervening before Pan's pride landed him in a heap of trouble. His friend was skilled and powerful, but he couldn't go against a Glory. "You said your piece, but that doesn't explain what you want."

Weld gave Pan a final lingering stare before turning away. "Where's Jade? Charity might not want to kiss me, but Jade will. That filly will jump at the chance to ride this stallion."

Cam glowered. "You're a disgusting pig," he said, unable and not wanting to hold back the words.

Card finally joined the conversation, rising to his feet, and closing on Weld. He invaded the other man's space, looming over him. "Cam is right. You are a disgusting pig."

"And seeking intimacy with your students is a swift way to see you expelled from your teaching position," Charity added. She smiled mirthlessly. "Please try it. It'll be amusing watching you fail since Jade is a thousand-fold more worthy than a jackhole like you."

Weld clutched his chest, feigning fear and hurt. "A jackhole? Expulsion? How horrible." He snorted, and the sneer returned. "You lot are such prudes. And who said anything about having intimacy with Jade? I was just planning on fragging her."

The table quieted, all of them shocked, but Cam didn't give Weld what he knew the other man wanted: outrage. Instead, he laughed, carefree and contemptuous, right in Weld's face. "You try anything with her, and she'll kick your nuts through the top of your head."

Weld replied with another sneer, which was maybe the expression he knew best.

Cam offered a cheerless smile. "You're a Glory, and maybe you'll make it to Crown, but you won't always have a greater Awareness than the rest of us. We'll catch you, overcome you, too."

Weld scoffed. "Oh, really. How do you figure? I got a Plasminia Tang same as you."

"But do you know how to use it? Did you Enhance all your Tangs to Crystal when you Advanced to Glory?"

Weld's flush was all the answer Cam needed. *Idiot.* All those advantages freely given, and Weld had wasted them. The man was about as sharp as a round boulder.

Still, Weld tried to barrel through on bluster. "Plasminia got me what I needed."

"Are you sure?" Cam asked.

"Look at my eyes." Weld stepped closer. "When Master Winder learns of your disrespect, you'll be lucky if he maintains your sponsorship at the Academy. You remember saying something like that to me?"

Cam recalled. It was about what he'd told Weld right before the man had been expelled from Light Squad. The question and this entire conversation also didn't matter. He was done with Weld. "You do what you want. Light Squad ain't taking any classes with you. You betrayed us with Nailing and Nageena. We aren't forgetting that."

Weld gave a dismissive shrug. "That wasn't on me. I barely survived Nailing and Nageena myself."

"Except we were cast into a different Realm," Card said. "And somehow you got to stay safe here in Nexus. The rakshasa Sages never harmed a hair on your empty head."

"Call me lucky then, but it don't change the facts. Y'all are behind me now. You'll always be behind me." Weld smirked again. "And hate me all you want, but I *am* the instructor of Kinesthia. Classes start in a few weeks. I'll expect you there, and I take a hands-on approach in figuring your strengths and weaknesses, just like Cinder Shade." He grinned. "That man was good with a sword. It's a shame he died."

With a doff of an imaginary cap to Charity, Weld left them, and the table remained silent upon his departure.

Seconds later Pan spoke, and his words reflected what was on Cam's mind. "That man is a stinking pile of shit."

Charity chuckled. "He is that, but language, my sweet panda-person."

Pan offered a hesitant smile. "Was I not supposed to curse?"

Cam laughed. "Curse all you want if you're feeling the need."

"I never expected to say it," Card said, not glancing up as he went back to eating his dosas, "but I'll be happy when we leave the school."

"Same here," Cam agreed.

Weld gritted his teeth on thinking about the just-finished conversation with Light Squad, of how those stuck-up prigs had looked down at him—again. It made no sense. He was a Glory, and a powerful one to boot, while they were merely Adepts. And yet somehow, they still thought they were better than him?

Frag them. Let's see how they act when I become a Crown.

Weld snarled inwardly. In the end, he'd make all of them bend the knee to him. It was a promise he'd made when Cam Folde had forced him out of his oh-so-precious unit, tossing Weld aside like yesterday's garbage. No doubt, everyone had likely thought that would be the end of Weld's ride, figuring he'd head home and never look to raise his head ever again.

But life had a funny way of working out. Weld hadn't kept his head down. Instead, he'd found a new liege, been shown a greater path to power, and it hadn't cost him anything more than a couple of worthless birds his father had kept as pets. Weld smiled at the memory. If that's what was needed to get what he deserved, then he would prove traitor to anyone who tried to hold him down. A prize was owed, and no one—not Devesh, the Holy Servants, or even the Empty One—would prevent him from receiving it. He was owed, and he intended on having it all.

Thinking on his bright and optimistic future had Weld feeling a mite better as he strode through the cafeteria, especially when he imagined how the so-called good Ephemeral Masters in Light Squad would pay for how they'd done him wrong. Revenge would be his, including on Jade, who had dared to think him unworthy of her company.

Weld snorted in derision. Jade would have been lucky to have a man like him, but instead, look what she'd done. She'd sided with Cam and his band of pricks. Well, she'd made her bed and when it was over, Weld planned on uglying her some so no man or woman would ever look on her kindly again. Same with Cam, but for him, Weld had a special punishment. The man had a meeting with fate that he'd never see coming. All it would take was cunning, planning, and quiet patience. Weld smiled, thinking on Cam's future. The jackhole wouldn't know what hit him.

But to ensure the arrogant prick's ignorance was why Weld bothered listening in even after he left Light Squad's table. Just a simple twist of Ephemera brought Card's words to him, as crystal clear as if he'd been standing next to the stupid noble.

They were leaving the Ephemera Academy, were they? Not a bad idea. And if the shoe had been on the other foot, Weld would have done the same.

But where were they going?

Seconds later, Weld smiled, easily reckoning the answer. Master Winder's newly discovered area that was heavy with Ephemera, the fallen temple to some Divine. Weld's liege had a spy in Sidewinder

Company. The rakshasas knew all about it. It was only too bad none of the brothers or sisters were in a position to steal it away from Sage-Duke Kazar.

But that didn't matter to Weld. Journeying to the temple might be the perfect way to ambush Light Squad, and if Saira showed, even better. Rumor had it she was a Crown again, but Weld's liege was a Sage. He could do her in.

Weld nodded to himself. He'd reach out to his liege and let him know what he'd learned. As he continued to muse over the matter, he grew ever more certain about the plan he'd concocted. Yes, this would work out quite well. His liege would surely see matters the same way.

Whistling cheerfully, Weld exited the cafeteria, winking at a pretty Novice heading inside and making her giggle. He continued to smile, nodding to those who caught his eye, pretending like he actually cared about the imbeciles. His feigned good cheer lasted until he reached his quarters. There, Weld reached into his chest of drawers and withdrew a simple globe.

Activating the *nomasra* with a touch, he spoke to his liege.

Following the unpleasantness with Weld, the rest of the day passed by well enough. Cam tried to keep himself and the others busy with training and studying, but late at night, he found himself alone in the library. Even Pan had retired for the evening, having headed home several minutes earlier.

But Cam had remained. There had been a book he'd finally found, one Professor Shade had mentioned last year. *The Warrior and the Servant,* a slim volume, and upon an initial perusal, it seemed to merely be a set of aphorisms dedicated to how a warrior should properly live their life. But the word at the title's end—Servant—had Cam intrigued. He thumbed through the book, wondering if Rukh and Jessira—the Holy Servants—might have written it.

His thoughts remained distracted as he walked the pathways of the Ephemeral Academy. Insects rustled, and a full moon lit his way, casting silvery light through a net of lacy clouds. The heavy summer weather draped unmoving across the land like a wet rag, and although Cam sweated, he largely disregarded the mild discomfort inspired by the humidity, even if he might often and loudly complain about it. As an Adept, it would take more than muggy weather to have him feeling too much on the wrong side of good.

He continued to read the book, able to see due to his Adept-Enhanced senses.

But a deep voice drew him out of his reveries as he neared the dorm hall. "Cam Folde."

Cam glanced around, quickly sighting Sial Shivein pacing toward him, and he waved acknowledgement, surprised anew at the near-human appearance of his one-time professor. Only Sial's height and bee-tled brow remained of his previous build.

"I haven't seen you in a while," Cam said when the Awakened turtle arrived. "Where have you been?"

"Master Winder has me working." Sial grunted. "No rest for a Glory, I suppose."

"What does he have you doing?"

Sial scowled. "Nothing enjoyable, but I do whatever he asks. I owe him too much to say no." He added a chiding note. "So do you and the rest of Light Squad."

Cam held off from glowering. Being told that he owed something to Master Winder wasn't true, and no one could tell him otherwise. Nevertheless, because he'd come to think of Sial as—not exactly a friend but at least a warm acquaintance—he disregarded the admon-ishment and his resulting annoyance. "What kind of work?"

"Lancing a boil. What else?"

"That's dangerous work," Cam replied, not sure what else to say. In truth, he wanted to ask why Sial was bothering with lancing boils under Master Winder's direction. Yes, the work was necessary and im-portant, but Sial had to have concerns about the Wilde Sage's methods.

"It is dangerous, but we've succeeded so far without any losses.

Even better, I was allowed to keep the last core he lanced. It's Adept-Staged, but a few more of those, and I should have enough Ephemera to Advance to Crown."

Cam's brows lifted at the surprising news. He hadn't realized Sial was so close to Advancing. "You feel the difference between certainty and doubt?"

Sial appeared puzzled. "Feel the difference?" A moment later, his confusion cleared. "I can see why you would say it like that, but no, I don't feel the difference. Not yet, but I'm close. It's different than the last time I was a Glory." He gave a grave nod. "Having your Plasminia Tang has made me so much surer about what I can accomplish. Thank you."

Cam shrugged off the compliment. "I only showed you how to use Plasminia. Everything else is your own work."

Sial chuckled. "Humility usually serves you well, but not in this instance. Accept my praise. Because of what I've accomplished, Master Winder is having many other Ephemeral Masters descend to Adept in order to gain a Plasminia Tang. It's already making a phenomenal difference in how far we can see ourselves progressing."

This, too, was surprise. From what Cam knew, the skill required to help an Ephemeral Master gain a Plasminia Tang was greater than any Crown possessed, and for whatever reason, Cam figured the same applied to Sages. Apparently not if Master Winder was helping his Ephemeral Masters gain them. Still, how had the Wilde Sage learned what Cam had thought only Professor Grey had known?

"Your confusion is understandable," Sial said. "Master Winder said that Professors Grey and Shade had many discussions with him prior to your disappearance to Hearth. How to create a Plasminia Tang was a focus of their conversations."

Again, it was information Cam hadn't known. He hadn't realized the professors had been teaching Master Winder.

With a start, he realized that a pair of Glories had been instructing a Sage. It sounded ludicrous, but then again, they really weren't just simple Glories, were they? Cam shook off his considerings, returning to what Sial had said earlier. "How is having a Plasminia Tang helping you and the others Advance?"

"With our other Tangs Enhanced, we're all much more powerful than we were prior. It gives us confidence and inspires us to try for more on the Way into Divinity. Confidence is often the difference between success and failure."

Cam smiled, gratified by Sial's words. Many people had been helped by what he had learned and shared, and through their work, many people could then be saved from the depredations of the rakshasas. It meant that his life had a brighter meaning and purpose than he'd ever expected, and the awareness caused that hidden ghost that told him he was just a no-good Folde to die a tiny bit more.

There was a question that remained, however. "If you're close to Advancing, why not go to the thickened area of Ephemera that Master Winder discovered?"

Sial nodded. "I know of the temple, and I'll go there when I'm sure to Advance." He shrugged. "Confidence is a large part of the Way into Divinity. I've had too many doubts before. I need to be as certain as possible if I want to succeed."

"Are you sure?"

"I'm sure."

Cam hid a frown of disappointment. The other man had trained Cam's unit, fought and bled alongside them, and having him with them at the temple would have felt right. Nonetheless, if that's how Sial felt, then so be it. Cam shifted the conversation. "What's it like? The temple."

"I've never been there, but Master Winder says it was originally commemorated to Devesh or a Divine, maybe Rukh and Jessira or William and Serena. Regardless, it's ancient. All that's left are a couple of columns." Concern lit his features. "It's not the easiest place to reach. The journey is arduous. It's best if you have a Crown to smooth the way. Rakshasas are known to frequent the nearby hills."

"We'll have Saira," Cam said, infusing his voice with certainty. He'd yet to hear from her, but she had promised to come back to the

Ephemeral Academy and guide them in their Advancement.

"Then you're a lucky man. Saira Maharani was a skilled Crown during her first life at that Stage. I can only guess at her abilities now."

"She'll be as powerful as a weak Sage," Cam replied.

"I suppose so," Sial mused, stroking his chin. A moment later, he smiled, clapping Cam on the shoulder. "Stay safe and safe travels. When Saira returns, you should ask for her help in retrieving Jade. I've heard that Sage-Duchess Salin isn't being cooperative."

Cam nodded. It was good to know. As Sial moved off, Cam called out to him. "You really should come with us." With everything Sial had done for them, it only felt right to make the offer again. "We have a new way of Enhancing that's faster than anything we've done before. We learned it in Hearth. Same with how we Advance. We can teach you on the way to the temple."

Sial grunted. "If Master Winder allows, perhaps I will." With that, he strode off, quickly lost in the dark.

5

The conversation with Sial lingered on Cam's mind throughout the next day, and his pondering eventually led him to thinking about the rest of Light Squad. They weren't back yet, and while it would be another couple of weeks before the matriculating students arrived at the Ephemeral Academy, he hoped it would be far less time for Jade, Saira, and Avia. He really wanted to get gone from the school, and that longing had him perseverating over the matter, even after he and Pan returned from lunch.

They were seated at their dining table, notes spread out before them and supposedly studying, but Cam couldn't get his mind off the missing members of Light Squad. He sighed, not realizing how heavy until Pan glanced up from his reading.

"What's wrong?" Pan asked, taking a mighty munch of his bamboo. "If you scowl any harder, I might be able to see your skull."

Cam blinked. He hadn't realized he was frowning so hard. "It's the others," he said after smoothing his expression. "I want them back. We need them. I don't want someone stealing the temple out from under us."

Pan chuckled. "Aren't you forgetting something?"

Cam considered the question, eventually shaking his head. "What do you mean?"

"Planning. We can't just leave the Academy without knowing what we need on the journey or even how to get to the temple."

Cam rolled his eyes. "Well if you're fixing on being pedantic, don't forget we also require the answer needed in order to Advance to Glory." His response had Pan grinning in that toothily cute way of his, and Cam had an idea as to why. "You're smiling because I used the word pedantic, aren't you? A large-coin word."

"And you're using those kinds of words more and more often every day."

Cam was interrupted from replying by a knock on the door. He glanced to Pan who stared back briefly before suddenly focusing again on his reading. "You aren't going to answer the door, are you?" Cam asked.

Pan shook his head. "I would, but I know how much you like to do it."

"I don't like answering the door," Cam said. "Not every time. And just as a matter of clarification, it wouldn't hurt you to stand up every now and then."

"Clarification is also a large-coin word."

Cam grumbled under his breath. On his way to the door, he poked Pan in his soft belly, eliciting an outraged squawk. He grinned, darting away before the panda could poke him back, and he was still smiling when he threw open the door. His expression transformed, first to shock and then delight. With a glad shout, he drew Saira into the room, hugging her close and spinning her about.

She laughed. "It's good to see you, too, Cam. Now put me down."

As soon as he did, though, Pan was the one hugging Saira off her feet, the three of them laughing.

"We missed you," Pan said.

"I can tell," Saira replied. "And I missed you, too."

Cam took a moment to study Saira. It had been over a month since he'd last seen her, and she looked well, at peace like he'd never seen her before. Her indigo-Haunted sclerae were bright and alive, and the constant strain and worry he'd grown used to finding on her features were no longer evident. He wondered what had changed. Was it her time in the Sinanes? Being around family? Or was it because she'd Advanced to Crown and been healed in ways he couldn't know? Or perhaps it was a combination of those things.

That seemed the most likely reason, but whatever the case, Cam was glad for her, and he said so.

Saira smiled. "Being home was a balm to my soul, something I'd needed for so long and never recognized."

Her words had Cam thinking about his own family, of how long it had been since he'd seen them. His happiness at seeing Saira dimmed some, but an instant later, he shook off his homesickness. Now wasn't the time for melancholy. "How long will you staying?"

"For as long as is necessary," Saira said, moving to join Pan where he'd already resettled himself at the dining table. "What are your plans for the future?"

Cam took a seat next to her, going on to explain his and Pan's meeting with Master Winder and the offer of this new place of Ephemeral concentration. "It's supposed to be a temple to a Divine, something from Maviro's history, but it's nothing but ruins now. All that's left are a few columns."

Saira frowned. "Rainen mentioned it to me when he was in the Sinanes. I'm surprised he told you, though. Not after you left his sponsorship."

Cam didn't miss her doubtful expression, and her reaction had him concerned. "You sound skeptical. Why?"

"Because this information came from Rainen. What's in it for him? Why not have his own people go there and Advance?"

"He said none of them were ready," Pan answered.

Saira shrugged, indicating her lack of reliance on such a likelihood. "I suppose it's possible, but he could have also waited until they obtained the required answer."

This time it was Cam who frowned. There had once been a time when Saira and Master Winder had been close, and while Cam knew she'd grown to doubt the Wilde Sage, he hadn't realized their rift had grown so wide. "You don't trust him?"

"I don't trust anyone from Golden. My time with Thor and at home reminded me of why I came to this continent in the first place. It was to grow powerful so I can serve others, not to serve myself. The Sages here don't believe the same as I do. I doubt many of them ever did."

Cam viewed her in surprise. Her statements reflected his own thoughts about the Sages of Golden. "So what happens next? You think we're better off going with you to Sinanes?"

"Undoubtedly. If nothing else, you'd be safer." She tossed him a wry grin. "And don't think I haven't noticed that you've yet to mention Charity. How is she?" Cam reddened, earning a tinkling laugh from Saira. "I'm sure my sister and several of my nieces will be disappointed."

"We've only kissed a few times," Cam said, embarrassed that Saira knew about him and Charity and unsure why.

"Kissed her a few times." Saira tsked, still smiling in an all-too-knowing fashion. "How scandalous. I'll have to have a conversation with that young woman."

Cam's embarrassment only increased, and he flustered about, searching for anything to change the conversation. Desperate, he withdrew the oval *nomasra* given to him and Pan by the Wilde Sage. "Master Winder gave this to us so we can communicate with him. Do you think we should use it?"

Saira's smile faded, and she lifted the *nomasra* from his hand. "I think not." Her indigo-Haunted eyes brightened, and a line of Ephemera flashed from her hand and into the pendant. With a satisfied nod, she handed the *nomasra* back to Cam. "It's linked to me and my mother now. Since I'm coming with you, there isn't anyone I would trust more than the two of us to see you safe."

"You're coming with us?" Pan asked, his hopeful tone a mirror to Cam's own feelings.

"Of course," Saira answered Pan, directing a warm smile toward him. "When do you plan on leaving?"

Cam grimaced. In truth, he wanted to be gone tomorrow, but Avia and Jade weren't back yet. "The sooner the better."

"What's holding you back?"

Cam explained. "And Sial said Jade might not have an easy way back to the Academy. Sage-Duchess Salin isn't being very helpful."

Saira pondered his words a moment before giving a sharp nod. "Leave it to me. I'll talk to the Sage-Duchess and Jade. I'll even scout the region around the temple and confirm Rainen's claims."

Cam stood, confused. The scouting he could figure—after all, Saira could fly—but how did she plan on getting in contact with Jade?

Saira tapped the side of her head, offering a chiding smile. "Telepathy through Spirairia."

Cam shook his head, abashed. He should have realized.

"We should practice more," Pan sent to him, sounding as abashed as Cam was feeling.

"I know, but with everything else, I just kind of forgot," Cam replied.

Saira laughed at their reactions. "Don't forget your skills. The flashy ones of throwing fire and lightning may seem grand, but it's the seemingly little ones—empathy, telepathy, healing, and creation—that make the world a better place."

"And practice balance, control, and focus," Cam added. "Balance leads to control. Control leads to focus which allows for better balance." He recited the teachings from Professors Shade and Grey.

"Exactly so," Saira said with a smile and a nod. "I'll have Jade back at the Academy by tomorrow morning. Sage-Duchess Salin owes me a favor. I'm sure she'll be happy to anchor line Jade back to the school. I'll also talk to Avia's father. Light Squad will be reunited soon enough."

The last bit of Cam's worry eased off, and he settled back on his heels with a satisfied smile. "That would be excellent."

Jade relaxed in her auntie's garden, luxuriating in the last of the day's sunshine while also enjoying the fresh fragrance of honeysuckle that permeated the air. The world without was a distant hum, shut away as it was by the high brick wall that perimetered the grounds. A hummingbird flitted from one flower to the next while a pair of butterflies danced amongst the limbs of the tall red maple that shaded the garden.

This was a lovely spot, and a lovely time of day to spend alone, and Jade closed her eyes, appreciating the space even though it was elsewhere that she wished to be. She imagined herself back at the Ephemeral Academy with Cam, Pan, and those she loved. Had it been her decision, she would have never left.

But it hadn't been, and it wouldn't be until Jade achieved the Awareness of a Glory or left Sage-Duchess Salin's sponsorship.

Either would do as far as Jade was concerned. She wanted her freedom and was tired of being trapped here. She hated how the Sage-Duchess had immediately anchor lined to Nexus and brought Jade back to Bastion. And it hadn't been due to benevolence either. It had been because Sage-Duchess Salin had been desperate to learn before anyone else what had happened to Light Squad.

Weeks of debriefing had followed in which Jade had gone over the events in Hearth in excruciating detail, only keeping private the information about Rabisu and the Presences who had interceded on Cam's behalf against the Rakshasa of Dissolution. While Jade was a born gossip, in this one situation, she had held her friends' secrets tight, honoring their privacy. Just as importantly, the events themselves made little sense to her. Had the voices truly been those of Rukh and Jessira like the rest of Light Squad believed? And did they truly have a special love for Cam? If they did, then the world would never again be the same.

Jade shivered as an exciting possibility occurred to her. What if Cam was their long-lost son? It was improbable, but so what? Just imagine if it was true. Jade grinned over the possibility, thrilled. Over time—brief seconds—her smile slipped away. Cam's past, whatever it might or might not be, didn't matter in Jade's smaller view of the world. For her, it was enough that the two of them were friends. By now, Cam had earned her love and loyalty many times over. In fact, everything good that Jade had ever achieved as an Ephemeral Master was because of

Cam and the rest of Light Squad. They were her brothers and sisters, her family.

Which made it all the more maddening that Jade had been brought back to Bastion. She missed Light Squad, and rather than being with them, she was stuck here, ordered back to this city by a Sage-Duchess who didn't actually care for Jade in the slightest. Only those with wealth or power—preferably both—captured the Sage-Duchess' affection, and since the death of Jade's father—it still felt wrong for him to be gone from this world—she had neither.

Even worse was this home where Jade had been forced to stay: Auntie Balaria's house. It didn't matter that the luxurious mansion had been purchased by Jade's father on behalf of his only sister and sibling or that he'd maintained it for years. He'd only ceased paying for the upkeep once Jade's uncle—Auntie Balaria's husband—had matured his tailoring shop into a thriving success.

But none of the years of care from Jade's father seemed to matter to Aunt Balaria. Selfishness and lack of gratitude ran deep in the woman's veins, ugly attributes made obvious by her regular queries about how long Jade would be staying in her home.

The truth was, Aunt Balaria viewed her niece as little more than a beggar and certainly not a beloved member of her family.

A howling from high above diverted Jade's attention, and she started, rising to her feet as she set her sight on the sky. A figure flew overhead, and Jade formed a True Bond to bring the person to greater clarity. She immediately grinned in joy and relief.

Saira. She'd come for her.

Jade continued to grin at her friend's unexpected and welcome appearance, and she stepped forward, prepared to greet the other woman even as Saira descended.

The back door opened, and out hustled her auntie and her two daughters, both of whom luckily took after their father in terms of their demeanor. Neither Alasha nor Polrin had their mother's sense of entitlement or her unwarranted arrogance toward anyone she considered a lesser.

"Who is it?" Polrin asked.

"*It* is a she, and she is a Crown," Auntie Balaria said, her tone waspish and urging. "Be on your best behavior."

Alasha scoffed. "You actually think we might have a chance at marrying her?"

Jade disregarded her family's irritating argument and kept her attention focused on Saira, who smoothly alighted close at hand. "Anyone tell you that you've got the silliest frown when you're flying?" Jade asked with a grin.

"Jade!" her auntie said, scandalized. "Show some manners."

Jade glanced back at her auntie and tried not to roll her eyes. "My manners are fine. This is Saira Maharani, the eldest daughter of Lysha Maharani, the Sage of the Sinanes. She's my *friend.*" She emphasized the last.

"Saira Maharani?" Auntie Balaria hastily smoothed invisible wrinkles from the pleats of her sari. "Then by all means, please introduce us."

This time, Jade did roll her eyes. As much as Auntie Balaria sneered at those of modest means, she was an utter sycophant when it came to those who had more, just like Sage-Duchess Salin.

Saira overlooked it all, chuckling warmly. "My mother might have mentioned my silly frown a time or two," she said in reply to Jade's comment about her expression while flying.

"She sounds like a very perceptive woman," Jade replied.

"More than you'd know," Saira said, her voice impeccably measured and collected, much like the woman herself. "It is good to see you."

"It's even better seeing you," Jade said, embracing Saira. When she pulled back, she made to ask why Saira had come to Bastion, but a clearing of a throat from behind them returned Jade's attention to her family. With a hidden grimace, she made introductions.

"It is good to meet the three of you," Saira said, "but do you mind if I speak to Jade in private?"

There was nothing her auntie could do but acquiesce to Saira's request, and she and her daughters departed indoors.

"This is a lovely garden," Saira said, glancing about in a slow circle, beautiful, elegant, and composed as always.

Beautiful, elegant, and composed. Those were excellent words by which to describe Saira Maharani, and the observation had Jade inwardly chuckling. And Cam had hoped to win this woman's heart? What a fool. He might as well have hoped to lasso the sun. No one Jade had ever met could measure up to Saira. No one except for Professor Grey, but she didn't count. She was of a standard beyond compare.

"It is lovely," Saira said with a firm nod, "but I also sense you're ready to be gone from this place."

Jade tamped down a sudden surge of hope. Was Saira here to free her from this prison of flowers? *Please Devesh, let it be so.*

Her prayer was answered with Saira's next statement. "Before coming here, I spoke to Sage-Duchess Salin. She is willing to anchor line you back to the Ephemeral Academy."

Jade clapped her hands in excitement. "When?"

Saira smiled. "Very soon. Just be ready. Charity and Card are already there."

"Wait here." Jade dashed into the house, off to pack all her belongings as quickly as possible.

The rest of the afternoon following Saira's short visit and the day after, Cam made sure Light Squad continued to focus on their training and sparring—weapons only and no Ephemera. Then came a period of practicing with telepathy and telekinesis, a long lunch break, and then the afternoon spent trying to bring their skills together as one. The last was actually their slowest and easiest session since going hard would only lead to mistakes and injuries.

Cam planned on having them go at speed later on, but for now, it was best to get their bodies and minds used to the proper movements.

Afterward, the four of them had a quick dinner, got in some studying in the library, and retired to Cam's and Pan's muggy quarters.

Charity grimaced upon entering. "It's so hot in here."

Card grunted agreement. "I prefer heat, but even this is too much."

Cam silently agreed, and he threw open the windows, hoping to air out the room that felt like a sauna. Of course, he wasn't sure what good it would actually do since the rest of the Academy was just as humid as their quarters. Sure enough, no breeze stirred the curtains, and the room showed no signs of relaxing from its sweltering feel.

With a mournful sigh over the mugginess and summer's stubborn refusal to relent, Cam got situated on the couch next to Charity while Card went to the dining table and Pan seated himself on the floor, munching on a stalk of bamboo. But rather than study, they ended up swapping stories from their childhoods.

"Then we dusted this rooster with flour and set him loose in town," Cam said, smiling in fond remembrance. "Maria and her friends shrieked, ran all over town, yelling about a killer ghost rooster."

"This is the Maria with whom you were infatuated for most of your life?" Card asked, a judging tone to his voice. "Scaring her doesn't sound like the most intelligent way to gain her interest."

"Charity would have appreciated it," Cam said, hoping he was right. He wasn't.

Charity shook her head, wearing a pained yet patient expression, as she patted his cheek in sympathy. "Please disabuse yourself of that notion straightaway."

A knock on the door thankfully interrupted whatever Cam might have been expected to say, and he went to see who it was.

For the second time in several days, he laughed in delight, hugged a woman close, and spun her about. This time it was Avia, and before he had a chance to set her down, she was crowded by the others who greeted her with similar joy.

They babbled at her, shooting questions too rapid-fire for Avia to answer. Cam got it sorted out by whistling sharply. "Settle down. She ain't running away from us. Give the fish a chance to breathe."

Avia pointed to herself and smiled. "I missed that. And I'm not a fish."

"No you're not," Cam agreed. "You're the fiercest fighter I know." It was only then that he noticed her eyes. "And you're also a Glory." The observation threatened to spill the others into asking dozens more questions, but Cam got them quieted, asking Avia to give them all the details from when they'd last seen her.

Avia shrugged. "There's not much to tell. I left the Academy as soon as I got back. After what happened with Nailing and Nageena, I didn't trust my safety here." She went on to explain about not wanting to Advance to Glory until she had all her Tangs at Crystal. "It was a lot harder to do it at Adept since I only had Kinesthia and Plasminia at Crystal during my time as Acolyte." She indicated Cam with a tilt of her chin. "And without the guidance of our illustrious leader here, I had to Enhance the rest of my Tangs to Crystal on my own, which went about as quick as a dolphin swimming with no flippers."

"Really?" Cam asked, perplexed. "My guidance was that helpful?"

His question quieted the room, and he glanced around. Everyone stared at him—not just in disbelief but like he was an idiot, even Pan. What had he said?

"You really are completely clueless," Charity said, giving him another sympathetic pat to the face, which had him jerking away. Before he could say anything, though, she made it all better by kissing the side of his mouth. "But your cluelessness is also part of your charm. We Enhanced best when you were around to instruct us."

Maybe so, but was it really that helpful? Cam hadn't recognized it at the time, but if the others felt the same way… Cam might have still commented, deferring the praise, but he caught Avia's eyes widen and lock on to him. Her nose twitched with excitement.

"What's going on?" she asked. "Did the world end and no one told me? Charity just kissed Cam, and he didn't react. At all."

Card grimaced. "The world ending might be better than what's actually going on. Those two are so utterly treacly. Too much affection, especially in private and even in public."

"Be quiet," Pan said to Card. "Not everyone is a grouch. I think it's sweet."

"It's something," Card muttered.

Avia clapped in approval, grinning happily. "I knew it. I knew it. I knew it. I just knew you two would make a great couple."

Cam eyed her in confusion. How could she have possibly figured on that since he hadn't known any such thing until just a few weeks ago? He glanced at Pan, wondering if he'd also known, and received a nod of confirmation. Even Card mumbled agreement. Apparently, everyone had known but him and Charity, whose shamefaced flush told the truth. She hadn't known either.

"I just thought it was harmless teasing," Charity muttered.

"Or maybe it was harmless teasing until we both realized it wasn't?" Cam suggested.

Charity narrowed her eyes, eventually shrugging. "Maybe so."

"Can we get back to catching up with Avia?" Card grumbled.

Cam chuckled. "Sure we can," he said, going on to give Avia a quick summation of what Light Squad had endured in Hearth, including at the end when Thor had killed the Jom-Strafe Crown, and the arrival of the two Presences, who had destroyed Rabisu. However, he left out much of the trauma and heartaches they'd endured, such as helping restore Nylara and gathering the thousands of dead. He didn't feel a need to ruin the celebratory mood.

"I missed so much," Avia said, her voice small. "All I did was work on Enhancing, met men and women who have no interest in romancing me as a person, and did whatever my father asked." She sighed, head dropping. "I wish I could have been with you."

"You did Advance to Glory," Cam reminded her, lifting her drooping chin. "And you'll get to Crown or higher. You'll even have all your Tangs at Crystal in just a few weeks, a couple months at the most." He grinned. "We have a better way for you to Enhance. It's something else we learned in Hearth."

Avia's eyes widened in conjecture. "I wonder why the professors didn't know about that method."

Cam knew the professors she meant. "Maybe they did, but it's something only Adepts and higher can do."

"That was my guess," Charity offered.

Pan and Card made similar comments.

"Whatever the reason, what's more important is that we survived Hearth," Cam said. "We became better Ephemeral Masters, and now we're home, and we have another chance to Advance." He went on to explain about the temple. "Saira is coming with us, and she's bringing Jade back tomorrow morning. Then we're off and out of here."

"You're leaving the Wilde Sage's service?" Avia asked, sounding surprised. "Even though he told you about this area of Ephemeral concentration?"

"Even then," Cam replied. "He's not the kind of Sage I want to be. I want to be like Thor."

"Like Thor?" Avia mused, staring off into the distance. "He must be someone extraordinary." An instant later, she refocused on the room, wearing a warm smile. "I'll come with you when you're ready to leave the Academy. Having an extra Glory is never a bad thing."

"Definitely not a bad thing," Charity agreed with a smile. "Even a Glory who's not a fish."

"You're right," Pan said. " I mean, Avia as an orca is fine, but if she was a fish, she would be even finer… or at least funnier. Funnier looking, that is."

Avia stared at him, appearing shocked. "That's impossible. Pan just made fun of me. He never used to do that."

"We're Light Squad," Cam said with a cheeky grin. "We do the impossible." Upon seeing Avia's look of confusion, he explained himself. "It's a phrase Jade coined from when we were in Hearth."

Once again, Avia wore a crestfallen expression. "I really missed so much."

Cam drew her into a hug. "You're here now."

6

The morning after Avia's return, Cam awoke well before dawn. He'd been unable to sleep very well given all the worries worming through his mind, and after tossing and turning for a while, he finally gave it up and wrenched himself out of bed, reckoning he might as well get some work done.

He spread a map out on the dining room table and spent the early morning hours prior to dawn studying the area near the temple that Master Winder was gifting to Light Squad. What was the best way to get there? What route should they take? The temple was in Maviro, and Cam traced the various roads leading to it, calculated the elevation changes and the ruggedness of the terrain. Eventually, he leaned away from the map, frowning in consideration. Based on his assessment, even with Charity's father anchor lining them as close as Master Winder said was possible, Cam reckoned it would still take them weeks of travel to get to the temple.

He rubbed his tired eyes, heaving a sigh. They'd need supplies for a rugged trek like that, but thankfully, Light Squad had the coin for it. Having two daughters of Sage-Dukes in their unit certainly would help with those kinds of costs.

Another sigh, and Cam rose to his feet, continuing to ponder what was needed as he tiptoed outside onto the balcony, quiet since Pan was still asleep. The world without remained dark and serene with only some crickets chirping as Cam stared into the lingering gloom, still sorting what Light Squad would need by order of importance.

In some ways, it all depended on Saira. Once she finished surveying the temple and returned to the Academy, they could figure on some final planning and packing before heading off.

The balcony door creaked open, and Cam flicked a glance over his shoulder. Pan had exited his bedroom and joined him on the balcony. "Did I wake you?" he asked the Awakened panda.

"I noticed the lights in the main room," Pan said, leaning his forearms on the railing. A second later, he exhaled heavily, features set in disappointment. "I hate this humidity. It doesn't bother me very much, but there's just something cloying about it that I can't stand."

"Isn't that something I should be saying? Not the cloying part since I'd never use a word like that. But the complaining about the humidity."

Pan grinned in his toothily cute way. "I thought I'd get it out first so you wouldn't have to, including the cloying part given your penchant for using larger words these days."

Cam laughed and gently clapped Pan's shoulder. A question occurred to him, though. "We never talked about our plans for what happens after we Advance to Glory."

Pan shrugged. "I hadn't thought about it." He cast a glance at Cam. "Do you have the answer."

Cam nodded. "I think I might. Or if I don't, I'm not far off. It's coming along, faster than I ever reckoned." He shrugged. "Who knew that constant danger could lead to Advancement?"

"It's the same for me and likely for the same reason: Hearth," Pan said. His eyes went distant, likely lost in thought about all they'd suffered in that Realm, all the times they'd almost died, the killing of people. His features cleared, but Cam could tell it took some effort. "It wasn't all terrible. We Advanced. We met a Sage who inspires us. Saira was rid of a rakshasa she didn't even know had infected her. And because of the hardships, I think we're all likely to answer the question needed for Crown quicker than anyone expects, even us."

Cam took in the words with a soft grunt, accepting them even as he remained troubled by what he'd seen and done in Hearth. The deaths of all those people in Nylara, the children buried under rubble, feeling responsible for it… even killing a wicked fool like Graft Pubber often left him feeling sick. Even several months of regularly practicing Saira's advice on how to deal with the trauma, he felt like he'd only achieved a snail's pace of improvement, and he wondered if he'd ever remember Hearth without being taken away by nightmares.

"I want to go to the Sinanes," Pan said. "After I Advance to Glory."

Cam breathed out in relief over the shift in conversation. Thinking about Hearth always had him feeling melancholy, and he was tired of that sad emotion. But thinking about the Sinanes fixed a wistful smile over his features. What was Saira's home like? Based on her descriptions, it sounded beautiful and fine. "I'd like to go there, too."

"Why can't you?" Pan asked, peering at him.

Cam shrugged, not wanting to admit a reason that would only set the little panda-person to laughing.

An instant later, he prayed for patience when Pan started chuckling, apparently having figured it out on his own. "It's because of Charity, isn't it?" Pan's chuckle became laughter when Cam didn't respond. "You like her. You'll go wherever she wants, even if it's to Maviro."

Cam protested. "It's not like that. Charity has duties and responsibilities. She can't just let them go."

Pan broke off from his laughter, but brightness continued to glint in his eyes, visible even in the dark. "And your duty and responsibility is to make her happy."

Cam sighed, disliking how often his conversations with Pan these days devolved into teasing about Charity. "You can be very irritating sometimes, you know that?"

"That's not denying what I just said."

"Let's talk about something else," Cam said, done with the topic of his future with Charity.

Thankfully, Pan got the hint. "I was serious when I said Hearth helped us Advance. I honestly think we'll all have it in us to reach Crown."

"I want to reach Sage and more."

"We both want that."

They fell silent after Pan's statement.

"When will you go home?" Pan asked, breaking the quiet.

Cam wished he could go home now. He missed his family and friends. It had been so long since he'd seen them, even longer from their perspective. "As soon as I'm a Glory. What about you?"

"Once I know what I'm meant to do."

Cam scowled, hating how Pan's people had convinced him that his only worth in life was enacting some useless prophecy of ancient mutterings. "You don't need to wait on that jackhole of a foretelling for your happiness."

Pan scowled right back. "I know that, but that doesn't mean the prophecy is meaningless. Besides, what about you?"

"What about me?" Cam did his best to rein in a surge of defensive irritation.

"Hearth was hard. Are you sure you're ready to head out again? It's going to be dangerous." Pan's tone softened. "There might be killing."

Cam shrugged, his flash of irritation already fading away. "We should be fine. Charity's father is going to anchor line us most of the way there."

"We'll still have at least several weeks of travel."

Cam grinned, not allowing himself to ponder the dangers they'd face for too long. "We wouldn't want our lives to be too easy, would we?"

Pan laughed with him, moving in for a quick hug. "Then we'll have to make better lives."

Following his early morning conversation with Cam, Pan couldn't go back to sleep, so he decided to practice his use of Spirairia. Although it remained difficult, he was pleased with how quickly his skills were recovering. It was like what he'd told Cam: Light Squad had suffered terrible misfortunes in Hearth, but they'd also achieved great successes. And it wasn't just in their Advancements or everything else he'd mentioned to Cam, but also the improvements they'd garnered when it came to focus, control, and balance, just like Professors Shade and Grey had taught.

An hour later, a rumble in his belly distracted him from his deliberations and reminded him of the time. The sun had risen, which meant breakfast was next on the agenda. Pan glanced to the bathroom, hearing Cam in the shower and hoped he'd be done soon. The man was starting to take longer and longer to get clean, which made absolutely no sense. Cam could quickly wash off whatever dirt and sweat had collected upon his relatively hairless skin and then send a wave of fire over his body to get anything he might have missed.

It was what Pan did, a far more elegant solution to keeping his fur clean than soap and water. Besides which, his skin itched something fierce whenever he bathed like Cam.

Pan grinned on thinking of his wording: *something fierce*. Cam's country dialect must be growing on him. Or maybe he just appreciated the sing-song nature of the phrasing.

His considerations about language ended when someone knocked on the front door. Pan sighed. Since Cam was still in the shower, it seemed he'd have to find out who it was, which was a shame. Cam always wore such a look of delight when he got over his grumbling and went to answer the door. And being a good friend, of course Pan would never think to steal away Cam's pleasure.

Sighing again, he rose to his feet, setting aside the bamboo he'd been distractedly munching on—a single stalk meant to tide him over until true breakfast, or second breakfast as his family used to call it. He went to the door and, upon opening it, gave a joyful whoop. It was Jade. Pan reached for her, hugging and spinning her about, just like he'd done with Saira and Avia.

Jade laughed as he twirled her about. "Put me down, you silly panda-person."

Pan did so, still holding her hands and grinning. "When did you get back?"

"Just now," Jade said, eyes shining as she smoothed down her hair and clothes.

She was quite fastidious when it came to her appearance, although Pan wasn't sure if anyone else recognized the fact, maybe not even Jade herself.

"Where's Cam?" she asked.

Pan gestured to the bathroom where running water could still be heard. "He takes so long to shower these days. Charity says so, too. She almost walked in on him the other day, but I'm not sure if that was intentional or not."

Jade chuckled, an evil lilt to her laughter. "Knowing Charity, I'm sure it was intentional. She teases our poor boy like no one ever could."

Pan's expression went flat when he realized that Jade didn't know about Cam and Charity. "She doesn't tease him as much anymore."

Jade's brow lifted, and her features bore a mixture of concern and confusion. "She doesn't? What happened? Did they argue?"

Pan offered a sly smile. "She doesn't tease him anymore because Cam likes it. So then it's no longer teasing. It's flirting."

Jade's confusion was replaced by burgeoning awareness. She clapped her hands, grinning wide and appearing both triumphant and ecstatic. "Tell me everything."

Pan did so, sharing what he and Cam had been doing over the past month.

"Not that," Jade said with an impatient wave of her hands. "I mean about Cam and Charity."

"Oh, them." Pan chuckled inwardly at Jade's intense expression. He'd known all along what she'd meant, but sometimes it was fun to pretend he wasn't quite as perceptive as he actually was. And why not? It was harmless fun that made his friends happy. They liked to poke fun at him about his innocence.

Pan went on to tell Jade about Cam and Charity's relationship along with Avia's return as a Glory.

"She's a Glory!" Jade exclaimed.

"Not only that, she's going with us to the area of Ephemera that Master Winder told us about. The temple. She'll be able to provide extra protection."

"It will be good to see Avia again," Jade replied with a fond smile. A moment later, her lips pursed in consideration. "How did Weld manage to stay at the Academy? Avia told everyone the truth, didn't she?"

Pan glowered. Weld Plain was a jackhole who had no business being here at the Ephemeral Academy. However, Pan wasn't stupid enough to voice what was on his mind without first casting a bubble of privacy around him and Jade. It was a skill Cam had helped him master since their return to Golden. "She did," Pan replied, "but all she could say was that Weld was present when Nailing and Nageena attacked us. He claimed that he managed to escape them by hiding, and his word was accepted even though he's a deceitful fragging traitor."

Jade gave a shocked inhalation. "Language, Pan."

"I'm sorry," Pan muttered, although he wasn't. What he'd said about Weld Plain was the exact truth. The man *was* a fragging traitor.

Jade rubbed the top of his head. "It's fine. I just hate seeing you upset."

Pan wasn't ready to let go of his anger. "I think the man is a rakshasa in hiding. I think at least two of the Sage-Dukes are as well."

Jade hissed. "Keep your voice down. We're in your quarters, but there are ways Crowns can hear through walls, even some Glories."

Pan understood her concern, although it wasn't necessary. "I made sure they can't." He explained about the bubble of privacy.

Jade frowned. "Really? I never noticed it."

"That's because you haven't been practicing Spirairia." The instant the words left his mouth, Pan knew he was being something of a hypocrite, and his ears wilted. "Cam and I haven't been either, and Saira sort of yelled at us about it."

"Saira yelled at you?" Jade asked in a tone of disbelief.

"Well, no, but you know what it's like to disappoint her."

Jade wore an understanding smile. "I do, and I felt the same way whenever Professor Grey called me out."

"I miss her."

Jade exhaled heavily. "So do I. Her and Professor Shade." An instant later, she shifted the conversation back to their prior topic. "Why do you think Weld is a rakshasa?"

"There are so many reasons," Pan said. "His presence at the same time that Nailing and Nageena entered Nexus. And his sponsor happened to have oversight of the island. That's too much coincidence to believe it was mere chance. His rapid growth as an Ephemeral Master. He was lazy and stupid when we knew him. How likely is it for someone to change so drastically as to now be counted a genius? And lastly his behavior. Master Winder says Weld Plain is a better person, but when we spoke to him just the other morning, he was no different than ever before. He is a pig and a jackhole. And for reasons unknown, several Sage-Dukes are protecting him."

All the while, Jade simply nodded agreement. "That's the only explanation that makes sense, and it also makes it doubly important for us to have protection when we go to that temple. I mean, what if someone else knows about it?"

"We think they do," Pan said. "It's why Charity is going to ask her father to join us. And if Sial also comes, we'll have two Glories, a Crown, and a Sage. That should be all the protection we need."

"Sial's here?"

Pan nodded.

"Good." In spite of her positive declaration, however, Jade frowned, clearly musing over the matter before a challenging glint lit her eyes. "Have you Enhanced all your Tangs? I already have mine at Crystal."

"We managed it a few weeks ago," Pan said with a dismissive wave of his hand, pretending like it wasn't of any importance.

Jade wasn't fooled by his attitude. She smirked, arms folded and wearing a knowing expression. "You realize that neither you nor Cam can keep your emotions off your faces, right? Your smug little pleasure is as obvious as your pretty black-and-white fur."

Pan made a mental note to work on controlling his facial expressions even as Cam finally finished his shower and strode out of the bathroom. He was naked as a lark, and his shriek of horror on seeing Jade in their front room had Pan howling with laughter.

After getting over his shock at seeing Jade—or more likely, the shock of having her see him utterly naked—Cam quickly got dressed, still embarrassed over the situation. As he pulled on his boots, he reasoned it wasn't too bad. It had just been an accident. Jade wouldn't make too much of an issue out of it.

Would she?

He groaned. Of course she would. He'd likely never hear the end of it, both from her and Pan.

Sure enough. "What's taking so long?" Jade called out from where she and Pan waited in the front room. "You don't have to wear so many clothes on my account."

"I'm ready," Cam groused, stepping out to join them.

"You look much better with clothes on than without," Pan said with a nod, although it didn't take much observational skill to see the smile hiding at the corners of his mouth.

Jade didn't bother hiding her humor. "You look good now, but has Charity ever seen you looking as dashing as you were a few minutes ago?"

Cam scowled. "That ain't any of your business."

Jade nodded along like he'd actually answered her question. "Which means she hasn't. I'll have to fill her in on the details."

Praying for patience as the other two chuckled away, Cam exited the quarters, trailed by their ongoing comments. He sought to shift the conversation away from his humiliating escapade, asking what Jade had been doing.

Thankfully, she took the bait—or at least chose to let him off the hook. "I was mostly just sitting around my auntie's house, bored to tears. Every once in a while, Sage-Duchess Salin would ask me about the Jom-Strafes or you or Saira… she'd pester me about everything to do with Hearth. It wasn't pleasant. If it had been my choice, I'd have never gone there. I couldn't wait to leave."

"There really wasn't anything else to do?" Pan asked.

"There really wasn't," Jade replied. "Like I said, I was bored to tears, and I couldn't wait to leave."

Her reply was about what Cam had expected. Jade didn't like Bastion, and she'd never bothered hiding that fact, especially her loathing of the city's nobles, many of whom had taken great joy when her father had fallen from Crown to Glory.

A moment later, Jade brightened. "But that's all in the past now. Pan was telling me what the two of you have been doing and this temple that Master Winder made available to us."

"It won't be easy getting there," Cam cautioned.

Jade shrugged. "Not much that's actually worth having is ever easy."

It was true enough, but Jade's nonchalance struck Cam as a mite too overconfident, and he felt compelled to caution her. "Don't forget that you'll need the answer to Advance to Glory if you want to make use of the Ephemera."

"I won't hold you back," Jade said. "And I know time is pressing. We all want to leave the school before the next academic year starts. I heard about Weld and how he's teaching Kinesthia this year."

Pan sighed, sounding despondent. "We literally just got back home, and we have to leave again. All because of that jackhole."

"He's not the only jackhole," Cam said, making sure to speak as vague as possible in case unfriendly ears were listening. "There are others. Some a lot more powerful. They protected him."

Jade nodded agreement. "Pan told me about that, too."

They exited the dorm hall into the damp heat. Cam rocked back on his heels with a disgusted groan. Inside had been muggy enough, but outside, the humidity felt like a punch to the face. The air was oppressive and uncomfortable, and it would only get worse as the day progressed. The sun was still low in the cloudless sky, but when it rose higher, that's when it would become sweltering.

Cam grimaced. He really couldn't wait for autumn.

Jade noticed his discomfort and offered him a sympathetic smile. "At least we're Adepts. The weather doesn't bother us nearly as much."

"Speak for yourself," Cam muttered.

"And when we're Glories, it will bother us even less," Pan added, talking over Cam. "As Sages, the weather won't bother us at all."

Further conversation was interrupted when a glad shout calling out Jade's name drew them to a halt. It was Charity, Avia, and Card, and the three of them hustled forward to hug her. Card stepped back after speaking a few words, joining Cam and Pan. Charity and Avia, though, remained with Jade, the three of them squealing with laughter.

Cam watched in bemused puzzlement as the women spoke over each other in ever increasing volumes, gesticulated wildly and acted as excited as children with an overwhelming amount of presents or sugar. Eventually, they settled down, and a sly look from Jade was followed by a peal of laughter from Charity.

"I think my secret has been exposed," Cam whispered as an aside to Pan, who promptly gave him a wide-eyed expression of disbelief.

"Did you say *exposed*?" Pan asked.

It took Cam a few seconds to realize what he'd just said. It was silly enough that he found himself chuckling along with his friend.

"Is it true?" Charity asked as the women rejoined them.

Cam feigned innocence. "Is what true?"

"You know what," Charity replied with a pout. "And here I thought I was special, but then you go and streak naked in front of Jade before ever giving me a peek at your goods."

The way she phrased the statement had Cam smiling, and he only smiled wider when he recognized how much it irritated her. Charity wanted him flushing, blushing, and acting like he'd been caught doing something naughty… although, that last part was sort of true.

Cam shook off the stray observation, figuring on finding a way to nip Charity's teasing in the bud. "Are you saying you want me to streak naked in front of you? Or that you want a peek at my goods?"

Jade and Avia groaned. Even Card and Pan did, and Cam glanced at them in confusion. What now? His attention went back to Charity, who wore an expectant and knowing leer on her face.

"Think about what you asked. You're not as clever as you think. Some with a dirty mind might think your questions were a subtle way of offering to streak naked in front of me, and also allowing me a peek at your goods."

Cam gaped. "That's not what I said, and you know it." He glared at the others. "You all know it."

"We do," Avia said, "but a wise leader also knows when to allow those who follow him to have their fun at his or her expense."

"She's right," Card said. "Now, can we please get some breakfast? I'm hungry."

Cam disregarded Card's complaint, his glower leaving as he contemplated Avia's statement. His followers? He had never considered Light Squad in that way, and that was for a very simple reason: it wasn't true. The members of Light Squad weren't his followers. They were his friends. He said as much.

Charity reached out to him, like she was fixing to pat his cheek, and he quickly jerked away. He hated when she did that. It was so condescending. However, she surprised him by completing her motion even after he'd pulled away, finishing by cupping his cheek instead of patting it. "We know we're your friends, but we also follow where you lead. In a way, that does make us your followers. Which is why we enjoy teasing you so much. We don't want you to forget that you are our friend as well as our leader."

It made a peculiar kind of sense, and Cam decided to simply accept Charity's statement rather than argue against it. He shrugged agreement.

"I'm glad to hear you say so," Charity said, sounding a pleased note. "Now, we could go back to teasing you about your nudity, but I think you'd prefer to lead us to breakfast. What do you say?"

Cam grinned, grateful to leave the entire streaking episode behind. "I'd love some breakfast."

"At last," Card said, sounding exasperated. "Can we go there now before the two of you start oversharing your affection?"

Cam flipped Card a rude gesture and stepped close to Charity, drawing her in for a quick kiss. "Thank you."

Charity didn't reply. She merely tucked in close to him, and they walked hand-in-hand to the cafeteria with the others following.

7

After breakfast, Card departed the cafeteria, leaving Light Squad behind but promising to join them at the Kinesthia field later on. For now, he had a task to complete, and he paced steadily toward what it entailed: a scheduled meeting with Dean Vorant Shoner.

With only a few others returned yet to school and with the hour so early, the paths through the Ephemeral Academy were largely empty. The summer sun shed warmth but clouds to the west promised a rainy relief from the muggy weather. Of course, what came after would be even more mugginess, but for a small bit of time, it would be vastly cooler.

Card grunted to himself. There was always bad that could come with the good and good that could come with the bad. Or at least the world largely seemed that way, an unshakable truth against which he saw no reason to complain.

Regardless, Card had always enjoyed a good thunderstorm, a gully washer as Cam would have named it in his backwoods way. As soon as the phrase crossed his consciousness, Card grimaced inwardly. He had a great deal of respect for the leader of Light Squad, but the man's

70

manner of speaking was of such poor form. Descriptive in an interesting way, but intonated in a way that had always grated on his hearing.

Another grunt. Everyone had their flaws. Card knew that he certainly did, and in spite of his many skills and talents, ultimately so did Cam.

However, that didn't include Cam's decision for Light Squad to leave the Ephemeral Academy and go to where their fortunes would be made. A wise choice, journeying to this area of Ephemeral concentration promised to them by the Wilde Sage. Certainly smarter than remaining here at the Ephemera Academy where Light Squad had faced so many unexpected dangers. Better to leave and make their own way in the world than live under the thumbs of those who couldn't necessarily be trusted.

This was especially highlighted by the fact that those in authority had chosen a miserable wretch like Weld Plain to act as their instructor, a stomach-turning proposition.

No. Leaving the Ephemeral Academy was the right choice. Besides which, what could they actually learn here at this point? Their skills were vastly superior to any other Adepts on campus, and the fact was, no other unit had ever pushed the bounds of what was considered achievable the way Light Squad had. They had truly accomplished the impossible.

In cogitating on the matter—

Another inwardly directed grimace. There he'd gone and done it again. Cogitating was one of Cam's favorite country words, and somehow, that backwoods dialect must have infected Card's own way of thinking. It was unfortunate and unacceptable.

As a result, Card took a deep breath and tried again.

On properly *considering* the matter, had this been his first year at the Ephemeral Academy and he'd heard rumors of any group with Light Squad's accomplishments and reputation, he wouldn't have believed it possible. It was too much, and many obviously doubted the achievements of his unit. Card hadn't missed the whispered conversations from those students and instructors still at the school. Their disbelief had been obvious, which was amusing since they didn't even know about the most awe-inspiring events of all: Light Squad had experienced the presence of the Holy Servants.

Card tried to constrain a joy-filled grin at what he'd been privileged to witness. It had been thousands of years since Rukh and Jessira had walked the green hills of Salvation or Hearth, and yet he'd heard their voices, felt their power, and even touched them when they wore their raiments of Professors Grey and Shade. All of Light Squad had, and it was all the more reason for him to defy his mother and remain in Light Squad, not out of mercenary self-interest alone but because Card had begun to think of the unit as his family.

It was the reason for this morning's meeting with Dean Shoner. He needed to watch out for the interests of his friends and family. They needed a second option in case the temple proved a failure. Asking the dean for a sabbatical would give them that option. It would grant Light Squad a chance to return to the Academy and continue their schooling if they failed to Advance at the temple.

Card's thoughts cut off when he reached the administration building, an unadorned rectangular structure of red brick and pale stone. The dean's quarters were on the third floor, and upon reaching it, Card briefly spoke to a receptionist before taking a seat and reviewing what he knew of Dean Shoner. The man was from Maviro, a Crown and a warrior. Tall and stoutly built, still fit. Married to a Glory, although his husband was said to be on the cusp of Advancing. Overall, the dean was a good person.

A moment later, the receptionist ushered him into Dean Shoner's office, a rather bland space. Functional was the best that could be said of the room as it was void of any decoration or art and only contained a few uninspired chairs and a bulky cherry desk empty of any papers.

"What can I do for you Cadet Wolver?" Dean Shoner asked after the receptionist shut the door and both men had seated themselves.

Card schooled his features to neutral before answering. "I'm taking an extended leave from the school."

Dean Shoner's smile cut off. "I'd heard rumors to that effect. Your mother won't like it."

"Yes, she has made her views about me quite clear. I am unwelcome in her house so long as I choose to live my life as I see fit."

Dean Shoner wore a tight-lipped expression of sympathy. "She can be difficult."

Card lifted his brows in surprise. "You know my mother?"

The dean appeared to carefully pick through his words. "I knew her briefly. A summer long ago in this very school."

Card's eyes narrowed in suspicion. The way the dean had spoken the words, there had been an undercurrent to them, one only used by former lovers.

His suspicion quickly became certainty, but he dismissed the newly gathered information. It was unimportant. Card had long grown used to his mother's predilections for taking on lovers based on nothing more than her needs of the moment or her flighty whims.

"You have my sympathy at having known her," Card said in reply to the dean's statement. "But my intentions remain unchanged. I wish to take a sabbatical. All of Light Squad wishes it."

The dean appeared surprised. "You've been charged to speak on their behalf?"

Card shook his head. "No, but I'll make sure they come by and ask for a sabbatical as well."

The dean nodded approval. "A wise decision in case your other options don't pan out the way you hope. You have my blessing."

Card breathed out in relief. This had gone far easier than he'd expected. In his imaginings, he'd felt sure the dean would have pressed his own advantage rather than readily acceded to Card's wishes.

Since that wasn't the case, and there was nothing more to discuss, Card rose to his feet and offered a handshake. "Thank you, sir. It's much appreciated." He left Dean Shoner and went to rejoin Light Squad, pleased at what he'd accomplished.

Card knew himself to be a fine fighter, but Cam was better, Avia was more dangerous, Jade had greater skills, Charity was more talented in the use of Ephemera, and Pan was their moral center. All that was true, but Card had his own unique talent, chief among them being his worldly understanding. He could serve Light Squad by protecting his friends from problems they didn't see coming.

Cam looked up, frowning in irritation from his reading of *The Warrior and the Servant*. Did Pan have to munch his bamboo so loudly? And chew so… vividly. Cam could picture every one of the panda's teeth puncturing the bamboo, over and over again.

A moment later, his frown transformed into an amused smile when he caught sight of his friend, his favorite little panda-person seated on the ground, legs splayed and brow sculpted in concentration over whatever he was reading. The adorable picture was completed by Pan's pink tongue sticking out of the corner of his mouth.

It was the evening of Jade's arrival back at the Ephemeral Academy, and after spending most of the day training, Cam and Pan had retired to their quarters with a plan on finalizing some studying before meeting the rest of Light Squad for supper. It would be their first real meal together since returning to Golden, and Cam hoped it would also be full of fellowship and fun even with Saira's absence.

Pan disrupted Cam's deliberations. "What are you studying?"

Cam displayed the book in question. There was a lot wisdom within the pages of *The Warrior and the Servant*, but oddly enough, he felt like much of it was familiar, as if he'd already read many of these teachings at an earlier point in his life and was only now recollecting them. Or maybe that was just because of the universal nature of insight and perception and how they were sometimes best seen in hindsight.

Whatever the case, Cam found comfort in the text, which steadily taught him a practical idea on how to become the kind of the person he'd always envisioned for himself. Sure, Pan might think the book a bit too basic and obvious, but Cam enjoyed reading it. Besides, he'd always reckoned himself a bit basic and obvious anyway—unlike Pan, who was an erudite and deep thinker.

Cam stared at his friend and curiosity swept over him. "What are you reading?"

"Not much of anything, really," Pan said with a disconsolate sigh. "I'm stuck. Nothing seems interesting."

"What's wrong?"

Another sigh. "It's the question on Advancing to Glory. I don't fully understand the difference between giving and receiving. I have some aspects—I'm almost there—but I'm missing something." His ears wilted. "What if I don't have the answer by the time we get to the temple?"

He sounded utterly despondent, and rather than offer meaningless words of affirmation, Cam set aside *The Warrior and the Servant* and slid off his chair. He went to Pan and drew his friend into a hug. "I'm worried about it, too. We can worry together. How about that?"

Pan shoved the top of his head into Cam's chin, going on to rest the side of his forehead against Cam's jaw, a sign of how upset he actually was. "The question is supposed to be one of the great blocks that limit an Ephemeral Master's growth. What if I fail?"

Cam leaned away from Pan, tilting his friend's head upward so they were peering eye-to-eye. "We might all fail, but what you achieve in life won't be the reason for how I think of you."

Pan's wilted ears perked. "How do you think of me?"

Cam smiled. "You know how. You're my brother." He stroked the side of Pan's face. "You'll always be my brother, and I hope that's how you'll always think of me, even if you become a Sage and I'm still an Adept."

Pan grinned, some life returning to his eyes. "That wouldn't be right. The prophecy says I'm supposed to support someone profound and wonderful."

Cam raised his brows. "And an Adept can't be profound and wonderful?"

Pan chuckled. "I see what you're doing. Thank you."

"Let's focus on something other than study," Cam suggested. Sometimes when Pan got to feeling bad about himself or his future, it was best if he did something that proved his competence or just got him interested in an entirely different topic.

"Like what?"

"How about using a True Bond to cast small blasts of lightning." It was a notion to which Cam had given plenty of thought recently.

"Why lightning?"

"Because it's an electrical discharge, a partially ionized plasma."

"An electrical what?"

Cam laughed. As expected, Pan's features had settled into an expression of utter befuddlement. Cam had a momentary feeling of triumph. Only rarely did he know something Pan didn't. "It's part of the information that the voices—"

"Rukh and Jessira."

"Right. Them," Cam agreed. "It's from the knowledge they gave me. Plasma is a state of matter, and it's related to Plasminia, just like solids are related to Kinesthia, liquid is related to Synapsia, and gas is related to Spirairia. They're all fundamental states of matter, and while I can create fire." He demonstrated his words by creating a white-hot flame on the tip of his index finger. "Fluid." The fire was replaced with a twisting drop of silvery liquid. "Or a gas, I like lightning." Electrical sparks danced along the knuckles of his hands, up his arms, and along his face, and he knew without having to look into a mirror that the lightning had flashed his eyes white. An instant later, he let the electrical sparks dissipate.

Pan viewed him in silent speculation. "I don't think I like how much more you know than me."

Cam smiled. "You should like it since I've been teaching all of it to you."

Pan brightened. "And you're even a good teacher."

Cam laughed. "Don't sound so surprised. I've got skills."

Pan gestured in Cam's general direction. "You have plenty of skills. Lots more than you give yourself credit for having."

Cam shrugged, never liking any proud talk about himself. He shifted the conversation. "All of us have our Tangs at Crystal, and when we get to Glory, the perfect Advancement that Rail taught us will come in handy. We might get to Crystal even quicker than Avia."

"She won't like that. She already feels like an outsider."

Cam frowned. He'd worried on that same possibility, and he made a mental note to ask Avia if she really felt that way. Of course, on considering it, he could understand why. She'd missed out on most of Light Squad's time in Hearth.

"Rail Gristle was an interesting fellow," Pan continued. "The way he walked, his gracefulness, even the way he spoke. I never saw the similarity, though, until we came home, but doesn't he remind you of someone?"

Cam recalled the strange old man from Hearth who seemed to know so much even while living as a hermit out in the middle of nowhere. Rail had made an impression, but who did Pan mean by his question?

An instant later, Cam made the connection, shocked he hadn't noticed it until now. "Cinder Shade. They're more powerful than they should be, more knowledgeable, and both of them have a way to their personalities that makes you think of a Sage." He caught Pan peering at him in speculation, and sighed. His friend would pester him until he voiced the final similarity. "And Cinder might be Rukh who was one of the voices who saved us in the Temple of Gates."

Pan settled back with a satisfied grunt. "Exactly."

Cam shook his head, not sure about the importance of the last part of their conversation, nor did he want to keep on jawing about it. Thankfully, there was one sure-fire method of getting Pan to talking about something else: feeding him new information. "You want to learn about the fundamental states of matter?"

Pan set aside the book he'd been halfheartedly reading and sat forward, wearing an intent expression. "I would very much like that."

Cam made ready to do exactly that, but he halted as an epiphany swept over him. A connection between Rail and Cinder. Connections. With a bolt, he realized that the answer needed to Advance wasn't about the difference between giving and receiving, but rather on how they were connected. Every one of the questions in Advancement had connections.

He sat back, stunned. Was it really that simple?

Maybe so, and he teased at the possibility, tugged at it, tried to work it out in his mind. But with each passing second, the understanding slipped free of his grasp. It was gone. He sighed in disappointment.

"What happened?" Pan asked.

Cam described his near-epiphany. "I was so close."

Pan nodded slowly, but he appeared distant, lost in through. "I never thought of it like that. I wonder…"

Cam didn't interrupt as Pan considered the question they both needed to answer. He only hoped that what he'd just said would ignite his friend's awareness and get him the needed solution.

"They're looking good," Saira noted.

Cam nodded agreement but kept his eyes locked on Light Squad, who were putting in a final training session at the Kinesthia field before heading out in a couple of days. Their unit was whole with Saira having just come back to the Academy a few hours ago, several days after Jade's own return. On top of that, she'd also confirmed that the temple was real and after gathering some final supplies, there was no reason not to get rolling.

Cam had many good memories at the Ephemeral Academy, and while he was a far better person because of the school, nothing was meant to last forever. His hours here were done, and it was time to live his life the way he wanted, to take the first step on a thousand-mile trek where he became the kind of Ephemeral Master he'd always visualized.

True, perhaps he'd never quite reach that goal, but as Professor Grey would have told him: the journey would be its own reward. And Cam was ready to stride onto that shining path.

Prior to that, however, he wanted to see how well Light Squad could manage without his direction. He had Charity, Pan, and Card sparring in hand-to-hand combat against Jade and Avia with the latter limiting herself to an Adept's abilities. Based on what he was seeing, his earlier fears about Light Squad not being sharp as a spear's tip had been vastly overblown. Everyone had kept themselves in fighting trim and done their best to maintain their Ephemeral skills, which was a good thing since in their upcoming travels, who knew if they'd run into rakshasas? It might even be likely given Light Squad's rash of bad luck.

Cam continued to study the unit, pleased with what he was witnessing. "Time!" he shouted.

The others pulled apart with Card bending down to help Jade rise to her feet. Other than Avia, all of them looked done for, but none of them were stooping low or gasping like a beached fish. Instead, they stood tall and straight, hands on hips, taking controlled breaths even as sweat poured off them in this typically sunny and muggy summer Nexus afternoon.

"Get some water," Cam ordered. "We'll go again in a few minutes."

"Are you taking part this time?" Charity asked, a challenging note to her voice.

A few months ago, Cam would have gotten his hackles ruffled at Charity's tone. But now that he'd gotten to know her better—although that wasn't the same as knowing her well—he simply grinned sharklike at her. "I'll be there, and you best be ready when we go hard at it."

Smirks and snorts of laughter met his words while Charity merely smirked. "That probably isn't something we should do in public."

Cam replayed his words, putting it together, and scowled. "That's not what I meant, and y'all know it."

His response only earned him more laughter.

Cam shook his head. When had he become so fumble-mouthed? Wasn't that Pan's specialty to make innocent quips that suggested something intimate? The answer to the first question arrived in a bolt. It was when he'd started courting Charity. For whatever reason, being around her made him talk like an idiot. Which meant that the best he could do for now was shut his mouth and let the situation play itself out. Soon enough, after a few final jibes from Jade, Light Squad drifted off to get water, and the matter was over.

"They have come a long way," Saira said, still standing nearby.

Cam nodded. It was true. Light Squad had progressed farther than he had ever imagined for them or himself. Professors Shade and Grey had thought different, but Cam had always been full of doubt. He'd always figured that with their Plasminia Tangs and True Bonds, they wouldn't show well until they'd Advanced to Glory.

But he'd been utterly wrong, and he'd never been more glad for it. "I doubt there's another group of Adepts as lethal as Light Squad."

"Given everything we survived in Hearth, is that a surprise?"

Cam shrugged, knowing she was right, but there was something to what she had said that caught his attention. "We?"

Saira offered a crooked smile. "Of course. I was with you in Hearth. I trained you during your first year at the Academy. I think I've earned the right to consider myself an honorary member of Light Squad."

"You sure you want to be associated with low-class folks like us? You being a princess and all, it might not shine too well on your tiara."

Saira blinked, frowning in confusion. "I'm trying to parse your sentences. The first one is easy enough to decipher, and just to be clear, you aren't low-class folks. If you were, my mother wouldn't be so intent in having all of you join the Sinanes."

They'd spoken about this before, but it still struck Cam as unusual. "Your mother really wants us?"

Saira huffed. "You're not a stupid person, Cam, so why do you ask the same question over and over again?" She didn't give him a chance to respond. "Going back to your statements about my reputation, I have the sense that you mangled a bunch of words together to make the barest sort of sense."

Cam adopted a dullard's expression. "What's mangled mean?"

Saira threw her head back and laughed, an unexpected reaction. The Saira who Cam had grown to know during his time at the Academy and more deeply in Hearth had been reserved and closed, sometimes painfully so. The most he would have expected from her in reaction to his joke would have been a polite smile. He'd never have expected her to laugh like she thought something he said was actually funny.

But this was a different Saira, a more relaxed version, and once again, it had him wondering as to the cause. Was it really as simple as going home and being back amongst those who loved her best? Or had the change occurred in Hearth, when she'd Advanced once again to Crown?

Either possibility might be true, maybe even both, but so was neither. And while Cam wanted to ask the reason for her change, he kept his mouth shut. Saira was a private person, and she probably wouldn't appreciate his poking.

Charity strode up to the two of them. "We had a discussion while we were guzzling water," she said.

"Guzzling?" That wasn't a word Charity ever used.

She smiled confirmation. "Guzzling. Consider it my attempt at imitating your lovely colloquialisms, like Victory used to."

Cam shook his head. "You're a lot softer on the eyes than Victory."

Charity's smile widened. "What a lovely thing to say, especially after that crude offer from earlier."

Cam briefly closed his eyes and prayed for patience. "You're never going to forget that, are you?"

Saira chuckled. "She would be wise not to, and with that, I'll leave you two alone."

Cam watched as Saira went to join the rest of Light Squad, and seeing her interact so well with them, it became obvious. She belonged in their unit and not just as an honorary member.

"She's different," Charity said, also watching Saira. "More easygoing or kinder."

"She was always kind."

"I didn't mean to imply she was mean, and she wasn't even cold. But she was deeply private, almost insular. She's been more open and outgoing since coming back from the Sinanes."

Cam grunted agreement, not having much else to say.

"I wanted to ask you something," Charity said, turning to face him.

"We're leaving in two days, and I was hoping we could spend tomorrow together. Just us. We could gather supplies and maybe go out to a restaurant for lunch and dinner."

Cam couldn't help but smirk some. "Are you asking me out on a date?"

"Not if you act like a jackhole about it."

Cam wiped away the smirk. "I'd love to spend tomorrow with you, only…"

Charity's eyes narrowed in suspicion. "Only what?"

"Two things, actually. First, I don't have money for lunch *and* dinner."

"I'll pay."

Charity always paid, and Cam didn't like it, knowing it was probably irrational, but not able to help how he felt about it. Nevertheless, he did his best to keep the feelings of inadequacy off his face. "Second, we're going out to dinner tomorrow night as a unit. It'll be our last night here at the Academy."

Charity's eyes lighted. "That's a wonderful idea. Date first, dinner with the squad after." She leaned in to kiss his cheek, giving it a soft pat as her expression firmed. "Now, let's get back to work. We need to know we're at our sharpest when we head into the wilderness." She seemed to add an extra sway to her hips as she sashayed away from him. A quick wink over her shoulder, and she continued on her way.

"Yes, ma'am," Cam breathed, not sure how he'd gotten involved with someone as dangerous as Charity Kazar. He smiled. Maybe it was because he just liked dangerous women.

8

"Our last day at the Academy," Cam said as he and Charity strode through the streets of Nexus. Given the day's young hour, the sun had yet to bake the world to boiling, and in fact, it was actually right pleasant. A soft breeze played about now and then, carrying the smells of bread baking and food cooking, and the company was nice, too. That is, so long as Charity didn't offer any of her condescending looks or pats of Cam's cheek. Of course, the cheek patting usually ended with a kiss, so Cam reckoned that maybe he shouldn't whine too much about it.

He glanced sidelong at Charity, wondering what he could possibly do to irritate her enough to get her to pat his cheek. Maybe he should comment on how nice she looked? And she did look nice. Better than nice. Striking. She had her red-hued dark hair braided and clustered under a wrap, and in the sunshine, her blue irises appeared brighter than usual amidst the sun-yellow of her Adept-Haunted sclerae and dusky skin.

"We need to find you more appropriate clothes," Charity announced through their telepathic link. *"That will be our first stop. It's something*

we should have done days ago, but better late than never."

Cam glanced at his garb. What was wrong with what he was wearing? It was part of the same set of clothing given to him by Master Winder upon his admittance into the Ephemeral Academy. And sure, he'd used them pretty hard, but none of them showed any worn patches or appeared threadbare. The worst that could be said about them was they were a mite shabbier compared to when Cam had first donned them.

Charity must have noticed his confused expression. She patted his cheek, but unfortunately didn't bother giving him a kiss. "You need proper clothes for when you meet my father," she said aloud. "Boots as well. Making a good first impression is important."

Cam frowned. Sage-Duke Kazar would be the one to anchor line Light Squad to Maviro, but just now, when Charity had said that Cam would be meeting her father, there had been an undercurrent of meaning, something serious, and he wasn't sure he was ready for that. Certainly not when he had only been seeing Charity in a romantic way for a few weeks.

Panic bloomed, and Cam did his all to contain it, trying to figure on why meeting Charity's father in *that* kind of way should have him feeling five different shades of terrified. His flittering thoughts wouldn't settle enough for him to reckon the answer, so he fixated on a simple question. "What kind of meeting do you have in mind for me and your father?"

Charity glanced at him, and a moue of disappointment creased her features when she recognized his suppressed terror. "My father knows about you, your history at the Ephemeral Academy, Hearth, everything but those voices at the end and the two of us as a couple. I never told him about either, and I won't until you're ready. Right now, he knows you as the leader of Light Squad, that you're a Plasminian Adept who will soon Advance to Glory. He sees you as a rising power, a young prodigy, and you need to look the part. How you're currently dressed just won't do. You look like a farmer in shabby boots."

Her explanation eased some of Cam's fears, but her final comment had him scowling. "What's wrong with a farmer in shabby boots? Where I come from, a person like that is worth respecting."

Charity rolled her eyes like he was a simpleton, which only increased his ire. "I know that, but as I said, making a good impression is important and that starts with your attire. It means that you cared enough to dress well for the other person's benefit. It's a sign of respect as well as good manners. After all, a farmer from your home wouldn't show up to a meeting with my father—or any noble—mucked in mud and smelling like a pigsty, would they?"

That wasn't the same thing, and she knew it. Cam was about to declare it so, but Charity silenced him with a finger to his lips. He grimaced in annoyance. She always did this when she didn't want him talking back. He shoved off her intruding finger, but she replaced it with her lips.

Then Cam couldn't talk for another reason, and he didn't want to. The wolf-whistles from the heavy crowds around them didn't bother him either. Her lips parted, and she flicked her tongue against his before pulling away. But now that the kiss was ended, Cam's annoyance only increased as he recognized what Charity had done. She'd quieted him with a kiss.

It was wrong, but before he could tell her off, she surprised him, ducking her head. "I'm sorry. I shouldn't have done that. Kissing you to shut you up is..." She huffed, appearing honestly contrite. "It's not the kind of person I want to be."

Cam's aggravation bled off some but not entirely and anger still suffused his voice. "Then why did you do it?"

Charity stared at the ground again for a few seconds, eventually shrugging and lifting her gaze. "I'm nervous. I'm allowed to be nervous, aren't I?"

Cam's scowl became a glower. Now she was twisting what had happened to make herself seem like the victim.

Before he could respond, Charity sighed. "I'm sorry. Again. That wasn't fair. I am nervous, but it doesn't give me the right to do what I did."

Cam continued to frown at Charity. He wanted to believe that she understood what she'd done was wrong, but what if she didn't? Or what if her apology was just another ploy? And what would that mean for them moving forward? Had he just made a terrible mistake by getting involved with her? Because if it was a mistake, it wouldn't affect just him. It had the potential of affecting everyone in Light Squad. Cam set aside the burgeoning questions, focusing on the most important one. "And what was it you did?"

"I put my finger on your mouth to keep you quiet, and when that didn't work, I kissed you. That was the worst, using our relationship against you like that." A heavy swallow. "I really am sorry."

She appeared so remorseful that Cam couldn't hold on to his ire, probably because he didn't want to, and it drained out of him. He hugged Charity, not sure if that was the proper thing to do, but he did it anyway. Having a relationship like this with a woman was new to him, and he simply went with what seemed right.

Charity nestled into his embrace, arms going around his waist and head resting on his shoulder. After a moment, she pulled back. "I also shouldn't have tried to turn my anxiety against you. Being nervous doesn't give me a special dispensation for acting the way I did."

Cam accepted her apology but remained confused by her behavior. It was so out of character.

They walked on a bit before Charity responded. "My father doesn't know about us," she said. "I told you that, but it doesn't mean he won't figure it out, or…"

"Or?" Cam prodded.

Charity exhaled heavily. "I just want him to think well of you."

Cam nodded acceptance, although inside he remained troubled. Charity's last statement hadn't been what she'd originally intended on saying, and they continued down the road, silent, with Cam continuing to ponder what Charity wasn't willing to tell him.

"Let's go to the tailor first," Charity suggested. "You need nice clothes even if it's not to meet my father."

This time, Cam didn't argue with her suggestion, nor did he question the why or the need. He just followed Charity, but he did ask about the matter. "You sure the tailor will be able to finish the work in time?"

Charity gave a firm nod. "Of course. Money can't buy everything, but it can buy a lot, including having a tailor and his apprentices moving a project up and working late to see it completed."

Cam grunted, recognizing anew how wealth had its privileges, including what many would consider unfair advantages. Then again, money wasn't the only way to measure a person's prosperity. He took himself as an example. He was an Adept, which back in Traverse would have meant he would have been a person worthy of respect and honor, wealthy in nearly all the ways that counted, including in the making of coin.

But what if in that fantasy life, his father and brother had remained on the sauce? Would he have been happier in that existence compared to one in which he'd never achieved Ephemeral Mastery, lived modestly, but his father and brother had managed to stop drinking? Who truly would have been counted as being wealthier?

Then there were those who were truly impoverished and would have thought either version wealthy. Cam certainly would have thought so back in Traverse, never figuring he'd achieve anything until Pharis had given him a kick in the pants and forced him back to school where Master Bennett had taken an interest in helping him out.

Cam smiled on thinking about his old instructor, and the recollection drifted his mind on to the other people from Traverse, people like Midwife Spenser and Master Moltin. They, too, were Adepts, but in a few weeks, Cam would surpass them all by Advancing to Glory. He was close. The relationship between giving and receiving felt like it was less than an inch beyond his figurative fingertips.

And he'd get there. No chance he wouldn't, especially when he'd made a breakthrough the other day. Answering the question wasn't about figuring on the difference between giving and receiving but on how they were connected.

"We're here," Charity said, halting before a store in a wealthy part of Nexus.

While the city's streets were generally clean throughout with no slums or truly poor sections, the stores here had better merchandise, and there was an increased sense of tidiness to the area. Same with the folks walking about. Most of them had their noses in the air, wearing clothes of a fine fit.

The same could be said about the tailor's shop, *Finely Crafted*. It stood bracketed by a bakery and a place to purchase groceries, with all three business tucked into a block-wide, fanciful, three-story building decorated with bracketed cornices, stone lintels, and wide transom windows. The floors above appeared to be residential, and Cam found himself wondering what it would have been like to grow up here.

"We don't have to do this if you don't want to," Charity said, drawing him out of his musings.

Cam took in her demeanor, the worry she emitted. "But it's important to you?"

She gave a solemn nod. "It is."

Cam smiled. "If buying new clothes for me means that much to you, then who am I to say no?"

Charity exhaled in relief. "Let's go inside."

She gave Cam a playful shove, directing him into a store filled with bolts of cloth, bins full of buttons, frilly lace wrapped around hangers, and hundreds of items that Cam couldn't name. The store smelled nice, too, a mix of potpourri and clean, untouched fabric.

A plump man with a pencil-thin mustache, slicked-back hair, and wire-framed glasses over Adept-Haunted sclerae came out from behind the large counter that bisected the store on the side opposite to the entrance. Black slacks hung from suspenders and a white shirt with a maroon vest stretched over the man's ample belly. He wore a welcoming smile as he approached them. "Charity Kazar. What a privilege and honor to see you again. I heard rumors about your demise and miraculous recovery. It's so good to know such horrific stories were utterly false. You are the picture of beauty and grace."

Charity accepted a kiss on each cheek. "It's good to see too, Master Jeffrey." She gestured to Cam. "Allow me to introduce Cam Folde. He's my… the leader of Light Squad, my unit. We're to meet my father, and he needs appropriate clothing."

"A pleasure to meet you, sir," Cam said, recognizing the reason for Charity's hesitation even as he shook hands with the tailor. She'd changed what she meant to say about their relationship.

"A pleasure as well, young sir," Master Jeffrey said, sizing Cam up. "And Miss Kazar is correct. You do need a better set of clothes." His eyes grew crafty as he glanced to Charity. "And how much time will I have to outfit this fine young Adept?"

"One day. We need the clothes tomorrow morning. Two sets. He'll also need boots."

Cam felt like an outsider to the conversation, and although he wanted to offer a comment, he had no notion of what to say. Seeing a tailor for a fitting was well outside his expertise.

"That's a lot to ask for in such a short time," Master Jeffrey said, "especially the boots."

"Money is no object," Charity said. "I'll be paying."

This earned her a sharp-eyed look from the tailor before his attention returned to Cam. "I see."

He drew out the phrase, loading it with shades of meaning that had Cam uncomfortable. Was it really that easy to see what was between him and Charity?

"I can take the measurements for the boots," Master Jeffrey continued, stroking his chin in consideration. "I'll send them to Master Daniel. My brother trusts me to do that much."

"That would be excellent," Charity stated.

Master Jeffrey clapped his hands, and his smile returned. "In that case, young sir, if you don't mind, please stand before the mirrors." He guided Cam to a trio of floor-length mirrors that were set in such a way as to grant a sight of his body from every angle.

Cam twisted about, not recognizing himself from all the different viewpoints. After all, how often did a fellow need to look at his shoulders?

"Stop admiring your backside," Charity said.

Cam shot her a scowl. He wasn't admiring anything. It was just strange to see himself like this.

Her comment, however, earned her another speculative look from Master Jeffrey. "Quite so," the tailor said. "Your backside is quite nice, but please stop twisting about."

Many measurements followed, including of Cam's shoulders, his chest upon a deep inhalation and exhalation, his thighs, waist, and worse, his backside. Having some stranger touch him around those parts had him fidgeting.

"Stop moving around," Charity chided.

"I can't help it. I ain't some farmer's prized animal."

He caught Master Jeffrey's mouth twitch as humor gleamed in his eyes. "Did you say ain't?" He went on to mutter something under his breath about handsome men who shouldn't talk.

"You're not a farmer," Charity said. "But if you want to think of yourself as my prized ox, then feel free to do so. Just let Master Jeffrey do his job."

Cam laughed. "You'd best hope I'm not an ox."

Charity frowned, puzzled. "What's wrong with an ox?"

"Oxen are castrated. They're kept around for draft purposes." Charity viewed him in quiet consideration, and Cam could just about read her intentions. He scowled. "And I'm not your draft animal either."

"How about a steer?" Charity asked with a teasing smile.

"They're also castrated." Cam sighed in exasperation. "How do you not know these things?"

"I wasn't raised on a farm. What about a bull? Would that make you feel better?

"It might."

All the while, Master Jeffrey continued to measure, muttering under his breath about yokels needing luck in courting the daughter of a Sage.

Cam might have glared at the man, but a recollection about the rules of courting occurred to him. It was about how prior to a woman choosing a beau, the man had to prove himself respectable to her family. He shot a wondering look toward Charity. Was that what this was about? Charity wanted him dressed respectably for when he met her father? That's what had her feeling so nervous about this meeting between him and her father?

If so, then Cam figured he should probably take a more active role in making sure that Sage-Duke Kazar wasn't disappointed when they met. He straightened as Master Jeffrey brought out some samples for the promised clothing. There were items that Cam figured might make for a comfortable outfit, but even as he opened his mouth to make that observation, Charity shook her head, and Cam kept his opinion to himself.

Quality clothing wasn't an area of his expertise, and rather than argue with Charity about any of the choices, he reckoned it might be better to let her make the decisions. Beyond the fact that she was paying for it, she was also more likely to know what her father might find of good taste.

It was just past noon when Cam ticked off the last item on their list, and he did so with relish, like the paper itself had been a sadist. "We're done."

Charity glanced his way. "And I believe the paper knows exactly what will happen if it causes you any further trouble."

Cam grinned. "It surely will if it knows what's good for it."

"I'm sure it won't ever forget," Charity replied before flashing him a honey-warm smile. "We just have one last stop."

Cam groaned. He was sick to death of shopping. It had taken hours longer than he would have liked, and worse, he'd already ended up being used just like the draft animal he claimed he wasn't back in *Finely Crafted*. Both of his rucksacks bulged like they were fixing to break his back. "What now?"

"Lunch."

Cam eyed Charity in suspicion. "Lunch where? Someplace fancy?" He didn't mind the fancy food, but he hated the fancy way of dressing a person needed in order to enter a restaurant that served that kind of fare. Cam wasn't fancy, posh, or whatever rich folks called themselves, and never would be. He was straightforward and simple, and if that wasn't good enough for Charity, then maybe—

"I was thinking of street food. It'll give us a chance to talk on our way back to school."

Cam's internal diatribe cut off. Not only did he prefer street food over any other kind, but he could even afford it. He wouldn't need Charity's… charity. He smiled at the word play.

"I'm glad to see you no longer want to bite my head off," Charity noted as they set off from the leather worker's shop where they'd made their final purchase. "When I mentioned lunch, you looked at me like I was going to ask you to drink bilge water."

Cam didn't reply at once because what was there for him to say? Any words leaving his mouth right now would probably be the wrong ones. It certainly seemed likely given the morning he and Charity had just had. Ever since her comment about meeting her father, he'd been tense and unable to relax, in spite of his best efforts.

Thinking through the situation from her perspective should have settled him, but it hadn't. Logically, he knew she had legitimate reasons for saying and doing as she had, but his heart didn't seem to want to listen. He kept on fearing what that meeting with Sage-Duke Kazar might truly mean, like some secret sense giving him a niggle of a warning he couldn't decipher.

He snorted derision at the notion. It was so stupid. There was no warning to decipher. Everything he was feeling likely just stemmed from his own feelings about his lack of self-worth that lie at the heart of nearly every bad thing from his childhood. Cam only wished he could make that rational understanding a proper certainty that his heart could accept. Everything would be better then.

And his inability had him frustrated, unable to react well at Charity's attempts at humor. She was trying, and he was being a jackhole. He didn't like it—his behavior toward her—but the truth was, beyond that strange warning, he also felt like it was long past time to clear the air.

Before he could speak, though, Charity took a deep breath, as if she were preparing for an unpleasant experience. "Our relationship is new to me, and…" She drew him to a halt, guiding him toward a quiet alley away from the crowds. "You need to understand. I made no secret of how I was raised, the expectations set upon me. What I was told to master and how quickly, who could befriend me, who I could trust— everything was laid out."

Cam had a dreaded inkling where this was going. "And the kind of person allowed to court you?"

Charity nodded. "You aren't a noble, but that isn't as important as you might think. Not to me."

Cam tried to listen without prejudice, but Charity's words were easy ones to say, but how true could they actually be? Most people wouldn't go against their parents' disapproval, which meant that if he didn't impress her father, whatever he and Charity had was only ever going to be a temporary bit of fun. In the end, they'd go their separate ways, and his heart would be broken.

He silently berated himself. He'd always known that would be the most likely scenario, so why had he been stupid enough to get involved with Charity Kazar? He wanted to smack himself, but prior to getting too upset, it was probably best to hear it from her own lips. "And your father? How will he think of me?"

"I want his first impression of you to be one of acceptance. That's all."

"Do I have a chance to earn his acceptance?"

Charity smiled. "He'll love you if he's as smart as everyone says."

Cam thought long on her response, eventually allowing that it made sense. "I guess that's alright then." He held up a cautioning finger. "But when we meet my family, especially Pharis, you better know the difference between a bull and an ox. I'd be mortified if you didn't."

Charity flicked her eyes over him, voice throaty, smirking. "And I'm sure you'll be very willing to teach me." Her amusement cut off. "Not that I wouldn't love learning just how you intend to instruct me, but there's more about my father you should know. He wants you tied to the duchy. He was even willing to have me seduce you to see it done. But it was never supposed to be anything other than a physical fling. Do you understand why?"

Cam had an inkling, and a fresh pit opened in his gut. He nodded, staring at the ground while doing his best to hold on to his wounded pride. Charity hadn't come out and said it, but it sounded pretty obvious that her family, especially her father, wouldn't approve of him, of his country way of speaking. If that happened, then where did that leave him and Charity? Nowhere, probably. He sighed. "If your father doesn't approve of me or accept me, I'll leave it alone. I won't make your time with your family hard. I'm the leader of Light Squad. That's all your father will see."

When he looked up, he found Charity gazing at him, her brow furrowed in confusion. "What are you talking about? Do you think I wouldn't want to see you anymore just because my father might disapprove?"

Cam's heart jolted with hope that he'd misinterpreted her words. "That's not what you're saying?"

Charity shook her head, pity for him evident. "No, that's not what I'm saying, but I just want you to be prepared if that's how my father feels. But even if he can't accept the person you are and approve of our relationship, I'm not leaving you." She took his hands. "We are together, if you want the same thing I do."

Cam stared at her intent expression, thinking over his past and his present and what he might want with Charity. He inhaled deep, realizing he wanted it all. But did she? "And what do you want? For me to be your beau?" At the end, his courage failed him, and he couldn't fully express what was in his heart.

Charity chuckled. "An odd word, but appropriate. Will you be my beau? Can I be your belle?"

Cam smiled. "I'd like that. We are courting, after all." He bent to

Charity, glad for how tall she was. He kissed her, holding her close and not caring if some hoots and hollers trailed into the alley. There was only Charity.

9

Charity had hoped that her apology to Cam would have smoothed over his ruffled feathers, and it mostly seemed to have been the case, at least based on the kiss he'd planted on her. But a nagging doubt lingered over the mess she'd made of their day. Or maybe she was simply judging herself too harshly. After all, there had been the kiss, and it had been a good one. She shivered inside, remembering the feel of Cam holding her. His strong arms and soft lips.

Didn't that mean the afternoon had been salvaged?

And yet, her earlier behavior, the manner in which she'd tried to handle Cam, that continued to bother her, especially because she knew the reason for it. It stemmed from something she'd struggled with most of her life: her general mistrust of others, especially their motivations. Growing up, most people had only ever wanted to know her because she was the daughter of a Sage-Duke. She'd learned early on to doubt whomever she encountered and build barriers to protect her heart from those who only wanted to use her. The few people she'd allowed past her protections had invariably betrayed her trust. They showed their true faces once they got what they wanted, and over time,

Charity had learned it was best to give everyone nothing of herself. Let them see the facade but not the woman and person.

Cam, on the other hand… he had been a difficult one to understand. When she'd first met him, he had seemed pleasant enough but not particularly special. Unlike Victory, she hadn't been charmed by Cam's country accent, and to say that he'd surprised her later on was an understatement. Charity had never expected Cam's dogged determination or his cunning as a battlefield commander and eventual skill.

However, once she realized how much she had misjudged him, she'd begun testing Cam, seeking to draw him into her orbit, just as her father had wanted.

It hadn't worked. Cam never wavered from his intentions on leading Light Squad and mastering Ephemera. That had been his singular focus with no other desires to distract him, and Charity was eventually forced to concede that Cam was that rarest of individuals. He didn't need or want anything from her. In fact, he had actually seemed afraid of what she could give him—still was afraid—which led to a startling recognition. Charity could actually trust Cam.

Thinking about the unexpected truth, Charity wondered what it meant for her. For them. And ultimately, what did it mean about her wants in life? Would being the belle to Cam's beau be enough for her? And if so, where would that lead them both?

She exhaled in irritation, unable to answer any of the questions, and she viewed Cam askance as they strode back to the Ephemeral Academy. He seemed oblivious to her turmoil, but that probably wasn't so. He had depths of awareness but also possessed the grace to leave a person alone if the situation required it. Like now.

Charity faced forward again, reconsidering what had her upset with herself. She'd treated Cam poorly, and the reason was because of her underlying suspicious nature. Which meant she needed to be more cognizant of how her past could color her future with Cam. He'd earned her trust, and she needed to explain herself and her intentions more fully moving forward.

As it was, Cam had probably thought she was ashamed of him. She'd certainly acted like she was, but that wasn't the case. So what if the noble houses of Maviro wouldn't accept him as he was? They would once he Ascended to Crown—and Charity had no doubt he'd accomplish at least that much. Then there would be gushing admirers aplenty.

"*Do you want to talk about it?*" Cam sent.

Charity smiled in appreciation. Speaking telepathically to him felt more natural than using their voices. "*I was thinking of this morning, and how I treated you.*"

"*That still has you bothered?*" He sounded surprised, like it wasn't of any concern to him.

His attitude had Charity scowling in annoyance. "*Yes, it still has me bothered.*"

"*Why? I'm not upset anymore, so why are you?*"

Charity didn't have an answer.

"*You know, after it happened,*" Cam continued, "*I was so worried about what it might mean.*" He offered her a wry grin. "*We ain't exactly lived similar lives. My small town. Your capital. My poor old man, drunk most every night. Your father, a Sage-Duke. We're different in a lot of ways.*"

"*We grew closer in Hearth.*"

Cam nodded. "*But that wasn't exactly a normal situation, was it? All that stress and danger—it had us bonding or we'd likely have died. But we're home now and those terrors are gone. What holds us together?*"

"*You mean other than you staring at my backside?*"

"*Your front side isn't too bad, either,*" Cam said with a shrug. "*And if I recall right, you and Master Jeffrey were the ones staring at my backside.*"

Charity chuckled, but pondering Cam's initial question wiped the humor from her face. What did hold her and Cam together? Without the incessant terror of the Jom-Strafes, would they eventually drift apart? It would only be natural, expected really. Then where would they be? Mere acquaintances like they'd been before Hearth?

Just thinking about it had Charity shivering in alarm. No. That wouldn't be their future. She refused to allow it, and she made a decision then, gathering her courage before her qualms and distrust could further speak to her. She would hold faith to Cam, and if the worst happened, then so be it. But it wouldn't be because her frets and fears left her hollow and always looking for a reason to end their relationship.

As soon as she made the decision, Charity felt like her breathing came easier, that she could more fully enjoy her stroll with Cam. Simple things like lovely flowers sold by the roadside merchants smelled lovelier, the masterfully carved bowls sold in a vendor's stall appeared more beautiful, and the feel of Cam's hand in hers felt more right than ever before.

"You've figured out your problem?" Cam asked.

"I think so," Charity replied, smiling his way. *"What do you want for lunch? I'm hungry."*

"I was thinking either aloo tikki chaat or puri bhaji."

"Puri bhaji."

Cam grimaced. *"Are you sure? It was under-spiced the last time we had it."*

Charity felt herself relaxing further as they discussed the merits of their various choices. It was especially humorous since the correct answer was actually boli. Then again, Charity knew that might just be her sweet tooth talking.

In the end, she allowed Cam to have his aloo tiki, and afterward, they returned to the Academy, still walking hand-in-hand and in a pleasant silence.

"I'll see you at supper," Cam said when they reached her quarters.

"See you there," Charity replied.

Before leaving, Cam kissed her again, not the smoldering kind like from earlier, but it was still nice. Charity licked her lips, enjoying the show as Cam strode off. His backside truly was fine, the way his cheeks flexed and relaxed. As she watched, a notion flitted through her mind of Cam personally demonstrating the difference between a bull and an ox.

"Stop staring," Cam sent without turning around.

"It's worth staring at," Charity replied, unembarrassed to have been caught even as a part of her—a large part—wanted to call Cam back.

She wanted to kiss him again. That and much, much more.

But it would also be a terrible mistake. They weren't ready for that. She knew it, felt the truth of the sentiment resonate within her heart. Instead, Charity held her lips shut by force of will, and fanning herself, she stepped into her quarters, needing a cold shower.

For their final supper at the Ephemeral Academy, Light Squad chose to eat at the Blind Pig, the restaurant where Cam had worked for a summer.

It had been four years since Charity had last stepped foot in the place, and she found herself smiling in wistful recollection at its unaltered homeyness. So many good memories here, and all of them from when she'd been invited to Light Squad's many victory celebrations during their Novice year. There remained the tables that appeared to have once been beer barrels, the flagstoned flooring of an indeterminate original hue, and plaster walls that were overlayed with dark wood paneling that would eventually become fashionable again at some point.

Of course, that point wasn't now, but it also wasn't of any import because in that moment, what Charity appreciated most was the Blind Pig's predictability and utter normality. In her life since joining Light Squad, something unchanged and familiar was to be treasured.

"This way," a member of the wait staff said, breaking her free from reminiscences.

Light Squad was shown through the Blind Pig's dining area, which was already filling with the usual clientele of hardworking laborers and young families, and into a private room. There, the restaurant's proprietor, Master Fringe Green, waited for them. The heavy-set fellow, flushed of face and with a red apron heroically stretching across his ample abdomen, greeted them with a smile, going straight to Cam and hugging him. "It's good to see you again, boy. But don't make dying a habit. Just some friendly advice from your old bossman." He grinned the entire time.

As did Cam. "Wouldn't think of it. If I ever end up a corpse, how will I ever get to eat the best chicken biryani in Nexus?"

Master Green threw his head back and laughed. "Never change, Cam Folde." With that, the proprietor said a few more words, introducing the wait staff, a pair of young men who had the features and early girth of being either his sons or nephews and who would be taking care of them tonight. The two men took the drink orders, which consisted of water for everyone, although Cam tried to insist that it was fine if others wanted alcohol.

"It doesn't bother me at all anymore," he said. "Have some if you want. Don't hold back on my account."

But no one took him up on his offer, which wasn't surprising. In spite of how much they might tease him, everyone in Light Squad had a great deal of respect for Cam and were also protective of him. They placed their orders and settled in for a fine meal and fellowship, discussing their many adventures. Meanwhile, throughout the evening, the wait staff were perfectly polite, unobtrusive, and efficient in carrying out their tasks. Charity made a note to tip them well.

Jade, who was their best storyteller, reached the part of their journey in Hearth where they'd encountered the village of Vacacy and Graft Pubber and his bandits.

"That fragging bastard deserved what happened to him," Avia said with a scowl. "I wish I could have been there."

"Be glad that you weren't," Charity murmured to Avia, head down as she mechanically ate her food. Killing Graft had been a necessary evil, but she still recalled the heavy thunk of her killing arrow slamming into Graft's flesh. The nightmares from that sound continued to haunt her like an angry spirit.

"But look how much you learned," Avia said. "How much you experienced."

"We also lost four years," Cam reminded her.

Avia waved it off. "You lost nothing. You survived for months, gained control of Ephemera in ways that I still lack, and soon you'll be a Glory like me." She finished with a grin, although no one else at the table was smiling. Avia's own expression faltered as she glanced at the others, likely picking up on their emotions about the matter. "I'm sorry. I've heard most of what you experienced, but I didn't realize it was that bad."

"You don't have to apologize," Saira said, laying a hand over one of Avia's. "But our life there was harrowing. You should be grateful you were spared."

Cam nodded agreement, continuing the story and the mood lightened when he told about Rail Gristle and his inexplicable vast skill and knowledge.

"He was… impressive," Saira agreed. "I don't think I've ever met anyone quite like him."

"Other than Professor Shade," Card said, for once not grunting.

Saira inclined her head. "Correct. Other than him."

Charity recalled what Cam had recently mentioned to her: that Rail moved like Professor Shade, spoke like him, too. Until he'd mentioned it, she'd not made the link, but it seemed obvious in retrospect.

The conversation continued, reaching the part where Light Squad learned to kayak.

"When I'm a Glory, one of the first things I want to do is run the rapids near Charn," Pan declared.

Charity smiled. Pan's love for water was unexpected, especially since early on during their attempts at kayaking, he had hated it. Only later had the fever of speeding down the whitewater taken hold of his heart, and he'd whooped with joy whenever they'd come across any rapids.

"I'd love to run those rapids with you," Charity said to Pan, briefly flicking her eyes to Cam. "I'm pretty sure I can even convince at least one of the others to join us."

Cam, overhearing her comment, gave her a wry smile—he'd loved racing the rapids every bit as much as Pan, probably more—before he pushed on to describe his near death experience in battling a Jom-Strafe Glory.

"I still don't know how he managed to defeat that thing," Jade said with a disbelieving shake of her head.

"It was already pretty badly injured by the time we fought," Cam replied, trying to throw off the compliment like he always did.

"Maybe so," Jade said, "but you still had no business killing a creature two Stages of Advancement over your own."

Pan shuddered. "I don't think I've ever been as terrified as when we found Cam floating in the water."

Jade grinned. "You can say that again."

Pan did so, and everyone chuckled, even Card.

Charity, however, grimaced after the humor faded. She didn't like that memory. "I'm just glad he survived and thrived."

Cam arched his brow in question. "Thrived?"

"You're stronger and faster than before," Charity replied. "You have more endurance, too. Same as I, and your hair is like mine now as well, and we share the same skin tone."

"Like the two of you are siblings," Saira noted, a teasing smile lurking at the corners of her lips.

Cam chuckled. "Devesh, I hope not. We sure haven't been kissing each other like we're siblings."

Charity's brows lifted, and she viewed Cam in surprised fondness. He used to flush and flinch whenever anyone mentioned any woman showing interest in him, like it shocked or embarrassed him. Or that he was unworthy of the attention or some disaster might occur on account of it.

Look at him now, though, showing utter disregard over confirming their relationship. He'd come far.

While Charity smiled at Cam, everyone else laughed—everyone except for Jade, who wore a worried frown, a comment evident on the tip of her tongue. However, she didn't voice it, and the discussion moved on to the rest of their time in Hearth. Avia spoke afterward, describing her years getting her Tangs to Crystal and any other interesting events she could recall. Most of those centered around swimming or playing in the water.

Unfortunately, like all good things, the dinner slowly wound down, and they departed the Blind Pig, heading back to the Ephemeral Academy as a group with Cam striding ahead with Pan, Card, and Avia while Charity, Saira, and Jade trailed behind.

"Avia is rooming with you again," Charity said to Jade. "It must bring back a lot of good memories."

"It does, but she's still a slob."

"Messiness is in her nature," Saira noted.

Jade laughed, but her heart clearly wasn't in it.

Silence settled over their small group, and Charity caught Jade viewing her askance. She waited for the other woman to speak, unsure why she seemed so reluctant to say what was clearly on her mind. The three of them were friends, grown close in Hearth, trusting one another enough to talk about anything. So why this reticence? Did it have something to do with Jade's repressed comment from earlier in the evening? About her and Cam kissing?

Charity considered it likely. In fact, if she was a betting person, that's exactly what she would guess to be on Jade's mind. However, quiet continued to reign, and it eventually led Charity to sigh in mild annoyance. "What is it?"

"I know you and Cam are a couple," Jade began, "but is it just a fling for you? It better not be."

Charity smirked inwardly, glad that her insight into the motivations of others remained intact. "We are a couple, but—" She swallowed back words that could be interpreted as being uncertain about how she felt about Cam since there was no uncertainty. At the very least, she wanted to be the belle to Cam's beau. "I like him, and I really want to see where it can go. I hope it goes far. We both do. It's not a fling."

"Be careful with him," Jade warned. "When it comes to relationships, Cam's afraid of his own shadow."

Charity didn't need the reminder. Hurting Cam was the last thing she would ever want to do, and she flicked her gaze to him, wishing he truly knew his worth. He had so many admirable attributes. He was a *good* person.

A good-looking one, too, and she couldn't help but trace his shape.

She'd always been attracted to tall, powerfully built men, especially if they were intelligent, and Cam was all of those things and then some.

"Close your mouth or an insect might fly in," Saira admonished.

Charity chuckled. "It's hard not to stare at him."

"Or lust after him," Saira said with a warm laugh.

"He deserves to be seen in that way," Charity said, feeling defensive toward Cam for some reason. "Not just lusted after but loved." As soon as the final word left her mouth, Charity felt a lurch in her stomach. Had she just said love? Was that what she felt for Cam?

Before she could bury herself in an introspection for which she was unprepared, Saira thankfully interrupted. "He does deserve it, and until now, his feelings have always been unrequited."

"Which is why you better not hurt him," Jade added in a forceful tone.

"That's the last thing I'll ever do to him," Charity said.

"Good," Jade said, not dropping the matter. "You know what would happen if you did?"

Charity wanted to roll her eyes at the dramatic threat. "Let me guess. You'll find a way to make me pay?"

Jade waved away her comment. "Sure, I'll make you pay, but the one you really have to watch out for is Pan. He's loving and kind, but if you hurt Cam, he'll end you."

Charity viewed the sweet panda-person, reminded of the aphorism regarding a kind person grown angry. She nodded. "I take the warning."

10

Cam stood in the doorway leading into his bedroom and checked to make sure he hadn't forgotten anything. During his four years away from Golden, all of his personal belongings had been sent back to his family in Traverse, and with only a month and a half back at the school, there had been neither the time nor the desire to collect anything new. The bedroom was as spare as if he'd never lived in it for what had truly been a momentous period of his life, nothing to indicate his presence here, no mark to mention that he'd ever existed. It felt wrong, but other than carving his name onto the beam holding up the ceiling, what else could he do?

The lack of material possessions made packing pretty simple—his clothes and whatever gear Charity had purchased on his behalf for the journey to the temple, and he was good to go. But still, shouldn't there have been something of himself impressed into the walls, floor, or furniture? Anything, even a ghostly sensation to tell some part of his story to a future occupant?

Obviously not and after giving the room a final look-see, Cam headed into the main living space where Pan appeared about done with his packing as well, tucking a small book about the nature of Devesh into a vest pocket.

The sight reminded Cam of something he'd missed, and he darted back into his room, grabbing the copy of *The Warrior and the Servant* that he'd purchased yesterday and left on his dresser. Professor Shade probably wouldn't be too happy if he didn't have the book memorized the next time they met, which was a strange sort of idea to have, but it also felt right. The rest of the world believed Professors Shade and Grey had died, but Cam reckoned—prayed, actually—that he'd see them again.

"Forgot something?" Pan asked when he stepped back out.

Cam nodded, briefly displaying the slim philosophical text before finding a place for it in an interior pocket of a rucksack. That way, it would be safe from weather and ruination. He straightened, taking in their main living area for what was probably the last time.

It had been and remained a warm, cozy space, both welcoming and comforting with the morning light streaming in, reflecting off the high-gloss shine of the dining room table and spotlighting the couch and high-backed chairs. More importantly, this was where he and Pan had become so much more than either of them could have ever imagined. Their time at the Ephemeral Academy had been filled with progression, maturation, and eventual acceptance of their worth as individuals.

And again, there was nothing to indicate all their struggles. The room and quarters would belong to someone else soon enough, and they'd never know a single thing about the man and Awakened Beast who had achieved so much within these walls. It was a stark reflection of an underlying truth: everyone was born, lived, and died—often alone and in pain—and were soon forgotten.

Feeling melancholy, Cam heaved a tired sigh, hating the moment's finality. "This is it then. The end of our journey at the Ephemeral Academy."

Pan pressed his forehead into Cam's. "Our time here is done, but this was always just a stopping point. Our journey isn't over yet. I think our best selves and lives are ahead of us. We'll have plenty of bumps and bruises but also joys and triumphs. We're not finished with life."

Cam smiled, glad for Pan's presence and how easily his friend could draw him out of his moods. "You're right. We ain't done with growing. Advance to Divine or death, those are our options."

Pan laughed. "Is that the new phrase for Light Squad? Instead of no chance?"

Cam grinned. "It's a good one, right?"

"It's a good something."

Their conversation fell silent as they stared about the living room.

"I'm going to miss this place," Pan said, his eyes welling. "I know we still have a future, but this room meant something. This was our home." Pan's voice quavered, and he blinked rapidly, trying not to cry. He failed, and Cam drew him into a hug. They embraced, tears leaking down Pan's cheeks, a couple of sobs, too.

Cam waited for his friend to collect himself and leaned away once he did. "We'll make another home for ourselves, better than this one. Full of family, friends, and children. Like you said, the school was always only a stopping point. These rooms are the same."

Pan sniffed a few more times. "You're right. It was always only a stopping point, but what a good stopping point it was." A moment later, he tilted his head at Cam, offering a thoughtful expression. "You think children will ever be in our future? Given all the danger we're bound to face, it doesn't seem likely, does it?"

Cam shrugged, wiping at Pan's tears and pressing a strained smile past his own sorrow. "Why wouldn't they be? I never figured on having little ones running underfoot, but it only sounded right after hearing about Pharis and her young 'uns. Who knows? Darik might even have some children now that he's married."

Pan grinned. "You yokeled on purpose."

Cam chuckled. Pan was right. He had used a backwoods word on purpose, but it had also served its purpose. It had gotten his friend to smile. But there was a certain gleam lighting Pan's eyes, a not-so hidden delight. The reason wasn't hard to fathom, either, and Cam closed his eyes, praying for patience, even while hoping the patience wouldn't be needed.

Unfortunately, his patience proved necessary.

"Anyone in particular you have in mind for the mother of your children?" Pan asked, mouth twitching with a repressed smile.

Cam opened his eyes, staring at Pan in mock-consternation. "You really think I'm going to answer that?"

Pan chuckled lightly. "Your lack of an answer is answer enough."

"And you're still not getting an answer," Cam replied, shooting his friend a scowl.

The teasing glint never left Pan's eyes. "I'm guessing the mother of your children will be the first woman you meet who knows the difference between a bull and an ox."

Cam gaped. He'd mentioned that to Pan in confidence. "I knew I shouldn't have told you about that."

Pan chortled, clearly pleased with himself.

"That's the last time I share a secret with you," Cam said, not having to feign annoyance.

His irritation must have broken through Pan's smugness because his ears wilted. "I'm sorry," he said, his expression one of honest contrition. "I didn't know it meant so much to you."

"Well, it did," Cam snapped. The room fell silent, Pan still remorseful, but eventually Cam breathed out a sigh, the anger gone. "It's fine, but this relationship is new to me, and I don't like it how you're always needling me about Charity. Let me figure it out some before you go making fun of it all the time."

"I really am sorry."

"I know." An instant later, a fresh occurrence had Cam scowling once more. "And you better not tease me when Charity is around. She'll cut you quick with that tongue of hers."

"Yes, I'm sure," Pan said, smiling again. "You'd know more about her tongue than anyone."

Cam couldn't help but laugh. "You're incorrigible, you know that?"

"It's part of my charm?"

"The fact that you have to ask should tell you everything you need to know."

They both laughed, but moments later, the room went quiet as they glanced around a last time.

Cam inhaled deep, exhaling slow. "It's time."

As one, they left the quarters that had been their home and shelter.

From Weld's vantage point sitting in a rocking chair on his front porch, he had a perfect line of sight to the Academy's main gates while the shaded balcony out back looked at Nexus' bay and the statues of Rukh and Jessira. The heavy sun burned down at an angle right into his face and the muggy weather that draped the world might have bothered those of lesser Advancement. But for a Glory, it meant nothing.

And since it meant nothing, Weld ignored it, lost in his thoughts and plans. He was closing in on Crown, not as fast as some reckoned, but still quick enough. He'd likely get it done within months of leaving the Academy. He grinned thinking on all the fools who figured he'd train a bunch of useless Novices in Kinesthia. Weld snorted. What a waste of his time. He had many tasks far worthier of his precious time.

Of course, there was that missing piece of surety that he needed in order to Advance to Crown. That and a massive amount of Ephemera, the latter of which was a problem, which got him scowling. His liege had promised many things, delivered on every occasion, but not recently when it came to giving Weld his due. Always there was some delay.

Do this. Do that. Just a few more months, and you'll have what I promised.

Frag that. Weld was tired of waiting. He'd done everything his liege had asked and some of it had been flat-out disgusting, downright distasteful, sometimes even dangerous. But Weld had done everything asked of him because he knew something no one else had seemed to believe. Weld had always known that Cam Folde would come back from Hearth. He'd never doubted the jackhole would find a way to survive Nailing's and Nageena's attack.

And being prepared for that eventuality was the reason Weld had done as his liege had demanded, all the while racing after the carrot of more Ephemera and Advancement like a hound going for a squirrel.

Well, that had been in the past, and Weld was owed for the work he'd done. The payment was past due, and it was time to collect.

Dark thoughts of what would happen if his liege proved a traitor swirled through Weld's mind as he considered his options. For reasons he didn't care to pursue, the idea of betrayal cast his thoughts on the statues in the harbor, and the reminder caused him to grimace. Every time he looked at the statues, he felt like they were staring at him, judging him, and finding him wanting.

Well, let's see what those statues had to say when Weld Advanced to Crown. Or better yet, when he Advanced to Sage.

He chuckled to himself. It was silly. Nothing like that would ever happen. Beyond the fact that statues couldn't talk, Rukh and Jessira were long departed from Salvation. They'd outgrown caring for this world, which was why in the end the rakshasas would win. Weld was sure of that. Fact was, everyone probably knew it, even prigs like Rainen Winder, but they just weren't brave or wise enough to face the truth.

Well that wasn't Weld. He had courage aplenty along with the wisdom to hitch his wagon to a rakshasa Sage who would help him rise to greatness.

Nodding at his future success, Weld sipped at his nearly boiling-hot morning tea, which was hot enough to steam. Of course, that didn't mean much to a Glory. Weld might be impressed if his drink had truly been boiling. For now, though, there wasn't any reason to even bother blowing on the tea to cool it down any or parcel it out in small sips. Weld just drank it straight, like it was lukewarm.

With a satisfied smack of his lips, he made to return to his contemplations on how to Advance to a Crown, but those deliberations cut off like a snipped thread when a sight he'd expected to see for the past few days came strolling down the road: Light Squad, geared up and heading out of the Academy. Based on their sourpuss expressions, they didn't plan on coming back anytime soon. And if he and his liege had their way, that time would be never.

Weld grinned at their hangdog faces. They had no idea. He smiled, cruel and vindictive, wondering in a desultory fashion if he'd ever have a chance to teach those arrogant bastards some instructions on pain before they were turned over to the Lord. He sure hoped so.

Having them know he'd been the one to do them dirty would be the final dish of his long-simmering revenge, especially for two in particular. Them two would pay the ultimate price today, this very morning, which would be a fine start to what was shaping up to be a truly lovely day. Everything was in place, and there was no way for them to escape.

Weld's smile widened.

11

After exiting the Academy grounds and collecting the clothes Charity had purchased for him, the rest of the walk through Nexus reminded Cam of a funeral procession. It made no difference that the world was bright and sun-filled. Underlying it all was the feeling of a gloomy cloud hanging overhead, something that dimmed the light, and it was for the same reason he'd been so despondent when departing his quarters. This was a leave-taking. This might be his and Light Squad's last time walking these streets that had come to mean so much to them, especially him.

Sure Cam hadn't spent many hours in the city itself, but he'd viewed it plenty from the Academy's grounds, and there was a familiarity to it that he'd miss. Just like he'd miss the school itself.

Charity, walking by his side, wore a stiff expression, and Cam recognized she might be feeling some of the same nostalgia that he was experiencing. He reached for her hand, hoping to bring her comfort, and she squeezed his in silent thanks. They walked that way for a while, but when Cam sought to release the hold, Charity held tight.

She glanced at him, her eyes soft and glistening. *"Don't let go?"*

Cam gave a tight-lipped smile at the questioning note at the end of her statement, wishing she felt more confident in his support. Of course he'd hold her hand. Wanting to offer her further proof, Cam lifted Charity's hand to his lips and kissed her fingertips. *"We'll take on the world together."* Her smile of surprised delight was everything he could have hoped to see.

"Thank you," she whispered.

"You're welcome," he whispered back.

They shared a private smile as they paced behind Saira, Pan, and Jade who had the lead while Card and Avia marched at the rear, the two of them sharing their own hushed conversation.

Cam was glad for it. Avia had yet to fully reforge her bonds with the rest of the squad, and doing it with the ever-grumpy Card was a great first step.

The streets narrowed in places, widened in others and Light Squad journeyed on. They entered a neighborhood of colorful homes and buildings with awnings stretched out over the sidewalks. Shadows pooled in places but the area remained lively and alert with young families walking about, many of them collecting at a glade on the edge of a cliff leaning out over the waters of Lake Nexus. And everywhere there were corner street vendors selling their aromatic wares from food wagons parked near statues of heroes—not just Rukh and Jessira but others such as Divines, Sages, and even those of lesser Advancement who had managed to achieve something remarkable in their lives.

Seeing it all, this clear example of folks living a normal and happy life, Cam redoubled his vow to see the rakshasas either brought to justice or ended.

Later on, the crowds thinned and quieted, but several blocks on, at a farmers' market, the raucousness returned. Light Squad pushed through the throngs of shoppers and merchants, and a few minutes later, they were through, back in a residential block. This one contained closely spaced homes, tall and with elaborate woodwork and gabled windows. It was a wealthier district of generally older people, all of whom were dressed in fine garb.

However, upon studying their clothing, Cam realized that what they wore wasn't as nice as the shirts and pants that Charity had purchased for him. Master Jeffrey truly knew his craft. Cam's new clothes were truly splendid, fit him perfectly, better than anything he'd ever worn. They hadn't even required any kind of adjusting, and as before, it had him wondering on the cost of something so fine. However, when he'd asked Charity, she'd told him not to worry about it, which of course only caused him to wonder even more

They strode on, and eventually Cam tossed aside considerations about the cost of his clothing when Light Squad reached an area where the buildings and homes thinned. He tensed then, and he wasn't the only one. Everyone seemed to feel the same way. They were closing in on the park where Nailing and Nageena had ambushed them, and Cam couldn't shake the worry of it happening again. And based on everyone else's tight-lipped expressions, they seemed to worry the same as him.

Charity spoke, seemingly trying to calm everyone's nerves. "My father has oversight of the city today."

"Merit's mother had it last time," Card muttered.

No one had much to say after that comment, and they hustled through the area, not slowing until they finally reached their destination: a white granite shelf, sheltered upon a black cliff and overlooking Lake Nexus.

Cam inhaled sharply at the sight, his breath stolen by the beauty. A harbor of aqua-blue waters smashing against black stone with rainbow-colored sprays resembling stained glass lofted high. And set like a perfect backdrop rose a vast city in alabaster stone and indigo roofs. Near the waters, a blessedly stiff breeze blew away summer's mugginess.

However, Cam's attention quickly centered on the man standing on the platform. Sage-Duke Kazar. Even without seeing his violet-hued sclerae, his Advancement was evident simply based on the weight of his existence, which pressed outward with a greater sense of reality than the stones upon which he stood. In this, he was similar to Master Winder, although possibly less potent. At least, that's the impression

Cam drew from the Sage-Duke.

Other impressions. Charity's father was of above-average height, slimly built, and clean-shaven. Handsome as well, and clad in dark clothing of an even finer fit than Cam's newly acquired garb. He possessed no weapon, which only made sense. A Sage was the weapon.

As they approached the Sage-Duke, Cam studied the man further, noticing where Charity got the shape of her eyes, her nose, and the perfect arch to her eyebrows. It came from her father, who was staring at her with a warm smile that never faltered even when Charity quickly shook her hand free of Cam's.

The Sage-Duke hadn't missed their connection, but he seemed to ignore it, stepping forward and drawing Charity into a brief hug while he continued to smile. "It's wonderful to see you again, child. Are you ready to come home?"

Charity peered at her father, frowning slightly in seeming study, but seconds later, her features cleared. "Can we can count on your overflight when we enter the temple?"

The Sage-Duke nodded. "Of course. The disaster from four years ago won't recur, either here at Nexus, Maviro, or the temple." He smiled wider. "Let's get you home. Your mother has a banquet prepared." He gestured, and the world trembled. From directly above the ground, a black line rippled and firmed, spun on its axis before widening to expose a doorway filled with a swirling rainbow bridge.

Seconds after it lit into existence, Charity was the first one through and following her at regular intervals of thirty seconds were Avia, Jade, and then Card. Next was Saira, and after her, Pan… but before he could enter, the anchor line faded away.

Sage-Duke Kazar offered a sickly smile of apology. "Sorry about that. I'm not as skilled with forming anchor lines as some."

He cast his hand, and once again, a black line rippled, flickering as a static noise sounded. The anchor line steadied for an instant before flickering and crackling again. Cam frowned at the Sage-Duke's inability to stabilize the anchor line. The black line eventually firmed, rotating to reveal a rainbow bridge extending into infinity.

"There we go," Sage-Duke Kazar said with a proud flourish and a grin as sweat beaded on his brow.

Pan gave the Sage-Duke a questioning look.

"Hurry now," the Sage-Duke urged. "As I said, I'm not as skilled as some at creating anchor lines."

Pan shrugged, stepping through. Cam made to follow, but before journeying to Maviro, he faced back one last time, staring the way they'd come, recollecting all he'd accomplished on this beautiful island. He'd never forget it. He stepped through the anchor line, glancing back one last time…

And saw Weld Plain smiling triumphantly from a dozen yards away, flipping him a crude gesture.

A horrified certainty filled Cam's mind. Light Squad had been betrayed. The image was swept away, and the anchor line consumed him.

Weld laughed uproariously as soon as he saw that self-righteous prig, Cam Folde, enter the anchor line. The fragging jackhole had even looked back one last time before stepping through, and the shock on his face had been beautiful to behold. It was just too good. Cam must have known right then and there that Weld had gotten one over on him and there was nothing he could do about it, not in this life or any other to come.

The fact was, Cam's fate was sealed. He was heading somewhere other than Maviro and Charity's soft kisses. Somewhere dark and ugly, and there wasn't no coming back from it. The man and his fragging panda were as good as dead, but first, he'd learn the meaning of pain, and maybe in the middle of that torture, he'd finally regret all of those times he'd spoken ill toward Weld.

"My role in this is complete," Sage-Duke Kazar said as soon as Weld sauntered over. "Tell your liege to never trouble me again."

"That was the agreement between you and my liege," Weld responded with an agreeable nod.

"Then our time together is done." Kazar turned away and gestured, no doubt fixing to create another anchor line.

"Hold on a moment." Weld knew his comment was a mite cheeky, but he also didn't care given his recent triumph.

The Sage-Duke glanced back, glaring hard, a contemptuous expression on his face. Weld ignored the other man's anger. He'd endured far worse and come out on top on every other occasion. This time wouldn't be any different.

"I know you've done what you promised," Weld said, "but I could use an anchor line, too. My time at the Ephemeral Academy is about done. I need to get gone, so if you don't mind too much, I'd be mighty grateful if you'd forge an anchor line out of here on my behalf." He winked at the poleaxed Sage-Duke. "If you do that, I'm sure I can put in a final, last good word with my liege." Weld grinned, knowing the expression was cocksure and not caring too much. What was Kazar going to do? Weld was protected, and if the Sage-Duke aimed on hurting him, he'd only hurt his precious daughter, too. Weld's liege would see her killed, and then he'd turn Maviro to rubble.

The Sage-Duke viewed him in disgust. "Your *liege* can see to it, traitor."

Traitor, was he? Weld wanted to laugh in the Sage-Duke's face, but that might be pushing the situation a mite farther than was safe. Still, as he reckoned matters, no insult should ever go unchallenged. "I ain't the one who just betrayed two Ephemeral Masters, including the man Rainen Winder was figuring would be the next Wilde Sage." The Sage-Duke's eyes narrowed, and the reaction had Weld grinning. "That's right. I heard it from Winder's own fat mouth." Kazar's disapproving stare became a scowl, which had Weld grinning wider. He imagined what the Sage-Duke was probably thinking just now, about what would happen later on if Rainen asked about Cam Folde. It was easy enough to lie to Crowns and Adepts, but to do that to another Sage? That wasn't so easy. Given that, Weld figured he might as well turn the screws a little harder. "And reckon on this: that same man might have been your son-in-law. Your daughter loved him."

Kazar's scowl turned murderous. "You lie."

Weld shook his head, not bothered in the least by the Sage-Duke's anger. "I ain't lying. Charity loved Cam, or at least she loved kissing him. If kissing was the same as fornication, she'd have been pregnant with his children five times over by now."

Weld's smug self-assurance abruptly ended when he found himself unable to breathe. The Sage-Duke held him by the throat, lifting him off the ground, choking him. Weld grabbed at Kazar's hand, unable to move it. Panic filled him. This wasn't right. Kazar couldn't do this. Weld had protection. When his liege learned what had happened…

The Sage-Duke brought Weld close, speaking soft and deadly. "Listen well, insect. What I did was for my duchy and my people. It brought me no joy. Whoever Cam Folde might or might not have been, he was ten times more worthy than a mewling serpent like you. Do not test me again."

Weld gasped when Kazar tossed him aside, grateful to be able to breathe and grateful no one was around to see his humiliation. He rubbed at his bruised throat, terrified but furious. "My liege will hear of this," he spat, working up the courage to scramble to his feet and glare at the other man.

Kazar smirked. "I'm shaking. Ask him to come tell me personally of his affront. He won't like my response. You'll like it less."

The Sage-Duke making light of the situation had Weld's fury surging, and he made a promise to himself. There would come a reckoning over what Kazar had just done. Weld promised himself there would be, and when it happened, he'd cut out the man's liver and feed it to him. For now, though, threats would have to do. "You ain't untouchable. Your daughter and duchy are at risk. My liege promised to leave them alone, but he can always figure things differently if I tell him to."

Kazar's smirk deepened. "So you control him, do you? Then maybe I should just kill you now and be done with it."

He paced forward, and Weld backed away in terror. All his prior cockiness was gone like a leaf blown away by a wind. Survival was his sole focus, and he spoke as fast as he'd ever done. "He won't hear it from me. Promise. Everything worked out good. You go your way, and I'll go mine. Ain't no need for you to even forge an anchor line on my behalf. I'll make my own way off of Nexus."

The Sage-Duke halted, his contempt obvious. "You truly are a coward, aren't you?" He shrugged. "In that case, who am I to deny your liege such a worthy follower? Where do you wish to go?"

Weld viewed the Sage-Duke with uncertainty. Was Kazar really offering to send him wherever he wanted to go? It would make his travels a whole lot easier. But still, even if Kazar forged him an anchor line, it didn't mean that Weld would ever forget what had happened here, especially that crack about him being a coward. Best to keep that to himself for now, though. "Send me home," Weld said. "It's time me and my old man had a long talk."

"You'll kill him."

It was a statement rather than a question, and Weld shrugged in dismissal. "Probably, but not until after the old man learns his place."

"And after that?"

"After that is between me and my liege." Weld had no intention of ever discussing his future plans with the Sage-Duke. No one needed to know about the boil eventually to be constructed in Charn. It suited Weld just fine that it happened to be near enough to Cam's old home of Traverse. He had plans for that town.

The Sage-Duke stared his way for a few seconds before speaking. "You plan on convincing your master to create a boil in Charn, somewhere close to Traverse. Either that, or one is already being constructed there. Your hatred of Cam Folde knows no bounds."

Weld kept his jaw from dropping by the barest of margins. How the fragging hells had the Sage-Duke figured that out? It wasn't the entire truth. Weld couldn't convince his liege of anything, but still, Kazar's guess had been close enough.

Kazar laughed in his face. "You're as obvious as you are pathetic." He gestured, and an anchor line circled to life. "Leave now. Go home. Settle matters with your father. Convince your master of your deepest desires. In the end, they won't matter. You'll always be a worm. And I'll gladly be rid of your stench."

Weld straightened his shoulders. He wanted to tell the Sage-Duke off, but now wasn't the time. He didn't have the power, but one day, he would. He'd Advance to Crown and then to Sage, and when that happened, Kazar would beg him to end his life.

With every bit of dignity that he could gather around himself, Weld stepped onto the anchor line.

Sial wasn't sure what was going on, but he knew it couldn't be right. What were Sage-Duke Kazar and Weld Plain talking about? The two of them were deep in conversation, but based on their demeanors, neither cared for the other very much.

So why were they talking? And what was the topic of their discussion?

Sial continued to watch from a distance, hidden under the shadowed boughs of a tree. He'd rushed here—to the only area in Nexus where anchor lines could be forged—intent on joining Light Squad on their trek to the temple that Master Winder had discovered.

Even with Saira and Avia, they might need his protection—plenty of rakshasas circled the surrounding hills—and he should have told them earlier about his desire to go with them. If he had done so, he wouldn't have had to run here at a sprint upon discovering that they'd already departed the Academy. Soft emotions, however, were hard for Sial to express, especially those involving the care he felt for another.

And he cared for Light Squad. In many ways, he'd never stopped thinking of them as his students. They were his pride and joy.

True, he'd not been the one to train them following their first year, but that was only because Master Winder had him wandering all over Golden and killing rakshasas. But that didn't mean Sial hadn't often thought about Light Squad. He had, and it was why he had come here in such haste, arriving only to discover something odd.

When he'd reached the area, there had only been Cam, Pan, and

Sage-Duke Kazar present. No one else. The sight had raised an obvious question: where was the rest of Light Squad? Then the Sage-Duke had said something to Cam and Pan before gesturing and creating an anchor line. However, this one had wavered like Kazar was struggling to control it and several seconds had passed before it firmed into existence. And when it did, Cam and Pan had entered it without hesitation. And following their exit from Nexus, the anchor line had surprisingly vanished, which made no sense.

Sial had been told that Light Squad meant to go to Maviro, to the Sage-Duke's palace, before journeying to the temple Rainen had offered them. So why had Kazar let go of the anchor line? Shouldn't he have stepped through it right after Cam and Pan?

Forging an anchor line wasn't easy, and if the Sage-Duke had already made one for the other members of Light Squad, a second one for Cam and Pan, then why waste the energy on a third? And he'd need a third unless he meant to fly back to Maviro. True, Kazar was powerful, and for him, forging a third anchor line wouldn't necessarily be a strain, but he'd still be feeling it for a few days.

Sial continued struggling trying to make sense of the situation.

Then Weld Plain had flashed into existence, apparently Blended and waiting until everyone else was gone. That's when he and Kazar began discussing matters, something secret given the warping of air that one of them had placed around the dais and which made eavesdropping impossible.

Not knowing what else to do, Sial had continued to watch, Blended now.

Things between Kazar and Weld became a little more interesting when the Sage-Duke grabbed the other man about the neck, lifted him off the ground, and said something to him before tossing him aside.

What had that been about? Nothing good for Weld as far as Sial could tell.

There had been more conversation, but this time Weld appeared humbled during their talk. Seconds later, the Sage-Duke gestured again and created a third anchor line. This one had a normal appearance, but

Sial's jaw dropped in worsening consternation when it, too, closed after Weld entered it.

What was going on? Surely Weld wasn't going with Light Squad to Maviro. That would be insane. They hated him. So why create so many anchor lines? Where were they all going? And why had Kazar done Weld such a favor, especially after choking him and flinging him away like a bug?

Everything about the situation seemed deeply wrong, even ominous, especially for Cam and Pan since Weld had waited for them to leave before revealing himself. Sial's concern heightened further when Kazar created a *fourth* anchor line, confirming in his mind the troubling oddity of the morning's events.

Sial retained his Blend and rushed away from the Sage-Duke, thinking deep and wondering who to trust. Something wicked had occurred this morning. Of this, Sial was certain, and he pondered who to tell about it.

Master Winder? That seemed the most likely option, but Sial dismissed it out of hand. The Wilde Sage cared only for killing rakshasas, not whatever had happened here at Nexus. And given his temper, especially if he felt like his time had been wasted, contacting him wouldn't be a good decision, at least not yet.

Sial shook his head. No. It would be better to reach out to Saira. He trusted her, could use her wisdom. Nodding to himself, Sial rushed away from the platform where the Sage-Duke still stood, heading for the docks and the ships. Given the ominous nature of this morning's events, he needed to get off Nexus and find a place to hide.

12

Sage-Duke Ahktav Kazar watched as the wretched Glory—a rakshasa of all things—prepared to enter the anchor line. How the filthy man strutted and preened, so proud of his meager accomplishments. Ahktav wanted to snap his neck.

But he couldn't. The Glory was protected to an extent, the representative of dangerous powers in this world—rakshasa Sages whose might and reach were growing ever more bold as the years went by. The awareness of their power had Ahktav wondering if Rainen was right about the Sage-Dukes needing a united front in their war against the fiends.

Until now, it hadn't seemed necessary, especially given the costs incurred by such a ghastly conflict. If threatened, the rakshasas had made it clear that they didn't believe in a just war where only those with Ephemera would fight one another and noncombatants would be spared. Rather, the rakshasas believed in a kind of conflict where everyone would be vulnerable to their malice.

Twenty years ago, they'd demonstrated their position when Borile Defent, the Silver Sage of Weeping, had completely wiped out a small town of two thousand souls. It was only thanks to luck and happenstance that Rainen had managed to track down and kill the murderous rakshasa before he could perform any further barbarous acts.

Nonetheless, the lesson had landed. If the Sage-Dukes ever came after the rakshasas in force, the monsters would enact a pogrom against every person they could slay. No one would be spared or considered sacrosanct. Hundreds of thousands would perish, the great cities enveloped in flames and ruin, and the continent awash in blood, centuries in recovering. And those were the best case scenarios.

It was because of those fears that Sage-Duchess Thens, and now Ahktav, had both temporarily bent the knee to the rakshasa Sages. It wasn't because of cowardice but rather due to measured doubt. Could they actually defeat the rakshasas? And in the process, could they save enough of Golden to make the victory worthwhile?

Ahktav wasn't sure on either question. None of them were, and none of them shared Rainen's certainty that war was inevitable and it was best to fight it now on their own terms.

Making such bold proclamations had always been easy for the Wilde Sage, legendary in his unchanging repetitiveness, and by this point, he was largely ignored. After all, Rainen didn't bear any responsibility beyond his own needs or those of his military units. He had no one else to serve and save, and after a war against the rakshasas, he wouldn't be the one helping to rebuild shattered lives, villages, and towns. All Rainen would do was fight and kill, what he'd always done in his long life.

Ahktav snorted in derision. No. The Wilde Sage would merely send his various companies—Sidewinder and others—into the heart of battle, but he'd never have to deal with the aftermath. That task would be left for the Sage-Dukes alone, and the ugly calculus of what would occur in a conflagration like that was why Ahktav was only staring after the Glory who'd mocked him rather than killing him like he deserved.

After the man departed, Ahktav let go of the anchor line and mused further over Weld Plain, a man whose skills were every bit as nondescript as his surname. Rainen had miscalculated with that one, believing him to be supremely gifted given his Advancement to Glory in such a swift fashion, especially following his expulsion and readmittance to the Ephemeral Academy.

Then again, none of the Sage-Dukes had seen through Weld's deceit, not quickly enough, at any rate. True, they'd had their doubts about him, but Weld's explanation about how Nailing and Nageena had simply overlooked him during their battle against a pair of impossibly skilled Glories seemed reasonable at the time, especially since he'd been found buried beneath the rubble of a fallen building and uprooted tree. And his statement for why he had been meeting with Light Squad—a desire to mend fences with his old unit—had also sounded likely, in spite of what Sage-Duke's Vail's daughter had said later upon her return to Nexus.

Indeed, there were other reasons not to doubt Weld's words. After all, a mere Acolyte couldn't have granted Nailing and Nageena entrance to Nexus. The rakshasas would have required the aid of a Sage-Duke, specifically the help of Marsula Thens, who had control and oversight of the island at the time. Her failure had been the more pressing issue. That and the questions raised by a pair of Glories—the instructors at the Academy—apparently able to hold off two skilled rakshasa Sages. The various issues had distracted everyone enough for Weld to largely escape notice.

The question as to whether someone might have turned traitor—Marsula or Weld—had been whispered but swiftly set aside. In the end, it had been determined that Nailing and Nageena must have devised some unforeseen means to enter Nexus at the same time that Marsula had anchor lined Weld Plain onto the island. Immediately afterward, two Glories had miraculously fought off the rakshasa Sages until help arrived with the only loss being that of Light Squad.

A political compromise at its worst that assigned no blame to any particular person and cast no shadow on anyone's integrity. Essentially a tragic accident was how it had been deemed, which in hindsight, was absolutely ridiculous. But wasn't history littered with similar situations? Of people believing what they wanted to be true and not seeing what actually was?

Regardless, it was why Weld had been allowed to stay at the school, and for a while, he'd been closely monitored. However, the wretched boy had done well, demonstrating competence and composure. In addition, not once had the stink of bad behavior attached to him even as he'd quickly Advanced, which the Sage-Dukes took as further confirmation of his improved nature and significant talent.

Marsula had also been closely watched, but she, too, had revealed no changes in her behavior. She'd even been instrumental in the destruction of several powerful boils, including the killing of a handful of rakshasa Sages in her duchy. Both Marsula and Weld had performed well over the years, casting no hint of treasonous behavior.

But then Nailing had reached out to Ahktav and the truth had been revealed. The Sage of Warring Thunder had united the rest of his kind well enough to threaten an individual duchy, and right now, his sights were set on Maviro. That is unless Ahktav did as Nailing bid and send two promising young Ephemeral Masters to Mote, to Hell. A simple-appearing *nomasra* would see it occur.

Ahktav shook his head. How had it come to this? He once again considered Rainen's exhortations that the Sage-Dukes forge a union, and for the first time, an inkling of doubt entered his mind. Maybe they should come together and put aside their machinations.

He sighed. Organizing nine men and women, who each thought they knew best wouldn't be easy. Putting aside such a difficult proposition, Ahktav considered the lie he'd been forced to commit toward his daughter, who clearly had deep feelings for Cam Folde. Hurting someone he loved was never pleasant, but at least it hadn't been difficult. In truth, Charity was a bit of a disappointment. No expense had been spared in helping her Advance, but here she was, still an Adept when at the same age, he had been a Glory.

The harder deception, though, would be when Ahktav had to address Saira Maharani. Lying to her would be tricky, and lying to her mother, the ferocious Sage of the Sinanes, Lysha Maharani, even more so. But one element that would be on Kazar's side would be the strain from creating a fourth anchor line in such short order.

A plan came together in his mind, an improbability that would be questioned and doubted, but with Marsula's support, it would hold, a mix of falsehoods and truths. Plus, Ahktav already had someone perfect on whom to blame for this disaster. He'd sensed the Glory's presence—Orthosial Shivein—and while Ahktav had initially intended on slaying him immediately for witnessing what he shouldn't have, the Awakened turtle had fled. Now, it was too late to hunt him down. Ahktav tsked to himself. He really should have killed the Glory when he had the chance.

Still, though, the turtle could yet serve, but it would be in some other capacity, that of a scapegoat. All it would take would be a few judicious lies and others would see to Sial's death without Ahktav having to lift a finger. Pleased with the hastily drawn-together plan, the Sage-Duke created an anchor line and headed home.

Charity had already recovered from the travel through the anchor line to Maviro when Avia stepped through. The other woman stumbled slightly, and Charity quickly moved to help. She supported Avia by the shoulder and arm and guided her away from the anchor line so the rest of Light Squad could arrive without any issue.

Avia offered a strained smile as she dealt with the nausea of exiting an anchor line, but within seconds, she had recovered. She nodded her thanks and withdrew from Charity's assistance, glancing about. "You have a beautiful home."

Charity flicked her eyes over the private plaza into which she and Avia had arrived. Attached to the Sage-Duke's palace, it was the only place in the city where anchor lines were permitted, and although she had been here so many times that the luster had worn off, Avia was right: the plaza was beautiful. It was a round space, decorated with scattered planters containing flowering ginger intermixed with yellow- and pink-hued blossoms, hanging baskets of red-hot cattails drooping to the ground, and arrangements of jasmine, whose aroma perfumed the air. And ringing the plaza like silent sentinels towered a squadron of red maples.

However, that was only part of the plaza's beauty. Beyond the trees, a half-wall of gray granite perimetered the space with paper vines softening the stone before they trailed down to red brick pavers that were laid out in a herringbone pattern that pointed inward toward a large fountain. There, a statue of gently smiling Jessira stood with her arms outspread, and from her hands, water poured forth, cascading in a gentle wash as droplets flung about, scintillating in the air as tiny rainbows. The spray relieved some of the summer heat, but it was the strangely shaped statues, odd creatures perched on the fountain's edge, that captured Charity's attention. One of the beings was small and doglike, another appeared to be an upright cat, and a third was a creature with the build of a bull. No one recalled what they might have been—perhaps an ancient type of rakshasa—but all of them bowed low to Jessira.

Moments later, Charity's examination of the plaza ended when others from Light Squad began joining them. Jade and Card followed by Saira, who stepped through the anchor line, which unexpectedly rippled and ended.

Charity took a halting step toward where the rainbow bridge had been. What had just happened? Where were Cam, Pan, and her father? The anchor line shouldn't have just ended like that. Charity continued to view the area in rising alarm, and the others appeared to share her concern.

"Does anyone know what's going on?" Jade asked.

Charity didn't answer. No one did.

A minute passed, and still nothing.

Saira broke the silent tableau. "Something's wrong. I'm going to call my mother." She withdrew a *nomasra* and spoke softly into it.

Charity couldn't hear what Saira's mother was saying, but moments later, another anchor line formed.

"Hold on," Saira said to her mother, explaining what was happening.

"Form a True Bond," Charity ordered Light Squad. "Move. Take positions." She indicated where she wanted them, placing them so they encircled the anchor line with overlapping fields of fire.

An instant later, Charity's father stepped through the anchor line, appearing utterly fatigued. He stumbled into the plaza, face pale with exhaustion, legs trembling like he could barely stand. Charity had never seen him so tired, not even after defeating a rakshasa Sage and lancing the monster's boil. Her father gestured, and the anchor line disappeared.

Charity made a noise of protest. What about Cam and Pan? Where were they? They should have come through by now.

"What happened? " Saira demanded. "Where are Cam and Pan?"

"Likely dead," Charity's father said. "The anchor line was wrested from my control."

Questions were shouted, one on top of another.

"How is that possible?"

"Who wrested the anchor line?"

"What did you do?" The last was a shouted demand from Charity.

Her father glared at her. "I did nothing. And if you children would stop your nattering, I'll explain." He inhaled deep, rising from where he'd been hunched over at the knees and tugging his shirt straight. Another breath, and some of his strength seemed to recover. "I've never experienced anything like it. I've always considered anchor lines to be inviolable, but apparently, I was wrong. Cam and Pan went through the anchor line, one after the other. Too closely spaced if you ask me." He grimaced, like their actions reflected poorly on them. "At any rate, it was then that I sensed a malevolent presence. It touched the anchor line and ripped it away from me."

Charity viewed her father in disbelief. Who could possibly do something like that? Her father was a powerful Sage and no being on Salvation should be able to steal an anchor line of his creation. In fact, she didn't think any Sage could contest the anchor line of any other Sage.

The blood drained from her face as the answer came to her. "A

Great Rakshasa?"

Her father gave a grim nod. "That's what I think. A male is what I sensed before I lost the anchor line."

"Coruscant," Saira said.

She was right. It had to be him. Simmer and Shimala were women.

"Why would he want Cam and Pan?" Card asked. "How would he even know about them?"

It was the same question at the forefront of Charity's thinking.

Her father shrugged. "That isn't so hard to answer. By now, you should know that no one in Light Squad is anonymous. You've accomplished too many things to remain unknown. I believe Coruscant either wants to ascertain how you've managed to stymie him so often or he's decided to take you off the board." He breathed out a tired sigh. "Coruscant is to me as I am to an Adept. Fighting him took me to my limits, but he bested me without effort."

Charity frowned at her father's explanation. It made a certain kind of sense, but a tingling in the back of her mind warned her that something was still amiss. She tried to piece her confused thoughts together. "If Coruscant could take away your anchor line, why couldn't he do that for any anchor line? Wouldn't it mean that any of them could potentially be compromised?"

"Not every anchor line," her father said. "Only the ones that he could know of in advance, ones that have a definitive time and place when they'll be forged."

Charity couldn't make the connection, and she continued to frown at her father, unable to figure out what he was trying to tell them.

Jade, however, was able to decipher the intimated meaning. "You mean like the one that was meant to bring us here from the Academy?"

Charity's father nodded. "That would be my guess. From what I understand, your leave-taking wasn't a secret. You even had a celebratory dinner over the event. Everyone at the school knew when you would be journeying and where. Given that, Coruscant must have had someone there who witnessed your departure and relayed the information to him." He hesitated. "After our battle, I recreated the anchor line to

Maviro, and just as I stepped through, I saw a Blended figure in the distance. It was just a flicker, but I had the impression of an Awakened Beast. A turtle."

"Sial?" Avia said, sounding as shocked as Charity was feeling.

Sial had been their instructor. He was gruff but fair, and she liked him.

Her father nodded. "Sial was once a rakshasa. Who is to say he isn't one again?"

13

Weld Plain. The man's name echoed in Cam's mind before the anchor line stripped away his concentration, and he found himself speeding through a tunnel lit by a kaleidoscope of swirling colors. His body stretched to tearing, and his consciousness frayed. Cold crushed his marrow, freezing him throughout. A shrieking whine overloaded his hearing, loud enough that he worried for his eardrums. He wanted to shut his eyes, plug his ears. The scent of oranges and almonds, faint at first, but eventually severe enough to have a bizarre kind of weight, bore him down, seizing his stomach with nausea.

This was unlike any anchor line Cam had ever traveled, and adrenaline and fear had his heart racing.

Then with an abruptness that left him vertiginous, Cam discovered the anchor line had ended. But the cessation of movement stole his balance, and he lurched forward, stumbling, falling on his elbows and knees where he landed upon a smooth surface as soft as a feather bed. There he stayed, his breathing uneven and ragged, eyes shut as he waited for his stuttering heart to slow. Many seconds passed, maybe minutes. He lost track of time, but finally, he felt stable enough to unseal his eyes and discover what had become of him.

A starry sky of iridescent nebulae and distant blue and white motes met his gaze, and a plethora of endless connections filled the void. Countless rainbow bridges pulsed in time to some vast, incomprehensible breathing. A tide of life flowed with each inhalation and every steady exhalation. Cam rose to his feet, awed by the sight and sensations. What was this place? Working off instinct, he delved his Source, forging a True Bond and…

His mind ceased functioning, unable to grasp or comprehend what he was viewing or even what he was feeling. Humility and the need to bend his knee to that which was most holy swept over him.

All is Ephemera and Ephemera is All. The phrase had never been more real than in that moment as a flood of perceptions cascaded over his consciousness, focused upon a Singing Light of indescribable beauty and serenity. Cam drifted, comforted to return to a peaceful oblivion before birth and existence, and he knew it wasn't wrong. It was right and good and true, everything for which everyone longed at the end of their life.

But Cam wasn't ready to set aside his burdens. Not yet. Responsibilities required that he remain alive, and with a shuddering effort, he flicked closed his view of the woven world, realizing he'd gone to his knees in prayer.

He blinked then, and the glorious starry sky returned, along with the blue and white motes, and when he studied them more closely, he saw they were doorways opening onto other vistas. Some appeared familiar: the city of Nexus with snow falling upon it, another of a much younger Cam and three youths—Jordil, Lilia, and Tern—entering a Pathway to Grace, and one in which Cam huddled on the ground as battle in the sky raged between the Wilde Sage and the Silver Sage of Weeping. Others made no sense, such as a celebration in which Cam greeted a shy boy and girl while Pharis and Charity looked on. There was another view that left him wanting to weep at the beauty within: a rustic Realm of dragons and peace and elves and dwarves. There were other views, too, but those were thankfully rare, leading as they did to places of emptiness where the Singing Light and hope appeared nearly absent.

Cam shuddered, forcing his gaze away from those dark and dangerous doorways. They reminded him of the anchor line in Hearth, and as if thinking about that Realm brought it into focus, there stood a view of Thor where the Sage of Loyalty held a crying child, comforting her.

"Cam!"

The shout distracted Cam from his observations, and he spun about, seeing Pan. His friend stood close at hand, appearing stunned but otherwise well enough. But where was the rest of Light Squad?

Cam went to Pan, hoping for answers. "What happened? Do you know where we are?"

"It's the Web of Worlds," Pan said, gazing about in wide-eyed wonder. "It's supposed to be a myth, but in every story, this is how it's described."

Cam frowned, calling forth everything he knew about the Web of Worlds. It was supposed to be the spiritual juncture where folks could travel from one Realm to another. It was also said that only the soul could make the journey here, but Cam felt solid enough. He even had his rucksacks and weapons.

He continued to frown, unable to make sense of the situation. He recollected then his last view of Nexus, of Weld Plain, and a snarl curled his lips. However, an odd question occurred to him, one that shoved aside his burgeoning anger. What if Charity's father had killed him and Pan? That would explain their presence in the Web of Worlds. It would also mean Cam's sense of solidity was an illusion. He patted himself. But if it was an illusion, he couldn't reckon on how to break it.

"Do you know what happened?" Pan asked.

Cam nodded. "Weld. I saw him right after I stepped onto the anchor line. He betrayed us."

Pan shook his head, glowering fiercely. "It wasn't only him. Sage-Duke Kazar was the one who fashioned the anchor line that brought us here."

Cam exhaled in disappointment. "Which means we have proof that at least two Sage-Dukes are conspiring with the rakshasas."

"But why?" Pan asked. "What's the purpose in bringing us here?"

The notion of figuring the answer died on Cam's tongue when he noticed the steady drumbeat approach of two distant figures, a man and a woman, their features obscured. He studied them, picking out details of their clothing. The man wore a long blue coat, buttoned over a white shirt and gray slacks. The woman wore an emerald-green sari laced in golden thread. And although Cam couldn't yet see it, somehow he knew a wine-colored *kalava* wrapped the man's left wrist while a black-beaded *thaali* hung around the woman's neck and she also wore emerald earrings to reflect the color of her eyes.

Cam knew them. Even from a distance, he recognized the man's graceful leopard-like gait and the woman's honey-blonde hair. *Professors Shade and Grey.* Both of them appeared solemn enough to be attending a funeral.

"How are they here?" Pan asked, his confusion evident.

"Hello, children," Professor Grey said once they'd drawn close. "It is wonderful to see you again."

"But we wish the circumstances were far better," Professor Shade added.

Cam filtered all the confusions twisting through his mind until only a single question remained, the one everyone in Light Squad had wondered upon. "Who are you?"

Professor Grey offered a warm smile. "You know us, child. You've known us for a long time. My truest name is Jessira."

"And mine is Rukh."

Upon hearing the declaration of their names, Pan shouted in triumph. "I knew it!"

However, for Cam, there was nothing but numbness. Rukh and Jessira. Jessira and Rukh. The Holy Servants. Was this real? Or was it just a wonderful dream?

A moment later, he shook off his doubts. This wasn't a dream. The beings before him truly were Rukh and Jessira Shektan. They lived, and Cam wanted to cry. All his life, he had hoped to experience something transcendental and virtuous, and here it was. The Singing Light he felt throughout the Web of Worlds also poured forth from the Holy Servants, from their eyes and very beings, luminescent and good.

Cam wanted to bow before Rukh and Jessira, but he wrestled his reaction into control. Their presence in this place and at this time had to be important, and it was best he learn what that might be.

Rukh and Jessira must have recognized the hardening of his resolve because the Singing Light emitting through them dimmed some, allowing Cam to regather his focus and think without the sense of holiness diffusing his clarity of thought. He straightened, ready to learn why he and Pan had been pulled to the Web of Worlds. "Why are we here?"

Jessira was the one who answered. "It is as you earlier guessed: betrayal. Some of the Sage-Dukes…"

"… have chosen to side with the Great Rakshasas," Rukh said, speaking on the heels of Jessira's words as if he were completing her thoughts. "It isn't new. It's happened before."

Jessira spoke again. "Too often, the hearts of people and rakshasas are easily corrupted."

None of what they were saying surprised Cam, but his earlier question remained. "But what about us? Why were we sent here?" His earlier fearful notion returned. "Are we dead?"

Pan gasped, like he'd never considered the possibility.

Jessira sighed, an aggrieved sound of regret. "It is because of Coruscant. He demanded that Sage-Duke Kazar send you to him, through a *nomasra* to maintain your physical forms, to the Realms of the Rakshasas where he, Simmer, and Shimala have made their homes."

Cam's mouth dropped in shock, and questions tumbled from his mouth. "Coruscant? Why? He wants us in Hell?"

"The Realms of the Rakshasas is more properly called Mote, not Hell," Rukh corrected.

Cam grappled with accepting that Hell was real and that Charity's father had intended on sending them there. The man must truly hate him. Was it because of Cam's relationship with Charity?

"It's not because of you," Jessira said.

Her soothing words brought Cam some relief, but the reasoning for the Sage-Duke's betrayal continued to circle in his thoughts.

"Is that where rakshasas come from?" Pan asked, returning the conversation to what was important. "From Hell, Mote, whatever?"

Rukh smiled. "A rare few, yes, but they are the exceptions. Rakshasas, you see, aren't exclusive to Mote. Their homes are many, including Salvation and Hearth. In truth, both of you are rakshasas. So is everyone from Salvation, Mote, and Hearth."

Cam shared a horrified look with Pan. They were rakshasas? Impossible.

"Your world was where the rakshasas fled when their original one began to fail," Rukh explained. "At the time, they were called demons, and they were. Over the years, we've battled them on many worlds, but Indrun and Sachi began the redemption of their people, back on their first world—on Mote—and William and Serena helped finalize that redemption on Salvation. It is just as we did for the Chimeras of Arisa."

Jessira took up the account. "The ones who remained on Mote had largely died out by the time the Great Rakshasas took up residence there. They brought it back to a certain kind of life, although the world is poisonous and can't maintain much of a population."

"But it serves their purpose," Rukh said. "Enough for them to field agents who recruit those from Salvation to their cause."

Cam accepted the explanation without question. If the Holy Servants said it was true, then it was true. "What about me and Pan? What happens to us?"

"For you, there is an opportunity amidst terrible danger," Rukh replied. "And we'll have to be brief in telling you. Holding you here is already stretching the limits of the agreement we made with the Great Rakshasas."

Cam frowned. Why would the Holy Servants have made an accord with the Great Rakshasas? He asked.

"For now, that's unimportant, dearest child," Jessira said.

Cam viewed her in uncertainty, latching on to the strange turn of phrase. "Dearest child?"

From Jessira, he empathed gentle humor. "That is who you are to us. You chose Salvation and your life there. Even after all the hardships you endured in your previous incarnation, you hadn't felt like you'd given enough. You wanted redemption, although you never needed it."

It was an answer that only spurred more questions.

"We cannot say anything more," Rukh said, speaking aloud and giving a firm look to Jessira who silenced at his reprimand. "We are here because there are three options facing you, none of them good." He gestured to the rainbow bridge. "Depart the anchor line, and you'll return to Devesh."

"Isn't that the same as death?" Pan asked.

"Not in the way you mean," Jessira said. "With death, your essence reunites with Devesh."

"I'd still rather not," Cam said, disliking that suggestion plenty. Theology aside, he wasn't yet ready to leave aside the burden of his life. He wanted to remain aware of himself, remain the person he was now.

Rukh nodded. "Then if you don't leave your mortal coil here in the Web of Worlds, you must go to Mote. Coruscant has extended his will and deemed it so."

"And we cannot prevent it," Jessira said. "The second option is for you go to Mote and attend Coruscant directly. But if you do, he will almost certainly seduce you to his service—through torture or some other means. And if he's unsuccessful, he'll slay you."

Cam balked. A future where he and Pan served Coruscant was one that didn't bear considering. But what else was there? Rukh had said there were three options and none of them were good. His heart sped up with trepidation. "What's the third option?"

Rukh exhaled heavily. "To still go to Mote but allow yourselves to be imprisoned."

Jessira continued. "In order to gain power, the rakshasas of Mote transform Ephemera into the selfishness of Nullity. By doing so, their bodies are similarly transformed, and to prevent their exteriors from reflecting the monstrous nature of their changed Sources, they must regularly remove the pollutants from their bodies, which they then discard into the Blood Sea, a world-spanning ocean of corruption."

Now, Rukh took up the explanation. "And underneath the ocean, there exists a prison. It's where rakshasas who failed Coruscant are sent. Understand, Mote is a world with only the barest traces of Ephemera, a dead desert compared to the lushness of Salvation or Hearth. The prison is even worse. It will feel as if it's bare of life and love."

"We can send you to this prison," Jessira said. "You'll be placed in an isolated cell, the beginning of your torment, deep underground, under the very floor of the Blood Sea."

Rukh added, "But there is hope. We can trick Coruscant into believing you've chosen to end your existence rather than go to Mote. The deception will allow you to remain safe in the prison. As we said, you'll be kept in isolation."

"Where you can still practice your skills. Use Spirairia—telepathy— to communicate with one another."

"And there will be one other you can befriend. This person can aid you, possibly even help you escape to Petala, the area of the Blood Sea that houses the Locus, the bridge leading back to Salvation."

"Who is it?" Cam asked, hoping for a name.

"We cannot tell you," Rukh stated. "For my purposes, this person cannot have any inkling that you were prepared to meet them. Your failure would be assured if you were to learn their name before the time is right."

It wasn't the answer Cam had expected to hear, but he shrugged aside his disappointment. If this is what the Holy Servants deemed necessary, then who was he to argue?

"You cannot be content in the prison," Jessira said. "Learn whatever you can. Master what you must. Your time in Mote can take you far. It can see you progress from Adept to Crown or even Sage when you return to Salvation. Study hard enough, and you'll also master the focus, control, and balance that you'll need in the higher Stages, more so than any other Ephemeral Master."

"But only if you stay alive, and discover the answers to Advancement," Rukh warned.

Jessira eyed them with fierce urgency. "When you have the answers, that's when you must escape. Go to Petala. Reach the Badlands, find the Locus. Cross the bridge you locate, and you'll go home to Salvation."

"But reaching the Locus won't be easy," Rukh cautioned. "There are many ways to die on the journey there."

Cam sighed, reckoning their decision wasn't much of one after all. "It sounds like you're recommending that we go to this prison."

"You will if that's what your heart tells you," Rukh said. "Does it?"

For once, it was Pan who spoke on their behalf. "It does." He offered an apologetic shrug to Cam. "At least it does for me."

Cam drew his friend into a hug. "It does for me, too."

Rukh nodded acceptance at their answers. "So be it. You've seen the Blood Sea before. I can show it to you again, if you allow. And the peninsula beneath which you'll be housed. The location of the prison."

Cam nodded. He and Pan needed all the information he could gather. "Show us."

He found himself on a finger of land, a broad plateau, hundreds of yards wide. It merged with knife-cut cliffs that fell to the sullen waves of a blood-red ocean stained with yellow streaks of what might have been pus. A sun, white as bone, shone from high above, a painful glare that cast shadows darker than night.

Cam did *know this place. He'd seen it in a dream, a terrible one sent by Shimala. Unlocking his knees, he forced himself forward, needing to know more about where he and Pan would find themselves.*

At the plateau's edge, where it met the incarnadine sea, spikes like knives splayed the waters in every direction for miles around. Strange moans seemed to emanate from the ocean along with a drifting wind that carried the stench of blood and decay.

Cam lifted his vision away from the grotesque waves and toward a distant range of mountains that rose with a blue and green glory. After all the harsh reds, their soothing color acted like aloe for his eyes. Life grew on the slopes of those rugged peaks and healthy-seeming water collected in high mountain lakes.

He looked in a different direction, finding another range of mountains on another continent. The spiked rises reared skyward, but their slopes had a strange gray quality to them, not exactly that of granite or stone. Cam peered closer and cursed at what was upon the mountains.

Webs formed of threads thicker than a wagon draped the slopes, and beneath them nothing grew but black trees with limbs crusted in white fruit.

The vision ended, and Cam was back in the Web of Worlds. Jessira held him upright, supporting him. He needed it after that horrible vision, and he clung to her motherly embrace, which felt like everything he would have wanted as a child.

Jessira held him a moment longer, cupping his face, scratching under his chin, and he pressed into the comfort of her hand. "Sweet boy," she said. "Have faith in that terrible place. The very nature of Mote will coax you to suicide. Do not listen to what it says. Remember your faith. We will always be with you."

Cam took in her words, silent and terrified. A world could convince him to kill himself?

"What about Nullity?" Pan asked. "You mentioned that."

Rukh grimaced. "It is awful, a true evil for those of a selfish bent." He sighed. "But it's also best if you experience it for the first time here where it is safe, rather than in that wretched Realm. This is Nullity. Prepare yourselves."

Cam took a deep breath. "I'm ready."

"You aren't, but so be it," Rukh intoned.

With an abruptness that severed his thinking, Cam found his head clamped in a tight grip. Agony shot down his brain, into his spine, and from there, it spread to every aspect of his body. But it wasn't a physical pain. Rather it was the suffering of absence—the deprivation of Ephemera.

He didn't know how long it lasted, but even a fraction of a second was too long.

"I am sorry," Rukh said when it finally—blessedly—ended. "But you needed to know the true meaning of Nullity. Mere description doesn't do it justice. It is the use of Ephemera in ways that should not be. Nullity is Ephemera—and a part of you—that won't ever return again to Devesh."

Cam shuddered. "And that's how the rakshasas become powerful?"

"Not on Salvation. On your world and in Hearth, they simply use Ephemera through malice. Only on Mote do rakshasas use Nullity." Rukh paused, seeming to peer into their hearts. "Are you sure about your choice?"

Unbidden, Cam recollected a vision of him with those two children—likely Pharis'. If he and Pan didn't do this, he'd never know the boy, never again see his sister. And since at least two of the Sage-Dukes had given over their allegiance to the rakshasas, what hope was there for Golden? They'd all die at the hands of the rakshasas.

Faced with such a possibility, Cam couldn't see himself turning tail. "I'm sure. Send me to the prison."

"We're both sure," Pan added.

"So be it," Rukh said, sounding simultaneously proud and sad. "As I said, Mote is a danger but also opportunity. Teach the rakshasas of Mote about Devesh. Teach them about all the different kinds of love, about what you learned in *The Warrior and the Servant*. Offer the rakshasas something better than the selfish teachings of their masters: Coruscant, Simmer, and Shimala. Who knows? In time, it may help lead to the overturning of that Realm."

"And always remember to keep your hearts open," Jessira added. "Maintain your faith and love for one another. In the darkness, cling to your goodness. Seek to create. That is Devesh's inspirational language written into all of our *Jivatmas*."

Her love flooded into Cam, and he bowed before her, feeling unworthy of her obvious dedication.

"Our time is nearly ended," Rukh said. "Pray at need. Don't be hesitant to seek Devesh's help. We will also help you as we can."

He flicked his fingers, and Cam's rucksacks were suddenly gone. Same with his weapons and the *nomasra* given to him by Rainen and that Saira had adjusted. In addition, the fine clothes that Charity had purchased had been transformed into a pair of drab gray pants and matching shirt with Cam standing in rough boots. He patted an interior pocket, discovering his copy of *The Warrior and the Servant*, but the rest of his possessions had been taken.

Pan did the same, drawing forth the book he'd earlier packed about the nature of Devesh.

Before he could protest the change, Rukh explained, "Where you're going, the people don't wear such fine clothing. You should also hide your true Stage of Awareness. Few rakshasas from Mote Advance past Novice. It would be best if you hid your level of Advancement. Use the skill you learned in Hearth and pretend to be Neophytes."

"A final piece of advice," Jessira said. "As a Plasminian, when you Advance to Crown, you can combine your Tangs into a unified whole. It may be a long time before such is of concern, but recall my words for when it happens. The knowledge on how is already within you, but it will require effort. It will require that you hold fast to your greatest needs and wants, to give everything you have. But doing so can potentially allow you to more easily Advance past Sage. Consider it."

Cam's mind went blank. It truly was possible to Advance past Sage? That had been the goal of Sages throughout history, and none had managed it in centuries or longer.

Rukh cleared his throat. "And as Jessira gave you a final piece of advice, I give you a final piece of knowledge."

Cam's mind was suddenly crowded with information about Mote, the three empires forged by the Great Rakshasas, the known politics of the place, the social structure of the prison… it was too much to take in, but given how rushed the Holy Servants sounded, Cam didn't think to question. He simply accepted everything he'd been told and learned. He glanced over to make sure Pan did the same.

"It's time to say goodbye now, children," Jessira said. "Go with Devesh and know that you will not be alone. You were never alone."

Rukh held Jessira's hand as they stared after Pan and Cam. The two youths swiftly departed, and he worried for them, replaying what choices he could have made that might have led to a better outcome. What could he and Jessira have done differently? In the end, there wasn't anything, and he set the wonderings aside. They couldn't know and predict everything.

Jessira breathed out in sorrow once Cam and Pan had become nothing but distant sparks of lights. "I wish he had never chosen this life for himself."

Rukh knew which of the two she meant. He loved the boy, too. "So do I, but his dharma is his to decide."

"Too stubborn for his own good."

Rukh brought her hand to his lips, kissing the backs of her fingers. "I promised to do my best to see him safe. Birch's mind is finally ready to see the Singing Light."

Jessira stared into his eyes. "Are you sure? There are so many Realms in the Anchored Worlds that require our help. Placing your sending in Mote… the distraction could cost us."

Rukh sighed. They'd already discussed this, but he also recognized why Jessira was bringing it up again. It was fear, not for him—although if his sending was destroyed, Rukh would be damaged for a time— but rather because of what his defeat might mean for the rest of the Anchored Worlds. Without Rukh's presence, Salvation and Hearth could both fall further away from Devesh and toward the Empty One.

But in the end, it would be as it would be. Rukh would do what he knew was needed and accept the outcome. He always had before and always would.

Jessira, though, had never done well at simply doing her best and allowing the final result to occur. For her, fear of the future and its attendant problems had always been a struggle.

Rukh kissed her softly. "It has to be done, and you know I'm the only one who can do it. Birch won't listen to anyone else. We have to take this risk. He has to listen to me if the boys are to have any hope of surviving Mote."

"And if Birch kills your sending? You'll be in his mind, in his world, which he has learned to control all too well."

"Then that is my karma. It will be as it is." Rukh shook his head, knowing what she was about to say, the gift they'd shared almost from their first meeting. "It cannot be you. Coruscant remembers your essence too well. He'll immediately sense your presence."

Jessira chuckled dryly. "Coruscant's defeat at my hands—a mere woman—was an unforgivable sin." She pressed herself close to him, resting her head on his shoulder.

Rukh embraced her, thinking about Mote. The boys would be in grave danger there. But if they succeeded, a fresh group of Divines could rise upon Salvation. They were sorely needed, and this time, as natural born children of Salvation, they could remain in the Realm when they Advanced to Heavenly Heathens. They could attack Mote.

Jessira chuckled at his unspoken thoughts. "William and Serena are still embarrassed by that ridiculous title."

Rukh laughed with her. "They should be. It's awful."

Their humor faded when Cam and Pan departed from their sight. The boys had entered Mote.

Rubbing her arms, Jessira exhaled a trembling breath and closed her eyes to pray. While she did so, Rukh continued to hold her close, breathing in the cinnamon scent that remained a part of her, even with their Ascension beyond a material form. He was glad for it. Inhaling her aroma had always comforted him.

Jessira opened her eyes, worry continuing to suffuse her features. "I'll hold the Anchored Worlds together if the worst comes to pass in Mote, which it will if Coruscant notices…"

"Zahhack never noticed me in Hearth."

"He was trapped behind the anchor line."

"And he would have bent every effort at rupturing it if he had noticed my sending in Hearth. He didn't. Neither will Coruscant. I'll be there for at most a few hours." Rukh grinned, a happy notion occurring to him. "I'll go as Rail Gristle."

Jessira remained dissatisfied.

"What?" Rukh asked. "You don't think I should appear to him as a lonely old man in a cabin?" He shrugged. "I'm just surprised no one from Light Squad noticed the similarity between Rail and Professor Shade."

"Cam might have. Our boy has always been observant."

"Hunters have to be observant, and in his first life, he was a supreme one." For a short while, their conversation fell into a comfortable silence, one that Rukh ended. "When all of this works out, Coruscant will have brought doom into his house. Mote could be stolen out from under him and the other Great Rakshasas."

"The last of our tasks will be done, and we can finally rest," Jessira finished, gazing at him, lips pursed and brow furrowed. "I wish I had your confidence, though."

"And I wish I had your mind for planning."

Jessira's mood didn't improve. "Offering a compliment won't ease my fears."

Rukh tsked. "So demanding. *Simply* intolerable."

Jessira rolled her eyes, chuckling lightly. "And on that note, Thor is nearing Divine. He can help us."

Rukh nodded, grasping her reasoning. "While I'm busy with the sending, you can touch Thor's dreams. Prepare him. He can help the boys escape Mote." He grinned again, tapping her forehead, knowing it would irritate her. "See. A mind for planning."

Another roll of her eyes. "And now comes the condescension even as you voluntold me for a task *I* devised."

"Voluntold? It's been a while since I heard you use that word."

"It's a portmanteau." A beat later, she sighed as if in apology. "I'm sorry, a portmanteau is a word formed by combining the spelling and meaning of two or more words."

Rukh frowned. Usually, he was the one who did the explaining about the definition of portmanteau. "I know what a—"

Jessira placed a finger on his lips, silencing him. "What you think you know doesn't matter, remember?"

Rukh laughed, glad that his wife could still surprise him.

14

Cam stumbled again upon exiting the anchor line, nearly running into Pan, and having to hunch over from the nausea. Breathing was a struggle, and nothing felt right. His heart beat irregularly. His muscles began clenching and cramping spasmodically, seemingly hard enough to break his bones, and he collapsed to the ground, mouth open in a rictus of a scream. What was going on? He'd never felt this way coming out of an anchor line before. His very marrow felt frozen, and the cold tightened in a crushing grip.

Minutes passed before fresh warmth entered his blood, heating him up. His muscles slowly unlocked and relaxed, and the steady beating of his heart told him he was still alive. One deep breath followed another, and the nausea eventually began tapering. A final breath, and the worst of it was over.

Cam opened eyes that had been shut the entire time and slowly rose to his feet. Pan was still on the ground, curled around himself but showing signs of life. Cam saw to him, helping his friend stand. Only then did he take in the chamber where they'd landed, a rough-hewn space of matte-black stone. A pair of wall-hung lanterns illuminated the area, emitting a light the color of pus and granting a view of a single barred door, dark like the rest of the room. Four rusted chains hung from an arched ceiling, and the ends looped to form nooses above a set of chairs placed directly underneath.

Those were the obvious details, but what became noticeable immediately thereafter was the lack of Ephemera. It had Cam gasping anew, but this was a different sort of suffering than what he'd just experienced coming out of the anchor line. This was a weakness of soul. Hopelessness weighed on his limbs, clawed at his mind, urging him to loop the nooses around his neck and kick off from the chair.

End it all, the despair seemed to whisper. *What is the purpose of living anyway? You're a no-good Folde. Everyone would be better off without you. Tern and Lilia would still be alive. Pan wouldn't be here. Take the chains—*

Cam refused the evil siren song, recognizing that it came from the deepest recesses of his consciousness, the wicked lie he'd lived with since Tern had died. He crushed its call. This wouldn't be his end, nor would it be Pan's, who appeared on the edge of abandonment. His friend needed him. They needed each other. Cam firmed his spine, got a grip on his despair. "We can do this," he told Pan. "Have faith. Remember what Rukh and Jessira told us."

Pan shuddered once, managing a nod, and the sense of hopelessness lifted a mite from his features. "What was that?"

"Mote. The Realm wants us to kill ourselves," Cam guessed, recalling the warning from the Holy Servants even as he indicated the chains hanging above. "The rakshasas want to help us on our way. It's evil, but it ain't a surprise considering who rules here."

"There's hardly any Ephemera," Pan noted. "How does anyone live with it?"

Cam stirred on hearing Pan's observations, nervous as he remembered the importance of keeping quiet in a place like this. He spoke to Pan, mind-to-mind. *"This is the prison Rukh and Jessira mentioned. We shouldn't speak like we aren't from around here. Don't use the names of the Holy Servants or Salvation. Who knows who might be listening or when?"*

"We're also supposed to be Neophytes," Pan sent back.

Cam nodded, doing the trick with his sclerae that he'd learned in Hearth. He glanced to Pan for confirmation. *"How do I look?"*

"Like a Neophyte."

"Good. So do you." Pan's sclerae had reverted to the whites seen in someone who hadn't yet started on the Way into Divinity.

"What happens now?" Pan sent.

"We wait." And just because he was feeling ornery, Cam took a seat in one of the chairs under the nooses.

Pan followed his lead, and an hour passed in silence, a time of stunned disbelief. Just a short time earlier, he and Pan been full of hope and wonder, surrounded by friends, with love blossoming between him and Charity, and all of them ready to Advance to Glory. So much to look forward to and all of it gone in a heartbeat.

Intellectually, Cam understood his life was vastly changed, but he wasn't yet ready to accept the truth about his situation. Rather, he kept praying, hoping this was a nightmare from which he'd soon awaken.

The door leading into the room creaked open, and he and Pan rose to their feet, confronted by a creature unlike any either of them had ever seen.

She was tiny, clothed in garb similar to Cam's and Pan's and had a fox's body, the head of a serpent, and an Adept's Advancement. The rakshasa—and what else could it be but one—flicked her tongue in and out, hissing slightly at whatever she tasted on the air. "You are un-expected," she said with a glare. "No one said you were coming. And it would have been a kindness if you'd hung yourselves."

Cam shared a bemused expression with Pan, not knowing what to say to the creature's declaration.

"Fine. You insist on living then," the strange rakshasa said with a sigh, displaying a pair of manacles. "I'm Warden Blythe. My word in this place is the same as Coruscant's, and I say this: turn around, put your hands behind your backs, and I'll put these on. Refuse, and I'll eat you."

Cam didn't want to do any such thing, but given how little he and Pan knew about the lay of the land here, he assumed it best to do as he was told. Besides which, while the rakshasa was an Adept, he reckoned they could take her if she tried to do anything untoward.

He and Pan did as the warden instructed, and a pair of manacles were quickly slapped over their wrists.

"Turn around," the warden ordered. Cam did so, just in time to see her twist her neck about until her head was aimed the opposite direction of her body. She shouted at the still-open door. "Worthless ones! Enter and see to these two."

Seconds later, two small birds—Novices both—flitted into the chamber, ascending to roost on the beams of the ceiling. They cheeped a few times, and Cam got the sense that both were males. One was plumed in lemon-yellow feathers except for a few that were green and blue on his tail and a small dusting of orange on the crown of his head, which was a hue similar to his parrot-like beak. The other one was mostly green, except for blue wing tips, orange collaring his neck, and red feathers on his crown.

The foxlike rakshasa stared at the birds, head swaying and a predatory gleam to her eyes. "You will take them to unoccupied cells. Separate them. Search them for contraband. Turn it over, or I'll eat you. Half-rations today for bothering me. Disobey, and I'll eat you." Not pausing a beat, she exited the chamber.

Once the echo of her footsteps had disappeared, the birds twittered with anger.

Their reaction lifted some of the shock suffocating Cam's thoughts. "Not a friend?" Cam asked.

"Not a friend," the green bird cheeped. "Hateful, she is."

"Cunning, too," the yellow one added, fluttering his wings in apparent agitation. "Wants to eat us." Once again, the bird fluttered his wings. "I am called Sprite."

"I am Kiwi," the other bird said.

Despite feeling silly at talking to a bird, Cam nevertheless gave his name, thinking it was the right thing to do.

Pan did the same, making an observation. "You're lovebirds."

"Lovebirds?" Cam hadn't heard of such a creature. Did it mean they were in love with one another?

His confusion must have been evident. "It's a type of small parrot," Pan explained. "They're usually found in warm forest environments."

"From a better world until we were sent here," Sprite said. "Warm and beautiful."

Curiosity nipped at Cam despite his horrible day thus far. "Why were you sent here?"

"A hateful man sold us," Kiwi said. "Enough talking. Follow."

He flew off, leading them into a narrow hallway carved from the same black rock as the chamber from which they'd just exited. The lighting in the corridor was similarly dim and dull, and they set off, manacles clanking.

But Cam's curiosity persisted. There was something sweetly innocent about the lovebirds, which he would have never expected to find in Mote. "Are you brothers?"

Sprite flew back, landing on Cam's shoulder. "No."

Kiwi decided to land on his other shoulder. "You smell good. Go straight. Take the third turn on the right."

They pressed on, encountering no one. A rivulet of water leaked from the ceiling, and Cam recalled what Rukh and Jessira had told them about the prison, that it had been built under the Blood Sea, the horrific world-spanning ocean formed from corruption.

Cam shivered, imagining the water's crushing weight. How long would he live if the ceiling cracked? Would his body be smashed to a pulp before he ever had a chance to drown? Or would the corruption itself dissolve him?

And isn't that what you deserve? You no-good Folde.

Cam scowled, abruptly angry at the situation in which he and Pan found themselves. Fragging Mote, and its stupid creepy voice—or wherever that voice was coming from. Whatever it was, it could frag right off.

The lovebirds led them through silent and empty halls, eventually guiding them to a place where the corridor branched into four different hallways. It was there that they finally encountered more rakshasas, a pair of wolves with the stout build of buffaloes and the white sclerae of Neophytes. The creatures snarled upon seeing Cam and Pan, but a single whistle from Kiwi got them to shut up. The green bird flapped his wings in agitation, and in spite of their intimidating visages and physical frames, the wolflike rakshasas backed right up to the edge of the corridor, heads lowered like they were bowing.

Cam studied them close, looking for what had them behaving so oddly. The rakshasas wore complicated expressions, a mingling of longing and fatal acceptance, which made no sense. With their build and dressed as they were—same as him and Pan—but free of manacles, they had to be guards or some such. But their reactions…

He asked Kiwi once they departed the wolves. "Why did those wolves seem so worried when you tweeted at them?"

The green lovebird didn't bother responding, but Sprite did. "Because of our Ephemera. They have none. Nor do they possess Nullity."

"If we aren't careful, we won't have any Ephemera either," Kiwi muttered. "Our Sources might drain. Who knows when, but it can all be gone. We'll be weak, unless we create Nullity—"

"Which we never will," Sprite interrupted. "We won't torture. We can't do that."

Cam put the information together with the last flash of information that Jessira had given to him and Pan in the Web of Worlds. "Only strength matters here."

"Obviously," Kiwi said with a derisive cheep. "And since you two are Neophytes, don't cause us trouble or we'll peck you."

Cam couldn't help but want to grin at the threat. Coming from a tiny bird, it was nothing but cute.

"Are all the guards Neophytes?" Pan asked.

"The only ones who aren't are us and the warden," Sprite answered. "But she's useless."

"Wrong," Kiwi trilled. "She's incompetent. It's why she was put in charge of the prison. Lord Coruscant can't waste an Adept, but he also can't use one that's incompetent either."

The explanation triggered another understanding for Cam. "And you ended up here because of your Ephemera? You're Novices, but your Mastery comes from Ephemera, which is why you work in the prison. How long have you been here?"

"You ask too many questions," Kiwi snapped. "How do you not already know all these things?"

"Who says I don't?" Cam asked with a shrug. "Maybe I'm just testing you."

"And maybe you're a spy," Kiwi muttered back.

Their conversation fell silent, and they proceeded through the prison. However, the trek took so long that Cam began wondering just how many prisoners were held down here. He asked.

"A couple hundred," Sprite answered.

"Then why is the prison so big?" Cam asked.

"Coruscant sends his least useful rakshasas here," Sprite replied. "The faithless, treasonous, and worthless, an entire city of them. They—"

"No more talking," Kiwi chirped, sounding angry. "We're here."

Cam halted, balking at a line of cages that stretched along either side of the corridor, each with a solid metal door as black as the stone into which they'd been bolted. Seeing them, a cold finger of dread slithered down his back. If the cells didn't have lights, then it would be like being buried alive in a cave.

The terror of the dark wasn't something he'd yet overcome, and the memory from Hearth—of fighting the Jom-Strafe, deep underground, hustling through a long tunnel with a mountain's weight bearing down on him… all those fears remained, and they inspired his imaginings in all the wrong ways.

Sprite flitted over to an already open door. The yellow lovebird trilled to Cam. "Come. This is yours."

Kiwi had flown over to a cell several doors down and called for Pan. "And this is yours."

With trepidation in his heart, Cam walked to the cell that Sprite indicated, peering inside. Based on the dim urine-colored lighting from the hall, he could make out a room with a ceiling barely tall enough for him to stand straight along with a single rotten cot and rank hole in the ground that he assumed was a toilet. Nothing else, including any kind of lamp or lantern. He'd be alone in the dark in there.

He broke into a sweat, panting, panic blooming. Rukh's and Jessira's advice emptied out of his mind. All he could think about was the terror of being trapped in the dark. "I can't go in there," Cam gasped.

Sprite flitted back to his shoulder. "I'm sorry, but you must," he said, his voice full of regret.

"You can do this," Pan sent to him. *"I'll be with you the entire time. Once the door closes, you can create a light with Ephemera."*

Some of Cam's panic subsided, and he closed his eyes, focusing on his breathing until he got himself under control.

He opened his eyes, finding Sprite peering at him, sympathy evident. "If you don't go into the cell, the warden will come. You don't want that."

"She'll eat you," Kiwi said, sounding less empathetic than Sprite.

"We're already in a lot of danger," Pan sent. *"We can't afford for the warden to take any special interest in us."*

"We're always in a lot of danger," Cam replied in a sour voice, going on to enter the cell.

The door closed as soon as he was inside. Once again, panic threatened to consume Cam's thinking. He stood stock still, eyes open but his gaze centered inward on his Source. He didn't Delve it, though. He just wanted to see it—had to—the crystalline nature of his Enhanced Tangs—swirling Plasminia, majestic Spirairia, serene Synapsia, and indomitable Kinesthia. Calmness entered his heart, and he was able to accept the darkness.

He reached out with Spirairia-Enhanced senses then, pushing his awareness past the metal door and discovering that Sprite and Kiwi had departed. At that point, he could have created a light for himself, but he wanted the cell dark. He needed to master his fear of it.

Before that, he recognized he better speak to Pan first. *"I'm fine,"* Cam replied, only now hearing the urgent pleas sent from his friend. *"Just give me a moment."*

Cam inhaled deep, accepting the dank and decay suffusing the air. This world, this place was a Realm given over to loss and despair, and perhaps he'd have felt exactly that way if he'd been alone. But he wasn't alone. He had Pan. They could always talk to one another, and no one here would know any different. Feeling a bit more settled, he fixed his mind on what was most important: how best to get themselves free of the prison.

The Holy Servants had vowed it was possible, and if Rukh and Jessira said it could be done, then regardless of how shattered his life might seem, Cam intended on fixing his hopes on that promise. He and Pan would get gone from this horrible place.

"What do we do?" Pan sent

While Cam had no way of knowing, he did his best to provide Pan some comfort. *"Rukh and Jessira said that escaping this place would require faith and learning. It'll be hard, but we're part of Light Squad, and there ain't anything we can't do. Hold fast to your faith. Hold on to your love for Devesh. Do that, and we won't fail. I know it."*

"I'm not sure I have that courage," Pan replied.

Cam didn't know if he had it either, but he wouldn't let any of his doubts leak across to his friend. Pan needed him to be strong, and no doubt there would come a time when Cam would need the same. He encouraged his friend, *"Then we'll have to share our courage. Whenever one of us is failing, the other has to lift him up. We can do this."*

"I'll try." Pan's words came out strained, quavering at the end.

It had Cam realizing just how difficult this must be for Pan. His friend had a good heart—brighter and softer than Cam's—but being buried in evil like this must be wretched.

"We'll get through this," Cam said, continuing to encourage Pan.

"We always have before, and we will this time, too. We've never failed each other. No chance we'll fail now. Remember, the others might be elsewhere, but we're still Light Squad, and Light Squad does the impossible."

"You really think so? You don't think this is too impossible even for us? We're in Mote. We're in Hell."

"I do," Cam said, infusing his voice with certainty. *"And Mote, Hell, whatever they call it, won't stand a chance once we get our bearings."*

The words seemed to encourage Pan, who shifted the conversation to a different topic. *"Why do you think all the rakshasas down here are Neophytes?"*

Cam had given that some thought. *"I think forming this Nullity that Rukh and Jessira mentioned isn't so easy. Ephemera is natural and good and right. Nullity isn't, and I think it takes a special kind of rakshasa with a special kind of selfishness to create it."* A fresh notion came to Cam. *"Speaking of rakshasas, what do you think about the fact that we're also rakshasas? You and me both. Everyone in Salvation. Same with Hearth. We're only pretending to be human and Awakened Beasts."*

Loathing filled Pan's voice. *"I hate that idea. It's disgusting."*

Cam shrugged, not caring one way or the other. *"If it's the truth, then it's the truth. But it doesn't change who we are underneath the name."*

"But rakshasas are evil."

"Their actions are. Or maybe our idea of what it means to be a rakshasa is wrong."

Pan made a disconsolate noise, clearly still unhappy at the idea of being a rakshasa.

"We'll be alright," Cam soothed.

For some reason, his words inspired a chuckle from Pan. *"Shouldn't I be the one supporting you? After all, you're the one afraid of the dark."*

Cam laughed. If nothing else, his time in Mote would see him never again afraid of dark, small places.

Coruscant had worn many names and titles over the long millennia of his existence, collecting them like clothing, and at this point, he no longer cared much about them. So long as he was given the respect and honor owed, any name would suffice.

However, he did enjoy his current one: Coruscant. A set of syllables that landed lovely on the tongue, and while the meaning was that of something bright and glittering, there was also an underlying aspect of danger and power to the word.

It was a fitting name and title for one of the Lords of Mote, and although Coruscant hated this world, as far as he was concerned, it was still far better to rule here in Hell than serve in some brighter Realm. Even better to rule some other place that he didn't have to share with his fellow lords, the surviving Sisters, who drove him to distraction with their various maladies of the mind. First, Shimala and her insane ravings and Simmer, a name that reflected her pot-boiling demeanor of repressed rage. Always on the edge of explosion, that one.

It was why Coruscant had ordered his Sages in Golden to transport these young Ephemeral Masters to Mote. They'd caused him enough trouble, and it was time to end their bothersome meddlings. Too many well-laid plans had been disrupted because of them, and what a coup if they could be seduced to do as he bid. He smiled.

Shimala would be furious since she'd often boasted about how she could bring the boy to her side. She had prattled endlessly about his potential, enough for Coruscant to have wondered for a time if she'd somehow created a link with the boy. If so, then she would have had him in hand by now, so obviously not, but likely not due to lack of effort on her part.

And then there was Zahhack, who would be even more aggravated by Coruscant stealing away the boy and the panda given how the Son's play for Hearth had been ended due in part to those two upstarts and their friends.

Of course, the actual instigators of that action had been Rukh and Jessira, which wasn't much of a surprise. Was there any plan or scheme concocted by Coruscant and his fellow Great Rakshasas wherein the so-called Holy Servants didn't find a means to bring it to wrack and ruin? Why couldn't they leave well enough alone, like they'd promised after the battles in Seminal?

And while Zahhack's deliciously ironic failure in the matter of Hearth would lessen him in the eyes of his dreaded father, in some ways, it brought Coruscant nothing but cold comfort. Rukh's and Jessira's defeat of someone who believed in the sanctity of strength stung all of them.

Coruscant pondered the Son of Emptiness and Zahhack's foolish willingness to play the puppet to his father's purpose. What idiocy. Coruscant wasn't interested in serving under the Empty One any more than he was interested in serving under Devesh. He was his own being, born and bred to conquer. That was supposedly how Devesh and the Empty One had begun their own reigns, so why not him?

But it would only come about through some heretofore unconceived defeat of the Holy Servants, who also had their plans. Coruscant's agents in Salvation had told him about Professors Shade and Grey. Thus had Rukh and Jessira named themselves there, saving these two wretched youths and others from Nailing and Nageena, a bending of the rules but not a breaking. Had they also aided them in some way in Hearth, another world of rakshasas where the Blessed Ones were forbidden to take an active hand?

Unlikely, but if true, it raised an obvious question: why were these students so important to the Holy Servants? No doubt, love was involved, but from whence did it stem? The potential of these youths, like Shimala believed? Probably in part, but Coruscant felt there had to be more to it than just that.

But what?

Coruscant didn't yet know, but the truth would soon be discerned.

It was why he currently wasted his time waiting on the arrival of Cam Folde and Pan Shun. He had other issues requiring his attention, but his instincts told him that none were quite as important as this one, of reckoning what Rukh and Jessira saw in the two youths.

While Coruscant waited, he paced the bounds of a broad courtyard conceived specifically for Cam and Pan, the better to calm their trepidations and fears. The open-air space was floored in tan flagstones, walled in red brick, and as lovely as any place in Mote. Flowering plants and fragrant shrubs exuded lush fragrances while gurgling fountains in various spots provided soothing sounds. A majestic statue of Coruscant occupied a corner, and all was as it should be, a perfect retreat for Cam and Pan.

But they never arrived.

Anger stirred in the Great Rakshasa's heart, but he crushed it. Emotions hindered proper understanding, and he needed to understand what had happened.

He cast his senses to the Web of Worlds, searching, discovering an echo of Cam and Pan. They had stood before Rukh and Jessira, talking to them for several minutes before embracing one another and simultaneously leaping off the anchor line's bridge.

Fleeting disappointment wisped across Coruscant's mind. So be it. Cam and Pan had chosen death rather than risking servitude under his rule. *Their loss.*

Coruscant called for Vel. There were other matters to attend, such as the old man's recent fatigue. He hoped it didn't mean his oldest friend was tiring of his life. It had happened before, and if it was happening again… Coruscant sighed. He didn't know what he would do.

15

After the day's hardships and tragedies—had it really only been a few hours? It felt so much longer—Cam hadn't expected to fall asleep so easily. Fatigue, however, weighed his eyelids, and he soon passed out on his cot, asleep in minutes.

The next morning or day or whatever, he awoke, slowly unshuttering his eyes and hoping…

He sighed. No. It hadn't been a nightmare. He was in a cold, dank prison in Mote, a place empty and dull of Ephemera. Minutes later, the grating of steel-on-steel had him sitting up and staring at the door where an oddly shaped panel he hadn't noticed until just then had been shifted open.

A gentle voice from outside the cell called out. "Anyone in there?"

Cam wasn't sure what was going on—everything about Mote was a mystery that he wished he didn't have to solve—but he replied to whoever had spoken. "I'm here."

"Oh, wonderful," the voice said, that of a female. "Sprite and Kiwi said we had two new prisoners, but they can be so flighty. Which only makes sense since they're lovebirds."

She chuckled warmly, an emotion that Cam hadn't expected to hear from anyone in Mote. Curious about who might be courageous enough to be friendly in this terrible Realm, Cam rose to his feet and moved to the still-open panel where he peered through the narrow opening. He sighted a woman—a Neophyte like everyone else—standing behind a wooden cart.

She was an unusual figure, matronly and different from any person he'd ever seen. Beyond being covered from the neck down in a loose-fitting tan robe, she had the head of a cow with large eyes framed with long eyelashes that gave her an innocent appearance. The rakshasa smiled, setting her hands on her hips. "There you are." She gave him an appraising glance. "Well, aren't you a handsome one?"

She spoke without a trace of mockery, but the warmth and openness of her voice had Cam frowning in suspicion. He had never expected to encounter kindness in this place, which meant the strange woman was likely nothing but a consummate liar.

He frowned inwardly. Or maybe he wasn't being fair to her. After all, look at Sprite and Kiwi. They weren't too awful. So maybe there was more hope to be found in Mote than he realized. It was worth bearing in mind, especially since Rukh and Jessira had asked him to tell those here about Devesh's love. They wouldn't have said that if there weren't people down here who might have the heart to learn.

That could come later, though, and Cam shook off his considerations, focusing on the strange woman before him. "Pleasure meeting you, ma'am. My name is Cam Folde."

"So polite, too." The woman indicated herself. "This one is called Tulip."

Cam smiled. "You were named after a flower."

Tulip cocked her head, confusion evident on her bovine features. "Is that right? What kind of flower is that?"

Cam's smile faltered. Did she truly not know about tulips? A moment later, he firmed his smile. "A tulip is a beautiful flower. Smells lovely, too."

"How do you know?" Tulip asked, blinking rapidly in growing

excitement. "Does Lord Coruscant have tulips? Did you serve at his estate? Did you fail him in some way? Is that why you're here?" She clutched her chest, blushing as a mortified expression stole over her face. "Listen to me prattle. It's none of my business. But this is." She passed him a tray containing a bowl filled with a foul-smelling mush, a lump of moldy bread, and a tumbler of cloudy water. The last fitted through a taller, narrower section of the panel.

Cam viewed the items on the tray in undisguised distaste. Beyond the flavor, which was sure to be despicable, was any of it even safe to eat or drink? The mold was bad enough, but the smell had to mean the food had gone bad. And the tumbler… what exactly was in it to give it that cloudy color?

Tulip noticed his disgust, and she scowled at him. "In Lord Coruscant's estate, perhaps you dined on finer fare, but you're a prisoner now. This is all you're going to get, and you only get it twice a day."

Cam replayed her words, not sure he'd heard them right. "Just this bowl of mush? Nothing else?" He'd starve even if the food was edible.

"And the bread and water."

Cam continued to stare at the disgusting fare. He shouldn't have been surprised at what the rakshasas fed their prisoners, but it still left him disheartened. Wasn't the lack of light, love, and Ephemera bad enough? Did he really have to subsist on this foul mush and probably starve while doing so?

It seemed so.

"If you don't eat the food, that's your choice," Tulip said, her voice kinder. "But I will need the bowl back. If you don't hand it over when I make my return rounds, you won't get any more food until you do."

Cam took the bowl, continuing to eye the food with a distinct lack of enthusiasm. But after a few more seconds of staring at it, he sighed. If this was the way it was, then he best simply accept it. "Thank you for the advice. I'll eat whatever you bring."

Tulip nodded, appearing solemn. "That would be for the best."

She appeared ready to move on, but Cam halted her before she pushed on. "There's a panda a few cells down from mine, a friend.

We came in together. His name is Pan, and if you have a way to get it, he loves bamboo." Tulip's head tilt of confusion was answer enough. "You've never heard of bamboo, have you?" Cam asked, not sure why he would have expected otherwise.

"I'm sorry to say I haven't. Does it taste good?"

Cam smiled, recalling the one time he'd given in to his curiosity and tried it. "It's terrible. Tastes like wood, but Pan loves it."

Tulip nodded, like Cam's words made sense, although based on her expression, they clearly didn't. "He must be a strange one."

Cam had never thought so, but oddly enough, although he'd only known Tulip for a few minutes, in speaking to her, he realized that she actually reminded him of Pan. It was her good-hearted nature. "I think you'll like Pan. He's kind, same as you."

Tulip smiled. "Polite *and* sweet. I'm lucky Sprite and Kiwi placed you on my docket."

Cam spoke to Pan, mind-to-mind, while they had their meal, and they shared impressions about Tulip, the truly disgusting food she'd served them, and what their futures might hold. It didn't mean they made much progress on figuring out the last, but Cam hadn't really expected that they would, not this soon. That answer might not come about for a long while yet to come, and their conversation petered out around when Tulip came around again.

Cam passed her his empty bowl, and she was gracious enough to talk to him a bit, but work eventually called her away, and then he was left alone in the dark. Now what? There was nothing to do. The cell was small; a tiny enclosure where no martial training could be practiced and with Ephemera's rarity, no skills could be mastered either. He wasn't even sure if he should Delve his Source. What if his Ephemera wasted away like Sprite and Kiwi had mentioned might be happening to theirs?

In Salvation, it would have been impossible since once a body incorporated Ephemera into their Source, it was with them for life. But Mote might be different, and he had no way of knowing without taking a risk he might quickly regret.

Cam's thoughts twisted into despondency and fear, and he sat upon his cot, mind locking again on his shattered hopes and dreams. Just the other day, his future had been so bright, but now look at him. Trapped and isolated in this cell, within this horrible Realm of depression, loneliness, and Ephemera's absence.

How long he sat there, he couldn't have said, but eventually he corralled his downwardly spiraling thoughts into control. His hopes and dreams had been stolen from him, but that didn't mean he couldn't have hopes and dreams. He lived. His body remained healthy, his mind sharp. The Holy Servants loved him, and he could do this. He could survive Mote and find a way to escape this place.

He didn't yet know how, but he'd learn. It was the only mystery that mattered, and while Rukh and Jessira had given him insight into what he had to do, Cam figured he'd have to calculate most of it on his own. They'd advised him to hold fast to his faith in Devesh, and while that kind of advice made sense, wasn't it also true that sometimes—many times—the prayers of a person went unanswered and their troubles never lifted?

Cam could speak on that since prayers hadn't done him a lick of good during his long years of drunkenness and physical frailty. A flash of remembrance swept across him, of tipping back the bottle when he would have done anything to relieve the boredom and pain of his existence. *Wouldn't a drink go good now? He should ask Tulip—*

He crushed the terrible idea. He had to keep his thinking crisp, if not for himself, then for Pan. They only had one another to lean on, and Cam wouldn't let feebleness of any sort be the reason they failed.

A moment later, he was shaking his head. Where had the sickness for wanting alcohol come from anyway? He hadn't felt that seductive desire in months now. In truth, he'd figured himself rid of addiction's hold. Sure, he never planned on challenging it by ever again having a drink of that smooth burn, but until coming to Mote, the very idea of drinking any kind of alcohol hadn't entered his mind in a long while.

He mentally shook his head. *Fool.* This was Mote, and if darkness followed light, then of course this was the place where his weaknesses would rise up again and try to drown him.

Cam might have lingered longer on his troubles, but Pan reached out to him. *"How are you holding up?"*

Cam appreciated the chipper tone in his friend's voice. *"About as good as can be expected."*

"You mean as good as can be expected since we're in Hell?"

There was a smile in Pan's voice, and Cam shared his humor, chuckling a bit. *"You know, I swear hell's bells rang when the warden found us in that chamber."*

Pan didn't laugh like Cam had hoped. Instead, he replied with solemnity. *"Hell's bells aren't something to joke about."*

Cam apologized. *"I know, but look at where we are. If we don't joke about it, then we might as well cry. We need a light in the darkness."*

"I know, but…" Pan sighed, the impression coming across their telepathic link. *"I guess I'm just tired."*

"I know you are. We both are, but we'll get through this."

"I hope so. I think so." Pan's voice brightened. *"We will because you had a good idea just then."*

"What idea?

"Bringing a light into our darkness. I just created a tiny Ephemeral light. It's enough to bring some light into this cell."

"You're not afraid of using up your Ephemera?"

"Why would I be afraid of that?"

Cam shifted about on his cot, embarrassed at his fear-fueled idea now that Pan had challenged it. *"After what Sprite and Kiwi said about their Ephemera, I was afraid it might actually happen."*

"That's not the way Ephemera works. We use our Sources to do the things we can—"

"But how? In Salvation, what we have in our mind and Source gets reflected onto the Ephemera in the rest of the world. That's how we can create a light in the darkness. But what about here? Where's the Ephemera

to do that kind of reflecting?"

Cam so very much wanted to be wrong, and he waited on Pan's response, hoping his friend would have a counter for his statements.

But Pan didn't, and silence fell over their conversation. Cam, though, couldn't bear the lack of talking. *"What are you thinking?"*

"I'm thinking I should let go of my light."

That hadn't been what Cam had been wanting to hear, and he exhaled heavily. *"You think we can run out of Ephemera, too?"*

Pan seemed to shrug. *"I don't know, but I also don't think it's a good idea to risk it."*

Again, their conversation fell quiet, and this time Cam wasn't in the mood to start it up again. Instead, he pondered deep about what he and Pan should do. Nothing immediately jumped to mind, but then Cam recalled what Rukh and Jessira had told them about mastering their skills. He glanced around his dark cell, unable to pierce the blackness. Even if there was light, the space was too small to train at fighting. And there wasn't enough Ephemera to risk using those abilities. However, there was still one skill that they could master.

Cam broke the hush. *"We need to practice Imbibing Ephemera into our Sources, even if we just Accrete it as slow as frozen molasses in winter."*

Pan didn't immediately agree or disagree. Instead, he asked a simple question. *"Why?"*

"Because Imbibing Ephemera into our Sources is about the only thing we can do here and about the only thing worth doing."

"We can't Advance, though. There's not enough Ephemera."

"That's not the point," Cam said, his excitement building. *"Let's say we learn to bring Ephemera into our Sources more efficiently. Let's say we also learn to Accrete more efficiently. What happens when we get home?*

Pan considered the questions for a brief time before sending a pulse of excitement. *"We'll be able to Imbibe all the Ephemera we could ever ask for and probably faster than we ever imagined."*

Cam nodded, although alone in the dark, there was no one to see. *"We won't need areas of Ephemeral concentration because the whole world will be that way for us. Who knows how far and fast we'll be able to Advance?"*

"But only if we have the answers necessary to *Advance."*

Cam challenged his friend. *"You have anything else keeping you busy?"*

Pan chuckled. *"Nothing comes to mind, but that might change if Tulip brings me some bamboo."*

Cam laughed with him. *"If Tulip ever brings you some bamboo…"* He shook his head. *"Wouldn't that be something?"*

"It's strange finding someone so sweet in this place," Pan said. *"That she would learn kindness in Mote. It's a miracle."*

"Miracles do happen," Cam agreed, although a niggle of doubt surfaced regarding Tulip. He made a mental note to test her when she next came around by viewing her in the woven world and using Spirairia to empathize her true feelings.

Tulip pushed her cart of empty bowls and tumblers through the prison's empty corridors, glad for the solace of quiet, which would end as soon as she reentered the populated parts of the city she called home. *The prison where I'm just as much a prisoner as those two I just served.*

In truth, the inmates down in the caverns under the Blood Sea were a mere fraction of those who lived here, the ones who had formed their own city and rough-justice society after their banishment from Lord Coruscant's estates. Over the millennia, their population had swelled to the tens of thousands, although once a century, Coruscant's legions would clear them out, a pogrom to halve their numbers since the lord couldn't countenance feeding such a vast number of those he considered useless.

The Day of Atonement was what those who lived on the surface of Mote named it. But for the dwellers down below, it was called Murder Day. And Murder Day was rapidly approaching, less than a year. Some of the prisoners would be killed as well, and for the same reason as the rest of the populace: they were useless to Coruscant's purpose.

It was something Tulip had always known she might live to see. She had been born here, had lived her forty years here, and expected to eventually die here. And not once had she ever seen the sun, which she wasn't sure actually existed. It sounded too fantastical. A shining globe so high above that a person couldn't reach it? She snorted at the notion. It was as silly as the idea of some divinity named Devesh loving His creation.

Love didn't factor much into Tulip's way of thinking. Only survival. It's all she recognized as being of worth, while thinking about the sun and love was pure foolishness.

Tulip continued on her way, but her thoughts drifted to other aspects of language that made no sense. Tulips, for one. The new prisoner, Cam Folde, had mentioned them. But those, too, were so far outside her experience that she couldn't fathom that such things were even real. Pretty plants that smelled good? What did that even mean?

Again, Tulip cut off her considerations. Flowers and tulips were beyond her reckoning, but what wasn't was the need to get free of the prison. Murder Day. Less than a year, and Tulip didn't want to die, which could very well happen. At her age, she'd be near the cutoff of those who would be killed for simply being too old.

It was with these thoughts in mind that Tulip began encountering more and more of her fellow rakshasas. First small groups of them, then scores, and finally hundreds, all of them sullen. And yet, despite their numbers, the corridors remained quiet. No one talked much in the Unnamed, their city. Instead, they kept their heads bent, avoiding eye contact with anyone else as they wandered the halls, often with no particular destination in mind.

Of course, there were more talkative groups here and there, but they were the exception that proved the rule. A few were bold enough to call out lewd comments to her, but Tulip simply had to show them the badge of authority pinned to her shirt, and they quickly let her be, going on to harass someone else.

Not that she blamed them much for their behavior. They'd never been given any hope or instruction that there was something better to life than simply fighting, fornication, and gambling. Of course, even if they had been told, it probably wouldn't have made much difference. The rakshasas of the Unnamed were, without exception, utterly lazy and their progeny, equally shiftless.

Which was sad. Tulip had once been just like the rest of them: worthless and without any plans for the future, but she'd been lucky enough to witness the work of one of Coruscant's legionnaires, an Adept. And seeing the woman's power had sparked a flame in Tulip's heart. Why couldn't she rise like the legionnaire?

The question had helped her realize that rakshasas didn't have to fall into the life into which they'd been born. *She* didn't have to fall into the life into which she'd been born. Tulip had dreams that led beyond an existence of dark caverns and vulnerability. She wanted something she couldn't even name. It might have been freedom, but she wasn't sure.

But whatever the case, Tulip wouldn't follow the path of every other rakshasa here. She had plans to improve herself, to find out if the sun and sky were real, to feel the wind on her face, and smell a tulip.

She cut off her dangerous hopes when she finally reached her destination, the kitchen area where a listless group of rakshasas used old rags to give the dishes she handed off to them a desultory pass. She held in a scowl at their laziness. It wasn't as if they had much work to do. Cook a mushy paste once a day, purify the water leaking down from the Blood Sea as best as possible, and clean the dishes afterward. That was it, and the rest of their hours were their own to fritter away, which they most assuredly did.

Setting aside her disappointment with her people, Tulip left the kitchen and went to Warden Blythe's office in order to give her report on the new prisoners. She knocked on the closed stone door. There was no immediate response, which was typical. Seconds passed, and while Tulip waited, she took a deep breath, preparing for what was to come.

She had to tell the warden the truth—as an Adept, the little fox-like rakshasa had a gift for seizing on lies—but what to tell her? What could Tulip say that would keep the warden's eyes off the prisoners? Those had been the questions Tulip had pondered ever since encountering Cam and Pan. A moment of further deliberation, and she had the words ready.

The call to enter finally came, and Tulip opened the door to the warden's office, a small, dimly illuminated room. Other than a large desk, the only furnishings consisted of a couple of lamps and a ratty chair.

Tulip bowed low at the waist to the warden, waiting until she was told to rise.

"What is your report?" Warden Blythe demanded, gazing at her with barely concealed impatience from behind her desk.

"The new prisoners are likely from Lord Coruscant's manor."

The warden flicked her tongue in and out, hissing slightly at whatever she tasted on the air. "Truth as you know it. Go on."

"They are useless traitors."

Warden Blythe's attention sharpened. "Explain."

Tulip held off from licking her lips, knowing it would give away her half-truths. This was where her plan might slip since Cam and Pan hadn't actually told her any such thing. But it made sense. The warden just had to believe her. "They spoke of flowers."

The warden fell back in her chair with a smirk. "Then you're wrong. They aren't just useless traitors. They'll seek to use you." The smirk became mocking. "Let me guess. They spoke of flowers and your name, wanting to make you feel better?"

Tulip kept her rising excitement in check. This wasn't part of her plan, but this way might work out even better. "Yes, ma'am."

"Then let them play their games," the warden ordered. "Be wise enough not to fall for their ploys. They think to elevate your hopes and betray them." Her expression became approving. "It is a well-documented way of creating a seed of Nullity."

There wasn't much Tulip could say to the warden's comment, and she replied with another, "Yes, ma'am."

"You're dismissed."

Tulip bowed low once again before backing out of the room, but even after she exited, she kept the triumph off her face. The warden thought Cam and Pan were ambitious despite their fallen status, that they sought to manipulate others in order to gain a seed of Nullity.

The warden was wrong. Cam and Pan were kind—Tulip could tell—which made them rarer than Ephemera. And the source of their kindness didn't matter much to her. The fact that they were kind was enough.

And in this regard, the warden was correct. The betrayal of kindness and trust could lead to the creation of a seed of Nullity, and that's exactly what Tulip intended on doing with those two.

16

Jade sat in bed, listening to the bluebirds singing. Their trilling floated into her quarters through the wide open windows along with the floral perfume of jasmine and chamomile from the nearby gardens. But underlying it all was the woody aroma of olive groves growing along Maviro's softly sloped surrounding hills. Sunshine, barely filtered by the gauzy curtains, poured inside, highlighting her room's decor, which was of far greater elegance than anything to which Jade could have previously claimed familiarity, even when her father had been a Crown. Against one wall rested a well-appointed chest of drawers, painted white and decorated with trailing vines and roses. In a corner diagonal to the bed stood a crowned armoire sculpted with marquetry. And in the area opposite, an arrangement of high-backed chairs with rich upholstery. Finally, there was the oversized bed itself, which was large enough for four.

Frankly, the lush furnishings were too much for Jade. She found them ostentatious and unnecessary, and even if that wasn't the case, in the moment, she wouldn't have appreciated them much anyway. Not when Cam and Pan were dead.

Jade continued to struggle with their demise. How could it have happened so quickly? It felt impossible, especially when her heart told her that all she needed to do was go down the hall to their rooms, that they were alive, and she'd find Cam meditating and Pan munching on bamboo.

But that was all in the past, and in the present, the brothers she'd chosen were gone. Tears streaked Jade's cheeks, and she swiped angrily at them even as a sob broke. She allowed the sorrow to last for a count of thirty before she shoved it down deep, not wanting to experience the grief for any longer than that. Cam wouldn't want her lying around crying over him. He'd want her out in the world, getting stronger and burning away any weaknesses. He'd want her to live, love, and find happiness.

And that's exactly what Jade planned on doing. Anger replaced her sorrow, and when she felt herself ready to face the world, she threw off the covers, got dressed, and flung open the door leading to her room.

She halted, unprepared for the sight of Card marching toward her down the hall, a determined expression fixed upon his face. With a sigh, Jade left the door open for him, settling herself in a high-backed chair, and when he entered, she silently indicated the seat opposite her own.

Just as she was about to ask him what he wanted, Card held up a hand, asking for patience. He closed the door, and she sensed when he forged a bubble of air—Pan had taught her how—to grant them privacy. Jade quirked an eyebrow, wondering what was on his mind.

Card spoke "We need to talk."

"I figured as much given you've created a bubble of privacy."

He grunted. "Nothing gets past you, does it?"

Jade rolled her eyes. "What did you want to talk about?" She tried not to snap at Card, but it was difficult. Her mind was a maelstrom of emotions—anger, frustration, grief—but Card didn't deserve any of that. In addition, Jade recognized that with her thin-skinned nature, accepting joking insults was still a work in progress.

Thankfully, Card appeared nonplussed by her annoyance, part of his charm. "I don't think Cam and Pan were killed like we were told."

Jade cocked her head, confused hope burgeoning while she waited for his explanation.

"What is the one inviolate law about anchor lines?" Card asked, going on to explain before she could guess. "It's that once an anchor line is formed, it cannot be superseded by the will of another. According to every theory I've come across, it's supposed to be impossible."

Jade wasn't sure if that was true or not. All her life, she'd worked hard at mastering her skills, but there were some classes that she had always found boring. Chief amongst them was the study of Ephemera's underlying principles. She was more interested in its practical application. However, just because she hadn't read much about the creation of anchor lines, didn't mean she'd blithely accept Card's statement without question. "Have you asked anyone else about this? Sage-Duke Kazar was pretty adamant that what you say *can't* happen was exactly what *did* happen."

Card nodded. "I asked Saira. She's gone to the palace's library to find confirmation of what I just told you."

Jade frowned. "I don't understand. Sage-Duke Kazar said it did happen." She knew she was repeating herself, but Card's declaration was so confusing. "Why are you doubting his word?"

"As I see it, there are four possible explanations for what happened yesterday." Card held up a finger. "First, the Sage-Duke let go of the anchor line for reasons of his own." Another finger. "Second, he let someone else gain control of it, again for reasons of his own."

"Hold on. How could he have done that with all of us watching. Saira was there." Jade didn't bother hiding her doubt.

"Saira wasn't there. None of us were. We were all conveniently here in Maviro. The anchor line was ripped away after we arrived. Saira saw nothing."

Jade grunted acknowledgment of his point. "Go on."

"Third, Kazar lost control of the anchor line. Fourth, he never had control of it to begin with. It always belonged to someone else. He just pretended to create it."

Jade shook her head. This still made no sense. "Is that last one even possible?"

Card hesitated, which was answer enough. "I'm not sure how, but I suppose it could happen, remote though it might be."

Jade nodded. If Card allowed for one remote possibility, then why not another one? "How much more remote would it be for Coruscant to gain control of the anchor line, just like the Sage-Duke said?"

Card's visage firmed, and his words came out heated. "That isn't a remote possibility. That is an impossibility." He hesitated, correcting himself a moment later. "It's not an impossibility, but it's so improbable. The odds are unbelievable, and I'm tired of unbelievable odds being used to explain disasters that seem to strike us."

Jade sat back, brow creased as she deliberated over Card's statements. "What you are saying? That Charity's father, Sage-Duke Kazar, lied to us? That he killed Cam and Pan?" She had to fight against abrupt rage. "Why? And what about Sial? He was there."

Card responded to her fiery tone with his usual calm demeanor. "First, we only have the Sage-Duke's word about Sial. And second, like I just said, he wouldn't be the first Sage-Duke to betray us. Nailing and Nageena gained entrance to Nexus when it should have been impossible."

Jade continued to work her way through Card's explanation, trying to find a flaw. Was there one? If so, she couldn't see it. But she was also wise enough to recognize her own limitations. The rest of Light Squad should know about this. Because if Card was right, then they had been betrayed again, and just like before, no one would be held to account.

"And you also have no reason to be angry with me," Card chided. "So why are you?"

Upon hearing his question, the last bits of Jade's anger snuffed out like a blown candle. "I don't know. Or maybe I do. Maybe I'm lashing out at you because Cam and Pan are gone. I'm sorry."

Card nodded his acceptance. "I feel the same way. The Sage-Duke is lying. He betrayed Cam and Pan just like Sage-Duchess Thens betrayed all of us. We can't trust him. We can't trust any of them. What he claims isn't an impossibility, but everything that happened is simply too convenient for me to believe events happened the way the Sage-Duke claimed."

Jade held quiet, not ready to reply, forcing herself to reconsider everything the Sage-Duke had told them, wrestling it through the lens of Card's explanations. A short while later, an idea occurred to her. "Coruscant isn't a Sage. He's supposed to be beyond a Divine."

"That's the only aspect of the Sage-Duke's explanation that gives me pause," Card admitted. "But Coruscant can't directly touch our world. Not well. It's why he and other Great Rakshasas work through their vassals. If they could influence Salvation more easily, our Realm would have already fallen to them by now. I don't think he could have overcome Kazar, even though the Sage-Duke says he did."

Jade pursed her lips. "What do you think we should do?"

"We should still go to the temple and Advance. But we shouldn't have Kazar with us."

"He won't go even if he could. At least not anytime soon." Jade stared off into the distance, still thinking. "With all the anchor lining he did yesterday, if rakshasas attack the duchy, he risks being too weak to defend his people." Her gaze firmed. "But Saira's mother might take us there. We should ask."

"Saira already made the request. Her mother agreed."

Jade eyed Card, impressed. "You have been busy."

A fleeting smile fled across Card's face. "Someone had to work while you were sleeping the day away."

Charity stepped out of the anchor line created by Saira's mother and struggled to control her gorge. She bent over at the waist, hands on her knees and taking shallow breaths. Traveling an anchor two mornings in a row wasn't easy, especially when her heart still grieved. Had it only been a single morning since Cam and Pan were lost? Surely it had been longer. It felt so.

Charity's unsettled stomach eventually eased, and she straightened.

The rest of Light Squad was already in place, and seconds later, Saira's mother, the Sage of the Sinanes, Lysha Maharani, joined them on a broad plateau overlooking a winding river canyon that extended into the distance with various secondary offshoots connecting like an arterial web to the main trunk. In addition, the rugged cliffs revealed ages gone by with the exposure of various lines of variegated stones of orange, red, yellow, gray, and brown. A stiff wind whipped grit and a mineral scent that had Charity sneezing.

"Allergies?" Avia asked. "I used to have them, too. Not so much since I Advanced to Glory."

Charity flicked her gaze to the other woman and lifted a questioning brow. "Is that your way of encouraging me to Advance?"

"Only if it actually works," Avia said with a cheeky smile.

"Can we talk about it now?" Jade asked Card, interrupting Charity's reply.

"We can talk," Sage Lysha said, her voice surprisingly deep. Or maybe it shouldn't be a surprise. Saira's mother was tall, strongly built, and had a commanding charisma that her daughter also possessed. An assertive voice was only natural for a woman like her.

"Talk about what?" Charity asked.

Saira addressed Card. "You didn't tell them?"

"I told you and Jade, but I didn't think I should tell anyone else in case Sage-Duke Kazar could somehow overhear our conversation."

Charity frowned. "What didn't you want my father to hear?"

Saira didn't answer, still speaking to Card. "You could have told them mind-to-mind."

Card's eyes widened as he stared at Saira before flushing, eyes dropping. "I forgot."

"So did I," Jade muttered.

Saira sighed. "You need to remember your skills. I went to the library to confirm your theory and expected you to handle the rest."

Charity had heard enough. "What's going on? What theory needed confirmation?"

Avia must have felt the same way. "And what didn't you want Sage-Duke Kazar to overhear? Why?"

Jade answered. "Because of what it might mean for Golden, for all of us."

Charity's patience snapped. "Stop talking in circles. What exactly were we supposed to know about my father?"

Card replied with an unambiguous answer. "I don't think he lost control of the anchor line. I don't think Coruscant ripped it away from him. I think whatever happened to Cam and Pan was intentional."

Charity narrowed her eyes at the bold accusation, especially since it led to a multitude of terrible possibilities. Her father had been cold and distant during her childhood, but she'd never doubted his love for his people or his hatred of rakshasas. "Explain."

Card did so. "I've studied anchor lines all my life and in great detail, the theory about how they can be formed, their uses, limitations, first principles. And everything I read indicates that what your father said happened isn't impossible, but so improbable as to be a meaningless difference."

"That isn't entirely correct," Sage Lysha said. "It can happen if a Heavenly Heathen, which is what we would guess of the Great Rakshasas, were to contest a Sage. They are a power beyond anything we know."

"And if the Heavenly Heathen were in a different Realm?" Charity asked, conflicted over what she was hearing. She respected her father, but she also couldn't let her feelings cloud her judgment.

Sage Lysha nodded. "It could still happen the way Kazar described." She held up a cautioning finger. "However, as young Master Card states: the probability is low. It would require a perfect storm of various happenstances."

Charity settled back on her heels, not sure what to think.

"If Charity's father didn't lose control of the anchor line, then how did this happen?" Avia asked. "What happened to Cam and Pan?"

Card stated four possibilities for how Cam and Pan had been lost, and none of them reflected well on Charity's father.

Charity grimaced, noticing the lack of denial from Saira and Sage Lysha, who appeared to agree with Card's assessment. She swallowed heavily, struggling with her floundering emotions. Like any child, she had wanted her father's approval, but since she'd rarely earned it, she'd settled for admiring his strength and steadfast commitment to Maviro. She found her admiration disappearing into slowly rising anger.

"Your father betrayed Cam and Pan," Card unnecessarily added.

Charity had already deduced the same. But the question as to why remained unanswered. Was it because her father disapproved of her relationship with Cam? Was it so unforgivable that she chose a relationship with a commoner? Had she doomed Cam somehow? She made to speak, but a slight quaver had her clearing her throat. "Why would he do that?" she asked, proud of the lack of inflection in her voice. "Does anyone know?"

"I would guess it has to do with the defense of Maviro," Sage Lysha answered. "I spoke to Avia's father. At the time you were sent to Hearth, Sage-Duchess Thens had many powerful boils in her duchy, but after those events with Nailing and Nageena, the boils were found under-manned and weakened. She was able to destroy them fairly easily."

Avia asked the question likely on everyone's mind. "She did Nailing's and Nageena's bidding upon a threat to her duchy?"

Sage Lysha nodded. "I believe so. As does Sage-Duke Vail."

Charity grimaced inwardly. If what Card believed was proven true, then the reason for her father's betrayal was almost certainly to do with fear for Maviro's safety. He cared for the duchy more than he did any of his children or grandchildren. Was that it then? Had the rakshasas threatened Maviro, just as they'd threatened Santh?

It sounded possible, even likely, but it begged the most important question: what had truly become of Cam and Pan?

Jade asked, and the others argued over the answer, their discussion twisting about in circular reasoning. Charity listened with only half an ear. By now, the shock had faded, and once she had a plan in place, she whistled sharply, ending the debate. "We can't learn why my father betrayed Cam and Pan or what actually happened to them. Not here and not now. Our best hope is to Advance. We can all reach Glory. We all have the answers or those who don't soon will. After that, we work on Advancing to Crown."

"I already have the answer for that," Avia noted, and upon seeing everyone's surprised expression, she flushed. "It was supposed to be a surprise."

Charity couldn't help but chuckle at Avia's embarrassed reaction. "Is there enough Ephemera here for her to Advance?" she asked Saira.

"No, but every little bit will help."

Charity nodded. "Then the rest of us who can Advance will do so. Avia gains more Ephemera and strives later on for Crown. We'll join her." And for the first time in Charity's life, she actually believed she could reach that lofty Stage. She had to.

"We need to force your father's hand," Jade said to her a moment later. "We can't stop at Crown. We have to aim for Sage. The only way Sage-Duke Kazar will answer our questions is if he has to."

"And if he doesn't?" Avia challenged. "What should we do?"

Jade's expression went flat and forbidding. "We do what we have to. Cam and Pan are family. We don't abandon family. Not now. Not ever."

"You're talking about a civil war," Avia reminded her.

"That's a risk I'm willing to take," Jade said. "If Sage-Duke Kazar did all this to protect his precious duchy, then putting it at risk is the last thing he'll want to do."

Charity disagreed. Threatening Maviro wasn't about attacking a vague idea or concept. It was about attacking a city full of good people. "We can't do that. Remember Nylara?" She reminded them of the fallout from the battle between Corona and the Jom-Strafe Crown. Thousands had died. "Cam would never want that."

Jade scowled, but in the end, she nodded agreement. "Then what do we do?"

It was Saira who replied. "We do exactly as Charity suggested. We Advance." She gestured to the river canyon. "The temple is distant. Several weeks past the base of this cliff and further down the canyon."

"Are we walking?" Jade asked.

"Unless you want me to fly you there," Sage Lysha said. "I can if you wish to hasten your journey."

Charity shook her head. "We need the time to firm our answers. Walking or flying, it won't matter. Advancing should be our focus. And after that, we Enhance and keep on Advancing."

"In that regard, I can help," Sage Lysha said. "There are occasional areas of Ephemeral concentrations that settle over the Sinanes. If I don't have any Glories who can reach Crown, and you've derived the proper answer necessary to Advance, it can be yours."

Charity viewed Saira's mother in surprise. It was a generous offer. Too generous. Charity narrowed her eyes. "What do you want in return?"

"Your service to the Sinanes, of course," Sage Lysha said as if the answer should have been manifestly obvious.

"For how long?" Charity asked.

Sage Lysha smiled. "Why don't you Advance to Glory first?"

It took three weeks of hard travel to arrive at the temple, and by the time they arrived, everyone in Light Squad had the answer needed to Advance. They'd camped for a night, and the next morning, each one began their attempt at Advancing to Glory while Saira and her amma watched over them.

The two women stood in the shadowed rubble of a ruined temple, gazing inward. At their backs, sunshine streamed into the river canyon, but the light didn't touch the building's porch-like entrance, which had been carved into the base of a cliff. Broad stairs led to a pediment, frieze, and cornice, but time and the elements had worn the sculpted stone to a blank slate. Inside, the deterioration continued where fluted columns, stout yet riddled with lacunae of missing stones, held aloft a domed ceiling decorated with ribbing, fanciful carvings, and a faded mural that Saira couldn't decipher.

The signs of decay were expected. After all, the temple was

ancient—lost to time until a relatively recent rockslide had exposed it to the world—and while no one knew its age, if forced to guess, Saira would have calculated it to be several thousand years of age.

None of that, however, currently held her attention. Rather, her focus was on the altar at the temple's far end. A dirty gray that might have once been white marble, it was also where Ephemera was at its thickest and the place Light Squad had Advanced to Glory. Only Avia remained there, Imbibing whatever Ephemera remained before they left.

The rest of Light Squad sat close at hand, cross-legged, meditating, and already Enhancing their Ephemera.

Saira caught her amma viewing her in silent speculation. "What is it?"

Amma shook her head. "Your friends are impressive," she murmured. "Glories for only a few minutes and already with all their Tangs at Gold."

Saira smiled, recognizing what her amma was truly considering: how to incorporate a Plasminia Tang into the Sources of the next generation of Ephemeral Masters. It wouldn't be as easy as she hoped, though. Saira and the rest of Light Squad had only managed it because of Professor Grey's teachings, and no doubt, that worthy woman was Jessira.

She replayed her words. *The rest of Light Squad.* Saira smiled afresh.

"You seem pleased," Amma noted.

Saira nodded, briefly pondering whether to tell her amma about the source of her amusement. Probably not the best idea. Considering herself a member of a foreign unit wouldn't go over well with the ruler of the Sinanes. Instead, Saira chose a different tack. "When I came home, it only took me weeks to Enhance all my Tangs to Crystal."

Amma tsked. "Yes, but you're my daughter. You're supposed to be exceptional." A beat later she added, "You *are* exceptional."

"Well, thank you," Saira said with a chuckle. "I like to think so."

They fell silent, the quiet interrupted minutes later by a distant shout in the vaults of Saira's mind. She frowned, turning her head away and concentrating.

"*Saira.*" It was Sial. Strain filled his voice, the connection clearly too hard for him to manage on his own.

But Saira could, and before their link was snipped short, she strengthened it. "*What's wrong?*"

Sial exhaled in relief. "*I've been trying to reach you for weeks now.*"

Saira frowned. Weeks? Sial contacting her had to be related to whatever had happened to Cam and Pan. "*What did you see? You know what I mean.*"

Sial told her, relaying how the Sage-Duke's anchor line had closed directly after she'd entered. Then how Kazar had created a second anchor line for Cam and Pan. That one, too, had closed. Afterward followed an unfriendly conversation between the Sage-Duke and Weld Plain. For a moment, Sial thought Kazar would kill the other man, but it hadn't occurred. Instead, the Sage-Duke had forged a third anchor line, this one for Weld, and finally, a fourth one for himself.

"*He saw me, I think,*" Sial said, his fatigue evident.

"*He confirmed it.*"

"*I was sure he'd kill me, but he never bothered chasing me down. He just left.*"

"*He is trying to do far worse.*" Saira informed him of what the Sage-Duke had told Light Squad, intimating that Sial was working with the rakshasas. "*Where are you?*"

"*I left Nexus right after you did. I've been moving around ever since. Right now, I'm in Warren.*"

"*Warren?*" Saira remembered it. It was a small town on the southern coast of Lake Nexus.

"What's going on?" Amma cut in.

Saira explained.

"Link me to this friend of yours."

"Where is he?" Charity asked, apparently overhearing the conversation and rising to her feet. "If he's a witness, then we need to keep him alive."

Saira's amma nodded agreement. "I need to talk to him."

"My amm—my mother wants to talk to you," Saira said to Sial.

Surprise and uncertainty laced his voice. *"Your mother?"*

Rather than explain, Saira simply made the link.

"Sial?" Amma began. *"You know who I am. Go somewhere private. I'll create an anchor line to your position. You'll come with me and the rest of your friends to the Sinanes. We'll keep you safe. We have more information about Sage-Duke Kazar than you know, but now isn't the time to discuss it."*

"You think the Sage-Duke marked me in some way." Sial made it a statement instead of a question.

"Unlikely. Had he done so, you would already be dead. No one could then contest his explanation for what happened to Cam and Pan."

"And the other Sage-Dukes would believe him?" Sial asked.

"Yes," Amma declared. *"They'll still believe him now."*

"But—"

"We don't have time for this," Saira said to Sial. *"We can go over the other points later."*

Sial dropped the discussion, telling them where to form the anchor line.

Saira nodded. *"I'll hold the connection in case anything changes."* She chewed her lip, worried for Sial, not knowing how much time he still had.

"What's going on?" Avia asked. She had just finished her work and the rest of Light Squad gathered close, all of them clearly aware of the tension.

Saira explained about her conversation with Sial.

Avia scowled when Saira finished. "That's our proof then, isn't it?"

"It is for me," Charity replied. "Three anchor lines wouldn't have exhausted my father as severely as he claimed. Four, though, would have."

"Unless he spent all his energy fighting Coruscant," Jade replied, sounding like she was playing rakshasa's advocate.

Amma chuckled. "We don't truly know the Great Rakshasa's might, but if it's what we suspect, then any fight Kazar could have managed would have been snuffed out within seconds. It wouldn't have been a long, drawn-out battle."

"Unless he can't touch Salvation like we suppose," Jade said.

Amma inclined her head in agreement. "True, but Sial's word still directly contradicts that of the Sage-Duke's."

"Then we better go save Sial," Card stated.

17

Hours and days of darkness swept by. They all blended into one another, and Cam lost track of how much time had passed since he and Pan had been imprisoned in Mote. It couldn't have been long, a few weeks at most, which he judged based on the length of his thickening beard.

Of course, it didn't matter if it had been two weeks or four. Life in the prison was cold, dark, and mind-numbingly depressing, and the worst aspect was the lack of stimulation. There were no sights or sounds to be had, and the only smell was the rank stench of his own refuse since the hole in the corner didn't drain his wastes away all too well.

Cam wasn't sure how long he could endure the solitude. He wasn't close to reaching his limits, but he also knew that there was only so much meditation a body could do and only so much conversating two people could share before they got to yelling at one another.

The only bright spot in his dismal life was Tulip, which was the literal truth. Viewing her through the woven world and empathing her emotions demonstrated that she had a hidden agenda underneath her kind smiles, wasn't as kind as she portrayed, but he could also easily overlook her lies since talking to her twice a day helped relieve the boredom.

It was with these cheerless thoughts that Cam finished off his mush, no longer noticing how disgusting it tasted. That probably reflected poorly on him, but it wasn't like there were any other options. It was either eat what was in front of him or grow even weaker than he already was. He needed whatever calories were offered. The same held true for the water he was given. It might have tasted like skunked sweat, but at least it kept the parchness at bay.

A knocking on his door's grate had Cam standing fast. Tulip was back, which meant the return of light for a short spell. Anything was better than the dark. Sure, Cam could have illuminated his cell, but he didn't want to risk losing any portion of his Ephemera.

He hustled to the door. "You're back sooner than I expected," he said just as Tulip slid open the grate.

"I'm efficient," Tulip said with a smile. "How was your food?"

Cam passed her his empty bowl, which he'd licked clean. "It ain't the best, but beggars can't be choosers, and neither can prisoners."

Tulip chuckled, a lowing sound, which made sense given her cow-like features. "I suppose not." She appeared to be waiting on him. "Your tumbler," she prodded after a moment.

Cam startled, muttering under his breath about his forgetfulness before hastily draining his water and passing the tumbler to her.

"I know you didn't get enough to eat," Tulip said, "but I might be able to find a way for you and Pan to get an extra helping now and then."

Cam smiled in gratitude, not sure what luck had brought Tulip into his life, even if he knew that he couldn't fully trust her.

He replayed his thinking and realized how cruel they might seem from Tulip's perspective. Being here in this prison wasn't exactly lucky for her. She probably hated it just as much as he.

"What's wrong?" Tulip asked, noticing the change in his demeanor.

Cam forced a smile. "Nothing. I just got caught up in the melancholy of being here."

Tulip gave him a tight-lipped smile of sympathy. "I know how that can be." She stared at him a moment longer, an undecipherable expression on her face, before she seemed to recollect her situation. "I better finish my rounds," she said, closing the grate.

Cam made his way back to his cot. By now, he'd memorized every inch of his cell and was able to navigate it without any light. He flopped onto his cot, wishing again for a blanket to ward off the chill.

"Do you want to meditate?" Pan sent to him.

Not seeing any other option, Cam figured he might as well. He took a cross-legged posture on his cot, and although the darkness was complete, he still closed his eyes. It only felt right to do so, somehow making the attempt more effective. He inhaled deep before exhaling slow, Delved his Source but didn't create a True Bond, just experienced it, soothed by the clarity it brought to his troubled thoughts.

He and Pan needed to find a way to freedom, and it didn't begin with worrying on loneliness and suffering. Those were the simple facts of their existence, and they couldn't change them. It was better to fix his mind on how to get free and get home.

Calmed by his reflections, Cam remained with his Source, still not Bonding to it but instead praying and feeling small. Minutes went by as he prepared himself for what was to come. He'd learned a trick during his long, lonely hours in Mote. A True Bond was no longer necessary for him to visualize the woven world. All it took was a simple twist of thinking where his mind's eye merged with his regular vision.

An instant later, the woven world flared in his senses—the bonds of life, color, and brilliance that linked this world just like it did in Salvation and Hearth. But in Mote, all was muted, not just the brightness of the strands but also their complexity. Single lines instead of vast tapestries and a wanness to every sensation, be it the Singing Light, the smell of spring flowers and rain, the idle summer heat, or the happy brightness of a child's innocence. None of that was present in Mote. Just this barest and washed-out expression.

And yet, since All was still Ephemera and Ephemera was still All,

Cam felt sure that the woven world here could still allow him to progress. He could still maintain his Source, increase it even by Imbibing whatever Ephemera was available.

He tried to do so, his usual pattern for meditation and growth in Salvation which had taken him far.

But like he had every previous time, he failed, and frustration bubbled under his meditative calm. Rather than fight it, though, Cam allowed it to happen, directing it so it washed through him. There was rage—a chronic kind that underlay his every thought since coming to Mote—along with the fevered ranting about how he didn't deserve what had happened to him, about how he'd suffered enough in this life, and then it was done. His anger receded in stages until it was gone.

Cam breathed slow and regular then, focusing on the peace of his Source and the barely visible woven world, simply existing within both. He was content, finding acceptance of all things: his life, his reality, and even this Realm.

Hours passed and nothing changed… until something did.

A strand of Ephemera twisted about, extending a limb to touch Cam's Source. He watched it with rising excitement but otherwise did nothing, afraid to even shift on his cot. What if the wrong movement or thought caused the Ephemera to flee?

As soon as the notion crossed his mind, the Ephemera did exactly that, and Cam desperately turned his attention away from it, focusing again on the acceptance of his existence.

Minutes passed before he looked again, and this time, he remained calm and with no expectations until the strand formed a deeper connection with his Source. Only then did Cam act. He Imbibed the Ephemera, a mere sip, but it was enough to have him smiling, not in triumph but in gratitude. He'd learned the first step in earning him and Pan their freedom.

Before he could share his discovery, a voice intruded in his mind. *"That was interesting. Who are you?"*

Cam stilled, not replying. The voice didn't belong to Pan.

"Are you there, boy?" the voice asked, that of a man. *"Can you not speak with your mind? Strange if you cannot given your ability to Imbibe Ephemera."*

Cam kept quiet. Should he respond? What if this was some trick? Although he had been largely ignored by the rakshasas during his imprisonment thus far, he had no doubts they wanted to torture him. When was the question, and the answer was one of his greatest fears.

"Fine. Remain silent then." The voice sounded both sad and annoyed. *"I offer friendship, and you'd rather hold on to your cowardice."*

Cam recalled then the advice given to him by Rukh and Jessira—that someone within the prison might befriend him and Pan and offer them aid. In spite of his doubts, he had thought it might be Tulip, but what if it was this other person? Courage unlocked his tongue. *"I can speak. Who are you?"*

The voice might have sighed in relief. *"I am glad to hear another voice after so many years. I'm even happier that you show some modicum of bravery."*

Cam wasn't sure he cared for the tone of whoever was talking to him. *"And if you were in my shoes, would you offer immediate trust?"*

The voice laughed. *"If I was in your shoes, I'd actually* have *shoes. Did they not take yours from you?"*

They hadn't, but Cam wasn't about to divulge that piece of information. *"You haven't told me your name."*

"I am called Birch Drang."

There was a pregnant pause then, as if the person speaking were waiting for the recognition of his name. But Cam had never heard of such an individual. Maybe he was famous here in Mote. But if so, why was he imprisoned? Or was he actually a prisoner? Worry shivered down Cam's spine.

Birch sighed. *"I'm already forgotten then. Not a surprise. I've been imprisoned for more years here than I spent above in service to Coruscant."*

Another prisoner then, or so Birch claimed, while also providing some tantalizing answers about his past. Cam needed to learn more.

Tulip hadn't been able to tell him much about Mote, Coruscant, or Nullity. Perhaps Birch could through subtle questioning. *"How long have you been imprisoned here?"*

"Many decades. Four going on five." Birch laughed. *"I'm old now, and the other rakshasas hate it, but their duty is clear: I am to be kept alive. The order comes directly from Coruscant."* He sighed again. *"I'm in the mood to talk. It's been so long."*

And he did so, telling about his life as a commander in Coruscant's legions, creating a seed of Nullity and eventually gaining the status of a Crown. He also spoke of the betrayal of his superiors when he and a cohort were sent to Salvation through the Locus.

"It is the truth of Mote: betrayal, murder, and torture are the best means by which we close ourselves off from Devesh and Ephemera. We focus entirely inward, initially transforming Ephemera into a seed of Nullity, and then growing that core. And the greater the individual's will to power, the greater the amount of Nullity they can create."

Although Cam was filled with dozens of questions, he kept quiet, content to listen as Birch explained the mysteries of how and why rakshasas gained power.

Birch gave off the sense of a smirk. *"Is it not ironic? Prior to my betrayal, I had also planned on betraying those under my command."*

"How?"

"Because the truth of Nullity is not one shared with the servants of Salvation. Those rakshasas from that Realm still use Ephemera, and their only purpose is to whittle away at the might of the Ephemeral Masters so that the Great Rakshasas can more easily conquer their world. Coruscant, Shimala, and Simmer will even use the death of their servants as fuel for their own growth. That was also my intention, at least on a smaller scale."

Cam considered what Birch had just told him. There was a truth to the man's—or rather, rakshasa's words. *"And that's when you were imprisoned? When you were found out for wanting to betray your subordinates?"*

Birch must have truly wanted to tell his story because he didn't hesitate in responding to Cam's question. *"I was imprisoned long before that. I was imprisoned in the emptiness of Nullity, but my fate as you're asking was actually sealed when I walked upon Salvation and felt for the first time what it meant to truly be alive. It was the same for nearly every member of my cohort. We couldn't have moved even if our clothes were on fire. We stood lost in wonder, rooted in place in a forest glade, surrounded by the fragrances of sunshine, life, and birdsong."*

He fell silent then, apparently lost in his reflections, and Cam had to prod him. *"What happened?"*

Birch sighed. *"What happened was that we found something we never knew existed, never knew could exist. And that was when we were betrayed by those who didn't feel the call of Ephemera. They slayed us, but as a Crown, I threw off my beguilement and killed them in return. I was the only survivor, the only one able to escape back to Mote where I was granted reprieve for reasons I don't know."* Birch went quiet for a time. *"I wonder. What was the point of it all? For us to experience hope and true life for a few brief minutes, only to have it stolen away before it could actually mean something?"*

Cam didn't have an answer for the rakshasa, but he empathized with Birch's situation… assuming it was true.

"Or maybe it was a teaching point from the Four," Birch mused. *"That anyone who seeks anything other than Nullity is a weakling."*

Cam latched on to Birch's words. *"The Four?"*

"They are Divines: Stipe, Fangold, Manchien, and Vel. Coruscant's lieutenants. They command his legions."

Cam pondered Birch's information. It explained much—again, assuming it was true—about the rakshasas, both here and on Salvation. It meant that Coruscant's forces might not actually be powerful, not if the first true breath of Ephemera caused so many to freeze in wonder. There might be hope for them, after all.

"Coruscant knows this," Birch continued. *"When he goes to Salvation, he'll leave his legions behind, growing more powerful when they're betrayed to their slaughter by Simmer and Shimala as he and the Four conquer your Realm."*

Cam stiffened with alarm. *"My Realm is this Realm."*

Birch chuckled. *"We both know that's not true. I told you: I was a Crown. The moment you spoke to me, you gave away everything. Cam Folde. There is also your friend, Pan Shun. Both of you Adepts. Charity Kazar. Light Squad."* Cam's alarm became fear, not for himself but for Pan, but before he could reach out to his friend, the rakshasa cut him off. *"You don't have to worry about me. I know how to keep quiet."*

He ended on an expectant note, causing Cam to grimace. He should have never replied to the rakshasa, but now he was trapped. *"In exchange for what?"*

Birch inhaled deep. *"I've been here for many decades, and I'm tired. Tell me of your life on Salvation. I want to hear everything—"*

"I thought you already knew everything."

Birch chuckled. *"I know the large-scale details, but not the important ones. What does an apple taste like? A pomegranate? What does the night sky look like? The dawn after a storm? I want to know it all."*

It wasn't much of a risk, telling the rakshasa what he wanted to know, but speaking to Birch hadn't sounded like much of a risk either. *"And by telling you this, you promise not to betray me or Pan?"*

"I vow it."

Cam carefully considered what to say. While Birch sounded genuine, he couldn't be trusted. *"You really think I'll tell you what you want to know? After all this talk about how you gain Nullity through betrayal?"*

"Betrayal only works if the party being betrayed doesn't know they're being betrayed." Honey coated Birch's words. *"Besides, I'll offer something in exchange beyond my silence."*

Cam doubted the rakshasa's word and worth, but he asked anyway. *"What's that?"*

"Two things. Training. I can finalize your education in the art of fighting."

Viewing his prison cell, Cam had no idea how any kind of training could take place. It sounded impossible. *"And the second?"*

"I can tell you how to escape this place."

Once again, Cam found himself stiffening, this time with repressed hope.

"I have your attention." Birch's voice was faintly mocking. *"Escape is what we both want and for the same reason."*

Cam couldn't let a remark like that go unchallenged. *"And what reason is that?"*

"Vengeance."

That wasn't why Cam wanted to free himself, at least not entirely. He wanted to bring Weld to justice, same with Sage-Duke Kazar, but that wasn't the same as vengeance. Cam said so.

"You're lying to yourself. Vengeance is a worthy pursuit of your aims."

"No, it isn't," Cam replied in annoyed distraction. It wasn't that he was opposed to vengeance, but that wasn't why he wanted freedom from Mote or how he wanted to live the rest of his life. Beyond that, Birch also claimed to want vengeance but against whom? Cam asked.

"My commanders, of course," Birch replied, although a moment later, he huffed. *"Or maybe you're right. I can't have vengeance against my commanders and also escape with you and Pan to Salvation."* Another huff along with the sense of a fierce scowl. *"So long as I can experience a world of sunshine and flowers, then I'll be content. That will be the extent of my vengeance. You promise me that, and I'll help you and your friend."*

Cam smiled in spite of his mistrust. *"A life well lived is the best revenge."*

Birch laughed. *"I suppose it is."* His laughter trailed off. *"Just don't preach to me about love. Love is naive and deceitful. We are selfish creatures, all of us, and we are meant to create our own happiness, not give it away to someone else."*

"You mean like with Nullity?"

Birch might have nodded. *"With Nullity, a true master requires nothing beyond themselves. They live for their own needs and happiness.*

It suffices and is also what makes us more powerful than Ephemeral Masters of a similar Advancement. Nullity is both a superior method of growth and a superior philosophy."

Cam refused to concede Birch's point. What was the point of power if it meant a person was forever alone? Because in the end, that was where Nullity led: an empty existence without meaning beyond self. *"And yet, the moment you felt a world of Ephemera, Nullity wasn't enough. You wanted what your superior model couldn't provide: the fragrances of sunshine, life, and birdsong."*

Birch didn't reply at once, and the silence lingered so long that Cam started to get worried. Had the rakshasa withdrawn his attention?

Just as he was about to ask, Birch finally replied. *"I take your point, but my earlier statement remains true. Love is naive and deceitful."*

"But it's also the source of everything you had never before experienced and wished you had."

"How so?" Birch asked, puzzlement riddling his voice.

"Because everything beautiful stems from Ephemera. How else do you think it comes about? What do you think Ephemera is? It's the act of creation, of naive love and hope, which are the greatest things."

Another lengthy pause before Birch responded. *"I can tell that you believe in your statements, but that doesn't make them true."*

Cam shrugged. Birch wasn't wrong. What a person believed to be true and what actually was could be two entirely different things. However, in this one matter, Cam knew he was right.

Another set of questions popped into Cam's mind about Birch. *"How did you know I Imbibed Ephemera? Have you learned how? And why bother if it's less powerful than Nullity? What are you using it for?"*

This time when Birch responded, he sounded discomfited, like he didn't want to explain himself. *"Having all of my rakshasas die, in the manner in which they did... for that fact alone, I was sentenced here. That's when I learned to Imbibe Ephemera."*

The answer didn't provide much information. *"But why? What's the point?"*

"Because it's the only thing that keeps me alive. Nullity is power, but

it also causes a person's body to fail, something I could correct outside the prison. In here, I found the only thing that could keep me alive was Ephemera. I'm keenly aware of it."

Interesting. *"Is that the same for all the rakshasas? The part about causing a person's body to fail? Even the Great Rakshasas?"*

"As far as I know."

Cam narrowed his eyes, contemplating what he'd just learned. It was a weakness that maybe no one else in Salvation knew about. And when he and Pan escaped this prison, it was something they could perhaps exploit one day.

As if thinking about him brought him forth, Pan spoke into his mind. *"What's happening? I haven't felt you this excited since we've been here."*

Cam quickly brought his friend up to speed on his conversation with Birch, and as soon as he did, Pan addressed the rakshasa. *"How do rakshasas procreate?"*

Cam blinked at the unexpected question, and he wondered what Pan had in mind.

Once again, Birch replied with clear reluctance. *"We can only procreate at those areas closest to the Locus."*

"And what is the Locus?" Pan asked, although he had to already know the answer since Rukh and Jessira had told them.

"The place where Ephemera bleeds into Mote. It's an anchor line to Salvation, and the means of our escape. Reaching it won't be easy, though. We'll have to travel the length of the Blood Sea. Underneath the ocean's bed, there exists another world: Petala, the Hollow Land, a dangerous place, and afterward, there comes the long length of the Badlands where Shimala houses her thralls. I can guide you through both places. You only have to accept my help. By the time I'm done, your skills will be diamond-hard."

From the outside looking in, trusting Birch might have sounded foolish, except Cam remembered Rukh's and Jessira's advice to do exactly that: to keep his heart and mind open. To trust in someone who could help them, a friend. He didn't believe in Birch—not yet—but he believed in the Holy Servants. *"How long do you think we'll be here? Before we can escape?"*

"You need to Advance to Glory. It's the strength you'll need to unlock the doors to your cells and survive Petala and the Badlands"

Cam frowned, further confused. *"What does Ephemera have to do with unlocking the cell?"*

"And why can't you do that?" Pan added.

"Because the doors to your cells can only be opened by a very special key, a Sage wielding Nullity, or—based on my best guess—Ephemera from a Glory. I lack the key, am not a Sage, nor am I a Glory-Staged Ephemeral Master. I barely have enough Ephemera to keep myself alive down here. It has to be the two of you."

Cam still didn't agree. *"Give us a few days to think it over."*

"Fair enough, but don't think too long." Birch chuckled. *"This prison isn't a safe place to ponder life's complexities. We might all be dead by the time you have your answers."*

18

Birch did as was asked by leaving Cam and Pan be for the next few days, and after the two of them talked it over, they decided to give the rakshasa a chance. They weren't stupid about it, though. There was still plenty about Birch to mistrust, and it wasn't driven so much by what the rakshasa had said but more about what he'd implied. Birch was a Crown, someone who'd created and mastered a great deal of Nullity, which meant he'd also mastered the art of betrayal and probably done plenty of evil in his life.

As a result, Cam didn't doubt Birch would prove false as soon as it suited his interests. For now, however, their desires appeared to align, and until that changed, Cam was determined that he and Pan would learn everything they could from the rakshasa. Rukh and Jessira had provided some information about Mote, but there was plenty more Cam figured that he and Pan needed to know, missing subtleties that could mean the difference between escape and death. They couldn't afford to overlook any information.

The very day they agreed to have Birch train them, Tulip came around to hand out the last meal of the day, and Cam eyed his plate of food, which had an extra serving of mush and water that was clear rather than cloudy.

Tulip winked when he viewed her in confusion. "Don't tell the warden," she said, heading off toward Pan's cell.

Cam shook his head. His worries over Tulip never receded—his use of empathy continued to demonstrate that she hid her true motives—but he was still glad for her presence. Sure, she was false in ways he couldn't quite determine, but her behavior still gave him hope. He'd expected the worst of the denizens in Mote, but maybe there was more to them than he'd originally guessed.

Continuing to muse on Tulip, Cam shoveled down his gruel, wondering what her hidden agenda might mean for him and Pan. Of course, he couldn't entirely hold that against her. After all, he and Pan had their own hidden agendas, but what had him concerned was whether Tulip intended on betraying them. Probably so, but what if he was wrong? What if she was actually good and kind? Or had that kind of capacity? Shouldn't he give her a chance? What was the worst that could happen if he did? And wasn't that pretty much the judgment he'd made about Birch? He'd granted the rakshasa some measure of trust while watching for betrayal and hoping for better.

Cam downed the rest of his food and water, eventually making a decision to give Tulip the same measure of trust that he'd offered Birch. He'd have to watch her through the woven world along with listening through empathy for whatever she said. Even then, he might not be able to fully decipher her truest intents, but hopefully, he'd have enough information to decide what to do for her.

When Tulip returned, Cam handed her his plate and tumbler, bowing slightly to her. "Thank you," he said, infusing his words with the gratitude he wanted her to feel.

She frowned in apparent confusion. "You don't have to thank me for doing my job."

"We both know giving me what you did is more than your job."

Tulip blinked rapidly, smiling slightly. "Maybe it is, but you deserve it. Both you and Pan."

Cam's jaw clenched, but otherwise he didn't react to the emotion wafting off Tulip: deceit. She didn't believe anything of what she'd just said. "I still appreciate what you're doing for us."

Tulip offered a final smile before shutting the grate and closing Cam's cell in darkness.

He exhaled in annoyed disappointment when she left. What was Tulip hiding? What was she lying about? He couldn't tell, which meant he'd have to remain cautious around her. And if she ended up trying to betray his trust? Well, he'd figure out what to do about that when it happened.

Returning to his cot and centering himself as best he could, Cam shoved down his lingering irritation with Tulip and reached out to Pan and Birch. *"We're ready to learn."*

The rakshasa immediately responded. *"You've made a wise decision."*

Cam discarded Birch's opinion. *"When do we start training?"*

"There's no time like the present. I'll test you."

A pressure built against Cam's mind, like someone was trying to gain entrance. He resisted.

"That's me," Birch said. *"Accept my invitation, and you'll be able to train in the way I promised."*

Cam wasn't prepared to do anything of the sort. *"What kind of invitation?"*

Birch huffed. *"The kind that gives you access to my mind, just like I'll have access to yours. We'll be equally at risk and open to one another."*

"No." Pan's refusal was without hesitation, and it mirrored Cam's own feelings.

"You don't trust me?" Birch asked, but he sounded approving rather than upset. *"Again, you show wisdom, but you should have never allowed me to into your thoughts in the first place."*

Cam's dark cell vanished, and he found himself standing alongside Pan in a rectangular arena floored in packed sand and with a ceiling that soared hundreds of feet above. Empty stands rose all about them, and sunlight the color of bone—cold rather than warm—beamed down, highlighting the empty space. A strange kind of quiet filled the arena and so did a musty smell that reminded Cam of a carcass rotted to bones and leather.

Where was this place? And how had Birch brought them here?

Sprite flitted through the empty corridors of the prison, darting from one rafter to another with a specific purpose in mind. He wanted to check on the new arrivals, Cam and Pan. They had seemed interesting when he'd first met them, but every time he'd gone to their cells, they were either asleep or talking to Tulip, which was strange.

Why talk to her? She was a rakshasa, no different than any of the others, but Cam and Pan regularly spoke to her with fondness and even trust.

Sprite had to warn them.

Plus, there was the book he'd noticed when peering into Cam's cell the other day. How had Cam smuggled in a book and why? Sprite had to know. He loved books. Nothing tasted quite as good as a good book. It didn't matter what it was about… well, he didn't like books about snakes, but otherwise books were wonderful!

Sprite landed on a ceiling rafter, cocked his head, and listened hard in case a rakshasa was close. Sometimes they tried to eat him or Kiwi. *Monsters.* The only way to survive in this terrible place was to always be wary of danger. And every rakshasa was dangerous.

"Where are we going?" Kiwi asked, having caught up.

Sprite briefly chirped at him, calling for silence. He thought he'd heard something.

Seconds later, Tulip trundled underneath, never bothering to glance up. Sprite waited until she was gone from both sight and hearing. Only then did he answer Kiwi. "I want to see what the new arrivals are doing."

"Why?"

Sprite cheeped in reluctance. Kiwi would only get mad, thinking it was too risky. He thought everything was too risky.

"Why?" Kiwi repeated.

Sprite fluffed his wings. Did he really have to say?

"I'm leaving if you don't tell me."

Sprite sighed. "Cam has a book."

Kiwi trilled alarm. "You want to go into his cell?"

"It's been so long since we've eaten a good book," Sprite cajoled.

"It's too dangerous."

"Then you stay outside and watch for danger." Having had enough of the conversation, Sprite darted off before Kiwi could argue. A few wingbeats later, he stood on a rafter, directly outside Cam's cell.

An instant later, Kiwi arrived. "What if a rakshasa comes along."

Sprite scoffed. "When do they ever come by this late?"

"Tulip might."

"She just collected the dishes from their final meal of the day. She won't be back for hours."

Kiwi tweeted. "I don't like this."

"You only have to watch for anyone coming," Sprite told him, pausing and eyeing Kiwi in challenge. "Unless you want to come in with me."

Kiwi twittered, wings fluttering.

Sprite knew it meant his fellow lovebird thought they shouldn't do something but could be convinced to do it anyway. All it would take was a small push. "If we eat the right book, just think what we can learn. It might be enough for us to Advance."

"Some books give me nightmares," Kiwi muttered.

"Do those two seem like they read books about nightmares? They have Ephemera. You felt it."

"I felt it." Kiwi spoke slowly, like the words were being pulled from his throat.

"Then let's go."

Not waiting for Kiwi's permission, Sprite flew down to the steel grate through which Cam received his tray of food and beverages. A hard shove scraped it open, the sound echoing and harsh in the corridor's quiet.

The noise had Kiwi chirruping in alarm.

Sprite hushed him, peering inside. Cam sat on his cot, legs folded with each foot on the opposite knee, unmoving, eyes closed and breathing deeply like he was asleep. Sprite trilled loudly, immediately darting away.

No response from within, and Sprite flapped back to the grate, discovering that Cam hadn't moved, not even an inch. He glanced at Kiwi, who remained frozen in place, roosting in the rafters. "Are you coming?"

Sprite flew inside, not waiting for a response. He alighted on the cot and gazed about, searching for Cam's book while also keeping an eye out for movement. With only the dim lighting from outside to provide illumination, it was difficult.

Kiwi landed next to him and whispered, "Where do you think it is?"

Sprite had a notion, but Kiwi wouldn't like it. "I think it's in his pocket." He indicated what he meant—a bulge pressing outward from Cam's chest.

True enough, Kiwi didn't like it. "We should leave."

"Not yet." Sprite hopped forward, careful and cautious. He flitted to Cam's shoulder, disregarding Kiwi's squawk of alarm. From there, Sprite climbed down to the pocket, but rather than reach inside, he tore it open from the outside.

The book, a slim volume, became visible, and Sprite gripped it in his beak, dropping it next to a still sleeping Cam.

Kiwi joined him. "We should eat it quickly."

Sprite agreed, and while he'd done all the hard work, he allowed Kiwi to tear into the book as well, and together, they consumed every last page and scrap. Once finished, they flew out of the cell, making sure to close the grate before resting in the rafters, both their stomachs bulging.

Neither spoke, both of them focused inward on learning from what they'd eaten. *The Warrior and the Servant* was the title of the book, and there was so much to understand, all of it wonderful. It had Sprite recollecting his life before Mote. The world into which he'd been born had been a place of warmth and beauty with green leaves, trees, and life, and he missed it… everything but the snakes. All snakes had to be rakshasas. How else to explain something that could walk without legs?

More wisdom seeped out of the book, the idea that very few things are correct in their most absolute sense but Devesh being the Most Holy was one of them.

The concept had Sprite tilting his head. How long had it been since he'd heard the Lord's name? How long since he'd even thought of it? Too long, and Sprite promised that he'd also remember how to pray.

But he also only had half the information, and his plans for tonight weren't yet done. Sprite disgorged what he'd eaten with Kiwi doing the same, and they fed again. Minutes passed, and while Sprite was far from figuring on what they'd just ingested—it would take them both weeks or even longer to truly understand the book's teachings—his greed had him wanting more. "Pan also has a book."

Kiwi sighed. "Let's go."

Cam spun about, furious at Birch. What had he done? Where—

Pan, remaining close at hand, appeared similarly mystified and upset, but what had Cam cutting off his thoughts was the lion-headed rakshasa approaching them from a far corner. Covered in tawny fur and heavily muscled, he wore only a loincloth and had the indigo-eyed Haunt of a Crown. This was Birch. It had to be. His stride held all the pride of a Sage.

Seeing a massive upright catlike creature caused a flicker of a memory in Cam's mind, there and gone again, but rather than worry over the remembrance, he forged a True Bond, separating slightly from Pan so they could attack the rakshasa from two directions if it came to that.

"What did you do?" Cam asked.

Birch halted, gesturing broadly. "I offered you training," he said, voice sounding like a growl. "This is where we'll train." He seemed to recognize Cam's anger. "Would you have agreed if I'd told you my intentions? That I wanted to bring you to an arena of our imagination? We created this place. All three of us. Our mindscape. Not me alone. And it can only be reached when the three of us are in agreement."

Pan growled. "We're not in agreement. Send us back."

Cam did a double-take. He'd never seen Pan so angry, although he shared his friend's fury.

"You had no right to bring us here," Pan continued.

Birch faced them, arms clasped behind his back and unperturbed. "Where exactly do you think this is? Do you think that's air you're breathing?"

Pan snapped at him. "I don't care. If you want us to trust you, then you have to treat us more fairly."

Birch offered a mocking smile. "Fair? Do you think it was fair that when I achieved a Novice's Awareness, I was sent to face Simmer's spiders. I fought them, watched hundreds die, and only after a year did I earn a spot in Coruscant's legions. Was it fair to watch my sire and dam put to the fire for disobeying one of the Four?" He snorted in derision. "Forget about fairness. It's a lovely concept if you're a child."

Pan had no response to Birch's statements, but Cam did. "You said this is our mindscape, a place of our imagination. What does that mean?"

"It means exactly what I said," the rakshasa replied. "It's an arena where I'll train you to lethality, which you'll need if you wish to survive Petala or even escape our prison. In return, you gain Ephemera and take me with you. I've decided you were right: living well will have to be vengeance enough, especially if I get to experience Ephemera as well."

Cam wanted to argue and ask more questions, but he also couldn't see the point. Best to simply accept what was happening now and learn the how, what, and why later. He shared a questioning look with Pan, who shrugged, apparently not knowing how best to proceed either. Cam grimaced. Not much help there. "What do you want from us?"

"I want to test you," Birch replied. "What weapons do you know?"

Cam considered whether to answer, but figured in the end that he had nothing to lose by doing so. "Sword and shield along with the spear and staff. We can also use Ephemera. Is that allowed?"

Birch smirked. "Anything that keeps you alive is allowed—the first rule in combat. But before we try with weapons, we'll see how you do in unarmed fighting." He pointed at Cam. "You first."

Cam vacillated on stepping forward, not wanting to engage without first understanding the rules. "How is the spar judged? A point system? And will you be limiting yourself to an Adept's abilities?"

Birch scowled in annoyance. "Of course I'll be limiting myself. That should be obvious. As for the rules, there's only one: concuss your opponent or render them unable to fight."

His words spoken, Birch advanced on Cam, who hastily got himself in position, forming a True Bond. The woven world came to life, wan and barely visible in this imaginary place.

Cam jabbed, testing the range, trying to get a feel for Birch's timing. The rakshasa shifted slightly, returning fire with a hard right. Cam blocked the blow on his shoulder and upper arm. He backed up a pace, but Birch closed the gap. The rakshasa shot for a single leg, went to turn the corner, but Cam defended, sprawling. He twisted free of the rakshasa's grip, took Birch's back, and got an elbow under the rakshasa's chin, sinking in a guillotine. Squeezed. An easy win.

But Birch wasn't done. He gripped Cam's arm, slicing a line of winrows with his claws.

Cam hissed, pushing the rakshasa away. A quick glance showed him the damage he'd taken. His left forearm was filleted open, blood pouring from the wound, muscle and tissue hanging.

His inattention cost him as Birch landed a looping left. It slammed home, and Cam felt his jaw shatter. He heard a distant shout from Pan, and that was the end.

Time continued, but Cam was unaware of reality. He lay stiff as a board, locked in place and wondering what had happened as he clawed the sky. It was a fleeting thought that came and went as fast as a spark from a campfire. Nothing else impacted his mind. Time passed.

"Fool." The voice had a rumbly quality. "You must always recognize the abilities of the one you fight. Closing with someone with claws is an idiotic decision."

Who was that? And who was he speaking to?

Slowly, Cam's awareness of the world recovered and his memory restored. Sage-Duke Kazar's betrayal. Rukh and Jessira. Mote. Every item returned, one by one, slowly, painfully. The lovebirds, meeting Birch, sparring against him. But then what?

Cam had locked in a guillotine, had the training match wrapped up. Only then did he recognize the pain in his left forearm and his face. He shifted his gaze, finding his arm flayed open. His jaw hurt, and Cam moved it around, eliciting a sharp, stabbing agony. Best to stop doing that.

"Can you stand?" It was Birch.

Pan faced the rakshasa, glowering fierce.

More awareness recovered, and with it a greater appreciation for the pain he was in. Cam groaned. "What happened?"

"You lost," Birch replied. "Recall the last moments of the match."

Cam tried to do so, but all his memories ended with the guillotine.

"You had the choke," Pan said, "but Birch has claws. He cut you open, and when you were distracted, he knocked you unconscious and broke your jaw." He glared at Birch. "You didn't have to do that."

Faster than thought, Birch landed a clubbing hammer fist. Pan swayed, struggling to remain upright before face-planting. Cam wanted to protest, but he could barely move, could barely think.

Birch stood over Pan. "My ways are not for you to question. Disrespect will not be tolerated. This is your only warning. Test me again, and you'll find much greater pain than this when next we train." He addressed Cam. "As for you, get up. Right now, or I'll gut you."

A single glance at Birch's unyielding face told Cam the truth. The rakshasa would do exactly as he'd stated. Protecting his forearm, which still bled profusely, Cam rolled over on his side and slowly clambered to his feet. His mind finally worked and rage surged into his thoughts.

He glared at the rakshasa, who stood implacable and uncaring while Pan breathed hard, clearly hurt and needing tending.

"He's fine enough," Birch growled. "You aren't. Imagine your arm hale and it will be so."

Cam wasn't sure how to do what Birch ordered, but he closed his eyes, forcing himself to believe that his arm and jaw were whole and uninjured. In the midst of his imagining, he heard Pan stir and sent a question to him. *"How are you feeling?"*

"I've been better," Pan sent back. *"You?"*

"I'll tell you later. We'll—" Cam broke off, surprised when his arm and jaw stopped hurting. He viewed his arm, shifting it about, examining it for the wounds Birch had inflicted and finding none. Moving his mouth elicited no pain, either. He was fine, but that didn't mean he wasn't furious. He spoke to Birch. "We're done here."

His comment earned him an uncaring shrug. "Learn from the lesson or do not. Your choice."

Cam's rage burned hotter, volcanic. He and Pan had been fools to think they could train under a rakshasa. "And you better learn your own lesson. When I say we're done here, I mean we're done. With all of it."

He focused on returning to the place of his imprisonment, and less than a blink later, he was back in the cold, damp darkness of his cell.

"We can't trust him," Pan said a moment later, apparently, having also returned to his own cell.

"We should have never agreed to his training," Cam agreed.

"Why did you leave the arena?" Birch asked, sounding befuddled.

"Shut up and leave us alone." Cam ignored any further attempts at communication from the rakshasa.

19

Birch frowned after Cam and Pan had left the mindscape. What foolishness. Acting out like children merely because he provided some necessary correction to their flawed techniques. He shook his head in disgust. Where was their pride? Their honor? To rant and rave over some mild pain? He couldn't understand or abide it. Inexplicable. Especially since there were ten thousand rakshasas who would have paid in blood for Birch's mentorship in combat, many more who would have begged to learn from him about life, power, and the best use of it.

But not Cam and Pan. Oh, no. Not those two arrogant pups, who believed themselves better than him, wiser and already well beyond his teachings. What conceit. Their obvious devotion to Devesh was understandable if misguided. Same with their feelings toward Rukh and Jessira… although in this regard, Birch could find some common ground with them. Anyone who Coruscant feared was worthy of emulation.

Birch nodded to himself. *Rukh and Jessira.* Yes, he would have been honored to learn from them, become like them, but he no longer knew what that meant. Who were Rukh and Jessira?

Originally, Birch had believed that the Holy Servants were nothing of the kind, that they weren't servants of anyone but their own power. A younger Birch had felt certain about it. After all, no one achieved Rukh's and Jessira's level of accomplishment without selfish devotion to their own needs. And to do so certainly wasn't evil. Virtuous self-ishness was the most obvious and proper methodology with which to experience the world. Rukh and Jessira had simply been more skilled and powerful than anyone in existence.

So Birch had long believed, but ever since he had first experienced a flood of Ephemera in that lovely meadow, his world had shattered and a festering doubt had taken root. That uncertainty had slowly gained strength during the cold, lost decades of his incarceration, especially when he'd discovered how to Imbibe Ephemera—clumsily and bro-kenly compared to Cam—but that was when his decline proved irre-versible. Skepticism had corroded his certainties, which was why he'd been unable and unwilling to voice a defense against Cam's arguments against Nullity. How could he when he no longer believed in it?

As he generally did whenever troubles polluted his waking mo-ments, Birch retreated into his mindscape, a place where doubts couldn't touch him. There, he entered a forest glade of singing birds and rustling animals, experienced a soft wind that carried the memo-ries of pine and perfumed flowers, and felt the cleansing wash of pure sunshine that poured down on him like a benediction.

Birch closed his eyes and turned his face to feel the warmth, throw-ing his arms wide, absorbing the blessing of this place that he'd only experienced for a few brief minutes before everything had become blood, carnage, and confusion.

"This is a lovely memory," a voice said.

Birch shot his eyes open, searching for whoever had spoken. He quickly discovered an old man standing close at hand and leaning on a gnarled staff. His skin, the color of rich soil, was as wrinkled as crum-pled paper, not matching his hair, which remained dark and thick. He wore an expression of equanimity with only the barest of smiles, and there was a solidity to him, something beyond that of the meadow itself, and Birch knew why. The answer came from the man's sclerae, which sparkled like a rainbow-refracted crystal. The man was a Divine.

A thousand questions rippled through Birch's mind, many of them centered on the identity of the man. Who was he? Not one of the Four—Birch knew all of them. And how was he here in Birch's mindscape?

No matter. In this place, Birch ruled. With a thought, shackles slammed around the man's arms and legs, wrapping him in heavy chains that were as weighty as Birch could imagine.

Feeling a bit more settled, he studied the being before him, wondering how he had entered Mote. And surely he wasn't native to Birch's home. This man gave off the aroma of Ephemera, and it was so pure that Birch found himself leaning forward, panting with want.

With a start, he collected himself and pulled himself together. A foreign Divine had invaded Mote, and he needed all his wits about him.

The man glanced at the bindings with a faint smile before returning his attention to Birch. "You don't need to fear me," he said, his voice warm and generous and without a hint of malice. "My name is Rail Gristle. I wanted to talk to you."

Birch wasn't fooled. This was a being of power, and he wanted something other than simple conversation. Right now, the man—Rail—wore a gentle demeanor, but it was merely a ploy. If he didn't gain what he sought, threats were sure to follow. After all, nothing in any Realm was ever given for free. "What do you want?" Birch asked, polite although he wanted to make demands.

"You have three paths ahead of you, Birch Drang. In the first, you continue as you have. Imbibe Ephemera in the way you have, maintain your life in the way you have, but where does it end?"

Birch grimaced. Yes, he knew exactly where that ended. An unchanging existence of dullness, not a true life, and one fated to come to its conclusion in less than a year with the Day of Atonement—Murder Day. "Go on. The second option?"

"Betray Cam Folde and Pan Shun and be killed."

"Is that why you're here?" Birch sneered, seeing now why this being had invaded his mindscape. He must have a special bond with the two young Ephemeral Masters. "Will you kill me then? Because those two certainly can't."

Rail shook his head. "I won't kill you, and while betraying Cam and Pan may allow you to escape the prison, do you honestly think Coruscant or the Four won't easily hunt you down?"

"I can survive Petala," Birch blustered. It had been his plan all along. Rumors spoke of a different world there, whispers of giant monsters terrifying enough to give even Coruscant pause.

"You would die. Petala is deadly and its guardians, fierce. They would destroy you in the blink of an eye, should you be discovered. And with the amount of Nullity you'll need to escape the prison, you'll stand out like a beacon. Staying in Petala is the same as death."

In the face of Rail's utter certainty, Birch couldn't simply disregard the warning. He shifted in nervousness. Was the strange old man right about those living under the Blood Sea?

"You can't stay in Petala," Rail continued. "You'd have to cross Lake Petala, journey through the Badlands in order to reach the Locus. You've been there before, but that was when Coruscant held your hand. We both know your chances in managing any of that on your own."

"None." The word slipped out in a whisper, and Birch's shoulders slumped. Nothing that Rail had told him was new information, but hearing it spoken aloud by someone else brought it into a focus that, until now, he'd largely avoided.

"As I said, you have three options in front of you," Rail continued. "In two paths, the outcome is certain. Only in the third option is the future unwritten."

"And what is that?"

"Accept Ephemera into your Source and replace your Nullity."

"To what end?" Birch asked, confounded. "By giving away my Nullity, I'll become a Neophyte." He sneered. "I think not."

"You've fought against accepting Ephemera all your life, but what has that gained you? Are you happy?" Rail peered at him like he was truly concerned over the answer. "The happiest you've ever been was in this glade when you first felt Ephemera in all its majesty. You've been chasing that sensation ever since."

Birch blinked, shocked at the man's insight. But that still didn't change the calculus of the situation. Rail Gristle was a danger, regardless of how kind he appeared.

"Replacing Nullity with Ephemera won't be swift, nor will it be easy," Rail continued. "And you'll have to learn fresh answers to the questions allowing for Advancement, but it's also the only path where hope exists because Ephemera itself is a byword for both hope and faith."

Birch didn't reply at once, caught as he was on those words: hope and faith. In his life, he'd caused so much pain, reveled in the torment of others, and never counted it is as anything of consequence. Hundreds had died or been put to the rack by his hand or because of his actions. What hope or faith was there for someone like him?

Rail glanced to the sky, which appeared to be darkening with swirling thunderheads, and his lips curled down.

So did Birch's. He had never imagined this glade in anything other than brilliant sunshine. So why were there thunderclouds now? They shouldn't be here.

Rail distracted Birch from his observations, speaking once again. "Our time ends, but listen to what I've said. You need not make the decision now, but listen to Cam and Pan. Apologize to them. Their ways are not your own, but their ways can lead you to a better path. Ask them about moksha. Meditate on what they say, and the answers to Advance through Ephemera will become apparent."

With that, Rail winced as if in pain before disappearing in shattering motes of light. However, his presence had a lingering heaviness, leaving Birch to ponder everything that had been said between them. He realized it hadn't been much, just a couple dozen words, and yet, the conversation had an import that demanded reflection.

Birch stared at the sky, lost in thought. What should he do?

The next morning, right after their first meal, Birch reached out to Cam and Pan. *"I have reflected on yesterday's events and see the problem. You think my training methods are too harsh."*

Cam listened without comment. He remained angry with the rakshasa, but emotions no longer clouded his judgment, and he was willing to hear Birch's explanation about his actions last night.

Birch continued. *"I'm sorry for my actions, but that is how I was taught. Here in Mote, we are trained in the crucible of pain."*

"The crucible of pain?" Cam cut in, not bothering to hide his derision even as he appreciated Birch's apology. He'd have never expected it of the rakshasa—any of them, for that matter. *"It sounds like an excuse for torture."*

"I'm not surprised to hear you say that. You are Ephemeral Masters, and Ephemeral Masters are weak compared to those of similar stature from Mote. We are so much stronger than your kind. Heed my teachings, and I can make you similarly lethal."

Pan joined the conversation. *"How do you know? Have you ever fought an Ephemeral Master?"*

"I fought you two," Birch said. *"Besides which, the truth is self-evident. Here, only the greatest and best manage to Advance and create Nullity. We are self-selected as warriors without peer."*

Cam scoffed at Birch's conceit. *"Your way of learning isn't about selecting the finest warriors. It's about finding the most fortunate rakshasas. Whoever survives the kind of instruction you believe best isn't actually the best. They're just the luckiest."*

"Untrue," Birch declared. *"There is luck involved in every endeavor. But in general, those with finer skills will shine through. Given that, I can say with confidence that Nulls are stronger than Ephemeral Masters."*

Pan got in a sly dig. *"You mean like how Coruscant is as powerful as Rukh and Jessira?"*

Birch didn't reply at once, but when he did, it was a muttered complaint. *"If the two of you could fight as well as you debate, we'd be free of our cells within a day."*

Cam had heard enough from the rakshasa. *"What do you want? We made our feelings about your training and you clear."*

Birch took his time in replying, and when he did, it was with a matter utterly unrelated to what they'd been discussing. *"Were you ever taught about the three Gunas?"*

Cam frowned, nodding his head and knowing the movement came across in his telepathy. What did the three Gunas have to do with anything? Birch had been going on and on about the superiority of Nullity and his way of training but now he wanted to discuss philosophy?

Even as Cam considered what to say, Pan spoke. *"We know about the Gunas. Why?"*

"I read about them once in a forbidden text. Over the decades, I've pondered their meaning. Since the two of you are Ephemeral Masters, perhaps you can instruct me?"

"That doesn't tell me why you asked about the Gunas," Pan said.

Birch replied in a wistful tone. *"I thought I'd be attracted to Tamas, to darkness and ignorance, but my heart led me to Rajas."*

Cam's eyebrows lifted in startlement. *"To passion and activity?"*

Birch nodded across their connection. *"In considering the matter, I believe that is how I conceive of Nullity."*

Once again, Cam discovered himself confused by the rakshasa. *"Didn't you agree that without Ephemera there can't be life or procreation? You even said it's why you're still alive five decades after getting tossed down here. Without Ephemera, you'd be dead by now, right?"*

"Your point?"

Cam would have thought it was obvious, but the rakshasa apparently needed him to spell it out. *"If your heart fixes on Rajas' passion and Ephemera is about life, then…"* He trailed off, waiting for Birch to figure the rest out on his own.

The rakshasa didn't, and after a short lull, he prodded Cam. *"And then what?"*

Cam sighed. *"Devesh help you. How can you be so smart and stupid at the same time?"*

Birch replied with an acid comment of his own. *"And how can followers of Devesh so regularly mock those without their knowledge?"*

Cam gaped. This rakshasa, who had carved his forearms to bloody ruin, busted his jaw, and knocked Pan unconscious, had just rightfully called him out for his behavior. It was discomfiting.

"*Well?*" Birch prodded.

"*Passion can't exist without life,*" Cam snapped. "*Nothing good can. Your heart wasn't leading you to Rajas because it reminded you of Nullity. Your heart led you to Rajas because it told you what you needed: Ephemera. Why else do you think you learned to Imbibe it?*"

Birch fell silent, appearing lost in contemplation, and Cam let him be. Eventually, the rakshasa replied. "*I've never viewed the Gunas in such a light. It gives me much to ponder.*" There came a hesitation next. "*We can form a different imaginary space, if you like. It's been a long time since I played chess with someone.*"

Cam had a flash of insight, something that was obvious in hindsight. "*You're lonely.*"

"*Very lonely. And I am sorry about yesterday.*"

The longing in the rakshasa's voice stirred Cam's sympathy. What must it have been like for Birch during all these decades where he'd been trapped and had no one with whom to speak? "*Give me an hour to meditate, and I'll play you.*" Cam patted for *The Warrior and the Servant*, which he read every morning. It should be right here. He frowned, patting all over his clothes. His fingers found the torn pocket. Rage nearly stole his ability to think. "*Someone stole my book!*"

A beat later from Pan, "*Mine, too.*"

Birch was laughing. "*It's the lovebirds. They're harmless, but those two are gluttons for books. They ate mine about the Gunas. It's how they learn.*"

The lovebirds had eaten his book? That's how they learned? It was utterly nonsensical, but Cam didn't have much time to think about the situation. The moment he agreed to play chess against Birch, the rakshasa became insistent they do so at once.

Cam agreed, but this time, the mindscape would be something he and Pan directed, and they created a space similar to the room where Professor Grey had taught them Synapsia. Birch glanced around the space, giving it an approving sniff before insisting on countless matches of chess and other strategic games. Hours passed, and Cam grew worried. Tulip was sure to show up soon with their second meal of the day.

Birch smirked at his fears, and Cam understood why when he re-emerged into his cell. Very little time had actually passed—less than half an hour perhaps—and the reason proved simple: in the mindscape, experiential time occurred differently. It could move either more swiftly or slowly.

In Birch's case, he'd spent most of his five decades of imprisonment in a state of slumber, coming awake for only the brief periods of the day when food was brought to him but otherwise experiencing only a fraction of the unspooling years. It was why he hadn't gone insane in his solitude.

In contrast, while playing chess, the many hours in the mindscape had translated to less than a single one in Mote. However, all the mental gymnastics still saw Cam exhausted, and he planned on sleeping a bit before Tulip arrived with supper.

Birch, though, had other ideas. *"Are you awake?"* Cam didn't reply, hoping the rakshasa would get the hint and leave him be. However, like a mosquito, Birch kept on buzzing. *"I know you can hear me."*

Cam sighed. *"Go bother Pan."*

"He already did," Pan grumbled.

Cam prayed for patience before opening his eyes. *"What do you want?"*

"The book I mentioned, the one that told me about the Gunas—

"What about it?"

"It also discussed moksha, but it never explained what it meant. Do you know?"

Cam grimaced. That's what the rakshasa wanted to know? He sat up, hoping this could be a short conversation but paused in his reply upon replaying the strange intensity in Birch's voice when he'd asked the question. *"This couldn't have waited until after I got some rest? It's that important?"*

"I'm not tired."

"I am," Cam growled.

Birch might have shrugged. *"With instruction, you'll get used to the mindscape. You'll learn to use it better. That's where I learned to Imbibe Ephemera, and the more time you spend there, the less it will fatigue you. We can squeeze in years of learning in only a few months. Time moves strangely in dreams, and that's what the mindscape is like."*

Cam perked. *"Will what we learn in the mindscape translate to when we're awake? Will our bodies know those things?"* If so, it would be a powerful means for them to greatly accelerate the mastery of their abilities.

"Yes and no," Birch replied. *"Yes, you can train in the mindscape, and for those skills strictly of the mind—the matters of Spirairia and Synapsia—what you master will be mastered. But for the fighting arts, you may know what to do, but your bodies will still have to be taught."*

Birch's explanation made sense, and despite his fatigue, curiosity had Cam asking another question. *"You say we need instruction on using the mindscape. We don't have anything like that in Salvation."*

The rakshasa offered a mental shrug. *"In Coruscant's legions, we're taught to look inward to improve ourselves, to search for weaknesses and either expunge Ephemera or transform it into Nullity. Following my imprisonment, I still did exactly that. Over and over again, but one day I wondered why. One day, instead of trying to transform the Ephemera I'd Imbibed in Salvation, I let it link to my Nullity, imagining the glade where my life had ended. That was the beginning of the mindscape: something external linked to self. I doubt anyone else has managed its creation. And yes, it is a powerful tool, and yes, I can teach you to use it. Whether you can create it for yourselves, though, is another matter."*

"Why is this so important to you?" Pan asked Birch. *"Training us, playing chess, learning our philosophy, the Gunas."*

Birch might have shrugged. *"Call it curiosity. I enjoy learning, and I want to learn if your kind of teaching is actually effective."*

Cam remained hesitant, and Birch seemed to recognize it. *"What else is there to do? We can only play so much chess. Why not train and learn from one another? And you can start by teaching me about moksha."*

Again was that intensity, and Cam frowned, wondering at the cause. He needed to know what drove Birch, and talking to him would hopefully give him greater insight into the rakshasa's true purpose. In the meantime, if Birch wanted to talk about philosophical and theological concepts, Pan could teach him. Pan liked giving those kinds of lectures and even had a professorial way about him when doing so. It was cute.

Sure enough, Pan soon began a portentous dissertation that had Cam grinning, although he tried to hide his humor.

"Moksha in its classic sense," Pan said, *"is our emancipation from samsara, the cycle of life and rebirth. But in modern terminology, we think of it as spiritual freedom from existence itself, or least the kind that is dedicated solely to the self."* He paused then, and if Pan had glasses, Cam didn't doubt the panda would have been peering over them at Birch, wanting to make sure the rakshasa understood what had thus far been spoken.

"Go on," Birch said.

Pan gave off the sense of nodding in agreement. *"Right. Given your Nullity, you are obviously dedicated to the self, which collides with a fundamental truth: the best way to achieve moksha is by expecting an outcome rather than fearing one. When dedicated solely to self, you will forever fear the future."*

It was the same advice that Rukh and Jessira had tried, time and time again, to impart to Light Squad.

Pan continued. *"But living with moksha as your guiding light allows for spiritual freedom, for passion to focus on the moment, and the acceptance in what will be. It is only when we fear the results that karma catches us."*

The squeal of metal drew Cam out of the conversation, and he glanced to the grate in his cell door, which had been cracked open. It was too early for supper, and he wondered who was out there.

An instant later, Sprite and Kiwi stood on the cell's threshold.

Kiwi, the green-feathered bird, fluttered his wings, squawking once. "Can we talk?"

"Promise not to eat us first," Sprite chirped.

Cam viewed the birds in confusion. "We can talk, and I promise not to eat you."

The birds flitted into the room, coming to rest in the rafters.

"We ate your books," Kiwi said, sounding defiant rather than regretful.

The simmering anger that Cam had come to chronically feel here in Mote tried to bubble to life, but he repressed it. "I know."

Kiwi flapped his wings in surprise. "You do?"

Cam nodded. "Of course."

"Can we learn from you and Pan?" Sprite asked.

"Why?"

"We want to become better than we are," Kiwi said. "We miss our home."

The entire time they'd been talking, Cam had viewed the birds through the woven world and empathed their emotions, and everything he felt told him that Kiwi and Sprite were trustworthy and sweet in their naivety.

Cam's fury lessened, removed itself, and he smiled at the lovebirds, charmed the same as when he'd first met them. "Why not? But first, why did you really eat my book?"

"Cam, who are you talking to?" Pan asked.

"You won't believe it," Cam replied.

20

"*The two lovebirds want to learn with us*," Cam said to Pan after he got Sprite and Kiwi to tell him their reasoning.

"*What?*"

Birch huffed. "*If you insist on speaking to other rakshasas, I'll leave you to it. We'll talk in the morning.*" He severed their connection.

The green lovebird chirped. "We ate your books because that's how we learn. And now we have many questions."

"*What are they saying?*" Pan asked.

"*I'll tell you later,*" Cam said to him. "You learn by eating books?" It's what Birch had told him early on after the theft of their books had been discovered, but at the time, Cam hadn't believed the rakshasa. It had sounded too far-fetched.

Kiwi tweeted. "It's much easier than reading."

Cam eyed the lovebirds, annoyed afresh and still struggling to believe that they'd actually *eaten* his copy of *The Warrior and the Servant*.

"Is the book true?" Sprite asked. "We remember Devesh—"

Cam cut him off. "What do you mean, you remember Devesh? How?"

"Because of where we're from," Sprite said. "We weren't born here."

"An evil man sent us here as a present," Kiwi added, chirping his anger. "He thought it would be funny since we know his heart is coal."

Cam had an idea what the birds were talking about. Sprite had made a vague mention about this when he'd first met him and Kiwi, but he needed more information this time. "Maybe you should start at the beginning. Where are you from and how did you get here?" He watched them through the woven world, seeking truth in their words.

Sprite, the seemingly brighter of the two birds, was the one who answered. "We were born in a better Realm, a world called Salvation."

Truth.

Kiwi trilled a mournful note. "It was beautiful."

Cam's annoyance died away, replaced by sympathy for the poor birds. "What happened?"

Both lovebirds drooped, neither responding until Sprite finally spoke. "Our father's wicked son gave us to a rakshasa Sage."

The truthful response had Cam confused. "Wouldn't this wicked son be your brother?"

Kiwi shook his head. "Our father isn't the one who sired us but the one who raised us. He's a human and has a human son." He chirped, indicating Sprite. "We aren't brothers of egg and blood, either. We are brothers of choice, and the wicked son stole us and gave us away as a present, the means by which he was able to obtain special training."

"The Sage then gave us to one of the Four," Kiwi said. "He sent us here, to see how long it would take for us to die."

"And here we've been for months. It has felt eternal."

Cam took in the information, viewing the lovebirds with empathy. If they were telling the truth—and he believed they were—they'd endured the same loss and betrayal as he and Pan. "I'm sorry."

Kiwi cocked his head. "Why are you sorry?"

Cam told him.

"We are alike," Kiwi agreed. "Which is why we wanted to know about the book we ate. Does Devesh really exist? We thought he did, but we've been here so long—or it feels so long—that we can't remember."

"Devesh does exist," Cam said. "The book isn't lying."

Kiwi chirruped. "You're a human rakshasa from Mote. How would you know about Devesh?"

Cam's instincts told him that he could trust these two, but speaking further to the lovebirds wasn't a decision he could make on his own. He quickly relayed what he'd learned to Pan. *What do you think? Should I tell them?*

Pan sent a pulse of conviction. *"I'll follow wherever you lead."*

Cam sent a nod of acknowledgment. In that case… he unclouded his Source, allowing his Adept Awareness to shine through.

The display had Sprite and Kiwi squawking in excitement, trilling in joy. They flitted about the room, visible in the light filtering through the grate and unable to remain still. Cam watched their antics with a smile, glad to have brought them some small measure of happiness.

The lovebirds landed on his shoulders, one on each side.

"You have Ephemera," Kiwi stated. "Just like us. I wasn't sure."

"You and Pan are Ephemeral Masters?" Sprite asked.

"We are," Cam confirmed.

Kiwi viewed him with a head tilt and a challenging gleam in his eyes. "What color is the ocean?"

Cam created an aqua-blue light on his fingertip. "Sometimes it's this color." The light became a storm gray. "Other times, it's this." The color changed to cerulean. "This is my favorite."

"He knows," Kiwi chirped, sounding astonished. "We're not alone."

Cam stroked the green lovebird's soft feathers, and some of his undercurrent of anger eased away. "No, you're not. None of us are."

Afterward, the lovebirds had a thousand questions, all of them related to *The Warrior and the Servant.*

Cam did his best to answer them, and on one occasion, he mentioned the truism of the sun always rising in the east and setting in the west.

To this, Sprite tweeted disagreement. "That's not true. There was a time when Salvation's sun never rose nor set. It just stood still in the sky."

Cam frowned. He'd never heard this story before, and he questioned Pan.

"They're right. There is a story about that. There was a time when Salvation's sun hung unmoving. It supposedly blazed like the unholy hells until a boy and his dragon set it into motion. And then Rukh and Jessira brought the world to full life."

Cam grunted in surprise. Who would have guessed that he'd learn a new story about Salvation here in Mote? Afterward, Cam farmed the questions out to Pan, who had better answers anyway.

Somewhere along the conversation, Kiwi offered a sorrow-filled tweet, saying, "I'm sorry you're imprisoned here with us."

"So am I," Cam replied. "Did I ever tell you I learned to Imbibe Ephemera?"

Kiwi stilled. "This isn't a trick?"

"It's not a trick." Cam told them how to view the woven world and Imbibe Ephemera.

Kiwi fluttered his wings, squawking a bit. "Can you teach us?"

"I'd be happy to," Cam said. "But it's getting late. Come back tomorrow night and practice with us then."

Kiwi sang high-toned notes, stating, "We'll come every night. We'll Advance."

Birch interrupted their conversation. *"Are you still talking to those idiot lovebirds?"*

"I thought you were going to sleep," Cam said to him.

"I was, but you and Pan keep babbling. It's impossible to rest in the midst of your prattling."

"Then stop listening in," Pan suggested.

Birch grunted.

"We spoke to him once, the rakshasa," Sprite said. "His words are cruel, but they also contain wisdom."

Cam viewed the yellow lovebird in question. "You can hear him?

Birch?"

Sprite tweeted affirmation.

"And you think he's wise?" Birch was many things, but that wasn't something Cam would call him.

Sprite cocked his head one way and then the other, almost like he was shrugging. "He's not wise, but he said something wise. He told us to doubt what we think we know; that doubt can be the greatest blessing."

Silence fell over the room as Cam considered Sprite's statements, feeling them resonate with his own beliefs about the nature of certainty and doubt.

A momentary epiphany flicked across his mind, and Cam held himself motionless, urging the understanding to make itself clear. The difference between certainty and doubt was a key question on the Way into Divinity, the means of Advancing from Glory to Crown, and if he could feel the answer…

The epiphany faded, and Cam sighed in disappointment. "On that note, I think we should get some rest."

The lovebirds trilled their agreement, promising to come back tomorrow before flying out of the cell and shutting the grate.

"*They're finally gone?*" Birch asked.

Cam rolled his eyes. "*Yes, they're finally gone. But to tell you the truth, if it came to spending time with you or them, I'd choose them every time.*"

"*That's a rather hurtful thing to say,*" Birch commented.

"*The truth can hurt.*"

Birch laughed. "*And here I was thinking you and Pan didn't have a cruel bone in your bodies.*"

"*Prepare to be surprised,*" Pan said. "*And Cam wasn't wrong about wanting to get some rest.*"

As usual, Birch didn't listen. "*Do you ever wonder why there aren't any lights in our cells?*"

Cam shrugged. "*To keep us miserable? Probably the same reason it's cold in here, why we don't have any blankets for our cots, or that we're expected to use a hole in the ground as a toilet.*"

"All that is correct," Birch said, *"but it's also a mistake on the part of our jailers. You see, the dark can also allow for quiet reflection. I spent most of my decades here asleep, but on the few occasions when I was awake, I reflected. And what I discovered was that the darkness is what came before. Everything begins in darkness and everything will end in darkness."*

Being stolen away and imprisoned in this horrifying place, a person might come to see Birch's viewpoint as being accurate, but Cam didn't think he was right, although he didn't have the right words to say why.

But Pan did. *"The darkness wasn't the beginning. Something didn't come from nothing. The Singing Light was the author of All. At least that's what I believe."*

Birch scoffed. *"Your belief is that of someone unable to face the harsh reality of existence. We are destined for emptiness."*

Cam had read about such an idea before, but he hadn't accepted it then, and he refused to accept it now. To distill reality to such a meaningless void felt like a betrayal of everything that he wanted for himself and others.

Pan spoke for both of them once again when he addressed Birch. *"If you believe that, then what's the point of anything? If everything begins and ends in absence, then why struggle? According to you, existence is a lie. Your life is a lie. What you're doing now is a lie. Give up now and let it go."*

"I've often thought of doing exactly that," Birch said.

"What's stopping you?" Cam asked.

Birch sighed. *"Ephemera. Every time I manage to Imbibe it, I feel just a little bit better and less desolate."*

"Then perhaps you should take that as a lesson," Pan suggested.

"Perhaps I shall. If nothing else, I'll reflect upon it."

"Then maybe you can reflect on it after Cam and I go to sleep," Pan suggested.

Birch chuckled. *"That sounds quite reasonable, my dear panda-person."*

Cam stiffened in alarm. They'd never told Birch about Pan's

nickname. *"How do you know about that?"*

"I am a Crown," Birch said, sounding both pleased and sly. *"We are linked. I know many things. And because we are linked, I will demonstrate how I know about the darkness."*

Before Cam could reply, he found himself clamped in a crushing grip. It was identical to what he'd experienced in the Web of Worlds as fiery agony burned through him, and when it let off, Cam fell off the cot, onto his knees, gasping. He desperately sought the comfort of his Source and the woven world. A harsh breath, and his heart slowed, having been hammering against his ribs. A final breath, and his emotions came back under control, the panic ebbing, replaced by fury and questions. Why had Birch done that?

"That is the meaning of Nullity," the rakshasa said, his voice grave. *"It is awful, but you needed to feel its force if you and Pan wish to survive Petala. And in the face of its emptiness, are you so sure it isn't the end and beginning of us all?"*

Pan shouted, but Cam didn't have a mind to listen. The fear faded, but the fury remained, ebbing when he noticed that the strands of the woven world sang more loudly than before, smelled fresher, and some of them had reached out to him, touching his Source, same as before, but he had a greater awareness of it. Curiosity replaced the anger. Threads of Ephemera that he hadn't noticed before were now apparent, and he watched, not pushing or pulling—only accepting—until the connection deepened. Then he Imbibed, a far greater quantity of Ephemera than before.

His rage simmered and fell away, unneeded right now. Cam exhaled in relief, grateful at its absence. He was tired of seeing red, even as he recognized that it also kept him alive in Mote. As he calmed further, the terror in Pan's voice penetrated his mind. Cam told him what had happened, cutting him off before he could rail further at Birch. *"It helped me gain Ephemera."*

Upon hearing his declaration, even the rakshasa sounded surprised. *"I lost Nullity demonstrating my truth to you. And you say that you gained Ephemera because of it?"*

Cam sent a nod of affirmation.

"Does this mean I was helpful?" Birch asked, a chipper tone to his voice.

"Unintentionally, but yes," Cam growled, anger rising once more at what Birch had done now that the shock was over. *"Hurting us isn't allowed. Stop doing it."*

"I know, but…" Birch sighed. *"If we escape this place—"*

"When we escape this place," Cam corrected.

"Fine. When we escape this place, you'll have to battle those with Nullity. That might be an attack they use against you. If you aren't pre-pared for it, we'll fail and die." Birch hesitated. *"Please don't shut me out again. I don't want to be alone."*

Cam grunted, not willing to make any such concession. *"We're done for now. Don't contact us. We'll contact you."*

He ended the link between himself and the rakshasa, his mind still roiling.

Pan cleared his throat. *"Did you really gain more Ephemera?"*

Cam sent a nod. *"I don't know how or why, but yes."*

A momentary silence fell over their conversation. *"I know it's wrong,"* Pan said, ending the quiet, *"but I'm glad you're here. I couldn't do this by myself."*

Cam gained courage from Pan's admission, which merely reflected his own emotions. *"I couldn't either, so we'll just have to do it together."*

Pan kept his eyes closed but was nevertheless able to view the wo-ven world through the lens of his Source. Seeing it had him shaking his head in awe. No matter how often he visualized it, the complexi-ty of Devesh's creation captured his breath. Every fragment of reality was united, down to the smallest mote of dust. Nothing existed with-out purpose, proving Cam's favorite aphorism: All is Ephemera, and Ephemera is All, and All was beautiful.

Of course, Pan knew that there was far more to reality than what was evident to his Adept-Staged limitations.

Cam, however, didn't seem to share as much of that restriction. Ever since yesterday and his exposure to Birch's Nullity, he claimed to be able to envision the woven world more readily and Imbibe Ephemera more easily. It had Pan wishing for the same—not because of jealousy but because of fear of failing his friend. Cam had stated that the increased pace might allow him to gather enough Ephemera to Advance to Glory sometime within the next fifteen years—assuming he survived Murder Day. Pan, on the other hand, had decades more ahead of him to reach the same Stage of Awareness.

It was unacceptable for both of them. Even if this Murder Day that Birch had mentioned and Tulip had confirmed wasn't set to pass within the next year, Pan couldn't ask Cam to wait on him for that long. While they didn't suffer physical torment in the prison, that didn't mean they weren't tortured. It was the agony of isolation, the loneliness of never seeing, hearing, touching or holding loved ones. Only a few weeks, and it had already left Pan feeling soul-deadened and empty inside, especially with the absence of Ephemera. It was a state of existence where he could imagine himself eventually not caring enough to eat or drink and committing a slow-motion suicide.

Pan believed it was all part of the rakshasas' plans. They didn't truly care whether their prisoners lived or died. The evil beings just wanted them to suffer in the worst way possible. Birch had told them that, and in this one matter, Pan actually believed the lion-headed rakshasa.

It was why he was currently contemplating reaching out to Birch. If the rakshasa placed the same torment on him that he'd used on Cam—the experience of Nullity—then perhaps he'd be able to gain Ephemera just as quickly as his friend. They could find a way to Advance swiftly enough to escape the prison before Murder Day.

But a willingness to trust the rakshasa in such a fashion had Pan frowning in distaste. He should ask Cam for his opinion before making such an important decision.

Even while he considered the matter, Pan kept his inner eye focused on the woven world where thin lines of Ephemera coalesced gradually, glacially with his Source. But he couldn't hurry the pace. Acceptance alone was the key. Trying to actively draw in more Ephemera would invariably draw in none.

Pan remained patient, and enough time passed for him to sense that the evening meal would soon arrive.

It was then that Birch delivered a sending. *"I truly am sorry for what I did to Cam. If you would give me a chance, I can explain my reasonings."*

Pan opened his eyes and pondered what he should do. It would be easiest to ignore the rakshasa but that also felt wrong. Didn't Birch deserve an opportunity to state his case? In addition—and yes, it was self-serving—hadn't he been thinking about reaching out to the rakshasa anyway? Nodding to himself, Pan spoke. *"You already explained yourself."*

"There's more to tell."

Pan wasn't sure he believed that, but he also felt it was only right to grant the rakshasa grace. *"Go on."*

Birch seemed to exhale in relief. *"The training I gave you was how I was instructed. I told you that, and I still think it's the best way to forge a diamond from coal. But I also know that you and Cam find it... repulsive, which is why I promised to be gentler in my teaching. Learn from me, and I promise, you'll become thrice the warriors you are now."*

Pan doubted it. He and Cam had been trained by Rukh and Jessira, the finest warriors of any Realm. What could Birch teach them that those two hadn't? Just as Pan was about to decline Birch's offer, he recalled the manner in which the rakshasa had fought: using his claws in an unexpected fashion, attacking when Pan hadn't been prepared. Pan cocked his head in consideration. Maybe there was something Birch could teach them. *"Why is this so important to you?"*

"Because when you escape the prison, in order to reach the Locus, you'll have to travel beneath the Blood Sea. As I told Cam, Petala is dangerous, and unless you're prepared, you will die."

That wasn't what Pan had been asking. *"Why do you care?"*

"Self-interest. If I teach you, then you can show me how to Imbibe

Ephemera more efficiently, and we'll escape together."

"And once we free you, why would you need us? You say you want to go to Salvation. Why can't you escape there on your own?" Of course, a larger question was whether Pan was willing to allow someone like Birch into their Realm. The rakshasa was a Null Crown, a walking disaster.

"I can handle Petala, but in the Badlands—the area around the Locus—Shimala will sense my Nullity. I need you and Cam to mask my presence."

Pan still didn't like it: Birch on Salvation.

The rakshasa seemed to sense his antipathy. *"Before you say no, allow me to make you a promise. Upon my Nullity, I will not harm you or yours. Ask your friend Tulip what that means."*

Pan would do exactly that, but he'd also ask Kiwi and Sprite. Tulip was friendly enough, but she was still a rakshasa of Mote, and while he hated painting people with a broad brush, he couldn't help but wonder if her kindness was a mask for other intentions. Cam was certain that was the case, saying he'd felt it whenever he spoke to Tulip while visualizing the woven world and using his skills of empathy. Pan hadn't noticed, but then again, Cam's abilities with the woven world were better than his.

"Let me talk to Cam first," Pan said.

"Fair enough. I await your word."

Birch cut the connection, and Pan formed one with Cam, quickly summarizing his thoughts about Ephemera and the recent conversation with the rakshasa. *"What do you think we should do?"*

"You're right about asking Kiwi and Sprite about this vow Birch made."

"Those two." Pan smiled. *"They're cute."* An instant later, his smile fell away. *"And Tulip? Should we include her?"*

Cam hesitated. *"Yes, but be careful with her. She has her own schemes."*

Pan nodded acknowledgment. *"Birch made a promise to me."* He told of the vow. *"Saying us and ours like he did… it might be enough to protect all of Salvation from him if we view ourselves as servants of our Realm."*

Cam nodded. "*It could include Hearth, too. I'm sure Birch would argue the point, but whether we agree to this or not, I'd want clarification on the wording.*"

"*And if we get it?*"

"*Then we let him do to you what he did to me and learn whatever we can from him.*" Cam shrugged. "*The rest is up to him.*"

"*That sounds about right.*" Now it was Pan's turn to hesitate. "*I wish we didn't have to think about people that way: as being untrustworthy.*"

"*So do I. But the Sage-Dukes and Weld taught us hard lessons. We shouldn't forget them.*"

Pan nodded, wishing that it wasn't anger alone that seemed to fuel his friend's desire for justice. That kind of emotion would eventually tear him apart.

21

It took some doing, but eventually Cam and Pan got Birch's promise worded to their satisfaction. It included a vow for him to never lie to either of them, to never bring harm to anyone from Salvation, and to also refuse the future orders of any rakshasas. Surprisingly, Birch had also agreed to burn out his Nullity and never seek to recreate it. He was apparently willing to start at the bottom of the Way into Divinity, as a Neophyte, and seek to become an Ephemeral Master.

Cam wasn't surprised by Birch's willingness to make so many compromises. Murder Day would fall on him just as hard as it would on every other prisoner. Knowing that, it wasn't hard getting the rakshasa to agree to whatever he and Pan wanted. And they had confirmation of the vow's integrity from Kiwi, Sprite, *and* Tulip, all of whom stated that an oath made on Nullity was considered unbreakable in Mote.

It didn't mean Cam trusted Birch, but it was a start. It was also why the same day they made the accord, Pan accepted an exposure to Nullity. It had been a terrible experience—far worse than from when they'd experienced it under Rukh, which Cam very well knew—and the poor panda-person had come out of it shaken and unable to speak.

Hours had passed before he could, and when he finally recovered his voice, he had steadfastly refused to talk about what he'd endured.

Cam hadn't pressed the matter either. He was just glad that the Nullity had given Pan a chance to Imbibe Ephemera more effectively. For now, that was enough, but moving forward, Cam had an idea for an even faster way, one using Plasminia. It was based on the teachings given to him in Hearth by Rukh and Jessira, but he'd yet to properly master that particular instruction.

Nevertheless, Cam had noticed that if he increased Plasminia's lightning-laced circulation, more tendrils of Ephemera attached to his Source. It was a hard piece of concentration, but anything to get them out of this hellish hole was worth trying. The next step, which was equally difficult, called for Cam to figure on how to keep all that extra Ephemera in place long enough to Imbibe it.

So far, he hadn't had much luck, which made the entire matter more than a mite frustrating and also why Cam and Pan had both accepted a few more times held under the grip of Birch's Nullity. Desperation fueled their choice, but it didn't help. The second, third, and even fourth experience of Nullity did nothing to improve their ability to Imbibe Ephemera any faster than the first time.

But working in the mindscape did. The way they experienced time's swifter passage there… it was enough for Cam and Pan to Imbibe even more effectively. Add in what they could do with Plasminia, and Cam figured they just might make it out of the prison before Murder Day. Having a path that would see them get free made all the difference in their days and nights. There was a reason to hope, a reason to strive.

And blessedly, it had nothing to do with the anger that seemed to simmer under Cam's every waking thought. The anger spurred on by every cruelty Cam had experienced: run out of Traverse by the so-called fine folks there, Rainen's callous use of Light Squad and nearly getting them killed, Hearth and all its dangers and murders Cam had been forced to commit in order to survive, Weld Plain and his stunning lack of punishment for what he'd clearly done, and the betrayal of the Sage-Dukes. That same rage kept Cam focused and driven, but it rose to a boil whenever he considered all those harsh and ugly matters too long. Which is why he did his best *not* to focus on them, trying harder to attach his mind to the hope granted him by Imbibing Ephemera, of freedom from this prison, and returning home. He knew the anger was divisive and would eventually ruin him, recognizing Rukh's and Jessira's wisdom of maintaining his faith and praying at need.

In that regard, what helped just as much as anything were the hours that Cam and Pan spent in the mindscape with Birch and learning his way of fighting. The lion-headed rakshasa's instruction wasn't as brutal as it had been that first time, but it was still plenty rough. Violence helped bleed Cam's anger, and although he and Pan endured plenty of batterings, broken bones, and pain under Birch's care, at least he knew the business of fighting.

There was also the other training—a gentler kind and one given over to strategy and tactics—that they underwent. But in this regard, rather than the arena, it took place in the space that reminded Cam of Professor Grey's classroom at the Ephemeral Academy.

It was only too bad they couldn't enter the mindscape without Birch. What he'd told them before about how he'd learned to create it with a combination of Nullity and Ephemera had proven true.

A creaking of the steel grate and a flapping of wings interrupted Cam's musings. Seconds later, Kiwi and Sprite alighted on his shoulders. The birds always arrived a few minutes after Tulip left for the evening, and in the weeks since they'd first flown into his life, Cam found himself ever more grateful for their presence. They were a bright light in his otherwise dismal world.

"What are you doing?" Kiwi asked.

"Just thinking about where I've been and where I'm going."

"You're leaving? But how?" Kiwi tweeted in alarm, flapping his wings, which Cam recognized was a sign of the lovebird's agitation.

"We're not going anywhere," Cam said, using his most soothing tone. "But you know we can't stay here forever."

Kiwi sighed. "I know, but I don't like thinking of when you and Pan leave us."

Cam frowned, not knowing what Kiwi was talking about. "You're coming, too, aren't you?"

Kiwi cheeped once, sounding disheartened.

"It's not that we don't want to," Sprite said, landing on Cam's other shoulder. "But we can't go to Petala. We've gone to the entrance that leads there, and…" He shuddered. "It hurts."

Cam frowned, not liking the notion of anything hurting the birds. His lurking anger wanted to boil to life, but he repressed it. "How does it hurt?"

"Like a snake eating us and being set on fire," Kiwi answered, a rather vivid description.

Sprite expanded on Kiwi's words. "The area near the tunnel is a cave, and it's harsh. It feels like Nullity."

"You've felt Nullity?"

Sprite chirped. "One of the Four, the person to whom we were gifted, made us experience it."

"And the area around the entrance to Petala feels like that?"

"The birds may be too weak to endure the tunnel," Birch cut into their conversation. *"Only Acolytes or higher can survive, and even better if you're at least an Adept."*

"Then how will you survive?" Cam asked Birch. *"You think you'll be at the Stage by then?"* Cam doubted it. The rakshasa had a further distance to travel than even the lovebirds.

Birch held silent for a moment. *"I said I'd rid myself of Nullity, but I'll keep enough to remain a Glory. I'll lose the rest on the Locus. Have no fear. I'll keep my word."*

Cam considered the rakshasa's explanation, eventually shrugging his acceptance. Perseverating over the situation wouldn't do him any good. He'd simply have to trust Birch. Besides, there was more information he needed to learn. *"The Blood Sea is a polluted place, and the pollution presses down on the tunnel leading to Petala, right?"*

"Correct," Birch said, *"If the birds can't endure the cave outside Petala's entrance, then they're highly unlike to survive the actual tunnel. It isn't the absence of Ephemera that is so harmful. It's the overwhelming*

pollution and sense of emptiness, which is worse than Nullity in its own way.”

"*The Son of Emptiness,*" Cam mused, recalling the anchor line in Hearth. "*I wonder if Nullity has something to do with him.*"

"*You know of Zahhack?*" Birch sounded surprised.

Cam nodded in distraction. "*We ran across him in Hearth, or at least that’s what Rukh and Jessira said.*"

Sprite hopped about, squawking and flapping his wings in excitement. "*You know Rukh and Jessira? What are they like? Are they actually birds?*"

Cam laughed. "*No, they aren’t birds, but they’re wonderful anyway.*"

"*They would make fine birds,*" Kiwi said with a firm cheep.

"*Rukh and Jessira are myths,*" Birch said, sounding dismissive. "*Or maybe not myths but something into which those of the higher Realms have poured their hopes and dreams so they don’t have to face reality’s great truth.*"

"*What truth?*" Cam asked.

"*The darkness is what came before everything.*"

Cam smiled. "*You’ve said that before, but how sure are you about it? What if your Lord Coruscant—*"

"*He’s not my lord,*" Birch corrected. "*I wouldn’t be imprisoned here if he was.*"

Cam waved aside the statement. "*What if Coruscant wants you to believe that about Rukh and Jessira? So you don’t see a better truth?*"

"*And what better truth is that?*"

Sprite was the one who answered, intelligent little bird that he was. "*That they are heroes, and we should all strive to be like them in some way.*"

A week later, Cam sat cross-legged on his cot, trying to get comfortable. He had meant to meditate and gain some greater understanding of how to Advance. In this case, it wasn’t figuring what was needed to reach Glory—he felt certain on that response—but on what it would mean to reach Crown: reckoning the difference between certainty and doubt. The answer seemed just past his grasp, so close and yet so far away.

He shifted on his cot, grimacing at its lumpy and hard-as-a-brick form. The truth was, the cot was worn down to the very fabric from which it had been made. The mattress was all but gone, and what remained was thin, hard, and coming apart at the seams. It was about the same for Cam's clothing and boots, even his body.

A month into his captivity, and he was falling apart. Day by day, he could sense his strength fading, his muscles wasting. And it wasn't his imagination either. According to Birch, what he was noticing was the passive nature of the Blood Sea in action. Its corrupting influence led to the dissolution of anything made from Ephemera.

Which only emphasized the need to get free of this place as quickly as possible. Murder Day was coming, less than a year according to Tulip, but Cam wanted to be gone well before then, with as much of his strength still intact as possible.

Setting his mind on what was needed, Cam concentrated inward and Delved his Source with his mind's eye. The bulbous potato shape that it had once held when he'd been a Novice had slowly transformed to a smaller, more condensed globe, although small protrusions still marred the surface. Focusing deeper, Plasminia became evident, laced in yellow lightning, which was a reflection of his Adept Awareness, and then there was the dense gas of Spirairia, the molten gold of Synapsia, and the airy firmness of Kinesthia.

For a moment longer, he considered what he wanted to do before resettling his attention on Plasminia. Unlike Enhancing, for what he currently required, he didn't need to slow the Tang. He needed it to spin faster. It was a simple trick of imagination, and once it started, Ephemera from without would be drawn to it like iron to a lodestone.

But in prior attempts, as soon as Cam tried to Imbibe what had Accreted, Plasminia would slow and the Ephemera would dissipate. He'd yet to make a successful go at it, but every day brought him a step closer. Maybe today he'd finally succeed.

Fixing his mind on that notion, Cam sped his Plasminia, watching the yellow lightning race faster and faster. Seconds later, strands of Ephemera crept closer, swirling in a slow-motion whirlpool. However, Cam kept his concentration on his Plasminia, speeding it even faster.

A notion came to him, something he'd not tried before, and he formed a True Bond. The burning anger he regularly felt ebbed away like it always did whenever he allowed himself to feel the gentle and creative-laden truth of Ephemera. In his distraction, though, Plasminia dipped its pace for a moment, less than a second, but it was still enough time for the Accreting Ephemera to waft away. Cam didn't let the loss dishearten him. He resumed Plasminia's rapid pace, rushing it in ever faster cycles until it became a yellow blur.

The entire time, he kept his True Bond, and his thoughts remained smooth and focused. Cam continued to spin Plasminia, preparing for the point when he'd failed all those other times. For many seconds, he maintained the process, doing nothing more than watch as Ephemera Accreted. There had been something in Rukh's and Jessira's instructions that might help him here, but prior to making the attempt, Cam shook out his muscles, relaxing as best he could. Only then did he reach out to the Accreting Ephemera, while at the same time he kept Plasminia spinning in a blur. His mind didn't separate, but there was a shift in his consciousness. Carefully, in a stuttering start, Cam performed two tasks at the same time: he Imbibed Ephemera and simultaneously caused Plasminia to continue racing.

Seconds later, his concentration shattered, and with a nearly screeching halt, his Plasminia slowed and the Accreted Ephemera dissipated. Cam's head throbbed from the whiplash, but he still smiled. Based on his rough calculations, in this one session, he'd likely taken in as much Ephemera as he might have otherwise gained in several days. It wasn't enough for him and Pan to Advance before Murder Day, but with the mindscape, there was every chance—

"You seem pleased."

Cam snapped open his eyes, gazing to the brightness from the open grate. Tulip had returned. Was it already time for breakfast? Had he spent the entire night meditating on Plasminia and Ephemera? And what had Tulip seen?

"What were you doing?" she asked.

Her question had sounded like nothing but sincere curiosity, but Cam didn't trust Tulip's motives. Whenever he viewed her in the woven world, there was that consistent pulse of deception in whatever she said to him. It was why Cam waved away her questions without really answering them, refusing to give her anything beyond the most banal of information.

Today was no different, and he opened his mouth, intending to do the same as always, but he halted before speaking. What if today he actually gave Tulip some measure of the truth? Would that change her fate?

Probably not, but why not try? He'd be careful and not give away too much.

"Have you ever wondered why Nullity is so hard to create while we're told Ephemera is everywhere?"

"That's only if we believe that Ephemera actually is everywhere."

Cam nodded. "I'm told it is. I heard it from an Adept."

"From when you served in Lord Coruscant's manor?"

Cam hesitated, not wanting to commit to a greater lie. "I never served in his manor, but an Adept told me the area near the Locus that Lord Coruscant controls is the best place for rakshasas to procreate. He said it was where Ephemera entered Mote."

"I see."

Cam shrugged, rising to his feet and approaching the door where Tulip held the tray with his supper. "It isn't like I have anything else to do, so I was hoping that meditating would help me see Ephemera. Maybe if I can… I don't know, touch it, whoever comes to kill us on Murder Day will spare me. They'd certainly spare you, wouldn't they? If you learned to Imbibe Ephemera like those from Salvation?"

"You shouldn't believe in such fanciful nonsense," Tulip said with an angry glitter to her eyes. "Salvation isn't real."

She passed him his food and tumbler of water and without further ado, slammed shut the grate.

Cam frowned after she left, not sure how to assess her response. The anger was understandable. She likely believed he was mocking her or trying to give her false hope in order to betray her later on or a combination of the two. It was the way of Mote.

Whatever the case, the conversation hadn't been a complete loss. He'd learned something from the conversation. Tulip hoped for a better truth than the one she'd always known, but for now, fear kept her trapped. Sadly, that was also the way of Mote.

After Tulip collected his breakfast tray and tumbler, Cam reached out to Pan and Birch, wanting to share what he'd learned. *"I figured out something important. It's something we'd be best off discussing in the mindscape."*

"Ooh. Something mysteriously important," Birch said with a chuckle. *"Will it delay our deaths?"*

Cam rolled his eyes at Birch's humorous fatalism. *"Just form the mindscape. The classroom."*

An instant later, Cam found himself standing in Professor Grey's classroom. The sun beamed brightness into the space, and an array of clouds like frayed cotton balls hung in a blue sky the color of Lake Nexus. Birds sang, and a cool wind promised autumn's relief from summer's heat. It was a beautiful illusion.

"What happened?" Pan asked, sitting on the ground and chomping on a stalk of bamboo.

"Yes," Birch asked. "What happened?" He reclined at the front of the room, on a chair built like a throne while delicately picking through a tray of meats and cheeses. Until Cam had imagined a charcuterie board, the leonine rakshasa had never heard of such a thing. A single taste of the cured meats and cheeses, though, and nowadays, whenever they were in the mindscape, he always had one in hand. In this, he was a lot like Pan, always munching on something.

Cam grinned at the unintended similarity, although the rakshasa probably wouldn't see the humor. He cleared his throat, gathering their attention. "I learned to Imbibe Ephemera using Plasminia," he said, explaining what he'd discovered.

Pan heard him out, asked for clarification, and two shakes of a cat's tail later, he was gone from the mindscape, yelling about how he wanted to try it out himself.

"The panda-person seems excited," Birch said.

"Wouldn't you be? All we have to do is master this skill, and we'll have our key to freedom. With the mindscape, we'll be gone from here well before Murder Day."

"Very true," Birch said, flicking through the charcuterie board before very deliberately choosing a single slice of cheese. He popped it in his mouth. "But it just means we'll die in Petala that much sooner."

Cam wanted to roll his eyes again. "We'll survive Petala, but there's more I need to know and master if we're to make our escape a reality."

"More skills from your famous patrons?"

Cam didn't answer at once, lost in thought. For the longest time, he had fought against the notion that Rukh and Jessira held him in any kind of special regard. Having that kind of belief had been a burden, the pressure of too many expectations. What if he failed to overcome his challenges? Especially given the advantages the Holy Servants had gifted him? What would that say about who he was as a person and Ephemeral Master? That he was weak and worthless, a confirmation of the most significant lie from the early years of his life?

"Patrons or however you want to call them, but yes," Cam eventually said.

Birch lifted his brows in surprise. "In all the time we've spent in the mindscape, you've always been careful about *not* claiming any special relationship with those two."

Cam shrugged. "Let's just say I've gotten used to the idea."

Birch offered a canine-filled smile. "I'm glad to hear you've finally accepted your fate."

"What fate are you talking about?" Cam asked.

"That you are Rukh's and Jessira's emissary on Salvation."

Cam grunted. Accepting that he was special to Rukh and Jessira was bad enough, but believing himself their emissary was even worse. He deflected. "I thought you said Rukh and Jessira were myths?"

"So I did, but even an old rakshasa can learn."

Cam regarded Birch, unsure if he was being serious. Had his heart truly turned? In their year thus far in the mindscape—and it had been that long subjectively—they had all learned tremendously from one another. Martial mastery from Birch in Cam's and Pan's cases, but what about the rakshasa? Had he learned Salvation's better philosophy?

Initially, it had been hard to accept that the rakshasa could learn anything of empathy, kindness, or patience. But over their time together, Cam had found himself laughing around Birch, listening to his counsel, and warming up to him. Trust, though? That was the hardest part of friendship, and he wasn't there yet with Birch. But he wanted to be.

The old rakshasa laughed, apparently recognizing the flavor of Cam's thoughts. "You are wise to hold on to your doubt. This is our mindscape, but we exist in Mote. Faithlessness is the byword for all who wield power in the Realm."

Cam nodded acceptance of Birch's advice. "I have to master my other skills. I'll be able to use them more effectively at Glory, but there's no reason not to get in some practice now." He paused a beat. "I need your help."

Birch grinned, sharp canines flashing and predatory. "And in what way can I help you?"

"I need you to test my will. Try to break into my mind. Make me see illusions." He lifted a cautioning hand. "But give me a chance to defend. It's meaningless if you simply overcome whatever wards I create."

"You need more than just a simple wall," Birch reminded him. "You need a Domain."

Cam grunted acknowledgment. Only Crowns and the rare Glory could properly create a Domain, an extension of their will where an

Ephemeral Master held utter sway and no mind-related attacks could penetrate. For Sages, it was said to be impenetrable. And while Cam wasn't a Crown—he wasn't even a Glory—what was stopping him from creating a Domain now? He couldn't see why not. He had the knowledge. All he lacked was the skill, but that could come about through regular practice.

He nodded. "Let's try it. Slow and easy, though. Give me a chance to work on creating a Domain."

"A Domain is a reflection of your will, but it does more than simply defend. It smooths away fear and any unnecessary emotions, thereby allowing your thoughts to run more quickly."

Cam smiled. He already knew this, but it was helpful to have the information stated back to him. Inhaling deep, he Delved his Source and created a True Bond. Next, he recalled the means by which a Domain was created. Normally, it would have been a complex weaving of Tangs, but with his True Bond, it was more about directing the output. Difficult but far easier than the alternative.

Nodding inwardly, Cam felt sure he could manage what was required. A heavy exhalation, and he focused his True Bond, imagining Ephemera pressing out of his skin, surrounding him, linking to the world without. His eyes narrowed as he sighted the woven world, the webs of connections. The entire time he recited a simple mantra: *control leads to focus. Focus allows balance. Balance allows for control.* Rukh's and Jessira's advice.

Several attempts later, he sensed when his Domain lit to life, an invisible extension of his will that gave the impression of denial.

Birch noticed it as well. "Impressive. Most impressive." He paced about Cam, seemingly assessing the Domain. An instant later, he attacked.

A pressure built against Cam's Domain, seeking entrance. He gritted his teeth, refusing to bend before Birch's attack, which came harder, a needling pain. Cam stiffened, the ever-present anger fueling his drive, and his Domain strengthened. He pushed back against the rakshasa's rising pressure, holding him off. A momentary reprieve, and

Cam breathed out, glared at Birch, furious, staring him in the eyes and refusing to lose. No chance he'd break.

A minute later, Birch relented, and for the first time since Cam had met the rakshasa, true admiration brightened his features. "I gave you everything of my own will, and you threw it back at me. Well done."

Cam accepted the praise, but in his judgment there was still so much more to accomplish. Forming a Domain on its own wasn't enough. "I can't just stand in place, though. I have to be able to form a Domain and use my other skills."

Birch nodded. "A static opponent is a dead one. But this was an excellent first step."

"Go again?"

Birch smiled, offering a mouthful of fangs. "So we shall."

The attack came hard and fast. Cam pushed his arms forward, defending, straining, but not backing down or quitting.

They kept at it until Cam finally cracked and couldn't keep going. He gasped, angry with himself as he collapsed after Birch's last attack. "I'm done."

"You did well," Birch said. "Now get some rest."

Cam wanted to, but there was still a final task to complete. He Delved his Source and created a True Bond, using it to help spin Plasminia ever swifter. And just like he had done in his cell, he viewed the woven world, which was evident, if waner, in this fabricated space. Still, the mindscape allowed for the work of years to be accomplished in months.

Not wasting a second, Cam forced his rotating Plasminia to spin faster, and slowly but steadily, thin lines of Ephemera touched his Source, drawn inward, Accreting. As before, Cam continued to watch as the Ephemera collected, accepting, not trying for more than what was coming to him, maintaining a relaxed posture. Once he felt prepared, though, he sought again to hold two thoughts at the same time. He swirled Plasminia while also Imbibing Ephemera.

However, like before, he only managed it for a few seconds before his concentration shattered. The Accreted Ephemera dissipated, his Plasminia crashed to a slower spin, and the whiplash caused his head to ache. Nevertheless, Cam grinned through the pain. He'd done it. He'd added Ephemera to his Source within the mindscape, which meant he and Pan could definitely Advance to Glory and escape this place.

"You learned something?" Birch asked, breaking into his joy.

Cam nodded, explaining what he'd done.

The rakshasa smiled. "Maybe we won't die in here after all. Maybe we truly will reach Petala." He gave a barking laugh. "Of course, that's when we're sure to die. The kaijus are ferocious."

22

Weeks after creating a Domain for the first time, Cam continued to master the skills granted to him by Rukh's and Jessira's instructions. He currently sat on his cot, eyes closed but seeking awareness of everything around him. The coolness of the corner that was farthest from the door, the drifting motes of dirt, the echoing sounds plinking through the prison's stone, and the taste of decay that lingered everywhere. And yet it wasn't his senses that brought him the information—not his eyes, ears, nose, tongue, or even his fingertips.

It was a mixed use of his True Bond and visualizing the woven world and deciphering the connections unifying reality. Or at least that was Cam's goal since the awareness he sought wasn't so easy to hold. This was Oversight, and with the skill, not only would Cam be more readily aware of what wasn't in range of his senses, but he'd also have greater understanding of anyone around him. He could sense Pan's Source from several cells away. Same with Birch's Nullity, but not when either of them were Blended. That might come once he Advanced to Sage, where nothing was hidden from Oversight.

Practicing through control, focus, and balance—as usual, that was the key—and thus far, the progress had been incremental but steady, still faster than Cam could have ever expected. All on account of the mindscape, and its time altering benefits.

Cam cocked his head and frowned. From down the hallway, a disturbance in the woven world impacted Oversight, a moving object nearing his cell. He focused upon what approached, gaining awareness of the strange shape: a tall, wide form melding with something square, and an instant later, he understood. *Tulip*. She was bringing supper. Shortly thereafter, the squeaking of the cart confirmed his discovery.

Smiling at his success, Cam rose to his feet, approaching the grate at around the same time that Tulip opened it.

She startled when she found him waiting for her, clutching her chest and blinking rapidly. "Oh, my. You scared me. I didn't expect you to be standing so close."

Cam smiled. "I didn't mean to scare you. I heard you coming, and I was hungry."

Tulip chuckled, passing him a bowl of tasteless mush and a mug of water. "Here you go then."

"Thank you," Cam said, ready to back into his cell, but Tulip remained in place, hand on a hip and staring his way. He faced her, head tilted in question. "What is it?"

She bit her lip, appearing to vacillate. "I was thinking about our conversation from a few weeks ago, when you told me about Ephemera being everywhere."

Cam recalled the conversation, and a slither of concern trailed down his spine. He wanted to trust Tulip, but she needed to prove she was worthy of it first. How she could manage that remained an uncertainty.

"Have you learned to see Ephemera?" Tulip asked. "Can you teach me?"

"What makes you believe I've learned?" Cam asked. "Or that I can teach you? It's only been a few weeks." He feigned a laugh. "I doubt the Ephemeral Masters of Salvation could even manage it so quickly."

She smiled. "I have a feeling you're smarter than any of those so-called Ephemeral Masters."

Cam didn't let her praise touch him, couched with deceit as it was. "What makes you say that? You said Salvation wasn't real. You were pretty firm on that matter."

"Maybe Salvation isn't, but Ephemera is real—I believe that much—and ever since you talked about seeing it, I've been wondering if that could also be possible for someone like me."

Cam frowned. There had been truth in Tulip's words that time. That and a wistful hope. "Someone like you? What do you mean?"

"A rakshasa from Mote. Can someone unworthy like me actually see Ephemera? Touch it?" She shook her head. "I don't see how. Ephemera is supposed to be from Devesh, and He never loved us. Why would He allow us to see His creation?"

She was wrong about Devesh, but now wasn't the time for a philosophical discussion. "You may be right about all that," Cam said. "But that still doesn't explain why you think I can see Ephemera after only practicing at it for a few weeks."

"But if you learned, could you teach me?" Tulip seemed to hold her breath, her eyes wide and beaming as she waited for his reply.

Cam refused to accept her reactions, though. This was Mote, and as she'd just said, Tulip was a rakshasa of this Realm. Deceit and betrayal were fixtures here. He had to be cautious. But he also couldn't deny her out of hand. After all, there had been her hope. Plus, Pharis had granted him grace by reaching a helping hand and forcing him out of his darkness and misery. How could he refuse to do the same for someone else in need? He leaned into empathy, feeling for Tulip's true wants. "Supposing I do learn to see Ephemera, if you wanted to learn, you'd have to do the same as me."

"And what's that?"

Cam indicated his rotting cot. "I mostly just sit there and pray to Devesh."

"Pray to Devesh." Tulip repeated the words like they were nonsensical.

Cam smiled. "Yes. I practice heresy since Lord Coruscant doesn't think any rakshasa should worship anyone or anything except their own will to power." He snorted derision. "Of course, he says that while also setting himself as our own personal deity. Hypocrite." He caught Tulip's expression of shock and laughed at it. "Yes. None of us are supposed to say such things, but what are they going to do? Put me in prison? Kill me on Murder Day?" He shrugged. "Lord Coruscant wrote my fate when he sent me here, and nothing I say, do, or think can make it too much worse."

Tulip viewed him a moment, like she was piecing together a puzzle. "I suppose that's true."

She departed then, and after she left, Cam considered their conversation. The entire time, he had been sensing Tulip through empathy, and she had emoted nothing but curiosity and hope, which had him praying on her behalf. He wanted to trust Tulip, but she had to prove herself worthy of it. He wasn't sure if she could.

A week after his strange interaction with Tulip saw Cam within the mindscape, seated upon the floor in the room that resembled Professor Grey's classroom back at the Ephemeral Academy. Each foot rested on the knee opposite, and across from him was Pan, his legs splayed and a bamboo stalk in hand. The morning sun was still rising, shining, and with the windows open, a cool breeze flitted inside. The scent of gardenias intermingled with that of cut grass.

The two of them stared at one another, each having managed to form a Domain, and now they tested them to see which one was stronger. They flung mental assaults at one another, utilizing Spirairia through their True Bonds to infiltrate the mind of the other. So far, it was an impasse. While Pan had greater skill in the use of Spirairia, Cam's will wouldn't relent. And he was also confident that in the end, he'd wear his friend down and win. It was how it always had gone so far, and he didn't see why this time would be any different.

Meanwhile, watching from a corner was Birch, one leg carelessly flung over one of the arms of his throne-like chair while he nibbled from a charcuterie tray. "How goes your instruction of Tulip?" the rakshasa asked.

"Slow," Cam replied. "Now be quiet. I'm concentrating." However, the reminder of the matronly-appearing rakshasa had Cam wishing that he could fully trust her. She acted like she wanted to learn—emoted that she did—but her intentions through the woven world still had strands of deceit crowding her thoughts like streaks of pus. Tulip had plans that didn't merely include learning to visualize Ephemera. There was more to her than that, and it likely had to do with betraying Cam in some manner. What that might be he didn't quite yet know.

Cam jolted, his attention returning to the contest when Pan thumped his Domain with a spear of thought. It nearly broke through, and while it wouldn't have done any harm—his friend's so-called attacks focused on imparting a desire to eat bamboo—it would have still been embarrassing and infuriating to lose this early since they'd only been at it a few minutes.

Pan quirked one of his cute grins. "I almost had you."

"Almost don't count for much," Cam growled.

"This is so boring," Birch announced. "Why can't we add some element of danger to the training?" His eyes widened, and he clapped his hands as if in abrupt and wondrous insight. "I know. How about if you let me throw Fireballs at you?"

"No," Cam and Pan voiced as one.

Birch sulked. "But this is boring. Can't we at least play chess while you attack one another's Domains? Or maybe throw spears at one another? They're sharp and pointy and lots of fun."

Cam had a better idea. "Why don't you join us? You can act as the third leg in our training. Whenever two go against one, they'll never know when the other one might betray them."

Birch chuckled, low and deadly. "Careful with thinking about betrayal. I might believe you're interested in creating a seed of Nullity."

Cam rolled his eyes at Birch's intentional misreading of his statement. "That's not what I meant, and you know it."

"It sounded like that's what you meant," Birch countered. "An impartial observer would agree with me."

"Cam's right," Pan said, interrupting their incipient disagreement.

"He's not an impartial observer," Birch sulked.

Pan talked over him. "It'll make all of us more nimble at defense and attack."

Birch huffed. "Fine. Let me just finish my food, and—"

Cam cast an irritated glance at the charcuterie board and imagined it gone from the mindscape.

Birch squawked like one of the lovebirds. "I wasn't done eating."

"You'll live," Cam replied, feeling no repentance over what he'd done.

Pan cocked his head at Birch, appearing simultaneously puzzled and mildly amused. "This is the mindscape. Do you really think that was prosciutto you were eating?"

Birch rose to his feet with a chuckle, flicking his hand and causing the chair to disappear. "Well played, my young panda-person. Using my own mockery against me." He cracked his knuckles and seated himself. "Now. Which of you wishes to taste the lash of my will?"

Bold talk, but Cam wasn't impressed. He tossed a challenging grin at the leonine rakshasa. "Prove you have what it takes."

Birch replied with a predatory grin of his own. "So I shall, young one."

An hour later, no one had yet managed to claim victory. Every time Birch attacked Pan, the weakest of their trio, Cam would turn on the rakshasa. Sure, he could have joined in and taken his favorite panda-person out of the game, but what kind of a friend would he be if he did that? And if Birch centered his attack on Cam, Pan would come to his defense. And neither of them had the skills to penetrate Birch's Domain. It left them stalemated, which was fine as far as Cam was concerned.

Training with Domains had done more good for him than he could have ever expected. Not only did it give him a defense against mental attacks—which were sure to occur when he went against Crowns—it also helped him fully set aside his self-imposed fears and doubts. He *knew* himself, his worth, which was far greater than that of a no-good Folde. That long-lingering lie of his uselessness had finally been burned to ash and swept clear from his mind. All because of the crucible of the training with Birch and Pan in the use of Domains and mental attacks.

Not only that, but the traumas that he'd witnessed and endured in Hearth had also been laid to rest. He no longer had to practice the techniques taught to him by Saira. All that remained was his rage, which he needed to both survive the prison and continue his progress. Reflecting on it, he inwardly shook his head. How strange it was that some of his greatest strides had taken place in these places of turmoil—Hearth and Mote. One, a world of seemingly endless danger and the other a Realm so deadly it was labeled Hell.

It had him pondering whether he could truly say everything in Mote was terrible. His living conditions, the dark isolation of the cell, and the food and water certainly were. But there had also been victories worth remembering. Cam had maintained himself here, held on to his sanity, gained the answer to Advance to Glory and nearly had what was needed for Crown, and formed an unlikely friendship with a rakshasa. Nearly as important, during his time in Mote, he'd also fully committed to mastering the gifts provided to him by Rukh and Jessira. He'd even learned to truly and faithfully believe himself worthy of their generosity and love.

And they loved him. He knew it, accepted it, and although the reason for it escaped his understanding, maybe one day when he asked, they'd tell him.

"It's time you learned more about Petala," Birch declared, apparently tired of their impasse and feeling like a lecture was in order. "It is under the Blood Sea, but that doesn't truly explain what we'll find there. We'll be walking on the undersurface of the Mote's crust. Gravity's perspective will shift, and when we look up at the sky of the Hollow Land, we'll actually be staring toward the world's core. There's a sun that never sets. It merely brightens and dims. There are titanic beasts and even plants that battle one another, and the deadliest are the kaijus, the most powerful of whom is Pelluraj, a monstrous, horned beast. He spews a fire that can destroy a city, and even the Great Rakshasas respect him. Getting past all these challenges will be difficult, and that doesn't even account for the Badlands."

"How did you get to Salvation the first time?" Pan asked. "If it's so hard reaching the Locus?"

"Ah, that. Coruscant controls a third of this world, and a good portion of his territory abuts the Locus. All of the Great Rakshasas have similar areas of control. I didn't have to deal with kaijus or Shimala and her thralls. In Coruscant's lands near the Locus, the lord forged an anchor line to send me to Salvation. He rarely does so, and after my own adventure in your world, I understand why."

Cam nodded. It was new information, and later on, he'd ask for more details. But for now, he refused to be deterred. "All this means is that we have to train as hard as we can. We can't slow down."

Birch shook his head. "You're wrong. You've been training harder than any rakshasas I ever knew, and if you don't slow down and rest your minds more regularly, you risk ruining yourselves."

Cam knew Birch spoke wisdom, but an obstinate, angry part of him didn't want to admit it. He shut off that reckless voice before it could speak. "We'll rest," he said, agreeing with Birch, "but what about our bodies? Outside the mindscape, we're weak. The prison's poison and lack of food—"

"—made us frail," Birch finished. "Yes, but I believe I mentioned that the creatures of Petala, the Hollow Land, can grow titanic. Rumor has it that their meat can cure nearly any infirmity. We only need to feed there, and we'll recover quickly."

"How sure are you about this rumor?" Pan asked.

Birch shrugged. "How sure can anyone be about a rumor? But it's also our only hope."

Cam continued to fret. In his time in Mote, his arms and legs had slowly emaciated. It hadn't even been two months, and he'd already withered and wasted away. But if Birch's rumor about the creatures of Petala proved true, then their physical weakness had a solution. And even with the lack of enough food, maybe they should be trying to get in some exercise? Anything to build up their stamina.

They couldn't Advance but have their bodies too weak to actually reach Petala. They had to regain some measure of stamina. There really wasn't any other option. Which meant that Cam's plan was clear. He'd continue learning all he could of Ephemera, controlling it as precisely as possible—focus, control, and balance—but he'd also work on his stamina. They all would. Strengthen their weaknesses rather than working on their strengths.

And then they'd break free of this place and restore themselves to freedom. He could almost taste it. The anger within seemed to rumble agreement.

A few days after learning about Petala and kaijus, Cam found himself facing off against Birch, ready to spar the rakshasa while distantly noticing that Pan, who had taken a break, was panting like a fish out of water. The three of them were training in their shared mental landscape of the small arena floored in sand, a place they'd taken to calling the Pit. Indistinct lighting left shadows in the corners, and the smell of cloves permeated the air, arising from somewhere and distracting Cam. Was the aroma real, or was it Birch's creation, something meant to throw him off?

Anything was possible since anything imaginable was possible in the Pit with the only limitation being their own conceptions. That was the nature of the mindscape, and they could do just about whatever they wanted to here. That included flying and fighting above the arena floor, sparring hard for hours with no need to face physical fatigue or even the need to breathe. But during the early months of their teachings with Birch—as they experienced time in the mindscape rather than the real world—Cam and Pan sometimes forgot that simple truth.

Still, they'd come far, and Cam viewed his instructor, the lion-headed rakshasa, in appreciation. Birch had also Advanced. He remained the same tough, occasionally fiery—but more often flighty—rakshasa they'd first met, and while he was still prone to fits of anger at any kind of failure, at least his heart was in the right place. What Cam most appreciated, though, was Birch's competitive drive, especially when it came to their martial training.

That unwillingness to accept defeat, to even allow the possibility of it, had rubbed off on Cam. These days, he wanted to win like never before and overcome regardless of the cost. He'd pay any price to return home to Salvation since being away was the same as giving free rein to all the traitors back home. The anger within stoked Cam to giving his all. He had to escape the prison and bring the evildoers to justice.

With those thoughts in mind, Cam stared and studied Birch from a distance of twenty feet, unarmed since, by now, he was the weapon. He didn't need a sword, spear, or bow. Close in or at a distance, his control of Ephemera would decide whether or not he achieved victory.

But that was easier said than done. Birch was brutal in his attacks, overwhelming in his use of force. Early on, he'd also been wasteful. Cam had noticed. A finer use of his Nullity—he was slowly losing that hideous source of power—could have allowed him to become even deadlier. Rukh and Jessira would have advised it. They would have told Birch that every movement and application of power should serve a purpose, both in the immediate sense and also in the three steps that followed.

As a result, while Birch had initially been unimpressed by Cam's early showings, over the time spent in the mindscape, that disdain had softened and changed. Sneers of superiority had transformed into expressions of surprise, especially on the day when Cam had thoroughly defeated his attacks. Surprise had become curiosity when those defeats became a regular event. Compensation came as Birch began utilizing the speed and power of a Glory, but even there, Cam would occasionally win.

And Pan—learning from Cam—had achieved victories of his own with both of them improving in leaps and bounds.

But eventually, so had Birch. He was a masterful warrior, and after months of observing his opponents in the mindscape, he'd deconstructed his losses and reforged his method of fighting into something truly lethal.

"Are you going to just stand there?" the rakshasa asked, breaking into Cam's musings.

Cam ended his deliberations by focusing on Birch's posture, his positioning, and the likely angle of his attack. It was a budding awareness of how the spar would play out before it even happened, largely lifted from Rukh, and a skill that could take Cam a far distance as a warrior. Oversight helped in a similar way, and gave Cam insight into what was coming his way.

An instant later, he was proven correct when Birch blasted forward, spurred on by his Nullity. Cam shifted aside. The rakshasa sped past, came around, sending a flight of arrows—invisible streaks of air. They shattered against Cam's shield. Gravity and boots of earth attempted to pin his feet as Birch attacked, hands glowing and a sword of compressed red fire alight in his hands.

Cam shattered the bindings, reversed gravity, and launched over Birch. As he passed over the rakshasa, he cast a mist of water over his opponent's sword. Steam billowed, fogging Birch's vision. Cam landed, thrust his hands, sending double hammer fists of air. It impacted the rakshasa's gut, doubling him over.

But Birch quickly recovered. He waved the fog away, sent a whip of fire and earth to entangle Cam's arms. Behind his attacks, he charged forward, seeming to fly, his sword aimed like a lance. A subtle admonishment to let his hands drop intruded on Cam's mind, the notion pressing against his Domain, trying to worm its way inside his thoughts.

Cam concentrated, and his sclerae flashed yellow. His Domain repulsed Birch's sending, and water and air lashed out to break apart the rakshasa's whip. Just in time, Cam raised a sword against Birch. However, his opponent was a master of the weapon, and Cam had to steadily give ground. He parried a thrust, blocked a slash, and evaded a follow-on vertical chop.

Retreating further, Cam bubbled the sand. A useless distraction that Birch expectedly ignored. The rakshasa strode forward, full of confidence and not paying attention to what was beneath his clawed feet. Cam smiled to himself. *Perfect.* He quickly forge-heated the sand, turning it into glass. Add in a film of water, and Birch slipped.

Now it was Cam who attacked, sword swirling in economical thrusts, slashes, and draw cuts. Birch raggedly defended, having no time to reset his balance. The rakshasa finally launched backward thirty feet, retreating to a shadowed recess of the arena where he recovered.

Seconds later, Cam was once again giving ground, and he scowled. He'd been so close. Rage had him momentarily seeing red, but he gritted his teeth and brought his anger to heel, using it to fuel his movements while his True Bond kept him focused on the fight.

Cam continued to defend, refusing to quit. Upon a slight break, Cam copied Birch by leaping backward twenty feet or more and letting go of the sword. He extended a hand, and fog billowed forth along with the deep-throated tolling of a bell. The mist and sound hid his landing. Another twenty-foot leap landed him near Pan, who appeared fit and ready.

Birch gave a sharp gesture, and the fog dissipated. "Running won't save you."

"Neither will standing my ground against a superior opponent." Cam shifted subtly.

"I'm ready," Pan sent, having risen to his feet and standing close at hand.

Cam didn't look at his friend or respond. Instead, he drifted to the side. Birch followed. Cam rolled under a slash. A jump carried him skyward. Birch followed, his leonine mane streaming behind him. They traded blows in the air and landed exactly where Cam had planned. The rakshasa's back was to Pan, who sent a single thrust of a fiery sword. It punched through Birch's chest, and he stiffened, hissing anger. The pain had to be excruciating. Cam smiled in grim satisfaction, knowing it from firsthand experience, having received the blow plenty of times in his sparring against the rakshasa.

However, Birch contained his scream of agony, merely groaning and slumping to his knees when Pan released his sword.

"Your enemy can find you at any time," Cam said, quoting one of Birch's teachings. Unsurprisingly, it was also one of Jessira's. She and Rukh had no compunction about doing whatever was necessary to win a fight or a battle, regardless of how ignoble it might seem.

"We did well," Pan said, grinning in that cute way of his, eliciting an answering response from Cam.

Birch grunted, regaining his feet, and rather than respond with anger, he smiled in pleasure. "You did well. I had discounted the panda after his defeat."

"That was only because you distracted me with bamboo," Pan said.

"It was only the vision of bamboo," Birch corrected.

Pan waved the words aside. "But it was bamboo. How am I supposed to fight when I see bamboo? It's my lodestar."

Cam threw a companionable arm over Pan's shoulders, victory granting him a sunny cheer. "You know it'll be years longer before you actually do? Eat bamboo, I mean. At least subjectively here in the mindscape."

Pan wilted. "I know. It's the worst part of being stuck in Mote."

Cam's brow lifted. "That's the worst part of being stuck in Mote? Not the imprisonment? Not the torture of being alone, of being locked away from our loved ones and Ephemera?"

Pan chuckled. "Well that part is also pretty bad."

"If you two are done, we have more training," Birch cut in, scowling some. Following a defeat, the rakshasa always made a point to defeat them in as brutal a fashion as he could manage.

Cam sighed and was on the point of agreeing, but an idea occurred to him, one inspired by Jessira's advice from the Web of Worlds. He shook his head. "No. We're done training. We won't be fighting you right now."

Birch narrowed his eyes. "Then what are we going to do?"

"It's like you told me the other week," Cam said. "We need to take time to rest every once in a while. Well, now is as good a time as any.

We should take a break and use the mindscape to create. The need to create is something Devesh put in all of us, and I'm thinking it's time we learned what that means for a rakshasa."

Birch appeared as distraught as Cam had ever seen. "I protest. I don't create."

Cam didn't relent. "You'll learn."

23

Cam had never tried his hand at any kind of drawing ever before, but in the days after he'd made mention to Birch and Pan of his intention that they practice on creation, he'd decided to give it a try.

Weeks of work in the mindscape had ensued, and right now, he was finishing up a piece, and he stepped back from his easel, viewing the oil painting with a critical eye and a disappointed frown. Even a man needing inch-thick spectacles could tell the results weren't good, about what a child holding a paintbrush for the first time might have managed. Cam sighed. Maybe he just didn't have it in him to get the lines and shapes to come out on canvas the way he had in his mind.

He sighed again before glancing around, immediately noticing that he wasn't the only one having trouble. Other than Pan's soft fluting—he'd always been good with the instrument—a heavy weight seemed to reign over the room that resembled Professor Grey's classroom. Outside, clouds shielded the sun and a chill wind moaned against the closed windows. In addition, heavy snow fell, and the thick flakes obscured the world without, which resembled the Ephemeral Academy.

The morose sight was unsurprising since the mindscape was merely a reflection of the emotional state of those who'd created it, and Birch was about as good at carving as Cam was at painting. The rakshasa currently stood before a heavy table, hacking away at a block of wood with an innumerable number of chisels, knives, and files flung about haphazardly on a nearby table. He even had a saw, but whatever he was fixing to carve was impossible to decipher. Maybe it was a bird?

"Creation is hard," Birch complained, throwing down a chisel in disgust.

"The bird isn't too bad," Cam said, trying to prop up the rakshasa's enthusiasm for art.

Birch glared at him. "It's supposed to be a tree."

Cam's expression went blank. "I see."

Pan gave up his fluting. "Maybe you should try something else."

"Maybe you should try something else," Birch mimicked in a sing-song fashion. "Easy for you to say, little panda-person. You're good at your art."

Cam smiled at Birch's irritation, which occurred about as regularly as a heartbeat. Besides which, Pan was right. They should figure out some other crafts, and he even had a notion of what to try next. He suggested it to Birch. "How about you let me work on carving while you give brush strokes a try?"

The rakshasa wore a pained expression. "But I'll get paint all over my fur."

Pan shrugged. "You could just imagine it gone. This is the mindscape."

The comment earned him another glare.

"What?" Pan asked. "You know I'm right."

"You know I'm right," Birch mimicked again with a huff. "Fine. But if my painting ends up looking as stupid as Cam's, I'm done with this so-called creation."

Cam didn't bother fighting the rakshasa on that point, although if it came to it, he would. The mindscape truly was too important to only use for training and fighting. They could accomplish so much more within it. But rather than argue about it now, he simply traded places with Birch.

A wave of his hand, and the block of curly maple transformed into mahogany. He'd heard once that it was easier to work with wood that had straight grains and not too many knots. Another wave, and the tools gathered themselves into a leather organizer. A final wave, and all the shavings vanished.

Cam stared at the block of wood, thinking on what he wanted to carve. What was hidden in the wood? What wanted to show itself? He tried peering inward, viewing it through the lens of the woven world and studying the connections and webs. His deliberations quickly had him lost in thought.

He wasn't sure how the woven world also existed here in the mindscape. It shouldn't be the case since this wasn't regular reality—just a figment of his shared imagination with Birch and Pan—and yet, the woven world and Ephemera *were* key aspects to the mindscape. The how remained a mystery, and whatever the reason, Cam was glad for it.

Gazing a little longer at the block of wood and the patterns of Ephemera—the sight, smell, taste, and feel of it—Cam got a glimpse of what might be hidden in the mahogany, and seeing it made him smile. It was something he'd read about once, and something no one had ever seen, but it was in his heart, and today, he'd bring it to life in this block of wood.

Cam set to work, beginning with a small carving knife and shaving a small groove upon the mahogany's surface. Another cut followed and so did many others. A meant-to-be smaller paring ended up carving a deeper groove than intended, and Cam paused, reassessing his plan. Eventually, a path forward became evident.

He set to work once again and Pan's fluting of a quiet melody helped him concentrate. He lulled into the work's flow, changing tools as needed but not always knowing which ones to use. Sometimes he was right, but most of the time, he was wrong. Still, the carving progressed, and the shape, crude and inelegant though it admittedly was, slowly took form.

It was her nose that became apparent first, then the rest of her features. He had less success with her mouth and chin, but it wasn't too bad. Next time would be better. Then came her mane of hair trailing down her neck, and wings that were only approximations of what he had in mind. Her legs and tail gave him no end of trouble.

But in the end, it was complete, and Cam stepped away from the table, excited at what he'd created even as he immediately saw where he could make improvements next time. And there would be a next time. The carving was crude, but this was his first attempt, and it wouldn't be his last. He had talent at this, which most certainly wasn't the case with painting. Painting had always been a mystery to him regardless of his best efforts and intentions.

Pan walked up to him. "What is it? A dragon?"

Cam smiled, pleased that Pan could easily tell what he'd carved. "Yes."

"What's its name?"

Cam didn't have an answer. While lost in the craft of carving, a name had never occurred to him.

By then, Birch had also wandered over, and he viewed the carving with a grunt of appreciation. "That's better than anything I ever managed." He chuckled in a morbid fashion. "If Coruscant ever saw this, he'd be livid. He hates dragons."

"Why does he hate dragons?" Pan asked.

Birch shrugged. "Probably because of Aia and Shon, the dragons belonging to Rukh and Jessira. Coruscant hates anything to do with those two."

Cam nodded. It made sense that Coruscant would hate anyone or anything allied to the Holy Servants. However, he hadn't been the only one trying a new form of art. He looked toward the easel. "You mind if we see your painting?"

Birch wore an expression of indifference, vaguely indicating for them to do so, like it didn't matter to him one way or the other. But Cam noticed the coil of proud satisfaction leaking through the rakshasa's uncaring façade. Birch was clearly happy with what he'd accomplished.

Cam hid a smile at Birch's obvious joy as he and Pan went to view the painting, a scene of a wildflower meadow in sunshine.

Pan inhaled sharply. "It's really good."

"You think so?" Birch asked, his voice unexpectedly shy and hesitant, so unlike his normal boastful or fatalistic self.

"It is," Cam confirmed. "Was this what you saw when you stepped into Salvation?"

Birch hesitated. "Not quite. Nothing is as lovely as that meadow. This is only a rough approximation."

"Well, it's a beautiful rough approximation," Cam replied.

Pan grinned. "Look at us. We've found our art."

"You already had your art all along," Birch grumbled, indicating Pan's flute.

"But now we've found ours as well," Cam said, "and it's worth doing."

"You might be right," Birch replied, his tone thoughtful.

"What do you think?" Birch asked, stepping back from his painting. In the past few months in the mindscape—only a few weeks in Mote—he'd worked hard at perfecting the scene from when he'd first stepped into Salvation, and during no part of that time had he ever demonstrated boredom with the process.

Studying the painting, even to Cam's untrained eye, there had been significant improvements from when Birch had first taken a brush to canvas. The scene was the same—a wildflower meadow—but whereas the imagery before had been static and somewhat dead, this latest iteration had life: movement based on the inclusion of a family of butterflies, a sense of wonder from the faint hints of sunshine, and flowers lifting their petals to the sky providing a feeling of joy.

"It's beautiful," Cam said.

Pan nodded, grinning in delight. "It would be perfect if you included a stand of bamboo."

Birch laughed. "When we go see the meadow in truth, I'll make sure to plant one. Of course, we'll be dead before then, but it's worth dreaming about." He pointed to Cam's carving. "How goes the dragon?"

"It's coming along," Cam said, leading the way to his table. He waited nervously while his friends viewed his carving. Just like Birch had been working to perfect his painting, Cam had been doing the same with the dragon. He didn't have a name for her—and the dragon was definitely a female.

Birch crouched low, examining the sculpture from all angles. "She's a bit toothy," he finally noted, indicating the fangs. "Her wings are somewhat stunted, and I thought dragons were supposed to be scaled. This one looks like it has fur."

"I like the notion of dragons as mammals, not lizards," Cam said, not appreciating Birch's criticism. He hadn't carped about the flaws in the rakshasa's painting, and he certainly could have. After all, the butterflies had been the size of sparrows, and the trees hadn't been nearly majestic enough.

Birch shrugged. "In that case, good job."

Cam flicked his eyes to Pan, hoping he'd have more encouraging words to offer. "You haven't said anything."

Pan perused the carving just as carefully as Birch had. "She is toothy," he eventually agreed. "And I think it's not just her wings that are stunted, but her tail, too. Do dragons have such stumpy tails?"

"It's a work in progress," Cam snapped, scowling and feeling defensive. He'd been proud of his progress, and for his friends to disparage his work had him flushing with irritation and embarrassment.

"I'm not saying it's bad," Pan said, laying a supporting hand on Cam's shoulder. "It's good, but there are areas of improvement you can make. That's all. You're almost there. Each time, you've gotten better. Just some final fine tunings, and you'll have her the way she deserves."

"It's certainly better than any of your paintings," Birch said. "All you have to do next time is shorten the teeth, fix her wings, and like our fine panda-person pointed out, lengthen her tail. Do that, and I'm sure we'll be singing your praises."

Cam tried not to let the criticism bother him any more than it already did, but it was difficult. He really had been pleased with his latest attempt. In a rush of anger, he waved the carving away, transforming the sculpture back to a block of mahogany. He glowered at the unshaped wood.

"Since Cam's throwing a tantrum," Birch announced, "I'll get back to my painting. You two didn't point it out, but the butterflies were too large and the trees too small."

Surprise replaced Cam's rumbling irritation. "You noticed that?" he asked the rakshasa.

Birch chuckled. "What kind of artist would I be if I didn't see the flaws in my work?"

Cam's surprise gave way to shock. When he'd first proposed that they spend some time learning to create, Birch had complained and complained about it, bitterly and at length. And yet here he was claiming now to be an artist of all things. Cam spoke an aside to Pan. "We're still in the mindscape, right? I'm not dreaming any of this, am I?"

"Dreaming what?"

Cam indicated the rakshasa. "This. Birch saying he's an artist and sounding serious about it."

Pan pursed his mouth in a studious expression. "I'm pretty sure we're in the mindscape, but you're right. That would be very much out of character for Birch. He always said he didn't have a single artistic bone in his body. Plus, not once has he mentioned how we're likely to die when we escape the prison."

"Very funny," Birch said, not appearing amused in the slightest. "We will die when we escape. But more importantly, mock my artistic soul if you will—"

"More importantly?" Cam asked.

"Yes, more importantly," Birch snapped. "Mock my artistic soul if you will, but know this." He stared Cam in the eyes. "I don't need coddling from my friends when it comes to my painting and neither should you when it comes to carving. We've only been practicing our art for not even six months. None of us have perfected our craft, and none of us ever should."

"I think you're right," Pan said. "We must be dreaming."

"Haha," Birch said, his tone dry. He gestured to the block of wood, still addressing Cam. "You've heard our critiques about your work. Take them to heart and don't be a whiny brat about them. Fix your flaws, and I'm sure we'll believe the dragon can take flight and kill us all." He chuckled. "Wouldn't that be humorous?"

"There it is," Pan muttered with a rueful shake of his head.

Birch grinned. "It's better than being cynical. Which would you prefer?"

"Neither," Pan replied.

"Don't be too hard on him," Cam said to Pan, viewing Birch in feigned sympathy. "I don't think the old-headed rakshasa can help himself. Given his decrepitude, he's probably locked in to those ways of fatalistic thinking."

"What's this about old-headed?" Birch demanded.

"Definitely decrepit," Pan said with a sage nod of agreement.

"I'm not old-headed, and I'm not decrepit." At Cam's and Pan's on-going sympathetic expressions, Birch scowled. "Just wait until the next time we spar. I'll show you old-headed and decrepit."

"I'm sure you will," Cam said. "Just be careful. You don't want to throw out a hip while trying to teach us a lesson."

Birch glowered in momentary silence. "You two are the absolute worst."

In the perpetual darkness of his cell, Cam focused his mind's eye on his Source. There wasn't much more he needed to Advance, maybe another couple of weeks—three at the most—and he'd have enough Ephemera Accreted. Pan was even closer, but then again, he didn't require as much to fill his Source to bursting. Cam, on the other hand— probably because he was a Plasminian—needed a lot more, which was why he currently had his Plasminia spinning faster and faster with a True Bond, ready to Accrete Ephemera.

The yellow blurring of Plasminia might have been distracting, but by this point, Cam had grown used to the spinning, even the crackling, whirring sound it made while doing so. Viewing what was required, he recollected the path that had brought him here. It had been three months since he and Pan had been snatched to Mote, and when they'd first arrived, despair had him certain that they'd never escape.

Over the days following that initial trauma, his hopelessness had given way to surefire certainty intermixed with despair. He'd been plenty furious in those first few days as well—still was—although he'd done his best to hide it from Pan, who needed his support and not his irrational raging. But somewhere along the way, his despair had fallen away like a discarded rag, and some of his fury had waned like heat ebbing from coals. He reckoned it was because he'd spent nearly four years in the mindscape with Pan and Birch, which meant that, rather than ruin him with loneliness, his time in Mote had actually deepened his commitment to his best friend and even given him a chance to make a new one in the old-headed rakshasa.

It meant hope had replaced his despair, an unexpected blessing. The rage for justice continued to burn, though. He hadn't and never would forgive his enemies. Some enemies just had to be put down, and at the top of Cam's list was Weld Plain. That man had earned the killing coming his way many times over, and the same could be said of Sage-Duke Kazar and Sage-Duchess Thens. But those last two wouldn't be easy adversaries. Weld might not be either. He had reputedly been nearing the Awareness of a Crown while Cam was only now putting together what he needed to Advance to Glory.

In the face of such a large gap in power, what chance would he have against them? The one advantage Cam could reckon was that by now, both he and Pan had the answers to Advance to Glory *and* Crown. They'd learned the latter answer together, part of the advantages of the mindscape where concepts could be more readily shared. And they were even part of the way to Sage, too. But would that be enough to face Weld? Even when Cam merged all his Tangs like Rukh and Jessira had said he could once he reached Crown? Could the two of them

Advance quickly enough when they returned to Salvation to put the fragging bastard down?

They had to, and they had to do it right quick. Cam hadn't forgotten the man's promise of bringing harm to Traverse. Worse, what if Weld had already made good on that threat? Or if he hadn't, how much longer would it be before he did?

Cam had to be ready. He had to be fully healed when he returned to Salvation, and for that problem, he had a potential solution. The potent food Birch had mentioned in Petala, but also another teaching from Rukh and Jessira. All it required was to wash Ephemera through every portion of his body, down to the smallest cell, and let it repair any areas of weakness. But doing so in the prison was a waste. Any healing Cam managed was almost immediately undone by the prison's toxic atmosphere.

"I think I should be ready to Advance by next week," Pan sent, breaking into Cam's musings.

"You're that close?" Cam hadn't expected that.

Pan laughed. *"I was Accreting Ephemera whenever you were carving."* A smugness took hold over his voice. *"It gave me an advantage."*

"Really? You could do that?" Fresh surprise laced Cam's voice. *"Even while playing the flute? Isn't that doing three things at the same time?"*

Pan seemed to shrug, pretending modesty. *"I'm talented."*

Cam laughed, imagining the cute grin Pan would offer after making such a boast. *"Then don't let me slow you down. I've got a few more weeks to gather enough Ephemera. Maybe a bit longer. Maybe a bit less, but we'll soon be gone from this place."*

Pan didn't respond at once. *"We're actually going to make it,"* he said after a few seconds, his voice full of joy and surety. *"We're going to break free of this place."*

"Ain't no chance we won't."

24

Birch reclined on the rotting carcass of his cot with his eyes closed while meditating. However, he wasn't without sight. His mind's eye was open, and he viewed the woven world, prepared to Accrete in the manner taught to him by Cam and Pan, both of whom had proven excellent instructors in their own ways.

Excellent warriors as well, although upon first meeting them, Birch would have never believed they had it in them. They had seemed so weak of will, unwilling to endure the pain and struggle required for greatness. And yet, they'd proven him utterly wrong. The heart of a ferocious warrior beat within both their unassuming forms along with the ability to accept his harshest instruction.

Of course, they had their own ideas on how to best learn from him and train, and Birch had to admit that their notions were superior to the ones in which he'd been inculcated. Theirs were more efficient, focused, and controlled, which seemed to be how both young men approached all aspects of their training. It had granted them greater, swifter, and surer gains.

And Birch wasn't so proud that he had refused to learn from the two youths, either. He'd listened to their philosophies, bent his mind to understanding and incorporating them into his own style of fighting. Unsurprisingly, he'd become deadlier for it.

Musing upon the matter, Birch considered Cam. He'd never expected to witness anything quite as ferocious as the human's desire to improve. He trained harder than anyone Birch had ever met, and the oddest aspect was how Cam didn't seem to recognize his level of drive. For the boy, he behaved like his approach to training was simply the way everyone ought to be.

Birch shook his head. That young man was going to be problem for many warriors. He already was, and as he continued to strengthen his Domain and perfect his Oversight, that difficulty would only increase.

Cam was also a good person, warm and generous if overly filled with a desire for vengeance, although he claimed his anger was aimed at wanting justice. The reasoning didn't matter to Birch. The more time he spent around Cam, the closer he found himself drawn to the young human, listening closely whenever he spoke.

Their relationship told Birch a truth that had become ever more obvious: Cam was a natural born leader, talented and charismatic with the rare understanding of how to get the most out of the people under his command. Witness his closeness to Pan, who likely wouldn't have ever fought for improvement nearly as hard as he had and did if not for Cam's loving support.

Loving support.

The bizarre phrase echoed in Birch's mind, and he recalled someone from his recent past who might have been said to have done the same for him, the strange Divine, Rail Gristle. Of course, Birch hadn't understood it at the time, but in hindsight, love and support *had* emanated from Rail. He'd only recognized it upon observing the relationship between Cam and Pan, of how they lovingly supported one another.

Birch wished he could join their circle of kinship, and he wondered sometimes why he didn't tell them what was in his heart, why he didn't tell them of Rail Gristle's advice. For some reason, whenever he wanted to, the words would freeze on his tongue.

Realizing his mind was drifting from the task at hand—Accreting

Ephemera—Birch chided himself, focusing again on the woven world. He had to be ready to leave. Pan and Cam were nearing their Advancement to Glory, only a few days for the former and few weeks for the latter.

However, the scraping of the metal grate in his door distracted him. Tulip had arrived with his breakfast, and Birch levered himself upright, squinting his eyes against the brightness. He hobbled to the door, cursing the pain and weakness that limited his every movement.

"Still alive, I see," Tulip said. To him, she didn't pretend the motherly concern that Cam and Pan said she offered to them.

"Still alive," Birch replied. In times past, when he'd been vital and dangerous, he'd have killed Tulip without a second thought for speaking to him with such disdain. The only reason he hadn't was because of the instant karma the Four would have visited upon him for doing so. Prisoners who harmed their jailers were immediately killed. Still, Birch sometimes—maybe even often—wished others viewed him with the fear they once had.

But the path of Ephemera, which had its own strengths, was his way forward now, and he set aside his childish longings without effort.

"Your food," Tulip said, shoving forward the tray of thin gruel and discolored water.

Birch sighed. Tulip also didn't give him the better fare and water that she gave to Cam and Pan, and he knew why. She wanted their trust, and while she'd yet to succeed, it wasn't for lack of effort. Cam had spoken to her about Devesh, Ephemera, and the possibility of Imbibing the latter, even told her about the woven world.

It was a mistake. Tulip would betray them all if she could. She was only pretending to listen with an open heart, and in the end, her true nature would manifest itself. Of this, Birch had no doubt. First and foremost, Tulip was a rakshasa of Mote, and that meant something. There was no openness to her heart. She sought to deceive Cam and Pan, but how to get them to see it?

Perhaps a direct method. Birch reached a connection to Cam and Pan, wanting them to listen in on his conversation with Tulip.

"What is it?" Cam asked.

"Just listen," Birch replied before addressing Tulip. "I know your ploy," he said to her. "How do you plan on executing it?"

Tulip frowned. "My ploy?"

"Cam and Pan."

"And how would you know about them?"

Birch cursed under his breath. She'd never mentioned the two Ephemeral Masters to him. So how indeed would he know of them? He thought quickly. "Other rakshasas have spoken of them. I am not forgotten. I was once a power."

Skepticism briefly laced Tulip's features before she offered a dismissive shrug. "I suppose someone must have told you," she mused. "Those two are Neophytes. They can't speak mind-to-mind." Her comments had a questioning quality to them, which meant she had doubts.

Birch snorted derision. "How else indeed?" A beat later. "So how do you plan on betraying them?"

"Why do you care?"

"Because I'm bored. I've been here for decades. I could use a diversion. Let me help you."

Tulip responded with a scowl. "Finish your food. I'll be back to collect your tray and tumbler." She made to close the grate.

"Wait." Birch wasn't yet done with the conversation. Cam and Pan needed to learn the truth about Tulip. "Thank you for all the years of bringing me my meals." He inclined his head. "I would dead by now if not for you, and as payment for what you've done, I truly would like to help you. I have nothing else to do. Tell me your plan with Cam and Pan."

"I know what you're doing," Cam said. *"You want me to see that Tulip is untrustworthy. It's unnecessary. I know she is."*

"Perhaps, but I don't like how much you've already trusted her with our futures," Birch replied.

A faint smile had creased Tulip's features. "Cam and Pan are kind fools, and maybe I'll still betray them. But not for now." She hesitated. "They have ideas about Devesh and Ephemera. Do you think any of it might be true? It's said you walked upon Salvation. What was that like? Was there really Ephemera so bountiful that the entire world glowed?"

Birch didn't reply at once. Tulip's question had tossed him backward in time, to his lovely glade where fragrances and sounds had bled comfort and sunshine beamed so bright it sang, where life had held a vitality he'd never known possible. He visualized the meadow more perfectly now than ever before. Painting the scene had helped him recall the memories that the many decades in this prison had stolen. He longed to return to his blessed place of warmth and nourishment. "It was all that and more," he whispered, lost in his recollection.

An instant later, he startled, discovering Tulip eyeing him with a tilted-head expression of bemusement. "I thought I knew you. I guess not."

With that, she closed the grate, and Birch found himself cast in darkness. But with the clear recollection of the glade, he remained bathed within the memory of sunshine.

"What was that supposed to prove?" Cam asked.

"Nothing, I suppose," Birch replied, still lost in his memory.

Tulip pushed her cart along the prison's empty corridors, lost in thought. It had been over a week since Birch had proposed helping her with Cam and Pan and a younger version of herself—even from just a few months ago—would have likely leaped at whatever scheme the Crown had in his devious mind. After all, Birch had been a respected and powerful member of Lord Coruscant's legions, and if anyone would know how to go about using Cam and Pan, it would be him.

Not that Tulip actually needed his help. Cam and Pan were so trusting, so easy to deceive, but having Birch's insight wouldn't hurt.

However, what gave Tulip pause was what it would mean to actually accept the lion-headed rakshasa's advice. There were many risks involved. In the midst of betraying Cam and Pan, it went without saying that Birch would try to betray her, too. It left Tulip in a conundrum, and in the end, she had decided to turn down Birch's offer, not merely because of her mistrust of his intentions, but more because…

Tulip sighed inwardly, hating to admit the truth. Somewhere during their months of captivity, those two—Cam and Pan—had wormed their way past her defenses, charming her with their smiles and kindness. Add in their stories about Devesh and Ephemera, and she no longer wanted to betray them.

She still might—she actually would if it served her purpose, but what if it didn't? There had been instructions in those stories from Cam on how to possibly gather Ephemera, and what if those stories weren't lies? What if she learned how to gather Ephemera? Could she not Advance in that way as well? Nullity didn't have to be her only path forward.

It went without saying that those of Mote would have scorned Tulip's way of thinking, but their views on the matter were easily ignored. In truth, why should Tulip ever care about the opinions of failures? If she Advanced to a Novice, then she would have worth for Lord Coruscant. His agents would notice her, and she'd be lifted out of the prison's pits and into the outer world.

That was worth the risk of waiting for Cam and Pan to show their true plans. And of that fact, she had no doubt. Those two had an intention beyond their soft words and teachings, and Tulip wouldn't make her final decision until she learned what it was. After all, this was Mote, and nothing good ever came from this Realm. That simple truth was paramount above all others, and Tulip could never forgot it. Should she lose herself in one of hope's many tendrils of a brighter future, some other rakshasa would see—the warden, most likely—and use it against her. Then she would be the one betrayed, serving as fodder and fuel for someone else's Nullity.

No. Tulip couldn't allow it. For now, she'd maintain a kind face for Cam and Pan. Let them come to trust her more and more, and she'd see where it led.

With those thoughts in mind, Tulip approached Cam's cell, plastering on a warm smile. "Good morning, young Cam. Here's your breakfast."

Cam approached the door with a glad smile of his own. "Good morning, Tulip." He inhaled the odor of the sludgy mush, sighing as if in appreciation. "Another lovely meal."

Tulip gave an amused chuckle at his wit, although at this point, she'd heard every quip imaginable when it came to the gruel the prisoners were fed. "We only serve the finest cuisine to our prisoners."

Cam replied with a low laugh, and Tulip watched as he took the tray, all the while maintaining the façade of a warm smile. And all the while thinking on Cam's true purposes and how it could serve her needs.

Cam thought long and hard about Tulip after she dropped off his breakfast. The meals she brought had been the only means by which he'd been able to mark time's passage during his incarceration, which struck him as strange: time's relativity. The days had gone by in a slow progression of unending dullness, at least at first, and yet at the same time, they had also breezed along more swiftly than Cam could have ever expected. Three months and three days. That's how long he and Pan had been incarcerated.

It felt simultaneously endless and yet at the same time, all too short.

Perhaps it had to do with the mindscape, and the many years he'd spent there—a little over four years—and he'd worked, struggled, and mastered much, including most of the learning that he'd received from Rukh and Jessira. In addition, because of Birch's tutelage, he and Pan had become far more lethal warriors than when they'd arrived. They'd done so well that the old rakshasa had grudgingly admitted that they might be strong enough to battle through Petala.

And that battle would be coming soon.

Not too much longer, and they could pick up and get gone, even take Sprite and Kiwi with them since a week ago the lovebirds had managed a breakthrough. Several months ago, they, too, had joined the mindscape and achieved the Awareness of Acolytes. It meant they could endure the pressures of the tunnel leading to the Hollow Land, barely so, but all the same, it was true. Cam grinned at the notion of Sprite and Kiwi battling kaijus. A silly notion when all he could imagine was them attacking a book.

His smile slipped when he levered himself off his ragged cot, set a small light above his head, and examined himself. Tulip would soon come to collect the dishes, but he still had time.

He grimaced at what he saw. A rough and ragged beard scrawled its way down his neck, and his boots had fallen apart to hard strands of leather. The same held true for his garb, which had rotted away to rags, barely keeping him clothed. Everything was decayed, which in hindsight shouldn't have been a surprise.

During their first month of imprisonment, he and Pan had often wondered at the lack of physical torture in the prison. At the time, they'd been glad for it, figuring that since they had one another, they could endure and survive the prison's confinement and loneliness.

But it turned out the physical torment had actually been present, insidious and ever-occurring. Within the cells, everything degraded, especially anything of Ephemera, including their bodies. Cam's teeth loosening in their sockets had been his first true warning that something was wrong. Then his limbs had wasted away, becoming noodle-thin and losing all signs of muscle tone and definition. Then had come the pain. Everything hurt, a splinter of agony infecting every joint, muscle, and nerve, all of them firing with pain, sometimes even at rest.

Cam shook his head. He was weaker now than he'd ever been, even under the thrall of Plasminia. Pan and Birch shared his affliction, and together, they were a trio of weaklings, and the only reason the lovebirds weren't similarly afflicted was because of the limited time they spent in the cells and the special meals given to those of the city itself. The food was actually grown adjacent and underneath the Blood Sea but well away from the water's poisons before being shipped to Coruscant's lands. And obviously, the prisoners weren't given that same food.

The physical debilitation burdening Cam and the others put a large hole in their plans for freedom. Once he opened the door to his cell, how could they possibly escape given their weaknesses? They'd have to avoid any kind of conflict if they wanted to get to Petala since none of them would stand a chance at battling even the meekest rakshasa, at least not for long.

It meant they would need help if they wanted to reach Petala, and thankfully, Tulip seemed willing. She didn't know their plans on breaking out of the prison, but she'd pieced together enough that—on her own and without their prompting—she'd begun slipping them better food with every other meal.

Birch remained distrustful of her motives, and Cam largely agreed with his judgment. While Tulip was kind, helpful, and generous, her mind remained conflicted, attached as she was to the teachings of Mote: of betrayal and Nullity.

And yet, she also tried to learn some of Cam's teachings. She told of how she sometimes tried to visualize her Source, laughing in self-deprecation while doing so, like it was all so silly. Nevertheless, underneath her humor, Cam could tell a part of her wanted to believe that there might actually be something to his teachings. Unfortunately, her mind's eye remained closed, and while that might someday change, it wouldn't be soon enough.

They'd have to leave Tulip behind, but Cam held on to the hope that, given all the instructions they'd poured into her, she would eventually master some element of their instructions. Maybe then she could Advance and find a way to escape this world. Either that or Cam could find a way to reach down into this hellish Realm and bring her to safety.

Thinking on it, he reckoned it strange that he'd ever come to trust Birch, who retained a good portion of his Nullity. However, as he'd burned it out, they'd realized the mindscape was becoming less effective. It apparently required some element of both Ephemera and Nullity in order to function, and as soon they'd made the discovery, they'd asked him to stop removing it. It was a selfish request, but one to which Birch had quickly acquiesced. He still retained enough Nullity to function as a Glory, and at the same time, he'd Imbibed enough Ephemera to reach an Acolyte's Awareness.

"Are you awake?" It was Pan.

"I just woke up," Cam said, dropping to do pushups. His limit was twenty, but when he'd started—back when Tulip had started bringing them better food—he hadn't been able to do even five.

"Do you think we'll make it?"

It was the very question that occupied most of Cam's waking thoughts. In some ways, it had been easier when he and Pan had first come to Mote. There had been no hope or expectations then, only the need to survive. Now it was different. Now, there *was* hope and there *were* expectations and failure would be a crushing defeat.

Which was why Cam refused to even consider the notion of losing to this fragging world. They would succeed because he and Pan had trained to their utmost. They had mastered every possible skill. They had the answers to Advance. They had done everything they could imagine might be needed in order to break free of this prison. And they either would or they wouldn't. The future would be as it was.

Unfortunately, Pan didn't have Cam's serene ability to view the future as a surety and not worry so much about failure. There were many times when Pan just needed to hear words of encouragement, and Cam was happy to provide that comfort. He answered Pan's question in the country dialect his friend liked so well. *"We ain't just going to make it. We're going to explode into the skies above Salvation and Advance to Crowns. Believe it."*

"Wouldn't that be something?" Pan said, sounding hopeful but otherwise unconvinced.

Cam scowled, abruptly angry at Pan's lack of conviction. But ranting at his friend wouldn't do them any good. Cam did his best to rein in the fury that seemed to lurk under his every thought. *"It won't just be something,"* he replied once his anger was leashed. *"It'll be the truth. We'll make it so."*

This time, Pan seemed to share the urgency and audacity of Cam's aspirations, laughing. *"Is that a prophecy? Have you become a prophet then?"*

Cam grinned, the last of his annoyance ebbing away. *"If that's what it takes to get you to believe, then sure. Consider me a prophet. In two weeks. That's when we'll get free of this prison, and after that, this world."* Even as he sent the words, a shiver of certainty passed down Cam's spine. They *would* get free of this prison and this world. *"No chance we won't."*

Pan must have taken heart from Cam's words. He fired off Light Squad's battle cry. *"No chance!"*

"What's this about no chance?" Birch asked, sounding sleepy.

Cam laughed, leaving it to Pan to respond.

25

Jade stared in longing and hope at the treasure of concentrated Ephemera that she held in her hands. Gifted to Avia a few weeks ago by her pod, it was a black pearl that was perfect for Light Squad's needs. Jade cupped the jewel, viewing it under the light of a tropical sun as she sat cross-legged upon the balcony extruding from her quarters in Solstice Palace, the home of Saira and her mother, the Sage of the Sinanes.

Even as she held the black pearl, Jade inhaled deep, reviewing what she needed to do today. After Imbibing enough of the Ephemera held within the jewel, she would Advance to Crown. Jade would accomplish her childhood goal and redeem her father's name. She had trouble believing all her dreams were about to come true.

And what a lovely place to see it happen. Solstice Palace had a graceful elegance—white towers, promenades, and blue tiles—that held Jade in a comforting embrace, but beyond the bold structure lay hills sculpted in a profusion of jasmine, lavender, and the lovely city of Tulara. The flora and buildings sloped down to the Arylyn Ocean where waves susurrated against the shore and sunlight set the water's

284

surface glinting like a million diamonds. Jade's gaze briefly rested on the oceanscape sight before her sight traced upward, catching a passing cloud that briefly shaded the world.

She tucked a lock of hair behind her ear when a tradewind gusted the perfumed fragrance of the jasmines and lavender. Her eyes closed, inhaling deep, she found herself smiling and glad for the lush fragrance and the restfulness of the Sinanes. The serenity had been a necessary balm following her father's death, the madness of Nailing and Nageena, and the terrible journey in Hearth. The smile slipped when she recalled that the peace here was an illusion. Jade hadn't forgotten Golden and the continent's betrayal at the hands of the Sage-Dukes. While she had been training, growing, and progressing over the past three years in this place of safety, the world continued to spin, and who could say how poorly other parts of it were doing?

Word regularly reached them in the Sinanes, rumors of ever-encroaching boils and towns falling to hordes of rampaging rakshasas and the Sage-Dukes who put out one fire only for another three to freshly appear. Then there was news about the traitor, Weld Plain. Whispers spoke about how he was soon expected to Advance to Sage. The prig had Advanced quicker than anyone had expected, and many Ephemeral Masters mourned that such a genius was also a rakshasa.

Jade snorted with derision. Weld was no genius. He was just a conniving traitor who happened to have been touched by fortune—the fortune of entering the Ephemeral Academy alongside Cam Folde. *That* was the source of Weld's genius: Cam's teachings with Plasminia. It had nothing to do with Weld himself.

And if he did become a Sage, then it would just mean his fall would be all the mightier. Jade would ensure it. She would also Advance to Sage and kill the fragging bastard. She snarled with self-directed anger just thinking about Weld, especially her prior infatuation with him.

An instant later, she cut off the incipient self-loathing. It wouldn't do her any good. The past was written. Only the present mattered, and in this present… her snarl became a smile of hungry anticipation. In the present, Jade was soon to Advance to Crown. While her sclerae currently held the blue Haunt of a Glory, on this very afternoon, it would glow indigo when she Advanced to Crown. Jade had the unwavering awareness required to both feel and know the difference between certainty and doubt. And she wasn't the only one.

The rest of Light Squad, all of whom had also come to the Sinanes along with Sial, were also soon to Advance. Jade was merely the first, and once they were all Crowns, they could begin the work of expunging the treason causing Golden's despoilment. It was work that required doing, and Jade and Light Squad were determined to see it done. Same with Saira, who considered herself a member of their unit and had the answer needed to Advance to Sage. The other woman merely needed to Imbibe enough Ephemera, and it would be so. And given their perfect Advancements, their power would be undeniable. Each member of Light Squad would easily be the equal of two or even three others of equal Awareness. Upon returning to Golden, they would be a force with which to be reckoned.

Light Squad. Thinking on the name had Jade scowling afresh. Light Squad was incomplete and in some ways, always would be without Cam and Pan. The scowl threatened to boil into a glower of rage. She would never forgive Sage-Duke Kazar for his treachery, and justice for Cam and Pan demanded that the man be brought low.

"That isn't the posture of someone preparing to Advance," Saira gently chided from where she sat quietly in a corner.

Jade glanced over her shoulder at the other woman, who had come to offer moral support. "Sometimes I do better when I'm angry? And shouldn't you be readying to Advance to Sage?"

Saira lifted her brow. "I'll achieve what I need as soon as you and the rest of Light Squad Advance. And if you truly do better when angry, then why are you stating it like a question?"

Jade's anger evaporated, and she found herself chuckling ruefully. How did Saira do it? Pierce through the heart of her annoyance? Was it her serenity? Or maybe it was simply because Jade respected Saira and wanted to be like her: self-aware and emotionally balanced.

Card could certainly do with some of that. The man grunted most of his thoughts, greeted joyous events with a shrug, and scowled at butterflies. Well, he didn't actually scowl at butterflies, but Jade could imagine him doing so.

"You're distracted," Saira chided. "Are you sure this is the right time for your Advancement?"

Jade shook off her thoughts about Card and focused on the here and now. "It's time. I've made my peace with everything we've endured, all my doubts, and found my certainty, the reason for it. It's in Devesh and the people I know and love."

Saira smiled, pleased. "Then it is time. Become your father's heir. Advance to Crown."

Jade gave Saira a firm nod before facing forward. She closed her eyes and lifted her face to the sunshine, inhaling again the fragrance of flowers, listening to the whisper of waves against the shore. Another deep breath, and she opened her eyes to the woven world, seeing the vividness of truest reality, the innumerable connections that linked Creation within an ocean of perfumed lights, lustrous sounds, musical scents, and a rainbow of tastes and touches.

A final breath, and Jade viewed her Source in her mind's eye before Delving it and forging a True Bond. With practiced efficiency, she guided her Ephemera, transferring it into that which was contained in the pearl, mixing them together, Imbibing and Enhancing whatever she felt capable of recovering.

Back and forth, on and on, and the Ephemera slowly filled her Source like a gentle rain falling on a parched landscape, reshaping it. Her Source rounded, became more spherical, beat in time to her pulse, and her Tangs brightened as she continued to cleanse the Ephemera she Imbibed. On she worked, firming her Source until—

Enough. She had reached her limit. There was no more Ephemera she could pack within her Source. Now came the most important step, and Jade paused a moment to steady herself. Once she felt prepared, she focused the entirety of her concentration on her Source, compressing it, working it, reshaping it, turning it over in her mind's eye like it was dough and she a baker.

As she labored, the answer required to Advance to Crown filled her mind. Jade knew it, felt sure of it down deep in the marrow of her bones, her recognition about doubt and certainty. She viewed the world as a ragged place where nothing was assured, but that wasn't where her heart resided. Her heart resided in the certainty of Devesh and of Light Squad. The awareness seeped out from her Source, along her arteries, down her head and neck, and through her torso and limbs. An instant later, her Synapsia flashed, brightening to a color she had always hoped to see but never expected: a vivid indigo clothed in a golden sheen.

Jade smiled and opened her eyes, knowing they shone with a Crown's indigo Haunt. But her Advancement wasn't yet complete. Returning to her Source, she Imbibed more Ephemera, pouring it into Plasminia. She would Advance that Tang, which would allow her to then help Advance the rest of them.

"How do you think she's doing?" Charity asked. She paced about her quarters, unable to sit still while Avia and Card remained focused on their game of chess.

Charity couldn't manage their level of calm, though. She strode back and forth, from the front room where the other two played chess, to her bedroom, and then out to her balcony, which overlooked the Arylyn Ocean. For once, the vista's beauty didn't capture her attention. Nothing about the waters, the lovely perfume of the many flower gardens, or the spectacular city molded over the surrounding hills captured her attention. None of it could restrain her, and she stalked back into her quarters and the front room where Avia and Card never once glanced up from their game.

Their serene lack of concern had Charity frowning. How were they so calm? Especially given that she was on pins and needles. Her insides trembled like a bag full of worms, and she wanted to bite her fingernails to the quick, even just run down the hallway and find out how Jade was doing. Would she Advance?

As soon as the question occurred to her, Charity shoved it away. *Positive thoughts. Positive thoughts.* She had to believe that Jade would have no trouble Advancing. Even considering the possibility of failure couldn't be allowed. *Positive thoughts. No negative ones. Jade will Advance.*

How could she not? After all, she had everything required to do so. She had Saira's gentle support, a black pearl full of Ephemera, and a clear understanding of the difference between doubt and certainty. There was no chance she'd fail.

Charity stumbled to a halt when Light Squad's phrase from Hearth echoed in her mind. She couldn't even recall who had first stated what became their battle cry, and she doubted any of the others could either.

And what difference did it make anyway? When the person who had led their unit was missing? Him and the finest panda-person in any Realm. Cam Folde and Pan Shun.

Charity missed them. Three years later, and she could still see Pan's wonderful, little smile, and most bitterly, she could feel Cam's arms around her. His kiss… she shivered. Thoughts about Cam were a bittersweet torture. They'd been so close to achieving a storybook kind of relationship, something truly wonderful, and her own father had stolen it from them.

She still loved Cam, and she likely always would. Even now, Charity struggled moving past him, no matter how hard she'd tried. And she had tried, including dinners with several young men who Saira thought might be a good match. Those dates, though, had proven disastrous. The first such individual had been pleasant but dull, the second a bit of a lech, and the third entirely too proud of himself. The fourth had an unfortunate overbite that would hopefully be cured if he ever Advanced to Glory.

Charity wouldn't ever know about that, though, just as she wouldn't truly know any of the positive qualities of her various dates—and they had to have them or Saira wouldn't have suggested the men as potential suitors. Unfortunately, Charity lacked the heart or patience to give any of them a proper chance.

On several occasions, she had even spent most of the dinner talking about Cam. She'd later tried to make it up to the overbitten young man with a goodnight kiss, but it hadn't made much of a difference. The kiss had been as platonic as kissing a plant, and the young man had later on complained about his mistreatment to Card of all people.

"Do you plan on wearing a hole in your rugs?" Card asked, not glancing up from the game.

Charity looked over at Card, wanting to make a face at him. Leave it to him to ask a jackhole question. It must be his nature. However, rather than give in to her childish impulse, Charity chose to slouch into an armchair, and from there, she viewed the chess match. "Bishop to g5," she said to Avia. "You'll pinch his queen in the next move."

Card glared at her, and Charity offered an innocent smile in return. "What? I'm sure Avia already saw the move."

"I actually didn't," Avia said. "But thank you."

"You're welcome."

Card gave one of his patented grunts. "I take it back. I'd rather you wore a hole in your rugs."

Charity corrected him. "You never said I should wear a hole in my rugs. You asked if that was my intention. It wasn't."

"So you've shifted your intention to helping Avia win?"

Charity shrugged. "I was bored?"

Another grunt. "You're nervous, and you shouldn't be. Jade will succeed, and after her, the rest of us."

Avia nodded. "The pearl has enough Ephemera for the rest of you to reach Crown."

"Assuming Jade doesn't waste any of it," Card said.

"She won't," Charity said, feeling sure about the matter.

It was true that any of them could have been the first to use the pearl that Avia had been given—they all had the requisite answer—but Advancing to Crown had been such a necessary and long-held dream for Jade that Charity couldn't imagine refusing her friend the first attempt. Jade needed this. She needed this success. And maybe afterward, Jade would fully and finally stop believing any of those lies she'd told herself regarding her purpose in life. Redeeming her father's name or saving some useless turd like Weld Plain shouldn't ever be the focus of her past, present, or future.

Two moves later, Avia took Card's queen and three moves after that, she had her checkmate.

"Well played," Card said, "even if you did have help." He sent a final glare at Charity, who gave him another innocent smile.

Avia grinned, pointing at herself. "Not a fish."

Card did a double-take. "I never called you one."

"But it would have been funny if you had. So I pretended you did."

Card frowned. "You two are so strange." He rose to his feet. "Let's go see how Jade is doing."

Avia wore an abruptly worried expression. "You don't think we'll distract her?"

"You're the Crown," Card replied. "Reach out and ask Saira."

Charity wanted to smack herself in the forehead. "Any of us could have done that."

"Which is what I did five minutes ago," Card said. "While you were wearing a hole in your rugs and helping Avia cheat. Saira said Jade was in the midst of her attempt." He halted, tilting his head as if hearing a distant voice. "Correction. She's finished the attempt. She succeeded."

Charity shot out of her chair, shouting triumph and racing for the door.

Weld strolled through the boil that was slowly coming to life in a remote valley where had once existed a small village, a place the rakshasas had destroyed several years ago. All that was left now were the broken remnants of cabins and homes. They leaned against one another like silly drunks, and although the corpses of those killed had been set alight on funeral pyres—while rakshasas believed in strength above all else, they weren't uncivilized—a burned-meat stench somehow still lingered.

Or maybe that was just in Weld's imaginings. He hadn't enjoyed killing all those dumb villagers, but what choice had he been given? A command had been received, and among the rakshasas, if a body didn't do as they were told, then that body would soon be dead.

Weld mused over the nameless village, still regretting his role in its destruction. It had stood in such a pretty setting. A mountain stream as blue as a Glory's Haunt burbled close at hand and rugged hills clothed in an evergreen forest and punctured in places by rocky prominences corralled the valley. And that didn't account for the people themselves. When Nailing had ordered Weld to scout the place, the folks had fawned over him, impressed by a Crown visiting their no-account village. More than a few women had batted their lashes, promising much with their shy laughs.

None of them had known the doom that Weld would bring, and he wondered how they might have greeted him if they had.

He grimaced. None of that mattered now. The boil had needed building, and this locus of Ephemera was a perfect spot for it. So what if a few villagers had needed removing to see it built? Not even the finest chef could make an omelet without cracking a few eggs.

Seconds later, Weld reached his destination, a blocky building constructed of stacked gray stone. It towered above the ruined village and nearby forest, seemingly faceless with no windows on any level. Only a solid wooden door, one wide enough for a wagon, broke the building's blank face. This ugly fortress contained the heart of the boil, and what the structure lacked in beauty, it would soon exceed based on the core planted within it.

Weld entered the building, gliding down a narrow hallway where the gloom was barely lifted by a couple of Ephemeral lanterns hanging from the walls. As he wandered deeper inside, he nodded to his fellow rakshasas, human and Awakened Beasts alike.

That had been the biggest surprise he'd learned since going over to the service of Sage Nailing and through him, Lord Coruscant. They'd told him true with none of the fragging lies about honor and service like everyone bleated about at the Ephemeral Academy.

Those kinds of statements—made by everyone from Professor Grey to Professor Werm—had always made Weld feel stupid and unworthy. And the instructors at the Academy had gone out of their way to treat him no different than the village matrons back home, who had reckoned he wasn't good enough to spend time with their daughters. Same with his father and his brother, who had thought Weld just wasn't good enough in general. Only his mother had seen his worth, and she'd be the only person back home he'd save when the time came to sweep away Golden's rot. The rakshasas to whom Weld owed allegiance would crush the Sage-Dukes and bring a better world to life, one based on strength and the willingness to rule.

Weld tightened his jaw, looking forward to that future because if there was one thing he was willing to do, it was rule those lesser than him, which meant most everyone. True, he was only a Crown, but in just a few hours, he'd become a Sage and then he'd be Nailing's equal. There would then come a time after that, though, when he'd learn all of Lord Coruscant's secrets. Maybe that so-called Son of Emptiness would tell them to him. Weld hadn't yet conversed with Zahhack, but it would happen, sometime in the future when serving Coruscant wasn't necessary.

But until then, Weld would do as he was told. He'd Advance, crush whoever got in his way, and make his enemies weep.

He scowled on thinking of his enemies. There were some that he hated more than any others. Light Squad, every member of them from Avia Koravail to that stuck up prig, Saira Maharani. Even—or maybe especially—Jade Mare, who should have known better than to think herself too good for the likes of him. In the new world Weld planned on fashioning, she'd beg to land in his bed.

But where were they? Rumor had it they'd hightailed it out of Maviro and headed to the Sinanes. It had been more than three years since anyone had seen either hide or hair of them, right after Weld had done Cam Folde dirty along with his prissy little friend, Pan Shun.

Weld smiled on thinking about their demise, and what they must have endured at the end. They'd likely been tortured to death in Mote, but even that wasn't good enough for Weld's vengeance. The boil he was helping build was hundreds of miles distant from the town of Traverse, but once he Advanced to Sage, he could take some time out of his day to go torch the place. He'd burn Cam Folde's past just like he'd ruined the man's future.

Weld's pleasure faded on thinking about the Sages who were the most instrumental in building the boil. Three of them: Nailing: the Sage of Warring Thunder, Cougrail: the Sage of the Bloody Claw, and Nageena: the Sage of Whispering Scales. All of them Awakened Beasts. The Crowns who owed them allegiance were no different, eleven of them ranging from a tiger to a falcon.

And none of them cared a whit about Traverse. Their focus was on Charn, the eponymously named capital of the duchy. Weld wondered if they'd even allow him to take his final revenge. He privately doubted it. Nailing had mentioned on more than one occasion that his vengeance should have been satisfied by what had already been done to Cam, and right now, going against the Sage's will wasn't smart.

But surely there had to be a way to make it happen.

Weld shrugged to himself. If it couldn't occur until Charn was a burned-out husk, then so be it. He could be patient. In the meantime, there was his Advancing to fixate upon. Satisfied by his plan, Weld swiftly made his way to his room, halting at the entrance.

Nailing waited within, seated on the bed. The Awakened buffalo's bulk made the space seem small, but what had arrested Weld's attention was the Ephemera pouring off a small globe resting on a small table next to his cot. He smiled. Nailing had fulfilled his promise, brought with him an Ephemeral treasure that would see Weld Advance to Sage.

"Are you ready?" Nailing asked, his voice a deep rumble.

Weld affected a cocky grin. "I was born ready."

Nailing snorted in mild derision. "Succeed, and I'll be impressed."

He'd be impressed, would he? "If you're impressed, how about you let me fly over to Traverse and give it a rakshasa's greeting?"

"No."

Weld made to argue, unable to help himself. "But—"

Nailing slapped him, rising to his feet with a glower. "Constrain your pride. The Lord might have gifted you with many resources, but you've yet to show the wisdom of his investment."

Fear had Weld bowing low even as fury coursed through him. "Yes, my liege." He hoped his bent-over posture hid the rage on his face.

Apparently, it did since Nailing readied to leave. "Come to me after you've Advanced. I'll have more tasks for you then."

Weld remained bowed, doing his best to control his rage. "Of course, my liege." Nailing left, and Weld straightened, making a private promise between himself and the Sage of Warring Thunder. *That will be the last time you ever humiliate me.*

26

Following their re-emergence into Hearth, life had often proven quite the challenge for Thor and his fellow Sages. During their time locked in the Temple of Gates, their world had been invaded by a powerful foe: the Jom-Strafes, predators who had conquered large swatches of their world. And unfortunately, thus far, there had been no room for negotiation with the monstrous creatures.

The Jom-Strafes had their own Sages, all of whom scorned diplomacy. Instead, they proclaimed the word of someone they named the Endless Emperor, a figure better known throughout the Realms as Zahhack, the Son of Emptiness. And Zahhack demanded that His followers operate under the philosophy of conquest with no quarter for negotiation.

Thor frowned upon considering the Endless Emperor. Prior to Cam's unit awakening him from his trapped slumber, he and his fellow Sages hadn't known their true enemy's name. Instead, they'd operated from ignorance, fighting to keep the anchor line closed that led from a dark and terrible Realm to Hearth, slowly losing a decades' long and desperate battle to the Son of Emptiness' wearying grip.

But Rukh and Jessira had slammed shut that wretched anchor line, which meant all that horror was now in the past. Just as wonderful, if Thor was correct in what he felt, then diplomacy with the Jom-Strafes might soon be available—whether they wished for it or not. In just a few hours or days, Thor had it within him to change his Realm's future.

It was why he currently sat within his study, cross-legged on a heavy, red blanket laid out over a large mattress upon the ground. The evening sun shone through the room's mullioned windows, reflecting off whitewashed walls, the bespoke desk and chair built to Thor's specifications—he was exceedingly tall—and the burnished shelves carefully organized by content. This room was where Thor was at his most comfortable and the only place where he could conceive of making this most important attempt.

Taking a moment longer to reflect on what would hopefully come to pass, Thor absorbed the view from outside: the city of Nylara, which remained far from recovered following the attack by the Jom-Strafe Crown. That, too, would change, not through today's attempt, but through the work of those who loved their home. And Thor would see them safeguarded and protected from those like the Jom-Strafes and their true master. Thor would never again fail them since he finally had the answer required to Advance further in the Way into Divinity. Thor comprehended the reason for refusal and surrender, down in his heart and through his soul.

Like all Sages, he had wrestled with the contradictory concepts and been unable to reconcile the two until he realized that the answer simply built off of his prior understanding of what had been needed in order to Advance to Sage. The revelation had slowly revealed itself, an epiphany that had begun during a heavy rain of all things. Jessira had also helped quite a lot. She'd spoken to him a couple of times several years ago, pointing him in the right direction, although he hadn't realized it at the time.

Finding the moment auspicious, Thor began his attempt. From his *null pocket*, he withdrew the cores of two Jom-Strafe Sages he had recently defeated along with a petrified mango, a treasure he'd created many decades past and that had slowly gathered Ephemera into itself. Thor studied the stony fruit, which had an orange-red hue and glistened like wet marble. On its own, the petrified mango was beautiful enough, but when viewed through the lens of the woven world, the fruit's greater secret was revealed as it glowed unnaturally bright, containing a similar abundance of Ephemera as the cores.

Together, the three items should be enough for Thor to Advance to Divine, and at that point, he would easily become the most powerful being in Hearth. He would then grant the Jom-Strafe Sages a simple choice: surrender or be slain, surrender or refusal. One way or another, their evil ways would be ended, and their people freed from their polluted philosophy.

Thor shook his head, having trouble accepting the wonderful future he could help create for everyone who named Hearth their home. And it was largely because of a group of young Ephemeral Masters who had come to his Realm as strangers and left as honored friends and heroes. He wondered how they were doing, especially the young man to whom he'd linked—Cam Folde. Where was he now and how was he faring? Thor hoped to learn some inkling once he Advanced to Divine. At that Stage, he should have the ability to penetrate the Realms, at least with his mind.

Realizing he was delaying for no particular reason, Thor resettled himself, closed his eyes, and Imbibed Ephemera. It flowed into him, waxing and waning, smooth and relentless as the ocean. All the while, he fixed his mind on his beliefs about refusal and surrender, feeling them to his depths, a circular rhythm to his labor.

Hours passed as Ephemera filled his Source, and he compressed it, smoothing out any final rough spots, perfecting the shape of a globe. On and on he deliberated and labored, a methodical process, slow enough for him to distantly sense the setting and rising of the sun. Another setting until at last... his Source flashed crystalline.

Thor's heart thrilled, and he woofed his pleasure, tongue lolling out as he grinned happily at his success. He continued to view his Source through his mind's eye, admiring its perfection, the rainbow hues glistening within. He woofed again. Thor could have stared at his Source for hours, but his admiration cut off when a familiar voice spoke to him from across the Realms.

"Congratulations, Divine of Loyalty," said Jessira Shektan.

Thor stiffened in surprised delight, not expecting her to contact him again so soon. She and Rukh were so far above him in stature and meaning, and he bowed low before her. *"Thank you, Most Holy One."*

Jessira laughed, warm and inviting. *"You misname me. I am a Holy Servant, and I am only holy for reflecting Devesh's Love. We bid you welcome to our small company."*

A second voice spoke, that of Rukh Shektan. *"And we wish our congratulations could be celebratory alone. But we need your help, Divine of Loyalty."*

Thor cocked his head in confusion. What could the Holy Servants possibly need from him? Their power was nearly absolute. Nevertheless, he didn't hesitate in offering his help. *"What can I do to aid you?"*

"We aren't the ones who need your aid," Rukh said *"It is someone else, one to whom you are bonded."*

Thor knew of whom they spoke. *"What must I do?"*

Saira had waited until the rest of Light Squad had Advanced to Crown before making her own attempt to reach Sage. She had wanted to be there for them, wanted to support their efforts, knowing how difficult it could be. Reaching Crown was often a barrier that many Glories couldn't overcome. But with the right support and help, it could be done, and Saira had felt compelled to offer that support. She could have never seen herself Advancing to Sage, which often required a week of seclusion, while her friends struggled or failed because of her absence. She would have never forgiven herself.

And her delay had proven absolutely essential. Charity had nearly failed her attempt at Advancing, and without Saira's presence, she would have. Instead, she had succeeded, all of Light Squad had, one after another. First, Jade, and the next day, Card, and finally Charity. Three Glories Advanced to Crowns in the same number of days.

Remarkable.

Only then had Saira felt content to lock herself away in her quarters and make the attempt to reach Sage. It had been two days of isolation except for her amma, who bore witness and offered support. Two days alone with her thoughts, her work, and her fierce determination, and two days later, success had been hers.

Saira had Advanced, just as she'd always dreamed, and she currently knelt in her quarters, eyes wide in wonder as she slowly extended her arms, turning them this way and that, like she'd never seen them before, and in a way, it was true: she hadn't seen them before, at least not like this. They glowed—her entire body did—with a lustrous illumination and countless connections of lights, songs, and floral smells that stretched from her to the world at large. How could she have believed her view of the woven world had been complete at Crown?

And what would her experience of the world be like when she Advanced Plasminia to Sage and from there, the rest of her Tangs? When she Enhanced them all to Crystal?

"You were successful?" Amma asked.

Saira, caught up in the woven world's wonder, could do little more than nod her head. She continued to view herself and her surroundings, made mute by the majesty of what had once been prosaic but now struck her as divine. It was as if she'd once been blind but could now see, deaf but could now hear, anosmic but could now smell all the wondrous fragrances of a million different flowers perfuming the air. She grinned when she considered food. If these were the changes to her other senses, then what about taste? When she had her favorite meal, would it be as if she'd been cured of ageusia? Saira didn't know, and she also couldn't wait to find out.

Amma chuckled, warm and knowing. "It takes time coming to terms with being a Sage. The first few days can be distracting."

Saira nodded once more, still unable to do much more than merely accept the sensations washing over her: warm sunshine, a cool tradewind, and the comforting scent of the briny sea along with a host of other impressions, so many and so varied. And this was to be her life from this point forward? Saira laughed in delight as brilliant exuberance bubbled through her.

Amma knelt behind her, hugging her from behind. "I have always been proud of you, but my pride is far less than my happiness at your joy."

Saira leaned into her amma's embrace, eyes closed, glad and at peace like she had never experienced. The world and its troubles could wait for a while. At this moment, there was only her amma's love and the glory of Ephemera. They remained that way for hours as Saira grew used to her new acceptance of the woven world.

Minutes later, a soft knock indicated the world's intrusion. Saira shifted out of her amma's arms, glancing to the door. There was no one there, and it hadn't been her sister, Dru, who sat silent sentinel in the foyer, waiting to be allowed into Saira's bedroom.

The knock repeated, insistent but soft and echoing, like it was heard from a great distance.

"Did you hear that?" Saira asked, moving to stand, glancing about for the source of the noise. Was this some aspect of being a Sage? Hearing distant sounds?

"Hear what?" Amma asked, also rising to her feet.

A third time came the knocking, and Saira spun in place, frowning. Where was the sound coming from? She cocked her head, waiting to hear it again. *There!* A fourth time it echoed, and still, she couldn't localize it.

Saira made to stride to a different location in the room, but her amma halted her, concern writ on her face. "What is it? What do you hear?"

"A knocking, like someone is at the door. Or some kind of door," Saira answered, her gaze locking upon her amma in worried confusion. "You didn't hear it?"

"No. I heard nothing." Worry now marred her amma's features. "You need to tell me what is happening."

"Saira Maharani?"

Saira frowned, lifting a hand and asking for quiet. She knew that voice. It belonged to Thor, the Sage of Loyalty. But how? It should have been impossible. Sages could speak telepathically across the world but not across Realms.

"Saira?"

"You hear something else?" Amma asked.

Saira nodded in distraction, her attention elsewhere. *"I hear you. Were you the one making the knocking sounds?"*

A sense of relief flooded across the connection. *"Yes. That was me."*

Saira frowned, mistrusting the voice speaking to her. How could it be Thor? More likely, it was some trickster rakshasa. *"And who exactly are you?"*

"Thor, once the Sage of Loyalty but now the Divine of Loyalty. We need to talk. Cam Folde and Pan Shun live, and they need your help."

Although Saira sensed nothing but veracity from this voice claiming to be Thor, she would test him first. Questions only he could answer. But if he spoke true and Cam and Pan were alive… it would be a miracle beyond expectation, and Saira's heart surged with hope.

"Do you know what this meeting is about?" Avia asked.

Jade shook her head. "I know Saira literally just Advanced to Sage, but that can't be why she called for us."

"I didn't hear anything either," Charity said. She flicked her Crown-Haunted gaze at Card and Sial, who marched far ahead of the three of them. The two men had already disappeared around a corner. "But it has to be important if she wants all of us present."

With nothing further to say, their brief conversation fell silent, and they strode through the largely empty residential halls of Solstice Palace. The corridors were wide, tan stucco walls that were decorated with lovely murals, frescoes, paintings, and sculptures. Even the rugs that softened the white marble flooring had a kind of artwork quality to them.

"Well, whatever it is, we'll find out soon enough," Charity said when they reached Saira's quarters.

The door was slightly ajar, which meant Card and Sial must have already entered. A quick knock, and Charity led the way into Saira's sitting area, which had an elegant simplicity to the furnishings and decor. Everything had clean lines with splashes of colored fabric from royal blue to carnation along with several bright paintings to enhance the otherwise neutral color palette of cream, gray, and taupe.

As expected, Card and Sial were already present, positioned on a pair of matching armchairs, leaving the couch and several other seats unoccupied. Saira stood before the mantel, lovely in a saffron sari and ruby earrings. A matching pendant hung from a gold necklace, but most arresting were her eyes. Her sclerae held the violet Haunt of a Sage, indicating her success in Advancing.

Charity made to congratulate Saira's success but halted when the other woman held up a restraining hand. Only then did she notice the tension and anguish lining Saira's features.

"I'll appreciate your warm sentiments when it's appropriate," Saira said, "but now isn't the time. We have a far more important topic to discuss. Please be seated."

Charity did so, settling on the couch alongside Jade and Avia. She glanced to Card, lifting a brow in question. He shrugged in reply, apparently not knowing the reason for the late afternoon meeting any more than she did.

Saira regathered their attention. "I called you here because I Advanced to Sage a few hours ago." She broke into a pleased smile that quickly faded. "It was then that I heard from an old friend—Thor, who is now the Divine of Loyalty."

Charity startled. That hadn't been what she had expected to hear from Saira, and she shared a wondering look with Card and Jade, the others who had also met Thor.

And now Thor was a Divine? Charity grinned, overjoyed at the rare and wondrous accomplishment of someone she had quickly learned to respect and love in the month of knowing him. Then again, her feelings for Thor weren't surprising. He was just that kind of person: loyal and loving, but fierce, just like his moniker and doglike appearance.

Saira continued. "Thor reached out to me because he learned from Rukh and Jessira—the voices in the temple were truly theirs—that Cam and Pan live."

Charity's smile wiped away, and the room fell to a depthless silence. Learning that Rukh and Jessira weren't simple myths should have brought her delight. It did, but the information impacted her far less than Saira's final words. Those struck her like a hammer to the head, and she rocked backward. Cam and Pan lived? How? Where had they been all this time?

The others seemed to share her shock, and Card was the first to regain his voice. "What happened to them?"

"It is as we suspected. Sage-Duke Kazar betrayed them. He did so at Coruscant's behest. Our actions in this Realm—of defeating his plans—earned his attention. Coruscant wanted Cam and Pan, even more after our work in Hearth, and he forced Kazar to aid in his desire."

"How did he force my father?" Charity asked. She flushed and cleared her throat. The answer didn't matter. "What did Coruscant want with Cam and Pan?"

"His intentions were to either break them to his will—have them willingly serve him—or kill them so they could no longer oppose his plans."

"Where are they?" Jade asked, cutting to the heart of the matter.

"Mote."

Charity gasped, and she gripped Avia's and Jade's hands, needing their support. They held tight to one another, all of them likely feeling the same horror. Cam and Pan had been sent to Hell? Tears welled in her eyes. What kind of torture had they endured over the past three years? What torment had they experienced while Light Squad had rested and blossomed in the Sinanes, carelessly gaining Ephemera and Advancing.

Fury filled Charity—at her father, the other Sage-Dukes and

Sage-Duchesses, Weld Plain—but she corralled it. There would be time for it later. "Then we have to go there, too," she declared. "To Mote. We have to get them back."

"And kill anything and anyone that gets in our way," Avia declared.

"That isn't as impossible as it sounds," Saira said. "Rukh and Jessira say that they were sent to a prison, and there is a chance that they can break free and escape."

"But three years of torture," Card said, voicing one of Charity's fears.

"Time passes differently in the Realms," Saira said. "Those closer to the Empty One experience its passage more slowly than those in the Realms closer to Devesh. Recall our months in Hearth compared to Avia's years here on Salvation."

"Hearth was closer to the Empty One?" Jade asked. "It didn't feel like the people there were worse than the ones here."

"With the anchor line in the temple, it was closer to the Empty One," Saira explained. "However, what is important is that while we've experienced three years, Cam and Pan have likely only been in Mote for several months, maybe as little as four or five. There is every chance that they haven't been broken."

Charity took heart from the other woman's words. "What do we do?"

Saira's gaze locked on her. "It will largely depend on you. When you and Cam shared that disgusting drink in Hearth, the one to heal from a Jom-Strafe's claws, it linked the two of you. Thor believes that connection should grant him the ability to bridge the Realms between you and Cam. You and Thor will be able to speak to Cam, but only when he's Advanced to Glory, which we have to believe he will achieve. And when he does, you must learn whatever you can to help us coordinate their rescue. Thor plans on bending every effort to eventually forge an anchor line between Salvation and Hearth and from Hearth to Mote. We'll go there and save our friends."

Charity furrowed her brow. That foul brew she and Cam had drunk had altered their appearance and improved their physical attributes, but it had also somehow linked them? Was that why his feelings for her had mellowed? Charity wondered if it had changed anything else about their relationship. Had his feelings for her merely come from that connection?

"It only linked you," Saira said, apparently picking up on her thoughts. "Any growth and emotional bonds the two of you formed were due to your own, shared choices."

Charity exhaled, breathing out a prayer of relief. She'd always wondered about how drastically Cam's feelings for her had changed. Knowing that it wasn't due to an outside influence was a blessing.

And none of it was currently of any import. "Can Thor do more than create the anchor line? Can he come with us?"

"No. There was some agreement made that Rukh and Jessira can never directly interfere in Mote or Salvation and none who've pledged themselves to their work at the Stage of a Divine or greater can do so either. Only we can go."

Charity nodded acceptance. Only minutes before, she'd have never expected to have had the aid of a Divine in any endeavor so not having Thor's help wasn't much of a disappointment. Besides which, Saira would be with them, and the rest of Light Squad were Crowns. They were powerful on their own. "What happens next?" she asked.

"Thor will let us know," Saira replied. "Be ready for his call."

Charity looked to the others. "We all need to be ready. Have equipment prepared. As soon as Thor tells me he can forge that anchor line, I want us on it within seconds."

Jade nodded. "We should share quarters from now on, stay in close contact all the time."

Saira smiled slightly. "I have plenty of room."

Sial raised his hand. "Do I have to share space with Card? He snores."

His comment elicited laughter from everyone but Card, who feigned a growl of annoyance.

Charity's humor ended. "I'm grateful for this, but I just want Cam and Pan home. That's all I care about."

"It's what we all care about," Avia said, hugging her.

"But what will they be like?" Card wondered. "Even at only four months in Hell, they'll need so much time to heal."

Charity viewed Card, surprised at his insight. He was right. Cam and Pan would have likely been brutalized in Mote. Who knew what injuries, both physical and spiritual, they would have suffered? "Whatever healing they need, we'll make sure they receive it."

27

Cam focused inward and visualized his Source, watching it closely as streams of Ephemera seeped into his lightning-laced Plasminia and from there, down into his other Tangs. With a twitch of will, he controlled the flow, careful so it didn't overwhelm his Source, parts of which threatened to deform as he Imbibed more of the Ephemera he'd collected on his skin over the past few days. Seeing the areas of potential weakness, Cam shifted to strengthen the walls of his Source, rounding it out, compressing it, smoothing as many extrusions as possible until he was finally satisfied.

The work lasted for hours, but there came a moment when he had time enough to pause and appreciate the shape of his Source. Starting out on the Way into Divinity, it had looked like a potato, all lumpy and deformed. But here it was now, nearly a perfect globe with only a few odd protrusions, but even that would change with his next Advancement.

Recognizing it was time to do exactly that, Cam inhaled deep and exhaled hard, imagining himself breathing out all expectations. *Do the work and the outcome is assured.* The words were Professor Grey's.

A last stabilizing breath, and he resumed his work, Imbibing and Enhancing the final quantity of Ephemera needed to completely fill his Source, every last bit he could compress into his Tangs. Plasminia held the most, and the rest held a relatively equal amount. All the while, he tightened the transitions between his Tangs so one day there wouldn't be any separations. All would be one, just like Ephemera itself. On he labored until his Source distended to bursting.

Now came the final step. Cam focused on his answer, what he recognized in both his heart and his mind as the difference between giving and receiving, the supposed first block on the way to becoming a Sage. More time elapsed, but there came an endless instant when his Source flashed and all his Tangs transformed into the blue Haunt of a Glory, gold-sheened and streaked with lacings of indigo.

Cam laughed in relief and triumph as fresh strength poured into him, like he could lift a mountain. It was an illusion, but for the few seconds while it lasted, he reveled in the feeling of accomplishment and fresh hope for the future.

"You Advanced!" Pan exclaimed, his joy evident.

"Only a little later than you." Pan had Advanced a week earlier.

"Better late than never."

"And now we can finally leave this place," Birch said.

Before Cam could reply, a familiar voice interrupted their conversation. *"Cam. Can you hear me?"*

Cam's eyes widened in shock. *"Thor?"*

Relief swept across the connection. *"It is I. I have been trying to reach you without respite for the past month. We have much to discuss."*

Cam frowned as distrust percolated through his mind. How could this be Thor? Sages couldn't communicate across the Realms.

"Cam?" It was Pan. *"Who are you talking to?"*

Cam's confusion and misgivings heightened. *"Thor. You don't recognize him?"*

"Who is Thor?" Birch asked.

"The Sage of Loyalty." Cam's frown deepened, and his suspicions hardened. The voice wasn't Thor's. This was a rakshasa practicing

deception, no doubt wanting to use Cam and his friends to create Nullity. His anger bubbled to life.

"*Are you speaking to someone else?*" Thor asked.

"*Pan and a rakshasa named Birch. Mind-to-mind like we are.*"

"*I see. They cannot hear me. Only you can. We are linked, you and I, and as I said, we have much to discuss.*"

"*What's happening?*" Pan asked.

"*Give me a moment,*" Cam replied to Pan and Birch before cutting off his connection to them. "*Who are you?*" he demanded of the voice, not bothering to hide his rage. "*You aren't Thor.*"

The voice didn't reply at once, seemingly pausing to collect his thoughts. "*I can see why you would be doubtful, but a little over a month ago in my time, I Advanced to Divine. The Realms are no longer a barrier for my thoughts, and I've been trying to reach you ever since. It's only in this moment that I succeeded. I assume it means you've Advanced to Glory. Congratulations.*" Warmth suffused the voice's words.

But Cam remained wary, his fury now at a slow boil. "*Prove you're who you say you are.*"

Thor seemed to sigh. "*At our first meeting, I had to flee from Shimala's sending. I've always regretted that, but Rukh expunged her evil from your mind. You awoke me in the Temple of Gates in Hearth. I battled a Jom-Strafe Crown on your behalf. You were the last of Light Squad to leave my world and return to your own of Salvation. And you have an irritating but understandable habit of wanting to pet my head and scratch behind my ears.*"

Cam didn't reply at once, but his doubts popped like soap bubbles, and his eyes welled. It was true. This was Thor.

The sense of a happy bark came across the connection. "*My time with you grows short,*" Thor said. "*I spoke to—*"

Cam cut him off, not yet ready to believe in the voice. "*How did you even know I was here?*"

"*Rukh and Jessira. They cannot actively touch Mote in any way, and as their agent—I made that choice after the events in the temple—I am similarly limited, but not to the same extent. I can talk to you. I can talk to Saira. I let her know of your situation.*"

"*You can talk to Saira because you're linked to her?*"

"*Exactly. I'm linked to Charity, too.*"

"*And can you actively touch Salvation?*"

A sad shake of Thor's head. "*I cannot. No agents of the Holy Servants not born to Salvation or Mote can do so. It was a promise extracted from them by the Great Rakshasas.*"

A million questions sparked in Cam's mind, but he latched on to what was most consequential. "*You talked to Saira. You let her know we're alive, and then what? What about Charity?*"

Thor seemed to swell with pleasure. "*And then they bring you home. Your friends, Light Squad, have also Advanced. All of them are Crowns, and Saira is a Sage.*"

Cam's mouth dropped. "*Everyone's a Crown? How? It's only been four months.*"

"*It's been over three years since you disappeared.*"

"*Three years?*" Cam slumped. Once again, he'd lost so much time. At this rate, his nieces and nephews would be fully grown by the time he met them. Again came the anger, but Cam shut it off with a flick of his will, full of despondency.

Thor seemed to understand his troubled thoughts. "*Time moves strangely between the Realms. Rukh and Jessira spoke to me about it. As a Realm travels further toward or away from Devesh, how time is experienced in relation to other Realms also changes. Because of that cursed anchor line, Hearth was falling away from Devesh, but now that it's closed…*" He shrugged. "*Regardless, it has been over three years for me and your friends.*"

"*And they've all become Crowns?*" Cam's Advancing to Glory didn't seem so impressive now. However, rather than linger on his envy, he quashed it. Life wasn't a race, and there was a more important issue at hand. "*Can you coordinate between me and Saira?*" His heart thudded faster. "*Or me and Charity?*" That would go a long way toward planning out what to do once he and the others jailbreaked the prison.

"*I can, but you won't be able to speak to anyone but Charity. You're only linked to her."*

Cam swallowed heavily, not the least bit disappointed. Today had been a day of miracles, and he imagined Charity standing in sunlight. The image reminded him of how much he missed her, how much he missed all of Light Squad. It was a large part of why he'd worked and worked and worked at Advancing in this hellish world. He wanted to get back to those he loved.

"Your friends are coming for you," Thor continued. *"I'm learning to open an anchor line between Salvation and Hearth, and from Hearth to wherever you deem the safest. It can only exist in one direction, though. You'll still have to journey to the Locus to get home. Give me a couple of months at most, and I'll see it done."*

Cam's heart pounded and his eyes watered as the enormity of what was happening landed on him. His friends were coming for him and Pan. *"We're escaping the prison today. This very evening. We can't stay here. Everything about this place is a poison. The longer we remain, the less likely we'll have enough strength and stamina to actually break free. We can meet the others under the Blood Sea. In a place called Petala, the Hollow Land."* He went on to explain what he and Pan had experienced over the past four months and the nature of their situation.

"I can sense what you mean." Thor sighed. *"I'm so sorry you and Pan have had to endure so much torment. It won't be much longer. I promise. I'll let Light Squad know of your situation. And I'll be in touch from this point on."*

Cam's eyes watered again, touched anew at having friends who'd risk Hell to retrieve him. *"Thank you, Thor. Thank Charity and Light Squad. Tell them I miss them. Tell them I love them."*

As soon as Cam shared a final few words with Thor, he reached out to Pan and Birch and explained what he'd learned. Their reactions were as excited as Cam's own, at least in Pan's case. Birch was understandably more muted. He didn't know Thor or anyone from Light Squad.

Afterward, Cam tested his ability to create the Ephemeral key needed to open his cell door. It was easy enough, although both Pan and Birch still struggled with it, failing nine times out of ten. Cam figured his own success was because of all the practicing he'd undergone back in Hearth when forging the key for the Temple of Gates.

Following that came hours spent Enhancing until Tulip arrived with his evening meal. Directly following supper, he, Pan, and Birch planned on escaping, reckoning it was best to try it at night, when the prison was at its quietest and everyone was asleep. Besides which, while Murder Day was still many months away, what if the rakshasas decided to move the date forward for some reason?

"You seem happier than usual," Tulip mentioned when Cam returned his bowl and tankard. She peered closely at him through the grate.

He had hoped that Tulip would have succeeded at learning to visualize Ephemera and Imbibe it, but a lifelong inculcation into the ways of Mote corralled her attempts, and Cam couldn't break down those teachings in just a few short months. It left him sad whenever he spoke to her, about how hard she worked at trying to earn his trust and never knowing that he saw through her overly happy and kind demeanor and was well aware of her deception and how it limited her.

"Just happy for the extra food," Cam said in response to Tulip's comment.

She viewed him a moment longer, focusing on his eyes, staring enough for Cam to curse under his breath. Had he forgotten to camouflage his Glory-Haunted sclerae? He didn't think so, but if he had, maybe Tulip had noticed. Was that why she was fixing her sights on him?

Eventually, Tulip nodded acceptance. "I'm glad to be of help." She clanged shut the iron grate and moved on.

Cam exhaled heavily. Whether Tulip saw anything or not, that didn't change his situation any. He, Pan, and Birch were getting gone as soon as Kiwi and Sprite arrived. And while he waited on them, Cam practiced his use of Ephemera, figuring it best to familiarize himself as best he could with his skills as a Glory.

An hour later, Kiwi and Sprite arrived, flittering around and chirping with excitement when Cam told them it was time to leave.

"We're really going?" Kiwi tweeted, barely calming enough to land on Cam's shoulder. "Truly? You're not lying?"

"We're really going," Cam confirmed. "Truly. I'm not lying."

Sprite alighted on his opposite shoulder. "We'll see the sun and fly in warmth and goodness?"

"Soon," Cam said, stroking the yellow bird's soft chest feathers. "Someday we will." He accepted an affectionate nibble of his earlobe, and when Kiwi chirruped, Cam offered him the same attention. He gave them both a final stroke before moving to the door. "Make sure the hallway is clear."

Kiwi gave a cheep as both he and Sprite launched themselves through the open grate, wings softly clapping as they flew away. Seconds later, they reappeared. "It's clear," Kiwi said.

Cam controlled a shiver of exhilaration. Their escape was about to happen. *I'm opening the cell,* he sent to Pan and Birch. *See you soon.*

"See you soon," they both sent back.

Cam formed a True Bond and created an Ephemeral key. An instant later, he had his cell door open, and he stared outward, heart racing, full of disbelief. *Was this actually happening?* After so many hopeless months, it seemed impossible. But there it was. The cell door was open, and there was nothing stopping him from exiting.

Nothing at all.

Cam took halting steps forward, pacing into the hall, pausing just past the threshold. And for the first time in months, he viewed something other than his cell. It was a dimly lit passage, stone-hewn and roughly shaped, but for him, it seemed like it might lead to paradise… or salvation.

But he'd never get there standing around like an empty-headed fool.

Cam got moving, stumbling on weak legs to Pan's cell. Seconds later, he had it open, and he viewed his best friend.

Pan had lost weight. He was no longer plump, and his fur was ragged with many bald patches. But he was still Pan, grinning in that cute way of his.

Viewing his best friend in any Realm, for the first time in months, Cam's underlying anger went to sleep. He reached for Pan, hugging him tight, his vision blurred with tears. "It's good to see you, brother."

"It's good to see you, too." Pan hugged him back, and for Cam, it was the best embrace ever.

"Does someone plan on letting me out?"

Cam smiled, breaking away from Pan. "What do you say about freeing our favorite, old-headed rakshasa?"

"We probably should. After all, he did promise me some bamboo."

They moved down the hallway, following Kiwi and Sprite, and several turns later, they arrived at Birch's cell. His door remained closed, but moments later, that was no longer the case, and Cam got his first look at the rakshasa who had become their friend.

Birch stood before them, gaunt, his ribs evident and his limbs as lean as twigs. He hunched over with a significant curvature to his back, and while his leonine features remained handsome, his fur was even patchier than Pan's. He cracked a smile, gazing at them with eyes clouded by cataracts. "Hello, boys."

"Hello, Birch." Cam reached for the rakshasa, hugging him close.

He stepped aside, allowing Pan to do the same, but they didn't have time for any further celebrating. Seconds later, they were marching through the corridor, guided by the lovebirds, the only ones who knew the way out of the prison.

Kiwi would occasionally flit back, chirping at them to go faster. "Someone might see us," he would say.

Cam certainly wanted to do as Kiwi said, and while his mind was willing, his body wasn't. He was weak. His legs occasionally trembled, and glancing over at Pan and Birch, he noted how they were struggling the same as him, possibly worse in the case of the rakshasa.

Nonetheless, they did their best to hurry along the empty corridors, Cam praying all the while that the hallways would remain unoccupied, and for once, luck was with them. No one was about to confront them.

Creeping minutes later, they reached a place where the corridor opened out onto a large atrium. Kiwi circled the chamber, playing lookout while Sprite stood perched on Cam's shoulder.

"Where's the supply room?" Cam asked the yellow lovebird. They needed fresh clothing, boots, food, and a number of other items if they figured on escaping the prison and surviving Petala.

"A few hallways past the atrium." Sprite indicated the open space. "We have to be swift. Someone might wander through at any time."

"We understand," Birch said. "This late in the game, we won't fail. Lead on."

28

The way across the empty atrium proved quick, and the space was blessedly silent except for the slapping of their hustling footsteps. No one was around to delay them, and they soon crossed the chamber and were rushing through an empty corridor. But none of them dared say a word since they still had a ways to go, and this area might be the busiest part of the prison. All it would take was a single individual to step out of one the various doors lining the hall and they'd be done.

But luck remained with them.

They raced on, took a left turn, then a right, sprinted straight ahead.

"Almost there," Sprite trilled from a dozen yards ahead. "Just a few more turns."

Cam glanced over. Birch was panting heavily now. So was he. Same with Pan, but not quite as much as the old rakshasa. Birch caught his gaze, nodding acknowledgement that he could keep up. Cam nodded back, facing forward. He'd have to trust that Birch wasn't lying. If the rakshasa was already reaching his limits, there wasn't much chance he'd make it out of here.

Both lovebirds halted before a door, wings clapping, keeping them suspended in the air.

"In here," Sprite said. "Quick."

Cam didn't have to be told twice. He dropped to his knees, lungs heaving, heart hammering. He shoved down awareness of the weakness urging him to rest. He'd lay down when it was time to take the final sleep.

Instead, he latched his concentration on the lock, piecing it together until he grasped the shape of the key. It required elements of fire and air mixed with absences filled by his will through telepathy. Simplicity itself. He got the door open, hustled through, and quietly shut it once everyone was inside. Only then did he exhale in relief, taking stock of their location.

They'd crowded into a small room and were pressed against one another. A dim lantern provided illumination enough for Cam to see the clothes, blankets, and robes haphazardly stacked on the shelves while cast on the floor were tarps, ropes, and even boots of various sizes.

They quickly exchanged the rags of their clothing for anything that fit them better. Feet were squeezed into whatever boots were at hand. Then they geared up, rolling blankets into tarps and tying them off.

"Where to now?" Cam asked Sprite.

"The kitchen. We need food. We can steal some there. This late, no one should be around."

Cam nodded, creeping open the door and peering in both directions. Empty still. "Let's go."

Kiwi and Sprite flitted past his head, and Cam darted after them with Pan and Birch following directly on his heels. Just a final stop in the kitchen, and if they had any kind of ongoing good luck, they'd be gone from this wretched place within the hour.

Now that they had clothing indistinguishable from the rest of the rakshasas, their travel slowed some, swift still but no longer at their previous breakneck pace. Nonetheless, they made their way hastily to the kitchen. A few others were about as they approached their destination, but they had their own tasks to perform, and Cam's anonymous-appearing group was left alone.

They entered the kitchen, a broad space with plenty of shelving and counters overflowing with pots, pans, and skillets and a large set of cookware set next to one another over a stove. From within them quietly bubbled the mush that Cam had long since grown tired of eating.

But his attention focused on who shared the kitchen with them: the serpent-headed warden and Tulip, who shifted about, a guilt-ridden expression on her face. Cam sighed in disappointment. He wasn't surprised by either of them being here, but he wished it might have been otherwise.

"Well, isn't this an interesting sight?" the warden began. "Three prisoners, including the great Birch Drang."

Cam briefly scanned about. Two doors stood on opposite corners of the kitchen area, the only means to enter. Both were closed, and he couldn't sense anyone else close at hand. Good enough.

The warden continued to grin, seemingly waiting for their reactions, likely expecting terror. Cam rolled his eyes in reaction to her overly dramatic countenance, trying to figure what they should do with her and Tulip.

"We can't let her live," Birch said.

Before Cam could stop him, the rakshasa extended his Nullity and crushed the warden's skull. Even as she fell and Cam stared in astonishment, Birch set the warden's body alight, burning it to ashes within seconds.

Cam watched in dumbfounded fury, turning his attention to Birch for answers.

The rakshasa shrugged. *"It had to be done. You know it to be true."*

Cam sighed, the anger departing as he recognized that Birch was right. He hated what Mote wanted to make of him: a killer. "Gather what we need," Cam ordered before turning his attention to Tulip, who gaped at him. "You should have listened when I taught you about Ephemera and Devesh." He let go of the control he had over his sclerae, allowing his true Awareness to shine through.

Tulip gasped. "You're a sovereign."

Cam recognized the term. It was given to those who achieved the rank of Glory in Coruscant's legions. He shook his head at Tulip. "I'm no sovereign. I'm an Ephemeral Master. A Glory from Salvation."

Her voice went meek. "Will you kill me then?"

"Must we?" Pan asked, strain in his voice.

Cam didn't want to.

"I can learn what you taught me," Tulip said, desperate. "I'll practice every day. Please."

It was the please that stilled Cam's actions. He couldn't kill Tulip. No matter how she might have sought to deceive them, he liked her too much. "Will you tell anyone what happened here?" He awaited her answer, viewing her through the woven world and reading her emotions.

Tulip licked her lips, terrified. "I have to, but if I'm unconscious, I can use that to save myself."

"You might be imprisoned anyway," Birch warned.

Tulip sighed, shoulders slumping. "It would still be better than death."

Cam nodded. "So be it."

"Wait." Tulip held up a hand, a different type of desperation on her face, this one containing hope. "Is it real? Ephemera. Devesh. Salvation. Is any of it true?"

Cam's tight-lipped annoyance with her relaxed. "It is. Learn what we taught, and someday, you might know it." Before she could respond, Cam flexed his will, and Tulip's eyes rolled. She fell to the ground, but Pan caught her just before she hit, easing her the rest of the way.

Cam viewed her in momentary regret, shaking his head. "Let's get what we need and go."

They gathered whatever food they could carry in their hastily constructed sacks, and Cam gave a final regretful glance back at Tulip before they headed out. Once again, it was Kiwi and Sprite leading the way while Cam, Pan, and Birch rushed after them, hunched over from their gear.

To reach the tunnel leading to Petala, they would first have to ascend higher into the city and pass through more populated areas. Within several floors, brighter illumination lit the way and the walls of the corridors became finer, formed of smooth stucco, tan and undecorated. Windows appeared with views opening into the city as well as the Blood Sea and its littering strands of pus. A palace rose in the distance, white and gold with rose tiles and slender towers.

"Lord Coruscant's home when he visits from the mainland," Birch explained, catching Cam when he gazed on the building. "The Palace of Beautiful Leaves—*Rone Orn Sion* in the old tongue. It's a copy of his actual home."

On they went, ascending closed stairwells and reaching an area where Birch began leading the way. He was more familiar with this part of the city than Sprite or Kiwi, and he hustled them down various hallways where they bowed low to rakshasas who were clearly of importance.

They reached a concourse a hundred yards wide, and from it branched a number of hallways with people of all types: rakshasas with the bodies of a goat and the heads of a jackal, others who slithered like snakes and yet had the torsos and arms of an ape. Some who were nearly human in appearance but had canines drooping down to their chins and lashing tails.

Cam held off from gawking as Birch swiftly led them through the area. The rakshasa took a corridor on the far side where they ascended a broad, open staircase and took an immediate left turn. The noises from the concourse silenced, replaced by the heavy panting of their breathing. Higher and higher they ascended, enough for Cam to feel the burn in his thighs, and he wondered how much longer it would take.

A left turn, and they paused, letting a large cluster of rakshasas pass by. The other group viewed them with mild curiosity, one of them muttering about unkempt servants. But as soon as they were gone, Birch hurried them onward, up flights of stairs and down hallways. They encountered more rakshasas—finely dressed and who barely glanced their way—but they never slowed, halting finally when they reached a locked steel door at the end of an empty corridor.

Birch indicated the lock, and Cam quickly keyed it open. Twisting the handle, they entered a closed stairwell.

"This should take us all the way down to the tunnel," Birch said. "There will be a small contingent of guards there. We might have to kill some of them."

Cam grimaced. They had already killed the warden, and in general, he didn't much like the notion of murdering those who were only doing their jobs. But what other option did they have?

Their small group took the empty stairwell and began what felt like an endless descent, occasionally passing closed doors and never speaking during their flight, not even Kiwi and Sprite, who had alighted on Cam's shoulders, serious as the rest of them. No one talked, and the only sounds were the slapping of their boots and their ongoing panting.

The stairwell ended at a tunnel-like area with a ceiling sheathed in a ring of black stones. Stepping through the portal-like structure, Cam stumbled, momentarily nauseated and cold.

"It's a static anchor line," Birch said. "It took us miles deeper underground."

Cam nodded acknowledgement, not sure of such a thing as a static anchor line even as he shook off the strange sensation of passing through it. They continued on their way, reaching another locked door, which Cam opened without any trouble. But upon stepping through, he paused at the threshold.

Before him extended a vast space illuminated by a plethora of lights. It had to be several miles wide and even longer with a ceiling lost in a haze that Cam realized was a cloud. His wonder only increased as he viewed the crops filling the area: corn, wheat, and rice growing on terraced paddies. A number of rakshasas walked the fields, inspecting the plants, pruning, and in some cases, harvesting.

"If anyone stops us, let me do the talking," Birch said, leading them into the gigantic chamber.

"Don't steal from here," Kiwi warned with a nervous chirp. "All grown food belongs to Lord Coruscant. If you steal any, your hand gets cut off."

They managed to get halfway across the room before someone finally stopped them, a horse-headed rakshasa with the body of a man. Powerfully built, he towered over them. "I am Foreman Jobe. Who are you? You aren't farmers."

Birch bowed. "We are servants from the kitchens, my lord. Some incompetents failed to bring the guards their food for the day. We are delivering it to them."

"I didn't hear about this," the rakshasa said. "Why didn't your foreman send word?"

"There was no time," Birch replied. "By the time the disaster was discovered, the foreman thought it best to simply send us with the supplies and the word."

The rakshasa rubbed his chin. "I see." Making a decision, he stepped aside. "This is most inappropriate. I will have words with your foreman. See to your tasks, and then come back to me." He smiled, thin and full of malice. "You will be lashed for the failure of your leadership."

Birch feigned a shudder before nodding. "Yes, sir."

They pressed on, and once they were beyond the horse-headed rakshasa, Cam asked about the foreman's final comments.

"He gave us hope that we could see about our duties without trouble."

Cam could figure out the rest. "And stole it away at the end. He hopes to create a seed of Nullity."

"And use that core to Advance," Birch finished. "Come on."

No one else stopped them, and they exited the cavernous space, entering a tall, rounded corridor formed of gray stone where several lanterns hung from the walls, emitting a dim light. A dank odor permeated the air, and the slow plinking of water from somewhere up ahead was the only sound.

The hallway ended, opening into a massive area that was smaller than the one with the crops but vast nevertheless. There, brighter lanterns and chandeliers illuminated the space, and a pair of curving corridors immediately branched off to the right and left before curling out of view. The dank odor was even worse here, and deeper in, on the far side of the cavernous room, a number of buildings clustered in front of a stone wall, blank-faced except for an inset steel door with a wheel. Dripping water manifested there, in front of what Cam knew to be the prison's exit and the tunnel leading to Petala.

Those were Cam's fleeting impressions, but the bulk of his attention was on the dead rakshasas, ten of them, armed and armored and resting in pools of their own blood. Their bodies lay around an old man, rotund but somehow frail in appearance, of light complexion, and with blue-gray irises. He stood centered amongst the carnage, wearing an expression of placid unconcern, but what was most striking were his sclerae. They were the colorless but rainbow-sparkling hues of a crystal. No, of a diamond. It was a color Cam had never before seen, but he recognized what it meant. This man was a Divine vastly more powerful than anyone he had ever met other than Rukh and Jessira.

"Shit," Birch muttered. "We're doomed."

The old man frowned at the leonine rakshasa. "You are known to me, Birch Drang. Watch your coarse tongue." He next addressed Cam. "You don't have much time. The next contingent of guards will be here soon. Get through the door leading into the tunnels."

Cam had no notion about who this old man might be, but if he was willing to help them get free, then so be it. However, curiosity locked him in place. "Who are you?"

"He is Velparn," Birch said. "One of the four Divines who rule under Lord Coruscant. And why he is assisting us is a question I'd love to have answered."

The old man smiled at Birch without cheer or warmth, and the heaviness of his Divine aura pressed upon them. Cam struggled to remain upright. Then it was over. "We all have our disappointments. Now, be swift. Exit this place before the next contingent of guards arrive."

Cam had no idea why the Divine was aiding them, but he also didn't care. Nor did he have time to figure it out. He nodded to the old man as he rushed past, the others following close behind. Hunkering down at the door, he knelt in the puddle, which stank like his yellow bile, and examined the lock. This one would require a more devious key, a mix of the elements, will, and even motion through telekinesis. Concentrating close, Cam worked to decipher what was required.

Minutes might have sped by, and from the branched hallways came the sounds of armor-glad guards approaching. Cam paid them no mind. The key was their only hope.

A voice, that of Velparn, whispered close at hand. "You are nearly out of time, and I can aid you no further."

Cam glanced back, unsurprised to find that the old man had disappeared. He returned his attention to the lock.

"Hurry," Pan urged. The guards were nearly upon them.

Cam disregarded the distractions and focused on the lock. He frowned in concentration, seeing the solution, and… there! He had it. With a breathy exhalation, he applied the key. Tumblers clicked into place, sounding loud in the silent room, and he winced at the sudden noise. Hopefully, the guards didn't hear any of it. Cam stood and spun the wheel. Large steel bolts retracted out of the jamb and into the door itself.

Yanking hard, Cam heaved the heavy door open. He urged the others inside. "Come on."

Pan and Birch rushed past with Kiwi and Sprite winging overhead. Cam followed right after them, just as the first of the guards appeared. They weren't looking his way. Instead, their alarm was focused on the dead guards.

Cam carefully closed the door. The light inside the passageway shuttered to a thin line and then utter darkness. Silence, too. He keyed the lock shut, and the quiet was briefly broken by the lovely sound of steel bolts hissing back into the jamb.

Only then did he exhale, laughing in ragged relief. They'd made it.

29

"I can't believe it worked," Pan said, standing close by in the tunnel's utter darkness.

"Me, neither," Birch replied, creating a light, which relieved the painful darkness bearing down on them.

Cam silently agreed with his friends, inhaling deep and grateful for the illumination. After the months spent in the grinding blackness of his cell, in this moment of joyous freedom, he felt like he could float away. Another part of him, though, wanted to huddle down and cry in relief. He shoved aside both notions. "Everyone alright?" he asked.

"Fine as a frog's hair," Pan replied with a warm chuckle.

Cam laughed in reply, appreciating one of his favorite sayings.

"We better hurry," Birch said. "The guards will send for someone to open the door. We must be well down the tunnel by then. Even better if we're out of it and within Petala."

The two lovebirds landed on Cam's shoulders, and Kiwi cheeped, sounding agreement to Birch's suggestion.

"Let's go then," Cam said.

He led them into the dark tunnel, which stretched out before them, seemingly endless and always descending at a shallow angle. No one was ready to talk, and the travel passed in silence. Cam glanced at Birch, who walked at his side. The rakshasa's earlier weakness seemed abated some, and he paced along with his shoulders squared, like their escape from the prison had given him fresh strength.

Cam shared some of that feeling, and Pan must have, too, since they were able to journey without pause, eating now and then on the go and sipping from canteens full of fresh water, which tasted clean and pure. The whole while of their journey through the tunnel, Cam kept an ear and his Ephemeral senses questing for anyone who might be coming after them. Occasionally, he would even hold a True Bond and use Oversight to gain further awareness.

So far, no one. *Perfect. Just let it continue.* While their group consisted of three Glories and the guards were said to be Novices, matters weren't quite so simple. Cam's group was still weak from their lack of food and the debilitating weakness inspired by the prison cells themselves. A fight against enough Novices would still do them in.

Thankfully, no one trailed after them. Either the rakshasas didn't care that they'd escaped, or it was taking them a good long time to find someone who could open the door leading to the Hollow Land. Whatever the reason, it was fine by Cam. The longer their lead, the better.

The hours sped by, and Cam found his mind drifting to what faced them in Petala. Birch hadn't been able to explain the Hollow Land all too well. It was supposed to be a world beneath the Blood Sea but what was the light source, this waxing and waning sun? How did plants grow? What kind of animals would they find? The kaijus, sure, but even those were a mystery. Birch only had limited information on the topic.

"We're nearing the end of the tunnel," Birch said, breaking into Cam's musings. The rakshasa gestured ahead, past his casted illumination and to where the tunnel brightened.

As a group, they edged toward the light, pausing at a doorway filled by a filmy layer that impeded their progress. It shimmered like a skin of water and gave them no sense of what lay on the other side.

"What is this?" Cam asked.

"The entrance to Petala," Birch unhelpfully explained.

Cam frowned at the rakshasa in reproach. He could have figured that out on his own. "I mean what do we do now? Do we just step through?"

Birch made to answer, but he must have changed his mind, clearing his throat. "I don't know, but I imagine so?"

Cam narrowed his eyes at Birch. "Are you telling me or asking me?

Birch grinned. "Both. And if you don't survive the journey, I'll be sure to tell Charity of your heroic end."

Cam sighed. Birch wasn't being particularly useful, but they also couldn't simply stand around the entrance to Petala and pick their noses. "I'm going through." He glanced at Kiwi and Sprite. "You two wait here."

He paced forward and pressed a finger against the shimmering film. It bent before the pressure he exerted, and he pushed harder. The film slowly gave way until his hand abruptly punched through, feeling like it was momentarily covered in a soapy layer. Then the sensation gave way to warmth. He wiggled his fingers, but the best he could make out was a vague motion.

Frowning, and seeing no other option, Cam took a single, wary step forward. He was through, but his equilibrium abruptly abandoned him. Up and down made no sense, no longer fixed in place. Gravity shifted, and he flailed about in a dizzied tumble, slamming into what had been the tunnel's ceiling.

He lay there, gasping. Vertigo held him still, and he closed his eyes from the nausea-inducing sensation.

"What happened?" Pan asked from the other side of the filmy barrier, sounding like he was speaking from the ceiling.

Not able to talk, Cam sent his reply. *"Stay where you are. Hold on."*

Minutes passed with him lying on the ground that had been the ceiling. But eventually, he felt able to view the world. Only then did he open his eyes, careful and cautious, levering himself upright in stages, making sure his disorientation was ended. He grunted, satisfied that he was fine and explained to the others about gravity's unexpected shift. He had no idea why it had occurred or the cause, and now wasn't the time to figure out the answer. *"Be careful. Don't go too fast."*

The others grumbled confused agreement but promised to do as he advised. Cam made his way further down the tunnel in order to give them room. He waited there, watching for what would happen.

Pan was the first one through. He spun and toppled just as Cam imagined he must have, thrashing about before plowing into the ceiling, which was now the ground. He lay there, gasping.

"It's something, isn't it?" Cam asked.

Pan groaned in reply. "Why is this world so wrong?"

Cam chuckled. If Pan could joke, it meant he wasn't injured. He waited then on Birch, who flailed ineffectually before slamming down onto the floor next to Pan.

After ensuring the old-headed rakshasa wasn't injured, Cam addressed him. "Did any of your stories tell you about this?" he asked.

Birch kept his eyes closed. "Of course they did. This isn't my first time in Petala. Now, if you don't mind, I think I'll lie here and never move from this spot."

The lovebirds flew through the barrier, having no trouble, but Cam still eyed them a moment.

"We're well," Kiwi chirped. "Where are we?"

"Petala," Birch said, slowly rising to his feet.

Even as the others continued to discuss the meaning of gravity's change, Cam wandered forward. He ascended a steep, gravel-strewn slope, discovering himself to be standing on a high-mountain plateau. He gasped over what he saw.

Petala was an entirely new world, lit from above by a hazy powdered golden light that wasn't quite like the sun. To his right marched a rugged chain of low-lying mountains, their granite shoulders clothed in conifer forests while to his left, a lazy river snaked through swampy valleys. Birds of every kind and what appeared to be flying reptiles—their wings as wide as sails—floated on muggy winds. The raucous cries of territorial animals shrieking their claims and fighting amongst themselves rang out from mist and heavy humidity. And everywhere extended a thick forest, its extent lost in the hazy distance.

It was too much to observe, and Cam wanted to retreat into the dark tunnel and its comforting enclosure. The months in the cell had shrunk his horizons, but he couldn't have moved even if he wanted. The Ephemera roiling through Petala, the Hollow Land, kept him in place. It was so much stronger than the prison, a flood compared to that tiny trickle. Still far, far less than Salvation or Hearth, but for now, it was enough.

Cam closed his eyes and breathed in the glory of being alive, of being free. They'd done it. They'd overcome their incarceration and came to this place where Ephemera was thick enough to feel like the blessing of sunshine. He bathed in it, luxuriating. Cam didn't even mind the roiling sense of Nullity underlying it all either, balanced out as it was by Ephemera. In this regard, Birch had been wrong.

At some point, the others arrived, and they, too, held still, frozen by Petala's tableau as well as Ephemera's lushness.

Birch broke the quiet, pointing to faraway waters the size of an inland sea, Lake Petala. It was even larger than Lake Nexus, and centered within it was a dune-covered island, appearing as vast as a continent. A lazy river many miles to their left appeared to lead in the direction of the lake.

"Our destination," Birch said. "The island is where we'll find the Locus."

Cam nodded. It was going to be a long, hard slog, but every step forward was a step toward their ultimate freedom.

They hiked all day with Cam leading the way since he had the most experience in journeying through forests and rough terrain—skills he'd gained in Traverse as a boy hunting with his father. They followed a broad animal trail, heading toward the river whenever possible, and trekking through an unfamiliar jungle of tall trees that Cam couldn't name. Their upper canopies were broad like mushrooms and set upon trunks that appeared stilt-like in comparison but were actually wide enough for a wagon to pass through. Downward lay a thick understory, which stole away any last light, shrouding the leaf- and detritus-strewn forest floor in a perpetual gloom and mugginess.

Cam wiped sweat that dripped down his neck. Even as a Glory, he couldn't quite ignore the humidity here, which was far worse than anything he'd ever experienced in Nexus.

Thankfully, there were also occasional breaks in the canopy where the shadowed murk and mugginess lifted. In those areas, they could more easily sight the strange golden glow in the sky—clearly the Hollow Land's sun. It remained undimmed for the many initial hours of their travel before eventually fading away to nothing. Even then a strange silvery-rose light radiated from nearly the exact same spot, duller and possibly meant to resemble a moon. There were no stars, though.

With the loss of illumination, they halted since using Ephemera to light their way seemed like a terrible idea. Plus, there were animals about, and even someone new to journeying through a jungle could have sensed their ill intentions. Creatures like the four-eyed deer that Birch had brought down in the very afternoon of their arrival—or at least that's what the antlered animal had most resembled. From up ahead on the trail, the deer had sighted them and rather than run away, it had charged.

Only the rakshasa's quick reaction had saved Pan from a goring. Hopefully, that kind of aggression wouldn't be the norm with every beast they encountered, but whatever the case, for now, Cam didn't want to challenge their good fortune. He wanted them through this jungle with no one the wiser.

They made camp in a small clearing barely more than three paces in diameter, and since the deer required cooking, Cam had them light a bright fire, reckoning it would drive away any of the nearby animals who might come around, sniffing blood and searing flesh. He also figured they must have long since outstripped anyone from the prison, so there was likely no harm from that front either.

As the deer continued to smoke over the flames—sizzling and popping, cooking quicker than was natural due to a skill gifted to Cam by Rukh and Jessira—he stared into the dark, seated next to Pan and figuring on staying up with his friend who had first watch. Birch lay in his rolls, having gorged his fill while the lovebirds roosted on the ground, not daring the jungle.

Pan nibbled on some meat. He preferred bamboo and root vegetables, but in this case, beggars couldn't be choosers. Besides which, the meat was filling, not just after the prison's thin gruel, but also in the way Birch had mentioned. Cam felt some aspect of the sustenance going to various parts of his body, healing him, filling out his gaunt form. A greater sense of strength filled him, and at one point, a rancid film had even coated his skin—probable impurities from the prison— which he'd burned off with a simple use of Spirairia.

Cam hadn't been the only one to experience such a drastic improvement. All of them had, but it was Birch who had gained the greatest benefit from eating the deer. A fresh spark filled the old-headed rakshasa's eyes, his color had improved, and his patchy fur didn't seem quite so ratty.

"Do you think the deer could have been on the Way into Divinity?" Pan asked. "I know its eyes were normal, but…"

"The deer wasn't Awakened," Kiwi said. "Sprite and I can tell these things. We will warn you when they are."

It was comforting to know the birds could help them in that way. A fresh notion occurred to Cam. "How many of the creatures in Petala are actually rakshasas? Are they all rakshasas?"

Pan shrugged. "You could ask the same about the animals and beasts of Salvation. Are they simply unAwakened rakshasas?"

"They aren't," Birch said, sitting up and having awoken sometime during their conversation. "Only Awakened Beasts can become rakshasas, so don't fear eating the venison on that account. Just remember: not everything that lives is a rakshasa, nor does everything have the potential to Awaken and reason. But your empathy and consideration are worth maintaining."

Cam viewed Birch in surprised speculation. The rakshasa was a lion, a great cat, a hunter of the savanna, and thinking on it, something stirred in the back of Cam's mind. He wondered what it must be like to race across the grassland, running as fast as possible. Just to feel the ground flowing beneath your paws and the wind rushing through your fur. He startled at the odd notion, shoving it aside. "It's odd hearing you talk about empathy when you're a hunter at heart."

"I was and still am a hunter at heart, but that doesn't mean I'll ever eat something that reasons. I'm not a savage."

Cam stared at Birch. "You surprise me sometimes, you know that? Not the savagery part, but about wanting to hold on to empathy."

Birch hesitated in replying. "I had a talk with someone early on in your incarceration. A powerful being, someone with the eyes of a Divine or higher. He entered my mind and spoke of my dreams and what I really want." The rakshasa shook his head. "Sometimes I think I might have imagined the entire thing." He barked laughter. "I mean, how could it be real? Why would someone so powerful bother themselves with a broken-down rakshasa?"

"He must have had his reasons," Pan said, laying a supportive hand on the rakshasa's shoulder. "You're more worthy than you give yourself credit for being."

Birch smiled wanly, staring at the ground. "You're a kind panda-person to say so. I'm going to be sad when you die here in Petala."

Cam chuckled. If Birch could offer up his fatalism, he wasn't feeling too badly. "What was this person's name?"

"Rail Gristle."

Shock tore through Cam. "Rail Gristle?" He wanted to be sure he'd heard correctly.

Birch lifted his head, surprise filling his eyes. "You know him?"

"We think he's—" Cam created a bubble of privacy. "We think he's Rukh." He went on to explain about their time in Hearth.

Awe suffused Birch's features. "You think a Holy Servant talked to me? Advised me?" He breathed deep, grinning in disbelief and wonderment. "One of them thought I was worthy."

Pan grinned at Birch in his cute fashion. "I also say you're worthy, so it must be true."

"But why choose me?" the rakshasa persisted.

"We've discussed philosophy and theology enough to know that Devesh chose all of us," Cam replied.

"That's a facile statement," Birch said. "There are countless beings whose existences are filled with torment and torture. They never feel His love. Where was He for them?"

Cam didn't have a good answer. "I wish I knew why He allows evil to flourish, but I can only tell you what I hope because to believe otherwise means that the Realms are just hellscapes with nothing good anywhere. I have to hope and believe that there is something that holds Him back."

"Maybe it's the Empty One," Pan suggested. "Maybe Devesh is powerful but the Empty One is His counter. They match one another, and it's up to us to determine the course of our lives."

"It's still not much of an explanation for Devesh's inaction," Birch said.

"I suppose not," Cam agreed. "There's never going to be a good explanation for evil and suffering. But like I said, all I can do is act in a way that I know is good and offer service so others don't have to suffer." The sentiment echoed in his heart, right and true, like he'd somehow known it all his life.

"I don't know about that," Birch replied, "but I will promise the two of you something right now. I know I'm weak, but I will never slow you down. I'll defend you to the end, no matter the cost."

Cam put his hand on the rakshasa's shoulder and offered him a smile. "How about we never have to find that out?"

Birch laughed. "I like that even better."

The night waned, and the silvery-rose light gave way to the powdered gold of what passed for the sun in the Hollow Land. Shortly thereafter, Cam got them moving again. They set off, burdened this time by the smoked venison they'd packed away. The weight they all carried was only slightly lessened when they discarded the thin mush they'd brought with them from the prison. There was no reason to carry something that wouldn't hearten and harden their bodies.

All day they hiked, struggling over roots and grasping shrubs as the animal trail thinned. The beasts they'd all sensed prowling around in the dark slunk in and out of view, but for some reason, none of them attacked like the idiotic deer from yesterday. Their small group pressed onward until the light they took to calling the sun gave way to the illumination they decided was a moon.

Following supper, Cam had first watch, and he sat on a stumpy log, staring out at the darkened jungle. He kept his senses alert, but a part of his mind also focused inward on his health. The venison had truly helped him heal, far more than he could have ever expected. His loosened teeth already seemed to fit more firmly in their sockets, and he had energy enough to send Ephemera through his body, healing the prison's lingering poison. In addition, with all their hiking, small muscle tears had formed along with areas where his bones, ligaments, and tendons had weakened. Cam healed them all and flexed his biceps, happy to see a fresh cord of muscle lining his stick-thin arms.

A soft rapping intruded on his work, and he frowned, not knowing what he had heard. He listened close for a few seconds, continued to stare at the jungle, feeling for movement. Nothing. The sound didn't recur, and he eventually shrugged to himself, resuming his healing.

There it was again, and Cam stood this time, moving to the edge of the firelight and searching about. He still couldn't localize the sound, but it happened again, a third time. Cam frowned, tilting his head in confusion when the lovely perfume of honeysuckle and hibiscus mingled in his mind. For an instant, confusion reigned, but then awareness of what was happening had him grinning wide.

"Thor?"

"It is I." Thor spoke into Cam's mind. *"Charity is linked to you now.*

I'll give you time alone."

"Charity?"

"I'm here."

Hearing her voice, smelling her scent, and knowing he and the others weren't alone… Cam had to hold in a sob. Charity sounded like she was crying also, and he found himself wanting to comfort her. *"I survived. So did Pan. Both of us. We Advanced to Glory, and we've even made friends. We're alive and free."*

Joy and astonishment came across their link. *"I can't believe I'm actually talking to you. I missed you so much."*

"I missed you, too."

"It sounds like you didn't just survive, though. It sounds like you thrived, just like in Hearth. Tell me everything."

Cam chuckled and went on to describe his time in Mote. *"The prison wasn't any kind of sunshine or rainbows. It was hell. The air itself was a poison, and our bodies withered. I think in another month, I'd have started to lose my teeth. As it was, I traded the hair on my head for a ratty beard. The worst was the confinement, though. Even with the mindscape, not being able to touch another person, not truly being with them…"* He shuddered.

"You don't have to say anything else." This time it was empathy and caring that surged across the link. That and guilt.

Cam's brow creased upon sensing her emotion. *"What happened? What's got you feeling so guilty?"*

"My father was the one who betrayed you. Maybe it doesn't have anything to do with me, but it feels like it should."

Cam grimaced, his simmering anger roiling. *"I've got words and violence I aim to deliver to your father, but what he did wasn't your fault. So get that notion out of your head."* He shifted the conversation, not feeling up to talking about Charity's guilt or anything else to do with his imprisonment. *"Tell me something else. Thor says you're a Crown?"*

"I am," Charity said with a nod. But she also wasn't apparently yet ready to set aside the discussion about his incarceration. *"We figured out early on that my father must have betrayed you. Sial saw it all. He*

saw my father create a new anchor line for you and Pan, and he saw Weld appear right after that."

Cam snarled, the rage abrupt. "*Weld. That man won't live long when I get back to Salvation.*"

"*I'll help you find him, but for now, we don't know where he went.*"

That wasn't what Cam wanted to hear. "*What do you mean?*" he demanded. "*What happened to him?*"

"*He disappeared on the same day we left the school. No one's seen him since.*"

"*If he's out there, I'll find him.*" Weld Plain had a destiny with a judgment that Cam personally planned on inflicting.

"*He might have to wait,*" Charity said. "*Some of the Sage-Dukes are traitors. My father and Sage-Duchess Thens have both aided the rakshasas. There might be more.*" She paused. "*I truly am sorry for what he did to you.*"

Cam exhaled heavily. Charity's guilt was wearying, but nevertheless, he summoned his patience and sent certainty across the link. "*For the last time, you did nothing wrong. You're blameless.*"

"*It's kind of you to say, but I still feel…*" Charity cut herself off. "*You don't need to hear this. You're the one trapped in Mote. I should be the one offering you emotional support. Not the other way around.*"

Cam agreed in silent irritation but kept his thoughts to himself. "*What happened after Pan and I disappeared?*"

"*My father said Coruscant ripped the anchor line away from his control. He said the Great Rakshasa must have had a spy at the school and blamed Sial for everything that happened, saying once a rakshasa always a rakshasa.*"

"*All of us are rakshasas.*"

"*What?*"

Cam explained what he had learned from Rukh and Jessira.

Shock and awe poured off Charity, and for a moment, she was held speechless. "*I can't believe you actually met the Holy Servants.*"

"*You met them, too. They really were Professors Shade and Grey. And we're also getting sidetracked. What happened to you after we left?*"

"Card was the first one to see through my father's lies. He'd read a lot about anchor lines—about how they're formed and how they're virtually impossible to steal away from the creating Sage."

"Card figured it out?" That was a surprise. Card was smart, but he wasn't cunning. He generally fell prey to ruses when it came to chess or any game of tactics and strategy.

Charity laughed. *"Well, it had me surprised, too, but Card has always been passionate about first principles. He convinced us of what must have happened, so Saira called her mother, who took us to the temple. We Advanced to Glory there, and while we were waiting on Avia to Imbibe Ephemera, Sial contacted us and confirmed what really happened. Afterward, Saira's mother anchor lined us all to the Sinanes, which is where we've been ever since. Then Thor reached us, and you know the rest. A month or so, and we'll be able to rescue you."* The explanation was spoken in a rush, and Charity finally took a breath.

Cam did some rapid calculating. Four months in Mote had been worth a bit more than three years in Salvation. So a few months over there should only work out to a couple of weeks over here. That's when he and Pan would see their friends again. A tingle of excitement coursed down his spine. But there was more to learn. *"What about on Golden itself? What's happening?"*

"We receive regular word," Charity replied *"But things aren't going well. The rakshasas are expanding their boils. Once we've saved you and Pan, we have to get back there. Sial already is there. He won't be coming to Mote. He rejoined Rainen, who was right all along. We need to go on the attack. The battle for Golden is only beginning."*

Cam smiled—not at Rainen being right—but the part about attacking the rakshasas. It was what he had been hoping to hear. No doubt, he and Pan needed to heal from their experiences here in Mote, but the people of Golden needed rescuing, and that would have to come first. A whisper from his conscience pushed him to wonder about what inspired him: the idea of helping others, or killing on their behalf? What kind of person did he want to be? How much did the ever-present anger still inspire him? And was it a rage for justice or vengeance?

"Cam?" Charity sounded strangely unsure of herself.

"Yes?"

"Thor has been able to expand his link, and I can sense how you look. Is this real?"

Cam sighed. *"It's real."*

A feeling of weeping came across the connection. *"I'm so sorry."*

Cam didn't want to talk about his physical infirmities. "*We'll get through it."*

"Are you sure?"

"I'm sure," Cam said, forcing certainty into his voice.

Charity didn't reply at once. *"I missed you."*

Unexpected tears blurred Cam's vision. *"I missed you, too."*

30

A couple of days following his unexpected and wonderful conversation with Charity, Cam found himself sitting on a boulder longingly eyeing his empty plate as Petala's sun slowly brightened. For breakfast, he'd just finished off the last of the fortuitous venison, gorging on it, same as Pan and Birch, all of them having regained much of their lost strength.

Maybe they should have budgeted out the food, but Cam didn't think it was the right approach. They needed to get stronger and they'd needed to do so as fast as possible. No one had disagreed with him, so they'd done what they wanted and eaten their fill at every meal.

And while they were still lean and scruffy, they were also far fitter than before, and if they continued to improve in the ways they had so far, Cam could see them all fully recovered within a few weeks, including Birch, whose spine had straightened some and his cataract-afflicted eyes had cleared.

But this was assuming they got more meat, which was why Cam stared at his empty plate in longing. "We need to hunt," he declared to the rest of the group.

"What about the vegetables?" Pan asked. "Those wild onions from yesterday didn't have as much healthy essence as the venison, but it was better than nothing. Why not harvest instead of hunt?"

Cam flashed Pan a grin. "This is where you need to figure on the power of *and*. We need to harvest *and* hunt. We can do both during today's hike."

Having said his piece, Cam called everyone to their feet, and they set off once again toward the river they'd spied early on, the one leading to Lake Petala. Canoeing down those waters was sure to be a sight faster than this endless trudge.

A plan in place, their small group followed a thin animal trail that bent around towering tree trunks and disappeared now and then in places where heavy thickets and brambles caught at their clothing. It made for slow going, with lots of twists and turns along with rises and falls out of a couple of narrow valleys where a pair of hills pinched together. By late afternoon, Cam reckoned they'd covered not much more than a couple of miles as the crow flew.

As he was mulling how to get them more swiftly to the river, Kiwi chirped in fear. "Something bad is ahead of us," the green lovebird said, indicating a distant clearing.

Cam halted their progress, studying the way ahead with Oversight. The skill didn't extend as far as the clearing, and he grunted in disappointment. "How can you tell something bad is up there?" he asked Kiwi.

"I can smell it."

"And the other birds told us," Sprite added.

Cam viewed the way ahead in worry. "Do you know what it is?

"A monster."

Cam frowned. That wasn't much of an answer.

"What do you want to do?" Birch asked.

Cam glanced at the old rakshasa. For a moment, he considered letting Birch make the decision, but he crushed the desire. Now wasn't the time for wishing and whining. They had to plan and figure what to do.

"We'll get a little closer, Blended. Make it seamless. I don't want anything seeing us." He next addressed the lovebirds. "Fly ahead and scout if you can. We'll be here. You can see us?"

"We can see you through your Blends," Sprite said. "You taught us well."

Kiwi cheeped agreement, and he and Sprite flitted off Cam's shoulders. He anxiously watched as the tiny avians darted through the heavy foliage. They were soon lost to view, and he settled in to wait, his attention clamped on the clearing.

In the watchful silence, Cam took inventory of their weapons. They had walking staffs that they'd fashioned early on during their time in Petala, but otherwise, nothing.

Well, that wasn't true. Their years of training in the mindscape meant that even unarmed, they had weapons at their disposal, just like proper Glories. He nodded to himself, forcing confidence into his thoughts. They could handle whatever monster was ahead. Same with whatever might be lurking in the forest.

While focused on what was ahead, Cam also made sure to keep his senses and Oversight open for anything coming up behind them or along their flanks. He didn't want to be caught with his pants down, staring straight ahead and never noticing some deadly beast stalking them until too late. An instant later, he was heartened to note Pan scanning their rearward surroundings as well. He had been about to make the order but was glad not to have to do so.

Oversight gave him conflicting information. Something large lay in the clearing, but he couldn't tell what it was. Moments later, the lovebirds returned, landing straightaway on his shoulders. Kiwi waddled over to his ear. "It's a monster, just like the other birds said."

That still didn't tell him much. "What kind of monster?"

"A giant. He's much taller than you."

"You know it's a he?" Birch asked.

Sprite nodded his head, an expression he'd picked up over the months. "We saw his bits and pieces."

"They were more like a log and boulders," Kiwi added.

Cam struggled not to laugh at the description of the monster's private parts. "What about the creature? What's it look like? Any weaknesses? Strengths?"

"He's strong," Sprite said. "His arms and legs are thick. Covered in white fur. His hair is braided, and he has a nest of horns on his head and sharp growths on his elbows, knees, and at the end of his tail. Like daggers."

Cam blinked in surprise. That was surprisingly helpful. "Any weapons?"

Kiwi chimed in. "I don't think he's smart enough to use one. He seems stupid. The whole time we watched, all he did was pick his nose."

"Kiwi is correct," Sprite said. "Flies buzzed around his mouth, and he moved his lips like a cow."

"You mean like a cow chewing his cud?" Pan mimicked what he was talking about.

Sprite chirped agreement.

Cam stroked his chin. "We have a creature who's taller than any of us. He's strong, and we'll assume fast, but likely stupid."

"His fur might have an undercoat," Birch said, appearing contemplative. "He might not be easy to cut or injure. There's something about the description, though…"

Cam waited for Birch to finish his thought, but the rakshasa remained lost in thought.

"Do we want this fight?" Pan asked. "What if this creature is Awakened?"

Cam hadn't considered that. All he'd been thinking about was how to kill the monster. Leaving the creature to his own devices hadn't occurred to him.

Kiwi chirped. "His eyes are yellow like an Adept's."

Meaning he *was* Awakened. This fight was unnecessary and wrong. Cam prepared to order them to circle the clearing.

"He also had a carcass with him," Sprite said. "A fresh kill. Like a bigger version of the deer you were eating."

Cam hesitated. "We could really use that food."

"I don't want to kill something Awakened just for food," Pan said.

"Neither do I," Cam said, "but—"

"It's a kaiju," Birch interrupted, sounding excited. "I knew the love-birds' description sounded familiar. That's how I was told they appear: white-furred, powerful, and many-horned. They can walk and run both upright and on all fours. This one must be young to be so small. He'll still be vicious and hard. If he sees or catches wind of us, he'll attack. That's their way. Kaijus are extremely territorial, even amongst their own kind."

Cam settled back on his heels, figuring on their next best step. The presence of whatever the kaiju had killed meant the fight was back on. True, they could still circle the clearing and avoid the creature, but he really wanted that food. And if kaijus really were nothing but vicious monsters, then they weren't really killing anything sentient. Or at least that's what Cam told himself, even as he figured on a way to make the attack less contemptible.

Something of his intentions must have shone through, because Birch cautioned him. "He'll fight well above his Advancement. He might only be an Adept, but he'll still be a challenge for the three of us, even as Glories."

"We'll best that challenge," Cam replied.

Cam crouched low, just inside the treeline. Birch was to his right and Pan to his left, and all three of them were Blended hard. The love-birds roosted in a nearby tree. No other animals were close at hand. It seemed possible that the presence of the kaiju had driven them away. Regardless, for now the birds seemed safe enough, and the meadow that held their target was quiet. Nothing moved or stirred, not even the wind, or even the kaiju, who lay slumped over and unmoving, eyes open, mouth gaping, and drool collecting on his chin. Cam only knew the beast was alive by the steady rise and fall of his chest.

And the lovebirds were correct. The kaiju was most definitely a male.

Cam shook his head at the beast's protruding manliness. Wouldn't it get in the way when he fought, swinging around like it was bound to do? It was also an obvious vulnerability and the only obvious one that Cam could spot. The creature was well muscled but sleek, appearing capable of explosive movements as well as great power. Upswept fangs like tusks curled from his lower jaw and his hands ended in claws longer than a bear's. Add in his barbed tail, and who knew what other powers he might have.

This wasn't looking to be an easy fight, and Cam wondered again if they really needed to battle the kaiju to begin with. The creature hadn't noticed them. Maybe they should just skirt this clearing and leave the creature alone. In most any other circumstance, Cam might have done exactly that, but the carcass of the dead deer lying next to the kaiju arrested that notion. He wanted what the beast had slain. It left his mouth watering just thinking of how far the meat would go to restore his fallen health.

"What do we do?" Pan sent.

Cam wanted to attack the creature from a distance, hidden in the forest's gloom. But a niggle of conscience wouldn't allow it. Could he truly just kill the creature? The kaiju was an Adept, and while it might not be Awakened, in his heart, it still felt like murder to simply slay it without…

Without what? Giving it a chance to fight back? Cam shook his head. No. That wasn't it. He wanted to give it a chance to declare itself. If it saw one of them and immediately attacked, then they'd have their answer. They'd know that the beast wasn't something with which they could reason. They could kill it then without remorse.

"I'm going to let it see me," Cam said.

"That is remarkably stupid," Birch said.

Cam firmed his jaw. He'd made his decision, and while he didn't like it much, it was what they were doing. He said as much. *"If it comes after me—"*

"When it comes after you," Birch corrected.

Cam shrugged. *"If it comes after me, rain hell on it and kill it quick."*

"Easier said than done," Birch muttered.

"Just be ready," Cam replied with a scowl, glaring at the rakshasa and earning a grudging nod of acknowledgment. Cam then met Pan's gaze, and they gently bumped foreheads. *"This is just another stroll in the park,"* he said in reply to Pan's obvious worry.

"The last stroll in a park took us to Hearth," Pan reminded him.

Cam affected a cocky grin. *"This one won't."*

He faced forward again, rising to his feet before Pan could offer a counter. Cam eased out of the forest, but the moment his foot hit the meadow, the kaiju surged to his feet, all sense of somnolence removed. The monster's eyes swiveled to Cam, and from them came swirling yellow fire.

Well that answered any question about reasoning with the beast.

The kaiju roared, a sound of fury and defiance, his arms thrust behind him. The creature's mouth filled with fire as well. Cam shielded hard. An instant later, the monster blasted his attack, a rumbling set of orange flames that braided together, one from each eye and the third from his mouth.

Cam was already moving. He ducked low under the flames.

Pan and Birch entered the meadow, unBlended and laying down their own assault. Gravity shifted under the kaiju, lifting him off his feet. The monster snarled, and returned to the ground. Pounding his chest, he roared again.

From Birch's extended hand arced a black light, one of his deadliest weapons. The attack lanced toward the kaiju with a dull moan, but the creature accepted the blow on his chest, barely wincing. Pan's follow-on assault of crackling lightning slammed into the creature, but the beast threw off the attack without flinching.

Only a few seconds had passed since Cam had entered the meadow, and a niggle of concern itched across his mind. They weren't holding back in hitting the monster, and so far, they weren't doing much damage.

Cam snarled. Then they'd just have to wear it down.

He fired off his own assault, a whip of water followed by fire. Water vapor fogged the meadow, and Cam surged at the kaiju, a glaive with a blade as blue as the waters of Lake Nexus forming in his hands. Somehow, the kaiju sensed his approach.

Cam firmed his shield but also increased his speed, trusting his greater Advancement to see him safe. He swept under the creature's swiping claws and rolled to his feet, standing behind the creature. He sliced his glaive across one of the monster's ankles.

The beast roared in pain. Cam was already diving aside, evading swinging claws and a tail meant to impale him. He was shielded, but after the kaiju had taken Pan's and Birch's attacks without any harm, he wasn't taking any chances. Cam backed away, placing himself so the creature stood centered between him and his friends.

The kaiju growled, slowly rotating, trying to keep the three of them in view, not exposing his flanks. No intellect lit the monster's Adept-yellow eyes, but there was a kind of cunning. Cam saw it and didn't figure on letting the beast figure out what to do next.

"Hit his flank when he faces me," Cam sent to Pan and Birch. Upon speaking, he feinted another run at the kaiju.

The creature turned to face his rush, unsteady from his weakened ankle. Pan and Birch immediately hit the monster with spears of air and lances of fire. The beast roared, fur smoking, wounded from Pan's flames. The beast stepped toward the panda.

Cam rushed the kaiju again, alert to a counter. The creature could be pretending to be injured worse than he actually was. Even as he made the consideration, the kaiju spun about, his eyes and mouth glowing orange. Cam braced himself, strengthening his shield. The trifold attack hammered into his protection. Gray webbing from his shield whined. Cam clenched his jaw, holding on. His vision blurred, darkened. His heart pounded. His shield edged on failure, but Birch brought relief, laying into the kaiju with a concussive series of black orbs. They impacted the same place as Pan's fire. And this time when the beast roared, it was in pain. Rivulets of blood stained and soaked the monster's fur.

Cam couldn't take advantage. He stood bent over at the waist, panting. His heart thundered in his ears, his lungs couldn't draw in enough air, and his muscles wanted to give way. But he took heart in spite of his weariness, fueled by rage, the notion of losing, of dying. They could do this.

The monster stared at Birch, taking limping steps toward the rakshasa. Cam and Pan hit the kaiju at nearly the same time, going after his flanks once again, which appeared to be where the beast was weakest. Pan's fire and air widened the wound Birch had created. The creature hunkered down, seeking protection from further damage. But Cam was there with his blue glaive, carving deep on the opposite flank. The creature tried to counter, but Cam was gone, leaping backward and covering a dozen yards.

Awareness of his impending doom seemed to flicker across the kaiju's features, but the creature wasn't done. The beast beat his chest and charged Birch, who seemed spent and barely able to move.

"Gravity," Cam sent to Pan. *"I'll go heavy. You go light."*

Cam held on to his True Bond, kept it from fraying apart by will alone, fighting past his weakness. He cast a line of trapping vines, a ruse, and as expected, the kaiju tore through them. Next, Cam worked gravity, weighing the beast down. The creature leaped upward, contesting Cam's attack just as Pan made the monster weightless. The kaiju launched skyward—thirty, forty, fifty feet, still soaring. A hundred feet.

The beast finally shrugged off Pan's attack, descending in a controlled fall.

Cam smiled. Off the ground, he guessed the kaiju wouldn't be able to defend himself as well. *"Kill him."*

The three of them lit into the kaiju, hammering weeping wounds from a distance. The creature remained airborne, weakened now, but they didn't let up.

"Keep him in the air," Cam ordered. Pan did so. *"Release him."* As soon as Pan let go of the kaiju, Cam grabbed the monster with gravity, making the beast's head ten times as heavy as normal. The kaiju bent over at the waist from the unexpected weight, accelerated, and

slammed headfirst into the ground. A resounding crack echoed over the meadow, the sound of a neck breaking.

Silence. Nothing moved or stirred. Cam heaved his breath, heart pounding against his ribs, wrung out from the battle, but elated at the conquest. He thrust his arms in the air, roaring with pride and anger.

Birch looked equally spent, hunched over at the knees and looking ready to fall over. He glared at Cam, who was still shouting his victory. "Oh, shut up. That was a stupid plan."

Cam didn't have any sort of rejoinder to offer since Birch was right. They should have ambushed the kaiju and used the forest to their advantage, attacking from different angles and always keeping themselves moving. Standing still had nearly killed all of them.

Well, he'd learned. The next time—and there was sure to be a next time—they'd crush the kaiju and never let the beast see what hit it. "It won't happen again," Cam said. "What should we do about him, though?"

"We can't eat him," Pan said. "He might have not had sentience, but he had Awareness."

Cam nodded agreement, and thankfully, Birch did as well, but for different reasons. "You're right. We can't eat him. His flesh is poisonous, just like the waters of the Blood Sea. Time and nature will see to his corpse… or another kaiju."

"But the deer he was feasting on should be fine?" Cam asked.

"As far as I know," Birch replied.

Cam grunted. "Then let's carve it up and get moving. The fight might bring some fresh monsters our way."

"Nothing but another kaiju," Birch said. "There were sure to be some who stayed to watch. They'd have seen us kill the creature who ruled this part of the forest. They won't test us. But you're right. We should make haste."

Quickly carving the deer with an intent on smoking it later, they circled out of the meadow and reentered the forest's gloom. Silence held sway, and Cam noticed the animals that had previously shadowed them, now gave them wary glances before disappearing into the underbrush. It didn't mean that Cam and the others wouldn't remain watchful, but at least the animals giving them a wider berth might grant them the peace to recover without further incident. The battle had taken a lot out of them, and none of them had the reserves to hold a Blend.

They trudged through the jungle, Cam in the lead, Pan walking alongside him, and Birch trailing after. For some reason, the lovebirds had decided to journey with the rakshasa, each one claiming one of his shoulders and tweeting their observations about the recent battle.

Cam didn't bother listening in. He remained glum and angry with himself about the kaiju and how he should have planned the battle.

"Your heart was in the right place," Pan said, interrupting Cam's internal diatribe. "But you're also right that we can't afford to take those kinds of chances. We're Glories, but we're weak."

And that was the crux of their situation. Their weakness. Even a single use of a True Bond had utterly taxed his stamina. Cam doubted he could have managed to hold or create another one during the battle, and it was no doubt the same for the others. Which merely emphasized their need to get stronger.

No. Not just stronger. They needed more strength *and* stamina.

"You're awfully quiet," Pan noted.

Cam shook himself out of his thoughts. "Sorry. I was just figuring on how we needed to improve ourselves." He explained his observations.

Pan nodded. "You're right. We need both of those things. And we'll have them, but worrying about it won't make it happen any faster. We'll get there. We have fresh venison. The last deer helped more than I expected. This one might go even farther."

Cam frowned at Pan in question.

"A kaiju was feasting on it. I don't imagine them eating anything that didn't have some measure of power."

Pan's explanation made sense, and Cam nodded, annoyed anew

with himself at not figuring it out on his own. He said so.

"Stop," Pan admonished. "You can't know everything. And you have to stop being so angry all the time."

Cam winced. "You've noticed?"

Pan smiled. "How could I not?"

"I noticed," Birch grumbled from behind.

"I understand why you're angry," Pan said, "but it's getting in the way of your joy."

"What's there to be joyful about?" Cam snapped, his annoyance transferring to Pan.

"We're alive. We're free. Our friends are coming to take us home. Those are blessings and they are worth celebrating."

Cam wanted to argue, but Pan's words penetrated through the haze of his rising anger, and he hung his head in shame. "I can't seem to let it go," he whispered. "It's always there. I'm just so angry all the time."

Pan hugged him. "I know. But you have to let it go. Become better."

Cam shuddered. "I'll try."

"That's all any of us can do," Pan said, grinning at him in his cute way. "And stop obsessing about things you overlooked. You're not perfect. No one expects you to be. I only figured out about the deer because I'm a genius."

Cam smiled wanly, glad for his friend's attempted joke. Anything to replace the shame and anger. "I wouldn't call you a genius."

"You're right. I'm a super genius."

Cam laughed at the ridiculous title, and the last of his annoyance fled. He drew Pan into a brief hug and kissed the top of his friend's head. "Thank you. And I don't know if you really are a super genius, but you're definitely the smartest panda-person I'll ever meet."

"And don't you forget it."

Cam sobered. "You're also the best friend I ever expected to have."

"We're not just best friends. We're brothers."

Cam recalled the conversation where he'd initially made the observation. It had been in their Novice year, which in the moment had felt so hectic and full of challenge. He smiled in bitter reminiscence. In hindsight, their Novice year had actually been fairly straightforward. There had been dangers aplenty, but none of these terrible betrayals and politics. Plus, Light Squad had been with them.

Thinking on his friends, he exhaled heavily. He missed them, and although talking to Charity had been wonderful, it wasn't enough, and nothing would be until they were all reunited. He mentioned his longing to Pan.

"I miss them, too," Pan said. "But we'll see them again. I'm sure of it."

"I know we will."

Pan did a double-take. "You do? I was just saying that to make you feel better."

Cam smiled. "We've trained ourselves to the best of our abilities. We've planned for what's needed. And we're learning from our mistakes. We'll succeed because failure isn't an option."

He caught Pan viewing him in doubt.

"It's true. We can't expect an outcome. After everything we've done, we have to be certain about it. And part of that certainty is not making an idiotic mistake like I did with that kaiju."

Pan groaned. "Not that again."

Cam chuckled. "Yes, that again, my fine panda-person." Hearing his own words triggered a question that he should have wondered about far sooner. "Say. Why do you still look like a panda? You're a Glory. Why didn't you change your appearance?"

Pan viewed him with an expression of surprise. "You don't know? It's because I like myself as a panda. It's who I am. Plus, I know how much *you* like me as a panda." He grinned. "And also, how could I be a panda-person if I'm not a panda?"

"You'd only be a person if you weren't a panda," Birch said, joining their conversation. "And that just won't do. It would shatter my sense of what's right in the world."

"Well, we can't have that," Cam noted.

"Then again, this is Mote," Pan said. "What's actually right about this world?"

Birch tilted his head as if in thought, and an instant later, he wore a bright expression, snapping his fingers like he'd just made a great discovery. "You're right. There is nothing right about this world. And that's why we're sure to die before getting free of it."

"Oh, shut up," Cam said, not in the mood for the rakshasa's permanent notion of their impending deaths.

Birch laughed. "You really want to deprive yourself of my brilliance and oratory skills?"

Cam sighed. "If only we could."

His comment earned another laugh.

31

The week following their battle against the kaiju passed without incident, but everyone remained alert and nervous. While no worrisome beasts came to test them, there were plenty of signs of death and battle throughout the forest. Every night, the sounds of creatures in conflict rang out, roars of anger and anguish, and the next morning, Cam and the others would discover puddles of blood thick with flies.

Everything in Petala seemed to be a constant state of strife, even animals that should have been small and docile. This included creatures generally cute and innocuous, like rabbits. On the night when they ran out of the venison they'd stolen from the kaiju, Cam managed to trap a rabbit that had the teeth of a predator and was the size of a small goat.

While they smoked the animal, Cam wondered about the Hollow Land. If the prey here was this deadly in appearance, then what did that mean about the predators? The animals other than the kaiju? So far, none of those more dangerous kinds of beasts had bothered their group any, although a pair of wolves the size of horses had patrolled close by a couple of times before deciding on an easier meal.

With those worried thoughts in mind, Cam poked at the rabbit, finding it about done. Unsurprisingly, though, the long-eared bunny was tough and gamey.

"It tastes as bad as the gruel in the prison," Birch noted. "But at least it helps with this." He gestured at himself in a vague kind of way.

Pan nodded. "Even the nuts and roots are helpful. Look at my fur. Birch's cataracts are almost gone."

Birch grunted. "The better by which to witness our imminent demise, my dear panda-person."

Cam chuckled at the rakshasa's comment, but he also surveyed himself. By now, whipcords of fresh muscle had reformed on his arms and legs, and during every day of hiking so far, he'd found himself able to cover the distance without as much fatigue. The same held true for the others. They still needed to eat what seemed like their body weight every day, which wasn't pleasant, but if it meant they'd fully recover before leaving Petala, then Cam would stuff as much food down his gullet as possible.

They settled in after dinner, and the next morning, they pressed on. However, as they drew close to an empty clearing, a sense of fear swept over Cam. Something was wrong, and he halted their progress. He peered ahead, huddling along the edge of the treeline, studying the clearing. Bathed in sunshine, it reminded him of the meadow where they'd fought the kaiju, but he couldn't reckon why, nor could he see the danger, not even with Oversight.

"What is it?" Birch asked.

Cam shook his head. "I don't know, but there's something wrong up ahead." He continued to study the clearing, trying to figure out what had triggered his alarm. But nothing seemed amiss. Everything was quiet and empty, and he stretched his senses, viewing the woven world. Still nothing, not even any wind to stir the wildflowers. He found himself considering the jungle past the clearing. Was there something lurking past the meadow? Was that it?

He couldn't tell. The jungle was impossible to survey, hazy with mugginess, and worse, just like the animals, the farther they'd pressed into Petala, the taller the trees had grown. They now towered hundreds of feet in height and several score in width at their bases with an abundance of underbrush that somehow survived on the thin light that reached the forest floor. The greenery made it impossible to see anything beyond a depth of twenty or thirty feet, including to his Glory senses which were muffled by the abundance of jungle life.

For a minute, Cam waited. But there remained no explanation for his ringing alarm.

Kiwi hopped close to him, tweeting softly in his ear. "Do you want us to scout?"

Cam allowed the little green bird to nibble his ear, and he stroked Kiwi's downy feathers, doing the same for Sprite when the yellow lovebird nestled close. He didn't want to put them in danger, but as fleet as they could fly, they might have the best chance of figuring out what was wrong with the way ahead. "Do it."

The lovebirds flitted off, darting into the jungle meadow. They soon reached the other side, and Cam watched them closely, viewing reality through the webbing of the woven world. So far, nothing. Just a kaleidoscope of connections—sight, sound, and scent—but no recognizable danger. Kiwi and Sprite flittered about the edge of the clearing, and still nothing.

"I sense the danger now," Birch said.

"We all do," Pan said, glancing about. His eyes brightened when he spied a stand of bamboo.

Cam had seen it seconds earlier, and he cautioned Pan. "Not yet."

An instant later, Kiwi and Sprite flew back across the meadow at speed, wings clapping. Cam's stomach hollowed. A shadow swept over the birds, some kind of flying animal with a wingspan equal to five wagons set next to one another. He gazed skyward, and his sight landed on a strange, scaled creature. A flying lizard. It screamed, the sound piercing the sky as it dove after Kiwi and Sprite.

The lovebirds flew faster. Cam stood, shouting, urging them to greater speed. "Hurry! Don't look back!"

"Come on!" "Fly!" Pan and Birch yelled.

Fear lodged in Cam's throat as the lovebirds raced toward them. He couldn't tell if they were going to make it.

They reached the foliage an instant before the flying lizard snapped shut a massive beak. It missed the lovebirds by inches, pulling up short so it didn't slam into the forest's undergrowth. It cawed in frustration, a sound that rose to terror when a massive snake fell upon it, a serpent that was as thick as a hundred-year oak and dozens of yards in length. Gray, banded in black, and with massive fangs dripping venom, the snake collapsed upon the flying lizard, flattening it to the ground where they fought.

"Move," Cam ordered as more snakes became evident. They had been Blended and were only now visible. They were everywhere, hissing to life, moving.

Cam led them at a dead sprint away from the meadow that was now full of massive snakes. They even tossed the remains of the rabbit to distract the serpents as more of them slithered or fell to the ground from overhead, writhing upon one another, hissing and chasing after them.

Cam glanced back, glad to see that the serpents were slow, but was there no end to their numbers? And just how broad was their range? And why hadn't they fallen straight down on his group while they'd been distracted at the clearing or even when they'd entered their territory? Cam didn't know, nor did he care.

He and the others just had to run. And they did, never slowing, cutting back and forth to avoid the snakes.

Minutes later, they seemed to have left the serpents behind, but even then, Cam wouldn't let them slow. A half-hour longer, he had them rush through the forest until the meadow was miles behind. Only then did they stop, Cam figuring they had to be safe by now.

"I hate snakes," Birch said, sounding both terrified and agitated.

"So do I," Pan agreed with vivid feeling.

Kiwi and Sprite hopped onto an overhead branch. "Snakes are the worst," the green lovebird declared. "So evil and ugly."

Cam nodded agreement, glancing at the two lovebirds. And freezing. Slithering across their branch was a smaller version of the same type of snake they'd just evaded. The serpent lunged.

Birch was there. A gesture, and he speared the snake through its head on a lance of air, where it hung suspended, mouth agape before Birch released it to fall to the ground with a hollow thud.

Cam viewed the monster, which had to be thirty feet in length. He shook his head in disbelief. How were they ever going to reach the lake with all these dangers to confront? An instant later, he tossed off his doubts. They'd get there because there wasn't any other option. Failure meant death.

"What do we do?" Kiwi asked, sounding mournful.

Cam considered the question. Could they Blend the entire way? Maybe, but not the lovebirds. They lacked the skill, and they'd been the ones who had been seen while scouting. He couldn't risk them like that again. He made a decision. "We still make for the river. Rafting to Lake Petala should be our goal and our plan."

"Wasn't that already our goal and plan?" Pan asked.

Cam shrugged. "It doesn't hurt to have some extra incentive, does it?"

"What extra incentive?" Birch asked.

"The slithery kind we want to avoid."

It ended up requiring several hours to skirt the range where the massive snakes roosted, and by the time they managed to leave the area behind, Cam and the others found themselves climbing a set of tall, rugged hills. To their left, the river they'd intended on journeying toward had carved a broad canyon that was lined on either side by steep rocky walls that were too vertical to easily descend. The towering trees of the jungle lowlands had given way to scrub pines not much more than ten or fifteen feet in height, and the humidity had dropped to a blessedly cool dryness. The land itself was silent except for a soughing wind that rattled tree limbs and stirred Cam's hair.

By then, the sun had begun dimming—only a few more hours of

daylight—and Cam studied the terrain for a place to hole up for the night. He made sure everyone was Blended tight, and they marched in single file with Birch bringing up the rear and Kiwi and Sprite perched on his shoulders.

But it was a hissing sound that snapped his attention back in the direction in which they'd come. A snake had followed them, its head rearing above the scrub pines, tongue flicking out. A Glory-Haunt filled the creature's eyes, which seemed to glare with malevolence as it sighted them. Its mouth opened, and the creature hissed louder, head lowering as it rushed forward.

"Go!" Cam shouted.

As one, they sprinted for any kind of safety. But where? Cam scanned ahead for an obstacle that the snake might not be able to scale. There! A steep rise, like a carved plinth. It had to be higher than the snake could rear. Cam sent his intention to the others, directing them. The lovebirds immediately lifted off his shoulders and flew to the top of the cliff, and seconds later, the rest of their group reached it.

Pan was the first one to scale his way to the top. Then Birch. Cam waited on the old-headed rakshasa, making sure he could make the climb. Satisfied, he readied for his own ascent.

A threatening hiss momentarily got his attention. The snake wasn't slowing. Its focus was locked on him, and Cam swiftly gauged the distance. It would be a near run for him to get to the top of the rise.

So be it.

Heart steady, fear absent, and True Bond in place, Cam took three steps back, ran at the cliff, and leaped. He grabbed at a rocky prominence and ascended by punching into the stone to make his own holds, climbing swiftly. Ten feet. Twenty. Forty. Fifty. Cam scrambled over the lip, rolling away just as the snake plowed nose first into the cliff.

Rocks chipped off, and boulders tumbled, smashing into the serpent, who shook its head at the stony deluge. But the creature merely hissed in annoyance rather than anger.

Cam rose to his feet and surveyed the nearby area, and what met his gaze didn't give him much hope. The cliff upon which they stood was isolated and far away from any other rises. The snake couldn't get to them, but Cam also couldn't see an easy means of safety. They were essentially trapped on an island with the serpent circling them like a scaled shark.

He then took a closer study of the fanged horror. It was similar to the others they'd encountered in that massive nest: gray with bands of black, but this one also had glittering scales that were crystalline and armored. Small horns flared off the crown of its head, and tufts of fur like a mustache extended from directly below its nostrils, down below its jaw and along its neck on either side. There, the fur faded away to fine hairs that reached halfway down its body. It also possessed a spiked tail and, strangest of all, a pair of stubby wings.

The snake hissed, and Cam felt himself flailing, wanting to fall inward in terror. With a flexing of his will, he threw off the attack—and the hiss had to be an attack, one directed at the mind. He firmed his Domain, blocking the sensation of fear, readying himself for what the serpent might do next.

It breathed out a mist, hazy and indistinct, and where it touched stone, the rocks eroded into slagged lumps. Birch was there. He gestured, and the poisonous mist dissipated.

The snake hissed again, a noise of frustration that rose to anger when Pan attacked the beast with lances of fire. All of them attacked—bolts of air, lances of lightning, and spikes of gravity to pin the beast in place. No damage. The creature's armored scales were too thick. Cam next tried to draw heat out of the serpent, but the creature tossed away his attempt with a contemptuous hiss.

It became an impasse, but Cam didn't trust it to last. He reviewed the terrain, seeking a way out.

"What do we do?" Pan's voice was steady, but it contained an undercurrent of terror.

"We die," Birch said in his typical fatalistic fashion.

Their conversation ended when the snake rammed headfirst into the cliff. Chunks of stone and boulders tumbled from where it struck. Again, the snake smashed into the cliff, and more of it came apart. If it maintained its assault, their place of safety would eventually be reduced to rubble.

Cam disregarded the assault, though. Getting off the cliff or killing the serpent was all that mattered.

"I wish the three of you could fly," Kiwi cheeped, sounding mournful.

Cam wanted to smack himself in the head. Of course. He and Pan were Glories, and Birch, with his mix of Nullity and Ephemera, had the skills and abilities of one. They couldn't fly, but surely they could leap across the river canyon, couldn't they? Cam believed it likely, even though they hadn't fully tested their new capabilities.

All they had to do was get down the cliff on the side opposite the snake, run to the escarpment, and jump the canyon. And even if they couldn't make the jump, they should easily be able to survive the fall into the water. And they had to make the attempt since staying here wasn't an option.

Cam's eyes narrowed, staring at the snake, calculating and having a realization. The snake represented both danger and an opportunity. A plan developed, and he explained it to the rest of the group.

"It should work," Birch said.

"Then we go on my mark." Cam stared at the snake, searching for a pattern and quickly finding one. The monstrous serpent hissed a long exhalation right before it battered the cliff. Cam gestured, holding the others in place, waiting. The hiss recurred. "Go!"

They leaped from the rise on the side opposite the snake, and from there, rushed to the river chasm.

The snake caught sight of them. It flicked its tongue and slithered faster. Cam allowed Pan and Birch to pull ahead, facing forward, but maintaining his awareness of the beast through Oversight. He knew how to feel the serpent now, and he kept his senses locked on it, judging its distance.

It closed but not quickly enough. He'd reach the river well ahead of it. Cam slowed his pace, taunting the snake. By then Kiwi and Sprite had flown across the chasm. Seconds later, Pan and Birch arrived at the cliff's edge and made the leap, looking likely to make it across. Cam slowed further.

For his plan to succeed, he needed the snake even closer for when he reached the canyon's edge. The serpent hastened with a final burst. *Perfect.* Cam did his best to speed his pace again. He raced to the river and launched himself into the sky, knowing he wouldn't make it across, having slowed too much. The snake's jaws clamped shut, the sound and pressure billowing into him, missing him by inches.

Cam spun in the air. He hadn't been interested in getting across the river canyon. He had been interested in killing the snake. The serpent had lunged too far, and its own weight forced it farther and farther over the cliff's edge. It hissed in alarm, but it was too late.

The snake was pulled downward, its fall accelerating in stages. Finally, its entire bulk slid over the edge, and the serpent smashed into the rocky shoals at the base of the cliff where its stout form finally gave way, bursting under the weight of its own body.

Cam smiled in satisfaction, shielding just as he slammed into the water. He sank like a stone but immediately began pulling hard for the surface. He breached the river and swam for the same shore as where the snake had crashed to its doom.

The others would figure out his plan when they saw the direction of his swim.

Cam had already set to carving the snake by the time Pan and Birch reached him. It wasn't easy work, but being a Glory taught by Rukh and Jessira, his control of Ephemera let him cut deeper and finer than if he'd been using the finest of knives. He looked up from the work when the other two arrived while the lovebirds held off at a distance.

"From now on, you have to tell us your full plans in advance," Pan said, his voice full of reproach. "You can't just order us about and take all the risks."

Birch nodded agreement. "Your plan worked, but it was reckless. You didn't have to risk yourself in the way you did. You could have simply created an illusion. The snake would have likely seen through it, but it could have done the same as actually placing yourself in harm's way."

Cam might have argued about the last. He'd actually considered an illusion, and against anything of a lower Stage, it probably would have worked. But probably wasn't good enough. The serpent had been a Glory, and who knew how well an illusion would have worked against it? After all, the kaiju they'd battled a little over a week ago had been a Stage lower in Awareness, and while there had been three of them pitted against it, look at how hard the creature had fought.

Pan continued to look unhappy. Angry even, glowering some.

"I'm sorry," Cam said to Pan, feigning an apology he didn't feel. While he didn't enjoy causing his friend any kind of upset, what had he actually done wrong? They were alive, and the snake was dead. What else did they want from him?

"You could have also used telepathy," Pan said. "You could have told us your plan at the speed of thought. We might have figured out some way to improve on it."

Cam's bubbling irritation halted. He hadn't thought of that, but would it have made a difference? Maybe, but so what? His plan had still worked out with no one injured. His annoyance flared to fresh life, but Cam recognized it this time. His conversation with Pan from the other day surfaced, about his anger. It was always there, and while in the prison, he'd used it to fuel his need to escape, thinking it stemmed from his need for justice. But now he understood the truth. He raged for vengeance, which wasn't the kind of person he wanted to be. The anger had served its purpose, but he no longer needed or wanted it.

Cam breathed out, unhappy with himself over how he'd snapped at his friends. Another couple of breaths, and calmness replaced the anger. A few more breaths, and his thoughts came clearer. Pan was right. He should have included the others in the plan. His lack of remorse became proper contrition along with shame. "I'm sorry," Cam repeated, this time truly repentant.

Pan sighed, still not accepting the apology. "Why did you risk yourself?"

Cam explained, and this time, he did use telepathy. Getting into the habit of more regularly communicating in that fashion might mean they'd use it reflexively in the future. *"Because we can't turn away from the opportunity that the snake presents."*

Pan cocked his head. *"Meaning?"*

"Meaning everything we've eaten here: the meat, nuts, roots… they've restored us much faster than any of us expected. What would happen if we ate the snake?"

"It was Awakened," Pan reminded him, speaking aloud.

"But what if it wasn't sentient?"

"It wasn't," Kiwi confirmed.

"Then the flesh might be of even greater aid," Birch said, stroking his chin. "Clever."

"There's a lot of meat," Cam said, indicating the massive serpent. "Enough for at least a week, and that's at triple rations."

Silence met his statement. For any other trio, the amount of meat represented by the snake might have actually been enough for a month, but ever since escaping from the prison, all three of them had appetites best described as beyond ravenous. They regularly ate three servings already, which meant with the snake, they'd be eating nine times the normal amount. Cam briefly wondered if the quantity was also part of why they were recovering so quickly.

"Then I suppose we should finish carving the beast," Birch said.

"I'm tired of meat," Pan said with a weary sigh. "If only we could have reached the luscious stand of bamboo back in that clearing." He spoke of the meadow where they'd encountered the nest of snakes.

"We'll get you some bamboo," Cam promised. "If we don't find any for you in Petala, we'll get you some back home in Salvation."

"Back home," Pan said, mournful and longing.

"Home," Birch repeated, but his tone was strangely dead, sounding uncertain.

Cam viewed the old rakshasa, who no longer appeared ancient and back-broken. Now, Birch appeared merely stooped with age, with an undefinable but unmistakable sense of power emitting off him, like he'd once been powerful and deadly and still retained enough of his former prowess to take down a foolish, younger male. But on speaking that single word just then—home—the weight of Birch's years seemed to drag him down.

"Is something wrong?" Cam asked the rakshasa.

Birch broke free of his thoughts and offered a faint but cheerless smile. "I'm just reminded of a story from my childhood. It's of someone who thinks to achieve something grand, and he does, but also immediately dies afterward. It was supposed to be a tragedy, which is how all of the stories from Mote end. The good ones, anyway."

Cam didn't want to think about how the bad ones ended. Instead, he gave Birch a brief hug, startling the rakshasa. "Your story won't be a tragedy. You'll get to Salvation, find your wildflower field, and there won't be any dying involved."

"So you say," Birch said, affecting a smile. "But someone will die. Someone always does. It'll probably be the two of you." He indicated Cam and Pan before glancing at Kiwi and Sprite. "And those two as well. I'll probably live long enough to set fire to your funeral pyres." He grinned the whole while, but for once his fatalism didn't have its usual mocking good cheer.

But Cam pretended like it did. "You and your grim predictions," he said with a forced laugh. "Now, let's get to finishing off this serpent. We've found the river, and I want to be boating down it before sunset."

32

Carving the snake took several hours, and by the time they finished, it was closing in on late evening. Cam judged the remaining light and reckoned there wasn't much left of the day, just enough time to hike a few miles downriver of the serpent's carcass. They could have made better time, but each of them were now carrying a hundred pounds of meat and dragging even more behind them. Afterward, they'd want to halt their trek since none of them much wanted to journey along the riverbank's uncertain footing during the darkness.

With the sun dimming and the moon yet to light the Hollow Land with its silvery-rose glow, they found a broad shelf well above a quiet cove and set up camp. The walls of the escarpment cupped them on three sides while a steep drop to the waters below maintained the fourth. Cam reckoned that it was high enough from the river to prevent any monsters from seizing them as a snack.

A steady breeze cast sparks from their campfire and lofted the scent of smoke, seared meat, and ash while the droning sound of crickets from across the water reached them in a familiar, comforting cadence. It was peaceful in the Hollow Land, possibly the first time Cam could recall any sense of serenity since coming to Mote.

However, the majority of his attention was on the searing snake steaks, enough for all of them to feast, and they were finally ready to eat. Upon taking his first bite, Cam discovered that the meat wasn't too bad, but what was even better was what the steak provided in terms of health. As he ate, every bit of Cam's lingering weakness seemed to drain out of him like the yellow bile from when he Enhanced Plasminia. The sense of strained tendons and ligaments to which he'd grown inured was healed with the creation of a True Bond and a wisp of Ephemera. Fresh strength infused his bones and muscles, and he noticed a significant change to his actual build. His whipcord musculature seemed a mite thicker. A few more days of eating snake, and he might have the same heft as when he'd first arrived in Mote.

The same improvement held true for Pan, whose fur had regained its prior luster and his stomach its pleasant plumpness. Birch, though, continued to show the greatest improvement. He walked with an upright stride now, his stooped back having straightened. At the rate the rakshasa was improving, it might not be too long before he resembled the powerful warrior Cam had trained against in the mindscape.

"I don't like eating so much meat, but that was satisfying," Pan said, patting his rounded belly.

The comment drew Cam out of his consideration about Birch, and he glanced at his favorite panda-person. "Are you too full to eat any bamboo?"

Pan laughed like Cam's question was utterly ridiculous. "I'll always have room for bamboo." His eyes narrowed, and he locked his sight on Cam in hopeful speculation. "You wouldn't happen to have some, do you?"

Cam chuckled. "Sorry, my friend. I don't."

"I don't have any either," Birch said, joining them next to the fire.

They sat in companionable silence for a while, staring over the water while the rest of the snake meat was slowly cooked into jerky.

"This is nice," Cam noted.

"It reminds me of when we camped along Brewery Highway," Pan replied. He sat up, appearing excited. "Do you remember when we first met?"

Cam laughed. "How could I forget? You came sniffing around my camp wanting food. You said something to the effect of liking the smell of what I was cooking."

"It was stew," Pan supplied.

"Right," Cam said with a smile of reminiscence. "It was stew, and you asked if I'd be interested in sharing some of it."

"I also played music for you when you had a nightmare."

Cam's smile faded to an expression of fond appreciation. "I remember. Thank you."

Pan shrugged off the comment. "Just being a friend."

Birch cleared his throat. "Sorry to end this sappy interlude, but we've been in Petala for a few weeks now. Do you have any idea when your friends will arrive?"

Cam shook his head. "Based on my best guess, it should be any day now. Hopefully."

The rakshasa grunted, appearing dissatisfied. "They won't be powerful enough."

Cam laughed, scornful of Birch's lack of faith in Light Squad. "What? Four Crowns and a Sage should be good to handle everything we'll face here. Trust me. Your prediction about our deaths won't come true."

"Life will find a way," Birch replied, sounding sour for some reason.

The conversation lulled afterward until Pan spoke, addressing the rakshasa. "What about you? Don't you have any stories from your past you want to share?"

Birch offered a bleak smile. "I'm afraid my youth wasn't full of friendship and sharing the road. If I tell my stories, they will only ruin the mood."

"Our time as fledglings was full of learning to fly," Sprite said, perched on one of Cam's shoulders. "It was wonderful," he added with a trill of joy.

Cam smiled at Sprite, running a finger over his soft head. Petting the birds always seemed to help him reach a state of peace and rid him of his anger, something he needed. "I wouldn't mind learning to fly."

"We will when we Advance to Crown," Pan said. "I'll be one of the few pandas to ever do so."

"And you'll be the first panda-person to do so," Cam replied.

Pan laughed. "That's right. The first panda-person."

"Our lives were wonderful until we were captured and caught," Kiwi stated from Cam's other shoulder. He chirped in annoyance at Sprite. "You couldn't keep from staring at the sky when you were supposed to be watching for danger. Idiot."

"We were caught by Father," Sprite said, sounding outraged. "Having Father find us wasn't a bad thing." He went so far as to hop over to peck at Kiwi, who quickly backed away, fluttering his wings and going to Cam's other shoulder.

He continued to flap in agitation, and Cam stroked the green lovebird's chest, trying to soothe him. "Easy," he said, his voice soft. "Y'all shouldn't be arguing."

Kiwi wasn't ready for that. He squawked at Sprite. "It wasn't a bad thing, but if we'd never met Father, then we'd have never ended up here."

Cam continued to stroke Kiwi's chest, not thinking too much about the green lovebird's logic.

Apparently, he wasn't the only one. Sprite had his head cocked to the side as if in confusion. "But Mote is where we met Cam and Pan."

"You also met me," Birch chimed in.

Both birds started at him, heads tilted. "And?" they said in unison.

"And that's also not a bad thing," Birch said, sounding aggrieved.

"It is a bad thing when you growl at us," Kiwi said. "And you growl a lot."

"Plus, you're a cat," Sprite added, "and cats eat birds."

Birch sputtered. "I am not a cat. I am a lion."

"But aren't lions a kind of cat?" Pan asked, eyes wide and sounding innocent.

Cam had to hide a smile as Birch's mouth opened and closed but no words came out. In the end, the rakshasa scowled. "I know what you're doing," he said to Pan. "You're trying to draw me into your conversation about good memories. Well, it won't work."

"It already worked," Cam told the rakshasa. "You're talking to us right now."

Birch's bluster transformed to a prim expression. "I was merely correcting the sweet lovebirds."

"Maybe so," Cam allowed, "but do you really think they needed correcting?" He nudged the rakshasa when he didn't respond. Birch hadn't been exactly happy back in the prison, but in Petala, the prospect of freedom seemed to terrify him. And most likely that had to do with a future of possible happiness, which wasn't something people of Mote ever expected. They were always fixated on finding the source of betrayal.

"You're allowed to enjoy the night and the fine company," Pan said into the silence when Birch still didn't reply.

"What fine company?" Birch said, his tone sour. "The lovebirds argue, you and Cam have a sappy conversation, and I'm compared to a cat."

Cam grinned. "Now you're getting it. Enjoy the night. There are no traitors amongst us."

"How do you know I'm not a traitor?" Birch challenged. "I could create an abundance of Nullity by betraying you."

Cam didn't doubt it, but in the years he'd spent with Birch in the mindscape, he'd come to understand and trust the rakshasa. Birch didn't seek Nullity. He sought his meadow and the serenity he'd experienced there. And while he'd never say so, he also longed for the contentment of unconstrained friendship.

"Tell you what," Cam said. "I'll leave you alone if you speak your truth on how you feel about being free of the prison."

Birch viewed him like he was an idiot. "I'm thrilled to be free of the prison. Why wouldn't I be?"

"Then laugh like you mean it," Cam said, really wanting Birch to take the lesson he was trying to impart, even though with his own issues regarding his anger, some might label him a hypocrite. "There's no one around to mock you. Let yourself feel joy. You deserve it."

Birch stared at him for a long moment, sighing. "Maybe some other time."

Cam nodded, accepting the rakshasa's decision. He'd come around.

The fireside chat broke apart shortly thereafter, and Cam went to his bedroll, meditating and Enhancing his Tangs. He'd quickly gotten them at Crystal—so had Pan—but now was the time to perfect them. Hours of effort later, he tucked in since in a short while, it would be his turn to take the watch.

A cloud swept across the face of the silvery-rose light that pretended to be a moon, and the world shadowed in a deeper darkness. An owl— or a similar bird—hooted somewhere in the distance while the river gently murmured as it rustled endlessly over smooth stones. Given the long day, and the fatigue weighing him down, Cam was quickly lulled to sleep.

He dreamed about the Ephemeral Academy and Charity, imagining walking its moonlit paths with her and kissing her.

Or at least he thought it was a dream, but then her familiar voice was present, drawing him out of his sleep. *"Cam? Are you there? How are you holding up?"*

Cam awoke, confused and his mind barely awake. *"Charity?"*

She laughed, throaty and teasing. *"Unless you're dreaming of some-one else you want to kiss."*

Cam roused to full wakefulness. *"Thor made another link?"* The answer was obvious the moment he asked the question. *"Never mind. Of course, he did."* A smile lit his features. *"There's only one person I'd like to kiss."*

"Pan is pretty cute."

Cam laughed. He'd missed Charity's humor. He'd missed so many things about her. *"Yes, he is, but I doubt his lips are as soft as yours."*

Charity chuckled, sounding pleased. *"Well aren't you sweet?"* The teasing left her voice. *"How are you really? You didn't say."*

Cam made to offer a banal answer, but he paused a moment, giving himself time for a proper self-reflection. What he learned had him furrowing his brow in surprise. *"I'm doing better than I have any right to expect. Better than fine, actually. Petala is as deadly as Birch promised, but we're figuring our way through its dangers. Thriving some."*

"Really?" Surprise laced Charity's voice.

"Really," Cam affirmed, going ahead and explaining about their improved health and what they'd encountered so far in the Hollow Land.

This time it was skepticism that colored Charity's voice. *"So, to regain your health, you only had to nearly die while fighting a kaiju of lesser Awareness and a nest of snakes the sizes of trees. Is that the summation of it?"*

Cam shrugged, sending a note of humor along the link. *"Not all of them were that big. Some were only as long as a sapling."*

"What about the dragon-snake? How big was it?"

Dragon-snake? Cam hadn't made the connection before, but Charity was right. The serpent they'd battled—had it just been today?—did have that sort of appearance. The idea had him wondering anew what it would be like to fly, to spread wings wide and soar from high above the ground. Or race the wind while running on fleet feet.

"Cam?" Charity asked, pulling him out of his imaginings.

"Sorry. I was just thinking. I'd never thought of the snake as being like a dragon until you mentioned it."

"It wasn't an actual dragon, was it?"

Cam laughed. *"Dragons aren't real. Not even in Mote."*

"Too bad. I like dragons." Charity paused a moment. *"And I can also tell you're stronger. You feel so much better than the last time we spoke."*

"Petala is terrifying, but it's been a blessing, too. We've been lucky."

Charity might have nodded. *"You're lucky in more ways than you know. Thor is almost ready. Give him another week, two at the most, and he should be able to create the anchor lines."*

Joy and excitement shivered up and down Cam's spine. They

wouldn't be alone. Light Squad was coming. *"We'll be waiting."*

Charity might have lifted an amused brow. *"Of course you'll be waiting. Unless you've already reached the Locus, that is."*

Prior to Cam's experiences in Mote and Hearth, he might have flushed at her teasing, but he'd grown past that version of himself. Rather than flush, he teased her back. *"We'll have a nice snake steak waiting for you. I'm sure it's not what you're used to eating, but even nobles have to rough it sometimes."*

"On that note…"

"You don't fancy snake steak?" Cam asked with a chuckle, glad to have come out on top for once.

"Not particularly."

Cam's humor faded. *"How are you doing?"* He should have asked her straightaway just as she had for him. Charity might have been safe in the Sinanes, but that didn't mean she didn't have her own stresses. Learning her father was a traitor, pushing to become a Crown, and bearing the weight of expectations couldn't be easy.

"I'm fine. I'm a Crown, and I'll soon get to see you again."

Cam didn't miss the omission. *"I notice you forgot to mention Pan."*

"That's because my joy at seeing my favorite panda-person goes without saying."

"Of course." It was a nice recovery, but her words settled some of Cam's lingering worries. After Hearth, his time with Charity had been short—measured in a few weeks—but they'd been full ones, at least for him. But what about Charity? What did she think? Especially since he'd been absent from her life for over three years now?

"I'm sorry my father sent you to Mote."

"I know, and you've done all the apologizing you need to do on that man's account."

"Still." She breathed out. *"I'll stop. Only because…"*

"Only because what?"

"I missed you, and you seem different now. Stronger, like you wouldn't even care about my flirting with you. You used to get so flustered whenever I did that. It was cute, part of your charm."

A longing tone filled her voice, and Cam understood the cause: the uncertainty about their relationship. He shared much of it. *"It's true. I'm physically weaker than I was, but I'm also stronger where it counts. And there's also no Realm where I wouldn't enjoy you flirting with me."*

Charity didn't reply at once, but when she did her voice had grown husky. *"Is that what you want? Me flirting with you? Well, aren't you the bold one? Just how bold have you become?"*

"You'll have to find out on your own."

"Won't that be interesting?" There came the sensation of Charity pressing close, whispering in his ear. *"Are you sure you want that?"*

Cam didn't back away. *"I'm sure."* The notion of kissing Charity and seeing just how far that might lead filled his mind. Some of it bled across the link.

Charity gasped. *"That's quite the vivid imagination."*

A reckless courage spurred Cam onward. *"I'm not hearing you say you wouldn't want the same."*

A pregnant beat. *"No, I'm not."*

"I can't maintain the link for much longer," Thor said, breaking into their conversation.

This time, Cam did flush, embarrassed at being caught out by Thor. Or maybe the Divine hadn't been listening in. He hoped that was the case. *"Understood."*

"Yes. Understood," Charity agreed, her voice also stilted and awkward. *"It was wonderful to talk to you,"* she said to Cam

"I wish we could do it more regularly," Cam replied. *"Maybe I should keep my mind open for when you reach out to me next."*

"Don't ever do that," Thor warned. *"Leaving your mind open means others can touch you if they know of your presence. Those would be people with whom you don't want any contact."*

"Then I'll be careful to keep my mind shut," Cam promised.

"See that you do. As Charity said, I should be ready to send Light Squad to you within the next week or two."

Cam wanted to bury his head. There went his hope that Thor hadn't been listening in, but at least the Divine had confirmed his fondest hope. It was one thing to hear Charity's promise that they'd soon be reunited but another for a Divine to make the same vow. Even better, a week in Salvation and Hearth would only be a day or so in Mote, so he and Pan should be able to see their friends by either tomorrow evening or the morning after.

"*I can't wait to see all y'all,*" Cam said to Charity.

"*We can't wait either.*"

"*I'll send them as soon as I'm able,*" Thor promised.

The conversation ended then, and Cam went back to sleep, smiling and fully at peace for the first time since coming to Mote.

Cam slept well the night following his conversation with Charity but any lingering good feelings faded away like a dream when dawn arrived, gloomy with mist and a gusty chill.

"I hate the cold," Birch grumbled as they packed away their supplies. "The only thing worse is when it's also drizzly." He glared at the weather. "Like this."

Cam felt otherwise about the cold, but he shared the rakshasa's distaste of dampness.

"Still think the river is a bad idea?" Pan asked.

"I do," Cam said, viewing the waters. During yesterday's adventures, he had noticed piranha the size of wolves patrolling the river, and just then, as if to confirm his concerns, a many tentacled horror—massive and black—slithered into view.

"I see what you mean," Pan said with a shiver, sighting the river monster.

Rafting the river had sounded like a good plan early on and from afar but it was far from good. Cam stared a bit longer at the tentacled thing, wondering at the creature's reach. "I don't think we should stay by the shore," Cam said.

Birch stared at the monstrosity for a moment, and without any further comment, he began clambering up the escarpment. They followed him, reaching the top and trudging onward the rest of the morning, dripping wet and cold, their breaths fogging. The rocky escarpment eventually crumbled apart, and the forest rose around them again, silent, still, and glum. They crossed a nest of streams that flowed down to the expanding river, watching for the tentacled monster.

Later in the day, though, the rain gave way to sunshine, and a warm wind breathed into the world, evaporating the water. Everything glistened and it might have been beautiful if not for the oppressive humidity that Cam had come to know and loathe.

They traversed a narrow valley, marching single file downhill along a rushing stream when Sprite stiffened from where he perched on Cam's shoulders. "There's something dangerous ahead of us. Something very dangerous."

Cam signaled the others to halt and stretched his senses, not feeling anything amiss. He glanced to Kiwi for confirmation. The green lovebird was busy cleaning his feathers, seemingly unaware of whatever had triggered Sprite's fear.

No help there, but that was often the case. Sprite was generally smarter and more aware than Kiwi. Cam glanced to Sprite. "What is it? Can you tell?"

Sprite cocked his head. "It's like the kaiju you fought, but this one is even more powerful."

Cam inhaled sharply. Another kaiju? And more powerful than the other one? They better avoid this one. "Can you tell where it is?"

Sprite chirped softly. "Downstream. Around that bend."

Cam cursed under his breath. "We'll have to go back and find another way."

A hollow thud cut off whatever else he might have said.

"It's coming this way," Sprite said, sounding on the edge of panic.

Kiwi finally perked, fluttering in alarm. "Something dangerous is heading toward us."

Cam wanted to roll his eyes at the green lovebird's delayed reaction. Instead, he hustled the others away from the stream. "Blend. Hard as you can." He explained what Sprite had told him, and they shifted deeper into the forest's gloom, doing their best to hide under ferns and shrubs.

All the while, the kaiju's thunderous footsteps approached. Onward the beast came, steadily, unhurried, like a slow-moving avalanche.

Pan hissed softly when a massive pair of feet came to a halt twenty feet away.

Cam took his friend's hand, trying to lend him strength and courage. Pan quieted, and they gazed upward.

"Don't move," Birch sent. *"If we run, he will chase us down."*

Cam nodded understanding, eyes arrested on the beast.

The kaiju was gigantic—fifty feet tall or more—male and similarly white-furred like the last one they'd encountered with a crown of jagged horns and dagger-like protrusions at his elbows and knees that were dark as ebony. They seemed to suck in the light, and a nest of red-streaked braided hair transitioned to bright white as it trailed down his back. His barbed tail rose slowly until it stood poised over his head like a scorpion's. A terrifying foe.

Cam's heart seemed to still, and he stiffened when the monster stared their way with his Crown-Haunted eyes. Their gazes seemed to fasten upon one another.

The creature whispered to him. *"We see you, weak creature of Ephemera. A walking feast is your only role. He and she will find you. We will make it so. Open, weakling."*

The words were followed by a glimmer of pain, like a needle stabbing into Cam's forehead, and a notion poured into him, one proclaiming that strength above all else was what was most important in life. Cam gritted his teeth against the intrusion, creating his Domain and shoving away the invading voice. The pain intensified, but Cam refused to relent, holding firm his will.

Minutes passed in the tableau, and a deathly silence filled the forest. Nothing stirred. Even the trees remained hushed, seemingly too frightened to rustle their leaves and fronds.

Eventually, the kaiju grunted, a deep and ponderous sound, satisfied maybe, before setting off upstream.

Cam had no idea what the kaiju had wanted of him, and why he had let them be, but he also wasn't about to look the unexpected gift in the mouth. Better to figure it out later. Right now, they needed to get gone, and they'd do so as soon as he couldn't hear or feel the beast's heavy footsteps.

Before rising, however, Cam checked with Sprite, who had the best senses of them all. "Can you feel him?"

The yellow lovebird cocked his head a moment. "No. He's gone."

Cam sighed in relief, and they swiftly hastened downstream, moving as far as possible from the departed kaiju, never slowing. They arrived at a cutoff from the trail, and Cam took it even though it meant a hard, scrabbling climb.

However, the change in direction proved a fortuitous blessing, ending as it did at a bare ledge. From it, the way forward could be surveyed. The river with the tentacled monster was only a mile to the west, while Lake Petala was still a several days' hike away. As for the Badlands, it remained past his line of sight.

With the sun readying to dim, they settled in, making camp. It was as good a place as any, especially with a trail winding down to the river's edge if they needed to make a quick departure. Cam continued to stare at Lake Petala, breathing a prayer, hoping that Light Squad would be with them before they had to journey across the waters to the Badlands.

"The kaiju left us alone for his own reasons," Birch said, coming up alongside him. "We need to be alert in case he follows."

"Why would he follow?" Cam asked with a frown.

Birch shrugged. "As I said, it would be for his own reasons."

Cam shuddered, recalling the words of the beast. He didn't like the idea of a creature so deadly having reasoning of any sort, especially any that had to do with him and his friends.

33

Cam glanced to the forest from where he sat at their cliffside camp-site. The animals were loud tonight. Insects droned, a regular rising and falling of noise, while large animals rustled against shrubs and underbrush, calling out and fighting. Most of the beasts gave them a wide berth but a few edged close, no doubt lured by the smell of the snake jerky. Cam watched them closely, his back to the cliff's edge, but a flash of his Glory-Haunted eyes got the curious animals to move on, including a massive tiger most recently.

He kept his attention on the cat, but it continued deeper into the forest, never slowing. Satisfied it posed no danger, Cam returned to his supper, stuffing his face with what he reckoned was at least several pounds of snake, his seventh such helping of the day. A distant part of his conscience figured he should pace himself, but there was no way to control his appetite, which remained ravenous. Once the meat hit his taste buds, there was no stopping until he was satiated.

And the meat continued to do him good. Rather than gaunt, he was lean now with cords of muscle evident. Now all he had to do was regain the rest of his strength, stamina, and bulk, and he'd be back to his normal self. Just another week at the pace he was improving.

"I'm stuffed," Pan said, covering a tiny belch.

Cam glanced over. "Really?"

Pan nodded. "Really. I'm also not getting as much out of the snake meat as I did initially. I think it means I'm nearly healed."

Cam frowned, surveying Pan, who appeared round-faced and plump. No ragged fur or areas of patchiness. And his little belly jiggled like it used to, and upon seeing that, Cam couldn't help himself. He reached over and poked Pan's belly.

"Hey!" Pan protested.

Cam smiled. "I had to do that."

"No, you didn't."

Cam chuckled. "Yes, I did. And I'm glad you've recovered, but I've still got a ways to go."

"You'll get there," Birch said from his place by the campfire, already in his rolls. "I have. It's wonderful. Now be quiet. Use your telepathy voice. Some of us need our beauty rest."

Cam snorted. "You'll be sleeping for a century if you're thinking it'll leave you beautiful."

Birch clutched his heart as if gravely wounded. "I was wrong. I won't die from the kaijus or terrible monsters here. I'll die from your cutting remarks."

Cam and Pan laughed while Birch turned his back to them.

"What happened back there?" Pan asked Cam after a moment of silence.

"Telepathy voice!" Birch reminded them.

Pan stuck his tongue out at the rakshasa.

"I saw that," Birch declared. "Very childish." He rolled back over to face them. "And since you're talking about the kaiju, I want to know as well."

Cam discussed what the Crown-Haunted monster had said to him, even the attempted breach of his mind. "I was able to keep him out."

"A good thing," Birch said. "Kaijus with that kind of power... it's best to avoid any interaction with them."

They spoke for a while longer until Pan and Birch decided to get some sleep. Cam had first watch, and he spent most of the lonely hours staring into the forest, pondering the many dangers of Mote: the Great Rakshasas, the regular rakshasas, the poisonous Blood Sea, and the many monsters of Petala. Salvation was a heaven in comparison.

And once his time on watch was done, he nudged Birch awake and slipped into his own bedroll. He fell asleep in moments.

Seconds later, however, he awoke, confused and unsettled.

This wasn't Petala. There was no jungle, massive lake, or creatures rustling under the silvery-rose light. Instead, Cam stood within a broad courtyard, floored with tan pavers that stretched to brick walls rising twice his height. Potted jasmines, curry plants, and gurgling fountains lurked in shadowed alcoves while the statue of a handsome man ruled the space from a sunlit corner. The sculpture was posed heroically—sword held aloft—and his visage held a commanding sneer.

Was this a mindscape? Had Cam somehow been pulled into one? He wasn't sure, but he also felt certain that, whatever this place was, it didn't belong to Birch. It belonged to someone far more powerful.

Seconds of patient waiting with only the chirping of insects to mar the quiet passed until there came a presence, felt before it was seen, similar to Rukh's and Jessira's but of a lesser quality.

A man entered the courtyard, ending all questions. Cam knew him without any need for an introduction. This could only be one person: Coruscant, the Great Rakshasa. The Sower of the Wind. The Far-Seeing General. The Wrecker of Hope. Dressed in simple white clothes and with a sword sheathed at his hip, he was of medium height and build, of pale complexion and had hair the color of straw. His intelligence was immediately evident, as were his striking hazel irises and the field of crystalline-diamond sclerae that appeared to contain all the colors of an Ephemeral Master.

Coruscant seemed to take in Cam's entirety with a brief glance, and his handsome face lifted in a paternal smile. The weight of his terrible regard and presence caused Cam's knees to buckle, and a desire to bow and scrape before this man swept over him.

With a surge of his will, Cam threw off the invasion, bolstering his Domain even as ongoing confusion and a thousand questions splintered his thoughts and circled his mind. What was happening? How was this possible? How had Coruscant dragged him into this mindscape? Was this even real?

Coruscant's paternal smile never left him. "So you are the one who gave me so much trouble on Salvation. I'd sensed that you died during your travels to my world. Clearly, I was misinformed. Rukh and Jessira were wise to harbor you, doing so in a way that didn't void their agreement with us. Cunning." He tilted his head. "So tell me, how are you still alive? And where is the panda?"

Cam didn't bother replying, focused as he was on forcing down his fear and maintaining the integrity of his mind. It seemed all those times where he'd trained to keep his thoughts locked away would soon be tested in ways he'd never imagined.

Coruscant knew that his attempt at levity and warmth had fallen flat. It was as obvious as the glower on the boy's face. No matter. It was to be expected. Winning the trust of those who had been taught all their lives that he—Coruscant—was evil personified would be no easy task, especially those like this boy, those for whom Rukh and Jessira had taken a special interest.

"Where are you?" Coruscant asked, although he already knew the lad wouldn't answer. Again, it was of no concern. He merely needed to keep the boy locked here, and the longer the better. The answer was sure to become evident, and then Coruscant would learn all of the youth's secrets, whether he willed it or not.

Coruscant wouldn't even require brutish force or threats of violence to obtain his needs. A more subtle hand, a patient one, generally served his desires, specifically, the feigning of weakness, which often led his enemies to view him as less threatening. Their fear would then abate until it was too late. At that point, Coruscant could then crush them to his will or crush them into oblivion. It all depended on his requirements of the moment. He'd even almost managed it with Rukh and Jessira, but near the end, she had seen through his schemes and nearly destroyed him for it.

Thinking on their fight didn't bear considering, and Coruscant shifted his attention back to the young man. He hid a frown. What was the boy's name? He'd forgotten. And how were his mental shields so strong? Coruscant bore down with his will, and a grimace of pain creased the youth's face, causing him to stiffen. *Good.* And yet, he also didn't break. Coruscant found himself appreciating the boy's strength of will. His mental shields truly were admirable.

But like a stony cliff worn away to sand by the endless ocean, the boy eventually broke, only a little at first, but wasn't that how it always was? And in this case, it was enough. Coruscant had the information for which he'd been searching. The boy's name and so many other details. They flooded forth. The youth's painful history. The first Pathway to Grace that he'd tragically delved. A dead friend named Tern. Years lost to alcoholism.

Coruscant scowled at the boy's weakness to drink. Pathetic.

Redemption, though, in the form of a Glory-Staged squirrel named Honor. The Awakened Beast had sacrificed herself on Cam's behalf. Coruscant's scowl became a reflective frown. Why would anyone do that? And why did those green eyes seem so familiar?

More information. Meeting a panda named Pan who played the pan flute. Coruscant snorted. A bit on the nose there. Or was that a cosmic joke of some sort? The Wilde Sage, Rainen Winder, sponsoring the boy and panda as students at the Ephemeral Academy.

The information cut off as the boy somehow managed to firm his barriers. Truly impressive.

Still, Coruscant had learned enough. "Cam Folde of Traverse, leader of Light Squad. And the panda is with you. So is one of my own, a traitor. Birch Drang." Coruscant frowned. "And two lowly Advanced birds. Why do you keep such worthless creatures around?"

The boy responded with a sneer of fury and defiance. "You've seen some of my past and present, but you haven't seen my future. You should have."

Coruscant smiled, intrigued. Was the boy a prophet then? Was that why Rukh and Jessira had spent so much time and effort on his behalf? "And what is your future?"

"My future sees me carve this Realm free of your influence. You will be ended."

Coruscant threw his head back and laughed in delight. The boy had courage. He'd give him that. "Many have tried to end me. Rukh and Jessira amongst them. They all failed. I still live."

"So do they, and compared to them, you are a flea."

Coruscant grinned at the insult. It had been too long since he had encountered someone who spoke to him without fear. The last to do so had eventually become one of the Four—Fangold. Would this boy have that same mettle? Doubtful, but it would be interesting to learn how far he might progress. To see what would become of him once Coruscant tore him apart and rebuilt him. Would he still be the same intrepid warrior he was now? Coruscant intended on finding out. He made to speak, but he cut off with a scowl. *She* was coming.

The boy smiled. "And now you won't learn anything else."

Coruscant's scowl deepened.

The lad, this Cam Folde, might be more clever than he realized. Perhaps he had also sensed her approach. And maybe that was the reason for his clever wordplay and defiance. It might have merely been a distracting ruse.

If so, it had worked. Coruscant no longer had the time to break through the boy's barriers. Instead, he needed to focus entirely on his own fortifications. The Merciless Deceiver approached, and the mindscape was where she was strongest.

Cam smiled at Coruscant's displeasure. Fragging jackhole was so sure of himself, but apparently Shimala was enough to freeze him in place.

Good.

Nonetheless, the low-throated chuckle of the Great Rakshasa posing as an old woman had him stiffening in alarm. He recalled the prior times he'd interacted with the Merciless Deceiver, and none of them had been pleasant. Not even the last occasion when Shimala's link to him had been ripped apart by Rukh. Still, witnessing her abject terror when confronted by the Holy Servant had been a true pleasure.

Cam smiled a bit, and the recollection of Shimala's fear helped him bring his own burgeoning terror under control. His mind cleared, anger rippled, but he controlled the reaction, burying his thoughts and emotions behind thick barriers, willing them to strengthen even further before Shimala fully arrived.

For this meeting, he needed utter clarity of thought. He masked his features, and a moment later, Shimala's chuckle repeated. It was the kind of laughter steeped in malice, and he turned around as an old crone with a grandmother's kindly visage and ancient eyes as ugly as sin entered the courtyard, strolling toward them with a gap-toothed grin of broken and blackened teeth.

Shimala.

Cam stared at her, his face studiously blank, wondering at her ugliness. Coruscant was handsome, and it was known that all Ephemeral Masters could change their appearance to a certain extent, especially once they Advanced to Glory or Crown. Surely Shimala with her swirling crystalline-Haunted sclerae could improve her looks some.

Something of his thinking must have been evident because Shimala glanced his way and winked. "You'll want to stop staring so hard at me, boy. I might begin wondering why." To make sure her point got across, the foul woman licked her lips in a lascivious fashion.

Cam bit back a grimace, earning him a mocking chuckle.

Coruscant broke the tableau. "If I'd known you were visiting, I would have set the table in the torture chamber."

Shimala waggled her brows at him. "You and me naked, little lord? We can have that sort of fun another time." She gestured to Cam. "What about your new pet? When can I try him? You don't mind sharing, do you? I promise not to break him. Much"

Coruscant snorted in derision. "It is your mind that is already broken, old crone. I remember your last days in Seminal."

Shimala scowled at Coruscant. "And I remember you begging for Jessira's mercy. On your knees, like a little lapdog."

Even as she insulted Coruscant, Shimala sent to Cam's mind. "*You remember me, don't you, boy? I remember you. You will be mine again. In this Realm, Devesh has no sway.*"

Cam felt a needle of her will try to intrude into his mind, but he threw it off with a surge of fury. How dare she? He straightened his shoulders and stared Shimala in the eyes, daring her to try again. Cam maintained eye contact even as she sneered and tried and failed again to breach his mental defenses. He wouldn't break and gibber before this heinous fiend. He wasn't a terrified boy any longer, and there was no chance she'd steal her way into his life and mind ever again.

"*How brave you are, child, but I remember your fear. The taste of it. The sweetness.*" Cam didn't respond, and Shimala smirked. "*You have nothing to say for yourself? Or maybe you can't. Telepathy is beyond a weakling like you.*"

"*I remember enough, and I know enough,*" Cam replied, sending Shimala images from their last time together, of when Rukh had made her cower in terror.

She roared at him in outrage.

"Enough!" Coruscant snapped, furious but likely unaware of the silent conversation between Cam and Shimala. "He is mine. Not yours. As is this place. Leave us now."

Shimala shrugged, appearing utterly untroubled by Coruscant's anger or Cam's insult. She maintained her insouciance. "Calm yourself, my young Coruscant. Before deciding what to do with this boy, we have matters to discuss."

With a scowl of disgust, Coruscant reined in his anger. "What matters?"

"The matter of my thralls, your legions, dear Simmer's creatures and our hopes for increasing them."

"I seek followers, not thralls," Coruscant stated. "And you ruin your hopes for more thralls when you regularly allow so many to be slaughtered in Salvation. But that is typical for you, isn't it? What did you do to your followers last time? How did you treat them?" Coruscant lifted a finger in the air, like he'd just managed to recall the answer. "Ah, yes. You killed so many with a *thaali*."

Shimala tittered. "It gave me endless pleasure to use something holy in that way."

"And yet, in the end, Jessira denied your victory."

"She denied yours as well." Shimala waved away his words. "And none of that is of any concern. It's old news, as they say in some Realms. Besides which, my thralls are far more competent than those long-eared louts."

Coruscant laughed in her face. "You honestly believe an unthinking thrall is better than a loyal retainer, someone who can do as they are bid even when unforeseen obstacles impede their paths?"

Cam listened without speaking, fascinated in spite of himself. There were so many historical references being bandied about, and he had no way to truly understand what they might mean. And while he realized he could now likely break free of the mindscape, there was no reason to do so. Not when two Great Rakshasas were stupid enough to speak of their plans while he was in a position to overhear.

Shimala gave Coruscant a canny expression. "Mock me at your peril, but you would be wise to follow my lead in this." She indicated Cam. "Your way will never see this child broken to your will. He has been touched by Rukh and Jessira. We all received similar reports, the training they gave him at that Academy."

"Is that why you're here?" Coruscant asked with a sneer. "Fear of this boy?"

"I fear no one, but I know about this boy. He was in Hearth for mere months. An Acolyte. But look at him now. A Glory already. He Advances too quickly."

Coruscant delayed in replying. "He is loved by Rukh and Jessira. That much is true, and he is mine. I brought him to Mote, to my territory. It is I who will find and break him."

"You don't have him?" Shimala asked, sounding surprised. An instant later, she cackled laughter. "You are such a simpleton. Everything is clear now. The boy is in Petala. He seeks to escape through the Locus. The moment he steps foot upon the Badlands, he'll be mine. I'll see it done." This time, it was she who sneered in derision. "And you honestly believe you can win?"

Coruscant offered a cheerless smile. "I'll have him in hand well before he steps foot on the Badlands. And even then, what will you do if he rouses Pelluraj or reaches the Locus? He'll be lost to you as well."

Shimala scowled, and that was all the information Cam needed. A plan came together in his mind. Shimala had correctly guessed at his location, and no doubt, she'd have the Locus tightly guarded. But with the right distraction, that cordon would loosen, and Coruscant had, either wittingly or otherwise, told them exactly how to do it. Pelluraj. The mightiest of the kaijus. If they could gain his attention and draw him to the Badlands, he could pull Shimala and her thralls away from the Locus.

Cam considered the plan. It was dangerous but it might also be their best chance to escape Mote. He nodded to himself, deciding it would do.

The conversation hadn't yet ended, though, and Shimala hadn't yet quit her smirk. "I will win, and I will steal this boy back to my side."

Coruscant didn't miss the statement. "Back to your side? And you say you knew of him in Hearth, but that Realm is denied to us." He frowned, speaking deliberately, like he was piecing together possibilities. "Which means what?" An instant later, he broke out in a knowing grin. "You were once linked to him but not any longer." He jeered at Shimala and cast a flicking-away motion at her. "Begone, old crone. You had your chance. Leave him to those of us with competence."

Shimala's smirk never left her visage, and she dipped a mocking bow at Coruscant. "Good hunting. We'll soon find out if your so-called retainers are better than my thralls." Her eyes landed on Cam. "And if you can make this follower of Rukh and Jessira your own."

With that, the mindscape dissolved.

Cam unshuttered his eyes, caught in a moment of vertigo. An instant later, he slammed shut the opening that had somehow been left ajar in his mind, wondering how it could have happened. He reviewed the day's events, seeking any mistakes he might have made, and he soon had his answer.

The kaiju Crown. For reasons of his own, the beast had wanted Cam's mind to remain open. He'd even said so. He must have somehow done this.

Cam shivered at the beast's frightening capabilities, enraged at how the kaiju had sliced an opening past his mental wards without him even knowing it. If that was the case, then what kind of power would Pelluraj—a Sage—have?

Until they encountered the monster, there was no way of knowing, and it was with these worries that Cam pondered what he'd just experienced. In spite of the breach to his defenses, nothing too terrible had happened. True, Coruscant knew of his past, knew of Traverse—knew too many details overall—but all told, it could have gone far worse.

And in some ways, it had actually been to Cam's benefit since listening in on the conversation between the Great Rakshasas had turned out to be useful. Coruscant and Shimala were powerful and deadly, but they also weren't unstoppable forces. They could be defeated, and both of them had their own weaknesses. Chief amongst them was their rivalry, and in Shimala's case, she also feared Pelluraj.

Cam considered again the plan he'd concocted in Coruscant's mindscape. What flaws was he overlooking? He couldn't tell, which meant he was too close to the situation. Glancing about, he noticed that Birch had the watch. The rakshasa sat with his back to the fire and was staring outward.

For a brief moment, Cam thought about discussing what he'd experienced with Birch, but no. Best to talk it over in the morning when all of them were fresh.

34

On the morning after his encounter with Coruscant and Shimala, Cam awoke just as the Hollow Land's strange sun came to life. A strong wind gusted, stirring the perpetual humidity but not driving it off, and in the distance, purple-tinged clouds without any silver linings promised the coming of a storm, a gullywasher as they'd call it back in Traverse.

Pan and Birch were both awake, and Cam figured now was as good a time as any to tell them what had happened overnight and what he thought they should do moving forward. He explained the situation along with his plan, and when finished, he glanced from Pan to Birch and back again, waiting for their responses.

They were being awfully quiet.

Birch was the one to break the contemplative silence. "You want us to use ourselves as bait and draw Pelluraj to the Badlands?" He sounded like he wasn't sure what to make of the plan, something beyond doubtful. But a moment later, the old-headed rakshasa offered a nod of acknowledgment and a sly grin. "You learned an enemy's weakness while not betraying any of your own. Well done.

Pan also grinned in his cute, toothy way and pressed his forehead to Cam's. "Birch is right. You did well." He addressed the rakshasa. "You both did. Without your training, Cam's Domain couldn't have succeeded. I'm proud of both of you."

Birch rolled his eyes. "I think that's quite enough of that treacly praise." The rakshasa appeared irritated, but Cam could see the pleasure in his eyes.

"It's not treacly if it's honest," Pan replied.

Birch responded with another eye roll.

Cam smiled at the interplay, relieved that the two of them saw the situation the same way he did. "I'm just glad it didn't go the other way, and Coruscant didn't figure out more than he did."

"I'm surprised he actually helped you, whether he meant to or not," Pan said.

Birch shrugged. "Coruscant and Shimala are Great Rakshasas, but they hate each other nearly as much as they hate Rukh and Jessira."

Cam had suspected as much based on the interactions between the two fiends. He clapped his hands. "Time's wasting. Let's get going. We'll eat on the trail."

They proceeded down the cliff on which they'd camped with Kiwi and Sprite pecking on acorns bigger than their beaks while the rest of them ate smoked snake. Cam imagined that every bite improved his strength and stamina some incremental amount and that every little bit of improvement was worth achieving. He kept viewing his arms, glad to see them muscled and filling out.

However, upon reaching the cliff's base, his self-reflection cut off, replaced by alarm when Pan shouted. Cam crouched down, tense, gaze darting about for danger. A moment later, he relaxed when he saw the cause of Pan's reaction: a stand of bamboo. He shook his head, calling a halt to their trek.

"Is he always like that when it comes to bamboo?" Birch asked while Pan harvested as many shoots as he could hold.

Cam viewed the rakshasa in disbelief. "Did you think he was joking when he made all those comments about bamboo?"

"I thought it was mere exaggeration."

Cam grunted. "It wasn't."

Pan harvested as much bamboo as he could carry, and they were soon off again while he munched loudly and contentedly.

"Is eating all that bamboo doing anything other than filling your gullet?" Cam asked when Pan showed no signs of slowing down.

"You mean is the bamboo providing healing like the meat?" Pan shrugged. "Not as much, but it's been too long since I've had any bamboo."

"At the rate you're eating it, you won't have any left by tomorrow morning."

Pan chuckled. "It's a price I'll gladly pay for having a belly stuffed full of bamboo today." He affected a portentous expression. "After all, a bamboo in the hand is worth two in the stand."

"That's a bird in the hand—" Birch said.

Cam desperately signaled the rakshasa, trying to cut him off before he could finish the phrase.

"—is worth two in the bush," Birch finished with a laugh.

Cam's shoulders slumped, and sure enough…

"What do you mean?" Sprite asked. "Why would a bird in the hand be worth two in the bush?"

Birch's expression went sickly. "Nothing. Just a mistaken turn of phrase. Forget I said anything."

Sprite continued to pester Birch for an explanation about what he meant as they traveled on.

The rakshasa lost his patience. "It's just a phrase. It means just be glad for what you already have instead of wishing for more."

Sprite silenced a moment, head cocked as he peered at Birch from his perch on Cam's shoulder. "I don't think that's what it means."

Birch flung his arms in the air, making an inarticulate noise before marching forward to join Pan.

"Do you know what it means?" Sprite asked, tilting his head and staring Cam's way.

"What do you think it means?"

"Does it matter?" Kiwi interrupted. "It's probably something predators believe. We don't have to know."

Sprite thankfully let the matter drop, and Cam quickly caught up to Pan and Birch, who had pulled ahead of him. They were talking about bamboo again.

"I think you'd eat that bamboo even if it caused you an upset stomach," Birch said. "Never have I seen someone so joyous at eating grass."

"It's not grass," Pan protested. An instant later, he corrected himself. "Well, it's a type of grass, but it's not like what cows and sheep eat. Bamboo is crunchy deliciousness."

"I'm sure it is," Birch said, his tone dripping with condescension. "If you're a panda."

"Or a panda-person," Cam added.

They chuckled, but Cam's humor fled when a soft rapping on his mental wards gained his alertness. *Thor.* He indicated for the others to halt, waiting for the Divine to speak.

"Light Squad is coming to you," Thor said.

"Now? You're sending them now?" Cam's heart raced with sudden excitement and anticipation.

"Yes," Thor replied. *"I'm sending them from Hearth. They'll arrive any second."*

"What is it?" Pan asked.

Cam didn't bother answering. Instead, he pointed to where a black line had split the world. Birch growled, claws out and ready to defend.

"It's Light Squad," Cam said to the rakshasa. Birch relaxed his claws, but his nose still twitched in agitation, for which Cam empathized. This was a large change for Birch. He'd be meeting new people and have to trust them when all his life he'd been taught to trust no one. "I know what you're thinking," Cam said, resting what he hoped was a comforting hand on Birch's shoulder. "We'll be with you."

Birch growled and shrugged off Cam's hand. "I'm not afraid of them."

Cam accepted the rebuke without anger. "As you wish."

By then, the anchor line had rotated, exposing a doorway where a rainbow bridge stretched to infinity. Out of it strode Charity Kazar, eyes sparkling with the indigo Haunt of Crown. A grimace of pain flashed across her lovely features. No doubt, she found the lack of Ephemera disconcerting. That, and the disorientation and nausea of traveling an anchor line across Realms.

Cam gave her space to recover, and while she did so, the rest of Light Squad emptied into Petala: Avia, Jade, Card, and Saira.

Cam found himself grinning wide and unable to speak. Light Squad. They were really and truly here. His eyes shone with unshed tears, and he didn't know what to say, and based on their expressions, neither did Pan, Charity, or the rest of their friends. They stood facing one another in silence.

It was a quiet broken by Birch who strode forward from where he'd been lurking in the back. "So you are the famous Light Squad. Cam and Pan have told me much about you. I'm Birch Drang. The one who kept them alive here in Mote. Introduce yourselves."

Charity addressed Birch with a warm smile. "Cam spoke highly of you." She inclined her head in a shallow bow. "Thank you for all that you've done for him and Pan."

The leonine rakshasa grinned. "It was a pleasure. They did well for me as well. I'd still be trapped in the prison if not for them."

The rest of Light Squad introduced themselves, but Charity had eyes only for Cam and Pan. After hugging her favorite panda-person and earning one of his adorable smiles, she faced Cam, scrutinizing him for the changes that had to be present. He'd been trapped in Mote for four months. That kind of imprisonment had to mark a person.

Indeed, based on their few conversations, she had expected to find him to be a walking skeleton, all skin and bones. Instead, physically he wasn't too different from when she had last seen him—a little skinnier, face slightly narrower, and beard much thicker. But otherwise, not much different at all.

But there were changes. His emotional exhaustion and the simmering anger lurking under his welcoming smile. And looking at Pan, Charity was sad to see the same changes present in him as well, not to the same extent but evident, nonetheless. Their emotions were understandable, and Charity pursed her lips in sympathy. In a better world, Cam and Pan wouldn't be filled with any such rage, but it burned within them, as obvious as a lit lantern in the dark. They wouldn't rest until her father and Weld Plain were brought to justice.

She did her best to set aside her worries. Those were concerns for another day. "It's good to see you again," Charity said, oddly hesitant and not knowing what else to say to Cam.

He laughed, drawing her into a hug. "Is that all you have to say to me? I'd have been sure there would have been some kind of comment to put me off balance."

"Maybe later," Charity said, her reticence melting under Cam's warm embrace, grateful that he didn't blame or hate her. He had said he didn't, but she hadn't been sure until now. Her arms looped around his waist, and she rested her head against his chest. It felt good holding him again.

They stood in an island of privacy until Charity pulled away. She smiled at Cam, bopping his nose. "You need new clothes. Those rags are about to fall apart." She slowly flicked her eyes up and down his body. "Not that I mind, but there are other women present. We wouldn't want you giving them a free show, like you did for Jade that one time."

Cam's expression went blank.

"The shower at the Ephemeral Academy?" Charity prompted him. "When you streaked her?"

Cam's face cleared, and he laughed. "Oh, that."

"And you do need new clothes."

Cam glanced at himself, flushing and apparently only now realizing how much of his skin was showing. Most of his thighs were exposed along with a good chunk of his chest and back and even part of a butt cheek.

Charity laughed, glad that some things about Cam hadn't changed.

"You can't hog him all to yourself," Avia said as she and Jade joined them. They hugged Cam before stepping back to make room for Card.

The two men shared a brief, manly embrace. "I can't believe you survived," Card said afterward. He had a smile plastered on his face, which was an occurrence as rare as snow in Maviro.

"I can't believe I survived either," Cam said, his Glory-Haunted eyes shining with happiness, which was a far better expression for him than the simmering anger that Charity had earlier noted.

Pan, Birch, and Saira joined them.

"What happens now?" Pan asked. "Do we camp here?"

The green lovebird Charity had earlier noticed trilled for attention. This must be Kiwi, and the little avian perched on one of Pan's shoulders while a yellow one—Sprite—sat on the panda's head. Charity examined the two lovebirds and grinned. They were so cute, nearly as adorable as one of Pan's toothy smiles.

"Charity was telling Cam he needs new clothes," Kiwi said.

"You can say that again," Jade said before addressing Cam. "What are you trying to do? Shock our eyes with all that skin? You already did that to me once."

Cam flushed again, which only caused everyone to laugh at his embarrassment.

Charity, though, decided to save her beau. She halted mid-stride. *Beau.* It had been so long since she had used the folksy word, and she smiled inwardly, glad to recall it. "Here," she said, pulling out a pair of rugged breeches and a fresh shirt out of her *null pocket.* "Why don't you go change?"

Cam gave her a grateful nod before darting off behind the bushes. Moments later, he was dressed more appropriately, and the same held true for Pan and Birch, who had also been given fresh clothing, in their cases by Saira.

"Now that Cam's backside is properly covered," Saira said. "We need a plan on how to traverse the Badlands."

"We have a plan," Cam said, "but first, are you weaker here than on Salvation?"

Charity knew what he was really asking, but it was Saira who responded. "You mean because of the lack of Ephemera?"

Cam chuckled. "Petala is like a lush oasis compared to the prison's desert."

Charity cocked her head. "That was surprisingly poetic. Have you taken up the literary arts?"

"Never," Cam said with a grin. "I like my way of talking too much. And don't worry. I won't talk any kind of lyrical if it ain't needed."

Card groaned. "And then you had to ruin it by speaking like that."

"I think his backwoods way of speaking is charming," Charity said.

"You always say that," Card replied.

"That's country way of speaking," Birch growled. "He was insistent on that being the proper descriptor of his vulgar accent."

"More like yokel," Card muttered.

Avia looked ready to add her opinion, but Cam cut her off. "We can go over the merits of how I speak another time." He went on to explain his plan about Pelluraj and how he intended on using the Sage-Staged beast against Shimala.

"It could work," Saira mused, her words reflecting Charity's own unspoken thoughts. "But we should test one these creatures. See how deadly they actually are."

Cam agreed with her. "We'll also learn how the lack of Ephemera affects your abilities."

"It's best to attack from a distance," Pan said. "That's how we defeated the one kaiju we fought."

Birch shuddered. "We were lucky when we fought him."

"Maybe so," Cam allowed. "But now we have four Crowns and a Sage to help us."

"This could actually work," Jade said, sounding simultaneously shocked and delighted. She clapped her hands. "It won't be easy, but it's doable."

Charity viewed the other woman in question. She hadn't realized Jade had been so full of doubts about coming to Mote. She'd talk to her later when it was just the two of them.

"And once you get back to Salvation, what will you do?" Saira asked.

"We'll Advance to Crown," Cam answered.

Saira's eyes widened in surprise. "You have the answer then?"

"We do. Both me and Pan."

"And Birch?"

The rakshasa shrugged. "I'm only an Adept, but I punch higher than you might expect."

Cam told them about Birch's abilities with Nullity, again going over the mindscape that he and Pan shared with the rakshasa and how it had allowed them to master the skills he'd been given by Rukh and Jessira.

"We'll need you at Crown as swiftly as possible," Saira said. "My mother should have a treasure. If not, Rainen might. He'll do whatever it takes to get another two Crowns battling with him. Salvation is buckling. The Sage-Dukes and Sage-Duchesses and their short-sighted vision and politics are a guarantee for the continent's demise."

Cam's brow furrowed. He'd clearly not been expecting to hear such dire news. "What about your home? The Sinanes."

Saira's lips tightened in unhappiness. "As Golden goes, so goes the world. The Sinanes will fall if we don't turn the tide."

Charity watched from her rolls as Cam marched the camp's perimeter, his back to the fire as he stared into the forest where insects made their usual racket and animals moved about amongst the thick shrubs and undergrowth. In the sky, she spied wheeling bats as large as eagles and wondered what kind of insects they ate. Were they the size of Kiwi and Sprite? Most likely so. Everything in Petala was larger than anything she'd ever encountered, and no doubt, the insects were of the same excessive size. Thankfully, they left Light Squad alone, apparently recognizing they weren't easy prey.

She continued to watch Cam, thinking about him, much like she had done ever since arriving in this strange Hollow Land. Upon learning he was still alive, doubts had flooded Charity's mind—not about coming here—mostly about where she fit in Cam's life. She wasn't sure about him any longer, his motivations, even his interests and dislikes. It had been so long apart for them, and he'd changed tremendously in that time, brief though it was for him, and she wasn't sure what that portended for the two of them.

What did Cam want? Charity could no longer tell. She lacked the easy ability to read him that she could once rely upon. Her skill at deciphering the subtle motivations that drove a person failed her when it came to Cam, and the loss had her wondering and worried.

Was Cam broken? On the surface, he looked largely unchanged, which was shocking. During their initial conversation, he had told her of his many infirmities of hair loss, muscular atrophy, and overall fragility. But seeing him now, it was hard to believe it had ever been the case. Cam was as tall as ever and while leaner, he was still nearly as powerfully built as before. He moved well, stalked rather than paced, and he also possessed a greater gravity, granted in part by the simmering anger she'd first sensed on their reunion.

Was his healing really because of the food here in Petala? Charity had eaten some of the snake meat, and while bland of taste and texture, it had left her pleasantly full. Otherwise, she'd observed no changes to herself or anyone else.

But apparently that hadn't been the case for Cam, Pan, and Birch. Based on their statements, the various meats, fruits, and nuts from Petala had quickly restored their bodies and repaired what the prison had ravaged. If true—and Charity had no reason to doubt their words—then she would count it a blessing. Cam and Pan deserved every kind of healing for what they'd endured.

Charity continued to study Cam for a little while longer before deciding she'd watched him long enough. It was time for them to talk, especially about what weighed so heavily on her mind. Taking a moment to create her scent of honeysuckle and hibiscus—mostly because the Cam she used to know liked it so much—she shifted out of her bedroll and rose to her feet, stepping carefully so as to not awaken anyone else.

She caught Cam smiling before she arrived. No doubt he'd scented her fragrance just like she'd hoped. He reached out blindly, and she took his hand, letting him pull her to his side.

"You smell good," Cam noted as they walked the camp's perimeter.

"Thank you," Charity said with a pleased smile at his words. "It's good to see you again."

Cam tossed her a grin. "You've said that already. It was actually one of the first things you said."

Charity arched her brow, mildly affronted. "Are you saying I'm not allowed to say it again? Because you're certainly allowed to say it back to me."

"It's good to see you again."

His words elicited another smile, one that faded as they continued pacing around the camp. This was it. It was time to confess. "I'm sorry."

Cam frowned, eyeing her in puzzlement. "Sorry about what?"

"That we didn't find you sooner. That my father betrayed you and Pan. That any of this happened to you."

Cam's puzzlement faded. "You mean my imprisonment." He shrugged. "The lack of Ephemera was the worst, but we got used to it. And your father made a mistake in letting us live. I'm sure that wasn't his intention, but it happened. And we'll pay him back for what he did." His eyes locked on her. "Do you have a problem with that? Pan and I are of one mind about this. Your father and Weld are both on our list. They die."

His vow wasn't surprising, but Charity still had to hide a shiver at his obdurate resolve. This was a harder Cam than the one she'd last seen, unforgiving and darker. She understood the reasons for the changes, but she still wept over them.

He must have sensed her turmoil because he drew her to a halt, hands on her shoulders as he peered at her. "I'm sorry if what I said bothers you, but this is the way it has to be. Neither of us—me nor Pan—can let this go."

Charity nodded. "I understand, and I won't try to stop you or even talk you out of it." She shrugged, helpless to explain what had her so upset. It also wasn't Cam's task to make her feel better. She should be the one helping him, but that would also mean asking him personal questions, and she wasn't sure how he'd react to her queries. Hesitating, she asked him anyway. "Did they torture you?"

Cam shook his head. "Not physically. It was much more insidious than that. It was the isolation that was worse than how our bodies wore down. They kept us in separate cells, in sheer darkness. Nothing to see or hear. Only smell and feel, and even then, there was only the cold and my own reek." He shrugged like it wasn't important, but Charity could see the pain in his eyes. "But at least I had Pan and Birch, and later on those two." He indicated the sleeping lovebirds, who currently roosted on Pan's belly.

She smiled. "They like you. How did they end up here?"

"Someone sold them to a rakshasa Sage, and the Sage gave them to one of the Four."

"Who sold them?"

"I never bothered asking," Cam said with a shrug.

"You should. Maybe that person should be on their list."

Cam smiled, still staring at the lovebirds. "They like perching on me. I think they find my shoulders comforting."

Charity squeezed his arm. "I like your shoulders, too, and for the same reason."

He cocked his head as if he were confused. "Is this some teasing thing you're doing?"

"Just me being honest. We weren't the same without you. Without Pan. Light Squad was incomplete, and we knew it. It's good being with you again, and I can't tell you how glad we are—how glad I am that you escaped that prison."

Cam smirked. "Why Charity Kazar, if I didn't know better, I'd think you *were* flirting with me."

Charity forced a throaty chuckle, recognizing what Cam wasn't saying. He wanted her to drop the matter about his imprisonment. "Is it working? Do you find yourself wanting to kiss me?" She pressed close, eyes lidded, voice husky, and she could tell from Cam's arms going around her waist that he wanted to do exactly that. Now, it was Charity who smirked.

"Is that an offer?" Cam asked.

"Only if you're brave enough to accept it." Charity pursed her lips, eyes closed, waiting for him to kiss her.

But Cam surprised her. His hands dropped from her waist, and he took a long stride away from her. "I would kiss you, but I'm supposed to be guarding the camp." He viewed her, a challenging expression of his own. "Maybe when we're alone, you'll still let me?"

Charity smiled, hiding her disappointment. What Cam said made sense, but there was a reluctance to his mannerisms that hurt. Had his feelings for her changed? "We'll see," she allowed. She strode away from him, and without having to look back, she knew he was staring at her. But what was he thinking?

35

The next morning, Cam roused early and looked over at Charity. She was still asleep, and he didn't bother waking her. He wasn't ready to talk to her again, especially since their conversation last night hadn't really settled his worries. They'd only raised fresh puzzles. While he'd never questioned that she would still care for him, he'd also never been sure where they would stand as a couple once he found out how much time had rolled by for her.

Those questions hadn't been present during their two conversations across the Realms, but from the moment he'd seen her again yesterday, they'd crept up on him like a foreign weed over fresh fields. And it all had to do with time and their experience of it.

Three years. That's how long it had been for Charity. Three years spent in the Sinanes. Three years to forget what they'd briefly shared as a couple. Three years to Advance to Crown. And given Charity's accomplishments and beauty, surely she hadn't lacked for suitors. Had she really turned them all down? And if so, why?

It seemed to be the case, especially given their conversation last night. But nevertheless, the doubts remained. With their time apart, why would she have bothered waiting for him? It wasn't even a matter of thinking himself unworthy, but simple human nature. Three years was a long time to go without companionship. So, with whom had she shared her life?

Cam recognized how his pettiness and jealousy didn't reflect well on him, but it was hard to let them go, to shove away the fears and imaginings. He did his best to do so. The fact was, Charity had come to Mote in order to save him, and that should tell him everything he needed to know about how she felt for him.

Wanting that to be his final thought on the matter, Cam stretched mightily and slipped out of his bedrolls. Overnight, mist had rolled in, fogging the surrounding jungle. No wind stirred the brambles and trees, and the animals were either asleep or had a notion of remaining quiet in Light Squad's presence. Either that or there were kaijus about.

Whatever the case, Cam appreciated the peace, and he made his way over to where Pan was bent over a pot, stirring whatever he'd fixed them for breakfast. Seated on a log and keeping Pan company were Birch and Card while Saira stood in the near distance, guarding their campsite. Avia, Charity, and Jade, however, remained in their bedrolls.

Cam leaned over to see what Pan had in the pot. "What are you fixing?" he asked, although the answer was probably some kind of snake stew. At least there were some seasonings. Cam scented paprika, cumin, and coriander along with garlic and ginger. If nothing else, the spices would make the stew more palatable. Cam was grateful for the healing gift of the food found in Petala, but he was tired of its blandness.

Gathering a bowl and blowing on it to reduce the heat—although as a Glory, a little fire couldn't hurt him much—Cam settled next to Card and Birch, both of whom already had their own dishes.

"This is actually pretty good," Card noted, having taken a bite.

"If it tasted like burned bamboo, we'd have still eaten it," Pan said. "The food we've found here is the only reason we survived."

"Things were that bad?" Card asked, taking another bite of his stew.

"Remember how tired we were after Dander?" Cam asked him.

Card nodded.

"Multiply that times ten."

Card grunted in reply, which had Cam smiling. He'd missed Card's grunting.

"The weakness wasn't the worst of it, though," Birch said. "There was that rain of snakes."

Card frowned at the old-headed rakshasa. "When you say rain of snakes, you mean like it was literally raining snakes?"

"They were falling all around us like scale-covered hail," Pan said. "Massive beasts, venomous, too."

Kiwi and Sprite alighted on Cam's shoulders, fluttering their wings before settling down. "Nothing is fouler than a snake," the green lovebird declared.

"Except maybe a cat," Sprite countered.

Birch growled softly in response.

"I said a cat," Sprite corrected. "Not a lion."

Birch gave the yellow lovebird a hard stare and a final harrumph.

"Anyway," Pan continued. "Most of the snakes were massive."

"How massive?" Card asked.

"The length of a tree," Pan answered. "Or at least as thick around as the trunk of one. Some of them were."

Card remained unconvinced, and he indicated the simmering stew. "And that's how big this one was?"

Cam shook his head, recollecting the battle against the fierce serpent. "This one was one of the smaller ones, but it was also probably one of the deadliest. It was Advanced. A Glory."

Card whistled appreciation. "That must have been a fierce fight. So how did you kill it?"

Birch grinned. "It was all on account of our illustrious leader. He's an utter lackwit with more courage than good sense." The rakshasa went on to explain how Cam had lured the snake into falling off a cliff.

Card laughed softly. "You're right. He's always had more courage than good sense. His lackwittedness… is that a word?" Card shook off his own question, addressing Cam. "What were you thinking?"

Cam shrugged, taking a bite of stew. "I was thinking we could use the meat. And I was also thinking that there was no way we were losing a battle to some stupid snake, no matter how Advanced."

Card cleared his throat. "Don't you mean no chance?"

Cam grinned at the reminder of Light Squad's mantra. "That's right. Exactly."

"And it wasn't sentient?" Card asked, taking a bite of stew.

Cam shook his head. "The lovebirds can tell when an Awakened Beast is also sentient. They said the snake wasn't."

"Mote is unusual," Pan said. "Or at least Petala is. Awakened Beasts here aren't all sentient. Sometimes they're just very powerful animals."

"And my plan also worked," Cam said, going back to how he'd lured the snake to its death. "The snake was a Glory, and we needed it dead. I'm not anywhere close to where I was physically prior to coming here, but I'm not far behind."

"Good enough to spar?" Card asked.

"No. We're too close to the lake," Cam replied. "The kaijus rule this place. If they hear us, they'll come investigate. We need to be quiet and careful."

"Quiet and careful are the bywords by which to survive the Hollow Land," Birch said as if offering sage advice. A moment later, his serious demeanor gave way to a careless grin. "Of course, as I have always told these four, we're likely going to die here anyway, so maybe we shouldn't worry about it so much."

"Don't mind him," Cam advised Card. "He's always like that."

"Most annoyingly fatalistic," Pan agreed.

Birch continued to grin. "I prefer to call it realistic."

Card briefly viewed the rakshasa before eventually grunting and going back to eating his stew.

Cam caught Birch looking his way. "Will he be doing that all the time?" the rakshasa asked, indicating Card. "Grunting like that?"

"All the time," Pan said, sounding mournful. "If you manage to get him to smile, count yourself blessed amongst both humans and Awakened Beasts."

"I smile when it's required," Card said, not looking up from his bowl.

"Smiling isn't a requirement," Pan replied. "It's supposed to be something you *want* to do, not something you *have* to do."

Jade had awoken during their conversation, and she stumbled over to the pot of stew. She sniffed it once, made a moue of distaste, but served herself a bowl anyway. She plopped down next to Cam. "Give it up. Even after Advancing to Crown, Card is who he's always been: a grump. That's never going to change. Even if he reaches Divine."

Card seemed to consider her words, giving a grunt of agreement before going back to his stew.

"A joyous one, he is," Birch muttered, appearing less than pleased.

But Cam felt otherwise, and he viewed Card with a smile. Yes, the man was a grump. Yes, he could be a pain with his grunts and attitude of superiority—although to be fair, that had faded some over time. However, what was most important to Cam was that Card was his friend. His brother. And he was glad to have his brother back in his life.

After breakfast, once everyone was up and ready, Cam viewed Lake Petala from the heights of the rise upon where Light Squad had camped. Even following the riverbank, which was crowded with thick jungle, he reckoned it would be a long slog.

He sighed, more than ready to be done with this part of the Hollow Land. "Let's get going." He made to stride in the direction of the river, knowing they'd want to maintain distance from the waters. He hadn't forgotten the tentacled horror he'd briefly spied a few days ago.

But before he could take five strides, a clearing of a throat hauled him short. "Where are you going?" Saira asked.

Cam wasn't sure what she meant, and he pointed at the river. "I was thinking we could follow the river to Lake Petala."

Saira chuckled. "You think we should walk?" She indicated the rest of Light Squad. "What do you say about flying?"

It took a moment for her words to penetrate Cam's thinking, but once they did, he shook his head at his lack of awareness. That's right. The rest of Light Squad had Advanced to Crown, which meant they'd also learned to fly. Cam's gaze went back to the jungled riverbank and Lake Petala. What he'd previously reckoned to be a few days of hard slogging was likely only a few hours travel through the sky. Of course, it had also meant he, Pan, and Birch would have to be carried like small children on a bed of air since they couldn't fly, but it was also a small price to pay. Then there were the flying monsters.

Saira must have recognized his doubt. "I understand the creatures here can be powerful, but they're wary of me. They veer away whenever they come close, especially the ones who can fly."

In that case… Cam grinned. "Who's flying me over there?"

It turned out to be Jade. She scooped Cam onto a bed of air, resting him so he faced forward while lying prone. Then she rose into the air, slowly, like she was getting a feel for carrying someone else. Once sure of herself, she called down to him. "Ready?"

Cam continued to grin. "Go fast?"

"Yes, sir."

Like a bolt, they were off. Cam threw his arms wide and whooped. The wind whipped over his face and through his hair. His clothes flattened against his frame, and the noise of their passage was a rushing sound, like waves breaking. He loved it, wanting wings of his own. He wanted to swoop and turn, do loops and spins, twirl through the air and race the sun. Nothing beat flying.

Sadly, the flight ended a few hours later when Jade alighted them on a small rocky hillock overlooking the lake. She set Cam on his feet while Charity and Card did the same for Pan and Birch. Saira and Avia, who had overflight control, landed a moment later. A harsh breeze gusted off the lake and waves crashed against the hill. Cold spray splashed high and mist carried, dousing them in droplets.

"It's clean," Pan said with a confused frown, licking at water dribbling down his chin.

Cam took a testing taste of the showering spray. The water was, indeed, clean, fresher than any he'd had since coming to Mote, having the flavor of a benediction, even compared to any of the streams and creeks they'd thus far encountered in the Hollow Land. He gazed at the lake, pondering the reason but unable to come up with any kind of answer.

Saira ended his considerations, shouting to be heard over the crashing waves. "We should rest here a bit."

Cam nodded agreement, gazing across the lake. Where were the Badlands? He sensed something distant, a place from which Ephemera drifted into Mote. But how far was it? No doubt, it would be a far longer flight than the one they'd just completed.

Charity moved to stand next to him, nearer than necessary. "I don't think I've ever seen you smile so much. What had you so happy?"

Cam feigned a laugh, although having Charity standing so close made him uncomfortable. He wasn't sure why, but maybe it was time to get over his discomfort. He didn't back away from Charity as he peered into her Crown-Haunted eyes. "What do you think had me smiling?"

Charity took his hands in hers and whispered to him, "I think we're in public, and if you step any closer, our friends might determine the answer to my question on their own."

"Then they'll learn," Cam said, still not backing off.

Charity quirked a sly smile. "Well, aren't you the courageous one? Most men I've known aren't. I like it." She looped her arms around his neck. "But are you sure?"

Cam tried not to stiffen. *Most men weren't.* What did that mean? His doubts, or rather his small-minded fears about their relationship, surged afresh. The jealousy washed over him, and he didn't know how to push it out of him. He remained frozen in place, unable to make the slight head tilt to kiss Charity.

Wolf-whistles from Birch, Jade, and Avia brought Cam out of his thoughts, and their leering grins gave him the excuse to quickly move out of Charity's embrace. He scowled while doing so, both in embarrassment and self-directed anger.

How could he have survived incarceration in Mote, the torture of darkness and loneliness, but the idea of kissing Charity was what drew such ugly emotions out of him?

Charity didn't seem to notice his crisis of conscience, and she patted his cheek, chuckling throatily. "I'm glad some things haven't changed."

Cam continued to scowl as she sauntered off to Avia, the two of them sharing a few words before glancing his way and breaking out in laughter.

"She does enjoy teasing you," Jade said, taking Charity's spot next to him. "You should be bolder when she does that. What's the worst that could happen?"

Cam didn't want to talk about it, and he tried to shift the conversation in another direction. "It's good seeing you again," he said to Jade. "How have you been?"

She gave him a look of disbelief. "Is that really what you want to ask? How I have been?"

He shrugged. "We haven't talked much."

"We talked all evening," Jade reminded him. "And stop trying to change the subject. If Charity wants you to kiss her, then you should kiss her. What's stopping you?"

Cam grimaced. "I don't know. Maybe it's not that easy for me."

Jade frowned. "Why wouldn't it be? Have your feelings for her changed? From what I saw before you ended up here in Mote, the two of you were well on your way."

Cam shot her a glare. "Well on our way to what? We kissed a few times, but that was three years ago for her and a lifetime for me."

Jade didn't back down. "So your feelings *have* changed." A moment later, her eyes narrowed. "No. That's not it. It's something else."

Cam didn't know how to respond. When Light Squad arrived yesterday, everything had seemed so bright and obvious. But then those doubts had begun, and now Charity had made that offhand comment—most men aren't—and his jealousy reared its ugly head, a sense of betrayal. Which made no sense and was deeply unfair to Charity. It had been three years for her, and a good person shouldn't want her pining after him for so long.

So what did it say about him that a part of him wanted her to feel exactly that?

Jade frowned. "I hope this isn't about your self-doubt again. You're worthy of Charity. Of anyone. Even Saira."

Cam huffed a forced laugh. "I know my worth."

"Then what is it?"

Cam didn't answer, ashamed of admitting the truth.

After a few seconds of deliberation, Jade's eyes widened in understanding. "Has she been with anyone else? That's what you're wondering?"

Cam stared at the ground, managed a brief head bob of acknowledgement, humiliated at how pathetic his reaction made him seem.

Jade forced him to meet her gaze, her eyes full of empathy. "Charity may or may not have had a few dates—"

Cam grimaced at the confirmation of his fears.

Jade scowled, irritated now. "Will you listen? Charity may have had a few dates, but she came here because of you. To be with you. That means something."

"What's that?" Pan asked, drawing Cam's attention away from his conversation with Jade, and he looked to where his friend was pointing.

A wave in the distance had breached the lake's surface as something large moved toward shore. A streak of red became visible.

Cam put aside any thoughts about Charity. He recognized that red fur. "Get us in the air," he barked to Light Squad. "Now."

No one questioned him. Jade reached for him while Card and Avia did the same for Pan and Birch. Light Squad launched skyward, a mile above the water. Moments later, the streak of red resolved into a Crown-Haunted kaiju. The creature dragged another of his kind out of the lake, dead, head lolling and terrible wounds scarring her neck and chest.

Cam hissed in dismay. *"It's the same one,"* he sent to everyone.

"The same what?" Jade asked.

"The same kaiju. We ran into him a few days ago. I recognize him. The red streak down his braids."

The titanic kaiju tossed the corpse upon the shore and sat down to feast. Flesh rended, a horrific tearing sound. The shoreline grew muddy with blood. The kaiju roared triumph when he ripped free the heart of his fallen foe, holding it aloft. He spied them then, stared their way, continuing to watch them and very deliberately took a bite from the heart. Cam viewed the kaiju in fascinated fear and disgust.

"What should we do?" Pan asked.

"We should carefully retreat," Birch said. *"That is a powerful Crown. We are no match for him, even outnumbering him as we do. He would destroy us."*

Birch was right, and Cam gave the order to depart. They moved out over the lake, away from the kaiju and his kill. But all the while, Cam sensed the monster still viewing them.

They flew for hours over the lake, cutting back and forth across the water in hopes of attracting Pelluraj's attention. The travel should have passed in boredom, but Cam remained tense. He couldn't shake the feeling that they were being followed, and he kept glancing back. He wasn't the only one feeling antsy, either. Jade, who continued to carry him, also regularly looked back.

But nothing worrisome met Cam's senses or Oversight. So what was it?

It was Saira who provided the answer. *"It the kaiju. He's Blended and following us. I think my presence gives him pause."*

"He's intelligent," Cam sent. *"He spoke to me when we met him the first time."* He recollected that one-sided conversation, which he'd come to believe was the reason for his vulnerability to the Great Rakshasas and their mindscape. In hindsight, it had also proven to be a fortuitous encounter. Cam wondered. Had that been the kaiju's intention all along? And if so, why?

"What did he say to you?" Saira asked.

Cam told them, also remembering the impressions he'd received from the creature, considering them afresh. *"From what I can best tell, his mind is geared toward a single drive. He wants to become stronger, and the easiest path is to kill others of his kind or anything that has Ephemera."*

"Can he follow us across the lake?" Card asked.

"He wouldn't dare," Birch replied. *"The lake belongs to Pelluraj. That is a beast that gives the Great Rakshasas pause. A mere Crown wouldn't pose the Stormlord of the Lake any challenge."*

"Stormlord of the Lake?" Cam asked. *"Is that Pelluraj's title?"*

"All kaijus are masters of the storm," Birch said. *"But there is only one Stormlord."*

"So maybe instead of flying across his domain, we should anchor line across?" Jade suggested.

"We can't," Birch said. *"The Great Rakshasas have a means to prevent anyone else from forming anchor lines in Mote."*

"He's right. I've tested it," Saira said.

Cam nodded. *"Which means we stick with the plan. We fly low enough to get Pelluraj's attention and use him to distract Shimala while we sneak into the Badlands. Pelluraj should also get the Crown to stop following us."*

"But where are the Badlands?" Jade asked.

Cam pointed without thinking. *"It's that way. Or that's what I'd guess since that's where I feel Ephemera coming into Mote."*

Jade frowned. *"You can feel that?"*

Cam nodded, while the others muttered about their lack of awareness of what seemed obvious to him. Then again, he'd always been more sensitive to the presence of Ephemera. He'd noticed it when Light Squad had lanced their first boil. Something to do with him being a Plasminian. He explained his thoughts.

Charity nodded. *"If you can feel it, then we'll trust your judgment."*

Her words seemed to end the conversation, and Light Squad flew in silence for several minutes until Charity drifted over to Jade. *"Let me have him. You've carried him long enough."*

Jade didn't give Cam a chance to disagree. *"Talk to her and figure this out before it ruins your relationship,"* she chided privately to him before passing him over to Charity on a raft of air and flying off.

Cam grimaced inwardly at Jade's words, mostly because she was right. Charity had dated a few men—kissed a few and perhaps it went even further. Why should he have ever expected otherwise? Especially with her thinking he was dead. She shouldn't be alone.

And yet, in that moment, he told himself that their relationship wasn't what had him truly bothered. It was the distraction of being carried by Charity, a distraction none of them needed. Cam needed to focus on keeping Light Squad safe and planning for what to do once Pelluraj found them. Or so he wanted to believe, although a part of him recognized that it was a lie.

"I can tell you're excited to be with me again," Charity said after a few minutes of silence. *"I can only imagine why."*

Cam grimaced inwardly. Charity must have figured something was bothering him, but now wasn't the time to be talking about it. He addressed her in a brusque tone, hoping she'd take the hint and let matters lie. *"I think you're the one doing the imagining."*

"I'm sure she's been imagining all sorts of vulgar things," Card said, having drifted over with Pan and picking up on their conversation.

Cam could have kissed the surly man for the diversion he provided.

"When you and Pan disappeared," Card continued, *"Charity wouldn't stop talking about the two of you."*

Pan perked, his expression bright and happy. *"Really?"*

"Of course," Charity said. *"You're my favorite panda-person."*

Card grunted, managing the gruff tone through his telepathic speech. *"Don't be too impressed. Most of her whining was about Cam. Even the few men she dated said the same. Sometimes, I'd even hear from them afterward."*

"Shut up, Card!" Charity growled, glaring fiercely at the other man.

But Cam silently hoped Card would keep talking, happy in a vindictive kind of way that Charity's dates had complained about him.

At the same time, though, guilt flooded through him at his sadly pathetic pleasure. Charity's relationships when she thought he was dead shouldn't matter. She had come to Hell itself to save him. Why couldn't that be enough? It should be. It had to be. Cam had to let go of his petty insecurities. Otherwise, that lie he'd lived with for so long—his unworthiness—would prove to be the truth. He would be unworthy of Charity.

Cam ignored whatever else Card had to say—and the man was saying a lot—reaching into himself, touching his Source and Ephemera, wanting it to heal his mind like it healed his body. *All is Ephemera and Ephemera is All.* The purity of Devesh's greatest gift poured through him, soothed his mind and his bruised emotions. And when it did, it was like a sun had bloomed inside him, lighting the dark recesses of his consciousness where the rot and rage written into his soul by his incarceration had festered and grown.

There was so much anger inside him. Cam had known it, used it to fuel his survival in Mote, but it was holding him back. He'd already known it, been called out about it by Pan, and he had to rid himself of it, especially since it was now pushing him to be jealous and covetous when he should simply be filled with joy and gratitude. Light Squad had come to save him. Charity was here for him. *Let it be enough*, he prayed.

The dark anger was no longer needed, and while it wouldn't so easily be set aside, Cam would work to heal himself and become the person Charity apparently believed him still to be.

In the midst of his troubling revelation, Card had kept on blathering, oblivious like he often was. *"Why those men bothered complaining to me, I don't know, but it was always the same. Cam this and Cam that. So tiresome."* He addressed Cam directly. *"And now that you're no longer dirty and covered in filth... no offense, but you were quite filthy when we arrived, and you still need a proper bath and a shave, but at least you're not scrawny like Charity kept carrying on about."*

Cam noticed Charity had her eyes closed, a tight expression on her face. *"Card, please, for the love of Devesh, shut up."*

"You're back to just being intimidating, especially with all your anger," Card finished.

Cam flushed. How had Pan and Birch put up with him if even Card had noticed his anger?

Card misunderstood the cause of Cam's embarrassment. *"You never knew? Everyone was intimidated by you."* He grunted a final time before drifting off.

Cam kept quiet as silence settled over him and Charity. He thought on what to say, wanting to respond with grace and understanding. He had to. If he wanted any hope of truly having a loving relationship with Charity, that had to be his focus, not his uglier emotions.

"I didn't ask Card to tell you that," Charity said, interrupting his ponderings.

The idea had never crossed Cam's mind. Such an emotionally twisted plan wasn't in Charity's nature. She was straightforward and honest.

"But I'm glad you heard it," she continued. *"It seems like you needed it."*

Maybe so, but Cam wished he wasn't the kind of person who *did* need it. *"I'm sorry."*

"Sorry for what?"

"For all of this. I wish I wasn't so angry. I wish I was a better person."

That earned him a fierce scowl. *"Stop doubting yourself. I didn't fall in love with you in Hearth because of your lack of self-worth. I fell in love with you because of your courage, strength, and good heart. Especially the last. You're a generous person. That's what I love most about you. That's why it never worked out with any of those other men. They didn't measure up."*

The response had Cam clamming shut his figurative mouth, and he reflected on the fullness of Charity's statement. She'd said she loved him and explained the reasons why. He only wished her words were true because right now, he didn't think he had a very good heart. His heart contained too much rage, and it had led to unbecoming jealousy. But there was a way back. There had to be. And Cam would find it.

Words came to him then, words that might light the way forward to healing. *"I love you, too,"* he said, believing it in that moment, feeling it. *"And I'm sorry for how I behaved today."*

"You don't have to apologize. You've been through more than I want to imagine. You survived Hell. We can't simply resume our relationship like nothing has changed. I shouldn't have pretended like we could." She gave him a tight-lipped smile. *"I'm the one who should be sorry."* Cam nodded acceptance, surprised by her sentiment and some of his anger possibly bled out of him. *"Thank you. Can we talk more after we're out of danger?"*

"As you wish."

36

Weld sat alone on a rocky precipice that overlooked Vivid Pass, the north-south waypoint that eventually ended at the small city of Game along the Charn River and from there to the capital of the duchy itself. A strong breeze gusted, tugging at his clothes, but it would take a far harder and colder blow to have him shiver. As a Sage, there wasn't much of anything from the natural world that could still touch him.

The morning sun glinted off the snow-covered peaks of the Diamond Mountains, although down in the valleys, life was already coming around. In a few more weeks, spring would bloom and green shoots would pierce the snowy powder. Until then, though, winter with its dry air and chill weather would hold sway.

Of course, regardless of his Awareness as a Sage, Weld didn't like winter. He never had. He never would. The cold wasn't for him. He liked his climate as mild and moderate as possible. In that regard, Maviro would have been perfect—temperate and never too hot or too cold—always ideal year round.

Thinking on the weather had Weld recalling that dumbass jackhole,

Cam Folde, who used to talk about winter like he was wanting to become intimate with it. Weld inwardly sneered. What an idiot and given how Cam's life had ended, that only proved the truth of the man's stupidity.

Musing on it got Weld to figuring about Sage-Duke Kazar. As soon as the work in Charn was done, and he was given free rein to handle Traverse, it might be a good time to go visit Charity's father. The man needed murdering. He'd earned it many times over when he'd choked Weld, talked down to him, and thought himself better. Let's see how he handled matters now that Weld was also a Sage.

True, battling Kazar wouldn't be an easy win. The truth was Ephemeral Masters were often more powerful than rakshasas of a similar Advancement and Weld wasn't yet a particularly powerful Sage. But life, fate, whatever anyone wanted to call it, seemed to have an eye on him. Opportunities arose when he least expected it, so why not an opportunity to become a powerful Sage and kill Sage-Duke Kazar? Or even Nailing?

Weld smiled, imagining the world trembling before him, everyone bowing and scraping to earn his goodwill. Even those from other Realms, like Coruscant, Shimala, and Simmer. If those three were the Great Rakshasas, then Weld would become the Greatest Rakshasa. Why not?

He wallowed in the gentle fantasy, using it as a pleasant distraction from the work to which he'd taken a break: the mind-numbing tedium of maintaining Nailing's great boil. It was a fortress from which the Sage of Warring Thunder planned on building out his strength and crushing Sage-Duke Zin Shun of Charn.

Weld snorted.

Nailing had all sorts of plans, schemes, and grand ideas, but until Weld had turned traitor, none of them had come to fruition. Weld had been key to the boil's ongoing construction. Three years he'd spent here, Advancing twice, but his time had otherwise been wasted. Worse, for reasons that made no sense, Weld hadn't been given command here. That honor had gone to Shilpa, an Awakened camel and another newly minted Sage.

Weld scowled at the slight. What was Nailing thinking insulting him like that? Whatever the rationale, it wasn't good enough to earn Weld's forgiveness. When he was done with Traverse and Kazar, he and Nailing would be having words. The Sage of Warring Thunder would explain himself, and if Weld didn't like the flavor of his language, then Weld would kill Nailing. Simple as that.

And Nailing's regular complaints that Weld hadn't Advanced all his Tangs to Sage better not be the reason for his disrespect. So what if Weld hadn't done as he'd implied he could when first joining the rakshasas? He'd Advanced Kinesthia, his Primary Tang, to Sage, along with Spirairia, the use of which had always come easy for him. Both were at Sage, which was one more than Shilpa had managed. She only had a single Tang at Sage and two others at Glory.

In truth, Weld was likely the most Advanced Sage in all of Salvation. He wasn't just a Sage Prime—someone with one Tang at Sage and another at Crown. Oh, no. He was so much more than that. He had two Tangs at Sage and the other two at Glory.

The bottom line was that there really wasn't any proper way to describe Weld's potential since there had never been anyone like him ever before. Sure his control of his abilities and skills was lacking, but that was easily solved through time and work. As soon as he had the inclination to fixate on his mastery, the world and his enemies better watch out. He'd crush them all. Weld nodded to himself. Soon enough, he'd outshine everyone and be sure they all saw it.

His future brilliance waited, but in the meanwhile, he glowered at his current status as the same question still intruded and ruined his good mood. Why had Shilpa been given primacy over him? The only reasons he could reckon were jealousy and fear. Nailing was jealous of Weld and feared what he'd become when he fully mastered his abilities.

Well, let the buffalo marinate in his jealousy and fear. Weld's time was coming. After Charn, he'd been promised Traverse. He only wished Cam was around to see what he'd do to his home and family. Or that Charity would arrive in time to see him end the life of her father. Then would come—

With a wrenching effort, Weld steered his thinking away from the dreams.

Once a day. That's how often he allowed himself to fantasize about his future glory. After that, he'd focus on his disappointments and use them as fuel to fire his ambition.

Accepting his present tribulations with as much equanimity as he could muster, Weld rose to his feet, using a blast of air to remove any clinging snow and dirt prior to flying back to the boil. He landed, taking in the sight, appreciating it, although he'd never mention it to Shilpa, who had been key to the boil's far lovelier design and layout. Whereas before it had been a rough fortress, now it was as beautiful as any building on Nexus. A line of dwarf cedars edged a crushed gravel pathway leading to a series of arched columns that supported a broad porch. Beyond that, the previously matte-black exterior had been transformed into shimmering white marble with wide windows that peered down into a green valley where had once stood a living village.

Weld frowned, noticing Shilpa standing on the stoop. She had once been a camel, but other than her long lashes, none of a camel's features could be spied in her appearance. The fact was, Shilpa was easy on the eyes. She also had the kind of tall, athletic build—not too small or big in the chest, but just right—that Weld appreciated. He wouldn't have minded getting to know her better, especially if it led to the bedroom. Too bad for her that she always slighted him, talking down at him.

"Nailing wants to see you," Shilpa said without preamble when he neared.

"Why didn't he send for me?"

Shilpa shrugged. "I am not one to question our liege."

Your liege, not mine, Weld thought.

He brushed past Shilpa, entering an atrium brightly lit by the streaming sunshine. The soothing smell of incense and floral aromas lingered in the air, and fine paintings and murals decorated white walls while long rugs softened the terra cotta flooring. Shilpa had once met an artist during her journey to Ephemeral Mastery, and the person had left an impression on her. Her every thought seemed to be about beauty and how best to create it for every sense.

Weld reached his quarters, which even he privately admitted were of rather poor taste in comparison to the boil's public spaces before sitting cross-legged on his bed and sending his presence to Nailing.

The Sage of Warring Thunder answered immediately. *"Shilpa tells me that the boil is ready. All it needs is a few final touches to Enhance the protections to the core. Nageena will see to it. She should arrive today."*

Weld didn't like Nageena, but he admired and respected the Sage of Whispering Scales. Early on, she'd worked at helping build the boil, and she cared for outcomes only. Not once had she ever spoken ugly to Weld when he didn't deserve it. In addition, if she was coming to the boil, then it had to mean that the battle for Charn neared. He asked Nailing if that was the case.

"In a few weeks, when spring warms the land, we'll sweep down," Nailing confirmed.

Weld mused on the war to come, but a fresh insight occurred to him. *"Why are you telling me this and not Shilpa?"*

"Because Nageena wanted your help with the core's final Rising."

"Me? Not Shilpa?" A thrill of excitement coursed through Weld.

"Shilpa lacks your power." Nailing appeared to pause, maybe thinking through what he wanted to say next. *"I also wanted to congratulate you. Consider this a reward for a job well done. I have been intentionally harsh with you. It was meant to put you to the test, and I'm pleased to say you passed. You've earned my appreciation and admiration. Well done. All you need do is master your abilities, and Coruscant himself will likely take note."*

Weld's heart thrummed. Finally, someone had noticed his talents and abilities. Nailing's praise had just saved his life. So long as he bended the knee when the time was right, Weld would make the Sage of Warring Thunder his first lieutenant. Either him or Nageena. Possibly both since they were so loyal to one another. He wondered if he could bring her to his side while they worked together on the core's Rising. He was a surging power. Surely, she'd see that and want to hitch her wagon to his horses.

Time would tell, but for now Weld was content. He metaphorically bowed to Nailing. "Thank you, my liege."

Rainen Winder paced alongside Perit Line through Sidewinder Company's encampment. They'd settled themselves into a narrow valley south of Game, a small town grown up along both sides of the Charn River and situated where Vivid Pass finished cutting through the Diamond Mountains before opening onto a high desert plateau. The weather in the higher elevations was likely to be brutal given how chill it was down in the valley where the wind howled and snow swirled into stinging particles of ice. Or at least they would have stung if Rainen hadn't been a Sage.

Perit disregarded the weather as well, although all his men and women who weren't Crowns huddled close to their fires for warmth or hustled about, getting their work done as swiftly as possible.

Rainen's eyes went to the Charn River, which flowed close at hand, clogged with ice floes that groaned and cracked against one another before making their way a few miles downriver to a waterfall where they plunged and broke apart with thunderous sounds that reached all the way to Game. There, down at the cataract's basin, the waters churned before sedating as the river made its way to the duchy capital of Charn.

That city weighed heavy on Rainen's mind. Nailing might have his sights set on it, having built a boil near Game. No doubt, when spring broke across the land in a few weeks—maybe sooner—the Sage of Warring Thunder would make his move. Rainen worried over what it would mean. Blood and death for hundreds of innocents went without saying, but what if Nailing's ambitions were even broader? What if he wanted more? What if his sights truly were set on Charn itself? Untold destruction would follow. The entire duchy could fall, all so the rakshasas could reign where Sage-Dukes currently did.

Of course, that likely wasn't Nailing's endgame either. The old buffalo also sought a way into Salvation for his true master: Coruscant, the so-called Sower of the Wind, the Wrecker of Hope, and the Far-Seeing General.

The Wilde Sage privately sneered at the lofty titles, believing that only those who doubted themselves required so many proud-sounding names, and he cared little if the Great Rakshasa had actually earned them. As far as Rainen was concerned, the less actually known about the fiend, the better for everyone. And the absolute best outcome would be if the Great Rakshasa was not merely trapped for all time in Mote, but if his power was somehow utterly snuffed out. The Realms would be brighter if Coruscant was bereft of puissance, well forgotten and disregarded by future historians.

Rainen pulled himself out of his worries and dreams when he caught Perit peering at him, concern writ large on the Crown's face.

"What can we do here?" Perit asked. "You know the numbers we face."

Rainen sighed to himself. He loved Perit, but he wished the man had it within him to Advance to Sage. Sidewinder Company was a potent force as were Rainen's other units, but there wasn't a single Sage within their ranks. And he could have used the help. Maintaining order on this fractious continent of conniving and backstabbing Sage-Dukes and Sage-Duchesses was difficult, grown nearly impossible in these, the latter years of his life.

The intransigence of the so-called leaders of Golden led to an intolerable yet immutable truth: the continent would fall if Rainen didn't find his heir. For a time, he had hoped it might be Saira—still hoped so since rumor indicated that she'd Advanced to Sage. And what a Sage she must be. Those same rumors stated that Saira had every Tang possible—Kinesthia, Synapsia, Spirairia, and even Plasminia—Advanced to Sage and Enhanced to Crystal. Rainen doubted any three Sages could withstand her might.

Another sigh. Unfortunately, he'd lost Saira's trust, and it was all because of that boy, Cam Folde. Rainen still believed that everything he'd done had been for the youth's betterment. The struggles and dangers he'd forced upon Cam. The boy had endured and overcome every task set before him, and the challenges had forged a diamond-hard warrior, one with an unparalleled will to win.

And if certain duplicitous and short-sighted Sage-Dukes and Sage-Duchesses hadn't allowed the boy to be killed, Cam Folde could have achieved the same as Saira. All of Light Squad—again rumor carried to Rainen of their achievements in the Sinanes—might have managed the same. They would have been unstoppable. Sages beyond Primes with Cam as their leader, guided by his strict morality.

If only Rainen hadn't lost the boy's trust and loyalty.

As it was, Light Squad was adrift in the Sinanes with no signs that they would ever return to Golden, even though the continent desperately needed them. Rainen needed them. Even as they were right now—four Crowns and a Sage, all well beyond Primes—fighting alongside Sidewinder or his other units… they could be the means by which Golden was saved. They could serve as the battering ram to destroy—not just this powerful boil in Charn's duchy—but all of Nailing's boils and his army of rakshasas.

And the notion of an army of rakshasas only spurred the occurrence of another question: just where and how was the old buffalo breeding his followers? Boils often occurred naturally, spurring the development of Awakened Beasts, but did every last one of them have to become rakshasas? If so, why? Those were questions Rainen had never answered to his satisfaction.

"Master Winder?" Perit persisted, interrupting Rainen's considerations, his face still lit with worry.

"We do as we must," Rainen said, flashing his most trustworthy Crown a warm smile. "And we'll win, just like we always have." He heaved a tired sigh. "It's just that some days I wish life could be simpler, not just for us as Ephemeral Masters, but for everyone, the regular folks who just want to live a life of peace. This could be a wonderful world if there weren't any rakshasas on it. Or better yet, if the Sage-Dukes and Sage-Duchesses would let go of their politicking and maneuvering. If they could simply accept what they have and lead for the betterment of all, rather than themselves." Another sigh, this one somewhat forlorn. "I'm tired of their fighting." On seeing the increase to Perit's worry, Rainen managed a wry chuckle. "But I'll be fine. Truly. Just remember that, sometimes, even Sages need to complain."

Based on Perit's ongoing studious and worried expression, he didn't share Rainen's humor. Still, the Crown offered a grave nod. "I think I know what you mean, sir, but to be honest, if you didn't have the world to save, wouldn't you be bored?"

The comment had Rainen laughing, and he clapped Perit's shoulder. "You might be right, my friend. So, let's go save the world."

The Sage of the Sinanes, Lysha Maharani, listened closely as her youngest daughter, Dru, reported on the grim tidings from Golden.

"The boil is said to house at least three Sages and five Crowns," Dru said, finishing her account.

"Triple all the rumored numbers, and you'll likely have a more accurate count," Lysha said with a discontented exhalation. She paced through her chambers, lost in contemplation, wondering if Golden's largely worthless Sage-Dukes and Sage-Duchesses would finally unite against this common threat. A moment later, she shook her head, annoyed at hoping for what was almost certainly an impossibility. Golden's Sage-Dukes and Sage-Duchesses would only unite when the sun died and the moon turned to blood. They were the wretched, final successors of far nobler ancestors, a living example of how even Sages could behave like rakshasas.

Lysha continued to pace, determining the response of the Sinanes. Dru's news seemed to have sapped the bright sunlight pouring through the open doors of the westward-facing balcony, and the information might as well have diminished the trilling of the evening songbirds currently settling in for the night or paling the lush scent of jasmines carried inside on a tradewind. All was lessened by what Dru had said and also what she'd left unsaid.

Lysha reached the balcony and stepped outside, reflecting still on how best to serve her people. Dru followed, and together, they stared at the aqua glory of the Arylyn Ocean, which glistened in the late-day sun. Lysha viewed the sight, recalling a story of how the waters had been named for William and Serena's home. Was it true? She'd always wondered, and if so, what had that home been like?

Not that it was of any real concern given the disaster unfolding on Golden. It seemed that Nailing had finally married his undeniable power to enough cunning to see him succeed whereas for so long, he'd utterly failed. Rather than directly challenge the powers who ruled Golden, the old buffalo had taken to birthing boils in faraway places— ones willingly overlooked by the Sage-Dukes and Sage-Duchesses— and there, he'd patiently and steadily grown them until at least one of them was sure to become a true menace.

It was all so avoidable. Nailing might have grown canny, but he wasn't some master of strategy and tactics. He wasn't Coruscant. The buffalo's plans were basic enough that if his foes could simply see past their own ambitions and address what they faced, they would have long since annihilated Nailing and his ilk.

Lysha found herself glowering at the night. The Sage-Dukes and their small-mindedness. Nailing's ploy was a self-inflicted tragedy since, in the end, if the Sage-Dukes and Sage-Duchesses merely bent a meager portion of their will to eradicating the boils, it would cost them far less.

But such wasn't the case. Instead, the corrupt rulers of Golden remained enraptured by their petty politics: who controlled which villages along the border. Who had the most beautiful palace. The most Ephemeral Masters under their banner—so wasteful. The fools dithered while the boils infecting their lands would eventually become impossible to overlook. By then, the price required would be one of irreplaceable blood and treasure.

Couldn't they see what was happening? Didn't they understand their peril? Especially since the other rakshasa Sages had fallen in with

Nailing. They'd made him their uncontested ruler, and if the Sage-Dukes didn't soon answer the destruction bearing down on at least one of them, it would be too late.

Which led to an inexorable question: how could it have come to this? What had changed for Nailing? In her previous encounters with the Sage of Warring Thunder, Lysha had come away unimpressed. Charge forth and lead with his horns, that had always been his stupid and predictable plan. But now… now, he schemed, not with anything approaching the sublime, but enough to become a challenge.

Another sigh. It seemed Rainen's warnings about the old buffalo were true.

"What is your response, Mother?" Dru asked. "Rainen asks for aid."

Lysha turned to face her daughter, making sure to school her features to stillness. It was a lesson for her youngest. A Sage, especially a ruler, could never display their dismay.

"And the Sinanes will answer. We will go to his aid. Seesha, Pravanthi, and Malian will accompany me."

Worry filled Dru's Adept-Haunted eyes. "That will only leave us with Sage Chervil to defend the Sinanes. He's…"

Lysha smiled. "Old?" Her smile widened at Dru's fleeting expression of guilt. "That is true, but he is still capable of defending the Sinanes. And he'll have the rest of our Crowns to help him hold the line until I return."

"It would be better if Saira was here," Dru said. "She's been gone a long time."

Lysha wanted to nod but held off from doing so even as she wished the same. Saira should have been here, home amongst family and those who loved her best. Or perhaps she was amongst family. It hadn't escaped Lysha's notice that Light Squad had the feeling of siblings who had chosen one another, and they were mighty. Children who'd Advanced to Crown at an age when most everyone else would have been greatly admired for reaching Adept.

Children like Dru, who was older than every member of Light Squad, except for her sister Saira. Lysha smiled upon thinking about her oldest daughter. Saira had always chosen her own path, and perhaps that was the reason for her success. Whatever the case, Lysha couldn't have been prouder of her achievements, but she was also still worried for Saira. It made no difference that Saira was a Sage because Lysha was a mother first, and it was a mother's prerogative to worry over her children, no matter how powerful.

"Saira has her own matters to attend," Lysha eventually allowed. "And if she's successful, our world will have two more mighty heroes to help defend those who can't defend themselves."

Dru frowned, not hiding her skepticism. "Cam Folde and Pan Shun. Do you truly think they're as accomplished as the others in Light Squad claim? From their descriptions, one would think that Cam Folde can breathe fire and grow wings."

Lysha chuckled. "Do not forget the special love they say has been demonstrated to him by Rukh and Jessira."

"The Holy Servants. Saira says they're real."

Lysha lifted her eyes. "You doubted?"

Dru shrugged. "How could I not? There has been no sighting of them for thousands of years, right after Salvation was said to have been reformed. All we have are stories of their greatness, and we all know how stories can be altered."

Lysha knew what her daughter inferred. The founding of the Sinanes had not been a peaceful event. It had taken blood and hard fighting, the killing of thousands of rakshasas who had once made the islands their homes along with the culling of those who had refused to bend the knee to Lysha's ancestors. None of it had been easy.

But that wasn't what the histories stated. The histories claimed that the Sinanes had been founded by those who chose to emigrate from Golden and other continents, settling here and establishing a place where goodness and equality of opportunity could flourish.

It was a mixture of truth and lies. Yes, the Sage-Duchy of the Sinanes in its current state had been founded by those from Golden, by figures lost to time: followers of Selene and Elliot, the first and last of Salvation's Divines. But those figures hadn't come in peace. They had come as conquerors, bent on eradicating the last rakshasas who followed the teachings of Zahhack, Rukh and Jessira's greatest foe.

Indeed, the so-called theological texts from the Son of Emptiness remained in Lysha's possession, and when she'd inherited them from her mother, she had shuddered in revulsion upon reading the wretched books. Selfish, brutal, and cruel were kind words when compared to Zahhack's teachings. No wonder Salvation had teetered on the brink of emptying of all life, saved only because William and Bartholomew—and later Serena—had saved the world, granting the space by which Rukh and Jessira had opened it to receive Devesh's Light.

Lysha's ancestors had kept the correct history, although even their records were incomplete. For instance, who exactly was Bartholomew? No one could say.

So, yes, Dru was correct. The histories could be altered, such as what was taught about the founding of the Sinanes, which had been a necessary war of conquest, but nonetheless, it had been exactly that: a war perpetrated by her ancestors on those who had previously ruled the islands.

And now, it seemed like Lysha and those descended from Selene and Elliot would have to return to Golden and save their ancestral continent from rakshasas. Lysha faced her daughter. "Regardless of the truth about Rukh and Jessira, call for a gathering of the council. The Sinanes go to war."

37

Light Squad cut a line across Lake Petala, racing a dozen feet above the water, surging heavy spray on either side of their passage. Sparkling rainbows glistened along the wavefronts of their passage, and the streaming wind and splashing water had Cam squinting his eyes.

Once they'd headed deeper into Lake Petala, the Crown kaiju following after them had finally given up the chase. With the monster no longer following in their wake, Cam relaxed and tried to enjoy the flight, even if it was still Charity who led the dance. They hadn't spoken much since she'd confronted him over his behavior, and he accepted the silence.

She'd said they'd talk more once the danger was over, and until then, he figured it best if he kept his mouth shut, his mind sharp, and his eyes on the lookout for Pelluraj.

The quiet also gave him time to think about his anger and frustration, how it had fueled his survival in Mote's prison but was now preventing him from being the person he wanted to be. A figurative sigh. He'd work on those troubles later—talk to Charity as well—but for now, he needed to focus.

An hour later, with no sign of the Stormlord, Cam glanced at the others, wondering how they were faring.

Card flew Pan across the lake, and the poor panda-person didn't appear happy, holding a white-knuckled grip on the bed of air that served as his transport. Meanwhile, Avia held Birch, and the old rakshasa wore a constipated expression of distaste and barely contained outrage. At least Kiwi and Sprite seemed to be enjoying the flight. They flitted alongside Saira, floating and diving, tweeting and chirping with effervescent happiness and excitement. They'd occasionally tire, and when they did, they would perch on Saira's shoulders or even her head, cocking their heads and peering about with bright eyes.

Distracted, Charity surprised Cam by dipping them low, skimming directly above the water where they carved a furrow across the lake. Spray soaked them, and they bounced around, buffeted by pockets of wind. Cam whooped in delight.

"You like that?" Charity asked, lifting them out of the water's reach.

"Absolutely love it!" Cam replied with a glad laugh. His reaction had him considering. How long had it been since he'd laughed like that? Surely when they'd escaped the prison, but that had been a fevered exultation mixed with a sense of unreality. This was different, though. This was because he was happy and there was no reason not to be.

Saira signaled from up ahead. *"I sense something powerful coming to the surface. It is beyond any of us. Ascend."*

They followed Saira as she lanced skyward, vertical, and while they climbed, Cam glanced down. A hazy white form slowly took shape under the water, rising, indistinct. There then came an endless moment where everything seemed to quiet in breathless anticipation…

Pelluraj breached the surface, white-furred, surging upward, higher and higher. Cam boggled at what he was seeing. The Stormlord was massive, larger than any ship, a literal moving mountain. More features became evident. Red braids, thicker and richer than the Crown-Staged kaiju that had been chasing them. The braids trailed behind Pelluraj, swaying hypnotically, and a glowing violet hue filled his sclerae. Gray spikes like broken barnacles extended in a ragged line down his back with similar jaggedly crusted features at his elbows. He continued to rise. Was there no end to him?

He finally fully breached the water, possibly standing, displaying legs like a wolf's with high ankles and bent knees and a knotted tail that ended in a knobby spike. Pelluraj continued to surge out of the lake, ever higher and higher.

Cam had a distinct sense of worry as the massive beast filled his vision. Perhaps they shouldn't have sought this monster's attention. But it was too late now. The Stormlord's eyes locked on them, and he roared.

"Brace yourselves," Saira cried.

Seconds later, a heavy wind battered them about, even at their height of several miles. That's when Cam's worry became fear.

"Flee!" Saira ordered. Light Squad raced away from the titanic kaiju.

But Pelluraj, the Stormlord of the Lake, continued to stare at them, his Sage-Haunted gaze containing a strange light. *"You sought me. And now you flee?"* he sent, sounding amused, his voice deep and echoing, thrumming with a strength to rival Coruscant's. The kaiju inhaled deep, his chest thickening even as the air around Light Squad seemed to thin.

Pelluraj roared again, and Cam realized that the first cry from the Stormlord had been a mere shadow of his power. This was the true night. Pelluraj's bellow could have shattered hills or overturned cities, and Cam's shield fared no better. It held for only a few seconds before ripping into tatters. Cam found himself seized in a guttural din that clicked and reverberated through and around him. Endless pealing that threatened to tear him apart. Had he still been an Adept, he doubted he could have survived the terrible noise.

Finally, it ended, but Pelluraj continued to view them as they flew away, calling out to them again. *"I see what you desire. Outlast my wrath prior to the Badlands, and perhaps you'll have it."*

A pit opened in Cam's stomach. They might have made a massive misjudgment in gaining the monstrous Stormlord's attention. The beast wasn't simply Awakened. He was intelligent and filled with a malevolent cunning. And surviving him was no longer an obvious possibility. Even at this distance, Pelluraj could still attack.

Cam thickened the air in front of his eyes. A simple trick learned from Jessira's teachings that brought the distant kaiju into tighter focus. As if the monster could sense his fears, Pelluraj's eyes brightened, and a grin creased his savage visage.

"*Shield!*" Cam cried, knowing it was likely futile. His shield hadn't done any good against Pelluraj's roar. What use would it be against his actual attack?

"*Keep going,*" Saira ordered. "*Tighten your formation. On me.*"

Light Squad responded immediately, shifting closer, flying only a few feet apart. Cam felt brief pride in their positioning. They hadn't come to Mote unprepared, clearly having long practice with the maneuver. The rest of Light Squad swept past Saira, who had slowed enough to allow them to do so. Once they cleared her, she threw her arms wide and created a shield. A wide green webbing spread out from directly in front of her, expansive enough to protect all of Light Squad.

Pelluraj inhaled deep once again before thrusting his head forward, mouth wide. Beams of crackling violet lightning arced from his eyes while from his mouth blasted a line of white fire that roared like a forest burning. The attacks combined into an ivory-streaked, violet inferno that slammed into Saira's shield and punched her back a dozen feet. She retained control of her flight, continuing to face the kaiju, but the assault didn't relent. Cam silently prayed for her, wishing her greater strength.

Maybe his prayers did some good because Saira stiffened under the weight of Pelluraj's attack, holding on, grimacing in obvious pain. Cam expected her shield to fail at any moment, but it didn't. It held. She held.

Cam gaped at Saira's strength. The amount of power in Pelluraj's attacks... how was she defending against it? He counted seconds that might as well have been hours before Pelluraj's fire and lightning finally guttered out and failed. The kaiju roared once more but this time in frustration. He glared again at their fleeing forms before falling back into the lake.

However, Cam could see Pelluraj wasn't done with them. His head remained above the water, and not once did his eyes unlock from them as he chased after, moving swifter than a shark.

"We are not finished, little pests," the kaiju proclaimed.

"We have to go faster," Saira urged. *"I don't know if I can defend against another attack like that."*

Light Squad accelerated, heading straight toward where Cam felt Ephemera drifting outward into Mote. Pelluraj kept pace, though. A violet mist surrounded the Stormlord, thrusting him forward as he cut through the lake, arms against his sides and legs extended behind. He was largely underwater, only his head breaching the surface.

Cam couldn't tell, but it looked like Pelluraj might even be gaining on them. He measured the distance to the Badlands, which felt so far away, and he worried. Were they going to make it there?

A howl on the wind reached him. *"Fools! What are you doing?"*

"Who was that?" Charity asked.

Cam smiled. The voice on the wind had once haunted his nightmares, but not after her connection to him had been torn apart. Even better, her presence was exactly what he and the rest of Light Squad had hoped for. *"It's Shimala,"* he sent to everyone. *"If she's angry with us, it means we're going the right way."*

"I guess it also means we'll see how well your plan actually works," Birch said. *"Either that, or we'll all soon be dead."* He laughed mirthlessly. *"Dead at the claws of Pelluraj or at the hands of the Merciless Deceiver. What a way to go."*

"Quite the cheerful fellow," Charity muttered.

"This is Birch on one of his good days," Cam said with a delirious laugh. They'd survived Pelluraj, at least for now. Now all they had to do was get him to the Badlands to fight Shimala and sneak away like mice during the battle.

As a plan, it wasn't much, but it was all they had.

Hours of flying, and not much changed. Light Squad soared high above Lake Petala and Pelluraj swam after them. The kaiju slowly closed the distance, but so far, he'd yet to attack again. In addition, the Stormlord's presence must have put everything that flew or swam to flight. Light Squad had the skies to themselves with no birds or flying reptiles close at hand, and even in the waters, other than some schools of fish that quickly retreated whenever the Stormlord approached, the lake was empty.

It got to be somewhat boring, and Cam's mind wandered. He tried calculating how close they were to the sky. Was it still miles above or was that just an illusion? It was hard to tell, but learning the hard way—by dashing their heads into whatever served as the ceiling to the Hollow Land didn't seem like a good idea.

Of course, trying to estimate the height of the sky led him to reflect upon the depth of Lake Petala. It sat below the Blood Sea, but how much stone and earth separated the two bodies of waters? And why was Lake Petala clear and clean when the Blood Sea was full of corruption? Shouldn't both waters be a muddy mix of both pure and filthy with some of each filtering out to each other?

And what about the wind and the clouds? Where did they come from? Or even the Hollow Land's storms.

He might have asked Charity, who still flew him, but he didn't want to interrupt her efforts. Her features were lined by a grimace of effort as sweat dripped off her face and she panted. He heard her pounding heart. Same with the rest of Light Squad's Crowns. Only Saira appeared unaffected, but for everyone else, the flight had them on the edge of their stamina, and the reason wasn't hard to fathom. It was the lack of Ephemera.

They had only a shadow of their might compared to what they could accomplish in Hearth or Salvation. Their weakness had Cam concerned. Light Squad had been flying for hours, inching closer to the Badlands, but with miles yet to go. But would they have enough left afterward to make it to the Locus, which was supposedly at the center of the Badlands?

As if she heard his concern, Charity spoke. *"I can't last much longer."*

Cam viewed her in concern, not knowing what to tell her and frustrated with his inability to help. Descending into the lake wasn't an option. They had to stay aloft. He stared in the direction his feelings told him the Locus lay. He still couldn't see the Badlands.

Charity cried out, and an instant later, they plummeted dozens of yards. Cam's heart caught. While the two of them could survive the fall into the water, neither could survive Pelluraj. Charity cried out again, her neck veins signaling her straining effort. Their flight leveled. But the Stormlord had taken note. The great beast viewed them with a malicious grin, surging his pace and closing the gap.

The rest of Light Squad descended, keeping their flight narrow and tight. Cam continued to spy ahead, desperate. Minutes later, a wonderful sight met his gaze. A sienna smear that steadily brightened, widened until it exposed a series of oddly undulating dunes that shifted in the wind. Not a single green thing grew. The Badlands. It stretched out in the hazy distance, only a few miles to go. *"It's not much farther!"* Cam shouted to everyone. *"Look."*

The view seemed to hearten everyone. Those flying redoubled their efforts, and Light Squad approached the barren land of undulating hills without halting. Glancing back, Cam noted that Pelluraj was no longer submerged. Still a dozen miles behind, the kaiju marched forth, the water draining off his shoulders, and his every stride saw him rising further out of the lake.

"Well done, little pests," Pelluraj sent. *"Flee to the Badlands but never return to my domain."*

Light Squad didn't need the kaiju's warning. They'd made it to the Badlands, and Saira indicated for them to descend. They did so, collapsing rather than settling with any kind of grace amongst dunes that reared like tall hills a hundred yards beyond the empty, red sandy beach of the Badlands. As soon as their feet touched the ground, everyone who had been flying bent low at the waist, heaving breaths, their pulses rapid and visible in the veins of their necks.

Kiwi and Sprite flitted about, chirping in concern.

"What can we do to help?" Sprite asked.

"They need rest," Cam told the lovebirds. "But they're likely not going to find it here. Tuck in." The lovebirds scrambled into a pair of his shirt's interior pockets. They'd be safer there. Next, Cam viewed the rest of Light Squad. Regardless of everyone's fatigue, they had to get going. Flying was clearly out of the question, but that didn't mean they couldn't run.

Pelluraj roared, and Cam's gaze snapped around to the great beast. Even miles away from shore, the Stormlord's every step shook the ground. And that distance didn't give Cam any comfort. The massive kaiju's attack could still reach them.

Cam gathered Light Squad, pulling them upright. "Come on. Up. We have to move."

A tickling in the back of his mind spun him about. A horde of shambling figures, thousands of them, humans covered in the red dust of the dunes, raced toward them. It struck Cam then. The dunes he'd spied from miles above hadn't been undulating with any kind of wind. They had been undulating with these rapidly approaching figures.

"Thralls," Birch cursed. A moment later, a sardonic smile lit his features. "It seems my bet about dying here is about to come true."

Cam scowled. He didn't have time for Birch's graveyard humor. Instead, he forged a True Bond, and the world brightened, all his senses heightened. His muscles twitched, and his thoughts accelerated. Calm and dispassionate, Cam studied the thralls, focusing on the grandmotherly figure flying at their head. Or at least she would have been grandmotherly if not for the mad rictus on her face. *Shimala.* Next, Cam viewed Pelluraj. Light Squad stood sandwiched between the two forces.

Thinking fast, Cam sought a solution for their predicament while the Badlands shook under the weight of the racing thralls and the rapidly approaching kaiju. Pelluraj roared out again, and Cam viewed the Stormlord, who had paused his approach, standing just off the beach. The kaiju's mouth was lit with a violet fire and his eyes were framed by lightning. Cam's eyes widened. Based on the angle of his aim, Light

Squad wasn't his target.

Cam gazed about, finally discovering what Light Squad needed. *"This way! Follow me!"* He led the others at a perpendicular angle away from Shimala and Pelluraj, and they quickly reached rocky soil, running faster on the firmer footing. It would still be a close-run matter as to whether they could clear both enemies in time, but in the distance, Cam had sighted a possibility. No more than a few miles away, there rose a series of stony dunes. Taller and with hearts of granite. Maybe they would be stout enough to shelter Light Squad from the brewing battle.

Pelluraj's attack crashed overhead with the din of a tornado and the crackling of unending lightning. Even from a hundred feet below, Cam felt the heat of its passage, the incinerating power the Stormlord generated. It was an assault made to crush the thralls.

"Shield," Cam ordered.

Pelluraj's attack landed, and the Badlands echoed with a peal of thunder that rang on and on. Sand blasted outward, moving fast enough to flay skin from bone. The world went gray and tan, and Light Squad huddled within their shields. The blistering sandstorm finally faltered and collapsed. The air was swept clean, far swifter than was natural. Cam glanced to the thralls, expecting them to be largely destroyed.

And yet, it wasn't the case. Shimala had protected her forces, using a shield similar to Saira's. A green webbing extended from her upraised hand, extending to surround her thralls, none of whom appeared injured.

A pause as Pelluraj seemed to judge the situation. An instant later, the kaiju made his decision and lunged for Shimala.

"Keep going!" Cam urged.

The two monstrous foes—Pelluraj and Shimala—reached one another, and the world was blasted apart in an escalation of lightning, fire, and sand. A concussive series of blasts echoed across the dunes. Shimala cried in rage, her cackling anger audible over the thunderous explosions.

"Awful beast!" she shouted. "Return to the lake."

Cam risked a glance over his shoulder. Shimala was fully engaged with Pelluraj, and although she appeared tiny and insignificant in comparison to the Stormlord, her blows were anything but weak. She floated at eye level with the kaiju, her attacks rocking his head about. Pelluraj snapped at her, missing by inches.

And splitting off from Shimala's forces, several thousand thralls surged after Light Squad. Given how spent the others were, battling them on open ground would be madness. The Great Rakshasa's creatures rapidly closed the distance.

Cam addressed Saira. *"I need you to cut them down if they get too close."*

"I'll see to it," Saira replied, drifting back to cover their rear.

Next, he spoke to Pan and Birch. *"Defend our flanks."*

They shifted into position while Cam remained on point. They had to reach those rockier dunes. There might be a natural chokehold where they could whittle the thralls coming after them. Cam had to believe so, or even with Saira's skills as a Sage, they might not survive the next hour.

38

Cam snapped his attention to the rear of their formation when the sound of a thousand forges burning at once erupted from where he'd last seen Saira. She was the source of the noise, and the fire erupting off her hands had incinerated a good portion of the chasing thralls. Several hundred, and their bodies dispersed as ash. However, her follow-on attack slammed against an unyielding webbed shield, dispersing.

The thralls apparently had access to either Ephemera or Nullity, and they came on in a tight formation, regular rows and columns, not even slowing down as they pounded through their ashen dead. Saira released her attack and sprinted away from Shimala's creatures. Once she had gained enough distance, she attacked again. But once more, the thralls shielded against her fire.

Cam grimaced. They might be in trouble. Their most formidable members remained fatigued from their long flight, and if Saira couldn't penetrate the thralls' shield, then what hope did the rest of them have? His mind raced as he sought a solution to their dilemma.

He studied the onrushing thralls. Dust billowed in the wake of their passage, clouding the sun while in the distance, Pelluraj's titanic battle with Shimala continued. Lightning, fire, waterspouts, and boulders the size of homes were flung about. A storm of sand blasted skyward, and the ground quaked. Even from a few miles away, Cam felt the constant change in gravity and concentration of air as the two monsters fought for supremacy.

A furious scream followed by a streak of light blazing across the sky caught Cam's attention. He focused his vision, sighting the cause. The streak resolved into Shimala. Pelluraj had launched her into Lake Petala. She hit the water's surface, skipping a dozen times, a hundred yards each occasion. Finally, her flight halted, and she lifted into the air, roaring her fury.

Cam put the Great Rakshasa out of his mind. An idea occurred to him, and he sent instructions to Pan and Birch. *"Change gravity behind us. One of you make it heavier. The other lighter. Random patterns. It'll slow the thralls."* Next, he addressed Saira. *"Be ready to kill them."*

All three sent acknowledgements, and soon enough, Cam felt the effects of Pan's and Birch's attacks. The thralls' rectangular formation broke apart, the rows undone as a few of Shimala's creatures launched skyward. Others stumbled and fell. Saira used the opening, attacking with a jagged course of lightning. The thralls shielded, but this one wasn't as sturdy. Saira's lightning sizzled and snaked into their formations. Dozens of thralls seized. Their muscles clenched, and smoke billowed out of their noses and burned eyes. They collapsed, dead and discarded. The other thralls never slowed.

Still, Cam saw hope. The formation was the key to the thralls' ability to withstand Saira's assault. Disrupt it, and they became vulnerable. Cam encouraged Birch and Pan to continue their assault.

"What can we do?" Charity asked.

"Keep running," Cam replied. *"All of you were flying for hours. You're exhausted. Save your energy. This isn't going to be a quick battle. From what Birch told us, it's a three-day run to get to the Locus. We can shorten it with flying, but I imagine we'll still be fighting the whole way."*

"The thralls are blocking us," Birch informed him. *"We need another*

plan."

Cam shot a long look at the thralls. He'd figured it was bound to happen, but he'd also hoped it wouldn't be so soon.

Fair enough. Cam had another answer for them, a trick learned during his years in the mindscape. Thrusting out with his True Bond—a mix of Spirairia and Plasminia—he slicked the ground, a sinuous line in random places. Enough for a misplaced step here and there. His sneakiness quickly bore fruit as a number of thralls stumbled, and many of them fell when Pan and Birch shifted gravity on them. Gaping holes in their columns became evident. Saira attacked with a blooming of fire that roared like a dragon's breath. Thralls lit like candles, bursting apart. This time, the stench of burned flesh carried.

"That stinks," Sprite piped up from his hiding space in one of Cam's pockets.

Cam smiled at the cute little bird's complaint. "Consider it the sweet smell of success."

"Sweet?" Kiwi squawked. "That isn't sweet. It's most foul."

Cam didn't have a chance to reply. Pan missed a step on the rocky soil. He stumbled, tried to catch himself, went down. But Cam was there. He darted to his friend's side, gathering him upright, and together they rushed to rejoin Light Squad, who had slowed down for them. The thralls were no more than several hundred yards distant, ranting and raving, matted hair flapping about. The ground shook under the pounding of their bare feet. This close, Cam could also see that they were clothed in nothing but dirt.

"What happened?" Birch asked.

"The ground shifted under my feet," Pan explained. *"I think it was the thralls."*

"It was definitely the thralls," Saira confirmed. Her expression had gone dark. *"If I block their attacks, I won't be able to counterattack."*

"How long can their Bonds hold?" Card asked, gasping and sounding like he was on his last legs.

"They're more likely to be using Nullity," Birch replied. *"They can last a lot longer than you and your Bonds."*

Cam's heart sank upon hearing the old rakshasa's statement. The thralls showed no signs of slowing or weakening. And while Light Squad currently maintained the gap between themselves and their foes, what about when their True Bonds failed? What then? *"Have any of you recovered enough for flight?"*

Saira had never lost her ability, and she indicated such. *"But if I'm carrying everyone, I won't be able to defend us against anything the thralls might do."* While she spoke, her breathing remained smooth and even, unlike Cam's.

He struggled with his wind, gasping. He'd thought himself largely recovered from the weakness of his imprisonment. He'd figured it was so following the seemingly miraculous improvement after feasting on the Glory-Haunted serpent meat, but apparently not. Same with Birch and Pan, and the rakshasa was the one having the most trouble.

As for the rest of Light Squad—Charity, Avia, Jade, and Card— they didn't appear any better off. Cam glanced back at the thralls, who showed no signs of slowing or weakening. He made a decision. *"Get us in the air,"* he told Saira. *"To the hills. We need a place to hole up and lose the thralls."*

Saira responded by lifting Light Squad into the sky. They rose, ten feet, twenty, fifty. The thralls gnashed their teeth, screaming in fury. Seconds later, Light Squad's flight stuttered, stalled. They descended.

"They're holding us down," Saira said, concern lacing her voice as Light Squad drifted toward the ground and the waiting thralls.

"Break their concentration," Cam ordered. He sent lightning, fire, and ice at the thralls. Shifted gravity on them, slicked the surface of the ground. The rest of Light Squad followed his lead. But the thralls shielded, shrugging off their attacks.

"Don't stop," Cam urged, never letting off his barrage. He continued casting coruscating lightning and plumes of white-hot fire. Anything he could manage. His True Bond thinned, frayed. He neared his limits but anger kept him in the fight. He refused to quit.

Birch cried out, unable to continue. Seconds later, Pan followed suit. Kiwi and Sprite trilled their alarm. The rest of Light Squad fought on, faces constricted with effort. Cam continued even as pain built in his chest. His True Bond threatened to snap, but by force of will and fury, he kept it intact. He wouldn't be the weak link that saw Light Squad die.

It must have been enough because with a cry of effort, Saira wrenched them free of the thralls. They burst upward, soaring. A hundred feet, two hundred, swiftly leaving the thralls behind.

Cam finally relented his attack and released his True Bond. He gasped, panted for breath, heart pounding against his ribs as he rubbed at a stabbing ache in his chest.

With Saira flying them, Light Squad soon left the thralls well behind, but even as Shimala's creatures were lost to sight, Cam had a feeling they hadn't seen the last of her monsters. The thralls had been much more skilled than he had expected, and he pondered what he'd learned about them.

First was his assumption that they were mindless. That might not be entirely true. They must have some kind of intellect, but was it the cunning of a predator or something that could reason? If the latter, then why did they have so little regard for their lives? He'd seen the thralls rush headlong into Saira's fire, not wavering in their attempts to get at Light Squad. Others had stomped their fellows to the ground whenever one of them fell, and the notion of aiding one another had never seemed evident.

His musings cut short when Saira began descending. They'd reached the rugged hills he'd spied earlier, and she carefully settled them down within a bowl-shaped hollow. Enclosed on nearly all sides by rough peaks resembling broken obsidian, several openings allowed entrance into the space, and by lucky happenstance, one of them pointed roughly in the same direction as the Locus.

Standing in the bowl, Cam could more readily sense the Ephemera billowing into Mote from the anchor line leading to Salvation. He had noticed it during their approach to the Badlands, but stopped paying it much mind once Pelluraj and Shimala had begun their battle.

Even now, he could see and hear the Stormlord and the Great Rakshasa's conflict as sheets of lightning coruscated from the sky to the ground and back again. Thunder cracked, the ground shook, and towering flames lit the clouds with a ruddy glow. Cam wished the Stormlord good luck in his battle. The longer the kaiju kept Shimala engaged, the better for Light Squad.

However, he was soon distracted from the battle when he noticed a bass-toned undercurrent. It was the steady drumbeat of feet pounding in time to a grunting chant. The thralls. They continued the chase.

"We can't stay here," Cam said, able to speak now that the raging din of conflict no longer made it impossible. "This way." He pointed in the direction where he sensed the Locus.

"How do you know that's the right way?" Jade asked with a frown. "You actually feel that's where Ephemera is coming into this world?"

"You can't?"

Jade shook her head.

Pan hesitantly raised his hand. "I can feel it a little."

"That's good enough for me," Cam said. "Let's go." He led Light Squad toward the proper exit, and they moved at a quick jog rather than a flat-out sprint. They needed to conserve their energy. There was certain to be a lot more running to do.

Moments later, Kiwi and Sprite emerged from Cam's pockets and flitted over to land on Birch's shoulders. The rakshasa grimaced, but it was all an act. Birch liked the lovebirds. Soon enough, he was talking to Kiwi and Sprite, stroking their chest feathers and telling them what good birds they were.

Cam glanced askance when Card moved to run next to him on his right.

The other man spoke. "How is it that after three years apart, you're still ordering us around? Shouldn't that be Saira's job? She's the Sage."

Card didn't sound or seem upset, merely curious, but the question had Cam thinking. He'd never really considered it before, but Card was right. After reuniting with Light Squad, he'd fallen into old habits of barking commands at them. But was it right, especially with everyone else at a higher Stage?

Jade, running to Cam's left, didn't share Card's doubts. "He leads us because he's the best at doing it. By far."

Cam glanced at the rest of Light Squad and received murmurs of agreement, including from Saira. Heartened by their trust, he faced forward and led them toward the beacon he knew had to be the Locus.

While they ran out of the bowl, Jade sent him a private message. *"Don't start doubting yourself again."*

"I'm not." Cam recognized why she might think so, but she didn't need to keep worrying about him. Honestly, her fussiness was a bit mothering. *"I know my worth. I just wanted to make sure everyone else is fine with my leadership."*

A bit of his irritation must have leaked across because Jade rolled her eyes. *"We're happy with your leadership, but you were also the one acting like a child when you found out Charity has seen other men. How was I to know the reason for that? Speaking of Charity, did you talk to her?"*

It wasn't necessarily any of Jade's business, but Cam answered her anyway. *"We talked."*

"And? Did you apologize? Because you needed to apologize."

Cam frowned, anger rumbling. *"Why is this any of your concern?"*

Jade grinned, not the slightest bit put off by his tone. *"As your adopted big sister—"*

"You're younger than me."

"No, I'm not. You were in Mote for four months. That was three years in Salvation." She gave him a smug smile. *"I'm older."*

This time it was Cam who rolled his eyes. *"Fine. You're older."*

"And as your adopted big sister, it's my duty to make sure you don't do something stupid and mess up what should be a wonderful thing between you and Charity."

Cam might have disagreed with her rationale, but he didn't have the heart. Besides which, Jade was right. *"Card said that she saw a few men," but he also said they complained about her.*"

"*Card told you that?*" Jade scowled, muttering under her breath, something to the effect about how Card should stay out of other people's private matters, which was pretty rich considering how she'd been interrogating him about Charity. She took a deep breath, seemingly gathering her patience. "*What else did he say?*"

"*He also said that she talked to them about me.*" Now it was his turn to offer Jade a smug smile.

"*And knowing she hadn't forgotten about you is what it took for you to overcome your childishness?*" She shook her head, giving him a look of derisive pity.

Cam scowled. "*I understand. I behaved poorly. I apologized. Move on. I'm not a complete idiot when it comes to relationships.*"

"*No. Just mostly an idiot,*" Jade said with a smile, and for some reason, it took the sting out of her words.

And although a part of Cam wanted to remain irritated with her, a larger portion couldn't help but laugh. He'd missed Jade's brutal but refreshing honesty. In its own way, it was even loving, similar to how Pharis, his actual older sister, might have advised him when it came to his relationship with Charity.

Jade snapped her fingers, like she'd just realized something important, and she viewed him wide-eyed and innocent. "Charity is also older than you, and so is Saira. Is that it then? Are you infatuated with older women?"

She had spoken aloud, and bat-eared Pan heard. He immediately joined them, a not-so-cute grin on his face. "What's this about Cam liking older women? Maybe it's true, but in the prison, all he could do was talk about Charity. The way he would go on about her."

"Really?" Jade swiveled about, facing Pan with an intense interest. "What did he say?"

Cam sighed. Here they were, trapped on Mote, sought by Shimala, chased by her mindless thralls, who apparently had the power of a Sage, weary to the bone, and yet these two—Jade and Pan—had the energy to tease him and gossip about his romantic life.

He wanted to stop listening when Jade laughed out loud over Pan's description of what happened when Cam tried to create a simulation of Charity in their mindscape—it hadn't gone well. He winced when the traitorous panda-person went on to describe the one poem Cam had tried to write about Charity. It had been his first attempt.

"He compared her smile to a crescent moon and her hair to sea-weed," Pan brayed.

Jade guffawed, and even Card cracked a smile.

Cam huffed, turning his attention to the ongoing battle between Pelluraj and Shimala. Their din was better than listening to Pan's stories.

39

Cam grimaced when Saira made her report. She'd ascended to the sky and scouted the still-chasing thralls, who were no more than ten miles behind Light Squad and closing fast. How? They shouldn't be able to cover so much distance so swiftly. They shouldn't even still be running. Didn't they ever rest? Eat or drink?

Apparently not.

Since Light Squad had landed on the Badlands two days ago, it had been two days of nonstop running and flying. Whenever Avia, Charity, Jade, and Card recovered, they'd fly hundreds of miles over a barren landscape, not stopping for any kind of rest or even sleep.

And yet, somehow the thralls would always close the distance as soon as Light Squad was back on the ground. Which led back to how. How were the thralls doing it?

It was a mystery Cam would have loved to answer, but maybe—hopefully—it wouldn't matter in the end. Light Squad was nearing the Locus, almost there. It couldn't be much more than thirty miles ahead. Which meant Salvation's shores were close, and there was no chance anything could stop them.

The one variable was Shimala. Did her battle with Pelluraj still rage? Cam couldn't tell. Not even Saira knew. But was that lack of awareness because of distance or because the conflict had ended? It was Cam's greatest concern. Shimala's presence at the Locus changed every calculation.

He tried to shrug off the worries, wanted to focus on his running. One step after another on the dusty plain that made up most of the Badlands. Keep going, even past the point of fatigue. If the others could do it, then so could he. Look at Birch. The old-headed rakshasa appeared to be moving on momentum alone, shambling along rather than running with glassy eyes and gasping uneven breaths, but he was still going. Pan didn't seem to be any better off and neither did the Crowns. Even Saira appeared weary.

Which was why Light Squad had to make sure they didn't have to battle Shimala's forces at the journey's end. Their chances against the thralls hadn't been good early on, and this late in the chase, it would be even worse. They had to get to the Locus before her forces reached them. And as matters currently stood, they should be able to make it. Assuming Shimala remained tied down with Pelluraj.

So Cam's thoughts circled even as the bright light of the Locus continued to heighten in his senses. By now, everyone could feel it, a lodestar tugging them onward.

The miles shrank. Twenty. Fifteen. Ten. Less than five miles to reach the Locus, and the rusty plain became a sea of ankle-high grass, as thick and luxuriant as any Cam had ever seen. It was the first sign of life in the Badlands. Small copses of trees became apparent, interspersed with wide fields of wheat growing tall at the base of terraced hillsides of rice.

Light Squad swept past them, and those who tended the farms—thralls by the look of them—never once glanced up from their labor as Cam and the others rushed past.

A mile, and by now the Locus was visible as a bright light beaming skyward, thinning to a nearly invisible line, broadening again where it formed the Hollow Land's sun. Cam hadn't been able to see the connection between sky and ground until now. He took fresh heart from the sight as well as the sense of tranquility washing out from the Locus. It wafted like an irregularly spaced wind of Ephemera, an intermittent breeze that bent the grass, crops, and greenery, spurring them to fresh life and growth even as they brought new strength to Cam's laboring run.

His stride smoothed and lengthened. Only a half-mile to go. He wanted to sprint the last. Just get it done. Not much further now.

And while the thralls had somehow managed to cut the gap even further, enough for Cam to easily make out their coarse features, it was too late. He viewed the baying, braying fiends and flashed them a vulgar hand sign.

"*Cam!*" Pan sent, sounding scandalized.

"*They deserve it.*"

"*It's too soon,*" Pan said. "*You only make that sign once we're safe.*"

A weighty presence cut off Cam's response. "Safety?" a voice on the wind mocked. "Is that what you children desire?"

Cam knew who it was without looking back. Still, he did so, and there she was: Shimala, floating ahead of her forces, pulling steadily ahead of them. The wind of her flight caused her tattered, white clothing to trail after her like a ragged cloak, and she smiled a skeleton's rictus, triumphant. But Cam could also see the strain underlying her effort. Battling Pelluraj and getting here so quickly, possibly empowering her thralls… all of it had taken a toll.

Fear didn't touch Cam. "*Keep going,*" he urged. "*She wants us slowing down and afraid. We're almost there. We can make it.*"

Just then, another presence unclothed itself from directly ahead of the Locus, and the smell of gardenias suffused the air. Cam cursed. *Coruscant.* Light Squad was caught between two Great Rakshasas. What should they do?

"These children are mine," Coruscant declared, visible now. He appeared unchanged from when Cam had encountered him in the mindscape: of medium height and build with pale hair and complexion and hazel irises set in crystalline-diamond sclerae. The one change was he now wore black armor that had a matte-black finish.

But his presence gave Cam hope. If the Great Rakshasas fought one another, maybe Light Squad could skirt their battle and escape into the Locus. Just like they'd done with Shimala and Pelluraj. It might work. It had to. All they had to do was reach the Locus, no more than a hundred yards away now, visible as a narrow bridge of white stone, its far end lost in a fog.

The rest of Light Squad must have latched on to the same idea. Without Cam needing to state the order, Charity, who currently had the lead, drifted right, curving wide and out of the direct line of sight between Coruscant and Shimala. It would take them away from the Locus, but it was also the right decision.

The Great Rakshasas charged headlong at one another, never wavering. But at the last moment, they took to the skies. The thralls, however, kept right on Light Squad's trail, a straight line that took them beneath the battling Great Rakshasas. With a surge, Shimala's creatures bolted forward in a strange stop-and-start fashion. And cut Light Squad off from the Locus.

Cam cursed, calling out orders for Light Squad to slow. They needed a plan of attack, and he scanned the thralls, quickly realizing that not every member of the horde were present to block Light Squad. Only about a quarter of them, while the rest had pulled back, standing still, swaying back and forth while staring dead-eyed at the battle between Coruscant and Shimala. However, that still left roughly a thousand thralls between Light Squad and the bridge leading out of Mote, plenty enough to pose a challenge.

His attention briefly went to the two Great Rakshasas, who flung attacks at one another with abandon. Coruscant carved the air with swords of ice and bolts of white hot air that screamed like a wounded animal. Thunder boomed, and the world shuddered. Shimala defended with a flick of her wrist, casting a shield. However, the webbing flared, buckled, and she grimaced. The watching thralls stumbled, and a number of them even collapsed, twitching or appearing dead.

"They're supporting her," Birch said.

The rakshasas' words confirmed what Cam had already figured to be the case, and he returned his attention to the waiting thralls blocking Light Squad's exit from this world. Shimala's creatures didn't advance. Just like the rest of their brethren, they held silent, swaying back and forth, snakelike.

Cam quickly formulated a plan. It would be quick and dirty, nothing fanciful since they didn't have the time for anything beyond a straight on attack. Shimala showed signs of buckling and was already down hundreds of her thralls. Coruscant seemed to be getting the better of her.

"We have to cut through them," Cam sent. *"Form an arrow. Saira at the tip. The Crowns at the edges. Me, Birch, and Pan in the center."* While Cam hated needing the protection of the others—he should be the one doing the protecting—now wasn't the time for false gallantry. The others were more powerful than him, and that's just the way it was. Once everyone was in position, he shouted, *"Charge!"*

Light Squad sprinted, and the gap between them and the thralls closed rapidly. Cam called out fresh instructions, and from a quarter-mile out, Light Squad launched crackling bolts of lightning and icy arrows into the waiting horde. The thralls defended, but their shield was weaker than before. Some of them went down. The rest rushed at Light Squad, a wave of maniacally screaming monsters.

"Hit the center. Break them," Cam ordered. *"Anyone between us and the Locus. Don't waste time on their edges."*

Light Squad did as instructed. Charity gestured, and thralls floated into the air. Jade finished them off with slugs of sizzling metal, a fusillade. Card was subtler in his assault. He caused the thralls to slip and fall on suddenly uneven terrain. When they did so, Avia sent spinning loops of air buzzing like a thousand saws that sliced the creatures apart. But it was Saira who acted as Light Squad's battering ram. She opened her mouth and howled, a high-pitched scream that shattered everything in front of her. The thralls broke like kindling.

For a brief moment, it looked like Light Squad might spear straight through the lines and columns of Shimala's creatures. Their attack certainly took them deep into the horde where their pace quickly bogged down. Then it became a battle of attrition: the thralls and their numbers against Light Squad's stamina.

Cam dimly noted the lovebirds tweeting in fright from where they'd resettled in his pockets. But he put them out of his mind and gestured. A green shield protected him. Just in time. A thrall smashed at him. The webbing flared, sparkling. Another gesture, and he held a white-hot double-bladed spear. He slashed out and killed the assaulting thrall. A third movement, and another protection formed, a round shield a pace across, smooth and glassy green in his off hand.

The world became a welter of noise, movement and chaos. Cam fought, slashing, thrusting. An outstretched hand with telekinesis crushed skulls, moved thralls about. One creature ducked low. Cam brought down his round shield, clubbing the thrall, followed by a hard stomp with a spike extruding off his boot that ended the monster.

Pan and Birch shifted to cover his flanks, moving in time with his steady forward pace. By now, they had battled and trained together for so long that they'd become a single unit. Thralls fell to Pan's staff and Birch's spear, and Cam settled into the battle.

No thinking was required. The only things he needed were the muscle memory and instincts honed from thousands of hours of fighting against Pan and Birch.

A whisper of noise, and Cam spun, cutting down a thrall that sought to backstab him. Another spin, and he bisected another creature. A slight noise and breeze, and he lifted his shield, catching claws from a screaming thrall. Birch stabbed the monster through the chest. All the while, Pan swirled his staff, clearing space. The thralls before him moved back, many falling. Cam and Birch were there to take advantage of the opening as quick thrusts ended the monsters.

Onward Light Squad pressed, continuing for the Locus, the bridge that represented true freedom from Mote. They killed anything that came close, and inch by inch, foot by foot, and yard by yard, they strained and struggled, gaining ground. Their goal wasn't far, only fifty yards.

But running for two days and being without sleep had taken its toll. Cam's True Bond frayed. The pain in his chest recurred. He slowed, unable to maintain the brutal pace, and the thralls seemed to take heart from his weakness. The monsters attacked with greater vigor. But Cam gritted his teeth, anger surging. Fresh strength coursed through him, and he fended them off. Telekinesis to pull thralls off balance. Small uses of gravity and shifting ground. Sword thrusts, bashing thralls with his shield, bolts of fiery metal when able.

Eventually though, the anger ebbed, and exhaustion weighed on his limbs once more. Blows began getting through his defenses. His vision blurred from a clubbing shot to his head. A slash to the thigh carved a furrow. Blood poured down his leg. It couldn't bear his weight, and he stumbled to a knee. A hammer blow to his gut, and his breath exploded. Lines of fire ripped down his shoulder from a clawing thrall. Cam gestured wide, and an arc of air bisected the monsters before him.

A brief respite, and Cam panted, heart pounding, exhausted and in pain. Pan and Birch stayed with him, all of them struggling. By then, the others had pulled forward, a small gap that the thralls swiftly filled.

Gritting his teeth, Cam rose to his feet. This wouldn't be his end, nor the end of his friends. He lifted his sword and shield, ready to kill. One of the creatures raging before him ducked low. Cam countered with a downward smash of his shield. Birch finished off the thrall, but took a stab to the thigh in the process. The rakshasa howled in anger and pain, struggling to continue forward.

Cam's hopes faltered. How would they make it through such madness?

Even as the question arose, the rest of Light Squad returned, clearing space around him, Birch, and Pan. Cam regathered his will when he realized how close they were to the Locus: no more than ten yards away. They only had to break through a few dozen thralls.

Cam readied for what was necessary, but with an abruptness that shook them all, the thralls died, all of them as one, falling like puppets with their strings cut. Silence settled over the battlefield. Cam stared around, blank of thought. What had just happened?

"Keep going," Saira shouted, her voice hoarse and sounding as tired as Cam felt.

Light Squad stumbled toward the Locus, the golden, glowing bridge, which swirled with an undercurrent of every color. The clean fragrance of lilacs reached him along with the tinkling of bells. A fragile feeling of peace and serenity drifted like a wind of healing.

But appearing at the entrance and blocking it was Coruscant. His fine armor was misshapen, torn apart in places and his handsome features battered. But he stood tall and unyielding, wearing an expression of triumph. He must have defeated Shimala.

Cam wanted to weep. Couldn't Shimala have held on for just a few seconds longer? Light Squad had almost made it out.

Coruscant addressed Saira. "You may be a child of clay brought to life, but you cannot best me. Not here, not now, not ever."

Before Cam could ponder the meaning of Coruscant's statement, Shimala screamed from behind them. "We aren't done, you and I." Bruises marred her grandmotherly features, her tattered clothing was rent to ruin, and she limped heavily, walking rather than floating or flying, but still, she'd arrived.

In his life thus far, Cam would have never expected to be glad to see Shimala, but in that moment, he most certainly was.

Coruscant scowled. "Give it up. One of your sendings has already recently been destroyed. Do you really want to see another one killed?"

Shimala grinned. "Come and find out. Or don't. It's true. I can't best you, but I also won't let you have my pets."

"Don't do this," Coruscant urged.

Shimala didn't listen. She attacked, forcing Coruscant away from the Locus.

Light Squad took the opening and sprinted for the bridge, Cam and Pan supporting Birch. Stumbling, they reached the Locus even as thunder cracked and the ground shook all around them.

Coruscant screamed in rage, the sound carrying over the din of his battle with Shimala.

Cam took a single step on the bridge, turning back just in time to see Shimala slump to her knees, facing him with Coruscant looming behind her. "Another time, boy," she said. An instant later, her head slipped off her neck as Coruscant cut her down.

The surviving Great Rakshasa glowered at him. "Run. Stay. Hide. It doesn't matter. In the end, I will find you again and break you."

Cam lacked the courage to answer Coruscant's challenge with defiance. Instead, he made the prudent decision to take the final step onto the bridge.

40

After Coruscant's final grim warning, Cam faced forward and did his best to shove the Great Rakshasa out of his thoughts. He limped. His body ached, full of bruises and cuts, and breathing remained a chore. Blood soaked his shirt and trousers from his many wounds, but his various injuries drifted to the back of his mind, seemingly unimportant when he took his first full step onto the Locus, the bridge leading to freedom. A sense of unreality layered over him like a fog, shrouding his ability to think. All he could do was stare ahead, unmoving and unable to see much beyond the tears fogging his vision. A shuddering breath led to a wracking sob. One after another. He couldn't get them to stop.

Pan was there, and they held one another, both of them crying, but Cam didn't know why. At least not at first, but slowly, steadily, his thoughts cleared. It was the weight of everything the two of them had endured, and it crashed over them, too much, and in that moment, all they could do was cry. So many memories and emotions, and Pan was surely feeling them the same way. All the troubles and turmoil they'd suffered in Mote, the lost dreams and aspirations, the never-ending fury of Sage-Duke Kazar's betrayal, the surety that their lives were to end in the bleakest of prisons on Murder Day, the fresh hope of possible freedom, the constant struggle to make themselves believe that they could actually fight their way to freedom, the forced belief that their success was assured.

And they had succeeded, but for Cam, rather than leaving him fulfilled, the accomplishment left him empty, like his mind had been purged of all the horrors of the past few months, but now he needed to fill it with something fresh and new. But what?

Cam knew what it should be—something about saving Salvation—but for now, all he wanted was the peace of no expectations, of stillness and quiet where nothing was needed or required of him and he could simply exist, with no one or anything bothering his tranquility.

But not long after, only a few minutes maybe, Cam gathered himself, pushing himself free of Pan's embrace. "How are you?"

Pan offered a wan smile. "We did it." He swallowed heavily, giving a final shudder before rolling a shoulder, wincing. "I'm fine. Bruised, but I'll heal. It just came over me, though."

Cam cupped Pan's face, kissing his forehead. "I know, brother. It hit me the same way."

"It came over me, too," Birch said. "Where is my hug?" He wore a mocking smile, but there was pain hidden in the depths of his eyes.

Cam wiped away his tears and laughed in spite of his turmoiled emotions. "Come here." He hugged Birch, feeling the rakshasa stiffen at first before settling into the embrace.

Kiwi and Sprite fluttered out of Cam's pockets and alighted on Birch's shoulders. "We'll hug you, too," Kiwi declared.

"Just what I needed," Birch said, sounding put upon. "Two lovebirds pooping on me." Despite his sour words, warmth and humor lit his voice.

Cam released the rakshasa, grinning as a notion occurred to him. "Looks like we didn't end up dying in Mote, after all."

Birch viewed him, wide-eyed with shock before throwing his head back and laughing. "You're right. We didn't. I suppose it means we'll probably die the moment we reach Salvation. That seems to be the way of the Realms."

"Probably?" Cam asked. "You've always been so certain about our deaths before, even about how we'll die. Now you're not?"

Before Birch could respond, Pan spoke. "We're all meant to die at some point. Salvation wouldn't be a bad Realm in which to meet our end and reunite with Devesh."

Birch deliberated, shrugging at Pan after a moment. "I suppose not."

The rest of Light Squad had gathered at a distance, granting them privacy, but Saira spoke. "Come. The bridge home awaits. Who knows how long it will take to traverse its limits?"

"Give us a chance to heal first," Cam said.

"Do you need help?" Charity asked, viewing them in concern. "Saira is good at healing."

Cam shook his head, addressing Saira. "I don't need any help. Neither does Pan. We can manage. But if you could see to Birch?"

Saira inclined her head. "Of course."

Cam forged a fresh True Bond, closed his eyes and focused inward, seeking out all his injuries, coaxing the ragged wounds to close, the inflammation to resolve, and the bruises to repair. Minutes later, he inhaled deep, no pain as his cracked ribs were healed. There was more work to be done, but it was best to do so in stages. He'd finish healing later. Cam opened his eyes.

Charity stood before him, staring close, curious. "How did you learn to do that?"

Cam smiled. "The teachings from Rukh and Jessira. We mastered most of them in Mote."

"There's more to learn," Pan added, having also healed himself. "Cam says that there are layers to the instructions and they'll become more evident when we Advance to Crown and Sage."

Card grunted. "I wouldn't mind learning what they taught you. Think you can teach us?"

Cam nodded. "I'm sure we can find the time once we get back to Salvation. And on that note, let's move."

They set off, and Cam felt like he could float to the Locus' nonexistent sky. Nothing weighed him down. He had no responsibilities, and he drifted to the back of the group. Charity stayed with him, and they walked in silence.

Cam recalled his behavior toward her, and some of his weight returned. He owed Charity a proper apology and explanation. *"I truly am sorry,"* he sent.

She quirked her eyebrows in question. *"Sorry for what?"*

"I was jealous before. I shouldn't have been. I'm not anymore."

Charity gave a sniff. *"You should have been jealous. There were many men who sought my hand. I'm quite popular. You should remember that."* She took his face in her hands, forcing him to meet her gaze, and a flicker of anger lit her eyes. *"But the way you judged me... I didn't appreciate it."*

Cam swallowed. Fighting thralls and kaijus wasn't as hard as this conversation. *"I know. And I'm sorry. I'll do better."*

She eyed him a moment longer, nodding. *"See that you do."* Anger still laced her words, but she reached for his hand.

Hesitantly, Cam allowed it. Charity gripped his hand more securely, and he breathed out a prayer at her forgiving nature. He didn't deserve Charity, nor did he deserve her easy acceptance, but he was grateful for both, and they walked in a comfortable silence.

While they strode along the bridge, Cam finally gave his attention to the Locus. Glowing silver piers, each one broad, square, and topped by caps and posts carved into the shape of a pineapple, held the span aloft, while down below drifted an impenetrable fog, quiet and mysterious. The pavers of the decking and the stones of the fancifully carved railings shined gold, but an iridescent sheen underlay their bright and buttery warm color. The trilling of birds—not Kiwi or Sprite—and the chiming of bells melded with a soft, Singing Light that beamed down like moonbeams on a perfect night. A steady wind, soft as a baby's breath, whispered steadily against them, fragrant with some aroma Cam couldn't name, but it was lovely and lush with Ephemera, richer than anything he'd experienced in Mote or the Hollow Land but still lacking the depth of what he recalled of Salvation and Hearth.

Nonetheless, Cam tried to Imbibe the Ephemera. He found it impossible, though, and frowning, he tried again. Another failure. Cam halted his progress, trying to figure what he was doing wrong.

"You've noticed that you can't Imbibe the Ephemera?" Charity asked.

"Yes," Cam replied, still frowning, trying to Imbibe again and failing once more. "Do you know what I'm doing wrong?"

Charity smiled. "It's not you, it's the Ephemera itself. It isn't for us. It's meant for Mote. We read an account about it, or rather Thor did. The Ephemera on the bridge can only travel to Mote. No one can use it until then. It's what keeps that Realm alive."

"Does the bridge have a name?" Pan asked, having slowed down to join them.

"Not that we know or that Thor learned," Charity said. "It's always just been called the Locus."

Cam listened with half an ear as Charity and Pan discussed the nature of Ephemera and the Locus, but most of his attention was given over to reflections about Thor. From their first meeting, he had been an inspiration, a living example of how a Sage should behave. Cam owed Thor more than he could ever repay. He wouldn't have escaped Mote if not for the newly minted Divine of Loyalty, and Cam hoped to one day see his friend again.

Light Squad continued their journey on the bridge home, walking for hours and hours, but hunger and thirst never touched them. At first, Jade found it odd, but then again, she'd never walked an anchor line like this one—or whatever the Locus truly was. Who knew what was normal here?

Dismissing the observation, she became aware of Light Squad's prayerful silence. During the initial part of their trek, their conversations had been exuberant and celebratory, but eventually all of that had died down. There were only so many ways to rejoice over their successes, and after a while, for the most part they traveled in a meditative quiet.

On they went, passing countless silver pilings and capstones that merged one after another, each one seemingly identical. Jade might have believed Light Squad was traveling an endless loop, but she also couldn't find it within herself to summon any caring. The bridge was mystical and lovely, reminding her in some strange way of her father's love. She missed him, but strangely enough, it was a fleeting emotion.

"This is restful," Jade said, breaking the quiet and addressing Saira, who strode close at hand.

"It is," Saira agreed, facing forward and smiling in her classically serene and self-possessed manner. "On this bridge, only the moment is of import. Nothing else."

Jade viewed Saira in consideration, wishing she could be more like the other woman. If Pan's grin made a person happy, then Saira's smile granted them calm, something Jade still needed to master. Too often, her emotions still got the best of her.

Witness her treatment of Cam. Sure, he had been an absolute jackhole when he found out that Charity had seen other men, but did Jade really have to bite his head off over his reaction? Probably not, no matter how much he deserved it, but more importantly, she hadn't seen Cam in years, and this was how she responded to his first troubles?

Her behavior to him sat like a jagged pill in her craw, and while Jade knew she should apologize to Cam, for some reason, the words didn't want to come out. It bothered her, and she couldn't express why. Cowardice wasn't the reason. What then? Was it was because she didn't want to ruin the serenity of walking this tranquil bridge? Maybe that was it. Maybe Jade didn't want to think about her past or her future. Somehow, while traveling this span, all of her concerns had washed away prior to having a chance to lodge in her mind, and she couldn't find it in herself to fight that restfulness.

Nodding to herself, Jade deliberated then over Saira's observation, swiftly realizing that, as usual, the woman was right. The moment was where Jade's thoughts wanted to abide; not any worries about what had happened in the past or might happen in the future. None of that had any meaning here, and Jade smiled to herself, thankful for Saira's explanation.

"Look," Avia said, pointing to one of the piers. She and Card had been pacing at the forefront of their group, but they had slowed to a halt for the rest of Light Squad, who gathered around Avia's discovery. The base of a pier held a faint carving. "It's *Muladhara*," Avia explained. "The Root Chakra."

Jade leaned in more closely, affirming Avia's finding and assaying the rest of the piers directly ahead. They had the same carving, which was the first change Light Squad had encountered in any aspect of the bridge's piers, railings, or capstones. She smiled at Avia. "Our fishy friend has clever eyes."

Avia grinned, pointing at herself. "Not a fish."

"But you still have clever eyes," Card said. "I didn't notice anything until you pointed it out."

"Of course you didn't," Charity said to him with an affectionate snort. "You wouldn't have noticed it unless it had to do with Ephemera."

"That's the thing," Card said. "It does have to do with Ephemera, or at least some part of what we thought of as Ephemera before Rukh and Jessira saved Salvation. Channeling Devesh's gift of Creation was far more difficult then. Stories talk about how people used His reflected Glory in their souls before learning to connect their souls with the world at large. Later on, they did all that and also opened Chakras, like *Muladhara* to unite their Inner Self with Divinity." He made a face. "So much work."

Birch sighed on hearing Card's words. "In Mote, it was said that the Great Rakshasas closed their Chakras in order to affect the world."

Jade wasn't sure how Chakras were opened or closed, and she didn't care to learn unless it offered a better way to Advance.

Cam seemed to share her disregard for the past, indicating the way forward. "Let's go. There are supposed to be eight Chakras. Maybe seeing the first one means our next goal is the second one, then the third one, and so on."

"That would make sense," Pan said with a nod, cute and cuddly like always, even after his trials in Mote and Advancement to Glory.

Jade wondered why he hadn't altered his form to one that was more human. Her eyes landed on Avia. Pan had once been infatuated with her, who was most definitely not a fish, but rather a powerful, intelligent woman of worth.

Light Squad continued on, and this time, Jade found herself striding alongside Birch. She'd barely spoken ten words to the rakshasa, and she viewed him sidelong. Birch was said to have been a Crown in Coruscant's legions, but he'd been imprisoned over some failure outside his control. Sometime during his incarceration, he'd become a follower of Devesh, or at least, he'd fully turned traitor to Coruscant by learning to Imbibe Ephemera. Cam even said that the leonine rakshasa had been visited by Rail Gristle, who had most likely been Rukh in disguise. But what had Jade's attention was that Birch was said to possess Nullity, the opposite of Ephemera. She wanted to know more about it. But how to breech the conversation?

Birch must have noticed her struggles because he chuckled in amusement. "I can tell you have something to say. Say it. I won't be offended."

Jade took the opportunity. "What exactly is Nullity?"

Birch smiled, wan and bitter. "At its heart, it is the betrayal of love and sharing." He went on to tell about how Nullity was created, its advantages of personal power, but its weaknesses as well. "Ultimately, a master of Nullity fights alone. They have no one on whom to rely." He nodded with his chin to Cam and Pan. "Those two are brothers. They fight for one another. They'd sacrifice themselves to see the other one live. That's a kind of power I didn't respect until I tested them in the mindscape."

"The mindscape?" Cam had mentioned that as well, but Jade wasn't sure what it meant.

"It's a place of shared imagination where we mastered skills and talents. You couldn't see it in Petala, but those two fight well above their Stage of Advancement."

Jade viewed Cam and Pan, who walked ahead with Avia and Charity. The Hollow Land had been a desert, and Mote was supposed to be even more barren. And yet, Cam and Pan had learned to live there? Thrive in some ways, Advancing.

She shook her head in disbelief at what they'd accomplished. In addition, Birch was wrong about one particular matter. Jade *had* noticed Cam's skills and Pan's talents, the control they exhibited. It was astonishing, and she couldn't wait to see what they could do as Crowns.

"The mindscape was also where I learned to properly Imbibe Ephemera," Birch continued. "I still have some Nullity left to purge, though."

Jade stared at Birch. She hadn't known that. He still had Nullity? Didn't that raise all kinds of unpleasant possibilities? "How do we know you won't betray Cam and Pan?" She didn't bother hiding her distrust.

"You don't, but they do." Birch gestured again to Cam and Pan. "They know my heart. There are no secrets between us."

Jade wasn't entirely mollified, but then again, Cam and Pan had shared a mindscape—a place of shared imagination—with this rakshasa for four years. If they trusted him, then she supposed she ought to as well.

"Tell me about yourself," Birch said. "Cam and Pan would often comment on the members of their famed unit, Light Squad, but that isn't the same as truly knowing you."

Jade wasn't averse to telling Birch about herself, at least up to a point. "What do you want to know?"

"Where did you go after their betrayal at the hands of Charity's father?"

It was an odd request, but Jade shrugged and answered anyway, figuring there was no harm in doing so. She spoke of her Advancement to Glory in the temple that Rainen Winder had gifted to them and from there, her journey to the Sinanes, going on to describe the islands and their beauty. "The Sinanes are like a dream," she said, voice breathy and mind lost in the recollections of swimming in the Arylyn Ocean, hiking to the summits of the many peaks scattered across the archipelago, and simply enjoying the music and plays of the capital's many theaters.

Birch quirked a mildly mocking grin. "I can tell."

In the past, mockery of any kind would have upset Jade, but the bridge's peace didn't allow for that kind of emotion. Plus, the lovebirds had landed on Birch's head, which made him look absolutely ridiculous. Jade laughed.

Birch rolled his eyes, like he could actually see the birds on his head, and he heaved a sigh, as if needing patience. "Why do they love roosting on my head?" he muttered, sounding like he was talking to himself.

"Because you let us," the yellow lovebird, Sprite, said. "And the view from up here is the best."

Birch sighed heavily again. "Some cats eat birds, but these two don't seem to know that. I don't think they have a single self-preservatory bone in their bodies." He said it with a scowl of annoyance, but the affection in his voice was clear.

And that affection for the fragile lovebirds released the last of Jade's antipathy toward the lion-headed rakshasa. She smiled at Birch. "Did you know about Pan's love for bamboo?"

Birch laughed. "Of course. He talks about nothing else."

Hours of walking ensued after Avia's discovery of the engraved Chakra, and Cam didn't know when the journey would ever end. The bridge seemed endless. They could have been treading its length for a day, a week, a month, or even a year, but time didn't seem to have meaning in the Locus. He wondered at times why Rukh and Jessira didn't contact him and Pan. Or even Thor. Was there something to this strange anchor line that prevented communication? Maybe there was some other reason.

Regardless, he didn't mind since along with time having no meaning on the anchor line, fears, hopes, or anger didn't touch him either.

Cam was grateful for the last. Only the moment counted, something he'd heard Saira mention to Jade.

Kiwi must not have felt the same way, though, because the little lovebird exhaled heavily, his impatience obvious.

Cam glanced over at the green avian. Kiwi and Sprite had been flitting around during their journey, spending time on Birch's head, with Pan, and generally going from one person to the next, gabbing nonstop questions. They'd joined Cam a little while back, landing on his shoulders and thankfully, staying quiet rather than nattering away with their queries.

Unfortunately, that silence didn't last forever. More recently, both birds had been regularly sighing every hundred or so piers.

"What's wrong?" Cam asked the green lovebird.

"This is so boring," Kiwi complained, sounding petulant.

Cam laughed. "What are you? A child? Next, you'll ask if we're there yet."

"Ask and you shall receive," Saira said. She had halted before a silver post, and at its base was a strange symbol that Cam didn't recognize. "It's *Vyapani*, the eighth Chakra," Saira explained, seeing his confusion. "I think it means we're nearly home. We've been seeing different Chakras as we've gone along. They've ascended regularly from *Muladhara*, the Root Chakra to *Svadhisthana*, the Sacral Chakra. Next came *Manipura*, *Anahata*, and *Vishuddi*. Afterward was *Ajna*, and most recently, *Sahasrara*, the Crown Chakra. *Vyapani* is the Chakra of the Soul, the last one. Hopefully, there isn't anything after this, except for home."

Cam figured Saira was right in her determination, and he lingered over her final word: home. Such a simple word. Only a single syllable, but it contained a wealth of meanings, all of them centered around love and obligations. While they'd been traversing the bridge, Cam had set aside his obligations for Golden, but he could no longer do so. His obligations for his home needed tending. From everything he'd been told, the rakshasas threatened to overwhelm Golden.

He took a settling breath. "Then let's go home. I'm ready."

Light Squad proceeded on, and shortly thereafter arrived at a place where the bridge's deck abruptly ended, stopping at an oval doorway wide enough to fit several wagons side-by-side and tall enough for someone thrice Cam's height. From it glowed an iridescent light, and through it wafted the Ephemera drifting to Mote. It flowed off the doorway in an unchanging stream that had a physical heft, billowing around and through Light Squad like a steady breeze. Cam tried again to Imbibe the Ephemera, and unsurprisingly, he failed once again.

Nonetheless, the excitement from when he'd first stepped onto the bridge returned. This was it. They'd done it. Journey's end. They were about to go home. Cam shared a triumphant grin with Pan before approaching the shimmering doorway. He glanced to either side of it and saw nothing but darkness all around. "What now?"

Saira answered. "According to Thor, we simply focus our minds on where we wish to go, and the doorway will send us to that place. It is easier for those of greater Advancement. I'll go first, to my mother. The rest of you follow but think of both me *and* my mother. Wait for a count of sixty between each individual." She called out the order of exit before addressing Cam, Pan, and Birch. "For you three, since you've never met my mother, think of not only me, but the rest of Light Squad. The greater links you have, the more likely you'll end up where you should. Is that clear?"

Light Squad voiced their acquiescence. However, prior to entering the doorway home, Saira gestured to Kiwi and Sprite, who'd settled on Cam's shoulders. "You two should come with me. The travel between worlds can be difficult. I'll smooth it for you as best as I can."

The two lovebirds flitted to Saira and landed on her fingers. She proceeded to tuck them into an interior pocket before facing the doorway. Pausing a beat, she stepped into it and disappeared.

Birch laughed into the silence left by her passage, sounding slightly delirious. "I can't believe we made it. We actually escaped Mote."

"Believe it," Cam said. "This is Light Squad, and we do the impossible."

"Damn straight, we do," Jade agreed.

The count of sixty was reached, and the next one through was Charity, but prior to making her way through, she faced Cam and quirked a teasing grin. "Kiss for good luck?"

He shifted about, conflicted. He'd behaved poorly toward Charity, and it felt wrong for her to so easily allow their familiarity and affection. Shouldn't she still be upset with him? He would have been, but then again, he was full of anger. Maybe that just meant she was better than him. It was likely true, and if so, he'd have to trust her judgment that he didn't need further punishing.

Cam reached for Charity and gave her a quick peck on the lips. She had other ideas, though, cupping his face and drawing him close so the kiss lasted longer. Her lips and tongue tasted of honeysuckle.

"That was nice," she whispered when she finally released him, her eyes glinting with mischief. She bopped his nose. "See you on the other side." She stepped through the doorway, leaving Cam wondering what had just happened.

Jade sidled up to him. "I hope you realize how lucky you are. And close your mouth. You look like an idiot."

Cam clicked shut his mouth, not needing to glance around to be aware of the knowing smirks from the rest of Light Squad. No one bothered saying anything, although they didn't have to.

The next one through was Card. Then Jade and Avia. Birch went through, leaving Cam and Pan alone on the bridge.

The minute passed quickly, and Pan quirked one of his cute grins. "I'm eating a mountain of bamboo when I get home. See you soon."

He was gone, and Cam was alone but he wasn't lonely. His life was full. He had friends who loved him enough to brave the depths of Hell on his behalf. How lucky did that make him? Probably the luckiest person in all the Realms.

Sixty seconds passed quickly, and he exhaled, overwhelmed with joy, giddy with excitement, smiling, and ready. One final step, and he'd be home. He could finally rest and be at peace.

In that moment, he glanced the way back, like he could see all the way to Mote. He had found Birch there, a good soul in that wretched

Realm. How many more were there like him, though? How many who only needed the reflected light to show them the way to greatness? There were probably more than he could count, and Cam made a vow to return and free them. Free those like Tulip from the tyranny of the Great Rakshasas. He didn't know how, but he'd see it done.

41

Nageena was young. She'd only been a Sage for a hundred years, but it was long enough for her to understand history's tilt and ascertain the importance of the war for Golden. This current battle would likely determine in which direction the continent would trend. Would it shift to the rule of the rakshasas or would Golden continue under the control of the vapid Sage-Dukes?

Glancing at the raging conflict from where she stood on a faraway cliff, Nageena wasn't sure. No one could be, and it was why she studied the battle so assiduously, searching for answers, studying the escarpment where rakshasas fought Rainen Winder's famed Sidewinder Company. Several days ago, the Wilde Sage had ambushed Nailing's forces and driven them away from their boil, all the way here, to the sea. The core had even been lanced, which had greatly weakened all of the rakshasas who'd counted on its constant flow of Ephemera to empower them.

Now the battle had become a matter of stamina. Who could last the longest: the Ephemeral Masters with their individually greater skill and power or the rakshasas with their massive advantage in numbers?

Staring down at the battle, Nageena had to believe it would eventually be the latter. Her kind would win. Their numerical superiority was simply too great to overcome, and the Ephemeral Masters had to know it. But they wouldn't simply roll over and die. And neither would the rakshasas.

The two forces fought on, unyielding and unflagging, as together they created a meat grinder for one another. That was the truest nature of war: death in the service of violence.

Of course, that didn't matter to the poets and bards who might chronicle this battle. Rather than focus on the dying, they would speak and sing about the heroic exhortations filling the air, the screaming fireballs hammering shields, and the explosions blasting craters into the ground. They might describe the shrouding of the midday sun by a fine powder of dust, lightning bolts hammering from sky to ground, and pealing thunder loud enough to shatter eardrums. But would they mention how all the raging noises and sights were in service to a simple proposition: the bloody-soaked killing of a foe?

Nageena doubted it. The supposed glory of the battle lingered longer than the many who would never again live. And that was where her mind focused: on the ground below where those of lower Stages fought one another to a bloody standstill. The rakshasas were taking far more losses, ten for every single member of Sidewinder Company they managed to kill, and if such deaths continued, Nailing's forces would soon be utterly crushed.

But that calculation was acceptable for the Sage of Warring Thunder since in the end, the purpose of his lower-Staged forces would have been fulfilled. They were merely meant to wear down Sidewinder's Ephemeral Masters so when Nailing and the other Sages fully committed to the battle, their opponents would be too fatigued and injured to put up much of a resistance. As matters currently stood, that outcome wasn't in doubt.

However, would that serve the needs of Nageena's true master, who wasn't Nailing or even Coruscant? That title belonged to the Empress of the Deep, the Sage of Hunger who had long ago been displaced from her home in the Sinanes by traitors and the deceitful. And the Empress of the Deep wanted revenge on those who had stolen the islands from her rule.

Several centuries ago, the means for obtaining it had come over her when the Sage of Hunger had fallen into a senseless state, a spell lasting three days. When the empress had awoken, a prophecy had spilled from her lips, one proclaiming some king from another Realm who would be the emperor to fulfill her revenge. He would drown the Sinanes with fire, lightning, and a tidal wave as high as a mountain.

Since that time, everything the empress ever did was in order to fulfill the prophecy. No doubt, it was why she had saved Nageena upon her Awakening as a frightened water moccasin, lost in the vast sea. The empress had found and taught Nageena, lifted her to Sage before returning her to Golden where she had been ordered to join and aid Nailing in his service to Coruscant. Something to the prophecy indicated that the Sage of Warring Thunder would play a critical role in finding the emperor the empress sought.

But was this battle part of that prophecy? Nageena couldn't tell. All she knew was that it seemed an utter waste, and she scowled at the senseless carnage. So many deaths for what was ultimately unimportant. What difference did it make who ruled Golden? Rakshasas or Sage-Dukes—they were all the same.

Nageena cocked her head in consideration. That wasn't entirely true. The Wilde Sage fought for freedom. He didn't want to rule others, which wasn't the case with the politicking Sage-Dukes and Sage-Duchesses, who could have ended this battle on their own terms if they could have simply seen past their own selfish interests. Or the conniving Sage of Warring Thunder, who wanted the world to bow at his feet and only his feet, regardless of his pious mouthings of loyalty to Coruscant. Nailing didn't want the Great Rakshasa in Salvation anymore than the Sage-Dukes or the empress.

"It won't be long before we get to kick some ass," Weld said.

Nageena glanced askance at her fellow rakshasa Sage, who stood at her side, clearly itching for the fight. The two of them, along with

Shilpa and Cougrail, the Sage of the Bloody Claw, were part of the reserves that Nailing planned on using to overwhelm Sidewinder and the gathered forces of Sage-Duke Zin Shun. Three fresh Sages thrown into the fray when the two Ephemeral Masters were at their weakest. It would be an easy victory, assuming, of course, that the other Sage-Dukes didn't surprise them by intervening and that Weld was actually worth his salt.

On that matter, Nageena had her uncertainties. Weld Plain had more potential than anyone she had ever encountered, which wasn't surprising since the man had two Tangs Advanced to Sage and two others at Glory. He was a potential powerhouse, but for now, he was also unskilled and raw, and that made him vulnerable. Worse, he was lazy and his courage was also in question. Nageena had read the reports of his behavior during the engagements when Weld had fought for the Wilde Sage. He'd been a coward then, carried to victory by the rest of his unit, Light Squad.

Nageena smiled to herself on thinking of those young warriors. Now, those had been foes who would have eventually been worthy to face her, particularly their commander, Cam Folde, who had been both fearless and frighteningly competent. No doubt he was dead at this point, which was a shame. She had wanted to question the boy herself, find out what he knew about those two unlikely Glories who had defeated her and Nailing.

Glories defeating Sages… it was ridiculous in hindsight and more so in the moment. Even more ridiculous were the rumors that those two had been Rukh and Jessira in disguise. Nageena had heard the whispers and discounted them without a second thought. The Holy Servants—if they had ever been real—were long dead and gone, their legacy ruined. Witness the pathetic Sage-Dukes who claimed to serve Golden under their auspices.

"When do you think Nailing will unleash us?" Weld asked, his violet-Haunted eyes glowing with anticipation.

Nageena had no chance to answer. A ringing gong heralded the opening of an anchor line. She frowned. Had Nailing called for reinforcements of which she wasn't aware? A rent in the sky swiftly appeared, and Nageena hissed. This wasn't an anchor line of a rakshasa's manufacture. The flavor was wrong. This had the taste of an Ephemeral Master. But who? Had the Sage-Dukes actually gathered their courage?

The answer came a split second later when a Sage and three Crowns exited into the skies above the sea.

The Sage of Whispering Scales quirked a smile at Weld. "Prepare to be unleashed, puppy. That is Sage Maharani of the Sinanes."

"We'll still outnumber them seven to three," Weld said with an obstinate thrust of his jaw.

Nageena lifted her brows in question. "You think so?" She shrugged. "I guess we'll find out soon enough."

Rainen Winder had lived many centuries and in all those vast number of years, he'd never expended himself as much as he had in this battle for the duchy of Charn. Nor had he ever taken so much damage. One of his eyes was bruised and shut, an ankle had been snapped, and one of his shoulders was dislocated. But those were the least of his injuries. He'd held his Bonds too long. Even now, they frayed, wanting to come apart, should have come apart, and when Rainen finally released them, he dreaded the price he'd pay in pain—the cost, the time spent in recovery, *if* he recovered. That wasn't assured, but there was also no room for doubt in Rainen's mind.

The moment was all that counted, and in this moment—this time when the afternoon sun lowered and the day's end might signal Golden's ruination—he would either give his all or see Charn eradicated. Self-preservation or save a duchy? It wasn't much of a choice.

Just then, he grunted, taking a blow to the back from some fragging Crown that must have been hidden. Either that, or the bastard had slipped in while he'd been distracted. At least Rainen's shield had deflected the attack. Too bad he couldn't retaliate. Chasing Crowns wasn't worth the effort, not if it left him open to a counter from Nailing or one of his Sages.

Matters might have progressed differently if the enemy Sages—there were seven of them—would stand still and fight. Instead, they kept shifting about, facing him one moment before darting off in another direction. And all the while, their Crowns pecked at Rainen, Sage-Duke Shun, and Lysha Maharani.

He had initially been heartened upon her arrival, but then Nailing had played his trump card, revealing four fresh Sages of his own: Nageena, Cougrail, Shilpa, and that wastrel, Weld Plain.

How in the fragging unholy hells had that boy progressed to Sage so swiftly? He had to be a genius. He certainly fought like one. What he lacked in refinement and control, he made up for with sheer power. Even now, he and Nageena battled Lysha, forcing her on her back foot.

Regardless, upon the entry of the four fresh rakshasa Sages, the battle, which had seemed winnable, became one of attrition again. Hours and hours of fighting, and unfortunately, Sidewinder Company couldn't help. Neither could Shun's forces. Both units—their ranks mostly containing lower-Staged Ephemeral Masters—had been forced to take shelter from the battle roaring near the ocean.

Rainen grimaced. He, Shun, and Lysha were losing.

An instant later, his grimace transformed into a predatory expression when he sighted Nailing finally holding still. The Sage of Warring Thunder was facing the wrong direction, and Rainen blasted him into a mountain. Nailing was temporarily out of the fight. And although Cougrail sought to take advantage of Rainen's supposed inattentiveness, it wasn't the case. Rainen was ready. He spun about and shielded against a blistering lance of light before countering with a screaming bolt of ice that impacted the other Sage and flung him away. For good measure, Sage-Duke Shun darted forward and hammered the rakshasa into the ocean.

Only then did the Wilde Sage relax the slightest bit, smiling at the brief victory and the momentary respite from the chaos all around. He glanced sidelong when Shun joined him, and together they floated off the coast of Charn, surveying the battle along the escarpment.

"I wish we had more Crowns," Shun sent.

Rainen grunted. He wished for many things, but Shun was right. Their lack of Crowns was one of their many weaknesses, a reflection of their overall lack of Ephemeral Masters. Somehow, the rakshasas always had more numbers to throw into the fray, although they used them mostly as a harassing force. Their blows barely hurt against Rainen, Shun, or Lysha, but they were distracting enough for Nailing and his Sages to attack and land considerable blows.

"We aren't going to win this," Shun added a moment later. The man looked shattered, and it was easy to understand why. The rakshasas had established a foothold in his duchy, one that he wouldn't be able to easily dislodge. Small towns and villages throughout his duchy would soon face grave danger.

And the other Sage-Dukes hadn't lifted a finger to help. Cowards, liars, and traitors, the entire lot. All of them feigning fear that Nailing had also planted a powerful boil within their borders. Rainen snorted with derision. Nailing was a single Sage, and while he was influential amongst the rakshasas, not even he had those kinds of resources. There were other rakshasa factions who didn't follow the Sage of Warring Thunder.

And those other factions hadn't and couldn't marshal enough resources into any other single duchy to threaten its survival. There were many rakshasas, but not so many Sages for that kind of an attack. Rainen knew it. Everyone did. All the Sage-Dukes and Sage-Duchesses needed to do was come together with a united front, and they could end the rakshasa menace. After all, other than the ones here, there were only fifteen other rakshasa Sages in the rest of Golden.

But that victory would only occur if the Sage-Dukes could ever see past their cowardice and selfishness, their politics. Which they couldn't and hadn't, not even when Rainen had begged them for help. None of them had responded, either due to weakness on the part of Avia's father or treason when it came to Kazar and Sage-Duchess Marsula Thens.

All this Rainen considered as thunder and lightning roiled the sky, hammering the escarpment, which cracked. A cliff slowly slid into the sea even as Lysha sent Weld crashing to the ground. Cougrail, having lifted himself out of the ocean, dodged vicious arcs of fire from the Sage of the Sinanes that trailed after him, but one caught him, a crushing blow that blasted him right back into the water.

Rainen smiled in satisfaction. The Sage of the Sinanes had seen Cougrail's attempted blindside attack coming the entire time.

"She's magnificent," Shun murmured.

Rainen nodded agreement. That she was, and of the three of them, Lysha was the least injured. Her power remained remarkable, and Saira was said to be her equal even though she'd only been a Sage for several months. Rainen wished Saira was here now. They could have used her help, although even her presence likely wouldn't have been enough to tip the balance. Still, any small amount would have been a blessing. Best if Saira brought Light Squad with her. Four Crowns and a Sage. Now that could have turned the tide.

The fracturing of granite returned Rainen's attention to where he'd flung Nailing. Stones and boulders rumbled in an avalanche as the Sage of Warring Thunder freed himself from the mountain into which he'd been blasted. He looked furious.

Rainen shrugged. The respite was over. Charn would burn and there was no turning that terrible ship around.

He made to rejoin the battle against Nailing, but three Sages joined the buffalo, and he slowed, frowning. *"Do you have enough to take those three?"* he asked Shun.

The Sage-Duke shrugged. *"We'll find out."*

Rainen readied to attack, but a sight and sensation high above had him halting again. An anchor unlike any he had ever experienced was breaching the sky. It wasn't of rakshasa make or that of an Ephemeral Master. It was something greater, grander, and everyone halted even while a last crackle of lightning and peal of thunder rattled the sky.

Rainen continued to stare as the anchor line formed, oval in shape rather than rectangular. It rippled, opened, puffing the nearby clouds out of existence, filled with an iridescent and golden light that sang. The feeling of Ephemera wafted from it, deep and rich.

The sense and sight of it… hope spurred within Rainen. He prayed that whoever exited the anchor line was coming to the aid of him, Shun, and Lysha. Otherwise, they were lost.

Weld snarled. That bitch! She'd slammed him into the ground like he was just some first-year Novice. And fragging hells if it didn't hurt. He felt around his chest for anything broken. His stomach and limbs, too. Everything seemed to be working, but his ribs ached something fierce. Same with his back.

If the core he'd spent so much time helping Rise hadn't been lanced by that jackhole Rainen, he could have taken her. She'd gotten a lucky hit is all. Weld was a powerful Sage. Every rakshasa said so. He'd beat that bitch next time.

Weld sat up with a pained groan, trying to see past the shroud of dirt his impact had lifted. A moment later, he measured out the crater he'd created and found himself impressed by its size. A large home could have fit in it, and he had to clamber out to see over the edge.

He stared upward then, at the one who had cast him down, but her focus was somewhere else. She was busy staring at Rainen and Sage-Duke Shun, the three of them possibly sharing a telepathic discussion. Still, although they hadn't been given a proper introduction, it wasn't hard to figure out who she was. Based on her features alone, she could only be one person: Lysha Maharani, the Sage of the Sinanes and the mother to the even greater bitch, Saira.

Well, frag them both. Weld was also a Sage, and he'd kill Lysha Maharani, and when he caught up with Saira, he'd kill her, too. He'd learn them both, learn them good and proper. They'd find out real fast that Weld Plain wasn't a Sage they should ever think of wiping off like he was dirt under their shoes. He nodded to himself. That's exactly how he'd arrange the situation. He'd humble her before breaking her.

But not yet. Weld's True Bond was starting to fray, and he hated the pain from holding it too long. Better to take a small break for now and see how matters played out. He chuckled a bit when Cougrail got his ass kicked. A serpentine fire had trailed after the Sage of the Bloody Claw—what a stupid name—finally catching him and tossing his dumb ass back into the ocean.

Weld laughed some at that before fully lifting out of his crater, looking for Nailing. The Sage of Warring Thunder was currently flanked by a trio of rakshasa Sages, and the trio squared off against Rainen and Sage-Duke Shun. Weld briefly glanced to Lysha and decided she could wait. Not that he was afraid of her, but joining the party with the Wilde Sage seemed a likelier use of his talents. Together, he, Nailing, and the other three should be able to kill at least one of the enemy Sages.

Just look at them. Rainen looked like he'd been beaten, broken, and beaten some more. An eye was swollen shut, distorting his whole face, while an ankle dangled, and he was holding an arm funny, like it didn't work right. As for the Sage-Duke, his features were similarly battered. Blood crusted his lips from a flattened nose, one of his hands was swollen and misshapen, and he seemed to strain at catching his breath, holding his side. Weld focused and heard the Sage-Duke wheezing like a blacksmith playing with his bellows. He chuckled. Old Shun probably had a few broken ribs. He was done for. All it would take was the killing blow.

Weld nodded to himself. Yes. Fighting his one-time master and sponsor and the Sage-Duke seemed a mite smarter than tackling Lysha just now. He might have still gone after the Sage of the Sinanes if Cougrail hadn't just gotten his ass handed to him. Or if Nageena was around to support him.

His smile became a frown. Where was that snake anyway? He hadn't seen her since early on when Lysha had arrived, attacking now and then, but largely absent. *Coward.* If she'd hadn't run off like an itty bitty insect, this battle might have already been over. Sidewinder would certainly have been destroyed if Nageena had only supported Weld and his fellow rakshasa Sages a mite more courageously. Had she done so, there wasn't any way Rainen could have anchor lined his unit to safety.

But she hadn't, and the Wilde Sage had anchor lined Sidewinder away from the battle. Which meant Weld would have to hunt them down and kill them… after his fun in Traverse, of course.

Just then, like she'd heard Weld's rough thoughts, here came Nageena. The Sage of Whispering Scales slithered out from behind a dark bank of storm clouds with the setting sun at her back. Blended and nearly unseen. Weld might have actually missed her if he hadn't happened to glance over just then, looking for Cougrail.

And Lysha hadn't yet noticed Nageena, facing the wrong way as the Sage of Whispering Scales approached from the other woman's blind spot, sinuous and slow. Weld watched, held his breath, and hoped. Nageena closed with the Sage of the Sinanes, accelerating at the last moment. Lysha must have sensed her. She spun about, catching a flaming sword on her shield. The webbing flared, deflecting.

Some aspect of the attack got through, though. Blood bloomed on Lysha's abdomen, quickly spreading. The Sage of the Sinanes backed away, grimacing. It was her first true injury.

Nageena didn't follow, speaking to Lysha. "Your land will be consumed in rain and ruin."

Weld frowned. What the hell was that about? He shrugged. Nageena was a strange one. Whatever was rattling in her brain pan made no difference to him. Now was the time to rejoin the battle.

As he ascended toward where Nailing and his Sages faced off against Rainen and Shun, a light high in the sky paused his flight. An anchor line, different than the usual ones, rippled to life over the ocean. Weld frowned. What the fragging hells was going on now? Had the fragging Sage-Dukes finally decided to fight?

42

Rainen threw fisted hands in the air and shouted in triumph when he saw who had stepped forth from the anchor line: Saira Maharani… and two lovebirds. He frowned momentarily when the little avians darted off, but his confusion quickly gave way to elation. Saira meant they might not be ruined after all. They simply needed her to—

The Wilde Sage's thoughts sputtered to a halt when Saira, who had taken a moment to scan the battlefield, accelerated across the sky. She moved nearly too fast for Rainen to follow, certainly too quick for an enemy Sage who had drifted away from Nailing. Saira attacked the reptilian rakshasa, ripping through his shield without any seeming effort, and cleaved him in two.

Rainen inhaled sharply, shocked to his core. He'd never imagined Saira to be this powerful, or any Sage for that matter. Killing a Sage was no easy feat, and yet, she had made it seem exactly that. Saira had simply flexed her will, created a white-hot sword made of Ephemera, and the deed was done. The enemy Sage's shield had lasted for less than a second.

Impossible, and yet it had occurred. Rainen paused, reconsidering the situation. Saira's actions might have rewritten the odds, not necessarily stacking them in favor of the Ephemeral Masters, but at least improving them. Or at least the odds would have been improved if Rainen and Shun weren't so badly injured. Both men were wrecked, and neither had much left to give. Saira showing now might not yet be enough.

Still, it was better than nothing. Six rakshasa Sages and their many Crowns against Rainen's forces. Even as he reassessed the situation, Saira was off again, easily driving away Nageena and rejoining her mother. The two women shared a heartfelt hug and a few inaudible words. A gesture from Saira, and Lysha's wounded abdomen was restored to full health.

The Wilde Sage looked to Nailing in silent speculation. What would the buffalo do? Retreat and give up the battle? Rainen hoped so. It would be better for both their sides and sakes if Nailing simply gave up and retreated.

However, the Sage of Warring Thunder was apparently unimpressed by Saira's appearance. He glowered at her and her mother, demonstrating no signs of good sense.

Rainen sighed. *Fine.* If Nailing wanted to continue this battle, then he'd receive his wish. Rainen would make sure the buffalo choked on it. The Wilde Sage firmed his spine, forced back any doubts, and only allowed thoughts of the victory to come. *There is no pain. There is no weakness. There is only success.* It was a mantra that Rainen repeated over and over again.

However, before the conflict could recommence, the anchor line pulsed again. Someone else was coming through, and Rainen waited, daring to hope it might be the rest of Light Squad. With them, this battle might actually be winnable.

He grinned wide, laughing when Charity Kazar stepped onto the field of darkening sky, regal as an empress. She briefly surveyed the skies, forged a golden staff and immediately went on the attack against two nearby rakshasa Crowns. They desperately defended against her, and their struggle drew in another of their allies. But even at three against one, the rakshasas were only able to stalemate Charity. Her use of Ephemera was just too skilled and controlled, too elegant. She slipped lances of fire, thrust a hand to block blades of ice, and took a heavy bolt of lightning straight on her shield without the slightest strain. An attempt to lock her in place was easily battered aside, and the use of gravity to weigh Charity down backfired on the enemy Crown, who plummeted like a stone.

Rainen shook his head in disbelief. He couldn't recall any Crown with Charity's skills nor a Sage as powerful as Saira. Watching them had his hope surging, and he clapped Shun on the shoulder, grinning wide. "We aren't dead yet, old friend."

Shun grinned in return, indicating Charity. "Should we help her? Maybe lift her burden by killing some of those pesky Crowns?"

Killing rakshasa Crowns sounded perfect. One of them had murdered Perit Line, Sidewinder's commander. The grief… Rainen scowled. No, he'd grieve later.

He went to nod in agreement to Shun's proposal but halted before doing so. His attention had fixed upon Nailing, the fragging bastard who'd written this tragedy. Fury had him seeing red. Nailing wasn't injured like Rainen, and he wasn't straining to hold on to his Ephemera. But he had to pay for what he had done. He had to die. "No," Rainen said, gaze locked on the Sage of Warring Thunder. "You go. I've got something else in mind." Grim and wanting blood, he called to Nailing. "Come on, Buffalo. You wanted this fight. Well, it's here. I'll make you choke on it."

Weld Plain couldn't believe it. What terrible deeds had he done to deserve this kind of karma? Saira Maharani and Charity Kazar had joined the battle. And following on their heels had come the rest of their brood. Fragging Light Squad. All of them: Card Wolver, Avia Koravail, and Jade Mare, and every one of them Crowns. Powerful ones, too.

That was bad enough, but then a strange figure, a leonine Awakened Beast, old and only a Glory, had entered the skies of Charn above the sea and cliffs. Saira had snagged the creature out of the air with a cord of Ephemera and set him on the ground.

The rest of her foul troop, though, had flown to Saira, ringing her and Lysha Maharani. Sage-Duke Shun had joined them, and together, they'd taken the battle to the rakshasas, killing four Crowns in a matter of moments.

Cougrail had burst forth from the ocean, taken one look at the pieces arrayed in the sky and fled through an anchor line. *Coward.*

Seconds later, another Sage died, and Weld reconsidered his thoughts about Cougrail. Maybe it was time he made himself scarce. But that lion-like rakshasa was close enough at hand. A little killing first before he got himself gone.

But the anchor line pulsed again, and from it came a panda, someone Weld knew all-too-well. He screamed in rage and frustration. That fragging bastard was supposed to be dead. Weld had been promised. And yet, here he was: Pan Shun, still alive and a Glory no less when he'd only been an Adept the last Weld had seen of him.

Saira set Pan next to the leonine rakshasa.

Weld snarled. If Mote hadn't seen fit to kill the fragging panda, then he would. And maybe it was more fitting for Pan to die this way anyhow, in pain and with his hope stolen just when he'd likely thought himself safe. Besides which, Weld had always wanted to watch the panda die, always wanted to be the one to apply the killing blow. Weld prepared a bolt of lightning, one that would incinerate the panda and his friend.

But then the anchor line pulsed again, and a final figure entered the skies above Charn. Weld's shoulders fell, and his attack drifted away as he gaped in stunned disbelief. Cam Folde. He floated in the sky, somehow able to remain aloft even as a mere Glory. Weld's previous howl of rage was nothing in comparison to the one he unleashed now. How was this possible? Why? What would it take to kill those two cockroaches? Could anything? Were they somehow invincible?

A trickle of fear coursed down Weld's spine, but he cut it off an instant later, recalling who he was and his purpose. He was Weld Plain, and he was a Sage. His destiny was greater than this battle. He would rule this world, and his enemies were only Glories. And if Coruscant hadn't seen fit to kill them, then Weld would.

He soared into the air even as Cam began to free fall. Whatever trick he'd used to hold himself in the air had failed.

And this time, Saira wouldn't be there to catch him. Weld would get to him first.

Just then, a trickle of Ephemera wisped past him, quicker and quicker, becoming a steady stream. What now? Weld paused, unsure what was happening. He glanced in the direction the stream flowed. It was going to the panda, who stood near the lion-headed rakshasa. Weld's eyes narrowed. Was Pan Advancing? It seemed so, and faster than should be possible.

Weld's eyes narrowed. He'd see that panda dead.

Cam had focused his exit from the anchor line onto Saira, just like she'd instructed. But wherever that happened to be, it wasn't the Sinanes. There were no peaceful islands of beauty like Charity and Jade had described. Instead, Cam found himself high in the air, amidst dark clouds and the feel of dirt clogging his mouth and stinging his eyes.

He spat, clearing his mouth. How was it so dusty this high in the air? And where were Saira and the others? Cam maintained his height for a few moments, floating on wings of air as he cast Oversight downward. His eyes widened.

What was this? A battle? Light Squad currently fought against a large group of rakshasa Sages and Crowns. Continuing to utilize Oversight, he gathered details, recognizing Nageena and Nailing. Of course, they'd be here. Rainen Winder as well. Peering further down, he looked for Pan, sighting him and Birch on a cliff near some sea. His senses next alighted on Weld Plain.

Cam's vision went red, and he could barely see past his fury. He had made a promise to kill that man, and it looked like he'd have a chance to make good on his vow, this very hour.

But first he had to wrangle his rage under control, which for now, wasn't of any use. He needed his full concentration for what was required. It also meant he had to release his True Bond.

Cam plummeted. Fear momentarily clenched his gut, but he wrestled it under control, ignoring it. He'd fallen like this before, back when Light Squad had entered Hearth. This wasn't anything new. He just had to get the work done before the sea made him wish for wings.

Closing his eyes, Cam began the process of Advancing. He spun Plasminia faster and faster until it became a blur, its blue-tinged lightning appearing as a solid bar of color. A vacuum formed, drawing Ephemera into his Source, slowly at first. Then ever more quickly. Cam drove the Ephemera into his Source, into Plasminia, a rush that became a river. Cam accepted every bit, clutching the answer needed to Advance in the forefront of his thoughts: the difference between certainty and doubt.

The river became an ocean. Plasminia bulged, distorted, couldn't accept any more Ephemera. But then the Tang pulsed, darkened to indigo, Advancing to Crown in a flash. But Cam wasn't done He sent the ocean of Ephemera deeper into his Source, starting with Kinesthia. Another Tang Advanced. Then Synapsia flashed to indigo and finally Spirairia. Cam Advanced, fully and completely, every one of his Tangs in mere seconds, all because of the gift and curse of being a Plasminian.

Finally, Cam couldn't accept any more, and then just as Rukh and Jessira had instructed, the greatest advantage of being a Plasminian became a possibility. His Tangs had an effervescence to them, their borders hazy. Cam could ignore the opportunity, but Jessira's advice rang in his mind, so he gritted his teeth, aware of what was required, accepting the task at hand, willing to give everything even if it broke him.

He compressed his Tangs, pressing them together, forcing them to fuse, pouring his body, mind, and heart into the effort. All his hopes, dreams, aspirations, and doubts. His love for Pan, Charity, and Light Squad. Love for his family and friends back home in Traverse, including any nephews and nieces he'd yet to set eyes upon. Birch and Sprite and Kiwi. Even the debt he owed to Rainen, which he had always recognized. The Wilde Sage had done much for him. His rage against injustice and betrayal as well. All of it, and just as Jessira had warned, it took his everything. The opposite of emptying his mind and body through meditation—this was an endless moment of concentration, of fixing on every part of his person.

But then, with an abruptness that had him figuratively stumbling, the pressure released as his Tangs merged, becoming a unified and singular whole. It spun as swiftly as Plasminia once had, lightning laced the unmovable heft of Kinesthia, the pliability of Synapsia, and the possibility of Spirairia. *All is Ephemera and Ephemera is All.*

Cam stuttered a disbelieving laugh, not having expected it to actually work. A final flare, and it was done. He had Advanced to Crown, and his single Tang was Enhanced to Gold. However, Cam still wasn't done. He imagined a waterwheel to slow his swiftly rotating and unnamed Tang. A burst of bile of every kind extruded from his pores, but Cam didn't need any of it. He flexed his will and burned off the biles before their stain and stink could collect upon him. Within seconds, his Tang had Enhanced to a perfect Crystal.

Now, he was done, and he opened his eyes and his senses.

The wind screamed past every pore. Every strand of hair provided information about heat, cold, and motion. This was true Oversight. The colors of the world shined bright, reminding him of the woven world while the smell of ozone hung heavy, mixed with that of powdered stone and the briny wash of the waters beneath him. Other sounds intruded, rhythmic and regular. Heartbeats. He could discern them without the need for a Bond. They were as clear as the ringing of a grand bell. More noises. The clatter of battle. The sound of insects scrabbling in the dirt. The moving clouds had a sound…

It was too much information, meant for a Sage's insight. Cam shuddered, closing his eyes and shutting off all his senses. Breathing deep, he prepared himself for what he needed. In the mindscape, he'd already mastered every skill up to Sage so utilizing his power as a Crown wouldn't be a new experience. He simply had to remember how to view the world with a Crown's insight.

Taking a few seconds, Cam readied himself. And this time when he opened his eyes, the surge of sensations didn't overwhelm him. This time, he laughed in delight. This time, his mind—Advanced to Crown just like his Source—adapted to the new information without any trouble, and the world was wondrous, scintillating, vibrating, and carrying the aromas of a vast field of wildflowers.

Cam continued to laugh, but the sea was quickly approaching. He Bonded his Tang and threw his arms out to the sides. His uncontrolled fall gradually arrested until he halted, a hundred feet above the water. He scanned the battle then, looking for Weld. *There.* His fear and fury momentarily spiked.

The fragging bastard was attacking his friends. He hammered away at Birch and Pan—also Advanced to Crown, pounding at their shields from where they stood before a cliff on unsteady ground. Cam's friends were doing their best to fight back, landing the rare blow, but it was hopeless. They were a Crown and a Glory battling a Sage, and there was no one around to help them. Saira and Lysha battled Nageena and two other rakshasa Sages while Rainen Winder and a Sage-Duke— both of them badly injured—had their hands full with Nailing, who appeared healthy and hale. The rest of Light Squad fought the remaining enemy Crowns.

Cam launched toward Weld. No chance he'd let the jackhole kill Pan and Birch. He clenched his jaw, pouring on the speed, focused on his hated foe, who had his back to him.

Weld cried out in triumph. A powerful blow had obliterated Birch's shield and crashed him into a rocky prominence. The old rakshasa struck with a sickening wet sound before slowly folding over at the waist and slumping to the ground. He didn't rise.

Cam screamed. More speed. Pan was barely holding on.

Cam knew that taking on a Sage wasn't a smart idea, but what other option was there? Pan was buckling. Any moment, his shield was sure to give way. Cam had to get there first. He had to—

Pan cried out. His shield had shattered. He stood defenseless, and Weld didn't hold back. A fireball slammed Pan into a boulder, plowing him through the stone, which powdered to dirt and dust. Cam's heart went to his throat. Pan lay face down on the hard ground, unmoving.

Get up, Pan. Please. Get up.

But he didn't. He simply lay there, barely breathing. Cam prayed for Pan, hoping he'd just been knocked unconscious, both him and Birch. Otherwise—Cam bit back the words. There was no otherwise. Weld Plain would die here today before he could hurt anyone else.

Seconds from arrival, Cam studied the field of battle, assessing. Shadows reached out from the escarpment, but he'd be able to see just fine. He surveyed, and the bare bones of a plan came together. He shifted his flight, making sure to have the setting sun at his back when he arrived. Any small advantage. Then there was the field of boulders. Weld would use the stones, flinging a fusillade, just like he'd done against Pan. Best to eventually bring the fight away from here then. Cam didn't think his shield would hold long against a heavy barrage like that anyway.

Weld saw Cam coming, and his mouth opened like he meant to say something. Cam didn't give him the chance. He cycled his Tang and attacked. Weld's mouth slammed shut, and he glowered, shoving aside the lightning sent against him, stalking forward. Cam pushed him back with howling ice spears that Weld took straight on against his shield. High-pitched impacts ensued, like trees snapping. The fragging bastard's defenses easily held, but Weld would have been better off evading.

And just like Cam had expected, the other man waved wildly at the field of boulders and retaliated with the heavy thunder of catapulted rocks. Cam smirked. Through Oversight, he'd seen the attack coming before Weld had even begun his extravagant gesture. He had all the time needed to decide how to evade, including assessing Weld's skills. Why had the other man bothered with a broad wave of his hand in the first place? Weld was a Sage, and a Sage shouldn't need such wasteful motions. And his use of Ephemera had been clumsy, nothing but brute force. Was Weld truly that lacking in skill? Even as an Adept, Cam could have done better.

The moment of decision arrived, and Cam spun through the incoming attacks. He moved in fits and starts. Darted a foot here, a yard there, fine movements to conserve his strength. Balanced, controlled, and focused. The boulders came close enough that Cam felt the wind and heat of their passage. They stirred his hair, nearly brushed against his clothes, but they didn't strike him. The last one whooshed by, and Cam used gravity to alter its arc. He spun in a full circle and flung the stone back at Weld.

Again, the man displayed a surprising awkwardness. He gestured—again!—and the boulder splintered into small fragments, some of which shattered against Weld's webbed shield. He should have simply dodged the attack. Nor should he have bothered pontificating, which he began doing. "You bested me a couple of times back at the Ephemeral Academy," Weld said, "but that was then. This is now, and now I'm a Sage, and you're only a Crown. You can't win. I'll end you, and then—"

Cam cut him off with a hail of small stones that left afterimages in their swift flight. As expected, Weld took them directly on his shield. However, camouflaged in the midst Cam's attack had been heavy slugs of superheated metal that screamed off his outstretched hands. They glowed white-hot, and Weld never noticed them. Not until the rounds crashed into his shield. Thunder boomed from the impact, a series of concussive blasts that shook the cliff.

Weld grunted under the series of blows, grimacing when a few of the rounds got through his shield. They didn't do much damage—it took a lot to hurt a Sage. Still, they'd sliced shallow lines across Weld's face and neck. First blood had been drawn, and it had gone to Cam.

"Is that the best you can do?" Weld demanded. "I cut myself worse shaving." He paced forward, shoulders thrust back, and glowering.

Cam responded by lifting two boulders imbedded in the ground behind Weld. While the other man wasted time posturing, Cam swung the rocks about, crashing them into Weld's knee. The idiot had foolishly dropped his shield in his moment of attempted intimidation.

Weld howled. The blow likely hurt like the unholy hells. And since Weld was standing so close to the escarpment, Cam buried him in it. Weld's cry of fury cut off as tons of stone rumbled down and collapsed over him.

Cam viewed the fallen rocks, their echoing cracks, and his enemy covered underneath it all. He hadn't killed Weld, but so far, he was less impressed than ever before by the supposed Sage's skills. Cam snorted derision. This was the man who had always crowed about his greatness, had always boasted about his strength and virility, and pretended to never have to work for his mastery.

And this was also a Sage who had allowed a Crown to hurt him so easily? Professor Shade—Rukh—would have been outraged at Weld's graceless use of Ephemera. Balance, control, and focus had been his bywords, and Weld lacked all three. Pathetic.

Weld blasted out of the fallen stone, covered in dust and dirt. "I'll kill you!"

Cam shrugged, not caring about Weld's threats. But his battle with the so-called Sage couldn't remain here, not with Pan and Birch still lying unmoving and near enough at hand to be in danger. He had to draw the fight away from them. Cam rose into the air, taunting Weld with a sneer. "Come on then, you little coward. Fly with me. Let's see how a rakshasa Sage does against a Crown."

Weld roared anger and launched after him.

Weld raced after Cam, intent on destroying the jackhole. Arrogant fragging bastard. Weld was a Sage. Nailing and Nageena had said he was powerful, and he was. He had felt the loss of the lanced core, was weakened by it, but he could still see to Cam's end. So what if the other man had gotten lucky with those metal slugs? Weld had already healed the small lacerations. He'd pay the fool back for that slight and so many others. He'd tear Cam limb from limb, and beat him to death with his own arms and legs.

Closing the distance, Weld even had a set of attacks all planned out, but Cam kept shifting about. He darted around in flashes, moving too swiftly to accurately track, even in the woven world. Weld scowled, unloading on Cam anyway. A rapid-fire set of screaming Fireballs. Cam twisted and turned, shifted and angled away. Every Fireball missed, trailing off into the sky or hitting the sea.

Weld glowered in frustration. How was Cam moving so fast? Evading everything? First the boulders and now the Fireballs. It was like the man had precognition and could see what Weld was fixing to do before it was done.

No matter. Weld figured he'd just have to shift gears.

He sent clouds of messages at Cam, fevered dreams of blood and torment through telepathy. None of them latched on, but Weld kept at it. This time, the dreams were of pints of alcohol.

That did it. Cam's lurching movements finally slowed. Weld smiled. He had him now. *Let's see him precognition his way out of this.* Weld flicked his hand, and a storm billowed. The clouds engulfed Cam, and from within, he spun about, struggling. Weld continued to smile. The clouds were lightning-laced fog, filled with nightmares made manifest. In this case, it was of Cam failing at the bottom of a bottle, helpless, while his friends died all around him. More lightning crackled, the ozone heavy and smelling like almonds. Ever more brutal nightmares appeared, and in them, Weld taunted Cam, cutting Charity into small pieces. Jade shook and shivered as small swords carved skin off her flesh. Traverse burned, and there was nothing Cam could do about it. All he could do was drown in his fear until someone with a kind heart ended his suffering.

Weld grinned, wide and vindictive, when Cam showed no signs of breaking free of his torment. He was done, and Weld approached his shaking and shivering form, figuring maybe it was time to put the old boy out of his misery. Weld entered the clouds, fixing to do just that.

Cam spun about, not looking to be in any sort of pain any longer. His sight fixed directly on Weld, and he appeared fully aware, his head tilted in consideration, entirely nonplussed.

Weld pulled up short, frowning. What was happening? How could Cam have overcome the telepathic attack so easily? Surely, he hadn't already formed a Domain? It had taken Weld most of a month to form the basics of one, and that had been as a Sage.

Cam's eyes glowed bright, the indigo-Haunt having flecks of violet, like he was part Sage. Weld watched, unsure what was about to happen.

"Is that the best you can do? I cut myself worse shaving." Cam mocked Weld with his words from earlier. "And thank you for the plasma." His eyes glowed even brighter. More flecks of violet. And from the fog a massive bolt of lightning speared into Weld, shattering around his shield coruscating endlessly, on and on. Weld stiffened, grunting, holding his shield in a rictus of effort. He never expected a Crown to—

The shield shattered, and Weld's rictus became one of pain. He screamed in outraged agony as the lightning coursed through him. It fried through him, setting his nerves alight. Everything burned.

The lightning bolt finally ended, and Weld sagged. He could smell his own burned flesh. Smoke billowed off of him, and everything hurt something fierce. With a concentration of his will, Weld created a fresh shield, but not before more slugs hammered him back and forth across the sky. Cam cut off his assault, darting away.

Weld let him go, focused as he was on his agony. This wasn't supposed to happen. It couldn't happen. Weld was a Sage. He was a man of destiny. Shaking off his confusion, Weld forced Ephemera into his body, repairing ruined flesh. Within seconds, the pain was tolerable, but the damage had been done. There was a lot of it. Still, he had enough of his Bond left to kill one miserable Crown. And that Crown stood motionless in the sky, a hundred yards away. Weld screamed after him. "Fragging coward! Face me like a man!"

Cam responded by glancing back and thin bolts of fire lanced from his eyes, arcing through the sky. Weld never slowed his chase, taking the blows on his shield. He grunted in effort, knowing that he couldn't keep on accepting Cam's attacks head on like that. They were just too strong. Which should have been impossible. But then again, everything about this fight should have been impossible, and a niggle of doubt crept across Weld's thoughts. He did his best to suppress it. The lightning bolt had been pure luck. There was no reason for him to be afraid of Cam Folde. He'd bested the man before. He'd best him again. That's what Weld kept telling himself.

Despite his best efforts, though, the doubt seemed to possess a life of its own. It reminded him of the past, from when Weld had first entered the Ephemeral Academy. Back then, he had been far better and stronger than Cam, but within months, the other man had overtaken him, increasing the distance with their Advancement to Acolyte. Plus, the fragging jackhole had plenty of courage whereas Weld retreated whenever the situation grew too difficult.

And as unlikely as it was to reckon, now might be one of those times. The rakshasa Crowns were being hounded. Nailing, Nageena, Shilpa and the other rakshasa Sage couldn't outlast Rainen, Shun, Lysha, and Saira. So maybe it was best to call this one a draw and fight another day.

Like he could read Weld's mind, Cam finally stopped his flight. By now, they were miles distant from the main battle, above the churning sea with no one around.

A steady wind whipped Weld's hair as he stared at Cam. His momentary fear was gone now. Cam had just made a mortal mistake, holding still like this. Weld readied an attack, one that Cam wouldn't be able to evade. "Finally decided to stop running?"

Cam smirked in that infuriatingly smug way of his. "That's rich coming from a Sage who can't catch a Crown. Most of your hair is gone."

Weld touched his head, feeling the bald patches. He wanted to howl at the mockery, but he controlled himself. No doubt, that's exactly what the man wanted from him. Weld forced a smile past his pain and fury. "I'll make it quick."

Cam's smirk widened. "I bet you say that to all the ladies."

Weld's smile became a glower of pure rage. This man. He thought he was so good and pure, so much better than everyone else. It was time to show him how wrong he was. "I changed my mind. I'm going to make it painful."

Cam laughed. "And I bet that's what all the ladies fear about you."

"Frag you!"

Cam shrugged, appearing unconcerned. "You can't win here," he said. "Look behind you. Your rakshasas are losing. I only have to hold you in place long enough for Saira and the others to kill your Sages. Then you die."

Weld risked a glance back. Nailing was in the midst of anchor lining away from the battle. One arm had been torn clean off and part of his face as well. Rents ruined his chest, spilling blood. If the Sage of Warring Thunder survived his injuries, it would be a miracle. Nageena and Shilpa were leaving, too, and the other Sage who Nailing had brought here was either gone or dead. Weld was alone.

Terror lit his insides. How had it gone so wrong, so fast?

Cam calculated. The plasma within the nightmare cloud had given him a chance to actually hurt Weld. He could have never created such a powerful lightning bolt on his own. And with all the concentrated energy still lingering in the atmosphere, discharged from the battle amongst the Sages, he could probably come close to replicating the lightning one more time. He spun his Tang, collected the plasma all around him. Waited. The timing was critical.

Turn just a little more, he silently urged Weld.

The other man did exactly that, giving his back to Cam as he stared at the battle between the Sages. Channeling the plasma and his will into his right hand, Cam unleashed a bolt of lightning that glowed like the sun and crackled the short distance between him and Weld. It slammed into the other man, wrapped around his shield, greatly weakening it but not getting through.

Weld spun around, glowering. "You fragging bastard. I'll kill—"

Cam hammered Weld with hot metal slugs. They exploded off his left hand and punctured Weld's shield with tiny holes. And through those imperfections, the lightning coursed. Weld stiffened, arms locked to his sides as he cried out in agony. His skin blistered all over and the rest of his hair burned off. Fresh smoke billowed off of him. The lightning ended, but Cam was already rushing forward. A white-hot sword laced with lightning forged in his hands. A single thrust to the heart, and it was done.

Yet somehow, Weld remained aloft. He glared at Cam, disbelief, rage, and agony in his eyes. Blood bubbled from his mouth. But then the energy and life went out of him. His limbs went slack, and he fell to the ocean, dead, confirmed by Oversight.

Cam sagged. He had hardly anything left.

43

Saira reached Cam as he tried to recover, slowing with a quickness that caused her hair and clothes to flare like sails. "You Advanced?" she said, smiling in relief and approval. "And you killed a Sage as a Crown. Congratulations. That is amazing."

"I got lucky. Weld might be a Sage, but he didn't have much control over his abilities."

"It's still quite an accomplishment."

Cam shrugged off the compliment. Killing Weld might be a great feat, but it didn't leave him feeling in any way happy or energetic. It had simply been a task that had needed doing.

And yet, some of his lingering anger from Mote might have ebbed out of him, and he hoped it wouldn't come back. He just wanted some peace in his life.

Even still, those clouds full of nightmares? Where had Weld come up with such disturbing imageries? The man had been sick in the head. If there had ever before been a doubt, it was a certainty now. Cam shuddered at the remembered visions. At least he'd kept Weld from killing…

Pan and Birch. Cam's gaze snapped back to the cliff where he'd last seen his friends. A quick focusing of his gaze brought them into sharp relief. Pan hunched over Birch, grief written large on his face, sobbing.

Oh, no.

Without another word, Cam shot off toward them. His last True Bond would have to last, and he gripped it tight, the pain in his chest aching fierce. How many times had he done this now? Held a Bond for too long? Three or four? Cam couldn't recall, but if there was a price to pay for doing so, so be it. He would gladly pay the bill when it came due. Just let him get to Pan and Birch. Speed was all Cam cared about.

Saira quickly caught up with him. *"My mother is a skilled healer,"* she sent.

Cam nodded acknowledgment, but kept silent, not having anything to say. He just hoped and prayed Birch would be alive to require healing. What if he was already dead? That was his greatest terror.

Seconds later, they reached Pan and Birch, and Cam stopped with an abruptness that made the world lurch in his vision. He ignored the nausea-inducing motion and dropped down next to his friends, landing with a heavy thud that raised a cloud of dust. Cam ignored the noise and dirt, focused on Birch. His heart dropped when he saw the rakshasa's injuries. Both his arms had been shattered, bent wrong in many places. His torso appeared caved in on the left, and his head was misshapen and swollen. Blood pooled beneath him. So much blood. An ocean of it. How was he still alive?

"Tell your mother to hurry!" he shouted to Saira. However, her stricken expression told Cam the truth about what she was seeing. There was no hope for Birch. He stared, helpless, not knowing what to say or do.

Cam looked to Pan and received a small head shake of negation. "He's in so much pain," Pan whispered, tears in his eyes. "I did the best I could to ease his suffering, but…"

There had to be something more they could do. Cam reached out with the last dregs of his True Bond, adding to Pan's work, helping Birch as best he could. Maybe it worked some, but he still felt so helpless.

The lion-headed rakshasa cracked open his eyes. "It looks like I was right about dying soon," he said, managing a smile at Cam through his pain. He coughed. "I wish I wasn't. Dying hurts."

Sprite and Kiwi arrived, flitting their wings to alight on Cam's shoulders, trilling in alarm.

"Can he be saved?" Sprite asked.

Cam stroked the yellow lovebird's chest. "I don't think so." Light Squad was supposed to have gone to the Sinanes, to a place of beauty and peace, not to a battle. Why did it always have to be this way? Disaster after disaster. Why couldn't Birch have experienced serenity and peace for just once in his life?

Sprite chirped his upset, hopping off Cam's shoulder and landing next to Birch. He cheeped, leaning close and nuzzling the rakshasa. Kiwi joined him.

"Can we ease his suffering?" Cam asked Saira, hating to see Birch in so much torment. "Can your mother help?"

"She's attending to our Crowns. Some of them were grievously wounded. Rainen and Sage-Duke Shun, as well. It will have to be me."

By then, the rest of Light Squad had reached them.

Charity crouched next to Cam. "I'm so sorry," she said, placing a comforting hand on his shoulder and kissing his cheek.

He appreciated her gesture, and he rested a hand over hers.

"What can we do for him?" Charity asked Saira.

"I lack my mother's skill," Saira said, "but I can smooth his passing. He won't feel anything. He'll be asleep."

"Do it," Cam ordered.

"Wait," Birch said. "Can you reach into my mind and see the meadow? I'd like my passing to occur there. I want to see it again before the end."

Cam gazed to Saira in sudden hope. Birch's one great desire in life was to return to the meadow where he'd first felt Ephemera and discovered a different possibility to his life.

"Open your mind, and I'll see it done," Saira said. She stared into Birch's pain-filled eyes, and shortly gave a firm nod. "I have it." An instant later, she cast open an anchor line, grimacing at the effort.

Saira must have pushed herself hard today and was likely nearing her limits. Nevertheless, the anchor line remained in place, a rectangular portal with a rainbow bridge leading to Birch's meadow.

"I'll carry him," Cam said, stooping low to lift Birch in his arms. He wanted to be with his friend until the end.

But Pan stopped him. "You're too tired. Let me."

Cam wanted to argue, but when he rose to his feet, he swayed, barely able to stand. Pan was right. He couldn't carry the weighty rakshasa. Nothing remained of his Bond, and the exhaustion was simply too much. Cam stepped aside, and Pan created a bed of air under the rakshasa, gently lifting him off the ground.

Cam made to follow after the two of them, but he stumbled, almost falling on his face.

Charity was there. "I've got you. Hold on to me."

"Thank you." Cam draped an arm over Charity's shoulders, leaning into her and letting her carry his weight.

"Come on." Charity guided him to the anchor line, following after Pan and Birch while the rest of Light Squad trailed after them.

"*I truly am sorry, Cam,*" Charity sent as they made their way to the anchor line. "*I know how much you cared for him.*"

"*He saved me,*" Cam said, his eyes welling. He wished there was a way to convey to Charity what he meant by that. Words weren't enough.

"*He saved both of us,*" Pan corrected.

"*We saved each other,*" Birch said.

Tears leaked down Cam's face. It was true. They had saved one another. None of them would have survived the prison or Petala without the support of the others. They'd done it together, as brothers, and today should have been a day of celebration, not tragedy.

They entered the anchor line, and Cam felt his body stretch. The world disappeared into a smear of light, and a shrieking filled his ears.

The next moment, he stepped into a sunlit meadow in the late afternoon. Warmth beamed down, and butterflies and bees flitted about amongst wildflowers grown waist high. A floral fragrance perfumed the air, mixing with the scent of the surrounding forest of pine. Somewhere close, small woodland animals stole about and frogs croaked. The rest of Light Squad exited the anchor line with Saira the last one through. But Cam's eyes were entirely on Birch.

The rakshasa rested on Pan's bed of air, propped up so he could see the meadow, and he gazed about in wonder and delight. "It's more beautiful than I remember."

Cam made his way to Pan and Birch, shrugging himself free of Charity. He went to his knees, taking one of the rakshasa's hands. Pan already held the other one while Sprite and Kiwi nested on either side of the rakshasa's mane, cooing softly. Light Squad stood at a distance, maintaining a silent vigil, which Cam appreciated. While they hadn't known Birch well, they recognized how important he had been—*was* to him and Pan.

"You made it back here," Cam said to Birch.

"I made it back," Birch agreed, his voice raspy and weak. "Promise to bury me. I don't want a pyre. I want to be one with this place. Part of the dirt that grows the flowers."

It was an odd request. A pyre purified and set a soul free. A burial was about worms and decay. Still, if that's what Birch wanted, he would honor the request. "We'll see to it," Cam promised.

"Thank you," Birch whispered. He spoke again, sending to Cam an instant later. *"Lean closer."*

Cam did so.

"I have a gift. My Nullity. You and Pan can use it."

Cam startled. Nullity. The few times he'd experienced Nullity, it had felt like he'd been drowning in darkness. He didn't think he could accept the gift. Was it even safe to do so?

Birch smiled. *"It won't be so bad. You're a Crown. My Nullity is at a Glory's Stage. Take it. Use it. Burn it up and Advance."*

Cam searched his knowledge from Rukh and Jessira. They'd left him information about Nullity, including how to use it, which actually wasn't much different than utilizing Ephemera, except everything was focused internally. In addition, according to the information from the Holy Servants, as a Crown, Cam likely wouldn't feel any effects of Birch's Glory-Staged Nullity. "*I accept.*"

"*Then take it with my blessing.*"

Cam stiffened as a strange intrusion entered his Source, a blackness like the anchor line in Hearth at the Temple of Gates. It remained separate from his lightning-laced, weighty Tang, drifting downward, resting at the bottom of his Source, a hard, cold nugget. There it remained, leaving him slightly nauseated at first until he got used to the sensation.

"It's done," Birch said, speaking aloud. "Use it well. I just wish…" A faint smile ghosted over his face. "I've received blessings enough. I shouldn't ask for more." He sighed, eyes staring over the meadow, and he breathed no more.

Cam sobbed, holding Birch, reaching for Pan. The faint sound of a Singing Light, the melodies merging in a lovely counterpoint, might have echoed over the meadow.

Pan reached for Cam's hand while they watched Birch's remembrance pyre burn. It was the very night their friend had fallen, and while they had buried the rakshasa in the meadow, just like he'd asked, it had felt wrong not to have some kind of fire. Sprite and Kiwi chirped from where they perched atop Cam's shoulders, and the four of them watched in silence as flames licked at the wood.

Crackling sparks and smoke lofted into the night sky, carried on a kind wind that also brought the calming fragrances of pine and wildflowers. The weather was warm, which wasn't a surprise. This part of Golden—an area south of Codent—was mild year-round.

Pan watched the fire with a pit in his stomach. He hadn't liked Birch very much when they'd first met, but he'd slowly come to appreciate and respect the rakshasa, and in the end, loved him like a brother.

But he was gone now, just at the moment that his life should have actually begun. It was so deeply unfair.

Pan wept, not just for his loss, but mostly for what should have been. Birch should have had a chance to experience Salvation, to see all its beautiful places and people. And he had been so close to doing so. Those last moments on the bridge leading home had been full of joy and happiness. Why couldn't that have lasted? Why couldn't Birch have known a day of love and peace? Why did he have to die at the very moment when they'd all thought themselves safe? Birch had been born a rakshasa of Mote, had died an Awakened Ephemeral Master of Salvation, and had never truly experienced the joy of living. It was a tragedy.

Continuing to weep, Pan wished he had an answer to what all this pain meant. Why did Devesh allow such sorrows?

Pan wiped at his tears, his sight going to Cam and then to the others gathered here. The rest of Light Squad stood silent vigil behind them, and even Rainen Winder had decided to attend. The Wilde Sage's injuries had his arm in a sling, his leg in a brace, and one of his eyes swollen shut. In this regard, he was like everyone else.

All of them bore wounds, including Pan, whose head throbbed from where that fragging jackhole, Weld Plain, had burned and blasted him through a boulder and into a cliff. How the man had managed to Advance to Sage was another aspect that often made life seem unfair. Pan was just glad that Cam had put the jackhole down. Birch had been avenged… although Pan wished his friend would have never required avenging.

"Are you ready?" Cam asked.

Pan nodded, swallowing heavily, unable to speak.

"Then it's time," Cam said. He subtly flicked his fingers, and the fire crackled more fiercely. The logs splintered, and the flames abruptly burned white hot. It only lasted for a few seconds, and then it was over. There was nothing left but coals and ashes.

Pan continued to stare at the glowing embers, numb with grief. Birch was truly gone.

Cam tugged him away from the remains of the pyre. "We should join the others."

Pan allowed himself to be led away, looking back one last time before facing forward. He firmed his spine and straightened his shoulders. He would continue to grieve, but now was the time to plan on what to do next. What that might be, Pan had no idea.

"I'm tired," Cam said, exhaling heavily. "We fight and fight and fight and just when we think we'll have a chance for peace, this happens."

"I was thinking the same thing," Pan replied. "What should we do?"

"My heart wants to go after Nailing straightaway and kill him. He was the reason for this battle. But we can't. We're too weak, and we need rest."

They reached the rest of Light Squad.

Charity stepped forward, peering up at Cam in concern. "What do you want to do next? Where do you want to go?"

Cam sighed again. "Nailing is still out there. Weld delivered the killing blow to Birch, but the Sage of Warring Thunder is the reason for all of this. And we've stopped his plans three times now. He knows me. What if he comes after Traverse? I need to be ready."

Rainen cleared his throat. "It will be a long time before Nailing recovers." He indicated himself. "I'll be months healing, and I would guess Nailing will need just as much time or more."

"But he's still out there," Cam insisted.

"Maybe so," Rainen replied, "But until Nailing crawls out of whatever hole into which he's hidden himself away, use the time to rest. Recover. You need it."

Pan viewed the Wilde Sage in surprise, not expecting his sympathy. Had something in him changed over the years? Or had he simply never recognized Rainen's capacity for compassion?

"I want to see my family," Avia said, speaking into the quiet. "It's been too long since I've visited my father or my pod."

Her comment spurred the others to say the same, even Card and Jade, whose relationships with their families were, at best, strained. Charity remained silent, apparently having no wish to see her father again which was understandable. Nonetheless, as Pan listened to their declarations of visiting loved ones, he wondered about his own family.

How were they doing? Did they miss him? Or were their worries only related to how he might fulfill the prophecy?

He scowled inwardly. He was worth more than that stupid prophecy, and he hoped his family believed it, too, but he accepted that they probably didn't.

"I'm going home," Cam said. "I want to see Pharis, Darik, and my dad. I want to see my nephews and nieces and my friends in Traverse."

"I'll go with you," Charity said. She directed what seemed like a frail smile at Cam. "If you'll allow it."

Cam stared at Charity, his gratitude obvious. "Are you sure? There's nowhere else you want to go?"

Charity offered a sarcastic chuckle. "Like where? Maviro? The Sinanes?" She shook her head. "No. I think going with you would be best. Unless you're worried what it might mean introducing me to your family." She offered a teasing grin, but Pan could see the effort it required of her. Asking to accompany Cam was harder than she let on.

Cam smiled at Charity. "Then I'd be honored to introduce you to my family. And I could also use the company."

"In that case, I'll go with you, too," Pan said.

"You don't want to see your family?" Cam asked, surprised.

Pan wanted to, but his heart still hurt over losing Birch. Right now, facing his family and their expectations… he wasn't ready for that. "I'll visit them some other time."

"What do we do about Traverse?" Cam asked Rainen. "What do we do if Nailing recovers faster than you think? I'm only a Crown."

Rainen waved away Cam's worry. "I'll watch over your town while I heal. If Nailing comes, I'll kill him."

"Where are we going after Traverse?" Pan asked Cam.

"How about the Sinanes?" Saira offered. "Come visit me there. Train with my mother. I promised to show the archipelago to you anyway."

"We should all go back to the Sinanes," Jade suggested. "It's become our home. Meet there in a week or so?"

The others quickly agreed to Jade's idea, and afterward, Cam addressed the lovebirds, smiling at them. "What about you two? Where do you want to go? Do you want to see Traverse?"

Kiwi was the one who answered. "Is it safe?"

Cam's smile faltered. "I don't know. Probably not. Not when a rakshasa Sage might want to raze it."

"Then can we go with Saira to the Sinanes?" Kiwi asked.

"Of course, you can," Saira replied, smiling fondly at the lovebirds. "My mother will love hosting you at the palace."

Pan held his tongue. He wanted the lovebirds to stay with him and Cam, especially with Birch dead. Having Sprite and Kiwi leaving, too—even if only temporarily—still felt like abandonment. A moment later, he sighed to himself, realizing he was being unreasonable. The lovebirds would be better off in the Sinanes where it was safe and peaceful.

"Then it's settled," Cam said, clapping his hands. Pan caught Cam smiling his way. "What do you say, my favorite panda-person? We'll go to Traverse, but before we get there, how about we find you a nice grove of bamboo?"

Pan set aside any lingering disappointment with Kiwi's and Sprite's decision and grinned in the toothy way he knew would make Cam happy. "Can we find a grove after Traverse, too?"

Cam laughed. "Of course we can."

"A word before you leave," Rainen said, and once he had their attention, he inhaled heavy, like he was bent on asking a hard question. "What happened in Charn can't happen again. The Sage-Dukes have failed their people for the last time. When you come back to Golden, will you help me rid the world the rakshasas?"

Cam answered. "We were already planning on it."

Semaraj was his name, the created son of Pelluraj, born from his father's will, along with a thousand others in his brood, half of them male and the other half female. Only a hundred of them had survived their first year, while the rest of them had been killed by their own brothers and sisters or by other kaijus. Ten years after and only Semaraj remained, and for the past hundred and twenty years, he'd slowly gained power.

Unlike so many of Pelluraj's children, he had never sought battle against his brothers and sisters. Fighting without the assurance of victory wasn't his way. While other kaijus regularly challenged one another—often to the death, no matter how much they might be outclassed and at the slightest provocation—Semaraj was wiser.

Early in his life, he'd learned a valuable lesson: patience. He'd learned to watch and wait, attacking those he was certain to kill and avoiding those who might pose a challenge. It was the route of a cautious warrior, and while some kaijus created many years later had quickly eclipsed Semaraj in might, where were they now?

Dead. They'd fought too freely, never backing down from a challenge. Meanwhile, careful and calculating Semaraj had continued to grow in power. He'd Imbibed enough Ephemera to steadily Advance his eyes, breath, and abilities, but just as importantly, Semaraj had learned to absorb and master the corruption that seeped into Petala and thereby become nearly indestructible. He'd achieved the very heights that his kind could reach with only Pelluraj himself standing higher.

Of course, it wasn't enough. It was never enough for any kaiju. Within the heart of every one of Pelluraj's sons and daughters beat the heart of a dominator, and Semaraj—no matter how others might consider him cowardly—felt no different. Living under Pelluraj's dominion was unacceptable, and ever did Semaraj think on how to overcome his father.

However, thought wasn't the same as reality. Defeating Pelluraj was an impossibility. It would be easier to master flight. In truth, the first and oldest kaiju was not merely more powerful than any of his children, he was also wiser and vastly more cunning. Pelluraj could trade blows with one of the Great Rakshasas and survive. He could outwit them at times as well, having nearly pushed to the Locus on more than one occasion.

In the face of such craftiness and power, Semaraj hadn't seen any hope for himself. Yes, he strode more proudly than any kaiju but Pelluraj, but all that meant was he was the greatest of slaves.

Then had come those strangers and their strange ways of thinking and even stranger memories. An opportunity had presented itself, and Semaraj had taken it. Why not? There was so much to gain. Freedom from Pelluraj's rule, from Petala itself and her corruption, which had made Semaraj's body strong, but also left him always requiring an abundance of Ephemera merely to stay alive. And that was the greatest reason to take the chance. On the other end of the Locus was rumored to exist the Realm of Salvation, the very source of Ephemera. By reaching that blessed land, Semaraj would become even more powerful than his father.

So, yes, why not? Why not when the only true dangers in Salvation would be weaklings who weren't kaijus, and therefore, of no concern? Why not when Semaraj's existence was so deeply proscribed by his father's whims? Why not when the only risk—a not entirely insignificant one—was that Pelluraj might notice Semaraj's encroachment? The father might kill the son, but that was always a danger in the Hollow Land, so why not indeed?

Semaraj had taken the risk, challenging fate and his future on the chance afforded him.

And it had worked.

The weaklings had distracted Pelluraj, just as he'd hoped, but they had also drawn Shimala into conflict with his father, just as he'd planned. And later on, she'd fought Coruscant's sending at the gateway to the Locus. Again, just as he'd intended.

And in the confusion, Semaraj, who'd been cautious and careful at all times, hiding when necessary, both from his father, and later the two Great Rakshasas, had entered the Locus, unnoticed and alone. He'd walked the golden bridge where Ephemera billowed like a wind, but frustratingly, it also refused Semaraj's every attempt at Imbibing. He'd eventually given up the attempt and walked the span, seeking its end. He'd finally found it: an oval doorway that glowed with every color. And beyond it was Salvation, Semaraj's destiny.

Taking a moment to stare back in the direction in which he'd traveled, Semaraj's memory took him along the long length of his life: his frightful beginning, full of hardships and never-ending challenges. His years and decades of weakness, of running from any challenge. His slow rise to power and eventual understanding that he'd never dominate Petala, not so long as Pelluraj lived. And finally, the lightning strike of clarity when he'd seen a different path forward, the one leading to this moment.

Semaraj grinned, sending a message to his father, not sure it would extend across Realms. *"Ware of me, Pelluraj, my father. When next we meet, I shall slay thee."*

The message was received, and Pelluraj replied, unimpressed. *"Try your best, cowardly child."*

Grimacing at the insult, Semaraj stepped through the doorway and into Salvation. He fell from a great height, but fear didn't touch him. His attention was elsewhere. Down below was a vast ocean, and since the fall wouldn't hurt him in the slightest, he focused on his other senses.

Like Petala, this world teemed with life and prey, but unlike the Hollow Land, Salvation was filled with Ephemera. Semaraj Imbibed, gorging. In a short while, he'd Advance.

A voice echoed in Birch's tired mind. He was ready to join the Singing Light and lay aside every pain and turmoil he'd experienced in his hard life.

"Are you sure you want to die?"

A golden-furred squirrel with green eyes appeared in Birch's mind's eye. He wondered how she could possibly be here when he was dead. Was death the same as life? If so, he was disappointed. He really wanted to rest. Or was this a mindscape?

The squirrel smiled at him. *"You aren't dead. Your heart stopped a few times, but you yet live. Barely so, and yet, it is so."*

Birch glared. The squirrel wanted something from him. It was the way of his life. Why else would she be here? Everyone wanted something from everyone. He frowned inwardly. Maybe not everyone. Not Pan and Cam or Sprite and Kiwi. But the squirrel wasn't them. She was a stranger. *"What do you want from me?"*

"My name is Honor. I have a proposal. Will you listen?"

Ephemera poured off her then, richer and purer than anything Birch had ever experienced, including the bridge leading from Mote to Salvation or even Salvation. He gasped, overwhelmed as he recollected. Cam had spoken about a golden squirrel named Honor, believed her to be Jessira.

Birch kowtowed before Honor, formal and overcome by her glorious presence. *"What is thy bidding, my Lady?"*

Honor laughed. *"Do not kneel to me. I am not your master. I am a servant. Look at me, Birch Drang. Do you wish to be a servant as well?"*

44

The morning following Birch's funeral saw Cam, Pan, and Charity flying miles above the ground, heading to Traverse while the rest of Light Squad were off to see their own families. The sun beamed down, harsh and unrelenting at the heights, and mist collected on Cam's clothes whenever they lanced into thick, fluffy clouds that reminded him of fog, while wispier ones simply frayed apart like torn clothing. The wind howled in the speed of their passage, and Cam loved every minute of it.

Flying through the skies of Petala had been a joyous wonder, even though he'd been carried. But soaring high above the world under his own power, the landscape below a gorgeous mix of forests, mountains, and rivers and the occasional quilt of fields and farms: it was perfect. Nothing in life was better.

Cam glanced over at Pan, who flew close at hand, doing loops now and then or just swinging back and forth, like he was strung from an invisible line. The whole while, Pan grinned in that toothily cute way of his. Cam couldn't help but smile back while he watched his favorite panda-person.

His sight landed next on Charity, but this time his gaze became appreciative. Until now, he'd never noticed the way flying pressed her clothes against her form, highlighting her athletic curves. He cut off his lust-filled appraisal as guilt crawled up his throat at what he'd been thinking.

It was only last night that they'd buried Birch and lit his remembrance pyre. Shouldn't he be grieving still? How could he smile or think about Charity like that so soon after his friend's death? Or even enjoy flying? And with so much suffering in Mote and Salvation, a part of him wondered if it there should even be room in his life for happiness.

Of course, that was being absolutely stupid, and Birch would have been the first one to tell him so. The rakshasa wouldn't have wanted Cam pining away, filled with sadness and resentment. He would have wanted Cam flipping a rude gesture to all their enemies, kicking their fragging asses, and loving life and Charity.

And if the roles had been reversed, Birch would have done exactly that—other than the loving Charity part.

Cam smiled in fond and regretful remembrance of his friend. He missed Birch, recognizing that grieving like a loon wouldn't be the best way to honor the old-headed rakshasa. Better if he gave himself fully over to wanting a life of happiness, of fixing his mind on *wanting* to be happy and healing himself of his anger. That would be the best way to honor his friend.

Nodding to himself, Cam decided to do exactly that. He didn't want his first visit home in far too long to be one filled with wishes and sorrow. For him, it had been two years since he'd last seen family, but for those in Traverse, it had been over seven. And for most of it, Pharis and everyone else had figured him to be twice over dead, first in Hearth and then in Mote.

Cam grinned when he imagined their reactions to him strolling into Traverse. *No.* When he *flew* in and his eyes glowed with the violet Haunt of a Crown. They likely had no expectation that he was still alive, and the shock of seeing him upright and breathing would only be matched by their amazement of his status as a Crown.

He dreamed about the joyous reunion to follow, but a movement caught his sight. Charity flew in wide arcs, back and forth, inward and away from Cam, arms at her sides and her legs straight back, smiling with an expression he couldn't quite describe. She seemed content, and he was happy to watch her, unashamed this time to appreciate how well she looked. Besides, he was allowed to look. Weren't he and Charity courting?

He wasn't sure. They'd never fully formalized their relationship again, but given everything else they'd told one another, it seemed likely. He'd have to confirm it with her. Someone in Traverse was bound to ask about their relationship, especially when Charity flirted with him, and she'd most certainly flirt with him. She might even go so far as to pinch his backside while they were out in public or plant a kiss on him, just to make him blush.

He wouldn't mind any of that. He liked kissing Charity, and he pondered anew how she could have overlooked his pettiness so quickly. It was probably because she was a better person than him, certainly more mature, which only emphasized how lucky he was to have her in his life. As for the flirting, especially if kissing was involved, that was sure to set tongues to wagging.

"Enjoying the view?" Charity asked. *"And I don't mean the landscape."*

Cam flushed, realizing only then that he'd been staring at Charity the entire time he'd been considering their relationship. Even as he made to apologize, Charity shifted, slowly rolling so her backside faced him. Cam watched, mesmerized, blurting out the first words that came to him. *"Can you do that again? But slower?"* He flushed again when he realized how his mouth had galloped ahead of his mind.

Charity winked his way. *"You mean like this?"* She rolled again, leisurely and deliberate, giving him a nice, long view.

Cam's mouth went dry.

"Your turn."

At first, Cam wasn't sure if Charity was being serious, but she made a get-on-with-it motion. However, he still hesitated. Was she really wanting a view of him from behind? Why?

"How can I tell how you look if you won't give me a proper view?" she added.

"A proper view?"

"You always wore a long jacket in Petala. I never got a good look at..." She flicked her eyes over his body. *"Your other attributes."*

Cam scoffed, laughing at her words. Nevertheless, he did a roll for Charity's benefit.

"Too fast."

Cam slowed himself, pausing when he was fully faced away from Charity. He flushed a third time, feeling faintly ridiculous. Women were beautiful, and it was easy to figure why a man would stare after them. Men, on the other hand, what was the appeal? Honestly. Men were hairy, lumpy, and often bearded. But if this was what Charity wanted, then who was he to deny it?

"Very nice," Charity purred, once he'd finished his demonstration.

Cam viewed her with uncertainty, wondering again about their relationship. *"We're still courting, right?"*

"Yes, Cam Folde. We are still courting." Charity shook her head, viewing him like he was an idiot.

Which was probably about right. *"I'm glad to hear it."*

Charity shook her head again. *"What will I do with you?"* Despite her words, she tucked in close, looping an arm with his, and they flew together, quiet and sharing a moment.

The silence lingered, pleasant, and there was no reason to interrupt it. On they flew, and Cam felt himself relax. For the first time in a long while, his heart was at peace, and he breathed out any lingering tension, glad that Charity was with him. He kissed her cheek. They flew in contented silence.

An hour or so later, Pan floated over to them. *"I think we're getting close."*

Cam frowned, wondering how Pan could know that. He'd never been to Traverse.

"I recognized it from all the times you described it to me," Pan

explained at the unspoken question on Cam's face.

Cam gazed ahead and downward, noting a cluster of ponds, small and glistening in the late-morning sun, their shapes familiar even from up above. And just past them towered a tall oak in the middle of a broad meadow, a lord of the forest. And over there was the large mound that he, Jordil, Tern, and Lilia used to climb, pretending they were Sages.

Staring ahead, Cam sighted Traverse's fields and farms, and he indicated for them to descend. They flew level with the surrounding trees. There was the town itself, looking every bit as small and nondescript as Cam recalled, nestled in a gentle curve of the Barr River.

His throat tightened. This was where he'd grown up, a place full of memories, both good and bad. This was Traverse. The name resonated in Cam's mind like the tolling of some bell calling him to warmth and safety. Cam slowed, flying now at barely more than a man could run, swallowing back a lump and wiping at some tears. Pan reached over and hugged him. So did Charity.

As low and slow as they were flying, folks who were out and about noticed them, pointing their way, shouting questions to one another.

But Cam's eyes were locked on one place alone: the small hovel where he'd lived for most of his life. There it stood, no longer decrepit but roofed in fresh cedar shakes, the falling-down porch replaced with something sturdier, and the walls exhibiting a fresh coat of white paint.

It was so tiny. How had he shared it with three other adults? Had it really housed them all?

He, Charity, and Pan alighted on the ground, and the neighbors and other folks—alerted to their arrival by the various other townsfolk—came out of their homes. Most didn't recognize him, and they bowed low, murmuring, "Welcome, honored Crowns." A few, though, did recognize him, and their words of welcome became shouts of disbelief, asking how he was alive, and wondering if he was really a Crown. A few asked if Pan was a rakshasa.

That earned a rebuke from Charity. "If he was a rakshasa, do you really think he would just tell you? More likely, he would kill you for asking."

Cam didn't bother listening to the replies. Nor did he bother answering the questions yelled his way. His eyes were on the front door, where his father, so old and frail now, stood alongside Pharis.

Again came the tears, and this time Cam didn't bother wiping them. He walked to where Pharis and his father waited, pushing through the crowd, slow at first, then faster. Within strides, he was running, covering the short distance in a blink. Then he was hugging Pharis and his father, all three of them weeping.

He was home.

The chaos of so many people shouting his name and wanting his time eventually broke through the haze of Cam's joyous reunion.

"I'll explain everything," he told Pharis and his daddy, glancing about and really seeing everyone around him for the first time. The neighborhood where he'd grown up was located in the poorest section in Traverse, and in that regard, nothing much had changed. These were people who didn't have much, but in really thinking it through, Cam realized they had enough. Everyone had roofs over their heads, clean clothes to wear, and enough food to eat. No child went to bed hungry.

So why had it felt so impoverished when Cam had lived here? He'd had the same things as everyone else, even if they'd been a mite shabbier.

The answer arrived like it often did from Pan, this time in the form of a question. *"Were these the people who called you a no-good Folde?"*

"That's about right," Cam said. Only then did he realize that while he'd had everything he might have needed from a material perspective, that wasn't the same as what was required when it came to matters of the heart and the spirit. He'd so often been treated like a pariah here, a no-good Folde, just like Pan had just reminded him, and those weren't memories that simply drifted away like leaves on the wind. Those kinds of statements had carved deep furrows into his soul, wounds and lies

that had taken a long time to heal. And being here again had reopened some of those painful hurts.

"Let's go inside," Pharis said. "I can tell you have a long story to tell."

Cam hesitated, but Charity urged him inside the house. "Go on. I'll take care of the crowd."

Cam gave her hand a grateful squeeze, a motion Pharis noticed based on the considering expression that stole across her face. "It's a long story, for sure," Cam said to his sister, indicating Pan and Charity. "They're both a large part of it."

"I can't wait to learn," Pharis replied, her eyes still sharp.

Cam viewed Charity a moment longer. She already had the crowd dispersing, and he found himself awed by her skills with people. How did she do that? If Cam had told the people that all would be explained later, they would have just shouted at him even louder.

"Go on. I'm fine," Charity said when Cam glanced her way again.

He nodded acknowledgment and followed his dad and Pharis into the home where he had spent his childhood with Pan trailing after.

Cam looked around. Nothing much seemed amiss. There was the front room and kitchen while a hallway led to the pair of bedrooms in the back. But the cots where Cam and his brother, Darik, used to sleep were gone, which only made sense. Darik had moved out after he'd married Widow Marlinth, who wasn't a widow anymore. She was Marlinth Folde now.

Cam's eyes narrowed. Actually, something was amiss but in a good way. Everything was clean and tidy, which had hardly been the case back when he'd lived here.

"It's good to see you, boy," Cam's father said to him, his eyes rheumy and weak and his breathing somewhat labored. His features had a perpetual sag, and his skin held a sallow complexion that Cam hadn't noticed until just now. Same with the prominent bulge to his abdomen. That didn't come from fine dining, not with spidery blood vessels marking the old man's neck.

Cam's face fell. He knew what was wrong. It was the drink. It had finally caught up to his father, killing his liver, and it would eventually kill him. His eyes welled. Destiny, karma, or fate was so monumentally cruel, like they were all conspiring to punish his father for finally making a good choice in his life when he let go of the bottle. "Daddy…" Cam didn't know what else to say.

"It'll be fine," his father said, patting Cam's shoulder. "I've lived a good life. Long enough to see two children married. And the third one's come back from the dead as a Crown." His words spoken, Cam's father began to cough, and he couldn't seem to stop. He coughed and coughed and coughed, and bright blood stained his spittle. Pharis helped him into a chair, handing him a fresh handkerchief.

"He started showing signs about six months ago," Pharis said. "There's no way to slow the progression. Now, why don't you tell us where you've been the last three years?"

Cam didn't reply, his sight caught on his father, wishing there was something that could be done for him. But even Saira's mother, as gifted a healer as she was, wouldn't have been able to help. He swallowed back a lump.

"Cam?" Pharis pressed.

He exhaled, ready to tell them where he'd been all this time, but before he could explain anything, the door to the house flung open, and in stormed his brother, Darik. "What's this about—" He halted seeing Cam and gave a whoop of delight. "Runt!"

An instant later, Cam found himself lifted off his feet as his brother swung him about. He hugged Darik back, and the two of them laughed. They continued to laugh even when Cam was placed back on his feet and registered that he was taller than Darik, more stoutly built, too, and his brother wasn't a small man.

"I think you're the runt now," Cam said with a smile.

Darik grinned. "That ain't what the ladies say."

"Lady," Pharis corrected, her tone aggravated. "That's what the lady says. You're married." She muttered under her breath. "How does Marlinth put up with you?"

"Why don't you ask her?" Darik suggested. "She'll tell you true."

Pharis wagged her finger at Darik, wearing an aggravated expression.

"Just be quiet, you. Cam was about to tell us where he's been this whole time he's been away."

Darik's humor fell away, and he turned to Cam. "That's right. Where you been, Runt?"

"I was just fixing to tell everyone before you blew in like a bad wind." Cam grinned to take the sting out of his words, and he went on to summarize what he and Pan had experienced. He glossed over some of the more unsavory and unsettling details. It didn't work too well since the family still gasped plenty, especially when he got to the part about Mote.

"You actually went to Hell?" Darik asked, his voice hushed.

"It's called Mote?" Pharis asked on top of him.

"Let the boy tell his tale," their daddy ordered.

Cam continued on, describing his imprisonment, of talking to Pan telepathically. That earned the fine panda-person, who'd been quiet this whole time, a wondering look.

"An Awakened Beast as a best friend," Darik said. "Ain't that something?"

"You wrote about Pan, but I never figured on meeting him," Pharis said. She startled. "And I don't have any bamboo saved anywhere."

Pan bowed to her. "Your warm company is of much finer sustenance."

Darik nodded in approval at Pan. "You talk real good. Are you the one who's been teaching Cam? He don't sound so much like a yokel anymore."

"Which is a pity," Pan said. "I love his drawl. So does Charity."

Three pairs of eyes locked on Cam, all of them wearing identical expressions of narrow-eyed speculation.

Cam cut them off, figuring it best to get it all out in the open. "Charity is the woman who came with us."

"The Crown standing outside bossing people around?" Darik asked. "She's right easy on the eyes, no matter which way she's facing."

Cam cut his brother off before he could say anything else. If Charity heard, he had no idea what she'd do to Darik. "She and I are courting."

The room broke out in shouted congratulations.

"I'm going to have another sister," Pharis said, clapping her hands in excitement.

"When's the wedding?" his father asked, leaning forward, hope writ large on his face.

"You did damn good, Runt," Darik stated, clapping Cam on the back. "If you ever need advice on how to please a woman in the bedroom, I'm your man."

Pharis smacked Darik's shoulder. "Don't be crude."

At that exact moment, Charity entered the house. "The crowd is gone, but I'm sure the mayor will eventually show up. It may take him some time, though. I placed a ward of antipathy around the home. It'll influence everyone who comes around to walk on by. They won't even know why they don't want to approach the house. They'll just leave." She shrugged. "It might not be my place, but I figured you'd appreciate the privacy."

Cam nodded his appreciation. "Thank you."

Charity graced him with a slight smile before addressing his father. "As for the wedding, we haven't decided on a date or even if it's going to happen." Next, she moved to stand next to Cam and beamed a brilliant smile at Darik. "And while I appreciate the offer, Cam doesn't need any instruction from you. He's never disappointed me in that regard."

Cam bit back a groan, wanting to do nothing more than creep out of the home. Silence met her declaration, everyone now viewing him and Charity in a different kind of speculation.

Darik eventually guffawed, breaking the quiet. "Nice try, but you two don't fool me. Cam ain't got it in him to lie about something like that. You two have never frag—"

He cut off, when Pharis clouted him upside the head. "Idiot."

Charity offered Cam a helpless shrug. "I tried."

"I kind of wish you hadn't," Cam replied, indicating Darik's ongoing mirth. Even his daddy was chuckling, while Pharis covered her face and shook her head.

Pan came over to join them. "At least they're laughing with you. They love you. Be happy."

Pan was right—as usual—and Cam viewed his family and their antics, joyful at being in this old house, back in this small town. His expression grew wistful and the anger underneath rumbled when he remembered Birch. He wished the rakshasa could have been here, too.

But that could never be, and now wasn't the time for sorrow or any kind of anger.

Cam forced a smile, focusing on the moment, wanting to savor it. It worked, and his smiled brightened. "I am happy. For the first time in a long time, I'm happy."

45

After a few more hours of catching up, Cam's father started to drift off. Pharis explained how he didn't have much energy these days, no doubt related to the damage done to his liver from his years of drinking. After putting their daddy down for some sleep, Darik and Pharis mentioned that they had to get back to taking care of their families. Both of them had a couple of children underfoot, and Cam promised to stop by and meet his nieces and nephews later on in the day whenever everyone was free.

For now, Cam wanted to show Charity his hometown. They asked Pan to come along, but he begged off, stating that they should have some time alone together. Making their goodbyes to everyone, Cam and Charity exited the house. Thankfully, no one was about since her ward of antipathy was still in place.

She made to remove it, but Cam held her back. "Leave it. I don't want a passel of people coming by and waking up the old man."

They stepped off the porch, and Cam had another notion on how to maintain his privacy. He created a Blend. This town was his home, and while he loved Traverse, his feelings for the place and its people were deep and conflicted. So many folks here had done him wrong, and he wasn't yet ready to talk to them or hear their proclamations of his greatness, and they'd do exactly that. How could they not? Cam was a Crown, and that meant something, especially out here in the hinterlands where only rarely did someone of his Advancement come by for a visit.

Cam wasn't willing to put up with any of that, the expectations of making peace with those who'd spoken so poorly of him and his family, the hypocrites who would now treat him like a conquering hero. For now, Cam wanted some time alone. He wanted to revisit Traverse without anyone bothering him. He wanted to see those who deserved his time, and that began with Jordil, Master Bennett, and Master Moltin. A few of the farmers who'd been warm to him over the years as well.

The matter settled in his mind, Cam guided Charity through the streets of Traverse in a slow stroll. The day was the kind meant to live and love, a perfect spring morning with the sun shining down, cotton-candy clouds decorating a sky so blue it ached, and a soft breeze to stir air that felt pregnant with budding life and possibility. Close at hand, the Barr River murmured, the sound mixing with the conversations of those who also walked Traverse's streets.

There were so many people that Cam recognized, some of whom he wouldn't have minded speaking to but not just yet. Everyone rushed about, busy with their work, which wasn't unusual, but there was also an intensity to their labor that he'd never noticed before. What was going on? It was probably nothing, and he shrugged it away as unimportant.

Cam slipped his hand into Charity's as they strolled. It felt so natural that he wanted to castigate himself again for ever doubting how she might feel about him. Or worse, for feeling jealous of her wanting happiness with someone else when she had rightly figured him dead.

She gave his hand a warning squeeze. "Stop."

He halted in the middle of the street and eyed her in confusion.

"You have that expression on your face. Every time you think poorly about yourself, you do this." She frowned furiously in demonstration before bopping him on the nose. "It isn't necessary."

Cam quirked a wry smile, not upset at being found out. It was actually somewhat of a relief to have his negative thoughts recognized and cut off so easily. Too often, he was both his own worst critic and greatest enemy. "Am I that easy to read?"

"You don't lie well," Charity said with a smile of her own. "It's charming, and it's also why I have so much fun doing things like this." She goosed him hard.

Cam yelped, rising off his heels. He glanced around furiously, wondering if anyone had seen.

Charity laughed. "We're Blended, you silly man. No one saw us." Just for good measure, she goosed him again. "Stop being so afraid of letting people know you like me."

"Goosing me in public isn't being afraid of letting people know I like you," Cam said with a scowl.

Charity tucked in close and grinned. "Now you did it. You just admitted that you like me."

Cam rolled his eyes. "I said it because I do like you. We're courting, remember?"

She laughed. "How could I forget?"

They strolled on, leaning close to one another with Cam pointing out people, buildings, and sights.

"That lane there leads to Farmer Gerald's farm. He's the one with the bull I told you about."

"The one that chased you and your friend?"

Cam nodded, laughing as he remembered every vivid detail of that terrifying afternoon from his childhood, back when he'd run for his life from the large and very angry animal. He sighed. "It was a good day."

"And a bull has all his parts intact, while a steer and ox don't." Charity arched her eyebrows. "You should be proud of me. I remembered. You don't have to worry about how I might embarrass you with my ignorance about farm life."

Cam wasn't sure what she meant at first, but then he recalled that conversation from what seemed like forever ago in Nexus. A few months for him but three years for Charity. He tugged her to a halt. "You'd never embarrass me for that or anything else."

Charity bopped his nose. "Good answer."

Cam rubbed at where she'd bopped him, not sure why she kept doing it. "Is this going to be a regular thing? You bopping me on the nose?"

Charity replied by drawing him close and pulling his head down to her. She kissed him, deep and inviting. Cam fell into the embrace, not caring that they were out in public. Their Blends hid them, and even if everyone could see, he doubted he'd care much. Charity's lips and tongue tasted of honeysuckle, and he couldn't get enough of them. His hands drifted down her back, squeezing her hips and holding her in place when her fingers curled into his hair. Cam wanted to lose himself in Charity, and his imagination ran wild.

Before he could act on his impulses, Charity pulled away. "We better stop. For now."

She sounded breathless, the same way Cam was feeling. His lungs heaved like he'd run a mile uphill. He managed a nod of agreement, his forehead resting against hers, unable to speak. They stood together like that for several minutes. Finally, Cam's breathing recovered, and he had them walking through Traverse again.

Soon enough, he was pointing out buildings and people again, wanting to focus on something other than Charity pressed tight to him. But it was difficult, nearly impossible. This was his homecoming, but all Cam wanted was to fly off somewhere with Charity and spend the day entangled with her.

However, a sight shoved that notion clear out of his mind: Lilia's parents. They walked on the other side of the street, appearing older and smaller, both of them hunched over, aging too soon and with more gray than black in their hair. Grief had carved lines into their faces, and guilt clogged Cam's throat. Both of Lilia's parents, but especially her mother, had always been kind to him. And look what he'd inadvertently brought to their doorstep: the death of their daughter.

"Who are they?" Charity asked, noticing where his sight had gone.

"Lilia's parents." Cam continued to stare after them, recalling their anger when Lilia had died, the blame they'd laid at his feet, whether rightfully or not.

"You should talk to them," Charity urged. "Go. They might not still feel the same way they once did."

Cam didn't want to. Fighting monsters and rakshasas was easier than what Charity proposed. But it was also the right thing to do, and if their rage hadn't slumbered any, he still owed them the opportunity to vent their feelings, regardless of how much it might hurt.

He nodded, and they stepped through the crowds, Charity's hand still in his. He dropped his Blend, feeling when she did the same, not bothering with the folks who shouted in alarm at their sudden appearance, nor their further exclamations at seeing who it was or that they were Crowns.

"Mr. Fair. Mrs. Fair," Cam called out to Lilia's parents.

They had already noticed the reactions of the other people around them and turned to face in his direction. Upon seeing him, recognition stole across their faces, along with grief and a wary regret and worry.

It was Mrs. Fair who stepped toward him, tugging her husband with him. "Cam Folde."

She stared up at him, and Cam did his best to maintain a calm facade. But Charity was right. He couldn't hide his emotions. Guilt—which he rationally knew wasn't his to bear but his heart couldn't seem to accept—etched his features.

Suddenly, Mrs. Fair was throwing her arms about him and hugging him, weeping inconsolably against his chest.

Mr. Fair was there as well, giving the two of them an awkward hug. It was he who explained the reason for Mrs. Fair's reaction. "You never deserved our anger or our hate, and what we did was wrong. We ran you off, not much more than a boy. We're sorry for that, son. Sorry for all you suffered."

Of all the reactions Cam might have expected, forgiveness hadn't figured in his guesses. Shocked at their responses, eyes welling and unable to respond, he merely held Mrs. Fair, letting her cry until she got herself under control.

After a few moments, she leaned away from him. "We are sorry, Cam," she said, tears still leaking down her cheeks. "You deserved better than what we did to you. What this entire town did to you."

Cam wiped at his own eyes. Forgiveness had a power he'd never measured or imagined experiencing in this way. It was a blessing, and the self-hatred built from that terrible afternoon of loss and blood, even some of his anger from Mote… they eroded like a muddy dam in a spring flood. "Thank you," he said, his voice husky.

Only then did Mr. and Mrs. Fair seem to recognize Charity's presence.

"Who is this?" Mrs. Fair asked. Cam made introductions, and Mrs. Fair smiled. "You came home a Crown, a great man, and brought back a lovely bride?"

"We're only courting," Cam corrected.

Mrs. Fair's smile became knowing. "Maybe for now, but not for long. We'll leave you two alone now. Let you see the sights of our humble village."

They left, and Cam watched them depart.

"How are you feeling?" Charity asked.

Cam shrugged, not really knowing how to answer. He'd hated himself for so long over what had happened to Lilia. To have her parents' forgiveness over the event, and even more stunning, their sorrow and regret over how they'd treated him afterward, had him stuck in a state of shock.

He and Charity spoke some more, but shortly thereafter, Cam's stunned amazement ended when a less pleasant set of people arrived: Maria Echo and her coterie of friends, including Suse Stump and Ingold Lord, a trio of women, married now, who had made Cam's life miserable throughout his childhood. Well did he recall their hateful jeers, which had only been made worse by his hopeless infatuation with Maria.

But that was also in the past. Cam wasn't the same no-good Folde he'd been fooled into believing of himself. He was a Crown, and if Mr. and Mrs. Fair had changed, then maybe these three had as well.

He studied them as they marched his way, noticing how the years had been kind to all three women, all of whom were Novices and carried a more mature beauty about them, especially Maria, who was more lovely now than ever before. However, she stalked forward while Suse and Ingold walked diffidently behind her, whispering to her, tugging on her blouse, and asking her to be kind of all things. Maria scowled at them in reply.

And the first words from her lips laid to rest any hopes Cam had that her heart might have softened over the years. "Well, well," Maria declared with a sneer. "The wastrel returns. Do you have some new murder to bring to Traverse? Some fresh tragedy?"

Gasps from Suse and Ingold met her statement. "He's a Crown," one of them warned.

Maria's sneer only became uglier. "Maybe he is, but first and foremost, he's a no-good Folde. A drunk and a curse to any who know him." She kept on with her harangue.

Cam had a momentary fantasy of silencing Maria's tongue. It would be quite easy, barely an inconvenience. And if nothing else, it would give him peace during his time in Traverse.

Sadly, it would also be wrong. He sighed inwardly as Maria kept on raging, but finally he couldn't take it any longer. "Are you truly this stupid?" He cut her off before she could reply. "It was a rhetorical question. You likely don't know what that word means, so I'll explain. I'll even use small words for your small mind. It means something related to the art of speaking and meant to influence it."

Maria drew in an outraged breath, while Suse and Ingold stepped away from her. Cam viewed them, seeing the tendrils of the woven world, which—unless he willed it otherwise—always filled his vision now that he was a Crown. He saw the connections between them and

Maria. There were only a few. Some frayed and others appeared torn in half. Suse and Ingold didn't like Maria much and only stayed with her out of loyalty and some fear.

"Think carefully about what you say next," Charity said before Maria could rage. Her Crown-Haunted eyes flashed. "I am not as patient as Cam. I won't bully or harm you, but if you continue to use your tongue as a knife, then I will dull it." Her gaze flicked to Suse and Ingold. "Including those of your friends. I know how you all treated Cam."

"Don't lump us with her," Suse cut in. "We were coming to apologize to Cam."

Ingold, always the follower, murmured agreement.

"You fragging cowards," Maria spat, shooting them a glare before redirecting her anger at Cam and Charity, cursing them fully.

While she ranted, Cam distantly wondered if Maria had always been this stupid. Or maybe she'd always gotten her way and never had to deal with the consequences of her actions. Either way, it made him think quite poorly of his younger self. How could he have ever thought Maria was beautiful when her heart was so ugly?

"And just because these two idiots simper before you, I never will," Maria finished, nostrils flaring and her face lifted in pride and daring.

It was then that Suse and Ingold stepped forward, faces bearing outrage.

"Shut up, you ugly cow!" Suse shouted, getting directly in Maria's face. "You're the reason we're still Novices. Your arrogance that you know better than Master Bennett or Master Moltin. We could have Advanced to Acolyte if not for you. All these years wasted listening to your advice. You're the wastrel, not him, you stupid pig. I curse the day you entered my life." She went so far as to spit at Maria's feet.

Maria gaped.

Suse faced Charity. "Do what you want with her, but please leave the rest of us and our families alone. We want nothing to do with her or her idiot face." Next she addressed Cam. "We truly are sorry for how we behaved toward you and your family. I know it might sound self-serving with you being a Crown and us being Novices, but it is the truth." She kowtowed then, her and Ingold both. "Please forgive us." Their faces remained pressed to the ground.

Cam had never wanted or needed anyone bowing so low to him, and he quickly drew Suse and Ingold to their feet. "You don't have to worry about me harming you or yours. That's never been my way." In that moment, he recalled what had happened just moments before: the unexpected forgiveness from Mr. and Mrs. Fair. He searched his heart for the anger and hatred he used to harbor toward Suse and Ingold.

Both were gone, though, evaporated over the years. He no longer hated Suse and Ingold for how they'd behaved as children. Rather, he pitied them. He took Suse's hands in his own and stared into her eyes, imploring her to believe him. "I forgive you, but do better with your children. Don't let them think hurting others who have less or are in pain is a good thing."

Suse stared back at him, eyes wide. "You forgive us? Truly?"

"I do, and I'd be grateful if you did as I advise." He wisped Ephemera to her, letting her feel the proof of his words.

Suse closed her eyes, inhaling deep, lips moving in a prayer. "Thank you," she whispered, eyes open once more. "And bless you, Cam Folde."

She and Ingold departed, a lightness to their steps, leaving Cam and Charity facing a still-stupefied Maria.

Charity viewed the other woman with a vindictive smile. "You were warned. Your tongue has been dulled, and all it took was you using it. Have a pleasant day."

She took Cam's hand, leading him away from Maria, who stood in a cone of isolation. No one stepped close to her, giving her a wide berth, like she had a disease. Maria gazed about, alone, shoulders hunched, and a confused expression of hurt on her face. Cam caught her eyes, and she straightened, pointing at him. "This is your fault!"

He sighed to himself, not angry with Maria's response but pitying it and her. Maria would likely never change, which meant her life would be one of bitterness and acrimony. After all, she couldn't receive forgiveness if she didn't first recognize why she needed it.

"That was an exciting conversation," Charity noted as they continued on their way. "Some might even call it interesting."

Cam shrugged. "Maybe in some other life, Maria will figure out how to become a better person."

Charity peered at him, her doubt obvious. "You really think so?"

Cam shook his head. "No, but I hope so, at least for her sake and her husband's or any children they might have."

Charity feigned a shudder. "That woman as a mother is a curse no child should have to endure."

Cam forced a chuckle, although he didn't really want to talk about Maria Echo any longer. "Let's go see some better people."

He led Charity through the streets of Traverse, both of them Blended again, and they arrived shortly thereafter at the village square. On the other side stood a familiar building fashioned of brick and wood siding: Master Bennett's home. Several dormers and a deep, wrap-around porch peered out over the village square, and like everything in Traverse, it seemed smaller somehow, less grand, although a younger Cam had once thought the home a grand dwelling. After a moment of introspection, he allowed that it still was. Size and expensive qualities weren't necessarily the measures of a home's beauty.

Cam directed Charity toward the house, halting well short of it as memories from the place swept over him. He recalled the many times when he'd trekked from his daddy's house to this home, how hard it had been as a Plasminian and a gentle walk of a hundred yards had set his heart to pounding and his lungs to straining.

How far he'd come. Nowadays, the pleasure of walking was like meditating, especially when shared with someone he cared about. Thinking on everything he'd been gifted, all the wonders, Cam sent a silent prayer of gratitude to Devesh for giving him an opportunity to heal, praying for others to receive the same blessing.

"This was your school?" Upon noticing his questioning gaze,

Charity explained herself. "You described it plenty of times. I feel like I already know everything and everyone here."

"This was my school," Cam confirmed, staring a moment longer at this place where he'd healed and grown so much. "Come on. Let's see if anyone is home."

They strode up the front steps to the porch, dropping their Blends. A knock on the door elicited an old man's quavering-voiced command to enter.

They did so, and Cam took a step inside and took a step back in time. Nothing had changed. He and Charity stood in a cozy space lit by an antlered-chandelier of Ephemeral lamps. A pair of well-crafted chairs huddled across from a frayed leather couch with a long table separating the seating. Several paintings—happily bucolic in the nature of farms, forests, and dells—decorated the walls.

But it was the wizened old man, bearded in white and seated behind a large, oak desk, who captured Cam's attention. Him and the wiry young man leaning over his shoulder. Master Bennett and Jordil Oil. They glanced up from whatever they'd been doing, both of them with Adept-Haunted eyes that went wide in startlement upon seeing Cam and Charity.

Cam viewed Master Bennett with nothing but love and gratitude, and he held the same for Jordil, but also uncertainty. It was because she'd wanted to help Cam that Lilia, Jordil's wife, had died. Was Cam still welcome in his oldest friend's presence? He wasn't sure. When Cam had been run out of Traverse, he'd never had a chance to find out what Jordil felt about him, and the few letters they'd shared hadn't spelled out much about any lingering feelings of anger or resentment.

Jordil's smile of dawning welcome and joy put to bed any of Cam's fears. "Cam." His voice throbbed with love. He stepped around the desk, embracing Cam in a hug, stepping back and making room for Master Bennett. "We thought you were dead, but then there were all these rumors today that you'd returned and were a Crown." He peered at Cam's eyes. "And here you are, and here you have." He grinned in delight.

Cam stared at his oldest friend, searching for the bitterness of loss. But thankfully, he only discovered serene acceptance. Jordil was a good person, and although Lilia's death had hit him hard, it hadn't broken him. Cam was glad for him.

"My boy," Master Bennett said, interrupting his inspection. "Come, sit, and tell us where you've been. We would have come to you, but every time we approached your father's home, the strangest notion of turning around and departing overcame our senses."

"Ah. That was my fault," Charity said. "I set a ward of antipathy around the house. I didn't want a bunch of people coming by and interrupting Cam's reunion with his family."

Master Bennett's gaze landed on Charity. "And who might you be, Miss…"

"Charity Kazar," she said, putting out a hand to shake with Master Bennett and Jordil.

"Kazar? As in the Kazars of Maviro?"

She inclined her head. "Sage-Duke Kazar would be my father."

Master Bennett's eyebrows rose and he eyed Charity in a fresh light, clearly impressed before addressing Cam. "You mentioned the members of Light Squad, but it was so hard to believe everything you wrote, even when your dean confirmed it."

"Not that we disbelieved," Jordil interrupted.

"No. Not that," Master Bennett agreed, "but it was still hard to reconcile. We remember you as a Novice, who could barely walk down the street unaided, and then we're getting accounts of your martial exploits and how you're hobnobbing with royalty."

Cam forced a chuckle, and while Master Bennett didn't mean any harm, his comment was still vaguely insulting. But those petty feelings were also unworthy, and Cam easily set them aside. Hopefully, it meant his anger was leaving him, and he responded to Master Bennett's comment. "That's not even the half of it. I have a lot to tell."

The four of them went to the seating arrangement in the front room with Cam and Charity sharing the couch, seated close enough that their legs touched. Their proximity earned another set of raised eyebrows from Master Bennett and Jordil.

"We're courting," Charity said, having noticed their awareness.

Master Bennett's gaze went from one of them to the other in momentary surprise and consideration. "I see. You truly do have a lot to tell us."

Cam gave an abbreviated account of his first year in the Ephemeral Academy, but even a shortened version took well over an hour.

Jordil was shaking his head only minutes into the explanation, and he kept on doing so at every new adventure. "I can't believe you lanced a boil."

Cam smiled. "There's a lot more to tell, like those first four years when we were thought to have died."

He told of Weld Plain's treachery, Hearth, and Thor but left alone the notion that the voices who had saved them from Rabisu were Rukh and Jessira or that he was favored by the Holy Servants in any way. The rest of the tale unfolded, and he spoke of Mote, battling kaijus, meeting Shimala and Coruscant, and returning to Salvation.

By then, dead silence had fallen over the room, and Jordil and Master Bennett stared at him, their gazes unblinking. Cam shifted under their regard, which held too much awe and even a hint of reverence. He was unworthy of either.

Master Bennett cleared his throat. "I can see the book from Fetch Devile served you better than I might have ever hoped."

Cam smiled in remembrance. Fetch Devile. It had been a long time since he'd thought about the man, whose book and instructions had saved his life. It had also been Fetch's aphorism—All is Ephemera, and Ephemera is All—that Cam had adopted as a perfect distillation of his philosophy and theology.

"What do you plan on doing next?" Jordil asked.

"I'm having dinner with Pharis' family and Darik's tonight," Cam said. He caught Master Bennett and Jordil sharing a strangely knowing look, but couldn't understand why, even as he empathed their doubt and humor. Shaking off the observation, he continued. "After that, I think we'll stay here in Traverse for a while. There's more to show Charity and Pan. Afterward, we'll rejoin the rest of Light Squad in the Sinanes. We have to Advance if we want to defeat the rest of the rakshasas."

Master Bennett shook his head, his expression one of sorrow and dismay. "You've set a mighty task for yourself. You don't think you've done enough in this war?"

Cam smiled again, this time faint and without humor. The rakshasas of Salvation were only the beginning. The larger war would include Mote. The promise Cam had made upon escaping Petala—a vow to those like Tulip—was to bring battle to the Great Rakshasas and end their reign. He wanted to see Mote freed from their tyranny.

Everyone would tell him it was a foolish endeavor, which is why Cam had never mentioned it to anyone, not even Pan or Charity. But there it was. All he needed to do was Advance past Sage to Divine and beyond. Thor had shown the way, so why not Cam?

46

Cam glanced out the windows, surprised at how late it was. The sun hung at a few hours past mid-afternoon, which meant he'd been talking to Jordil and Master Bennett for hours, and while Charity had made a few contributions to the conversation, she'd largely remained silent throughout. He smiled at her in appreciation, grateful that she'd never once complained about being bored. And surely she must have been, at least to some extent.

She smiled at him in return, seeming to understand the reason for his expression.

Still, it was time to head home. Cam rose to his feet, prepared to make his departure. "We've been gone a long time, and I want to check in on the old man and Pan."

Master Bennett and Jordil both hastily rose to their feet as well. "Of course," Master Bennett replied. "We've kept you here long enough." Next, he addressed Charity, wearing an apologetic expression. "Please pardon our ramblings, young woman. I'm sure you have better things to do than listen to us babble on and on for so long."

Charity smiled at him. "I honestly didn't mind. I've been told a lot about Traverse and the people Cam loves. It's nice to see the reality matching the description."

Cam chuckled. "On that note, it's time to leave." He halted when a great idea occurred to him. "Do y'all want to stop by and have dinner with us?"

Jordil laughed. "Do you really think you'll be able to have a quiet evening with your family tonight?"

Cam frowned, unsure why that wouldn't be possible.

"You are a child of Traverse," Jordil explained. "Pharis read your letters to everyone who would listen. We all heard of your exploits and victories, your leadership of Light Squad, and Advancements. Everyone who once called your family no-good Folde quickly found a reason to change their tunes."

Cam grimaced, seeing what Jordil had meant. "And the hypocrites are going to want time with me."

Master Bennett took his hands, giving him a sympathetic smile. "You're a Crown, my boy, and as Jordil said, you're a child of Traverse. They don't want to just talk to you. In a way, they want forgiveness from you."

"And why is that Cam's responsibility?" Charity asked. She didn't sound angry, but there was a challenging note in her voice. "Why should Cam have to assuage their guilt? They made their beds. Let them sleep in them."

The room fell silent as Master Bennett and Jordil eyed Charity in nervousness. Right now, she looked like a fierce lioness ready to defend her cub.

Cam hid a grimace of irritation. He didn't need or want anyone's protection, and he pulled Charity away from Jordil and Master Bennett. "It's fine. If the folks here want something from me, I can at least listen."

The emotional temperature cooled, and Charity inclined her head to Master Bennett and Jordil. "My apologies. In the time I've known Cam, I've found him to be nothing but honorable, generous, and caring of others, even when they don't deserve it. He is worthy of far more than he often recognizes, but he's also been betrayed by too many people. No one, especially those who treated him so shabbily, should dare demand anything from him."

Master Bennett held up his hands like he was trying to placate Charity. "You won't have an argument from me, but that is his decision, is it not?"

The temperature would have risen again, but Cam placed a hand on Charity's shoulder, arresting whatever she might have said. Master Bennett was right. This was his choice. "You really think that's what they want? I ran into Maria Echo. She wasn't exactly generous in her praise toward me." He explained their brief interaction. "I actually feel sorry for Tormick Echo for having married her."

Jordil shook his head, staring at the ground and muttering, "There's something wrong with that woman. Her mind isn't right."

Master Bennett nodded. "Forget Maria. She isn't representative of the rest of the families who ran you off."

Cam mused. Maybe Master Bennett was right. Besides which, he'd already forgiven Ingold and Suse, received forgiveness from the Fairs. So what were a few more people to add to the tally? "I'll talk to them. Just tell me when."

Master Bennett cleared his throat. "They've already planned a feast in your honor." He smiled, abashed. "It's tonight."

Cam sighed. He should have known. That must have been why everyone was rushing around that he'd noticed earlier. He only wished he'd been listening in on their conversations. Then this whole feast in his honor wouldn't have come as such a surprise. "What time?" he asked.

"In a few hours. At twilight. The whole village is turning out."

Cam nodded acceptance, although he still wasn't looking forward to the feast tonight. He'd really just wanted a quiet meal with the family, but apparently even Crowns didn't get all their wishes. "I guess we'll be there then. See y'all tonight, but I really do want to check on Pan and my dad like I mentioned."

He and Charity set off with Jordil and Master Bennett following them onto the front porch to see them off. Cam halted, though, when he saw what was going on. During the time he'd been talking to Jordil and Master Bennett, the village green had filled up with tables and chairs and tents. Families were bringing in food, and young children ran around while their parents gossiped.

Cam eyed the scene in antipathy.

"Should we Blend?" Charity asked.

Cam shook his head. "We can't always be Blended." Seconds later, his resolve was tested when they entered the village green and folks halted whatever they were doing, bowing to him. "Or maybe we should Blend," he muttered.

Charity chuckled. "It'll be fun. You're the returning hero. Just imagine how much the hypocrites will hate it."

Cam grunted, not having it in him to share her amusement, just wanting to get through the square as swiftly as possible.

Just as they crossed the green, someone called out. "Cam Folde!"

Cam spied the speaker, Pivot Stump, a tall, heavy-set man who was trending toward having the same roundness and receding hairline as his father, the mayor. And skulking behind him was Barth Lord, Pivot's friend and sycophant, who'd always been nondescript and remained so.

Both men had been nothing but jackholes toward Cam when they'd been children, and their welcoming smiles had him grimacing inwardly. *Fragging hypocrites.* Pivot and Barth had never liked him and no doubt, their current smiles were as fake as their intent, which was just to be seen with him. Anything to impress the people.

Still, Cam held a leash to his irritation, recalling what Suse and Ingold, the wives of these two men had said to him only hours earlier. He plastered a neutral expression on his face and briefly inclined his head toward the approaching duo. "Pivot. Barth."

Pivot's smile flickered before reforming. "Look at you, Cam Folde. Returned to us as a hero. A Crown." His eyes went to Charity, and he bowed to her. "And with a woman more beautiful than any who has ever walked the streets of Traverse."

A vindictive streak lit inside Cam. "Allow me to introduce Charity Kazar, the daughter of Sage-Duke Ahktav Kazar."

The instant the words left his mouth, Pivot and Barth were tripping over themselves trying to bow and scrape to Charity.

Cam chuckled darkly to himself, but he quickly tired of the spectacle. "What do you want, Pivot?"

Pivot's smile fully fell away while Barth laughed nervously. "What do I want?" Pivot repeated. "I just wanted to welcome you home, Traverse's favorite son." He gestured toward the village green. "My father would have come, but he's overseeing the celebration on your behalf. That's all I want."

Barth, still laughing nervously, hesitantly stepped forward, gaze flicking to Pivot, like he was asking the other man's permission. "Ingold told me what you said to her. I wanted to thank you for that. It meant everything to her." He held his hand out, an offering of peace. "And I wanted to let you know she isn't alone in her feelings. I treated you bad, and I'm sorry for that."

Not bothering to glance at Barth's hand, Cam's attention instead went to the woven world and his skill with empathy, which told a person's true intentions far better than any words or expressions they might offer. And what his talents told him—the emotions, smells, sights, and tastes linking him to Barth—was that the other man, as mousy and insecure as he was, spoke true and sincere. More, this offer of his had brought Barth to the very edge of his courage. Inside, he trembled in terror, honest in his recognition of how poorly he'd treated Cam and wishing he could take it back.

Cam's dislike for Barth melted. How could he hate someone who was trying so hard to make right what he'd made so wrong? He smiled at Barth, mustering every bit of warmth he could manage and shook Barth's hand. "It's good seeing you, Barth. Tell Ingold I said hello." He addressed Pivot, whose honesty and remorse wasn't the same as Barth's. "Tell your father I look forward to the celebration. We have to go."

He took Charity's hand, and they departed from the two men,

who continued to stare after them, whispering in what they probably thought was a quiet fashion, but the words carried to Cam's Crown-Advanced hearing.

"Can you believe he forgave me?" Barth asked, sounding stunned. "And did you feel the power coming off of him? Off both of them?"

"I felt it," Pivot said, his voice less enthusiastic.

Barth didn't seem to notice, though, and his voice went rapturous. "And he's ours. From our town. Our blood. Us. Our very own Crown." His voice went higher, like he'd just had a fantastic notion. "What if he Advances to Sage? Just think how amazing that would be!"

Charity must have been listening in as well because she laughed. "I think you have a new devotee."

Cam rolled his eyes. He'd never wanted anyone in awe of him, especially anyone from Traverse. "Just what I needed."

Cam could have done without the celebration in his honor, but any chance for him to simply fly off on his own—a notion that had been whispering in the back of his mind—was snuffed out when his daddy learned about it. In his father's way of reckoning, the fine folks here had this coming. Karma had bitten them bad, especially since they'd always treated the Foldes as being barely a rung higher than pond scum.

Now look at them. Willing to bend the knee before one of his children. Someone who had achieved something grander than anyone else from this humble hamlet.

"My boy battled rakshasas," his daddy had said. "He's rubbed shoulders with the sons and daughters of Sage-Dukes and earned their respect. He's a Crown. Well ain't that something special? And what have their children done in this life? Nothing, that's what. Let them eat crow."

Cam might have wished that his father had a better reason in mind for attending the festival, but he also couldn't fault him much. His daddy hadn't lived an easy life, lost himself for a long spell in drink and poor choices, but in the end, all of his children had grown up alright when no one had figured they would. So, if his daddy wanted to thumb his nose at those who'd spent their lives doing the same to him, who was Cam to argue?

Those were Cam's thoughts as he paced alongside his father, Charity, and Pan through the darkened village. Not a candle was lit, and all was quiet except for the crickets and critters in the surrounding woods. A summer breeze, easy and clean, blew off the Barr River, and the earthy aromas of farms and fields carried through the unusually empty town.

Cam frowned. Where was everyone? Surely they hadn't all gathered at the village green already? He stretched his senses and realized they'd done exactly that.

"Are you ready?" Pan asked, pulling Cam out of his thoughts.

"Ready to show them what a no-good Folde can manage?" Cam's daddy asked with a grin.

Cam just wanted to get this over with, and he grunted in reply.

Charity elbowed him. "Please don't. I've heard enough grunts from Card to last a lifetime."

They turned a corner and entered the village green where they were met by an eruption of cheers. Everyone truly had gathered here with enough tables, seating, and food for all. A number of Ephemeral lamps had been strung on ropes throughout the green and its perimeter, lighting the space to brightness. The smell of roasted meats and vegetables filled the air, and Cam's stomach growled. He'd missed lunch.

"What are we supposed to do?" Cam asked.

"I think we go there first," Charity said, indicating the far end of the green, where Mayor Stump had gathered with some important and rich townsfolk on a low stage. They beamed, grinning wide and clapping like maniacs, as if the cheers were directed toward them.

"*Smile,*" Charity sent as they strode forward. "*Wave to the crowd.*" She took her own advice, and after a beat, Pan and Cam's daddy did the same.

Cam rolled his eyes, hating the attention but did as Charity suggested anyway. He waved desultorily to the crowd and plastered what he knew was a pained smile on his face.

"*Stop it. You look constipated,*" Charity said. "*Smile naturally.*"

"*I can't when I feel like an idiot.*"

"*You should try,*" Pan said. "*The moment you agreed to this celebration, it became for the people of Traverse, not you. This is what they need.*"

Cam realized that—once again—the fine panda-person was right. "*You're pretty smart, you know that?*"

Pan winked at him. "*I know.*"

Cam exhaled and imagined the tension exiting out of him, pretended he was relaxed and loose. His smiles and waves became more natural well before they reached Mayor Stump, who directed them to join him on the stage. There, the mayor presented Cam with a piece of paper, an award of some kind, and gave a long-winded speech that seemed mostly about himself rather than Cam. Mayor Stump finally wound down when the crowd began to hiss.

Then it was Cam's turn. He hadn't expected to have to say any words, but he managed to fumble through a hastily concocted speech without embarrassing himself too much. Charity even gave him an approving nod, while his daddy smiled like he'd never heard anything finer in his entire life.

"Now what?" Cam asked once he stepped off the stage.

"Now you greet your loyal subjects," Charity said. "Come on." Taking his hand, she led him into the gathered crowd. Pan joined them, and together the trio of Crowns made their way through the throng, shaking hands, talking to folks, and even kissing a few babies.

"He kissed my girl," one mother exclaimed. "She's blessed." From that moment on, everyone wanted their children kissed by Cam, and even better, by all three Crowns.

It took a long while getting through it all, but there came a point when they reached Pharis and her husband, Farmer Marcus, a man with hair gone to gray early. He was a decade older than Pharis and a widower prior to their marriage, and Cam gave the man a brief hug, thanking him for all he'd done for Pharis.

Farmer Marcus shuffled his feet, staring at the ground momentarily before lifting his gaze to meet Cam's. "With all due respect, sir, your thanks ain't necessary. Pharis is the one who saved me. She's my life's greatest blessing, she is." He indicated two children, a boy and girl, who were hiding behind Pharis' skirts. "I'd never have had these two rascals if not for her."

"Come meet your uncle," Pharis said, tugging the children forward. They had her smile and eyes and wore identical shy and tentative expressions. "This is Camford. He's named after you," Pharis said, indicating the boy. "And this is Pheala."

Cam bent low to them, offering each of them a handshake. "Hello. I'm your uncle Cam."

Camford, the older of the two, shook his hand, his features firming. "I was named after you. Does that mean I'll become a Crown?"

Cam smiled. "Is that what you want?"

Camford considered the question for a few seconds before nodding vigorously.

"I want to become a Sage," Pheala said, brave now that her brother had shown her it was safe to talk to the stranger who was their uncle.

Cam faced her. "I know a few Sages. The best was an Awakened Beast, a dog."

Pheala pointed to Pan. "Like him?"

Pan bent low to her, smiling in his cute way. "I'm afraid I'm a panda bear. I like bamboo." He leaned forward, pretending to sniff her. "Do you have any?" He kept sniffing, inching closer. "It's my favorite."

Pheala chuckled, and she began to squirm and laugh when Pan's furry face was pressed against her cheeks. He continued to sniff around her, and she laughed harder, grabbing Pan's face and holding him still. "You're silly. I like you."

Pan flicked his ears and grinned. "Life's too short to be serious all the time. And I like you, too."

"I like her," Camford said, indicating Charity. "She's pretty." An instant later, he darted behind Pharis, burying his face in her skirts.

Everyone laughed, which only had Camford squirming deeper into his mother's skirts.

Cam took pity on the boy. "I'm glad you think she's pretty," he said. "I think she's pretty, too. Do you want to meet her?"

A furious shake of Camford's head was followed by an indistinct mumble as to whether Cam would be marrying Charity.

Cam glanced at Charity, wondering if it was too soon to be thinking about those kinds of matters. "I'm not sure," he eventually allowed.

This got Camford pulling free of Pharis' skirts. "Why not? She's beautiful."

"Sometimes beauty isn't enough," Cam said, thinking of Maria's ugly heart. Thank Devesh that Charity wasn't anything like the other woman.

Charity knelt in front of Camford. "If we do get married, you have to promise to come to the wedding."

Her words inspired Camford to fully pull away from his mother's skirts, and his features went solemn. "I promise to be there."

"We'll all be there," Pharis added.

"I'll bring bamboo," Pheala declared.

Pan feigned being overwhelmed, a hand to his heart. "Bless you, child."

They laughed again before moving on, but not before Pharis got a promise out of them to come to her house for breakfast in the morning.

Soon after, they discovered Darik and Cam's daddy. Cam observed them from afar. The two of them and Marlinth had been seated at places of honor close to the mayor's stage, and they were busy accepting the congratulations of many well-wishers. Cam scoffed. "Most of those people never wanted anything to do with my brother or my daddy back when I lived here."

"I hear you," Pan said, "but they do now. And maybe it's because they're trying to be better people. Be charitable."

Cam rolled his eyes. "Yes, oh wise Sage."

Pan grinned in that cute way of his. "Give it enough time, and I'll get there."

"We'll get higher," Cam said. "Birch's Nullity will help us shorten the time."

Pan's expression soured to sorrow. "I miss him. I miss the lovebirds, too."

"So do I," Cam said, wishing once again that the leonine rakshasa was with them. He'd have loved this gathering. But since it could never be, Cam reaffirmed his promise to destroy the ones who had killed Birch. Not just Nailing, but all like him, including the Great Rakshasas.

"Enough of that, you two," Charity scolded. "This is supposed to be a celebration. Come on. Let's say hello to your father and brother." She looped her arms with them, pulling them forward.

Cam gave an exaggerated sigh. "Yes, dear."

"Will she always tell us what to do?" Pan asked.

Cam mentally shrugged. *"Maybe? Probably?"*

"In that case, you should go ahead and marry her. She's already acting like your wife."

Charity harrumphed. *"I heard that."*

47

The feast lasted well into the evening with plenty of drinking and dancing, and while Cam didn't do any of the former, of the latter, he found himself a popular figure. Lots of women wanted a turn with him on the cleared area that served as the dance floor. Everyone had a grand time—Pan playing flute with the other musicians and Charity also a highly sought-after dance partner—but eventually the celebration ended, and Cam led Charity and Pan back to the house where he had grown up.

They whispered as they made their way inside, making sure to keep quiet since Cam's daddy was already fast asleep. Charity took Pharis' old bedroom, while Cam and Pan hauled out their bedrolls and settled in the front room. They were both asleep in moments, all of them waking up early the next morning and going over to Pharis' place for breakfast. It wasn't anything fancy—just eggs, toast, and fried potatoes—but it was home cooking, shared with family, including Darik's, which meant it was just fine.

"What do you want to do now?" Pan asked after they left Pharis' home.

"I want to show y'all the rest of the town," Cam said, including one place in particular.

He led them along Traverse's brick-lined streets, and based on the clanging ringing out from his workspace, Master Carlson, the town's hardworking farrier, was already hard laboring. Cam nodded to some folks who dipped their heads his way, which seemed to be the way of the town. Everywhere he went, people paused to greet him in some fashion, which he didn't mind as much as he had yesterday. Following the feast and dancing, only a few people still stared at him in awe.

"Where did you say we're going?" Charity asked when they exited the walls surrounding Traverse.

"You'll see," Cam said, leading them to a bend in the Barr River where a weeping willow leaned out over the water.

Shrubs crowded the base of the tree, and based on a quick inspection, no one would figure there to be any room under the willow. But Cam knew the secret way past the bushes. He shoved aside the limbs of a rhododendron and squeezed inside, pushing forward, wincing at branches and brambles catching at his clothing. He smiled to himself, though. This had been a lot easier to do when he'd been smaller.

He eventually reached a clear area nestled under the arms of the willow. Opening out on a view of the Barr River, it was a small space but large enough for four children to dream. The water softly lapped the riverbank, and the world seemed to sway as he fell back into his memories. So much had happened to Cam in this secret hideaway. From this spot, he recalled the times spent skipping stones with Jordil and Tern, laughing at something clever that Lilia had said, the silly discussions that had once seemed so profound, or just lazing away a summer day.

Charity and Pan had followed him inside, the three of them barely fitting.

"This is where we used to hide so we didn't have to work," Cam said without turning around.

"You and your friends?" Charity asked. "Jordil, Lilia, and Tern?"

Cam nodded. "This is where it all began." He described that summer afternoon of blue skies and puffy clouds when Lilia had asked him, Jordil, and Tern if they wanted to dive a newly discovered Pathway. "We'd have been the first, and we figured it meant we'd be mighty."

He had told the story before to both of them, but this had been the place where it had all started for him, his Way into Divinity, which made it seem fresh and necessary. Charity took his hand while Pan leaned into him on the other side, resting his head on Cam's shoulder.

"It's peaceful," Charity said. "I can see why this place would be special."

Cam hugged them both, lost in reflections of what might have been if they'd never gone on that Pathway. Lilia and Tern would still be alive.

"We can't change the past," Pan said, somehow guessing at his disturbed thoughts. "We shouldn't want to. It only leads to heartache."

Cam smiled at his friend. "How'd you know what I was thinking?"

Pan gave him his inimitable grin. "Because that's what you tend to do: you brood."

Cam laughed, recognizing the truth in Pan's statement. "Sometimes I can't help it."

They stood there for a while, reflecting on all that they had experienced together in Light Squad before eventually departing. Cam glanced back at the willow, grateful for the tree and the secret space under its limbs where he, Jordil, Lilia, and Tern had spent so many hours. He exhaled, breathing out, and it felt like some peace stole into his soul, replacing the simmering anger he'd built up while in Mote.

"There's another place I want to show you," Cam said. He led them back into Traverse where they cut across the village to a different exit where a cobblestone road led into Marnin Forest and its cool shadows. "It's probably quicker if we flew," Cam said when the road became a gravel path. He recalled the last time he had made this journey, it had taken most of a day.

They lifted in the air, and Cam searched for landmarks, quickly finding what he was looking for. There was the cutoff, and a couple hundred yards further along, a rivulet that emptied into a larger stream.

They set off with Charity flying close. "You're taking us to the meadow, aren't you?"

Cam shouldn't have been surprised that she figured it out. He smiled. "I think you know me too well."

She offered a tight-lipped smile. "Pan was right. You do brood, usually over what you did wrong or can't change."

Cam didn't reply. They'd already arrived, a minutes-long flight for what had been hours of hiking as a youth. They alighted next to the stream where sunlight glistened and shadows dappled the water. Golden and silver fish, no larger than his hand, swam in the eddies and shallows. And the water endlessly murmured over submerged stones.

But—now as before when he'd been fifteen—what held Cam's attention was the small clearing across the bank. Wildflowers waved in a gentle wind, and where the Pathway had once stood, there now grew a young cedar, looking likely to become a giant of the forest. Otherwise, the clearing was so prosaic with nothing unique to distinguish it from any other woodland meadow.

But for Cam, when he viewed the sight, his mind went back to the past and to how much his life had changed and the price needed for the supposed glory that had everyone in Traverse bowing to him.

"This is where it happened?" Pan asked. "Your first Pathway to Grace?"

Cam nodded, expression tight with pain, reflecting on the foolishness of his youthful self. "We were so sure this was the only way a body could Advance. Diving a Pathway." He shook his head. "We should have all died in there."

"Why are we here, Cam?" Charity asked. She hesitated, taking his hand. "You weren't to blame for anything that happened here."

Cam wasn't sure she was right. It had been his idea to come to the Pathway but her question had him thinking. Why was he here? Was it a calling to see the clearing again? For reasons he couldn't rightly explain? Or maybe he just needed a walk down this part of his past. There were so many mixed emotions from this meadow. Without it, nothing he'd achieved in life would have likely happened. And without it, two of his closest friends from childhood would still be alive.

But like Pan had mentioned earlier, he couldn't change the past and shouldn't want to. Better to accept that and view the meadow without allowing the bitter recriminations of his youthful mistakes continue to haunt his present. He'd fixed his mind on forgiving himself many times in the past, but being back at the meadow, this time, the understanding seemed to anchor itself more firmly in his heart.

"This is where my life began," he said to Charity. "This is where I began my first steps on the Way into Divinity, and I'm glad for it. I wasn't always, but being with you and Pan, I'm happy for who I've become." He took her other hand in his. "And I'm glad you could come see my home and the places that made me."

Charity shook her head. "These weren't the places that defined you, Cam. This might be where you started your life, but you were defined through hardship and heartache. I saw most of it. And you've come out of it a good person."

Cam gazed at her, inhaling deep and exhaling slow. She was right, just like Pan so often was. More of the anger seeped out of him, and he was grateful.

They returned to Traverse a short while later, and Cam introduced Pan to Jordil and Master Bennett. There was also time to visit Midwife Spenser and Master Moltin and later on, they had dinner at Darik's home.

That became how they spent the next few days: Cam showing Charity and Pan about and getting reacquainted with the village of his birth. They also had many lunches and dinners to attend since most everyone wanted to host the three of them for a meal. In truth, they could have eaten five times a day, there were so many invitations, but Cam culled the numbers, making sure to always have time for his family and friends. It wouldn't have done him any good to come home to Traverse and not spend as much time as possible with those who meant the most to him.

On their last night in Traverse, after Charity had already gone to bed in Pharis' old room, Cam and Pan sat out on the front porch, gently swaying back and forth on a pair of matching rocking chairs, viewing the darkened and hushed village. Diffuse beams of light, silver and ethereal, shone from a half-moon that streamed through a scattering of clouds while the stars lighting the heavens' firmament twinkled. Crickets chirped, fireflies lit the air, and the occasional spattering of conversation and laughter drifted on a whispering breeze that wafted the fragrances of rose and lavender. It was a lovely night.

Cam wished Birch could have been there to see it. The old-headed rakshasa would have loved it. He'd always wondered about the beauty of the night sky.

He made the observation to Pan, who sighed. "I miss him. I miss the lovebirds, too. I hope they're happy in the Sinanes."

"I'm sure they are. They're with Saira. She'll take care of them."

"I know she will. She's a good person." Their brief conversation listed to a halt as they stared in contemplative silence at the bucolic village. Pan spoke again. "I've had to use Saira's healing meditation every night since we came back to Salvation."

Cam had done the same. Sorrow over Birch's death—the tragedy of it—clung to him like ragged webbing, and he wouldn't be rid of it with a simple shake of his arms and legs. It would take time, but being home with his family and friends had helped. So had Saira's meditation, and he figured the combination was the reason he'd made so much progress at taming his perpetually bubbling anger. It was down to a simmer now, no longer roiling, and there were even times when he felt its blessed absence. He longed to be rid of it altogether.

However, he hadn't realized Pan had shared any of that emotional pain. "I didn't know you were hurting so bad. I'm sorry."

Pan shrugged. "It's not like you and your rage, but…" He exhaled heavily. "I'm tired, just like you. I want peace and tranquility, but I'm afraid that's not what our future holds. Birch seemed to realize it. Maybe that's why he was always talking about dying."

Cam snorted. "Birch always talked about dying because he was afraid of hope and wanting a good life."

"He deserved both."

"Yes, he did. And so do we. You especially." Cam viewed his best friend, his brother. "We have battles still needing to be fought, but when it's done, we'll get to lay down our labor. We'll have peace. War won't always be our lives."

His words didn't seem to comfort Pan. "More fighting then. Always more fighting." The panda shook his head. "Why do we always have to wait to be happy? What if we could be happy now? Some say that every moment is a blessing and should be lived to its fullest. What do you think?"

Cam didn't have an answer. Pan's statement was a nice enough sentiment, but it was also a luxury only granted to those who lived in a world at peace. That wasn't Salvation or Mote. The rakshasas were out there. Nailing wouldn't quit just because of this one defeat. He'd keep coming. So would Coruscant, Simmer, and Shimala. None of them would stop until they got what they wanted: dominion and domination of Salvation and making the place the same as Mote.

Abiding, happy and content, while that happened wasn't Cam's way. But how to get Pan to see it? Was there even a way? Cam wasn't sure, but he made a suggestion, hoping it would bring his friend some peace. "How about this: you let me worry about gaining justice for all those hurt by the rakshasas, and I'll let you call me out if I brood too hard?"

Pan shook his head, facing him. "Worrying about justice all the time is no way to live. Justice is a vague concept. With your anger, it's simply vengeance wearing a prettier dress."

Cam laughed, unable to help himself. The phrasing wasn't typical for something Pan would normally say. "Where did you read that?"

Pan grinned. "Birch said it to me."

"Birch?"

Pan nodded. "It was in his book about the Gunas."

"The one Kiwi and Sprite ate?"

"That's the one, and that was one of the concepts in the book: about justice and vengeance, and how passion—Rajas—needs a reason.

Vengeance isn't a good one."

A stirring of annoyance flickered to life, but Cam squashed it. The conversation might be uncomfortable, but Pan wouldn't have stirred it up if it wasn't important. So rather than give in to his irritation, Cam considered their discussion in a fresh light, eventually grunting acknowledgment. "I can see why vengeance would be a dark reason for wanting justice."

He hoped that would be the end of the matter, but Pan wasn't done yet. "Then what will be your reason for fighting? Is it only going to be worrying about justice and vengeance?"

"I didn't say it was just for vengeance. I said it was for justice."

Pan eyed him, the skepticism obvious. "You need to tell yourself the truth about why you want to defeat the rakshasas and the Sage-Dukes who betrayed us. It isn't for justice alone."

Once again, the annoyance flared, and once again, Cam snuffed it out, glad at how easily that ability came. The week spent in Traverse had truly been a balm for his soul. And with his fresh quietness came the need to find a fresh perspective. "I'll think on it," he eventually said to Pan. "I'll find a better reason."

"I'm going to hold you to it," Pan said, his words a solemn vow.

48

The next morning came far too soon. Cam didn't want to go. There was a serenity to Traverse, of being home, surrounded by family, that he missed and didn't want to lose. Cam could feel himself healed, down deep in his bones and through his soul. He'd reconnected with his family and friends and was content even if it was time to rejoin the world. Nailing and the rest of the rakshasas still had to be crushed.

Nonetheless, even as he promised to come back as soon as he could, the heartache already creeping over him never eased. He made his goodbyes amidst a bunch of crying and vows to return sooner than eight years.

"You got yourself a good woman," his daddy said, indicating Charity. "Don't frag it up. Get yourself married before your old man has to take his final sleep."

Cam promised to do his best while Charity hid a smile and snigger in the background.

Pharis hugged him. "Come back safe. I don't care if you never make it to Sage. Just come home." She wiped away tears.

Cam hugged her, squeezing her tight for just a moment before bending low to talk to Camford and Pheala. "It was good meeting you two." He hugged them both. "Take care of each other and your momma. Listen to what she tells you. She's one of the wisest people I know and coming from a Crown, that means something."

Camford nodded solemnly, vowing to do so, while Pheala sniffed and hugged him again.

Next came Jordil and Masters Bennett and Moltin.

"It was good seeing you again," Jordil said, giving him a hug. "We'll be missing you."

"Take care, lad," Master Bennett said, hugging him as well.

"Next time you come by, I'll let you borrow a book I found," Master Moltin said, shaking Cam's hand vigorously. "It's about men and women—Immortal Great Souls—perpetually reborn into a fantastical city where they have to travel deep into a terrible Realm and fight in order to save their true world."

Cam smiled and nodded at Master Moltin's enthusiasm. His one-time instructor loved books about the fantastical.

Finally, it was Darik's turn, and he simply lifted Cam off his feet. "Take care of yourself, Runt. And listen to Dad. You have a fine woman next to you. Don't frag it up. Marry her, if she's willing."

"Take your own advice," Cam said with a laugh when Darik set him down.

"I did," Darik said with a grin as he displayed his wedding band.

A final few farewells, and Cam lifted off the ground, waving a final goodbye to his gathered family and friends before joining Pan and Charity, who already hovered high in the sky.

"Did you have a good time?" Charity sent to Cam once they had cleared Traverse's fields.

Cam smiled. *"I had a great time."* He glanced at Pan. *"What about you? You ever think of going home to the Diamond Mountains and seeing your folks like we talked about?"*

Pan considered the question for a moment, shaking his head. *"I'm not ready."*

"Why not?"

Pan shrugged. *"The prophecy. I guess I'm still angry about it. Whether my family meant it or not, I spent most of my life convinced that fulfilling the prophecy was my only worth in life."*

Cam pursed his lips in understanding.

"Maybe one day you'll forgive them," Charity said.

"Do you think you'll ever forgive your father?" Pan asked her.

Charity shook her head. *"That's different, though. My father is a traitor. Your family was merely misguided."*

"Misguided," Pan mused. *"It still hurt."*

Cam gave his friend a mental hug. *"It won't always hurt so bad. And when it doesn't and you're ready, I'll be with you."*

Pan smiled, and even mind-to-mind, he managed to do so in his infectiously cute way. *"I'd like that."*

"How about after we Advance to Sage?" Cam suggested.

Pan refused to commit. *"Maybe."*

Charity cautioned them. *"Advancing to Sage isn't easy, nor is it likely to be quick."*

She was right, but she was also wrong. *"I have Birch's Nullity,"* Cam said, wishing that it wasn't the case. He'd rather his friend was still alive. *"We'll have the mindscape."*

"The mindscape?" Charity asked. *"Can anyone else join?"*

Cam shrugged. *"I don't see why not, and with it, we should be able to condense five years into five months. We'll Advance faster than you know."*

Charity shook her head. *"That still won't be enough time."*

"It is if seven of us are sharing the experience," Cam said. *"Then five years becomes thirty-five. It'll work. Back in Mote, that's how Pan and I Advanced. We figured out what was needed to Advance to Crown together. We taught one another in the mindscape. Teaching goes faster there because it's not just words but concepts we share, something beyond telepathy."*

"And Saira is already a Sage," Charity said, quickly connecting the dots. *"She could teach us."*

Cam smiled. *"Exactly. We'll all be Sages by summer's end."*

"You really think so?" Charity asked, still doubtful.

Cam nodded. *"Just wait and see. We'll get there."*

There wasn't much more to say after that, and they quickly picked up speed, the wind whistling as they whipped through the sky. A pair of red-tailed hawks floated on thermals, shrieking in startlement when the three of them raced past. Clouds ripped apart in the wind of their flight, and the ground below might have been a blur of greens, grays, and browns had Cam still been an Adept or even a Glory. But as a Crown, everything was crisp and distinct. He pondered how it might appear once he Advanced to a Sage, and not just the typically visible world, but the woven one, too.

Then they were over the ocean, a vast and seemingly endless plain of rolling waves, cresting whitecaps, and blues of various shades: indigo, cobalt, and cerulean. They swept over a number of uninhabited islands, some of which appeared to be forested emeralds amidst the sea's sapphire, and others grew nothing but scrub and cacti, resembling a desert's desolateness. They also came across pods of dolphins leaping and playing, and Cam reminded himself to ask Avia if the creatures got along with orcas.

All the while, they kept a steady heading, traveling all morning and afternoon, finally stopping for the day upon an isolated island with the evening sun heralding night's fall. There, they set up camp, and a small fire was soon crackling merrily. Supper consisted of fish from the sea and some hardtack and dried vegetables that the villagers from Traverse had gifted them for their travels.

Afterward, Cam sat on the beach, staring at the ocean and the night sky. Moonlight scintillated on the water, a reflection of the uncountable stars in the heavens. The waves susurrated against the shore, regular and hypnotic, the melody melding with Pan's soft fluting. Cam was soon lulled to peace, and his mind drifted, relaxed as he thought of nothing but the quiet of the night.

Charity, who'd been taking a walk further along the beach, returned to camp, dropping down next to him. She tucked close, like it was right and natural, and he put his arm around her shoulders. "It's so beautiful here," she said. "Serene. I wouldn't mind taking it easy getting to the Sinanes if this is what we have to look forward to at every day's end."

"How long do you figure it will take to get to the Sinanes if we keep today's pace?" Cam asked her.

She shrugged. "Four or five days. There's no rush. We can send to Saira that we'll be late. Let's just enjoy the quiet."

Cam smiled agreement, kissing the top of her head. *"Quiet sounds mighty fine."*

A few days later, the three of them coasted down to a small jewel of an island where they intended on halting their travel for the evening. They made camp on the golden sands of a crescent-moon cove where the Arylyn Ocean's bright blue waters glistened under the dying sun. At their backs spread a thick jungle and beyond the trees, there rose a single rugged mountain. Clouds like pearls draped the summit, while the shoulders bore a clothing of forest. The rocky peak cast a shadow over the cove.

"We should get to the Sinanes by tomorrow afternoon," Charity said, pulling Cam from his observations about the island.

Cam merely nodded acknowledgement, content to hold hands with Charity as they strolled in a comfortable silence, alone on the beach since Pan had wandered into the jungle, looking for bamboo. A stiff wind blustered, pulling at their clothing and rifling through their hair, and the gentle wash of waves rolling against the soft sand sounded like a lullaby.

Charity halted their walk and pointed to the horizon where the sky blazed with pinks, plums, and violets. "Let's watch the sunset."

Gulls soared over the waters, twisting and turning, and Cam had a vague notion of joining them. He loved to fly, but after the hours spent in the sky, he was tired. Besides, he wanted to share this moment with Charity.

They watched in quiet as the sun lowered. The first tip dipped below the waterline, then another small segment. Minutes later, it was over. The sun was gone, and twilight reigned over the island.

"We should head back," Cam suggested. "Pan will start wondering where we are."

"He can send to us telepathically," Charity reminded him. "Besides, I wanted to talk to you about something."

A niggle of worry wormed through Cam's stomach over whatever she wanted to discuss. Charity sounded serious, looked that way, too. "What is it?"

"What do you want for yourself? What makes you happy? Because I want that for you. You need it."

Cam blinked. Since coming back from Mote, while he wanted a future without fighting, of serenity, he'd never given much thought about happiness. He'd always figured any joy he had would be fleeting and not really available until he saw to the end of the rakshasa menace. What was the point when they were out there looking to do harm? Cam took Charity's hands in his, not sure how to answer since she clearly had a notion that he ought to be looking for happiness sooner than what he reckoned. He stared at her, pondering the words to say and settling on the truth, explaining his reasoning.

Charity shook her head, a sad smile on her face as she cupped his cheek. "That's no life. You deserve happiness. Now, not in some future. You've given enough. What do you want for yourself in order to be happy?"

What do you want for yourself? The question echoed in Cam's thoughts. He might have disregarded it, but Charity's expression was so intense and honest in her worry for him. He had to consider the question and give it proper weight. What did he want? A quick answer occurred to him. He wanted to find out what courting Charity might mean, fully and truly this time. While for some that might just be an excuse to fool around, Cam wasn't built that way. And neither was Charity.

But would that make him happy? Or did he need something deeper and more meaningful with her, marriage like what his daddy and

Darik suggested? Cam wasn't sure, and the uncertainty ate at him, spiraled through his heart. He imagined himself married to Charity and what that would mean for her. He had a war to fight, so how could he drag her into that? It wouldn't be fair. Charity had her own wants and desires, her own happiness to find.

So where did that put them? And what if there was someone already out there who liked the same things Charity did, laughed at life in the same way she did, and wanted something other than battling rakshasas? Would that make her happy? Was Charity's question her way of asking if there was anything more to Cam than his war against rakshasas? And was she wanting to know where she fit into that war?

"You're being awfully quiet," Charity said.

"I was thinking."

"About?"

Cam explained.

Charity shook her head. "None of those things are what you want for happiness. They're about what you think *I* might want. So again, what do you want?"

Cam still didn't have an answer. "Other than killing rakshasas?" He could only shrug helplessly. He wanted Charity, but in what way and why? It sounded wrong to not know the answer to either question.

Charity sighed, appearing disappointed. "Let's go back and see how Pan's doing."

Again, they walked back in silence, but this time it wasn't hand-in-hand, and the silence wasn't so comfortable. Rather it was heavy, pregnant with tension. The entire time, Cam continued to ponder what he wanted in life, and what that might mean for him and Charity.

Pan either didn't notice the tension or was kind enough to ignore it, and following a light meal of fruits, vegetables, and cheese, they settled in for the evening. Cam took the first watch and still deliberated on his future. Even the next morning, he did so when they resumed their trip.

His conversation with Charity lingered in his mind, long into the morning and throughout the afternoon. So lost was he in his thoughts, that he found himself surprised when they arrived at Tulara, the capital of the Sinanes, which breached the horizon in a startling suddenness.

Cam inhaled in startled wonder.

Tulara was gorgeous, consisting of steep hills of tree-shaded roads that bent and swept down to the aquamarine waters of a harbor where many boats and dhows were anchored. Deeper within the city, a plethora of fountains and plazas along with frescoed buildings of ornate architecture provided further beauty while further out, sculpted green hills, their slopes covered in a lush abundance of flowering shrubs, cupped the capital. And centered upon a hill overlooking it all rose Solstice Palace, the home of the Sage of the Sinanes. Made of marble, it resembled a white flower with blue tiles shaped like rose petals to serve as the roofing. A bevy of elegant towers—linked together by fanciful arcades—rose in various places like stamens.

It was magnificent. Tulara was every bit as stunning as Nexus but even larger, and Cam found himself overwhelmed by all there was to see. "I didn't expect it to be so… much."

He didn't realize he'd spoken aloud until Charity addressed him. "There are books about Rukh Shektan's home city of Ashoka. I'm told that Tulara was created to as closely resemble his home as could be managed."

"I can't imagine how Ashoka could be more beautiful," Cam said.

"It's more than beautiful," Pan said. "It's perfect." He pointed to a distant slope. "That hill is forested in bamboo."

Cam laughed. "You would notice something like that. But you're right, it is perfect. Or at least close enough that it doesn't matter."

"They're waiting for us," Charity said, indicating a number of figures waiting in one of the Solstice Palace's many courtyards. It was Light Squad. "I sent word ahead about when we'd arrive."

Cam viewed his friends. It had only been a little over a week since he'd last seen them, but he found himself grateful anew for their presence.

"You really think your mindscape can have each of us reach Sage?" Charity asked as they descended.

Cam shrugged. "There's only one way to find out." He paused a beat and grinned. "Hard work. We do that, and there's no chance we'll fail."

His answers elicited groans from both Charity and Pan.

"Hard work is your answer to everything," Pan complained.

"That's because it's usually the right answer. Besides, you complain now, but I bet you won't be complaining half as much when we Advance to Sage."

Pan's brow furrowed. "Why would I complain about Advancing to Sage?"

"Exactly. You wouldn't. Now, what do you say about having a reunion with our friends?"

Pan grinned in reply.

They alighted on the ground then, and the rest of Light Squad joined them. From atop a balustrade, Kiwi and Sprite launched themselves, chirping loudly before landing on Cam's shoulders.

"I missed you," Sprite said.

"We both missed you," Kiwi clarified, "but I missed you more."

Cam grinned, rubbing the chest feathers of the lovebirds. "I missed both of you, too." He addressed Light Squad, smiling wide. "Now, what did y'all do during your homecomings? No reason to be shy. Speak up."

Card groaned. "Not your drawl. It's worse than ever."

"Ain't it wonderful?"

"I still think it's charming," Charity said, kissing his cheek.

Jade pretended to boggle her eyes. "I do believe the world ended. Charity just kissed Cam, and he didn't flinch or flush."

Cam heard Jade's statement, but he wasn't listening. *What did he want for himself in order to be happy?* Charity's question. And the answer came to him, arriving like a bolt and shattering all his doubts and fears. Charity had risked her life for him, breached Hell on his behalf. In the face of such willing sacrifice, worries about what might or might not be fell away. He drew Charity into his arms and kissed her deep and full. The hoots and hollers of the rest of Light Squad were music to his ears. *"I want us,"* he sent to Charity. *"That's what I want for myself, in order to be happy."*

Charity offered him a teasing smile. *"And assuming I want you, what happens next? Marriage?"*

"Yes." The answer wasn't so hard once he stopped prying at every other possibility. Marriage to Charity was what he wanted. *"That and more."*

Charity cocked her head in question. *"What else?"*

Cam grinned. *"I want to discover what makes you happy."*

She smiled slowly, in dawning pleasure. *"Good answer."*

GLOSSARY

Alset: A Divine who achieved her Awareness through deep thinking and study.

Avia Koravail: An Awakened orca who is the adopted daughter of Sage-Duke Kelse Vail of Saban.

Badlands, the: A vast desert in Petala.

Barth Lord: Young man from Traverse. He is a friend of Pivot Stump.

Bender White: An Adept and merchant from Portage (in Hearth). Light Squad buys a sailboat from him.

Bendrill: An Adept Purified Master.

Birch Drang: A Crown from Mote.

Borile Defent: The Silver Sage of Weeping. Presumed to have been killed by Rainen Winder.

Bounded Seas: The oceans surrounding Hearth.

Braver Highway: Leads from the duchy capital of Charn along Bastion Lake and from there, down to the duchy capital of Codent.

Brewery Highway: A north-south road that runs from south of Traverse, curls south of the Diamond Mountains, and ends at Coal Pass.

Cam Folde: A Plasminian from the town of Traverse.

Card Wolver: A young nobleman from the duchy of Chalk. He comes from a long line of accomplished Ephemeral Masters.

Carver's Gorge: River gorge and rapids in Hearth.

Chandra: One of the only two emperors the continent of Golden has ever had. He is the great-grandson to the other emperor, Guptash.

Charity Kazar: A young noblewoman who is the daughter of Sage-Duke Ahktav Kazar of Maviro.

Coal Pass: Cuts through the southwestern Diamond Mountains and leads to Vivid Pass.

Corona: The Sage of the Fiery Sun. She was once an instructor to Sial.

Cougrail: The Sage of the Bloody Claw. Allied to Nailing at Surelend.

Crowns of Light: Rulers of Hearth in the absence of the Sages.

Crown Corun: A Crown of Light from Hearth.

Crown Parment: The Crown of Justice in Hearth.

Dander: Town-village where Cam and Pan originally Advance their Tangs as Novices. Later on, it is the site of a large battle where Cam Advances to Acolyte.

Darik Folde: Cam's brother. He's following in their father's footsteps at drunkenness.

Einton: A Divine who achieved his Awareness through deep thinking and study.

Ephemera: Mystical and mysterious particle that permeates all aspects of Creation.

Ephemeral Academy, the: The finest school on the continent of Golden on the instruction of Ephemera.

Ephemeral Master: General term for those on the Way into Divinity.

Erock Molde: An honorable Glory of the Purified Masters from Hearth.

Eveangel Grey: Jessira pretending to be a Glory and an instructor at the Ephemeral Academy. She taught Synapsia.

Farla Wearing: A Glory and Purified Master who captures Light Squad.

Farmer Sigmon: Kind-hearted farmer in Traverse.

Fetch Devile: Plasminian from a wealthy family in Maviro. Cam heals himself based on the instructions in Fetch's autobiography.

Gob and Nona Felt: Husband and wife in Dander.

Golden: A continent in the world of Salvation. It is where the Nine Duchies are located.

Gordeon the Crown: A historical figure. He was a Crown who was killed shortly after Advancing to Sage.

Gorn Higin: A short, stocky nobleman from Valkin, a place near the city of Chalk.

Graft Pubber: Owner of a store in Vacacy upon Hearth.

Great Rakshasas, the: The first rakshasas. Their Stage of Awareness is presumed to be Divine.
- **Coruscant:** Also known as the Sower of the Wind, the Wrecker of Hope, and the Far-Seeing General.
- **Simmer**
- **Shimala:** Also called the Merciless Deceiver, Mother of Lies, and Corruptor of Innocence. She is seen as an old crone and might be the greatest of the rakshasas.

Guptash: One of the only two emperors the continent of Golden has ever had. He is the great-grandfather to the other emperor, Chandra.

Haunt: The color of an Ephemeral Master's sclerae. It denotes their Stage of Awareness.

Honor: Jessira pretending to be an Awakened squirrel who gave Cam a tremendous gift in a Pathway to Grace.

Ingold Lord née Brest: A young woman from Traverse. She is a friend to Maria Echo née Benefield.

Jade Mare: A noblewoman and daughter of a fallen house from the duchy of Bastion.

Jame Solver: An Adept and Purified Master in Hearth who helps capture Light Squad.

Jordil Oil: An Adept from the town of Traverse. Widower who was married to Lilia Oil and remains a childhood friend of Cam Folde.

Kahreen Sala: A young noblewoman from an exceptionally wealthy family in the duchy of Bastion.

Lake Petala: A vast lake in Petala.

Light Squad: It is the squad in the Ephemeral Academy in which the members are sponsored by someone other than a Sage-Duke. It was also known as Squad Screwup.

Lilia Oil née Fair: A Novice from the town of Traverse. Married to Jordil Oil and childhood friend of Cam Folde.

Lord Font Queriam: A Crown and was the dean of the Ephemeral Academy during Light Squad's Novice year.

Locus, the: The area in the Badlands of Petala through which Ephemera wisps into Mote.

Maria Echo née Benefield: A beautiful young woman in Traverse with a heart of coal. Her family is wealthy.

Marigold Spenser: Old midwife and healer in Traverse.

Marta Lightwell: The daughter of Surelend's mayor.

Master Bennett: An Adept and teacher of Novices.

Master Carlson: The town farrier of Traverse.

Master Moltin: An Adept and general teacher in Traverse.

Mayor Amale Lightwell: The mayor of Surelend.

Mayor Gard Singer: The mayor of Dander.

Mayor Long Stump: The mayor of Traverse.

Merit Thens: A young nobleman and the son of Sage-Duchess Marsula Thens of Santh.

Mote: The Realm of the Great Rakshasas. Also called Hell by those from Salvation.

Nageena: The Sage of Whispering Scales. Allied to Nailing at Surelend but her true mistress is the Sage of Hunger.

Nailing: The Sage of Warring Thunder. He is a servant of Coruscant.

Orthosial Shivein: An Awakened turtle. Once a rakshasa and saved by Sage-Duke Kelse Vail. He was the Kinesthia instructor at the Ephemeral Academy during Light Squad's Novice year.

Pan Shun: An Awakened panda from the Diamond Mountains. He is the focus of a centuries-long prophecy.

Pathway to Grace: Strange locations or emanations where entire worlds can be found and where Ephemeral Masters can quickly gain Ephemera and Advance.

Pelluraj: A kaiju Sage from Petala. Also called the Stormlord of the Lake.

Perit Line: A Crown and commander of Sidewinder Company.

Petala: A strange, inverted world underneath Mote's Blood Sea. Also called the Hollow Land.

Pharis Folde: Cam's sister, and the oldest of the siblings. Married to Farmer Marcus.

Pivot Stump: The son of Traverse's mayor. He is married to Suse Stump.

Placido Werm: A Glory and an instructor at the Ephemeral Academy. He teaches Spirairia.

Prahlass: A historical saint who prayed so devoutly that he achieved an Awareness beyond Sage, becoming a Divine.

Purien Folde: Cam's father. He's known as Traverse's town drunk.

Purified Masters of Hearth: Name given to Ephemeral Masters in Hearth who serve under the Crowns of Light.

Rail Gristle: Rukh pretending to be an old man living near Carver's Gorge in Hearth.

Rainen Winder: A Sage without attachment to a city. He is the sponsor of Light Squad. He is also known as the Wilde Sage.

Regim Baid: An assistant to Mayor Gard Singer of Dander.

Rizfam: The flute master who taught Pan.

Sage-Dukes, the: There are nine of them and they rule the nine great cities on Golden.
- **Sage-Duke Ahktav Kazar:** The Duke of Maviro.
- **Sage-Duke Dorieus Arta:** The Duke of Chalk.
- **Sage-Duchess Josie Salin:** The Duchess of Bastion.
- **Sage-Duchess Karmin Berjeak:** The Duchess of Corona.
- **Sage-Duke Kelse Vail:** The Duke of Saban.
- **Sage-Duke Knarl Pune:** The Duke of Codent.
- **Sage-Duchess Marsula Thens:** The Duchess of Santh.
- **Sage-Duchess Shah Pharin:** The Duchess of Twine.
- **Sage-Duke Zin Shun:** The Duke of Charn.

Saira Maharani: A powerful Sage from the island-nation of Sinane.

Salvation: The world of *The Eternal Ephemera*.

Shilpa: A rakshasa Sage. Originally a camel.

Sholl Singer: An Adept and member of Sidewinder Company.

Sidewinder Company: A powerful unit of Ephemeral Masters who are under the control of Rainen Winder. They range in Awareness from Novice to Crown.

Smoker Rest: A Glory and headman from Boldest, a small village in Hearth.

Stages of Awareness: The Awareness of the Stage is seen in the sclera, and this is also called a person's Haunt.

- **Neophyte:** Not really considered a Stage, and sclerae are white.
- **Novice:** First Stage and sclerae are red.
- **Acolyte:** Second Stage and sclerae are orange.
- **Adept:** Third Stage and sclerae are yellow.
- **Glory:** Fourth Stage and sclerae are blue.
- **Crown:** Fifth Stage and sclerae are indigo.
- **Sage:** Sixth Stage and sclerae are violet.
- **Divine:** Seventh Stage and sclerae are diamond.
- **Heavenly Heathen:** Rumored Eighth Stage.
- **Holy Servant:** Mythical Ninth Stage.

Surelend: Village nearly the size of Traverse southeast of Corona, and it is where Light Squad destroys their first boil.

Suse Stump née Marline: A young woman from Traverse. She is a friend to Maria Echo née Benefield.

Sutter Dampa: A Purified Master from Hearth.

Tern Shorn: Cam's childhood friend from Traverse, who died while diving a Pathway to Grace.

Thor: The Divine of Loyalty. From Hearth.

Tormick Echo: A young man from Traverse who is reputed to have a way with women.

Tulip: A rakshasa from Mote.

Vacacy: A crappy town close to Carver's Gorge in Hearth.

Victory Arta: A young nobleman and the son of Sage-Duke Dorieus Arta of Chalk.

Vivid Pass: Final north-south pass that eventually ends at the small city of Game along the Charn River.

Warren: Village on the southern coast of Lake Nexus where Light Squad disembarked while journeying to Surelend in *Blood of a Novice.*

Way into Divinity: General term for those who wish to Advance their Awareness of Ephemera.

Weld Plain: A rakshasa Sage, who thinks very highly of himself.

Zahhack, the Endless Emperor: The name used by the Jom-Strafes for the Son of Emptiness.

ABOUT THE AUTHOR

Davis Ashura is a bestselling author, a full-time practicing physician, and a one-time woodworker. His motto has generally been, *"Try it. The worst you can do is fail."* It usually works out—except when jumping out of airplanes. Davis is best known for his *Castes and the OutCastes* trilogy, which is part of the *Anchored Worlds* universe, a set of linked epic fantasy series.

His books are hopeful in nature. He likes to write about heroes who see themselves as servants first. Heroes who fall in love and become partners and make time for family, friendship, and fellowship. His characters are folks with whom it would be fun to have drinks and dinner, but who could also handle any trouble that might crop up.

Davis is married and shares a house with his wonderful wife who somehow overlooked his eccentricities and married him anyway. Living with them are their two sons, both of whom have at various times helped turn Davis' once lustrous, raven-black hair prematurely white. And of course, there are the obligatory strange, stray cats (all authors have cats—it's required by the union). They are fluffy and black with terribly bad breath. Additionally, there is the rescue dog— gnarly-toothed, beady-eyed, and utterly sweet.

Visit him at **www.DavisAshura.com** and sign up for his newsletter to learn the latest information on his books or simply follow him on Facebook, Instagram, or Twitter.